OXFORD LIBRARY OF
AFRICAN LITERATURE

General Editors

E. E. EVANS-PRITCHARD
G. LIENHARDT
W. H. WHITELEY

1. The Bagre shrine, fixed in the neck of the central granary, which projects through the flat roof of the compound

THE MYTH OF
THE BAGRE

JACK GOODY

OXFORD
AT THE CLARENDON PRESS
1972

Oxford University Press, Ely House, London W. 1

GLASGOW NEW YORK TORONTO MELBOURNE WELLINGTON
CAPE TOWN IBADAN NAIROBI DAR ES SALAAM LUSAKA ADDIS ABABA
DELHI BOMBAY CALCUTTA MADRAS KARACHI LAHORE DACCA
KUALA LUMPUR SINGAPORE HONG KONG TOKYO

PRINTED IN GREAT BRITAIN

TO

GLYN DANIEL

AND

HUGH SYKES DAVIES

PREFACE

I N presenting this 'myth' and its translation, I want to offer thanks to my collaborators, in whom I have been singularly fortunate. Benima Dagarti, an enterprising LoWiili whose experiences as a soldier led him to look outside the community rather than within, first helped me write down this myth, which he had learnt from his father's brother, Naapii. I made a rough translation on the spot and I have to thank Romulo Tadɔɔ for all his assistance at this time. In typing out the myth, I had the interest and help of Joan Warmbrun of the Centre of Advanced Studies in the Behavioral Sciences at Palo Alto; later the West African Research Unit and African Studies Centre at Cambridge came to my aid. I have been assisted by Meyer Fortes's deep knowledge of Tallensi language and behaviour, for in many ways these are similar to those of the LoDagaa. In the later stages I have been greatly helped by Kumbɔɔna Gandaa, teacher, trader, politician, statistician, a convert to Islam, a scholar in all he does. It was in his company that I attended my first Bagre ceremony in 1951; it was his presence in London (and his willingness to give up his very limited free time) that enabled me to get the text out of my field-notes and into print. And it was with him that I returned to Birifu in December 1969 and January 1970 to see part of the Bagre being performed once again. On this last occasion we were able to record a version of the myth, but I have not used it in this book: the present text has been in my hands for nearly twenty years and I do not wish to delay its publication by the very considerable time the new version will take to transcribe.

Although I have spent several years working on this material, I am fully aware that there are many gaps. I have tried to avoid filling these from my own imaginative experience and have preferred to stick clolsey to the text and to its exegesis by the actors themselves. Further interpretations of my own I will offer in due course. The trouble with so many accounts of the myths, cosmologies, and thought of non-literate societies is the failure of the editors to distinguish news from views. I have tried to make this distinction as clear as I possibly can.

I owe a debt of gratitude to the Crowther-Beynon Fund of the University of Cambridge.

JACK GOODY

St. John's College, Cambridge
March 1970

CONTENTS

LIST OF PLATES

REFERENCES AND ORTHOGRAPHY

(i) I have given all cross-references to the myth in the following form:
W. (White Bagre) or B. (Black) followed by line number.

(ii) For books, I have used the system adopted by the *American Anthropologist* and many other journals (references in the text).

(iii) For references to my field notes I have given the page numbers in brackets; the notes are deposited with the West African Research Unit in the University of Cambridge.

I originally wrote down the text using the script suggested by the International African Institute. I have subsequently made changes, specific and general, on the advice of K. Gandaa; in cases of disagreement I have nearly always followed his spelling. However, I have used *ng* instead of *ŋ* since the latter refinement seems an unnecessary extravagance in a language of limited circulation. I have also used *h* as a modifier to eliminate the use of diacritics, e.g. *bh* represents what appears to be an implosive *b*; *sh* represents *ʃ*. Most African languages suffer from too great an attention to phonetic values which discourages their transcription and reproduction.

In the notes I have abbreviated the names of two commentators on the text as follows:

K. G. for Kumbɔɔno Gandaa
R. T. for Romulo Tadɔɔ

In giving local words I use LW. for the LoWiili dialect of Birifu and LD. for the LoDagaba of Tom.

PART ONE

INTRODUCTION

1

THE LODAGAA AND THEIR INTELLECTUAL CLIMATE

I DID not go to Africa to seek out a 'simple' society, nor indeed did I find one. The material tools, of course, were elementary; with the aid of an iron hoe the LoDagaa gained a living from the poor tropical soils of the savannah country of West Africa. By Eurasian standards, productivity was low and remains so today; there is no plough or wheel to assist them and the long dry season limits the extent and type of farming that is possible. But as far as intellectual activity is concerned, the LoDagaa were far from simple, savage, wild, or primitive. They lacked, of course, the advantage of writing, though its restricted use was known in the main towns of the region. But their language was as subtle and expressive as ours; though it obviously lacked a specialist vocabulary for absent specialisms, there was inevitably a greater shared knowledge of what existed.

I make this point at the outset because even anthropological readers are only too ready to assume a great divide between 'primitive' and 'civilized' thought, between 'mythopoeic' and 'logico-empirical' modes, between the wild and domesticated varieties. For other readers this general impression may be reinforced by the 'myth' presented in this book. It is a view that requires a major revision.

The search for differences in communicative systems and in intellectual processes is an important field of comparative sociology, and I do not wish to play down the real variations that exist. But the radical dichotomy that lies at the basis of such sociological and anthropological thinking, as well as behind popular belief itself, seems to me entirely unacceptable, a relic of academic colonialism that still pervades so many of our 'humanitarian' fields of study. My knowledge of LoDagaa language and culture was far from perfect, but I did not personally experience any of the major problems of communication that such a dichotomy would entail, certainly as far as the logic of human discourse was concerned. While the Bagre myth differs from our own forms of discourse, being more particularistic in its ethic, for example, I do not find it intrinsically more difficult to understand than Masonic rituals or the Christian Bible. Neither Bagre myth nor Christian Bible are capable of any simple explanation; there is no master key that will unlock all secrets: no simple clue that will enable the reader to break the code. No more so here than in any other literary creation; all have to be judged according to similar standards, for there is not one set of rules for 'primitive' myth and another for the works of Sartre, Lawrence, or T. S. Eliot. My understanding of the Bagre text is no less and no more than my understanding of the Bible or of any other complex work of literature.

This myth and this ritual appear to have been composed by the LoDagaa of northern Ghana, or by a very similar people. The conditions under which they live are of course radically different from those of a townsman of Western Europe. The country they inhabit is part of the savannah zone that runs across West Africa between the rain forest of the coastal regions and the desert mass of the Sahara. Half the year, from October to March, it is very dry. This is the time when the Bagre ceremony is performed and when most 'calendrical' rites take place. During the six months from April to September, people are hard at work in their farms and this activity takes priority over all except the most urgent ritual needs; even burials are severely shortened, and the subsequent funeral ceremonies take place after the beginning of the dry season, when the harvest has been gathered in.

The harvest consists of the cereals, guinea corn (*sorghum*), millet (*pennisetum typhoides*), and maize; in addition there are a host of less important crops, ground-nuts, yams, sweet potatoes (*ipomea batatas*), cow peas (*vigra sp.*), bambara beans (*voandzeia subterranea*), frafra potatoes (*coleus dysentericus*), okro (*hibiscus esculentus*), and a number of other cultigens. Some wild plants too are a basic constituent of man's food, notably the baobab, dawadawa, and the shea. It is the ripening of the shea fruit that marks the beginning of the major sequence of Bagre ceremonies, each of which releases the new members from a prohibition placed upon eating one of the new crops, though these are not treated in any very systematic way.

These various crops are farmed in distant bush farms as well as immediately around the mud-built compounds that have been described as small forts—for they are completely enclosed, with a small parapet around the flat roof; except for the byre, where the animals are herded at night, the only access is by means of a wooden ladder to the roof.

The house is divided into a number of apartments, each containing an adult man, his wives and children, though a man with several wives will have more than one such unit. Each apartment includes a long room (*kyaara*) at the end of which stands a huge granary with its neck projecting through the flat roof. It is in this long room that much of the communal life goes on; in the wet weather women prepare food at the fireplace at the foot of the granary; in the heat of the sun men gather there to drink beer. This is the room used for the Bagre performances and it is in the neck of the granary that the Bagre shrine is built.

Off the long room are the women's sleeping and storage rooms, and it is here that the shrines to the hill and water spirits, the beings of the wild, are built against the inside wall. The opposite end of the long room to the granary opens on to a courtyard where most of the cooking of food and brewing of beer is carried out. From the walled court, a ladder leads to the rooftop, the surface of which is divided up according to the ownership of the rooms below. A shrine room has its section of the roof set apart for sacred purposes; each sleeping-room has its corresponding roof space where the inhabitants sleep during the dry season; the roof of the long room is where the grain is threshed and laid out to dry. And the rooftop as a whole is the favourite sitting-place on warm nights since it catches the evening breeze. Consequently, when the sun has set, parts of the Bagre ceremony take place here and it is on the rooftop of adjacent compounds that spectators sit late into the night, drinking beer, watching the dancing, and listening to new and old favourites being played on the xylophone.

From the rooftop one descends by another ladder to the area in front of the byre door, an outside yard that is kept clear of crops. Apart from this space there is only a narrow path in the growing season between the walls of the house and the tall stalks of the maize and guinea corn, which on the fertile soil that surrounds the compound rise above the level of the rooftop to some eight feet. The dominating feature of this open space is a tall shade tree, under which stands a mortar for pounding grain, some logs for resting on and a number of outside shrines, usually found clustering around the entrance to the byre. Apart from housing the cattle, sheep, and goats, the byre is the most sacred room in the house, for it is here are kept the wooden ancestor shrines, carved to every man who has left a son to survive him.

The group that farms together and has its own granary is a small one, consisting of a man and his direct descendants (an extended family), or a couple of full brothers (an expanded family), or more usually just a man, his wives, and his young children. It is this farming group that plants, harvests, stores, and distributes the food it grows. But it does so always within a wider network of kinship ties. Several closely related units of this kind will commonly share one of the mud compounds, though as these domestic groups constantly grow and divide in the course of their development, one finds dwellings of different sizes; in the near-by area of Lawra these dwellings may accommodate up to a hundred people. Elsewhere the compounds are smaller, but the male inhabitants are still linked by patrilineal ties to those living in adjacent houses. Up to a dozen such houses will form an agnatic lineage, the numbers of which trace their descent to a common ancestor five or six generations back. Each lineage sacrifices to its common ancestors, sometimes individually, sometimes as a group, and it is these unifying bonds of descent that men see as dominating their behaviour to other members, leading to active help in farming, in marriage payments, and formerly in war, as well as placing restraints upon aggressive acts within the clan. Descent provides the ideology of much common action.

These lineages form the basis of the organization of the Bagre society, to which the recital I have written down belongs. Each lineage decides when it will perform the ceremony, roughly at intervals of four or more years. But they get help from similar groups in the same settlement. For certain purposes the help of lineages that belong to the same patrilineal clan is required. But lineages from different clans also play an important part. Indeed the whole settlement is actively involved in an intricate web of reciprocal and supporting services.

In any one settlement, these named patrilineal clans, such as Kpiele or Kusiele, may be represented by one or more lineages. They are extensive, dispersed units, supposed to have common prohibitions (against eating certain foods and performing certain acts) and common acquisitions (such as arrow poison, medicines, and guardian spirits). They stretch into many neighbouring settlements, even to ones which speak languages that are not intelligible to the LoDagaa. In this context common descent is seen as overriding cultural identity.

Besides these numerous patrilineal clans, each individual belongs to one of four matrilineal ones. In Birifu, where this version of the myth was recorded, matrilineal clanship nowadays plays but a minor part in social life, although in the other area I worked (around Tom) all movable wealth was transmitted within these groups. For example, a man's livestock goes to his uterine brother or to his sister's son. While this form of inheritance is not now recognized in Birifu, there is evidence that in some parts of the settlement people had been pulled into the system of matrilineal inheritance practised by their neighbours.[1] Interestingly enough, the myth includes an explanation for matrilineal inheritance which is couched in terms of the resolution of father–son tensions and the use of inheritance to protect the security of the aged. In this respect it does, in a limited way, what Homer did more extensively, preserve in oral narrative the customs of an earlier time.[2]

The settlement I speak of is a named area, such as Birifu or Tom. It consists of 300 to 3,000 people whose dwellings are scattered unevenly over the agricultural land. In the large majority of cases, the settlement is identical with the area under the jurisdiction of an Earth shrine (*tengaan*) at which representatives of the clans sacrifice together on regular occasions as well as in times of trouble. The Earth shrine is as crucial to the social life of the LoDagaa as are the lineage and clan in a different context. For it again places certain obligations, certain restraints, upon those who dwell on its surface (or skin, *gan*, of the earth, *teng*). The foremost prohibition is placed upon the shedding of each other's blood. Should this occur, the settlement is said to 'spoil' and a heavy sacrifice has to be made before things are put right. The same is true of suicide and of a number of other acts, like sexual intercourse out of doors; though it was by observing the animals that (the myth relates) woman first learned about the reproductive act, to imitate

---

[1] I have tried to explain how this could occur in 'Inheritance, Social Change and the Boundary Problem', *Comparative Studies in Kinship*, London, 1969.

[2] See M. I. Finley, *The World of Odysseus*, New York, 1954: 26.

them is to fall into sin, for it is associated with extra-domestic
sex.[1]

The Earth shrine is primarily concerned with the settlements
of men and the land they cultivate, while the surrounding bush
(*wiɔ*, or *mwo*, grass) is the domain of the beings of the wild
(*kɔntɔme*), whose herds are the animals hunted by men and whose
crops are the trees and fruits of the woods. But the opposition is
not complete. The Earth shrines themselves are situated in uncul-
tivated groves, untouched by the hoe; the sabbath is a day of no
hoeing. Moreover, men farm in the 'bush' as well as around their
dwellings. On hunting expeditions, too, they come into contact
with the denizens of the wild, with the buffalos they kill in the
myth and the revenge of whose calf is an index of man's ambival-
ence towards the slaughter of living things, an important factor in
totemic beliefs.[2] On the other hand, since communications have
to be established with the beings of the wild, the shrines to them
are found in sleeping-rooms and occasionally, in the compound
yard, in small houses of their own. But the general association of
these beings with non-human territory, especially the rivers and
the hills, links them to the rest of the supernatural order. It is they
who are the main intermediaries in communication between mankind and other agencies, so that the possession of a shrine to the
beings of the wild is an essential attribute of the diviner, whose
function it is to reveal the ways of gods to men. Indeed it is with
precisely this theme that the whole Bagre recital begins. After the
invocation of a number of supernatural agencies, it recounts how,
against the background of various misfortunes, the younger of two
original brothers was worried by a dream and went off to consult
a diviner about what should be done. As a result he was told that
the difficulties might be overcome by performing the Bagre, which
involves the initiation of new members through a series of ceremonies carried out over several months of the dry season.

Variations upon this general pattern of social organization are
found throughout the Dagari-speaking peoples of the north-west
of Ghana, as well as among neighbouring groups speaking other
languages. In the pre-colonial period there were no chiefs, although

---

[1] Having learnt from the animals, man then dissociates himself from them.
See the Black Bagre, line 1955. Further references will be shown simply as B.
(Black Bagre), W. (White Bagre), followed by the line number.
[2] See Goody 1962: 120, for a further discussion of this point.

men of power and influence played important roles from time to time. There were consequently no continuing boundaries connected with the limits of jurisdiction of an individual chief or of a council of elders; the only 'frontiers' were those of the parish or of one of its segments (a minor ritual area), which roughly corresponded to the territory inhabited by the local section of a clan.

Since there were few human boundaries, social intercourse flowed relatively freely between neighbouring parishes. People attended each other's weekly markets in the six-day cycle. They did so to buy produce like chickens and grain that were in short supply or were less expensive; and they did so too for social reasons, to drink beer, meet girls, talk to friends, or visit relatives. For while most marriages took place within the parish, some were made outside, leading to (or arising out of) ties of kinship and affinity. Social intercourse between neighbouring parishes led inevitably to disputes, which in their turn led to fighting and raiding, since there was not the same moral and religious pressure towards peaceful settlement that existed within the ritual area. But the flow of communicative acts took place against the background of common cultural elements, anyhow as far as neighbours were concerned. In a spatial sense, culture changed in the manner of linguistic dialects; the poles might be far apart, but at any intermediary stage the customs of adjacent parishes would be very similar, similar enough to enable them to attend each other's funerals, markets, and festive occasions.

In this situation, there were no 'tribes' as such; although on some occasions settlements did place themselves in more inclusive 'groups', the way they did so could differ according to the context. Permanent 'tribal' names therefore arise out of the needs of the observer rather than the actor, so that, while basing myself upon local usage, I have had to adopt my own designation for descriptive purposes. The group with which I am dealing here, consists mainly of the inhabitants of Birifu, whom I identify as the LoWiili. They are surrounded on the west by the LoBirifor, across the Black Volta, on the north by the LoDagaba and on the east by the DagaaWiili. To this complex I give the name LoDagaa, a combination of the two words they often use to indicate cultural direction and affinity.[1] Some fifty miles to the south lies the Muslim market town of Wa, established many centuries before. Some ten miles

[1] See Goody 1956: 16, for a more extended discussion.

to the north, up the road that runs parallel with the Black Volta, which forms the western boundary of northern Ghana, lies the small administrative centre of Lawra, founded in 1907 when the British extended their influence over the north-west.

The advent of the British has inevitably led to changes in the way of life. But owing to the paucity of crops for sale, these changes have been less marked than one might expect. Apart from the relief from war, famine, and disease (anyhow in their earlier forms), the most radical of the new influences on village life has been the intro-duction of the school and the church. In the last thirty-five years the Roman Catholic Church has spread rapidly in many parts of the area, leading to the abandonment or modification of some magico-religious practices. But the picture is very patchy. In the LoDagaba area around Tom, north of Lawra, where I spent some nine months in 1952, mission influence was quite strong and the Bagre ceremonies were rarely performed. Among the LoWiili on the other hand I met no Christians at that time and the Bagre continues to have a vigorous life to this day.

The other main instrument of change was the school. When I lived in Birifu, a primary school had recently been started and the two teachers were sons of the late chief (an office introduced by the British); at an earlier stage they had been sent to school in Lawra and had subsequently gone on to a training college. Characteristic-ally, both were members of the Bagre society, for their father had insisted upon their being conversant with 'traditional' as well as 'modern' ways; indeed the dates of the Bagre were occasionally arranged to fit in with school holidays, and counter-adjustments in the return to school were also not unknown. This participation continued after the chief's death and I myself witnessed the wife of one of the teachers (later the local District Commissioner) suc-cessfully come through her initiation. Besides the general attach-ment to traditional belief, children who attend school are seen to be as much in need of supernatural protection as anyone else, a belief which they actively share.

The attachment to traditional belief was not at all inconsistent with a vigorous commitment to social development and I joined in many discussions with the educated few about what could be done, given money and independence. Independence came, as well as some external help. But when I visited Birifu in 1966 I noticed surprisingly little change. On a purely external level it is difficult

to alter a local mud-built compound by adding improvements in
the shape of a tin roof; it is not the kind of structure you can tamper
with. But more importantly the basic system of production by hoe
agriculture has changed little, so that the base is lacking for any
extensive change on the local level. Although some five hundred
children, possibly half from Birifu, must have been through the
local primary school since it first started, none of them save 'drop-
outs' remained in the village to farm, apart that is from the chief,
who was the son of his predecessor; even the present teachers were
from other settlements and did not live in the village. In Birifu,
the Bagre still continues to be performed; indeed its influence is
spreading in some rural areas to the south and west, among the
peoples of the Wa district and across the river in the Republic of
the Upper Volta, for like many similar cults in the area, the Bagre
and its myth are not confined to one settlement, tribe, or people.[1]

I have yet to describe the physical appearance of Birifu itself.
The settlement is sited on a stretch of the left bank of the Black
Volta, just below the 11th parallel north of the Equator. The land
near the river is little cultivated, since it is subject to flooding.
Further away the terrain is better and a small part of the total area
even has the advantage of a permanent supply of water, a spring
at the foot of a sharp escarpment. A few houses stand on the flat
top of the scarp, including my own, which looked down over the
plain inhabited by the Chaa and Ngmanbili clans, across towards the
River Volta and the Ivory Coast. But in many parts the surface of
this plateau was almost barren of earth and showed only the bare
surface of the flat, reddish, laterite rock underneath.

Clearly Birifu was an old settlement site. All the present clans
claimed to have migrated from different places in the south about
five generations earlier, though no reliability can be placed upon
this time scale. Previously, they claim, Janni lived here; these are
the Dyan now living around Diébougou in Upper Volta. The
remnants of their compounds, recognizable by the tessellated
floors, are scattered throughout the settlement. Whether the Dyan
were also responsible for the round pits hacked out of the laterite
for water storage and the extensive but simple forms of hillside
terracing, I do not know. At all events, the site has been in continuous occupation over many centuries, partly because of the

[1] For details of its recent spread I am indebted to the Bagre film made in
Haute Volta by G. Savonnet and to Mr. A. Jangu of Wa.

excellent water supply which makes possible some elementary
irrigation. In this feature Birifu is well favoured by comparison
with her neighbours, though the over-all density of population is
not very different.[1]

This then is the physical setting of Birifu. Its social life revolves
mainly around agriculture. But while a woman's domestic round
continues along largely the same lines throughout the year, the
men are fully occupied in the growing season from March to
October but have much more time at their disposal during the
dry season. Some of this period is spent in house-building; much
time is devoted to rituals of various sorts. Of these pragmatic and
ritual activities, the most popular are the communal ones. Even in
the wet season people join each other in farming parties, sit for
hours at funerals, visit the weekly market, and of an evening go to
drink beer at the house of one of the regular women brewers. But
probably the most talked-about and rejoiced-in part of social life
is the series of Bagre performances, associated with 'the deity of
meetings', of coming together. For here, in the long, warm even-
ings, there is the music of the xylophones, the poetry of the myth,
the dancing of the young, the conversation of the old, and plenty
of beer, food, and girls.

This then is a sketch of the social and intellectual setting within
which the Bagre is performed and the text recited. In the following
chapters I first try to give an account of the organization of the
Bagre society, then to discuss some features of the myth and finally
to present the text, translation, and notes. With texts and rites of
this length and complexity, there is an enormous amount one could
add by way of comment and analysis. It is now nineteen years
since I first took down the Bagre recital; while much remains to
be done, the first priority must be to record the facts as I understand them. In the many discussions of African thought, African
symbolism, African religion, even the expert often finds it difficult
(sometimes impossible) to distinguish news from views, the con-
struct of the observer from the concept of the actor, latent from
manifest interpretation. In the Bagre text we have a document of
African provenance which in length and complexity far surpasses
anything so far recorded from the traditional, oral cultures. Its
publication at least provides a base for the examination of the

[1] I have estimated the density as 330 per square mile of arable land, the
Lawra district as a whole having a density of 81 (1948). See Goody 1956: 27.

intellectual processes of these societies. This base is lacking in those pictures built up by a process of question, answer, and creative interpretation, a process that often tells us more about the recorder than the recorded, more about Paris and Oxford, Dakar and Accra, than the villages of the West African savannahs.

Bibliographic note

For those wishing to pursue any aspect of LoDagaa culture, a bibliography is available in the second edition of my book *The Social Organisation of the LoWiili*, London, 1967 (1st edn., 1956). The other main sources are Henri Labouret, *Les Tribus du rameau Lobi*, Paris, 1931, and J. Goody, *Death, Property and the Ancestors*, Stanford and London, 1962.

The work of M. Fortes on the Tallensi is the most relevant to the study of the stateless peoples of the area, especially his forthcoming account of Tallensi religion, which will no doubt make as significant a contribution to comparative sociology as his two earlier volumes, *The Web of Kinship* (London, 1949) and *The Dynamics of Clanship* (London, 1945).

2

RELIGIOUS ACTION AMONG THE
LODAGAA

To understand the Bagre myth, and the Bagre ceremonies with which it is associated, one needs to know something more of the religious system of the LoDagaa.

There are a number of ways of describing such activities. One can analyse the actors' relationship with the supernatural, the structure of the pantheon itself, the acts and concepts associated with communication between man and god, the network of symbolism involved in ritual acts, and finally the interaction between 'religion' and social structure. All these approaches are contributory ways of understanding, yet all are in some respects liable to mislead. For the LoDagaa, as for most non-literate peoples, religion is not a boundary-maintaining system; there is indeed no word that comes anywhere near a translation of 'religion' or 'ritual'. We find a range of institutionalized practices centring upon the communication between men and gods (widely interpreted); there is no religious system *per se*.[1]

What exists, exists in change as well as in continuity. Certain facets of religious practice, notably the medicine shrines, are particularly subject to change (of the kind we may call organizational change) because they tend to offer specific returns which they later fail to produce. Their built-in obsolescence results in a degree of turn-over, or at least in fluctuations in their popularity.

Another change occurs in the relative importance allotted to the various constituents of the pantheon, and in the actions associated with them, at different times. These changes occur over the shorter as well as over the longer span. From the actor's standpoint, the shape of the supernatural world changes according to the divinity

[1] I was encouraged to find that the same point was made by Father Girault in his perceptive outline of the religion of the LoDagaba and the LoWiili, where he writes: 'il est utile de mettre en garde le lecteur contre le préjugé courant de trouver ici un ensemble de croyances cohérents, capable de constituer un tout entrant dans des cadres ethnographiques' (1959: 330–1).

he is propitiating. For wider social groups, too, different agencies come into prominence at different times of the year depending upon the ceremonies being performed. Bagre, as we shall see, is oriented more towards God than any other religious activity of the LoDagaa. But there is also a longer-term swing in the relative position of even major elements in the pantheon. I know of no other way of explaining the quite large differences that one finds among the inhabitants of quite a small area, e.g. the different position of 'gods' (*ngmime*) and 'beings of the wild' (*kɔntɔme*) among the LoWiili and the LoDagaba. However, the most striking illustration of the change in emphasis occurs with regard to God himself. Seligman's 'otiose high god' is after all the being who has created the world and all that therein is, the all-powerful, even if he does not care to exercise that power. Therefore he always remains a potential source of supernatural strength when others fail. And one form in which he may make such a come-back is in a transient cult, such as that of *Naangminle*, 'the little God', which was very popular in the Voltaic region during my stay there in 1952.[1]

Religion then is more dynamic than many analyses suggest. There is an ongoing process of continuous creation of religious concepts and behaviour; indeed the religious field seems to be the most productive, creative, changing of any aspect of the activities of pre-industrial man.

This is partly because of the many options which religious practices and concepts are able to leave open, since they are rarely constrained by empirical considerations. The conceptual ambiguity that Gluckman discovers in law has here a yet fuller rein; indeed ambiguity, as with the conceptualization of the soul, is essential in order that the concepts should 'work' at all.

Consequently we cannot expect too much sharpness of definition

---

[1] I have discussed the entire text with my friend, Kumbɔɔno Gandaa (now a convert to Islam) on several occasions and I give his comments in footnotes, especially when he disagrees with me.

K. G. comments: 'The *Naangminle* of Leo in 1952 cannot be compared with *Naangmin* (God). The word *Naangmin* is used figuratively there. Indeed Gaziere from the chief's house at Birifu was nicknamed "*Naangminle*" by women in the house long before the appearance of the Leo *Naangminle*. This is because Gaziere was persistent in his demands. So when we were young, and feared to call him by such a derogatory name we translated it literally as "short god". Hence "short god" became Gaziere's nickname. The *Naangminle* of Leo was given this name because his powers were subordinate to that of God.' But 'the little God' is surely a refraction of God in the way that other shrines are not.

in these realms. Where we get greater precision from an individual, it may well be that individual's own gloss on the basic set of beliefs, the society's lowest common denominator. But this again is an inadequate way of putting it. The fact that our own religious concepts are encapsulated in holy writ and that we have continual recourse to the 'authority' of books in our search for knowledge may bias the approach we make to the religion of non-literate societies. We look for a definite dogma, a set array of knowledge, an over-reaching system; we hunt for a key to an intricate and interlocking mechanism; we look for something that 'makes sense' of the very discrepancies and ambiguities that are the essence of this conceptual domain in oral cultures.

For there no ultimate authority exists; there is no Holy Book, no dictionary of terms, no encyclopedia of concepts. Authority lies in usage, in communication; and common usage is a sounder basis than the explications of the specialist, often elicited at great length by a series of questions posed by the inquirer, rather than arising naturally out of his communications with gods and fellow men. This is an area of discourse in which informants, especially *the* informant, can be a dangerous indulgence—at least if one is trying (perhaps in vain) to specify some of the over-all parameters of LoDagaa (or any other) religion. There is no secret knowledge, not even a standardized myth like that of Bagre, which can unlock the religious system. For there is no defined, unchanging body of knowledge to unlock. But rather a series of particular constituents, of which the Bagre myth is one, built into different shapes with the bricks of common usage.

Even so the metaphor is clumsy. A basic concept like *siura* (LD. *sigra*), which I have translated as 'spirit guardian', or an agency like *ngmin*, 'god', has many modalities; one is trying not so much to find the key as to follow, to ravel, a mass of threads, to explore the varieties of meaning, the many types of ambiguity.

Here I want to try to outline the religious activities of the Lo-Dagaa, bearing in mind these problems and bearing in mind too the inventiveness and thoughtfulness of man at all levels of 'civilization'.

The Earth shrine (tengaan)

As far as any particular settlement in the region is concerned, the most important focus of religious activity is the Earth shrine, because it is in its worship that the settlement or parish emerges as a social unit; the name itself, *tengaan*, means literally the 'skin' or 'crust' of the earth. A general prohibition exists upon shedding the blood (*zɨɨ kyiru*) of another resident in the same ritual area, on pain of heavy sacrificial offerings and a fine of cowries.

The Earth shrine itself is located in a grove situated in a central part of the settlement where sacrifices are carried out by the Earth priest (or master of the Earth), his assistants and patriclan representatives, who constitute the nearest approximation to village officers that are found in these acephalous societies of the West African savannahs.

Apart from the parish, most settlements are subdivided into minor ritual areas, which roughly correspond to the land occupied and farmed by each of the patriclans that live there.

The compounds themselves are also protected by the Earth shrine, since stones from its grove are placed in the foundations of every house and constitute an element in other shrines. But sacrifices to the Earth can be made anywhere by building a little mound of earth (*tingser*) by the side of the path leading to the shrine. And the same mound can form an altar for propitiating distant ancestors, whose shrines are not known or have 'turned to dust' through the action of white ants; for the dead were anyhow buried within the earth.

The ancestors (kpiin)

Inside the house the main shrines are to the ancestors. Each man who leaves behind a male offspring has an ancestral stick, in rough, human shape, carved to his name. This shrine is created during the series of funeral ceremonies, at the end of which it is placed in the byre of the house where he lived. A woman has a secondary type of shrine made in her name and this is eventually transported back to her natal home by her clan sisters.

The ancestors are clearly dead humans, transformed into spiritual agencies, whose jurisdiction extends to their lineage kin and, in limited ways, to their matrilateral descendants. Their custodianship and worship is basically a matter for groups defined by patrilineal descent and little takes place within the compound of which they are not formally apprised by the residents. Birth, marriage, and death all fall within their orbit.

Medicine shrines (tiib)

Outside a LoDagaa house stand a number of shrines made from sticks, stones, and clay. These are mostly what I have called 'medicine shrines' or *tiib*; the word is cognate with *tii*, 'medicine' and *tiɛ* 'tree'; for most medicine the roots, leaves, bark, and twigs of trees are essential constituents.[1]

All such shrines lead outside the compound with which they are physically linked, because they have been acquired by a particular individual in return for 'payments' of various kinds. A few of the shrines, such as that to Nako Hill in the Ivory Coast, are linked to outstanding natural features that form places of pilgrimage. All have a history of migration, of acquisition, either from within or without the parish.[2]

They have been inherited, acquired at the instruction of a diviner, or sought on the initiative of the present owner as a remedy for some social, psychological, or physical misfortune.

Two such shrines are referred to in the myth, Bari and Base. The first shrine, made of dried sticks, sometimes stands at the entrance to a house; it is one that a neophyte has to salute before he can climb in. For some people Bari (or Bara) is more than a medicine shrine as it seems to be identical with the patriclan shrine of the person reciting the Bagre, the shrine of the Kpiele of Kyaa. This clan shrine (*dogro tiib*) is also known as *Gankye*, the call that members shout out as their poisoned arrows speed towards their prey. For this group there is a very close connection between the shrine and the clan's success in hunting and in war.[3] The second shrine, Base, is situated by the door to the byre where it is passed as one enters to approach the ancestor shrines; its power relates particularly to witchcraft.

The shrine Base is found in houses throughout the LoDagaa area, though it again serves different purposes depending on the particular group to which it belongs. Among the Nambegle of Tom (LD.), it belonged to the lineage as a whole; it was a *kpartig* (or *kpartib*, meeting) shrine, where all gathered because it was there that the grandfather had made a promise to sacrifice if he

---

[1] K. G. agrees that *tii* and *tiib* may have a common derivation but doubts that this is true for *tiɛ* (pl. *tiir*), tree.

[2] With the exception of a few that have come into being locally.

[3] See Goody 1962: 110; also 2623, where it is linked with birth as well as the bow.

2. The entrance to the byre, where the ancestor shrines and guardian spirits are kept. On the right is the clan shrine, with its gourds containing hunting and homicide medicine

3. An outside shrine to the wilds and to the beings that inhabit them

should beget children (*be na fu sããkum kõ nuɔr ti dog yi*). It was a patriclan possession (*dogro bume*) concerned with birth (*dogfu iɔng*). What is a clan shrine for one group is likely to be a medicine shrine for others in the community.

The beings of the wild (kɔntɔme)

The agencies I have so far described, though of great importance in LoDagaa culture, play but a very minor role in the Bagre myth, though a greater one in the rites themselves. The beings of the wild (*kɔntɔme*), however, are central to the myth.

Unlike other supernatural agencies, these beings are portrayed concretely, in speech and in sculpture. Their shrines consist of a representation of a male and female being and they are spoken of as dwarf-like creatures of human appearance; in West African English they are often known as fairies or dwarfs.

These beings inhabit hills, rivers, and trees.[1] They are for the wilds (*wiɔ* or *mwo*) what humans are for the cultivated areas over which the Earth shrine (*tengaan*) has sway. Their flocks are the wild animals (B. 2322), their crops wild fruits, and it is they who are acquainted with the qualities of the different trees required for man's medicines. Indeed, while they are 'the beings of the wild' they are also the transmitters of man's culture, for, as the myth relates, it is they who first showed him how to cultivate the land, to cook food, to make iron, to shoot with bow and arrow, showed him in fact all his major accomplishments.

These agencies are the immediate originators of man's culture. While God created man, it was the beings that taught him most of what he needed to know. The Bagre thesis on this point is repeated in other contexts of social life. All knowledge of supernatural agencies comes from them. It is to them that the diviner appeals in order to be able to tell his client what to do. It is by them that people are taught new supernatural techniques and acquire new shrines, often (it is said) by spending time with them in the wilds.[2] And originally it was they who passed on to man their technological accompaniments.

---

[1] At the beginning of the Black Bagre the younger of the two original men meets both the river beings and the beings of the woods (B. 41, 133).

[2] The idea is a recurrent one in West Africa. For the Ashanti, see R. S. Rattray, *Religion and Art in Ashanti*, London, 1927, pp. 38 and 26, where they are described as 'the speedy messengers of the gods'.

The story is told in the Bagre but another version, probably derivative, was told to me by the same individual from whom I recorded the myth. I relate it here because of its statement concerning the relationship between beings (*kɔntɔme*) and guardians (*sigra*).

When man and woman first came to earth, they sat amidst a group of trees, the *gwo* (dawa dawa), the *sigtir*, the *taantir* (shea), and so on. They had no house and no food. So they slept on stones under the tree, the *sigtir* first. And there they found food.

One night the woman said to her husband, 'Why do we come to sleep in this tree when there is no food growing here? Look at that shea tree or dawadawa with its food.' The man said nothing. She repeated this question for three days. Then one day the man said, 'Let's go to the shea tree'. So they went there and left the *sigtir*. By midday they had nothing to eat and nearly died and they thought of returning to the *sigtir*. Before they did so, the woman took a shea nut and ate it and found it sweet and she climbed up and they ate. But they were not satisfied and so returned to the *sigtir*. However, they could no longer find the food that had been there before; then they had found meat and everything at the bottom of the tree. So every day they had to go out and collect the fruit of the shea. But after three weeks it was finished. Then they saw some grass growing—it had seed. So they went along and started to cut it and one of the beings of the wild said:

'That is my food which God gave me.' When he said this, the woman stopped.

Anya na i in bundiri a Naangmin kum. O baa yil lɛ ka pɔɔ bar

And the being said, 'cut it', and she did so.

ka kɔntɔmo lɛ yil ka ngmaa ko ngmaa bar.

And he said 'What did you eat before?' The man replied

O yil ka buon yia dong di a kɔre zaa. A deb yil ka,

that they used to eat at the foot of the sigtir.

ka sigtir pule bɛ dong dirɛ.

The being then said, 'Wait and I'll show you how to farm.'

A kɔntɔmo yil ka vɛ̃ ka n wül fu, a kob ba ma kob.

He took the man along and told him how you can farm the grass

Ti tɛro deb kyeni, ti yil ka le fu na tuɔ̃ ko a mwo

we have eaten.

anyi wa diã.

He took a large stone, together with charcoal and let a fire burn for three whole days, took out the stone, broke it so the earth fell away, leaving the core. He took this home and put it in the forge, put it on the fire and then beat it till it bent. Then he made a hoe and put it in water so it boiled and the iron became strong. As the water cooled, he took it out and used it to cut a branch off a tree. This he took back home and carved into a hoe handle, made a hole in the end and fixed on the blade. Then the being said to the man, 'Watch what I do. The trouble all comes from your wife. She wants food so badly. If you work hard, you'll get food to give her.' So he showed him how to cultivate the soil and made the woman plant the seed. When she'd finished, he showed him what to do. 'When this grows and is ready, they cut it.' When this had been done, the being showed them how to pound the grain and make porridge. This she did and gave the food to her husband.

As he was about to eat, he thought, and then said
A lɛ song a bɔɔ ko di, o tɛra tiero, p̃ãã yil ka a

that at the foot of the [tree], the stones that lie there,
sigtir pule, a kusibɛ ala na gã,

we will always give them food. He then gave food to
ti na ma ina bundiri iɔng. Ti p̃ãã i iɔng

each of the stones. They finished eating. They took the stone,
a kusibɛ zaa kpo. Ba'a di baari. Ti p̃ãã de a kusir,

and went to bury it in the farm.
p̃ãã kyeni ũũ a puo puɔ.

This is what they call sigra (LW. siura).
A lɛ na so ba buɔlɔ a ka sigra.

Another text on the guardians seems to refer to the clan 'guardians':

If they saw a trader, they would take him to the guardian
Ba la nyɛ a yɛra, ba na bɛ la kyeni a sigra iɔng,

and kill him.
ti ku.

The time referred to was the period of the Bagre performance and other sources tell of the killing of strangers at these places of the guardian spirit, though it was a relatively rare occurrence.[1] The narrator continued:

The guardian, he is the earliest of all. He looks after
Sigra in dɔ̃ɔ̃nio sob. O lɔ nu kaara

everybody. They know that if the cowherd looks after
nibɛ zaa kpo. Ba bɔɔn ka naa kyiinɛ na ma kaar

the cattle, when they kill a cow, he gets the head.
bumzaa, ba la ku naab, o le so a zu.

But a person is not a cow that can be killed to the guardian.
Ti nir be i naab ka be na nyɔ ku a sigra iɔng.

So it is that when they find a single individual, they take
Lɛ na vɛ̃ ka ba mãã pɔɔ a ni boyen kyeni

him and kill him, saying that this is food for the cowherd.
ti ku ti yel a naakyiinɛ bundiri n'anya.

To the concept of the guardian I return after considering the other major elements in the pantheon.

Gods (ngmimi) and *deities* (weni)

The Bagre myth centres upon the tripartite relationship of man, God (*Naangmin*), and the beings of the wild. As I have stated, the other supernatural agencies that play so important a part in the normal religious activities are almost entirely neglected. The ancestors and the Earth shrine, though they are the recipients of sacrifice in the course of the Bagre ceremony, are scarcely mentioned. Of the many medicine shrines so liberally scattered in front of people's houses, Bari and Base are referred to only in passing, as is that standard trickster of LoDagaa folklore, the spider.

But apart from God, that is *Naangmin* or chief god, there are other gods (*ngmimi*, or *weni*, deities) which stand in a subordinate position to God, though in a superordinate one to man.

It should be remembered that among the LoDagaa God has no altar, no shrine, no point through which communication can be effected. People 'call the name but do not know him'.[2] But gods

---

[1] K. G. doubts this. 'The killing of human beings at Bagre runs counter to the very principle of the Bagre myth. If such a story is true, it must be a different *sigra* . . . Bagre prohibits the shedding of blood'.

[2] On this quotation, K. G. comments: 'I do not think God is not known. They know Him and identify Him as above all other supernatural gods. He may not be idolized but that is because God is everywhere—in heaven, on earth,

or deities do have shrines, especially *saa ngmin*, the rain god, to which a special part of the roof is often devoted. They are regarded as having a filial relation with God, but then so (in the last analysis) are all created things, and both supernatural and material phenomena fall under this category. Nevertheless the use of the same name does appear to imply a closer association than with, say, the beings of the wild.

This situation does not indicate any absolute dominance of the beings of the wild by the gods. Indeed the first are said to teach, and therefore to 'own', the latter (*kɔntɔme wiili ngmin, bɛ lo so*); of course, they have nothing to teach God. 'What the beings teach and it helps you (mankind), that's what we call god' (*a kɔntɔme na wiil ko'o sɔɔni fu, a le na ti ma buola a ngmin*).

The *ngmime* (gods) again play little part in the day-to-day activities in Birifu (LoWiili), though they have more of a role among the LoDagaba. The 'rain god' has a special position; so too does the Bagre deity (*Bo wen*). Otherwise the LoWiili only appear to use the concept as an alternative term for other agencies, in their role as beings subordinate to God or Fate. The position is made clear in W. 5254–60 where a neophyte asks about the relationship between God and god. The reply is

> 'we follow
> God.
> He is the senior
> but we can't see him.
> It is a god
> who comes down to people.
> That's what we call god.'

Similarly the beginning of Black Bagre lists an array of gods, a key to which is provided towards the end (a great feat of organization in a work of oral literature). The gods are then revealed as

etc. His powers are passive, not active as those of the other demigods. He has no revenge but takes his child when the time comes for him to die. That is why no appeal is made to God until the last resort. The other gods are vindictive; when you offend their ways they punish you for it. It is little wonder that when a person is ill or dead they first try to find out whether the death or illness is caused by the vengeance of the other gods, or whether it is natural—that is, according to God's will. If no cause is found for the death or illness, it is presumed to be God's will and the sufferer in the last resort appeals to God in desperation, e.g. "What have I done to deserve such treatment from God?' (*Bonu kã i ka Naangmin fɛrɛ ma nya?*).'

beings of the wild or agencies of other sorts. The only gods that emerge as agencies in their own right appear to be *Naangmin* (God), *Saa ngmin* (rain), and *Bo wen* (the Bagre deity).

We can now consider the position of *Bo wen* in the pantheon of agencies and in the set of shrines, the material correlatives of the supernatural agencies. The shrine is set in the neck of the granary, and consists of a small mud mound usually with a shell from the river (*man*) and a stone from the hill (*tong*), the two main abodes of beings of the wild. But even non-initiates may have shrines of the same type in the same place. These are normally for fertility (*dogfu tiib*), but if a man is a senior initiate and goes to kill a Bagre fowl there, then the shrine is for *Bo wen*—because he owns all (*o lɔ so a zaa*).

The Bagre deity looks after the granary and its contents, after all 'things of the hoe', which are so necessary for the performances themselves.[1] Bagre may be seen as a funeral (p. 36), but it is about birth, fertility, health. It was described to me in the following terms:

The initiating of members comes through farming.
Bɔɔ nyɔɔb yin kɔb zie.

If you don't have (crops), you cannot perform Bagre.
Fũũ ba tɛrɛ fu kã tuɔ̃ nyɔɔ Bɔɔre.

Every kind of crop they'll store in the granaries.
A kɔb bom zaa ba ma iɔɔn boori.

There is a stone that they put down so it looks after
A kuur ka ba ma de bin ko kaar

all the food, then they can take out some food from the
a bundiri zaa; ka ba maa ir a bundiri a boor puɔ

granary and perform Bagre. The stone that watches
ti nyɔɔni a bɔɔr. A lɛ na kuur na zĩ gu

over the food so they can initiate the neophytes,
a bundiri ka ba de nyɔɔni a bɔɔbil,

it is good that he sees those neophytes.
a shɔɔn ko nyɛ a bɔɔbil.

[1] In the Nambegle lineage of Tom (LD.) the *Bag ngmin* (i.e. *Bo wen*) is only brought up to the neck of the granary at the time of the Bagre dance; otherwise it is kept in the byre at the foot of the ancestor shrines. This I was assured was the 'god who descends' (*ngmin ka sigra*) (2404).

Well, because of this they call the head of Bagre,
Lɛ zũ, a la na vɛ̃ ka ba buɔla Bɔɔr nikpɛ̃ɛ̃,

Bo wen (the Bagre deity).
Bɔɔ wen.

The main axes

The main axes of LoDagaa religion are two. Firstly there is the association and opposition between the Earth and the ancestors. Sacrifices to these agencies occur at the beginning of every Bagre ceremony.

The other axis is the Earth and the Heavens. It would be easy to oppose these two in some simplistic way. They do contrast in terms of the Below and the Above, Earth and Sky. But the complexities of LoDagaa thought are not to be neatly encapsulated into some trivial diagram, some elementary opposition.

God, Sun, Sky, and Rain are a set of linked concepts, at least etymologically. Of the LoDagaa in the Ivory Coast Girault writes that, 'Le nom de Dieu est *Nãmwin*, appelé tantôt *Mwin* . . . *Mwin* ou *Mwina* est le soleil et son idée est inséparable de celle de Dieu. En aucun cas on ne peut parler d'une identité, mais plutôt d'une même localisation, puisque la résidence de Dieu est le ciel: *sa* ou *salom*' (1959: 332). Among the LoBirifor, *wen* is used for both god and sun. For sun the LoDagaa in Ghana use the etymologically related form of *ngmitong*—the *muto* of Girault, which he translated as 'the strong sun' (1959: 333). But I have myself never heard the sun identified with God or any other deity; the etymological connection is denied at the conscious level.[1]

But God is often located in the *salon*, sky, translated by Girault as 'voûte obscure' (1959: 337), or in the above (*saazu*, 'firmament d'en haut'), both of which terms he derives from *saa*, 'voûte céleste'. More commonly, *saa* is rain, thunder, lightning.[2] The word also refers to the rain shrine (in full, *saa ngmin*) found in many LoDagaa

---

[1] K. G. agrees but notes that the Isala of Tumu use the term *wiɛsi* for both sun and God.

[2] K. G.: 'In Birifu, *salon* can sometimes mean clouds, though the more usual word is *zuzue*. *Saazu* means "in the air" rather than "in the sky"; *saasuɔ*, the rain's knife, is the rainbow. The word *saa* is used for thunder and lightning in the following way:
saa tana—it thundered (lit. the rain shouted).
saa nyiurɔ—there is lightning (lit. the rain flashed).'

houses where it takes a whole variety of forms and is universally of great significance in oaths and similar procedures. The killing power of lightning is something the LoDagaa fear greatly and a death from 'rain' is always attributed to some major offence against the shrine.[1]

The polarity between Earth and Sky is also a sexual polarity. As the myth relates, the Earth is female and fertilized by the male rain from the sky (B. 455). God too is male, and even has a 'wife' (B. 646).

To return to the theme of the major axes of LoDagaa religion, the Earth (shrine) and God emerge as more general categories, or explanatory principles, than the other agencies of the pantheon. Nor are they confined, in their more inclusive usages, to the Below or the Above. For example, my learned friend Bǒyiri once said to me when we were discussing deities (*wen*), '*a zaa in ten-gaan*', 'it's all the Earth shrine'. While *wen* and *ngmin* are linked with the Above, with God, they are also Below in a sense that God never is. He created the world and then distanced himself; he cannot descend again just because he is all-powerful, as is vividly explained in the myth (W. 6050). But others can. The god who descends cannot be God; it is the Bagre deity.

The Bagre deity is thus Below as well as Above. It has a material manifestation which inevitably includes earth. It is here, as well as there. So too are the ancestors; they are in the land of the dead (*kpime teung*) which is also the place where God resides (*Naangmin teung*); but they are also where their shrines are.

The problem of location is solved in two ways: firstly, by move-ment between here and there: at funerals and at sacrifices to their shrines the ancestors are spoken and thought of as being near at hand; as at All Saints, the souls of the dead revisit the living. Secondly, by means of concepts such as the soul, which allow of multiple essences, multiple presences.

For supernatural agencies, like human beings, have life (*tɛra nyɔvuɔr*); the myth illustrates this when it humorously portrays the reactions of the Earth to being struck by human beings making their sacrifices on its surface. In this sense, even the dead ancestors could be said to have life. In any case it is only one of the dual

---

[1] God is closely associated with the rain and the myth speaks of God's rain-drops (B. 4467). It is significant that when man tries to build a shrine to com-municate with God, it is a rain shrine he builds (B. 3532).

aspects of the human persona that dies a physical death; the other continues to exist, and to inhabit both the Above and the Below, as do all supernatural agencies.

Man too, though essentially of the Below, has his window on the Above. Not only do communications come to him from the universe of supernatural agencies, but some of his number visit there and come back to earth. Whereas for most of mankind death is a journey from which we do not return (except unseen as spirits), some come back as visible ghosts (*nyãākpiin*). But more important are those living men who have gone and come back. In the Black Bagre it is the younger brother (*tɔ ble*) who with the aid of the spider (*selmunder*) climbs upwards to see God and returns to earth with a child, 'God's child' (B. 482).

The guardian spirit (siura)

Before I discuss the main problem that the Bagre myth raises for comprehending LoDagaa religion, I need to return to the idea of the guardian spirit (*siura*, LD. *sigra*) that I touched upon before, since this is important both in the myth and in the ritual.

These tutelaries work on two levels. Any individual may have a spirit guardian, who can be an ancestor, a medicine shrine, or other agency. Some clans provide a guardian for each child at a ceremony that occurs at about the age of three months. It is this ceremony that is in effect duplicated (in its ritual elements) during the Announcement of Bagre when the neophytes are taken before the ancestor shrines and are made to flick shea butter on them three times (*tɔna*).

But each clan also has 'a place of the guardian' (*siura zie*) which serves the clan as a whole. It is here that the bells given to each Bagre neophyte are buried in the earth; bells are one of the main means of communicating with the supernatural world. When the Maale lineage performed their Bagre in Birifu, their elder, Depep, took a pot of beer to the place of the guardian and prayed before the ceremony first began. In Kyaa, on the other hand, they first addressed the ancestors, who were, for Bagre purposes, the guardian spirits. A man approaches the shrines and flicks shea butter on them. Someone has to do this for each neophyte; a diviner is usually approached to find out the name (or at least the matriclan) of the man who should do it (425).

In Kyaa 'the place of the clan guardian' is in the scarp above the riverain plain. It is a slight shelter in the rock, where the exposed chalk contains saline minerals that the cattle come to lick. It is from this slight cave that the ingredients are dug for making white-wash and for this reason it is known as *Bɔɔ pla*, the white hole.

Men go there at various times to seek help. My friend Benima had gone there with his father, Na, who was troubled with prob-lems to do with fertility (*dɔɔb*, birth). Subsequently, at the general thanksgiving festival (*bagmãã dãã*) that is held every year, they returned there to kill three fowls and so 'take out the mouth', that is, pay a return gift for what had been received. This, then, is the place of the guardian for the whole local section of a patriclan (*ti sãã [yiri] siura zie ti ko*) and it is to there they go at Bagre-time to bury the neophytes' bells.

Such a site is often of great importance to a clan in its migration history, for the place of the guardian contains perhaps the essence of clanship. It was here that in former times lone strangers were sometimes sacrificed to the 'herdsman' who looked after his flock.

The Bagre myth in LoDagaa religion

In translating the Bagre myth of the LoDagaa I was constantly struck by the fact that its whole tone and content was much more 'theistic' than I, as a non-initiate, had experienced LoDagaa religion, and as I had obliquely described it in *Death, Property and the Ancestors*. I am not aware that my description was unduly conditioned in this regard by my own 'world view', if it can be described by such a term. Indeed the writings of British and French administrators such as Rattray, Tauxier, and Labouret, and the outline of LoDagaa beliefs presented by R. P. Girault, a French missionary of the Catholic faith, are not basically at odds with what I myself reported.

But the myth of the Bagre society is different. The creator God, common throughout Africa, is perhaps still a *deus otiosus*, but his position in the pantheon is more important than other religious activities would suggest.

This is the paradox of LoDagaa religion. If we look for the supernatural agencies that play the major part in the thought, con-cepts, and behaviour of the LoDagaa, these are certainly the Earth and the ancestors. These are the two focal points, what one might call the ritualization of the principles of locality and of descent

(Goody 1957: 103). In this respect, my own analysis of the LoDagaa certainly supports Fortes's study of Tallensi religion and the work of other observers of the pagan peoples of the savannah region.

God (*Naangmin*), the cognate of the Tallensi *Nawun*, plays a small part in day-to-day activities. There is no altar at which one can offer him prayer or sacrifice. He has little or no influence in the current affairs of man. An oath to God is worthless. A man who has lived a full life and has died of old age is said to have died 'God's death', because no maleficent agency has cut short his life. It is doubtless for these reasons that Fortes translated *Nawun* as 'Heaven' or 'Fate'; God is the ultimate cause.

From the standpoint of acts of worship and everyday usage, I would not begin a description of the pantheon with a description of God, as Father Girault chooses to do in his essay on their religion. There he writes:

Il est incontestable que c'est l'idée de Dieu qui domine et 'coiffe' l'ensemble de la religion des Dagara. Elle est tellement ancrée en eux qu'il ne leur viendrait même pas à la pensée de mettre en doute son existence. La vie quotidienne en est imprégnée et, au milieu de l'ensemble complexe de fétiches et de superstitions, Dieu émerge toujours et a sa place nettement à part; le reste, ce sont les *tibè* (fétiches); Dieu est seul à ne pas être représenté par un fétiche (1959: 331).

He sees an opposition between God (*Nâ-nwin*) and fetish (pl. *tibè*), though the latter are 'l'expression matérielle des relations de Dieu avec les humains' (p. 333).

This is a very different view of the religion of the LoDagaa than emerges in my account of their funeral ceremonies or, I suggest, in everyday life as I, and others, have observed it. Indeed the view of Father Girault brings the LoDagaa into a much closer relationship with studies that have been done of the religions of the southern Sudan, especially that made by Evans-Pritchard among the Nuer.

Which of these views is correct? The question, though natural, is misplaced. It would seem at first as though the view that all supernatural agencies were emanations of God, and the polytheistic approach, where God is a residual figure, were at opposite ends of the spiritual universe—monotheism as opposed to polytheism. But this is not altogether the case. In the first place, the uniqueness of God is perhaps less significant, and less established, than Girault suggests. God is opposed to 'fetish' (a tendentious translation) only because he has no material counterpart; the Christian crucifix could equally be described by this term. But more usually the word is applied to 'medicine shrines' and would exclude the ancestors as well as the Earth, even though they have altars at which their worship is pursued. Moreover, while God is the creator, creation does not necessarily imply uniqueness; though the parallel is not exact (God builds, *ir*; man begets, *dɔɔ*), the ancestor that founds a lineage is not to be separated from his offspring. Indeed the term *Naangmin*, 'head *ngmin*', is itself an index of this lack of uniqueness.[1]

Father Girault sees the Bagre as a dedication to God, for he identifies *wen* or *ngmin* with *Naangmin*.[2] The myth makes it clear that, firstly, the Bagre rites are not immediately directed towards God, but towards other agencies; and, secondly, that these agencies, described as *ngmin* or *wen*, include the beings of the wild. Moreover it is important to insist that not everyone becomes a member and not all LoDagaa have the Bagre; it is not in my view intrinsic, nor is it seen by the actors as being so, though its importance is certainly stressed in the myth (W. 4555).

Nevertheless, when this has been said, it remains true that the whole myth of Bagre is very much more theocentric, in the way Girault desires, than is the experience of everyday religion. God is not the centre of attention; the beings of the wild are the main agency concerned.[3] But this orientation is seen as the weakness not the strength of Bagre. The beings pretend to have the secret of life and death, but it is God who is the creator; the beings of the wild, who taught man many things, have also deceived him.

This theistic orientation is not peculiar to Bagre but is found in many of the shorter stories that it is convenient to label 'folktales' and which LoDagaa children (and some adults) are only too

---

[1] Though *na* can mean 'chief', the LoDagaa did not traditionally have chiefs in the usual sense. *Na* was applied to a leader in a whole variety of activities and its usage was essentially relative to a particular context of social action.

[2] If this were so, it would no longer be true that one did not sacrifice to God. To the Bagre deity (*Bo wen*) one certainly makes such offerings.

[3] K. G. queries my emphasis here. 'In the myth we do not know how the first man (*tɔ ble*) was created nor how all other beings and creatures came into existence. But it is common knowledge that they were created by God (*Naangmin*). To these various creatures God gave each their various powers, except to innocent man in his natural state. Had these creatures not tempted and polluted man's mind, there would perhaps have been direct communication between God and man. However, the myth tells us of the invasion by the *kɔntɔme* of man's life—teaching him both good and evil, only to deny it later before God.'

delighted to tell. Like most ethnographers, I collected a mass of such tales, though I rarely heard them recited in a natural context.

In a collection of seventy-nine such tales, the main actors were people and animals; the only supernatural agencies to appear were God (in eight tales) and the beings of the wild (in five); the Earth, the ancestors, the medicine shrines, none of these were introduced. The collection may not be altogether typical; it came largely from children, who are the main tellers of tales. But the agencies that appear provide a surprisingly close parallel to those in the Bagre myth. In other words, the powers to whom the LoDagaa appeal in sacrifice, prayer, and oath are not those with which either myth or folk-tales are concerned. This fact suggests that we need to rethink radically the role of myth in relation to cosmology and to culture. In itself, it is no charter for the system of religious action, much less the key to culture.

How do we explain the partial character of LoDagaa myth and folk-tales? It would be inappropriate to look for an explanation in particularistic terms, for we find a very similar situation in another group in northern Ghana whose culture, society, and traditions are very different. The Gonja were organized as a state and their religious practices were much influenced by Islam. However, their stories have a surprisingly similar array to those of the LoDagaa in that of all the supernatural agencies at their disposal only God and the beings of the wild (the jinn of Islamic tradition) play significant parts.

The two contexts in which God stands out are both ones of considerable verbal elaboration; they are narratives of varying degrees of formality, elaborateness, and standardization. They are also, in part, didactic situations; in the Bagre the rites and their background are being 'explained' to the neophytes; in the folk-tales, the old are addressing the young, or the young are repeating among themselves what they have learnt. It is particularly important to remember that, despite the accepted idea of the storyteller entertaining the multitude, these tales are largely directed to, or recounted by, the young. Such is also the situation in the other parts of northern Ghana in which I have worked and Father Fortier says of the Sara tales that he collected . . . 'dans chaque famille aussi, le père souvent, et plus encore les femmes — tante ou grand-mère — transmettent aux enfants les histoires de *Sú*, ou des contes modernes' (1967: 45).

The prominence of God in these contexts seems related to their verbal and didactic nature. In this way Bagre resembles, partially at least, the universalistic churches of Eurasia, for it provides a general 'theological' umbrella for the innumerable medicine and other shrines that individuals possess. God emerges as an explanatory principle rather than as an active ingredient of LoDagaa religion. His position, as an otiose God, is a function of the problem of evil. As the creator, he is good and omnipotent. If he were to continue in his primordial role, our problems would not exist. With his aid, disease, evil, and misfortune could be banished. This is the clear, explicit message of Bagre (B. 5361).

But misfortune does exist and hence God is not among us. We have to deal as best we may with other agencies, who are in a sense creatures of God, inferior to him, yet not simply manifestations or refractions of him; for they carry on an independent existence, come into conflict with him, reject his ways, and yet are more potent as far as mankind is concerned because they are with us materially and have not distanced themselves from us in the way God has.

It is this ambiguous position of God, omnipotent but powerless, that adds one dynamic aspect to the religion of the LoDagaa, as well as of many other peoples of the western Sudan. For given this situation, there is always the possibility of drawing God back into the human situation. This is how I interpret the argument of part of the Black Bagre, as well as the phenomenon of 'the little God' to which I have already referred, and the continuing movement of peoples like the LoDagaa into (and out of) the world religions like Islam and Christianity. The LoDagaa invariably identify *Naangmin* with the Allah of the Moslems and the Jehovah of the Christians. There is no problem here; it is only his role that differs in these religions, partly because they are literate, and are therefore more concerned with explanation, and partly because they are more universalistic, and are therefore less concerned with particularistic features like ancestors, totems, and local shrines or Baals.

But there is another aspect to the Bagre myth, which is especially significant as it is the only extensive text of this kind to emerge from Africa. Whether you look at the cosmological aspects of the Bagre, or at its symbolic content, or at the position of God, you find that the Bagre myth takes up a special position. This position is not wrong, but on the other hand it is not right. Or rather it is partial. It provides the solution to no cryptogram, breaks no code; it is only part of the total picture.

Perhaps the clearest indication of this is that the society is itself an association in which all need not join; secondly, it belongs to a category of secret societies which, while more permanent than the healing cults, are nevertheless on the move from one group to the next and finally, though the LoDagaa have this long, explicit systematized, cosmological myth, neighbouring societies do not. Which leads me to conclude that myth (in the sense in which I use the word) does not have the central role in human cultures that Malinowski, Lévi-Strauss, and others have assigned, but is in many ways peripheral, changing, the sort of thing that mankind can take or leave. The function which writers and anthropologists have alike assigned it seems in part a reflex of the greater fragmentation of beliefs in industrial society; these authors appear at times to be harking back to a state of greater certainty of myth, classification, and structure than their present situation can offer.

3

THE BAGRE ASSOCIATION

AMONG people whose social life and religion I have briefly outlined, the Bagre association holds an important place, both because
of its performances and because of its myth. But in contradistinc-
tion to some of those who have analysed 'initiatory' procedures in
other parts of West Africa, I would stress at the outset that this
cult does not seem intrinsic to LoDagaa culture. I mean by this
that in any given locality membership is voluntary;[1] there are
LoDagaa communities where it is not performed, nor is it confined to any one 'people', any one cultural, linguistic, or ethnic
group. Of the settlements in which I worked, it was of great
significance in Birifu and of very little in Tom, anyhow at the time
I was there, partly due to Christian influence.

In Birifu the three years 1950, 1951, and 1952 saw the performance of the long series of ceremonies by at least one lineage or clan
sector during every dry season. On each occasion the ceremonies
occupied the attention of most of the senior men in the community
over many weeks, drew large numbers of people (from without as
well as from within the parish), and huge quantities of grain and
fowl were consumed.

The name

In referring to this sequence of ceremonies, I have used the term
Bagre throughout, since this is the most common form in which
the word is found among the Dagari-speaking peoples (Labouret
1931: 461; *baghr*, Girault 1959: 334). But in fact the form used in

---

[1] Although the myth stresses the importance of entering Bagre because

> 'If you are not a member,
> you'll never hear
> about your grandfathers'
> affairs' (4552–5),

in fact this is not altogether true. Bagre not only represents an esoteric form of
knowledge, little used even in ritual affairs, but it is quite possible to be learned
without it.

Birifu is Bɔɔre, following one of the regular sound shifts that occur in this dialect.

The root is the same as the Tallensi *boyar*, which Fortes translates as 'shrine' (1949: 6). In Birifu its meaning is best brought out by recourse to the words of a LoDagaa: 'If you dream on the mat (*fũũ zan a seung puɔ*), you go to a diviner, who will tell you which shrine (*tüb*) [or other mystical agency] is troubling you. He will then *buu* a *bɔɔ*.' This last phrase can be translated as 'look what sacrifice needs to be made', or 'find out the mystical cause'; indeed the diviner is known as a *bɔɔbuuro* (LD. *bagbuura*). When you are told what is wrong you sacrifice a fowl to the shrine, an action for which the LoDagaa use the phrase *o maal a bɔɔ*, 'he makes good the mystical trouble'. The term *Bɔɔre* or *Bagre* used as a title for this association is recognized as being of the same root as an ordinary sacrifice because in both cases 'they kill fowl' (A. 41).

The distribution

The Bagre association is found among the Dagari-speaking peoples of northern Ghana and the adjacent parts of the Ivory Coast and the Upper Volta. That is to say, local 'lodges' occur in settlements belonging to the various peoples of the LoDagaa cluster, namely, the LoWiili (Fr. Oulé), the DagaaWiili, the LoDagaba (Fr. Dagari), and the LoBirifor. It has also spread to Dagaba (Engl. Dagarti) groups and to some LoWilisi (or 'true' Lobi) communities in the vicinity of Gaoua. But the distribution is uneven and it is important in some communities and not in others, its appeal varying over time like that of medieval saints of the Catholic Church.

Other societies of this general kind are found among the same peoples (occasionally in the same settlement), notably the Gyoro or Dyooro described by Henri Labouret (1931). Neither the Gyoro nor the Bagre are associated with masks.[1] But these so-called 'secret societies' are widely distributed through the savannah country of West Africa, and the secrecy of the rites is often reinforced by the use of masks, voice disguisers, raffia dresses, and other ways of pretending that man is something other than he ordinarily is.

In northern Ghana such associations are characteristic of the

[1] In Gaoua the Bagre appears to make use of a mask on the shrine to *Bo wen*; such masks are current among the LoWilisi.

western part, an area that has other material features which link it to the Mande culture area,[1] most obviously the flat-roofed house and the xylophone. Some associations, like the Sigma of the Vagala and of other Grusi groups, make use of animal masks; other masked societies used to be found among the Moslem groups in the western Gonja town of Bole, a probable indication of Ligby and Senufo influence. In other words, such societies are found among pagans and Moslems alike, in both acephalous and state systems, though never I think among the ruling groups in these states, a fact of importance in political terms.

The Dirt Bagre and the Oil Bagre

The Bagre association has two major sects, only one of which will be found in a particular parish. In Birifu, when the time comes to whitewash the initiates, they are painted in white stripes. It is this procedure that gives its name to one of the sects as well as to the first and main set of entrance ceremonies, both of which are known as *Bo pla*, the White Bagre. This form of Bagre is also known as the Dirt Bagre (*Bo diɔr*, LD. *Bo deɣr*), the term 'dirt' having a double reference here to the chalk dug from out of the earth, and to the state of impurity of the neophytes, which is given greater stress in this sect.[2] In the adjacent parish of Babile, the ritual takes another form, known as *Bo kãã*, the Oil Bagre. The difference between the two forms lies primarily in the way the neophytes are marked during the *Bo pir* (Whitening) ceremony, when they are set aside from ordinary human company. At this time the Oil Bagre uses the fat prepared from the shea nut to rub on the arms and bodies, though whitewash is put on the face itself. The Dirt Bagre, on the other hand, uses the whitewash to cover the whole body of its would-be members in white stripes, though the whitewash is in fact referred to as 'oil'.

The act of whitening also appears in closely parallel ritual contexts, especially at the burial ceremony when a widow (and to a lesser extent a widower) is covered all over—not simply painted in stripes. Bagre, I was told, 'is [like?] a funeral'. And as in a funeral, the whitewash does not simply set one apart; it purifies you of

---

[1] For an account of such ceremonies among the Bambara see Zahan (1960).
[2] The situation is more complex than this brief statement allows. The neophytes are not so much impure in themselves as (like children) standing in danger from the impurity of others. This is why they cannot sleep with women.

your sins (such as forbidden sexual intercourse), it protects you from misfortune (e.g. the return of the ghost), and at the same time it has the power to harm or to kill the wearer, if he fails to confess his sin.[1]

There are some other differences between the two sects. Whereas in the Dirt Bagre the neophytes are forbidden to attend markets or funerals until the very end, in the Oil Bagre they are taken around the market before the performances are finished. This opposition between the two sects forms part of the instruction given to the neophytes in the course of the ceremony itself (W. 4441). And it is stressed even more in informal contexts. For the initiates of the Dirt Bagre say they stand in fear of the others because their prohibitions are less stringent (they are said to permit sexual intercourse) and their performances more hurried; they only decide to perform Bagre when they see the size of the harvest (2641). Nevertheless such opposition is of a strictly limited kind, for the adherents of the different rituals attend each other's performances as well as interacting in other contexts of social action. As the myth again suggests (W. 4430), attendance at different rites may lead to an assimilation of ritual forms and hence to further differentiation and diffusion among the lodges of the same sect. This process is recognized by the actors, for two lineages will speak of themselves as having the same Bagre medicine, that is as having obtained the ritual from the same source, accounting in this way for the similarities in their performances. At the same time they recognize that even lineages that make such a claim may differ in other aspects of their procedures, as is the case with the Naayili and Kyaa patriclans of Birifu. The process of ritual differentiation is a continuous one.

Other associations

There is another society of this general type that has special relationships with Bagre. Just beyond Babile lies the LoDagaba settlement of Tanchera, which is the local centre for the performance of *Dɔɔro*, a cult that is probably associated with the important Gyoro ceremony that occurs in the Bakye area of the Ivory Coast

---

[1] K. G. comments: 'The whitewashing of the widow or widower after the funeral (*guɔ yɔɔra*) is to restrain him or her from doing anything rash, such as committing suicide. This period gives him or her the time to reconcile the inevitable with the evitable. However, in Bagre the whitewash restrains a person from going against the rules laid down (e.g. against sexual intercourse).'

(Labouret 1931: 414). These performances, which again take place mainly at night (and where fire is strictly forbidden), have to be carried out before people see the first whitewashed neophytes of the Bagre, that is, before the guinea corn is cut. Bagre (*Bo pla*) is also performed in Tanchera and I attended parts of both sequences there over a six-day period in October 1950. The same people participate in both and visitors are welcome to the esoteric part of the ritual, which includes characteristic songs, dances, and dress.

I make this point to emphasize that these associations rarely serve as indexes of cultural identity. Like Rotary Clubs and Masonic Orders they transcend local and tribal affiliations. Although at any one time a group obviously either does or does not practice a specific cult, the influence of these associations is seen as capable of extending or contracting. In Birifu the story is often told of how the Dagaba of Jirapa to the east tried to adopt Bagre. When they 'killed' all their initiates, they were unable to revive them since they had used clubs rather than medicine for the purpose. A more recent incident of the same kind was said to have occurred in Biro, on the southern boundary of Birifu. The grandfather of the present headman arranged to perform Bagre but four people were killed and he was told to stop. The reason given for their failure was that, when beginning the Bagre recital, they addressed only the ancestors, the guardian spirits, and the Earth shrine, omitting to call upon the beings of the wild and the (Bagre) deity that play such a central role in the ritual. This reasoning brings out the importance of exact memorization and the correct performance of the ritual, a matter which is constantly brought to the attention of the initiates.

There is one further cult in Birifu which resembles these. It is that of the Night Cow (*tinsɔɔ naab*), which involves the discovery that the cow is really a bull-roarer. The cult has implications for health and well-being, but plays only a very minor part in the social life of the LoDagaa and like Vukãlɛ (Goody 1969: 137) it has little to do with the pantheon of supernatural agencies. It seems as if it were an association on the way out and while it is not exclusively for the young (like Vukãlɛ), adults do not take it at all seriously, even though it does involve the killing of fowls (526). Given that these associations and cults are mobile over time and space, one would naturally expect to find them on the way out as well as on the way in.

Reasons for joining Bagre

Just as there is decay, so too there is revival and expansion. I myself met two elders from Birifu who had made a journey of about 100 miles southwards into Gonja in order to revive Bagre in a LoBirifor settlement where it had not been performed for a number of years.

There are many reasons for the spread and contraction of these cults. But from the actors' standpoint what counts is their success or failure in promoting and maintaining health (in the widest sense). It is often ill health, or the fear of ill health, that leads a person to join himself or to enter his child. In fact, a person does not join but is 'caught' (*nyɔ*) by Bagre, a state which is revealed by the diviner when he is approached on that individual's behalf. Either because of a diviner's diagnosis or in order to prevent a future misfortune, the individual's father will have him made a member when a suitable opportunity arises. If for example a child has a guinea-worm which will not get better, then his father goes to consult a diviner. If the latter attributes the sickness to *Bagr ngmin* (say the LoDagaba, who do not use the term *wen*), you should spurt water on the child. For 'the Bagre god has caught you' (*Bag ngmin wa nyɔ fu bin*) and the child must be made a member when the ceremony is next performed. Thus the specific reasons for putting anyone into Bagre are largely 'medical', to 'ward off trouble' (see B. 1346).

Not everyone belongs, for the expense is heavy (requiring much guinea corn and many fowls) but its membership covers some 75 per cent of the population. Initiates enter at all ages. It is generally the case that the richer the family the earlier the age of entry, reinforcing the idea that it is regarded on one level as a kind of insurance. And since it is the responsibility of the father (or the husband of a married woman) to look after the health of his dependants, it is his responsibility to see them through the Bagre.

It is the health aspect, too, that means there is a wide age-range among the neophytes. For example, the Chief of Nandom (Lo-Dagaba) was an old man when he became a member. He had a sickness that 'troubled him every day; his skin was hot', but when he became initiated the disease was cured. This transformation occurred when the whitewash was put on. As in funeral cere-monies, this act is equivalent to making an exculpatory oath, usually to the Earth from whence the chalk comes (Goody 1962: 58).

People become neophytes not only when they are ill or after they have recovered from sickness, but also beforehand, in order to prevent the onset of disease (53). Joining after a recovery from sickness is probably the result of a conditional oath to *Bo wen*, made either by the neophyte or by someone on his behalf, which promised that he would become a member if he came through successfully. The same point concerning health is made by Labouret, who attended many ceremonies.

Celles qui se font initier viennent généralement d'être malades et désirent éviter une rechute. Quelquefois aussi, une consultation du devin les a averties que, pour échapper aux dangers les menaçant, il est indispensable qu'elles s'affilient à la secte du Bagré (1931: 461).

He also stresses two other points that my observations confirm, namely, the mobility of the cult and its character at once local and yet international.

Cette confrérie n'est pas purement villageoise, d'ordinaire le prêtre qui instruit de nouveaux adeptes en rassemble de dix à trente ou davantage, appartenant à des agglomérations voisines.

Regarding its mobility, he says that all his informants were agreed that 'this association came from the East, that is, the Northern Territories of the Gold Coast [Ghana], from whence it spread with various modifications', among different linguistic and cultural groups, being especially characteristic of the LoDagaba ('Dagari') and the Wiili ('Oulé'); the LoBirifor of Gaoua in the northern Ivory Coast adopted the cult about 1870 and knew the name of the man who had first introduced it and why he had done so.[1]

[1] K. G. comments: 'The frequency of Bagre performance in each sector depends on the ability of the head of the family to carry it out and also on the call of *Bo wen*, which is manifested by unknown disease in one of the non-initiates in the family. Thus in about 1929 *wen* descended in our family and wanted us to perform the Bagre. Unfortunately, according to my father, I was the victim of *wen*, and hence our house had to perform the Bagre again although it had been done a few years back. Similarly in 1939 *wen* descended on our house and demanded a performance. This time Teungdire became the victim of *wen*. The sickness brought by *wen* is normally unknown but usually took the form of a feverish ailment.

'The reason for joining is not necessarily dependent on the descent of *wen*. It is to educate all and sundry in that which brings peace and prosperity. The

The functions of Bagre

If the initial reasons for joining are largely 'medical', the reasons for continuing to participate are mainly social. Each grade of membership has various duties, and progression through the society is a matter of some pride to the individual. The performance of the ceremonies themselves, the food, the beer, the music, the throng of dancers, the subjection of the neophytes to ordeals through which one has successfully passed—all is a source of pleasure to the initiated.

There is another important role that Bagre plays. People aim to perform the main part of the ceremony when the moon is full, for the dancing is a special feature of the rites. The senior spectators sit round and drink from the large pots of beer, while the younger ones dance *Bo bine* up till the performance of Bagre Day, and after that it is *Bo sior* as well.[1] For all it is a time of relaxation and enjoyment. Men and women will sit on the rooftop conversing and drinking beer, simultaneously out of the same gourd if they are on friendly terms, while the young use dancing as a means of courtship. My friend Kpaari deliberately went there with the intention of securing another wife (a good dancer attracts a lot of attention, though some of this is unwelcome and associated with wizardry) and claimed that most marriages were made at this period (45). Bagre is the time for enjoyment and courting.

One minor function of the Bagre is to act as a 'friendly society'. When I visited the aged Tɔntɔl, one of the oldest men in Birifu, he was lying naked on his mat, with only a thin cloth as a cover.

Naayili clan have had several performances through the years but only on these two occasions were they compelled to do it because *Bo wen* had manifested itself. In fact the reasons on medical grounds are rare.' We perhaps need to differentiate the reasons why individuals enter from those that lead a clan sector to undertake a performance; these usually happen at fairly regular intervals.

[1] K. G. comments: '*Bo bine* is the dance danced at Bagre. It is also the name for the tunes played at ordinary dances, known as *diɛn*: *N kyiera diɛn zie*, I am going to the place where *bo bine* is played.

'*Bo sior* is the period from *Bo tīnsɔɔ* to *Bo gyingyire*. The same dance, *Bo bine*, is played continuously for the three days, but at a slower tempo. In Birifu, at ordinary dances (*diɛn*), the *bo bine* is played first. The dancers dance their fill; towards the end of the night *sior* is played to round off the dance. In Lawra (LoDagaba) it is the other way round. They start with *sior* (LD. *sɛbri*) and finish with *bine*.

'In Bagre both dances are played interchangeably depending upon the mood both of the players and the dancers, but more *bine* is played in Birifu while the reverse is true in Lawra.'

My companions advised him that as he was a senior member of Bagre, he was entitled to *bo foba*. These clothes, consisting of a smock and baggy trousers, are bought with money collected by the neophytes; what they get is divided into half, one lot going for clothes, one lot to the Bagre 'mother', that is the organizer. Mainly these purchases are used for draping round the funeral stand of a member, especially a poor one, for funerals are always an occasion for display and if you do not have, you borrow. But the living too can wear the clothes; indeed, I was told that since the clothes were *tiib*, that is, bought with money collected through a shrine, they were good to wear as a protection when one travelled abroad, but this use was not generally accepted (154).

Finally, moving from the realm of manifest to latent functions (or rather from functions that are actor-based to those that are observer-based), the integrative aspect of these ceremonies requires some consideration. While such remarks must remain largely impressionistic, I noted that of the two communities, Birifu with Bagre and Tom virtually without, the former is very much more 'integrated', in terms of the making of political decisions, both under party politics as well as under colonial rule, in the resistance to missionary influence, and in general tone. While one cannot relate this difference directly to the performance of Bagre (to which in any case there could be many functional alternatives), it is the case that those ceremonies require the constant and intimate co-operation of the patriclans into which the inhabitants of the settlement are divided.

This co-operation takes place on a number of different levels. In the first place, the main meals are divided out by patriclan. Portions are given to all the patriclans living in the parish and each group eats somewhat apart from the others. No ceremony is complete without the participation of all segments.

Secondly the lineage performing the ceremonies requires other segments to undertake specific services. Certain of these, connected with the ancestors, require the help of other lineages of the same clan. In this case elders from the non-participating lineages address the shrines and carry out the sacrifices. In other cases, a joking partner (*bo lɔnluɔrbe*) is needed to 'make hot things cool'; such partners are always from another clan.

Thirdly, every clan has a number of relationships which are of an occasional kind, but which take on a reciprocating character.

The group invites one or more clans to provide the Speakers to recite the Bagre myth.[1] Another group provides the xylophones that are played in the room. With yet another clan one is accustomed to divide one's share of Bagre produce.[2]

Finally, the ceremonies themselves are organized by a group of elders from the whole parish, who consult together (but do not always agree) about how the performance should be carried out and who should provide the Speaker during the important parts of the ceremonies—acting on behalf, as it were, of the clan that has been specifically invited. The Bagre performances thus require the interaction, over a long period in the year, of the major segments of the parish at all levels, among the elders, the adults, the young men, and even the children who flock to watch the dancing. Conflict as well as co-operation is the result, but the interaction is close and continuous.

Ritual services: change and exchange

The network of services performed by other groups includes acting as the Speaker, at least for the invocation and on other important occasions. When Maale carried out their Bagre in 1950, it was the senior initiate in Kyaa, Bɔyiri, who spoke to their neophytes—*o la so a nuor*, 'he owns the mouth', even for prayers to the ancestors. For Naayili (Wuurader's lineage), the same services were performed by a lineage in their own clan sector, though in earlier

[1] K. G. comments: 'If Naayili are performing the Bagre, they may hire (*yar*) Kyaa to be the main instructors at the Bagre. If Kyaa have not got many leading Speakers, they invite ones from other sectors to help, or even from Naayili itself. Yinkwo and Doyeri from Naayili were always invited to help, even if they were not hired. In this case the helpers are not entitled to a share of the Speakers' lot but because of their services they are normally given something'.

[2] K. G. comments· 'Until of late there were only a few persons with the big xylophones in Birifu suitable for the Bagre room: Gandaa, Terkoder, and some others. Similarly there were very few people who could play the tunes in the room. So during Chief Gandaa's lifetime his xylophones were always hired for the occasion. Although technically two xylophones (*gyil berɛ*) were supposed to be provided, the chief normally sent for four for the Bagre tunes and a smaller one (*gyil bil*) for the ordinary dancing.

'In addition to the hired instruments, any other player can bring his own xylophones but he is not entitled to payment. Each neophyte pays one live fowl for the xylophones and another for the drum (*bo kuɔr nuɔ*). In addition he gives enough malted grain to brew beer (*gyil dãã*) which the hirer gives players assisting him at the ceremony.'

years their partners had been another clan, that is, Baaperi. These arrangements are known as Bagre joking partnerships, at least when outside the patriclan.

A different set of partnerships exists for the sharing of meat. Kyaa share with Naayili (for they have the same Bagre medicine), while Baaperi share with Yongyuole. But the year I attended the Baaperi Bagre, they refused any longer to share in this way, for reasons that were obscure to me. Because of their refusal, the senior men of Kyaa and Maale, Bŏyiri and Depep, would not attend their performances; 'if you reject your partners (*dibzie*, place of eating), you spoil (*sɔ̃ɔ̃n*) the Bagre'. The result was that Baaperi entered into a new partnership, while Yongyuole were discussing what to do. The critical time would not come until Bagre was performed in their own section, but meanwhile the problem was talked over on sundry occasions. I heard one suggestion that they should share with Kyaa, but another man present pointed out that Kyaa was already sharing with Naayili and they would only get a return of half of what they gave (906). The calculation of reciprocity was quite specific.

I mention this point in order to make it clear that, as with the exchanges of services in funeral ceremonies (Goody 1962: 65), partnerships of this kind are subject to many pressures to change. At any one point in time such arrangements look permanent enough; but new alignments are constantly in the process of formation.

The reasons for these changes are many. Firstly, reciprocity in food depends largely on equality of numbers. When one group increases, it receives less by way of concrete benefits from its earlier partners (906). Secondly, disputes and disagreements over other matters are reflected in the Bagre partnerships; if another type of debt remains unsettled, you may refuse to meet your Bagre obligations. This is the point where political considerations of various kinds enter in; and the result of such a withdrawal may be that the allies of one's former partners boycott the proceedings, as happened with Bŏyiri and Depep at the Bagre ceremonies of 1950. Non-attendance at ceremonies is one of the most common ways of expressing disapproval. As with resignation from committees, others are sure to ask the reason why. But in any case to attend a ceremony that one believes is being wrongly performed is to invite mystical trouble (Goody 1962: 104).

Recruitment

While the Bagre association is organized on a parish basis, its ceremonies are conducted on a lineage level. Any year the performance is arranged by a particular clan sector such as Naayili or Kyaa (or one of their constituent lineages), and only members of that group can become neophytes. This number can include female as well as male members; even if they have married out, women retain membership of their natal clans for this and other purposes. There were forty-two neophytes at the Bagre held by Maale in 1950, including the wife of Bizɔɔla, a teacher from the house of the late chief. While the father has the responsibility of putting a daughter through Bagre, he will be reimbursed by the husband since she has now joined another household. For both sons and daughters, the father (known in this context as the *Bo ma* or 'Bagre mother') has to collect the very considerable amount of grain and chickens required for the performance. But this responsibility changes over time depending on the bridewealth status of the daughter. The LoDagaa pay bridewealth in a series of instalments, the largest of which is made when a woman has borne her husband two or three children and has therefore 'built his house'. When this payment (*doɛ̃*) has been made, the woman becomes one of 'our housepeople' (*lieb a ti yirsob*); 'She observes our taboos (*kyiiru*) and we will induct her into our Bagre.'

It might appear as if the woman has now become a member of her husband's lineage, and this certainly is one meaning of the phrase *lieb a ti yirsob*. But she still remains a member of her natal group for some purposes and at her final funeral ceremony it is to her father's people that her ancestor shrine is carried by her clan sisters. I should add that the observance of one's husband's taboos occurs earlier in a marriage and is a matter partly of religion, partly of respect, partly of convenience. A woman observes these taboos while she is pregnant 'because of the child inside' (2788); for the child will belong to its father's patriclan as well as to its mother's matriclan. But a woman who wishes to show respect to her husband may well observe his prohibitions at other times; there is nothing to stop one observing extra prohibitions; it is only the minimum that is laid down.

In Birifu there is no set order for the lineages or clan sectors to perform their Bagre. In 1950 the Maale and Baaperi sections were in action; in 1948 Kyaa had performed; in 1949 there was nothing; in 1951 Naayili (Wuurader's lineage) and Kyaa (Konkyol's lineage) had theirs. In 1952 Ngmanbili proper decided to hold their performances. The question is left to a particular lineage because they have to decide, on the basis of preliminary inquiries, whether there is enough grain, fowls, and potential initiates to perform it successfully. The actual choice of initiates will rest with the sponsors themselves, since it is they who have to produce the grain. These individual decisions are crystallized at the first ceremony, the Asperging of the Initiates (*Bo puɔru*) which is also known as *Bii yir*, Choosing the Children. The particular house at which the Bagre takes place is an ordinary compound known as the *Bo yir* (the house of Bagre), which is special only in that it has the Bagre shrine (*Bo wen*) in the neck of the granary that protrudes through the roof and must have a long room (*kyaara*) large enough for the performances 'in the room'. The head of this house is known as the *Bo sob*, the owner of Bagre. He has to be a senior member, otherwise he would not possess the Bagre shrine and its 'medicine'.

Bagre roles

The senior men in Bagre (there is at least one from each clan sector) are known as the Bagre Speakers (*Bo nɛtuuri*), those whose mouth (words) you follow. It is they who recite (*kaabena*, a verb used only for ritual speech, prayer; or *kɔɔra*) and the neophytes repeat the lines after them. In the White Bagre, the Speakers do all the reciting, while the others follow. But in the Black Bagre, as the myth explains, they are not the only ones who do so. Anyone who has learnt the words may be asked to take a turn (W. 4430).[1] Among the LoDagaba, the senior Speaker, the one who starts the Bagre, is sometimes known as the *zangbaalsob*, the owner of the *zangbaal* or top slat of the xylophone, which often lacks the usual gourd hanging underneath as a sounding box. The same slat is also called '*paaro ziɛ*; *o'paarena* describes the regular rhythmic beating of this slat, which acts as an accompaniment to the melody, especially when there is no second xylophone being played. As the Speaker recites, the rhythm is beaten out, for example, on one of the

---

[1] K. G. comments: 'Permission is first granted and when he accepts to lead he has to thank the person giving him permission as well as all those people inside and outside before continuing from where the recitation left off. He does not actually sit on the stool but stays at his place. Usually the reciters stand when the Black Bagre is chanted.'

wooden troughs used for feeding pups. This man is known in Birifu as the xylophone player (*gyil kpiere*). In the Black Bagre, he also shakes a rattle to the rhythm of the verse. The rhythm differs substantially in the White and Black recitations, the former being slow and measured, the latter being quick and chanted.

The accompaniment is especially important in the invocation with which the White Bagre begins, for this is a kind of greeting or prayer. First the Speaker taps (greets) the Earth shrine (*ngmɛ a tengaan*), then he taps on the gods (*ngmɛ a ngmin zu*), then on all the ancestors. This invocation is repeated at various times in the Bagre recitation, forming a general appeal to supernatural agencies.

'The owner of the slat' is also known as *semaansob*, owner of the farm (2236), who was described to me as the *tengaansob* (custodian of the Earth shrine) within the Bagre. He will take the leg of the sacrificial fowl normally reserved for the Earth priest, for example at the opening ceremony. He takes it to the lineage of the Earth priest, who first accept it, then give it back, saying ' If you want to eat it, do so; if you want to throw it away, do so.'

The 'Bagre mother' (*bo ma*) is a name used for any senior member from whose house people are becoming neophytes (167).[1] But it also refers more specifically to the owner of the house in which Bagre is taking place. Some restrictions are placed upon all 'Bagre mothers', for they cannot both sleep with their wives and eat Bagre food. The domain of the family and the domain of the fraternity are kept apart by this prohibition, and the same split is given explicit recognition in the text, where the conflict of obligations to kin and colleague is brought out in the discussion of the way in which the game killed in the Bagre hunt is divided (B. 2480).

Finally, there are the guides (*bo kyiine*, lit. herders). It is the guide's responsibility to watch over his neophyte and to see that no harm comes to him. For this reason he has to avoid certain actions. In the Final Funeral Ceremony, persons standing in various relationships to the dead man (all of them 'orphans') sit round his quiver, which is his material representation. At one point they draw out the arrows and keep them. If a person who at that time is acting as a guide does this, he should at once go and bury the arrow in a swamp. If he puts the arrow in his own quiver he might kill an animal which his charge would eat; if the neophyte did so, he would die (3083). He has been brought into contact with death.

---

[1] As, for example, in the song on p. 100.

The grades of Bagre

There are two main stages of Bagre, the White and the Black. Those who have passed the first grade are known as *bo pele* (sing. *bo pla*); those who have passed the second grade are known as *bo sɔɔli* (sing. *bo sɔɔla*). Alternative names for the second graders or senior initiates are *bo kyuurdem*, referring to the skin bag acquired on this occasion; or *gan dem*, referring to the leather bottle used to hold the marked cowries. There is another stage which one must reach before a son or daughter is initiated; persons who have passed this stage are known as *bo tĩĩ dem* (or *kyüli dem*), referring to the Bagre medicine that they now possess.

The ceremonies that I describe later relate mainly to initiation into the first grade. There is only one ceremony for the second grade, which lasts a single night. Junior members (*bo pele*) have to act as assistants or guides to the new entrants. Each neophyte also requires the help of a senior member in the most crucial rituals. Only they can perform the major roles in Bagre and only they can act as sponsors (*bo ma*) of new entrants; indeed, to be a sponsor a man has to reach the third stage of 'owner of the Bagre medicine' used to kill and revive the initiates.

In addition to these two grades, there is also the category of non-initiates (*dakume*), which includes those who have not yet been initiated, or those who are forbidden to join the society.[1] Finally, there are the new entrants themselves who are in the process of going through the ceremonies (*bobil*, little Bagre members); these I refer to as neophytes or novices. Members are known generally as *bo kari*. While women can become members, they can only be first graders, except in very special circumstances.

Bagre equipment

The material equipment is given to the neophytes at the Whitening Ceremony; it consists of a small round gourd (*kuɔr*), an iron bell (*gbelmɛ*) and a skin bag (*wuo*) in which to keep them; however, the gourd is destroyed at the end of the Bagre dance. Initiation to the second grade leads to the acquisition of a leather bottle (*gan*), together with some marked cowries, another skin bag (*bo kyuur*). The Bagre medicine (*tĩĩ, kyiili*) itself is acquired during

---

[1] The same word is used in connection with other such associations (e.g. Dyooro and the Night Cow).

every ritual series, since each man wanting to enter his housepeople has first to get the medicine.

Apart from the medicine, this equipment is similar to that employed by diviners; the bell is always associated with the beings of the wild and is used to call upon them to assist in the fact-finding process. But in the Bagre the only time the 'divinatory' apparatus is used is at the end of the Bagre Dance and at the death of a senior member. Even this is a mock divination and the tools that are given to the initiate resemble those given to Masons when they are made members of a lodge. Among the LoDagaa, Bagre is not in fact an initiation into a diviners' association, such as exists in parts of Gonja (in Busunu, for example); it is concerned to offer some protection (as the myth insists at the very beginning) against the misfortunes of life, *dune non, kure piime*, the biting of scorpions, the taking of one's life, a brand of protection not offered by other 'deities'. These mystical problems are the very ones that are raised at the beginning of the recitation; they worried the elder of the two 'first men', so that he could not sleep and went off to consult a diviner, who showed him the way, the Bagre way. Parents are under great pressure to do their best for their children by providing them with ritual prophylactics. By entering Bagre, the text goes, 'we seek a head that sits on our shoulders'. Not only is knowledge acquired but also protection against death, disease, and similar misfortunes.

This medicine is used in the gravest of the rites of the White Bagre, that in which the neophytes are killed and then revived. Here the latent function of slaughter and resurrection, of death and rebirth, is similar to that found in many other such performances, from the cult of Osiris to the Order of Freemasons. But from the actor's standpoint, the ritual has a different, manifest function: it bears witness to the concern about death and disease, and about the possibility of overcoming death which the Bagre medicine holds out. This is a concern not about the after-life (though ideas on this are expressed in the course of a funeral), but about death as the end of life and as the punishment for, or result of, wrong-doing.

In the second recitation, the comfort that the Bagre medicine offers to the neophyte in its promise of resurrection is shown to be illusory, but membership of the society may still ward off death and disease, even if it cannot repair the ultimate damage they do.

And for the actors, or at any rate for their sponsors, it is this comfort that is in the long run more important than the opportunity to eat one's fill, to meet one's peers and kin, and to advance one's status in the community, though these considerations are all relevant to the analysis of such performances.

An individual's Bagre bag is returned and destroyed at his burial ceremony; so too is the medicine and the other accoutrements. And whether the dead man had a diviner's container or a Bagre container, his colleagues will sit at the foot of the funeral stand (*paala per*) on which his body rests and proceed to divine (*buura bɔɔ*).[1] The interlocking nature of divinatory and Bagre procedures and concepts is apparent in these acts. Though it was repeatedly denied to me that Bagre was an association of diviners, the word for divine is *buura bɔɔ* (or *bag*), finding the cause of the mystical trouble; that is to say, the only word for 'divine' or 'diviner' incorporates the word *Bagre*, and the Bagre society does involve divination on these formal occasions, though never at other times.[2] For ordinary divination, one uses the *kɔntɔn gan*,[3] not the *Bo gan* (or *kpo*) of the Bagre. It is the *kɔntɔn* or beings of the wild that guide the diviner and they are the ones (the topic receives a great deal of theological attention in the Black Bagre) who guide the Bagre. Thus my friend Bŏyiri's remark to me, early in our acquaintance, was very significant. 'The container of the beings of the wild', he remarked, 'is the more important. The *kɔntɔme* own the Bagre (*so a bɔɔ*); it is they who seize the neophytes (*bɛ nyora bobil*)' (402). I was told this at Daazie's burial. On the second day, a representative of each lineage in the clan sector gathered at his feet to

---

[1] The Bagre divination is carried out at the foot of the funeral stand by the senior members present. They will divine three times with the Bagre container (*Bo gan* or *yuon gan*, outside container) and three times with the being's container (*kɔntɔm gan* or *diu gan*, room container). Money is collected and shared among the other clans of the parish, though not by the dead man's group (504).

[2] K. G. notes that the diviners' invocation is also repeated in the Black Bagre, though I did not record it in the present instance. 'They often greet the strangers in the crowd, asking for a quick mind and a tongue that does not falter. They go on to greet the outside creatures (that is, the other shrines outside the house) and then the inside ones. They greet the hills, the rivers, the Earth shrine in their own village and later greet similar beings and things in the neighbouring settlements. Thus in Birifu they would greet Babile, Tugu, Tanchera, Kwŏnyŭkwŏ, Meto, Manduor, Gbetuor and similar places before starting the actual story.'

[3] *Gan* .. skin; both *gan* and *kpo* refer to the leather bottle in which a diviner or a member keeps his cowries.

'divine' with his Bagre container. One man was handed the leather bottle and shook out two cowries at a time until they landed favourably (one up, one down). The container was then handed to the next man, who did the same. This was not true divination: the participants are essentially 'taking out the dream', that is, separating themselves from the memory of a man with whom they had performed these acts in the past. In other parts they throw the cowries on the first day of the burial ceremony and continue every morning and evening for the three days it lasts (2473).

When the body has been interred, the Bagre container is also buried, and a chicken is given to the man who does it and a hen to those who 'divined'. The leather container holding the Bagre medicine is placed in an ant-hill, so that it will be utterly destroyed by the termites (2473). At this time three fowls are killed, roasted, and distributed among the second graders present.

At the second of the major funeral ceremonies, the Hot Funeral Beer, beer is specially brewed for the senior members of Bagre, the *bokyurdãã*. The joking partners take some of the top of one of the pots (*bɛ vuona a nuɔr a dãã iɔng*), throw some cowries and then take a gourd full of the beer to the ancestor shrines.

At the Final Funeral Ceremony of a Bagre member there is more divination with the *kpo*. When they throw the cowries (*loba libie*), they sing a catchy Bagre song (*bɛ ngmiɛri bagr*), in which they salute various categories of diviners.

They greet all diviners that use the stick (*dakuorsob*);
Bɛ puri a bagbuuri zaa

They greet the owners of books with their pens (those who divine with books),
bɛ puri a gandem ni bɛ magdaali

they greet those who read the sand.
bɛ puri a biir ngmiɛrɛ.

They also salute a number of animals and places connected with divination and with the beings of the wild. They greet the *bur lani*, a fish that swims alongside a canoe, which it can sink with a bone; a fish that listens to what is being said (in the boat and elsewhere), and tells it to the River, where the beings live.

They greet the River Volta, *na man*, chief of rivers. And they greet the hippopotamus (*'yen*) and the stinging fish (*man garka*).

The whole greeting corresponds to the opening invocation of an Ashanti diviner, which acknowledges the major categories of supernatural being, of the natural world, and of former practitioners, before going on to deliver the message.

Bagre prohibitions

A wide variety of prohibitions is placed upon those undergoing the initiatory rituals. Some are general restrictions placed on the behaviour of all who attend. For example, there is a prohibition on 'fighting' (i.e. quarrelling) during the course of the ceremonies, an example of the widespread institution of 'ritual peace' found on such occasions. Another general ban is on sexual intercourse, a ban which also obtains in hunting and in war. In these essentially male activities, the 'dirt' that comes from sleeping with a woman has a damaging effect on the individual; but the point is also that medicines are frequently seen as being weakened by the sexual act.

Other actions are prohibited during a specific ceremony, for instance the drinking of water or beer out of a calabash from which someone else has just drunk. The most important of these specific taboos are those on eating certain new crops. These foods include both wild and domestic varieties, namely the shea fruit, bean leaves, beans, yams, and bambara beans. Before the appropriate ceremony has been performed, the neophyte is forbidden to eat them, on pain of heavy fines and even expulsion from the proceedings.[1]

The food taboos are thus progressively raised as the performances go on, somewhat in the manner discussed by Radcliffe-Brown for the Andamans (1922). But the items prohibited are not always ones that have any great importance outside the context of the Bagre itself. From the actor's standpoint, some of them, such as the shea fruit, are prohibited because when they are ripe they indicate the time for beginning one of the performances.

If these prohibitions can be said to indicate 'ritual value' (and I hold no brief for this particular formula), they do so only partly in relation to the objects tabooed. They also emphasize the 'ritual value' of the fraternity itself, whose procedures are thereby set aside from those of the daily round (the sacred set off against the profane, but again the formula obscures as much as it reveals), and made perhaps more awesome as well, especially since the break-

---

[1] The list given in the White Bagre includes guinea corn, ground-nut soup, and chicken.

ing of a prohibition is thought to entail severe supernatural sanctions. For the actor, certainly, the taboos have more than emblematic significance, though this is reasonably seen as one of their latent functions.

Finally, there is a category of prohibitions which one acquires as a member of the fraternity itself. One rule of this kind is the prohibition on resting a gourd from which you are drinking on one of the grass rings used by women to support a pot of beer on the head. Such prohibitions mark off a member of the society from the mere uninitiated; like the Masonic handshake, they quietly identify members.

The Bagre calendar

As the myth relates, the timing of the Bagre ceremonies usually turns upon the ripening of the new crops that are forbidden to the neophytes. When these are ready, there is a danger that the novices may do wrong by eating the forbidden food before the appropriate ceremony has been performed. Hence the organizers make haste to arrange for the malted grain to be collected and the beer to be brewed so that the ceremony can be held two days later.

The first ceremony, the Asperging of the Neophytes, has no specific season. I have known it done in August although the main sequence of rites does not begin until the following June. Indeed it is often combined with the first of the main series, that is the Announcement of Bagre, which takes place when the fruit of the shea tree is ripe. This ceremony is associated with the legend of the large fruit-bat who came across a shea fruit after a quarrel with his mate about sexual intercourse, which had been refused. Because of his help in discovering the first of the new crop, the fruit-bat is the foremost in the category of 'Bagre animals' (B. 3702). Most of the other 'Bagre animals' (W. 4583) are also associated with the timing of ceremonies but in a more specific way. Some recurrent aspect of their behaviour indicates the time of year when a rite should be held.

The Announcement of Bagre is followed soon afterwards by the Bagre of Beans (in fact, of bean leaves used for soup). There follows a gap while the major crops are harvested and the ceremonies begin again in early December with the preparation of the medicine, followed by the Whitening Ceremony. The remainder continue at intervals of a week (that is, a six-day week) and are completed by mid January, the ceremonies in any one sequence normally starting on the same week-day each time.

In the following table I list the ceremonies that took place in or near the settlements in which I lived during the years 1950 to 1952.

The Bagre timetable

	Birifu 1950–51		Elsewhere
	Baaperi	Maale	
1. Bo puɔru (Asperging the Neophytes)			
2. Bo wuur (The Announcement of Bagre)			
3. Bo biong (The Bagre of Beans)			
4. Bo tīī dãã (The Beer for the Bagre Medicine)	1/12	They did not do it this year as they had done it last.	
5. Bo pir (The Whitening Ceremony)	7/12	8/12	Tugu 2/12 Tanchera 3/12 Babili 13/12
6. Kengmir (The Beating of the Malt)	19/12	16/12	
7. Bo siɔr (The Bagre Dance)	25/12	31/12	Tanchera 27/12 Tugu 25/12 Nadoli 19/1
8. Bo tuur (Bagre Gifts)		3/1	
9. Bo gbelmɛ (Bagre Bells)	6/1	12/1	
10. Tiib puru (Bo paal dãã) (Thanksgiving)		17/1	

	1951–2		1952–3	
	Birifu		Gwo	Birifu
	Naayili	Kyaa	Bekuone	Ngmanbili
1.	8/5	} 5/7		
2.	2/5			
3.	29/6		25/6	
4.				26/11
5.				2/12

This is the sequence of ceremonies that I describe in Chapter 5 and that are discussed in the first part of the myth, the White Bagre. The White Bagre begins with a visit to the diviner, which is what usually prompts a father to enter his child. The Asperging of the Neophytes is referred to straight away (W. 45). This is followed by the Bagre of Beans (W. 209), when they eat the bean leaves. Then they eat new yams (W. 364). This leads on to the Ceremony of the Bean Flower (W. 557), which is connected with the old guinea cock and his mate; now beans are eaten. They had, however, omitted to perform the Announcement of Bagre (W. 741), which is associated with the large fruit-bat and his mate, and with the prohibition on shea nuts, which are made into butter. They measure the grain for beer (W. 1081) and return to this ceremony.

When the harvest is in and the dry season upon them, the Whitening Ceremony begins (W. 1600). This involves collecting 'shea oil' (whitewash), fibre, and a small gourd. After the Whitening Ceremony the neophytes collect grain and are given detailed instructions as to how this should be done. It is at the Beating of the Malt that they start to collect fowls (the text referring to this ceremony appears to begin at W. 2226).

They discuss the Beating of the Malt in some detail (W. 2440). But the being of the wild interferes and they start on the performances for Bagre Eve, which is that part of the main ceremony of the Bagre Dance where the neophytes are killed. The neophytes are indeed killed but the elders are unable to revive them. It appears that the Beating of the Malt has been omitted (W. 2925). The being of the wild awakens the neophytes, but they had to return to the Beating of the Malt (W. 3037), with its communal hunt for wild animals. This is followed by the Bagre Dance (W. 3481). Food is prepared and the neophytes are killed (W. 3828). There is still some problem about waking them (W. 4259) but this is done and the appropriate Bagre songs are sung (W. 4352). The instruction is continued (W. 4367) and this ceremony ends with the day called Bo Gyingyiri (W. 4963). A week later there is Bagre Bells (W. 5501) when the bells given to the neophytes are washed. There is another hunt and more confessing and questioning before the ritual sequence ends with the hope that initiates will go on to the second grade, the Black Bagre. The text of the Black Bagre is not itself connected with the ritual sequence nor with the ritual calendar.

4

THE BAGRE MYTH

The recitation of Bagre

IN the previous chapters I have outlined some facts about
the Bagre association and discussed some aspects of its role in
the communities where it is found. But from the standpoint of the
present volume the most important aspect is the recitation of the
Bagre 'myth', which constitutes a unique feature of this particular
society. In contrast to other continents, Africa has few recorded
myths of this kind, if by this word we refer to a text of the actors
rather than the observers, and certainly none of this length or span.
In this chapter I discuss some aspects of the recitation and the
form it takes.

The Bagre ceremonies are accompanied by the recitation of the
'myth' which serves as a guide to the ritual processes, an explanation of these procedures and a placing of them in a cosmological
scheme. The myth is recited in the Bagre room, away from the
ears of non-initiates, and it is generally done before as well as
during a ceremony. The White Bagre, which contains the order
of service, is recited three times up to the point where the particular ceremony is described.

It is usually the senior of the second graders who begins and
who recites at least the invocatory passages with which the myths
commence. In the White Bagre he is known as the Speaker (*bɔ nɛ-
tuurɛ*). In the Black Bagre, the senior man sits on a three-legged
stool (*da kɔɔ*) though the reciter is said to be 'in the chair' (*kɔɔ zu*).
When he 'leaves the stool', another member has to take up the
chant, usually one of the elders, but in fact any second grader,
however young, may carry out this task, as is explained in the
myth itself (W. 5541). The 'owner of Bagre' has some initiative in
whom he 'hires' to be in the chair. This option was once compared
in my presence to the act of bringing help to the farm. If you have
a close friend (*ba*) and you know he needs help, then you may offer
to bring a party to work on his land; or a man may himself indicate
that such help would be welcome. In return he provides a large

meal and plenty of beer as a recompense.[1] A man who is arranging Bagre may make a similar request to another patriclan (or perhaps more than one) to provide the Speakers; this does not mean that others may not join in or even initiate the proceedings, but they do so on behalf of the invited group who are the ones entitled to share out whatever is due to the chair.

A premium is placed upon a correct rendering of the myth, though clearly variations creep in and become an accepted part of the recitation. Prestige is accorded to those who can recite the myth and their achievement is rewarded not only by general acclaim but also by special allocations of food and beer, which are said to be 'for the chair'.

A much higher pay-off comes when the Bagre is taken up by another community or when a settlement has forgotten the rites and wishes to perform them again. Here the stated reward is said to be one horse and 100,000 cowries, though this sum does not all accrue to the individuals themselves. Once again this contingency and the related payments are quite explicit in the myth (W. 4379).

The actual recitation is done by a single individual sitting on a chair, who chants the short phrases that constitute the 'lines' of the text as I have recorded it. Each line usually contains two stressed syllables and an indefinite number of unstressed ones, but in a chant of this kind, which does not suffer from the constraints imposed either by a strict musical accompaniment or by the formalizing pressures of written composition, a certain degree of flexibility is present.

---

[1] K. G. notes that the farming metaphor is also used when one reciter hands over to another. 'For example, if my "father's brother", Yinkwo, was tired and wanted someone to take over he would say:

Kumbɔɔnɔ yee	Kumbɔɔnɔ,
maa dɔɔ fu	I brought you forth,
ti ziɛ bibiiri	but today
faa nye nuɔri	you have seen the plot
ban ngmaa kuma	they cut for me
kã kɔ bɔ̃ɔ̃ gu	and I've hoed in vain.
fũũ i bie	But if you are a good lad,
kakuor bie	a real farmer's son,
de n nuɔra	relieve me of my work
kɔ ti tani	and hoe part of it for me.

The term *nuɔri* identifies the verse with the strips of land allocated to farmers in a competitive gathering; *kɔ*, hoe, is identified with the recital; *kakuɔr bie*, a farmer's son, is the boy who is able to recite the verse.' The metaphor is quite explicit.

The rhythms are different for the White and Black Bagre, the latter being faster and more complex. The recitation is accompanied by a rhythmic beat (again different in both parts). If a sacrifice is being made at a mound, then those present all take a small stone which they beat against one on the ground. If it is a sacrifice to the Bagre deity, then the sacrificial knife beats out the rhythm. At one stage in the ceremony known as the Beating of the Grain, the initiates sit on the roof of the house holding calabashes of water, representing the beer into which the malted grain will be transformed; each man taps the half-full gourd in time with the chanting of the White Bagre.

The Black Bagre has a different rhythm, often beaten out with two old xylophone sticks, whose rubber tips have been worn down with use, upon a wooden plank (*kpambirɛ*) that covers the entrance to the byre, or upon the hollowed-out trough (*baa leung*) used for feeding young pups. The reciter, the *kɔɔ zu sob* himself, often holds a rattle which he shakes in the proper rhythm. Some members may accompany him and others too may beat the dog-trough. The reciter chants a line of the myth and this is taken up by the whole assembly. Indeed each recital has to be carried out three times, although time is sometimes saved by two men reciting at once.

The language of Bagre

Henri Labouret describes a special language that is used by Bagre members in the Ivory Coast to communicate with one another; it is formed by adding certain standard syllables to each word, such as English children use in 'eggy-peggy'.[1] The added prefix (*numbum*) makes the language almost unintelligible to outsiders (1931: 465).

The use of special languages is just one of the mechanisms of disguise that characterize such societies, others being the use of masks,[2] of voice-disguisers,[3] and of other forms of concealment

[1] Girault also mentions a secret language of Bagre, but in connection with ordinary funerals. Although I do not understand all the sentence he gives, the majority of the words are not secret nor are they of the kind suggested by Labouret (1959: 352).

[2] See B. Holas, *Les Masques Kono* (Paris, 1952). A good example of the masks 'disguising' men as ancestors appears in Achebe's novel *Things Fall Apart*, London, 1958, p. 81.

[3] See H. Balfour, 'Ritual and Secular Uses of Vibrating Membranes as Voice-disguisers', *J. R. Anthrop. Inst.* 78 (1948), pp. 45–69.

such as darkness, closed rooms, and special forms of behaviour. Where such languages are not of the 'eggy-peggy' variety, they may be borrowed from neighbouring peoples. The secret language of the Gyoro society of the Bakye area apparently belongs to the Grusi group (Labouret 1931: 428); the secret language of the Dogon appears to have Mande or Mossi connections (Leiris 1948: 19).

The Bagre of Ghana has no special language that I know of; the text of the myth is in everyday speech. Nevertheless there are some modifications. Firstly, there are certain formulaic modes of composition that characterize the two myths. When an action is described, it is usually done in three (or at least two) phases. The first indicates that the action is about to take place, the second that it is taking place and the third that it has taken place. The following example is taken from the Black Bagre (B. 173).

> Does it please you?
> He said it does so.
> So he spoke
> and when he'd done so . . .

The other linguistic modification consists of words that are special to Bagre. The following are some examples of these usages (2618):

   i. *sambar ata*, in a trice, at once, e.g. *sambar ata ka n'i*, or in ordinary speech, *n na ina pampaana*, I will do it right away. The latter part (*ata*) means thrice in ordinary speech. One cannot use the normal word, *gbaa* (times), in Bagre.
  ii. *aro* (the LoDagaba word) replaces *gbor*, for canoe.
 iii. *o zin kpib* replaces *o zin gbile*, he sits quietly.
  iv. *man gbulu* (or *kpul*) is the big river, the Black Volta (i.e. *man*), or rather a special part at Lawra (1522).
   v. *kolingwiɛ* is *wagya* or *mwo puɔ*, that is, the far bush. When the white man first came they called him *kwolī* or *bong* (slave) because they did not know from whence he came.
  vi. *mol mol iɔng*. When you see the path and there's nothing to stop you, then you have an easy journey (*mol*, cheap).

The transmission of Bagre

At each of the ceremonies of White Bagre the appropriate section of the myth is recited to the initiates, for it provides both

a mnemonic for and an explanation of the rites that are being performed.

The memorizing of these myths is enjoined upon the new initiates
and rewards are offered to those who succeed in this task. Apart
from the prestige that accrues to him, a Speaker is given special
allocations of food, beer, and money. The neophytes are encouraged, when they become members, to go and watch other
Bagre performances, outside their own lineages and settlements,
so they may get to know how to recite (W. 5209). Yet it is clear
that more systematic methods are needed to learn a work of these
dimensions, some 12,000 'lines' in all. Such instructions were in fact
given, but essentially on a household basis. Benima told me how
he had been the favourite of his grandfather, Napii, who had
taught him the Bagre line by line. When the sons of the late chief
of Birifu, Gandaa, returned home in the school holidays, the old
man would call his younger 'brother' Yinkwo to assemble the boys
in the rooftop hut and get them to repeat whole sections, line by
line. Then he would test them, one by one, to see what they had
learned.

Clearly there are many individual differences in ability and
application. In fact very few of the initiates remember anything
like the whole myth. Those that do become the future Speakers.
In 1951 I travelled a hundred miles south, to a LoBirifor community in western Gonja, and met there, by arrangement, Yinkwo
and another elder from Birifu who had been called to revive the
performance of the Bagre rites. They stayed many weeks, instructing members, sacrificing fowl, and were certainly well rewarded
for their knowledge. Whether they received the horse and 100,000
cowries laid down in the myth I do not know. But their mission
was successful in that they used their knowledge of rite and
myth to teach another community the ways of Bagre.

The translation of Bagre

There are many ways of doing a translation of this kind. At
this point I am primarily interested in LoDagaa thought, in their
network of meaning, in what is somewhat vulgarly but fashion-
ably described as their 'code'. In most translations of oral texts
one learns as much about the translator as about the translated.
My aim is the effacement of the translator, though I cannot hope
to attain that goal. To this end I have been through this text with

three LoDagaa, with Benima, who recited it, with Romulo Tadɔ, who helped translate, and with Kumbɔɔnɔ Gandaa, who from his unique vantage point considered every word. Although it has taken me a long time to complete, I am simply the mediator. One's first task is to present a faithful text and a literal translation, as a base for the discussion of codes, meanings, and thoughts. For the great difficulty in communicating an understanding of the thought of non-literate peoples is the lack of adequate texts. Everything is mediated by a literate interpreter, the extent of whose contribution is rarely clear. For this reason one can rely upon little of the basic data for the study of *la pensée sauvage* and the reader has to be doubly careful of the analyses based upon them.

In order to minimize my own intervention I have tried to keep as close to the original as possible. This aim brings several difficulties. Firstly the range of meaning of LoDagaa words is obviously different from the approximate equivalents in English. But I have nevertheless tried to give a particular LoDagaa word a constant rendering in English since this enables the reader to follow the flow of the original, even though it may produce a flatter translation than would otherwise be the case. I have also tried to keep the flavour of the formulaic repetitions. Again, what may seem awkward and over-extended in a written form would not seem so orally when the repetitions can be used either to impress a point upon the audience or, more usually, to mark time in the narrative flow and perhaps give the reciter the opportunity to recall and organize the passage that follows.

Another difficulty in the translation arises from the fact that there is some movement between direct and indirect modes of speech during the course of a single passage.[1] And a third is that the pronoun 'he' is often ambiguous; I have sometimes replaced this with a more specific reference in order to assist the reader.

It is interesting that these problems of translation were those that Meillassoux and his collaborators found in presenting the original and the translation of the Soninke legend of the dispersion of the Kusa (1967). I do not claim to have solved them, since

---

[1] Meillassoux remarks of the Soninke tale he translates that 'le style direct n'existe pas. Lorsque le narrateur fait parler un personnage il lui applique la troisième personne du pluriel *i* sans que les pronoms personnels relatifs aux autres personnages ne lui soient rapportés' (1967: 8). A similar use of the pronouns of the third person plural appears to occur in LoDagaa.

no solution is possible. But I have tried to reproduce the style and content of the original in so far as this is feasible.

The characters in Bagre

The main human characters in the myth are the younger and elder 'brothers' or companions, who were the first men and ancestors of all those now living. It is the adventures of the younger one with which the narrative is mainly concerned, for it is he that visits the beings of the wild, and then God himself. And it is upon the struggle between the three that the myth turns. In the Black Bagre mention is made of the elder brother accompanying him to heaven; this only seems possible if he is to be identified with the spider who spun a web on which the younger brother could climb up to heaven.

When he gets there, the younger brother meets God who gives mankind a hoe (B. 4264) and a child; in this God is helped by his wife, 'the wise old woman', while the younger one is assisted by the 'slender girl'. But it is the beings of the wild (the being, the being's child, and the small being) who teach mankind most of what they know, though it is a snake (a boa) who shows the slender girl how to copulate.

The other humans are 'God's child' or Napolo, who was created in heaven, and Der, who arrived as the result of watching the snakes. In addition the first pair had 'Number Nine' and ten other children. Outside this family stand the two specialists, the diviner and the smith. Apart from the participants in the Bagre, whose roles are dramatized in the myth, and the Earth shrine, who makes one speech, the remaining characters are all animals: the buffalo child who tries to avenge herself on humanity for the death of her mother, the cats and the flies that help to create 'God's child', the Bagre animals that announce the time when the ceremonies should be held and are included among the elders; especially important are the fruit-bat and the guinea fowl. The animals mentioned as elders of Bagre are the following:

the large fruit-bat, who tells time for the Announcement of Bagre;

the belibaar bird, whose flight from east to west proclaims the arrival of the dry season, the time for the guinea corn harvest;

the kyaalipio bird, who tells the time when the girls should get up to fetch water to make the beer;

the large frog, who is not discussed with the others, but is presumably the one that appears in the narrative of the Black Bagre (B. 94);

the damdamwule bird, whose song informs mankind that it is too late to plant guinea corn;

the crown bird, who sings at midnight, so men can tell the time to feed the fasting neophytes;

the featherless cock, who tells the time to get up for farming;

the old guinea cock, who tells men when to perform the Ceremony of Beans.[1]

Other animals are mentioned only incidentally; the hawk ('God's creature') who kills the dove that Napolo thought he had himself shot (B. 1890); the antelope hit by the younger one before he deprives the buffalo child of her mother (B. 2311) and who is described as 'the heifer' of the beings of the wild. Other wild animals are mentioned very peripherally in connection with the skins offered by Napolo to the buffalo-girl when he takes her as a bride, namely, roan, duiker, lion, and three kinds of antelope. God himself is surrounded by animals, by dogs (as is the diviner, B. 1226), leopard, lion, elephant, duiker, and hippopotamus (B. 512).

The neophytes themselves set out to hunt wild animals after the Beating of the Malt. Then they are taught which are for Bagre and which for the house (see p. 113. But these Bagre animals are part of the ritual rather than the myth. The main participants are not animals but human and supernatural beings, the younger one (who is representative of mankind), God and the beings of the wild.

---

[1] In the Black Bagre (B. 3702) 1, 5, 6, 3, and 2 are listed.

5

THE BAGRE PERFORMANCES

Asperging the Neophytes (Bo puɔru)

THE first ceremony of all is 'the Asperging of the Neophytes', when those proposed for membership are introduced to the shrines that will protect them. It is a little-publicized ceremony. The senior members (especially those who act as Speakers), junior members (especially those who act as guides), and the neophytes all gather at the house chosen for the Bagre performances, generally the largest in the lineage, but one which has a shrine to the Bagre deity in the neck of the granary. This ceremony should be started in the dry season, when the dawadawa (*Parkia oliveri*) flowers; this is a tree whose long pods hold a sweet yellow powdery fruit used for culinary purposes. But the performance rarely takes place when it should, mainly because of continuing uncertainty about all the food that is needed. In my own experience the commencement is delayed as long as possible and usually combined with the next ceremony, the Announcement of Bagre which is carried out when the shea fruit, whose nut is essential to make the fat or 'butter' used in the Bagre ritual, is ripe.

In 1951, the first steps in the performance of Bagre were taken on 8 May, when the Naayili elders called the prospective neophytes together and warned them not to eat the shea fruit. Already this was late, for the fruit had ripened and it was feared that some of them might have eaten it. The full performance was further delayed because of the shortage of fowls; so many had been killed off by Newcastle disease that sacrifices were difficult to carry out. Fowls are essential in order to 'asperge the neophytes' (*puɔra bobil*), for they all have to be taken into the byre, where the ancestor shrines rest. This year, the elder of Kyaa refused to start the Bagre, though strongly pressed by his clansmen. But Naayili decided to begin, even though they could not carry out the full rite at this time because of the fowl shortage (610). When Naayili took this decision, one segment of Kyaa (Dirɛ's 'room') decided to go ahead on their own, as they had strong grounds for doing so. There is no real reason why any segment cannot start in this way and why other members of the clan sector cannot send neophytes to be initiated by them (755): Bagre, food and all, is shared by the whole clan sector (771). Nevertheless the action taken by Dirɛ was clearly a threat to the authority of the head of the sector who had taken the decision not to begin at this time; in the end he was forced to follow suit.

Naayili in fact carried out the asperging proper on 20 June, on Wa'a (or Birifu) market, the day on which many such performances take place (790).[1] At this time the neophytes were taken to the byre where water and ashes were spurted over them by members of another lineage of the clan, people not directly involved. The ancestral shrines that lean against the wall in a corner of the byre are treated in a similar manner. An elder from a non-participating lineage mixes some of the water with earth (*tene*), here qualified as the Earth shrine's earth (*tengaan tene*), and the mud is put beneath the ears of the neophytes, on their chests and in between their first two fingers and toes. Then they are handed their 'Starting Fowl' (*tîîtîî nuo*) which they will look after until the next ceremony so that it produces chickens to use in the performance. This fowl is treated in a special way, for it has to be cut with a knife between the toes and on the joints of the leg, as well as at the back of the neck. It is as if a pretended sacrifice were being made of an animal that had been marked in the same way as the neophytes, for when it has been dealt with it is thrown aside (*loba*) as if it were being used as an omen, to see which way up it would fall. But the chicken does not in fact have its throat slit and is kept until the Bagre of Beans, when it is given to the Speaker to kill to the Bagre deity; it is the Speaker who now owns both the fowl, known as *Bo nuur*, and the eggs it lays.

At the same time the first prohibitions are placed upon the neophytes. They are forbidden the shea fruit, whose nut will be used to make fat; they are forbidden beans (*biong*) whose leaves will be made into soup at the Bagre of Beans (*Bo biong*), and they

---

[1] K. G. comments: 'The Birifu Market is Wura Daa, i.e. Wura's Market, though the pronunciation degenerated into Wara Daa and later into Wa'a Daa. Wura Daa used to be a very big market but, as legend relates, blood was shed in a fight and the payment to satisfy the market shrine was not made. The market has since dwindled. In 1940 it was revived by the late chief Gandaa, who provided the necessary sacrifices, but things did not return to their earlier state.'

are forbidden to eat *sense*, the small cakes of bean flour which are fried in every market. They are also forbidden to accept a gourd of beer from which someone has already drunk. All these prohibitions cease at the Bagre of Beans.

The spurting of water from the mouth is clearly a gesture of cooling and blessing, similar to the Asperges of the congregation in the Christian Church. This is made clear by the use of ashes which, as in other rituals, have the power to make hot things cold (Goody 1962: 69). When they have been dealt with in this way, the neophytes are sent home. If a candidate subsequently reports having had bad dreams, he will not be initiated unless a diviner is first approached to find out what is wrong. As in many other ceremonial contexts, the rituals test the candidate concerning his relationships with things supernatural.

On both the occasions at which I was present, the shortage of fowls meant the postponement of some sequences in this ceremony and a merging with the one that followed. I have no way of telling how often this happened but my impression is that the LoDagaa are more concerned with seeing that each phase is carried out rather than attaching it to a particular ceremony. This was certainly so in 1951.

The announcement of Bagre (Bo wuur)

The asperging of the initiates is followed by a ceremony announcing that Bagre is about to be performed. As we have seen, these two ceremonies are sometimes run into one another; it often happens that they are performed later than they rightly should be, since the requirements of grain and fowls are considerable and a lineage does not know until a late stage whether or not it can raise the amounts needed. So the beginnings of the ritual sequence are marked by some procrastination, considerable discussion about the manner and timing, and a certain amount of competitive jockeying for position, since an individual does not wish to admit to his inability to provide for his dependants and at the same time does not want to take on, publicly, more than he can manage.

As so much food and beer is required to perform a Bagre sequence, a great deal of firewood is needed for its preparation. Birifu is densely populated by savannah standards and women may have to travel several miles to get the fuel they need. So for any major ceremony of this kind, preparations have to be made well in

4. The Collecting of the Malt (*kei zuur*) before the first of the Bagre ceremonies. On the left sit the members, on the right the neophytes

advance, indeed in the preceding dry season. But though everybody guesses what is going to happen, a formal announcement is none the less made, when the ancestors and shrines are told and when the neophytes are introduced to them. In explaining this my assistant compared this ceremony with that announcing a girl's first pregnancy when everyone is already well aware of her condition.[1]

Each ceremony is preceded by the brewing of beer and two days before it begins the malted guinea corn is collected up and measured out (*bɛ yongna kɛɛ*). On this day all the neophytes dress up in their finery, the girls being draped in various cloths and carrying on their heads the personal 'shrine basket' (*tiib pele*), so carefully decorated with cowrie shells. Dressed up in this fashion, they make their way around all the houses in the neighbourhood, announcing

> Come out on the third day,
> *Ka(i) yi yi datɛra,*
> come and take the flour.
> *wa dɛ zɔ bar.*

The reference is to the fact that flour is placed on the Bagre shrine (*wen*).

Naayili measured out their malt on 26 June, Wa'a market day, and the brewing started on the morrow; the ceremony itself begins two days later when the beer is ready. The measuring of the grain is a formal affair. In the evening, the elders of the lineage assembled on the rooftop of the Bagre house, together with the senior men of other lineages of the same clan, and a few representatives of the other descent groups in Birifu. The neophytes were mostly young boys (my assistant's son had not yet been weaned) and women up to forty years old. The differences in age indicate the different values placed by men upon male and female lives respectively.

It is the close but non-participating lineages that actually did the measuring though it is more usually another clan who is described as the joking partners of Bagre, since they can do what the participants cannot. The neophytes sit in a line with their piles of corn in front of them (the children of one mother sharing the same pile) and the elders take a basket into which the grain is forced down and then emptied out on the rooftop again.

---

[1] I would note that when earlier I described this ceremony I understood that it should be performed at all first pregnancies, but the White Bagre suggests that it is confined to initiates.

At this time, the Bagre joking partners address the initiates, giving them their current prohibitions. They must not drink the water collected for the Bagre beer and they must not fight or have sexual congress until the beer has been drunk. They are also told what new crops and fruits are forbidden, and that they must not drink from a gourd which someone else has already touched (*bε bε nyuur kuõ tikye kora bε*). For, they are warned, those that break these prohibitions will not be accepted as candidates.

The grain is later returned to the houses from whence it came so that it can be turned into food and drink for the ceremony. But immediately after the measuring the elders entered into a long discussion about the difficulties of obtaining fowl. Eventually they descended to the byre. There the ancestor shrines were first swept with *kõ kõ* leaves, which are associated with the beings of the wild; sometimes strophantus leaves (*yebe*), used in the making of arrow poison, are taken instead. The elder of the other lineage group then addressed the Earth shrine and the ancestors, who were asked to watch over the brewing of the beer and not to break the vats by their presence; on most major rituals the ancestors are expected to turn up and in the Final Funeral Ceremony they are also spoken of as coming to drink the beer they had enjoyed during their lifetime.

After this introduction to the Earth and the ancestors, the neophytes were brought into the byre in order of age, the younger ones carried by daughters of the house, often reluctantly, for even at an early age these shrines are used as a threat by their elders (798). Sakpi's four-year-old son burst into tears when he was about to go in, but nevertheless he did as he was told.

When these rites were finished, the elders did what often happens on such occasions—made use of their meeting together for other purposes; they went over to the shade of a tree outside the house in order to divine the reason for the death of the late chief's horse, which had died suddenly. Meanwhile a few others walked a mile or so to the Bagre house of the close lineage who had acted as joking partners in order to carry out for them the same ritual services as they had just performed. Before going they also made a sacrifice which is directly relevant to Bagre. A small mound of earth was scraped together on the path leading in the direction from which their forefathers were supposed to have come; this is the *teng kori sɔr*, 'the road to the old country', where sacrifices are made to the ancestors of those who came first to the settlement. A similar sacrifice is made before other ceremonies, for example, before the Bagre Dance, and it is intended to secure the benevolent participation of the Earth and the ancestors in the rites that are being performed (233).

The ceremony proper took place on the 29th. At about 10 a.m. the elders from the neighbouring clan sectors arrived at the Bagre house to which they had been called. They took the neophytes off to the road leading to the Earth shrine where they built a small pile of earth (*tiungser*) on top of which a stone is placed. An elder of the non-participating lineage that carried out the reciprocating services offered prayers as he struck it with another stone, and then killed a fowl for every initiate. If any of these are not accepted, then that person's affairs have to be looked at more closely.

After the sacrifice, the senior Speaker present (old Iiru from Baaperi) began to recite the *Bo kaab*, the invocation with which the Black Bagre myth begins. This he did in rhythmic phrases (the 'lines' of my text, which are simply spatial representations of rhythmic periods), constantly punctuated by the striking of a stone on the Earth shrine. He finished and another Speaker started. Each phrase he declaimed was immediately repeated by a third. For the whole piece had to be recited three times, and this device was a way of saving time—the young children were now getting restless as they had fasted the whole of that day.

When the address to the Earth shrine was complete, the neophytes were taken to the other main focus of LoDagaa religious action, the ancestors. They were led into the byre and the invocation was repeated again, with the Speaker beating the wooden shrines of the ancestors instead of the altar to the Earth. The other main difference was that the person addressing the ancestors (Pinpuo) was from another lineage of the same clan, not an outsider. In terms of congregation, the Earth is universal, the ancestors particularistic.

Finally the initiates were called back again into the room one by one. The 'owner of Bagre' sat on the left of the ancestor shrines holding in the palm of his hand some shea butter, which he had taken out of a small pot. This oil he uses to create a relationship of custodianship between the ancestors and the neophytes, a relationship known as *siura* (or *siwee*; LD. *sigra*) in the myth.

The shea butter (*kã*) for this ceremony is made by the women in

a long and complicated process that takes many days. The other
main necessities for the ceremonies are also made by women, as
the text records:

> She takes the shea nut that turns to oil,
> *o dɛ kyuon ka lieb kã*
> she takes the malt that turns to beer,
> *o dɛ kei ka lieb dãã*
> she takes the corn that turns to food.
> *o dɛ kyi ka lieb saab*

Although not quite so time-taking, the technological processes
are as complex, more so perhaps, than those of the men—except
that of smithying. As Childe noted of the 'neolithic revolution',
many of the more complex discoveries and inventions of barbarian
science were associated with the work of women rather than of
men (1942: 56).

When the oil has been prepared, the husband will tell his wife
not to let the children get hold of any before the ceremony. 'Don't
let my neophytes do wrong (*song*).' For the proper time approaches
(*zie tolana*), and 'the fire should'nt blaze up,' as the text repeatedly
declares (e.g. W. 643).

In the recitation these two roles of the women are frequently
stressed. The 'wise old woman' is acquainted with all the technological processes and understands the secrets of childbirth; she it
is, as the wife of God, of 'Adam' (the first man, the elder one), and
of the present performer ('the mother of Bagre'), who instructs the
young girls ('the slender girls' of the myth) in their basic tasks.
But she is also responsible for seeing that the neophytes don't run
into danger ('spoil') by taking foods that are at present tabooed.

The shea butter that is manufactured in this way is used for the
special purpose of *siura*, the creation of a relationship of spiritual
guardianship, discussed earlier. The neophyte takes the oil in his
left hand, flicks it three times towards the ancestral shrines and
puts the remainder in his mouth. The initiates are ritually fed
(*tona*) with the oil, in one of the gestures of pretence (*tun*) that so
often mark the communications between man and god (Goody
1962: 60).[1] A special relationship is thus brought into being and
then sealed by the sacrifice of a chicken for every neophyte.

---

[1] K. G. comments: 'In Birifu the verb *tũɔna* is used for the criss-cross marking
on the face. The senior members (*bɔɔ kɔɔra*) will say: " *Yɛ tũɔ bɔbɔ a kãã*", or ask

In 1952 the Naayili clan had thirty-eight novices and on this occasion their fowls were brought out in front of the byre and divided into six piles, one for each of the five constituent lineages (only one of which was carrying out this ceremony, namely, the lineage of Wuurader), and one for the patriclan sector of Kyaa, with whom Naayili customarily shares (*puon*) and who were themselves performing Bagre the same year.

When they withdrew from the presence of the ancestral shrines the neophytes were first taken up to the roof and then down into the Bagre room (for there is no direct access to the interior of a LoDagaa house) where they were later given a meal of porridge (*saab*), ground-nut soup (*bule zier*), and beer (*dãã*). The first food is given to the second-graders (the *bɔɔbɛrɛ*, or senior members) who also receive the top of each pot of beer, the *nɛ dãã* or 'beer of the mouth'. The 'middle beer' (*dãã sɔɔr*) is given to the neophytes and the 'dregs' (*dãã per*), the name given to the bulk of the pot, is taken to the rooftop to be divided out, together with soup and porridge, among the five clans in the ritual area.[1] The host clan, Naayili, kept its share on the rooftop and divided it among the constituent lineages. The other clans took their portions and each sat together under different shade trees that stood in front of the compound.

Even married women consume the food with their natal patriclans. Only a few very senior women were called over to eat with the question *Yɛ tũɔ̃ na a bɔbɔ baari?* In the second stage of whitewashing, the guides are told: *Zɛ a bɔbɔ a kãã*, or asked: *Yɛ zɛna a bɔbɔ a kãã baari?* Here *kãã* is used figuratively for whitewash.

'Another action, which is akin to the presentation of the child before the ancestral shrines, is *tɔ*; in Bagre this is done when the fast of the neophytes is broken, before they can eat or drink for the day: *Yɛ tɔna a bɔbɔ baari.*

'This action involves the cutting of a small piece of food by the guide and raising it in front of the neophyte's face, 3 times for men, 4 times for women, and then throwing it away to the gods. He follows this by passing another bit of food under his arms and again throwing it away to the gods. This ceremony precedes the eating and drinking of the Bagre food and drink.

'The same action is done to a child (*fu tɔna a fu bie zie*) but with shea butter and medicines. It is carried out first thing in the morning before he or she takes anything solid.'

[1] Like all the food distributed on these occasions, the beer is subject to snatching (*aro*) by sister's sons (*arbile*) and by their children. I was invited to drink a pot that had been snatched in this way (by an educated member of the chief's house, a fact which was probably instrumental in the success of this gesture). He was a senior member (*bo sɔɔla, gan sob*) and there was some discussion as to whether this category was entitled to drink the beer intended for first-graders, though there was no doubt that non-initiates like myself could do so.

the clansmen of their husband (not with the married sisters of the clan). This was the one occasion among the LoWiili that I saw men and women eat together from the same bowl (though it occurs in certain LoDagaba settlements), and it happens only when the husband's kin are certain that the woman will stay in the house and when she has finished childbearing. Of such a woman they will say '*o in daba*', 'he/she is a man', and '*o in a* (or *lieba*) *yirsob*', 'he/she is (or has become) a member (or owner) of the house'.

When the food had been divided by patriclans, the elders returned to the Bagre room where the food was laid out in two lines for the initiates, who demonstrate to the neophytes how they eat all together at one time (like 'hawks', the myth says).

At the time of the Announcement of Bagre, communication is established with the 'god who descends'. The initiates and neophytes go to the roof of the house where the Bagre is being performed. There they pretend to throw something with their left hand, an action described as *bɛ yuana* or *bɛ tuura*, the latter meaning literally 'they follow'; in this context these words are used for communication with *tiib* (shrines) and with supernatural agencies generally. The actions carried out here, and later on Bagre Day, are clearly those referred to in the passages of the myth that speak of the descent of the god (e.g. W. 104):

> it was the deity
> that has come
> from the front,
> that is pointing
> with the right hand,
> that has come
> to stay here

The following day the same procedures were repeated once again. On the path outside the house, the Bagre was recited at a mound but on this occasion no chickens were killed. Nor were any killed in the byre. The meal consisted not of ground-nut soup (*bule zier*) but of soup made from bean leaves which was now permitted to the neophytes. For they were now released from some of the earlier prohibitions placed upon them, on cakes made from bean flour, on shea fruit, and upon sharing a calabash of beer.

This ceremony of *Bo wuur* is also known as *Bo Biong* (920), the

Bagre of Beans, the Beans in question being the black beans. The neophytes are now allowed to go their own ways until the series of ceremonies that take place after the major crops have been harvested. The first of these also has to do with beans, this time the white beans, being known as *Ben puuru dãã*, the Beer of the Flowering of the Cow Peas, or alternatively as *Ka puuru dãã*, the Beer of the Flowering of the Guinea Corn (920). Both the guinea corn and the cow peas flower at the same time. This is also the season when the first yams (*kpir nyie*) can be dug, the remainder being left to grow.

The ceremony that I have described took place at Naayili. Six days later, on 5 July, a similar ritual was performed in Kyaa, which has the same Bagre medicine, that is to say, it was obtained from the same source. Nevertheless there are certain differences between the two performances. The principal one of these has to do with the food eaten on the first day. In earlier times, it is said, a bachelor did not have any porridge at Bagre since he had no wife to cook it; for the grain that is measured out is taken back to the neophyte's own house to be turned into food and beer. But they took pity on these bachelors and it was decided that no one should eat porridge on the first day but only drink flour mixed with water (*zɔ kuõ*), the mixture that is often offered to strangers when they arrive at a house from distant parts. After that the flour is taken home and brought back the next day as porridge. Although Bagre explicitly extends kinship ties outside the kinship context (as, for example, in the division of meat, W. 3343), the dependence of its ceremonies on the individual hearths of its members is stressed throughout the proceedings. There is a constant interaction between the public collection and consumption of food and its private production and preparation.

At the Asperging Ceremony, Kyaa had been unable to kill the necessary fowls to the ancestor shrines. This sacrifice was therefore transferred to the present occasion and they began the morning by killing some fifty-five chickens on behalf of their thirty-one neophytes.

At the same time the elders discussed various cases where Bagre prohibitions were said to have been broken. Two of Kobaa's sons had been heard quarrelling, but the complaint was dismissed when they explained it was only an argument over some food in a gourd. But another lad was judged to have been in a fight and his father was fined 600 cowries and two fowl, which were to be sacrificed to the Bagre deity.

When Kyaa made their sacrifice to the Earth they killed a fowl for each initiate and also offered some flour, some shea oil, and a small pot of beer. Afterwards, in the byre, the recital was again carried out and more chickens were killed. The neophytes were then allocated their own beer to drink and led into the byre where the Starting Fowl (*tiitii nuo*) was treated in the manner described for the previous ceremony, since Kyaa had started that phase without sufficient chickens. At the same time the ancestors were called upon to keep the neophytes from getting ill and to guard them till all is over (*o ta vɛ̃ ka bobil wa in baalɛ; o na tuur a lɛ na na ka ba ti yi*).

The main meal was now laid out and the neophytes went into the Bagre room where they were told the story of the bachelor, before being given the flour water to eat, and more beer to drink. At the end of the row in which the food was laid out, a special pot (*do tangale*) was reserved for the owners of Bagre medicine, the second-graders. All this beer, described as *dãã bhaani*,[1] is kept for ritual purposes, as is made clearer in the rites of the following day.

The neophytes are now ritually fed (*tona*), to break their fast. This is done with flour, which they put on the backs of their hands. They take some in their mouths, then spit it out, first to one side, then to the other and let what remains fall on the floor of the room. As with all rituals of pretence, these acts are carried out three times for a man and four for a woman.

On the second day, 6 July, Kyaa carried out the same prayers (*kaab*) as before, addressing Earth and ancestors. Then a meal was prepared of porridge made from the flour (*zɔ̃ nyaaru* or *zɔ̃ haama*) of the day before. This is consecrated food (*saab bhaani*) which is consumed by the neophytes in the room and by the patriclan on the rooftop, and is otherwise given only to those with whom they share, namely Naayili (who, it will be remembered, had given them food of a similar kind) and Yongyuole, each of whom received three gourds.

The fowls which had been killed and divided on the previous day were now given out as cooked food in the same way. A second quantity of soup and porridge was referred to as the 'food for dividing' (*saab puon*). Each patriclan, including those who had

---

[1] Or *dãã mani*, designated beer.

shared the consecrated food, was given four calabashes of porridge, four bowls of soup, and four small pots of beer, together with some chicken.[1] Thirdly, there was the 'food for women' (*pobo saab*); a calabash of porridge and a proportion of the rest of the food (including one fowl) is given to the paternal lineage (*pɔɔ sãã yidem*) of every woman who is being put through Bagre as a wife.

Finally food and beer were put aside for special categories of people present, the strangers and the Speakers (who received two small pots). Meanwhile sister's sons playfully insisted upon their rights to snatch, either from the clan carrying out the Bagre, or from those who had been given a share.[2] In this way a network of particular and generalized exchanges among clans and individuals is established as an intrinsic part of the ceremony of, the one in which the majority of those who attend are most involved.

That and, for the young, the dancing. After the members are replete with food, the xylophones begin to play and all present, both men and women, join in the Bagre dance, which always has an element of courting in it. A fine dancer attracts much praise, and a man who puts on a vigorous show may find one or more girl admirers joining in just behind him, close relations as well as potential wives or mistresses.

Even when the xylophones are not playing, the girls will gather round in a circle at the side and dance and sing to the clapping of hands (*nuri ngmeb* and *kaaro*). They do this largely for their own amusement, but one elder told me that they also do it to attract the attention not only of local men but also of any traders (*bõ yero*) who may be in the neighbourhood or have lost their way in the bush, so that they will bring the salt needed to make the Bagre food. It is important, as at funerals, to maintain the tempo of the ceremonies as long as they last and this is helped by the continuous playing of the xylophone and clapping of hands.

Salt and cloth were probably the only two 'necessities' the LoDagaa obtained from outside the region. They knew how to

[1] At least Naayili, Yongyuole, Kyaa, and Ngmanbili divided in this way. Baaperi (of whom only two members were present) got a half-share and Puriyele (only one present) a quarter.

[2] K. G. comments: 'The word used to describe the right of a sister's child to get a pot of beer, fowl, etc. during such performances is *aro*. This is a hunting term. If someone shot an antelope and another does so later, the first is presumed to be the killer and the second (if he is from a different patriclan) is entitled to the foreleg (*o lɔ ara a bɔɔ*). If it is a dog that helps in the killing, then the foreleg belongs to his owner.'

make a salt from the ash of certain grasses, but it did not have the flavour of the salt purchased from traders. Imported salt came from two main sources. A small quantity was washed from the sands of the Black Volta at the Gonja town of Daboya and found its way to the Wa market. The town of Wa, forty-five miles to the south, was the major focus of large-scale economic activity for the LoDagaa, and most of the traders who passed by were on their way to or from that town. The main traders in salt came from the north bringing the rock salt from the Saharan mines and these were mainly Mossi traders belonging to the Yarsi group, who were of Dyula origin and travelled widely throughout the Voltaic area. Indeed the LoDagaa word for trader (*yero*), the Mossi word for Dyula (*Yarsi*), and the word for Mossi in a number of languages in the region all have the common root of 'trade'.

Traders gathered at the near-by settlements of Kwõnyũkwõ and Babile, where a few of their tribesmen were found even in precolonial times. The pedlars among them attended any local gathering like Bagre to sell their wares, which included 'Mossi cloth' (the LoDagaa have none of their own). But their task was always a dangerous one, as the early administrative records make clear. Acephalous peoples like the LoDagaa and the Tallensi might attack individuals or caravans going through their settlements, largely for booty but sometimes (in the LoDagaa case) for an offering to the spirit guardian (*siura*). And an additional reason for the ambivalent attitude towards the traders, whose goods they wanted but whose presence they did not, was the fact that they were identified with the centralized states who either raided them directly or else traded in the products of such raids. Indeed trading and slaving were hardly to be separated.

The preliminaries are now complete. The main series of ceremonies begins with the next, the Ceremony of Beans, which is normally carried out about the time of the main harvest, early in December.

The Ceremony of Beans (Bo biong)

In 1950, the year before the ceremonies I have just described, the Bagre was performed by two lineages in Birifu, by Ngmanbil-Maale (whom I shall call Maale) and by Baaperi. The first of these carried out the Ceremony of Beans on 1 December, which was Nakwol market day, the Day of No-Hoeing, a day associated with the Earth. It took place at the house of the 'mother of Bagre', a man called Zuko, where representatives of all the other clan sectors in Birifu proper were gathered together, that is, Kyaa, Baaperi, Naayili, and Yongyuole. The first part of the ceremony was taken up with a sacrifice made necessary because of certain acts that had been committed at the previous Bagre performance. Since this is the first major ceremony of the ritual complex, it is also the occasion when outstanding matters have to be settled. Indeed Bagre had not been held in Birifu for the last three years because the following debt remained unpaid.

Three years before, the late chief of Birifu had detected some bad medicine (*tū faa*) in a pot of beer which had been sent him to drink. He swore by the Bagre deity, by the ancestors, and by a medicine shrine called *maalseb* in order to try to discover who had wanted to do him wrong. On the very day that the neophytes were washed, a certain woman died, the wife of a friend from another lineage. Divination confirmed that she had tried to kill the chief and at her funeral all her gourds, pots, and clothes were destroyed in front of the medicine shrine. Her sons had then to provide four cows to be slaughtered there. All this wealth had taken three years to accumulate. Now sacrifices had to be made to the Bagre shrine and her sons had to produce a further payment of a cow, sheep, goat, and six chickens for sacrifice to the Bagre deity (*Bo wen*) at the altar placed in the neck of the main granary that projects through the flat roof of every house.

A preliminary discussion about the action to be taken was held at the foot of a nearby boabab, the shade tree for the compound. The head of the house made a little pile of earth, placed a small stone on top, then tapped it with another pebble. This was at Zuko's house, but in fact most of the main ceremonies were held at the neighbouring compound of Depep, the government head-man from the same lineage, since his provided more room for the neophytes, for the initiates, and for their numerous guests.

Bonyir, who had been 'hired' as Speaker from the neighbouring clan sector of Kyaa, addressed the shrine in short, staccato phrases, after each of which Zuko gave two taps with the stone. When he had finished speaking, Zuko grabbed a small chicken, held its head back with the thumb of one hand, and with the other took a knife and slit its throat. A few of the tail-feathers had been plucked and placed on top of the stone, an offering to the shrine, and over this the blood of the chicken was allowed to drip before the bird was cast aside to see which way up it died. Such a procedure is always carried out before any larger animal is killed, in order to find out whether the supernatural agency will accept the offering; for of all the animals killed in sacrifice, only the fowl is used both for downward as well as upward communication. Both chickens were killed in this way and both expired on their backs, favourably. Bonyir laughed out loud, partly from relief and satisfaction, for the major sacrifice could now proceed.

First of all a small goat had its throat cut and was left lying on the ground. The elders moved off to the byre to make a sacrifice to the ancestors, those to whom the chief had made an oath. Two more chickens were killed and then a sheep. When they came out the elders declared that these offerings were not sufficient and a boy was sent back to fetch another goat from Red Hill (Tanziiri), which was the clan sector of the dead woman's husband. Two more chickens were killed, one falling favourably, the other not, but the sacrifice of the goat continued.

All these sacrifices were part of the 'greeting' (*puuru*). When they had been completed, the main offering could be made and the assembled company went to the Bagre shrine in the large granary. This particular shrine consisted of a small mud projection built on to the granary, flat on top, about six inches high and eighteen inches square. On the side away from the granary was a shallow hole, on the right of which were two crystalline stones stuck in the dried mud.

The participants sat in a semi-circle and Zuko tapped the shrine with a short stick, as Bonyir addressed the deity. Four chickens were killed before the cow itself was slaughtered outside the house (for it was too big to drag up to the rooftop).

This sacrifice was a preliminary to the ceremony itself. As at the other performances the neophytes bring a fowl to kill to the Bagre deity. In addition they spend a good deal of time in the long room of the house listening to the White Bagre, which is recited up to the point in the ceremony that they have reached; this is their 'instruction'.

At the opening ritual various taboos were laid upon the neophytes, against quarrelling and against sex during the course of the performances themselves (e.g. W. 1972). Such taboos are widespread in such ceremonies for fighting and sex are often seen as disruptive and polluting elements in this kind of context. Asceticism is demanded of the neophytes; sex pollutes all those who take part even in ordinary times; it is especially polluting when an individual has been whitewashed, for then he is in a similar state to a widow, whose whiteness not only symbolizes social separation and sexual abstention, but is a test of whether or not she has kept her word.

At the same time the initiates are taught certain food taboos that apply throughout. The prohibitions on food are the most evident of all, though those on sex are the most severe. As far as food is concerned, almost none of the major crops can be eaten until the neophytes have been formally released from the prohibition. Yams (*dioscorea*) are prohibited until shortly after the Bagre of Beans, when 'they shake the yams' (*bɛ miiro nyii*); the elders speak in the room and then give the neophytes yams to eat (W. 400). Beans are treated in a similar way, being freed at *Ben puru*, though as with yams there is rarely any separate ceremony involved; the release is effected at one of the other performances. But both are mentioned in the text of the White Bagre itself (the yams at line 364, the beans at line 667), the release from beans being referred to as the Ceremony of the Bean Flower and connected with the story of the guinea fowl quarrelling with his mate. At the Ceremony of the Beans, the prohibition on soup made from bean leaves is lifted (W. 221). At the Whitening Ceremony, the neophytes are given ground-nut and vegetable soup (*bule*), which otherwise is not eaten until after they have been initiated; apart from this they eat only *yɔɔvaar* soup made from pumpkin leaves.

These food taboos function at a variety of levels. At the beginning of the ceremony, a blanket taboo on new crops exists and these prohibitions are progressively raised as the crops in question ripen and the neophytes run into the danger of eating the forbidden fruit. In the myth it is the bean leaves that first come ripe (W. 221), then yams (W. 364), then the shea fruit (W. 784); a fruitbat struggling with its mate lets a shea nut fall to the ground for man to pick up; in this way we know the time has come for the beginning of the opening ceremony of the year, the Announcement of Bagre (W. 758), a ceremony which should occur earlier in the ritual sequence. What is important here is that the taboos on food are lifted only with the aid of the Bagre society, by means of a communal ceremony which saves the neophytes from the fire that is approaching them (W. 1869), though it is also true that it is the association that imposes the taboos and conjures up the fire. The crops affected are some of the major food crops and it is clear in the myth that the Bagre deity assists in the production of the crops required in the performance of the rituals, as of course do other agencies. The interdependence of rites and crops is made manifest throughout. So too is the dependence of the neophyte upon his fellows, for large quantities of grain are collected from kith and kin (and especially from parents) for the performance of the rites which 'help', indeed 'save', the new members.

But even as diacritical features of the passage of ceremonies in the ritual complex, the punctuation marks of religious time, the food taboos have a special force. Since so much of Bagre is concerned with eating and drinking together, the lifting of food taboos is a public act in which all members engage. The junior grade of initiates are often laughed at in the myth because of their love of eating. It is the White initiates that are constantly referred to as 'hawks' or as 'the greedy ones' and it is food they are always said to think of when they are called to the Bagre house. It is the seniors, the Black initiates, who have to remind them that Bagre is not just for fun but has to do with serious problems that affect mankind in general and this community in particular (W. 1252). And it is they too who have to insist on first being offered the Bagre food and drink; the top of the beer belongs to them (W. 1225) and the way that this is offered and received is an essential part of the Bagre ritual (W. 445). Thus while the seniors are reserved, the juniors are encouraged to eat (there are special Bagre ways of all eating together); it is the neophytes who have not only to reject food, but have also to contribute food and drink for the rest to enjoy, as a condition of their entry into the society.

The commensalism, the inter-dining, and the fasting all help to validate the ceremonial sequence, since these are public declarations of commitment as well as acts of considerable psycho–physiological significance. The Bagre of Beans is the first ceremony to emphasize this aspect of the ritual sequence, though it plays a much larger part in the main ceremonies where the neophytes are inducted into the society by being separated from the community even to the extent of being 'killed'. But before these rites can take place, the proper medicine has to be prepared; this is the task assigned to the next ceremony.

The Beer of the Bagre Medicine (Bo tɩɩ dãã)

Whenever new initiates are brought into the society through the White Bagre, beer is also brewed for the members themselves at a ceremony known as The Beer of the Bagre Medicine (*Bo tɩɩ dãã*). At this ritual first-graders (White initiates) or second-graders (Black initiates) are given the Bagre medicine (*kyiili tɩɩ*), which they have to have in order that their children may become members.

The performance takes place shortly after the Bagre of Beans and before the Whitening Ceremony. In 1950 Baaperi held it the week (six days) before.[1] Beer was brewed, the xylophones brought out, and fowls killed to the Earth shrine (that is *sɔr puo*, on the road leading to the shrine), to the ancestors, and to the long-necked gourd in which the medicine is kept (*kyiili*): the medicine gourd is kept in a skin bag that hangs from the rafters of the byre. In these sacrifices the lineage is assisted by the usual group that carry out reciprocal services on such occasions and this in turn is rewarded with portions of the fowls that have been killed.

At this ceremony the senior members prepare the medicine (*bɛ ma vuulena a tɩɩ*) that will be used to kill and revive the neophytes in the room at the Bagre Dance.[2] The neophytes are not themselves present and the performance is essentially a private one. But it is an essential precursor of the dry season ceremonies where the aspirants are first separated from the community by being whitewashed like widows (the Whitening Ceremony) and then killed and revived during the course of the Bagre Dance; indeed the medicine is essential both in the death and rebirth of the novices.

The Whitening Ceremony (Bo pir *or* Bo byor)

The Whitening Ceremony takes place when the guinea corn is cut. Then the neophytes have their arms and head painted, though not to the same extent as those shown in Labouret's pictures of similar ceremonies among the LoBirifor of the Ivory Coast (1931: Plate 31), where they appear like living skeletons.

In 1950 this ceremony occurred early in December, that is, just after the guinea corn had been harvested. For the LoDagaa sorghum is the major crop and for this ceremony the new corn is

---

[1] Maale did not hold such a ceremony this year as they had done it last year (A 1).

[2] The verb *vuuli* means singe, as in the process of singeing the feathers off a chicken.

made into beer and porridge (*ka ziɛ saab*, red sorghum porridge). The neophytes are prohibited from drinking beer made from the new grain until the Whitening Ceremony formally releases them. On this day they all drink the Beer of the Mouth (*nɛ dãã*), so called because they are now silenced. But no member may drink it if he has already touched ordinary beer that day, nor may he drink it before the fowls have been sacrificed to the Bagre deity.

At the Whitening Ceremony the neophytes are taken out of circulation until the Bagre Dance that follows some weeks later. They no longer sleep in their own houses but in the compounds of Bagre elders. They are painted in thick white stripes, on their faces as well as their bodies, which not only cuts them off from the rest of humanity, like a widow at a funeral, but also places severe restrictions on their behaviour. Right from the beginning they are forbidden to fight between themselves and to sleep with their wives, or indeed with any woman. Now they can no longer use their 'lying mouths' for speaking but only for eating (W. 1950). At the same time, they draw a line in whitewash from the nose to the back of the head, that is, *bɛ tuɔn fu*. The invocation to the Black Bagre addresses the 'god with the mark between the eyes' (*ngmin nyɔtuɔn*); in the key at the end, this 'god' is revealed as the younger one of the two original men (B. 5252). Meanwhile, the elder brother is referred to as 'the striped god' (*ngmin sɔr goba*); these are the white stripes painted on the black body. The third of these mentioned in the Black Bagre is *ngmin par pla*, 'the god with the white arse', which is later revealed as the male fly and its mate who play a part in the creation of mankind, that is, in the birth of Napolo, 'God's child'. The reference is to the whitewash painted on the neophyte's arse with the words, 'That is your sitting arse' (*a par zinano ni anga*), although they are not allowed to sit in a room but only outside (*tiɛper*, literally at the foot of the tree, 3158) until the following ceremony. It also refers to the dust they gather through sitting on the ground. Unless the neophytes observe all these taboos, the healing virtues of the whitewash will be ineffective— and if their sins are found out, they will be punished by the elders as well as by the Bagre deity.

From now until the Dance the initiates are highly visible, painted in whitewash and going round compounds begging for grain and seizing fowls. During this whole time they are jeered at and abused by all and sundry.

5. The neophytes after the Whitening Ceremony, carrying their gourds. The photograph is taken from Labouret's account (1931) of the LoBirifor version from Upper Volta; in Birifu the painting is less pronounced

6. The Bagre guides watch over the whitewashed neo-phytes during their period of separation (1970)

In 1950 the Whitening Ceremony began at Baaperi on 7 December, that is on Nakwol market day. The Maale headman, who was conducting a parallel series of rites, was prevailed upon to postpone his own performance till the following day so that people could attend both. This market day is the one set aside for the Earth shrine and all hoeing is forbidden; consequently it is a day often used for ritual performances. Shortly before, I had encountered the neophytes walking round from house to house, telling everybody that the performance was due to begin in two days' time, an announcement that is constantly mentioned in the recital of the White Bagre. On these occasions visits are sometimes paid to settlements as far afield as ten miles away to let them know of the approaching ceremony.

In the morning the neophytes assembled, with the guides carrying the baskets on their behalf. They are taken into the room for instruction, where the White Bagre is recited up to the point in the ceremonies that they have reached. The neophytes later go up to the rooftop to eat and then return to the room.

Meanwhile, a large crowd gathered at the house where Bagre is being performed, mainly to drink, dance, and converse. When I arrived at about 7 p.m. the xylophones were being played with great vigour by the two best players in town. These were the smaller xylophones (*Lo gyil prumo*)—though still some four feet in length —which are used for the Bagre performance and are sometimes known as the *Bo gyil*. When any senior man arrived he was presented with a pot of beer by the one in charge; other men soon gathered round to drink and talk, while the younger ones joined in the Bagre dances (*Bo bine*) which are best enjoyed when the moon is bright.

The neophytes and their guides stayed in the room until 11 p.m. when the headman fired off two or three shots from his gun. They came out and climbed up to the roof; the dancing stopped as the spectators made their way home. Apparently the long stay in the room was because some trouble had been unearthed. The neophytes have to be in a state of ritual purity before they are whitewashed; that is to say, if they have broken any of the Bagre taboos they should confess their fault beforehand, otherwise they may undergo dire hardships. On this occasion one neophyte was suspected of sinning because his wife had run away.

When I reached the Maale Bagre at 4 p.m. on the following day the initiates and their helpers were making the head-bands (*zumuur*; LD. *zumiir*) that they wear after being whitewashed.[1] These head-bands are made from fibre (*byuur*) and chicken feathers (from the sacrifice) which are rolled together on the thigh. They are used in two other circumstances; the bands are tied round a widow's head for the duration of the funeral ceremonies and they are also used to cure headaches; both mourning and medicinal functions are relevant here. As people remarked on more than one occasion, 'Funeral and Bagre are the same' (A 1; 929); it is not that the neophyte is buried like a corpse, but rather that he is tested (and cured) like the survivors. The fibres are bound round the head of the neophyte before the whitewashing takes place; it is another test (W. 1916).

During the making of these bands the novices are supervised by a guide, for they can neither eat nor drink until food is specially prepared for them in the evening. When the sun sets, the food is brought out to them, together with a small pot (*dul prumo*), used only on these occasions and containing about a quart of beer. The neophytes consumed their beer and millet porridge on the roof and then returned to the room. Meanwhile the xylophones were playing *bine* (the Bagre dance) outside; people were dancing to the music but only sporadically, since there was not much beer available to encourage their steps and quench their thirst.

At Maale the neophytes stayed even longer in the room than they had done at Baaperi the previous night. The xylophones played *bine* continuously while, on the rooftop and in the courtyards, fires were lit to keep out the cold; Bagre members finished up the food the neophytes did not want. Shortly before dawn gunshots announced the emergence of the neophytes, who climbed wearily to the rooftops and lay down to sleep.

Once again the delay had been caused by a neophyte who had done wrong. It was discovered that he had slept with his wife the very night they started to brew the beer for the present ceremony. He was told off and made to wear a special head-band made from *siong myuur*, the kind of reed used for weaving sleeping-mats, which made him a figure of ridicule wherever he went. At the same time one elder reported seeing two neophytes having a fight and it was agreed they should be fined both in cash and

[1] Only in this clan section are these bands put on upstairs; in others it is done in the room.

in kind (that is, in chickens), the fines going to the Bagre Speakers.

It is at this time that the neophytes receive their Bagre accoutrements. Firstly there is the skin bag (*bo wuo*) in which they will keep their gear.[1] Then there is the small round gourd (*bo kuor*); one I saw had a little handle (*ya*) but usually they are quite round. To this is tied an iron bell and some chicken feathers from the sacrifice. The noise of a bell is always a means of communicating with supernatural agencies, usually the beings of the wild. In the centralized societies of the regions, a chief is often preceded by a man beating a double bell-shaped gong to announce his presence (or sometimes to deliver his orders, like a town-crier). But here the ringing of bells is a form of prayer, used by many diviners. On Bagre Eve the bells are shaken violently in an attempt to establish contact with the Bagre deity. The bells they acquire are tied inside the lid of the gourd and this has to be carried around by the neophytes until they are released at Bagre Dance. During this period the gourd, likened to a large hen's egg, has to be carried round with utmost care for

> if it breaks
> your head will split (W. 2022).

It is broken, formally, when the neophytes have successfully emerged from the ritual sequence.

After the meal, the neophytes are closely questioned and then stripped, bathed, and whitewashed. From then on they can no longer speak; if they do so, they receive a cuff on the head. Nor can they dance until the whole sequence is finished. If they touch anybody else's possessions (other than the clothes one is wearing), these will no longer be usable and at the final ceremony such possessions should be burnt and any animal killed. It is especially non-initiates who are in danger from the neophytes; if such a person touches the head of a new entrant, he will die. In Lawra, the neophyte can touch nothing belonging to a non-initiate and if he has something to give another person, he will put it on the ground and walk away.

After the Whitening Ceremony, the initiates have to go round to every house and beg for grain, as well as for money. They take

[1] This is the ordinary skin bag men carry over their shoulder, except that it cannot be made of goat.

with them an old basket (W. 2101), which is normally carried by a female guide (a substitute one) who accompanies them; they also carry a guinea corn stalk as a stave, a stick otherwise used only by widowers when they are whitewashed during the funeral ceremonies for their wives.

The instructions for collecting go into minute detail of how the neophytes must perform the normal human acts of drinking and excreting (sex is forbidden) away from the guides, since the sexual intercourse that senior members have had may compromise the position of their charges.

At this time the restrictions placed upon the neophytes are many; the previous prohibitions on fighting and sex are again enforced. The additional taboos were summarized to me as follows:

1. You don't speak with anyone (i.e. strangers) (*fu bɛ yel yeli ni nirɛ*).
2. You don't walk on the main paths (*fu bɛ dere sɔre*).[1]
3. You don't meet anyone (*fu bɛ turi nirɛ*)—i.e. you always turn aside (*pila*).
4. If they cook porridge, they always turn it over into a calabash (so that you eat the bottom first) (*bel wa mon saab, ba ma lieb a saab vol a ngmaan puo*).
5. A cow must not touch you (*naab bɛ tuɔr fuɛ*).
6. A dog must not touch you (*baa bɛ tuɔr fuɛ*).
7. When they give you a guinea corn stalk (*kakɛr*), do not hit anything with it: otherwise that thing will spoil.
8. Do not put your gourd within reach of a child.
9. Do not sit in a room (*fu bɛ zinɛ diumi*).
10. No one who gives you food must have had sexual intercourse (*nir bɛ gan a irɛ deɔr ti irɛ bunderi kofu*) (3157).

Having learnt what to do, the neophytes start off in a group, but each takes a different path. When one arrives at a house, he stands twenty yards away offering a mute and distant appeal (which can also be seen as a threat), while the guide goes forward with the basket to collect whatever grain is forthcoming. Only one neophyte from each house, or rather from each 'Bagre mother', makes such

---

[1] K. G. comments that this rule avoids coming into contact with persons who have had sexual intercourse the night before; it is also thought that ghosts (*nyāākpime*) take the main paths on their journeys between the living and the dead.

a visit to a compound, and he expects to collect from every man who has his own granary (that is, who farms cereals on his own behalf). They continue to collect until the Beating of the Malt (*Kɛngmir*), after which they get chickens in a similar way.

The stick is carried not only as a support but also to ward off the dogs who are accustomed to snap at strangers approaching their domain. If they have to strike the dog, I was told, it may die when the guinea corn is next cut.

The neophytes are given millet or guinea corn, and some of this is used for their own food; they eat three times a day, in the morning, noon, and evening. Since they cannot buy beer, they have to have it brought to them. I was at a house one day where two sons and a daughter were being put through Bagre; one of the sons was a schoolboy and his sister was the wife of a teacher. All three were sitting disconsolately on the roof of the compound, keeping away from all other houses, their eyes downcast, their demeanour humble. All were covered in white stripes, the girl with white rings round her nipples, and about her waist a thick cluster of leather bands (*gamie*). I was in the company of her brother-in-law and as we approached he started singing an abusive song:

Neophyte, come get your corn.
bɔɔ, bɔɔ, wa de kyi-ee

Fatty, fatty, come get your corn.
vara, vara, wa de kyi-ee

It's the children's hot food you take and eat,
bibiir sa tulu ka fu ire dire

So you've got enough courage to go through the rites.
ka par wa tãã ka fu nyɔɔr bɔɔr

Your guide's vagina is as wide as a hippo's den.
bɔɔ kyinɛ paar hee na iɛn bɔɔ nɛɛ

Your penis (or clitoris) is as stout and scaly as the lizard on the 'koo' tree.[1]
ka bɔɔ yɔbir (gyɛmbir) kpĩrkpĩr (gyira, garu) na koo bandaa

At this the young wife smiled, but soon resumed her solemn bearing and with the help of the guide her brother-in-law sent some beer over for her to drink. Anyone can (and does) abuse the neophytes during this period, though this is usually done by

[1] This tree is a favourite place for lizards.

children and by joking partners. It is explicitly a test of their self-control, to ensure that they can bear insults without responding.

The day following the whitewashing, when the neophytes have finished collecting, they return to the Bagre house and in the evening enter the room for more instruction. When this is over, other members come in numbers to throw (*loba*) money to the neophytes as they sit in the room. In return they are provided with pots of beer; Bagre ceremonies are always accompanied by much drinking.

The next day the neophytes disperse to their various houses and spend the morning collecting grain. When they return, they sit under a near-by tree until evening and then go to sleep outside or else up on the rooftop. They can talk among themselves and in the same house, but not to others. If one of them dies at this time, it shows that something is badly wrong and the individual is buried without a funeral ceremony; he may for example have slept with his wife and failed to confess. Even over the next two or three years and especially before the first rains fall, the death of any neophyte may be assigned to Bagre (W. 5837); to die with the whitewash on one's body is a yet more direct indication that the ordeal has claimed a victim, and hence such a death is particularly to be deplored. Essentially the Whitening Ceremony involves a test, an oath as well as a purification, and thus prepares the neophyte for the events 'in the room' that occur during the Bagre Dance.

The Beating of the Malt (Kε ngmir)

The Ceremony of the Malt is said to be performed three weeks before the Bagre Dance and three weeks after the Whitening Ceremony. In 1950–1, Maale held it on 16 December, one week after the Whitening Ceremony, and two weeks before the Dance itself. The performance leads to a certain lifting of pressure from the neophytes, who are now allowed to speak to people, though not to rejoin their domestic groups. They still go round collecting for the major ceremony of the Bagre Dance, though it is now fowls instead of the grain they have been seeking over the previous period; for this the guide is a small boy carrying a chicken basket. They beg or seize the fowls (W. 2245), which are later sacrificed to the Bagre deity. Once again detailed instructions are given to the neophytes on how to obtain the maximum number of chickens without actually causing open conflict (W. 2290 ff.).

The guinea corn collected during the previous period is used for the Bagre Dance, though the elders have themselves to make a major contribution in addition. Some is given to those who played the xylophone in the room. The late chief of Birifu, Gandaa, had himself been a great player at such ceremonies and always took his xylophone along, even when he could no longer play. Each neophyte would then send one basket of malted grain to the chief, who would provide a pot of beer for every man who played in the room (A 11).

The ceremony begins with a sacrifice to the place of the guardian spirit of the clan; Naayiili, for example, sacrifice at a particular baobab (*tuɔ*) in Sonkye. In the case of Kyaa, they sacrificed two fowls to the White Cave in the scarp above their farms and also sent a man to a hill near Lawra to bring back some earth which was made into a ball to put at the foot of the ancestor shrines; in this context the ancestor shrines and the guardian spirits are sometimes said to be the same (946).

At the ceremony itself everyone gathers at the Bagre house, the Speakers, elders, guides, second-graders, and neophytes; they all walk towards the river or swamp and seat themselves in an open field (*gbangbala*, W. 3046), each guide taking with him a handful of the guinea corn ears that the neophytes had been given on their earlier rounds. As they seat themselves in the field—each neophyte with a guide and second-grader, the Speaker recites the White Bagre from its beginning up to the account of the present stage of the ceremony and the congregation repeats his words line by line. This is done while the guides thresh a small quantity of guinea corn with sticks (W. 3184). The senior members take some grains of the guinea corn, put them in a container (nowadays a bottle) and say that they will change it into something else. Secretly they substitute some malted grain and display it to those present (1498 and W. 3195).

The congregation then moves to the 'swamp' itself where each second-grader dives into the river with his neophyte and they are allowed to bathe and swim for a while. Afterwards the congregation returns to the Bagre room where the White Bagre is recited three times. While this is happening the guides count the money that their neophytes were given during their rounds.

After the recital the neophytes are allowed to break their fast. While they eat and drink, the guides tell their second-graders the amount of money each has collected and the Speaker interrogates each second-grader about these amounts. The second-grader looking after the oldest neophyte (*Bo kpɛ̃ɛ̃*) is asked first, and so on down to the most junior. On the first two occasions fictitious figures are given. But in answer to the third question the right amount is finally quoted, a pattern of behaviour that also occurs at funerals and at marriages. When giving their returns, the members display their command of the vocabulary of numbers, trying to complicate ordinary usage by combining them in various ways. The following examples give an idea of this:

a. 2,000 less 100 (1,900)
   tur ayi vuɔ̃ kuba

b. the big 20 (20,000)
   lizer kpɛ̃ɛ̃

c. 3,560 less 5 (3,555)
   tur ata ni kɔɔru nuu dɔɔl
   lizɛɛ ata ngma nuu

By late afternoon the ceremony is over and the neophytes have their evening meal and are whitewashed once again. They receive further instruction in Bagre matters, especially in the wild animals that are associated with the cult (W. 3436) and how the meat should be divided if an animal is killed (W. 3328). At the end of the ceremony the neophytes and their companions go out on a ritual hunt with throwing-sticks and guns. The meat of certain special animals that they bring back is forbidden to non-initiates; it is Bagre meat. If they kill none of them on this occasion, they must do so later to pay their debt to Bagre, or rather to its senior members (W. 3472). The first such animal they kill after their initiation belongs to the association (W. 3428). This act, it is said, will take away the 'dirt' of the neophytes (W. 3431); a constant theme of Bagre is the attempt to reduce the pollution of the new entrants, though only for the period of the performances, since purity is an unnatural state.

Some wild animals are prohibited by the cult (W. 3436), others preferred (W. 3448); the text gives four of each, the pairing indicated by the numbers is my own suggestion and not one on which I would put much weight.

Prohibited (House)	*Preferred* (Bagre)
1. boar	2. rabbit
2. porcupine	1. duiker (*wala*)[1]
3. grass-cutter	4. partridge
4. guinea fowl	3. squirrel

The most important aspect of the hunt, as far as the text is concerned, has less to do with classification than with social relationships. Like most of the simpler societies, the LoDagaa prescribe certain modes of distributing the meat of animals, whether that of domestic animals offered in sacrifice or celebration, or that of wild animals killed in the hunt. The distribution follows the main lines of social obligation. In states, the local chief has his share; elsewhere, as among the LoDagaa, the meat is distributed along the dominant lines of kinship, descent, affinity, joking partnership, and friendship; certain main portions go to close kinsfolk, especially to the father and mother. But the Bagre society replaces ties of kinship with ties of association (or rather incorporates the one in the other), even to the extent of providing its own 'father' and 'mother'. The Bagre mother is the one who sponsors the neophyte; the Bagre father is the Speaker. At the same time the father of Bagre is the rain, the mother the earth, and together they produce the crops that are needed for the performances (W. 4770). Because of this conscious realignment, the whole process of distribution has to be redefined in terms of the association and, as usual, the myth does this by dramatizing the difference between the two methods in a conflict situation.

When the Beating of the Malt has been performed, the neophytes can talk to people again, but they are still abused by all and sundry. This treatment continues until the main ceremony, known as Bagre Dance. This is the central performance of the whole series, when the new members are relieved of their restrictions, killed and revived by means of the Bagre medicine, and are formally inducted into the association. This is the occasion that most of the population associate with the performance of Bagre.

[1] The antelope here is *wala*; the roan antelope given to the beings of the wild for their medicine is a *wal piel*, a horse-like antelope that is the counterpart of the stallion given by other clans when such medicine is transferred to them (W. 2693). Later we are told that it is the beings from the river that get the stallion and those from the hill the 100,000 cowries (W. 5390). On another level, the stallion is used to transport the aged to the ceremony and the 100,000 is used to buy grain (W. 4821).

The Bagre Dance (Bo siɔr)

The main ceremony of the whole sequence is known as *Bo siɔr* (LD. *Bag sebr*), the Bagre Dance (W. 3481); *siɔr* is a more athletic kind of dance than the *bine* that has formed the main dance up till now and it is accompanied by the larger xylophone (*gyil bɛrɛ*), which is played inside the room.

I should add that great store is set on the production of these instruments for the ceremony. They represent a considerable investment of wealth and some return payment is always given on occasions such as these. At the Bagre Dance a special pot of xylophone beer (*gyil dãã*) is placed by its side; into this a playing stick is dipped and the beer is then thrown away.

The grain for this beer is provided by the 'Bagre mother'. In 1950, the Baaperi 'headman' sent a large basketful (*pɛsõ*) of malted grain to the owners of the xylophone two days before the Bagre Dance was due to be performed, on the day known as 'the collecting of the malt' (*kɛɛ wuur* or *kyi wuur*). At that time some instruction is given to the initiates and a start is made to the brewing of the beer which will later be given to the owners and players of the xylophones and the drums (*kuɔr*) that are used. My assistant, for example, received two pots of beer (some eight gallons in all) for playing during part of one night. In addition each neophyte brings two fowls, one for the owner of the xylophone and one for the owner of the drum. Usually these fowls are taken from the gifts given to the neophytes when they have been successfully brought back to life. Like other gifts, they must travel outside the lineage performing the Bagre (122).

The people providing the xylophone on this occasion were the household of the late chief, Gandaa. This important figure had built up the chiefship of Birifu from nothing and had become a wealthy as well as a prolific man—he had some 200 children. His wealth was derived partly from medicine shrines, partly from the farming contributions of the residents of Birifu, and the remainder from a variety of other sources. He was himself a great player and kept several xylophones in good condition so that they could be brought out at funerals and other ercemonies. Indeed it was expected that people would ask for the chief's xylophones and these requests provided him with a small income which together with the money from playing at ceremonies and funerals helped to maintain his vast household. At the time of the 1950 Bagre he had been dead for six months and the elder of Baaperi, who was one of his 'headmen' and whose sector was adjacent to that of the chief's lineage, accepted the xylophones as before. But in the other clan sector performing Bagre that year, that of Maale, the elder and 'headman', Depep, borrowed xylophones from two other places, both in Kyaa. Consequently he had to divide the grain into three and sent only a small basket (*pɛlɛ*) to the chief's house. This they refused, saying that they had always sent Maale a full basket on these occasions. This statement was no doubt true, but the appeal to tradition probably concealed the fact that before the creation of the chiefship instituted a redistributive system through the centre, the basis of Bagre exchanges was a reciprocal one, with adjacent units performing these services for one another.[1] Depep's action was almost certainly a reversion to an earlier pattern, in opposition to the policy of centralization which colonial overrule, like the national overrule to which it gave way, made inevitable in one form or other. I heard Depep later apologize to the Naayili elders, saying that he was forced into this by Bonyir of Kyaa; as his Bagre joking partners this clan has a great influence in such matters. Nevertheless it should be added that they are unable to force their views upon their partners unless the latter are willing to accept them, for they exercise only moral pressure.

My assistant at this time was the son of the late chief and he had made plans for the Bagre Dance some time earlier. He had his Dane gun repaired so that he could shoot it off when the neophytes came out of the room after successfully passing through their ordeal. Furthermore he reckoned on taking his father's xylophone to play in the Bagre room: 'My father was always asked to take his

---

[1] K. G's comment presents a slightly different view. 'After the chief's death his xylophones were allowed to decay and none of his sons could play as he did. Depep therefore hired the xylophones of the best available player, Nikara, who was a sister's son of Gandaa'. K. G. insists that a similar situation existed with regard to the late chief, who 'did not allow chieftaincy to interfere with customary rites. If his xylophones were hired, it was because they were the best for miles around. Players from Nandom, Jirapa, and the Ivory Coast all came to him to purchase xylophones. Hence he was always busy making these instruments almost all the year round. He was the only player for the room as well as for the outside Bagre tunes and he played all the time until he went home. So his xylophones were not hired because he was a chief. During my father's lifetime, when his clan Naayili had their Bagre, he normally used his xylophones in the room but he still hired Depep's instruments as well as those of Tekoder, and these men were always given the traditional baskets of malt as well as the fowls.'

xylophone to every Bagre performance in Birifu.' But things did not
work out as he anticipated. His gun was repaired and he shot off
so much powder that he thought he would get a sheep from the
'Bagre mother'. For the xylophone his lineage received only a
portion of the total amount, a large basket of guinea corn, for
reasons I have explained. Kpaari was so annoyed about this that
on Bagre morning, when he 'swept' his sister-in-law with a guinea
fowl, he beat the bird so violently against the stool she sat on that
it died. People do this when they are dissatisfied with the Bagre,
for example, because they have not been given enough beer;
otherwise they allow the guides to save the birds which are needed
for distribution. In this connection it is also significant that the
Bagre Speaker from the late chief's house, who had held a position of *primus inter pares* when the chief was alive, no longer had
quite the same control and complained that Maale were making
many mistakes in their performance.[1]

The Bagre Dance takes place over three days, preceded by the
Bagre for Bambara Beans when there is some playful dancing;
the other days are Bagre Eve, Bagre Day, and the End of the
Dance. When the beer, which has hitherto been guarded by women
neophytes, is ready, the ceremony proper can begin.

Day 1. *The Bagre for Bambara Beans* (Bo singbile)

In Lawra (LoDagaba) the first day of the Bagre Dance itself
is sometimes known as *dãã paal*, 'the beer filling'. The neophytes
and spectators stand round the vats and sing '*Dãã paal, dãã paal*'.
The small pots are then filled up, and thereafter an initiate is
forbidden to use the word *paal*, to fill. A member will say instead,
'*Pur a dãã ka a shɔɔ a ngman*, pour beer till the brim is reached';
whereas a non-initiate will say, '*Pur a dãã paala ngman*'. By means
of such circumlocutions one knows who is and who is not a member.

I attended this ceremony in Baaperi on 30 December 1950. On
this day the guides cook all the food crops that have been forbidden
to the neophytes, that is bambara beans (*singbile*), black and white
beans (*beng pla, beng sɔɔla*), and yams (*nyu der*, water yams, for

---

[1] K. G. comments: 'Each "Bagre mother" hires a "Bagre father" to come and
perform the Bagre for them. If Kyaa have Bagre and hire Naayili to act as their
Bagre fathers, then Doyeri would organize it and he is to blame if anything
goes wrong. Similarly if Naayili invites Kyaa to act as their "Bagre fathers",
then Bonyir has this role. Again the influence of my father in these matters was
negligible. If anything it was because he himself was well versed in the myth.'

nyu war are not prohibited). All these are cooked for the neophytes and divided out among neighbouring clan sectors.

The taboo on bambara beans gives rise to a joking situation between members and non-members of the association. The latter can thieve the beans but members cannot. It is a perpetual joke at this time and I, as a non-initiate, was often urged to steal some, though I was also told a story of a lad whose 'penis became sick' through doing so. The situation is not dissimilar to that of a sister's son snatching from his mother's clan, though the action here is described as thieving rather than snatching.

Day 2. *Bagre Eve* (Bo tisɔɔ)

It is after dark that the food is eventually divided out, and around the Bagre house little fires are lit to roast the yams. When these are ready, the guides and their neophytes sit in separate groups; the former have two yams each, which they cut into four, one part for the neophyte, one for themselves, one for the Speakers, and one for general distribution. A group of people sitting near the house (all this part of the ceremony took place outside) collected the central slice of each yam, cut it into two and placed the parts in separate baskets. One of these baskets was to be divided among the four main patriclans while the other was divided among the three constituent lineages of Ngmanbili. When the yams had been shared out, some were put inside for roasting on the following day.

It was now fully dark and the neophytes were called around the pots of beer that stood outside. Some of the beer was poured into small pots that were carried off to other houses, so that it could not be stolen by the non-initiates. The neophytes brought the gourds acquired at the Whitening Ceremony and they were hung on a guinea corn stalk and suspended in the beer. The Speaker then shouted out, 'Let the neophytes come' (*a bobil ba wa*). They came forward and cried out, three times, 'the beer is full' (*dãã paal*), and afterwards, '*Hoas, hoas, hoas*', which was again repeated three times.

Just before dawn they cry to the Bagre deity who is believed to descend among them; 'the god who descends', and the whole problem of two-way communication between god and man, is a constant theme of the Bagre myth (W. 104). The neophytes have been sleeping on the rooftop of the Bagre house, huddled under their light cloths or lying close to a smouldering log. At cock-crow they are woken up by the Bagre elders and rushed off to the east side of the house where the first rays of the sun are rising. From here they are hustled back and forth, across the flat roof, looking for the descending god. They go to his shrine built in the neck of the granary where they kill a small fowl, but this time it is refused: *Wen, wen, wen zɔɔra, ho, ho, ho,* they cry. The fowl appears to be the offspring of the Starting Fowl with which each neophyte is endowed at the opening ceremony (W. 3630). When the sun has risen, they all go down to a point on the path that leads westwards to the river where it is crossed by another track. There, at this point of intersection and dispersal, they kill a fowl on a small raised pile of earth, which serves as an altar both to the Earth shrine and to distant ancestors (Goody 1962: 245). As they do so, they cry out a prayer, repeating each phrase three times:

> Path, take the fowl,
> *sɔr dɛ nuo,*
>
> path, refuse the fowl.
> *sɔr zɔɔr nuo,*
> *ho ho ho.*

After that they are all fed with beer, porridge, and soup that now includes beef (W. 3620). Later on that morning they return to the room where a fowl is killed to the skin bags (*bo wuɔ*) they acquired at the Whitening Ceremony. Before the sacrifice is made, the guides, initiates and Speakers chant a number of songs, of which the following is an example:

> The Bagre bag's fowl will hit you,
> *bo wuɔ nuɔ pɔb yɛ*
> *A wuɔ nuɔ na pɔb*
> *A wuɔ nuɔ na pɔb*
> *Hãã hãã*

For the word 'fowl', the names of all the forbidden foods are sub-stituted one by one, that is, yams, beer, and beans. The song is sung three times to the accompaniment of drums, made from gourds (*kuɔr*), both big and small. The bags are taken from the neophytes and hung on a house-post.

Another song is chanted, insisting again on the same uncer-tainty that had characterized the sacrifice to the 'path'.

> The bag refuses the fowl,
> *wuɔ zɔɔr nuɔ wɛ*
>
> the bag accepts the fowl.
> *wuɔ de nuɔ wɛ*
> *ho, ho, ho-oo.*

When the offering has been made, those present break into another song, which is again repeated three times:

> The Bagre bag strikes the fowl.
> *bɔɔ wuɔ ngme nuɔ yee*
> *bɔɔ wuɔ ngme nuɔ*
> *na kpaa kpaa kpaa*
> *na kpai kpai,*
> *hey hey hey.*

Now that the bags have been dealt with, the neophytes are given a meal and await the most critical part of the ceremony. For this is the night when they are killed and brought to life again. Indeed, it is actually claimed that they die and are saved (*bɛ ko ti siung*).[1]

The attempt to build up tension among the neophytes is clear from the text of the White Bagre. A headband is again tied around each neophyte (W. 3762); the notion of confession is again insisted upon (W. 3758). The medicine is formally carried into the room and is sprinkled with water as it comes (W. 3809). Later on all lights are extinguished, the Speaker roars, and in the middle of the room stands the pot of 'poison' with an arrow in it.

First of all the neophytes receive lengthy instructions which once again call upon them to confess any breach of Bagre discipline, lest the medicine fail to work and not bring them back to life. The confession takes place in front of the medicine, whose power is indicated by the further spurting of cold water over it (W. 3875). A red cock is sacrificed to the medicine, which is addressed by the usual Bagre invocation (W. 3908). The senior members are then told to put their hands in their bags and bring out the leather bottles (*gan*) used for formal divining (W. 3949). Sitting next to their respective neophytes, the first-graders untie the bell from the gourd that each one has carried and these parts of the gear are placed in front of them (W. 3981). In this ceremony it

---

[1] In Lawra, at this time, all ancestral shrines are brought into the Bagre room and a cow is sacrificed to them, to be eaten by initiates alone (A 10).

is said of the gourd that 'the big hen's egg hatches today' (W. 3970), for it plays a major part in the ceremony. The metaphor of the egg serves to stress the careful way in which the gourd must be treated, for it is equivalent to a person's life.

The seniors then cast the marked cowries from their leather containers to see whether they may go ahead (W. 3987). When this has been determined, the bell is taken by the guides and the gourds are lowered in the beer in which an arrow rests, making it appear as though everything was covered in arrow poison. Each neophyte is flanked by both a senior and a junior member—the latter being the usual guide. The gourds, filled with the 'poison', are handed back to the senior members who place them in front of the nostrils of the neophyte. First of all the Speaker (the Bagre 'father') tries the poison himself, roaring out as it gets near his nostrils that it is too strong for him to bear (W. 4017). The xylophone strikes up and the medicine is poured out into broken pots for the neophytes. The situation is rendered yet more threatening by the throwing sticks (or cudgels) that are now brought into the room (W. 4073). Further tests are made and the lights are put out. When the strophantus seeds have been ground up (W. 4136), the Speaker places his own medicine gourd in front of him, shakes his rattle and orders the senior members to take their sticks and seize the neophytes. In the myth, the neophytes are now in tears, but the tension is broken by laughter and the guides whisper to their charges, telling them to lie down. Throughout this performance, hunting terms are used to describe what is happening. 'They are poisoning the arrows (*ba zɛl a lɔɔ*)', the members declare, as they prepare the pot that stands in front of the neophytes. In fact it contains only beer, but in it has been placed an arrow and some roots. The arrow is of course assumed to have been poisoned with strophanthus (*yebe*) while powder from tree roots is an essential constituent of all medicines. The beer is then poured into the round gourd given to each neophyte, though first the senior members taste it to see whether the mixture is poisonous enough, roaring out as they do so.

No incident better indicates the climate of mixed belief and disbelief that marks such ceremonies. Here the LoDagaa are behaving in somewhat the same way as the Masons of contemporary Britain (some million in all), who are also 'killed' and 'revived' during the course of their initiatory procedures. It is not that one lot 'believes' and the other 'disbelieves' in the procedures through which they are being led. On a formal, theological level the Bagre ritual does appear to offer its members a means of conquering death, which is later revealed as a sham. But few of the neophytes really accept the threats of the Speakers at their face value. For most people a certain scepticism modifies more extreme forebodings. But in any case, there is never a complete gap in knowledge about these matters between members and non-members; snippets of information invariably leak out, friend whispers confidentially to friend, and, above all, one of the informal roles of the guide is to tell the neophyte what to expect. Thus the whole ceremony has an air of acting about it, though this is only one element in a complex whole which proceeds in an atmosphere of compounded belief and disbelief.

While the initiates are 'killed' and 'revived', their progress is punctuated by a number of songs which form part of the text (W. 4194). These songs vary somewhat as between local parts of the society, but within one group they are relatively fixed. New songs are often created for playing outside the Bagre room and after hearing of one incident bringing discredit on a neophyte, my assistant turned to me and said, 'I must make up a song about that in the room'. The satirical sanctions in these songs serve to reinforce the more formal authority of the elders and the more distant authority of supernatural agencies.

But the basic songs are fairly static, though one hears different variants at various times. One sequence went as follows. When the neophytes were 'killed', they sang:

A big question lies on the floor,
soor bala gã teung yee

a big question lies there but no one can solve it.
soor bala gã teung ka sooro ba ka

The songs sung in the room refer to the actions taking place. When they revive the neophytes, they sing (W. 4199):

Death kills,
kũũ ku na yee

but *Bo wen* saves us, so death can't kill.
bɔɔ wen faa bar ka kũũ ta kuɛ

and then:

> We've pulled the witch's old tooth.
> *sɔɔr nyin koro ka ti vir kpiru*

After this the members call for a reward for all they are doing:

> Bring us the hundred,
> *yɛ wani kuba yee*

> bring us the hundred to pay for the neophytes,
> *yɛ wani kuba ka ti lɔb bɔbɔ*

> bring us the hundred.
> *yɛ wani kuba yee*

> You Bagre mothers, bring us the hundred because the first wasn't enough.
> *bɔɔ ma minɛ yɛ wani kuba an ba ta*

The revival of the neophytes is still problematical, despite the earlier rehearsal under the aegis of the beings of the wild (W. 2457). Indeed the present situation dramatizes the conflict between God (or god) and the beings which forms a central theme of the Black Bagre that follows. For the first suggestion from the junior members about reviving the dead novices is that they should

> 'enter the room,
> take the bells,
> and the things of the beings,
> and shake them and see'. (W. 4261–4).[1]

The juniors fail and the seniors take over; after again calling for confession, they shake the bells and roll their tongues in the ears of the dead (W. 4342), as the beings had done on the previous occasion (W. 2680). While the role of God (or god) is not specifically stressed at this point, that of the beings is clearly equivocal since one of them deliberately led men astray by intervening when they were discussing God and declaring that 'he was God in the Bagre house' (W. 2462–4).

Directly they have been brought to life again, the neophytes are warned not to tell the secrets of Bagre to outsiders, even to the Oil Bagre members (W. 4464), and they are encouraged to learn the myth themselves (W. 4391).

---

[1] 'Things of the beings' appear to qualify rather than to supplement the bells.

When the instruction is finished for the time being, the guides throw burning brands outside the room (W. 4494). It is of some interest to see what different interpretations an act of this kind can generate. I thought at first that this was a symbol, perhaps of rebirth, but also a sign of their rejoicing and a challenge to the world outside. For non-members seize upon the brands and try to toss them back again into the room. However, my collaborator drew my attention to the similarity between this ceremony and the annual fire-festival of Moslem communities in West Africa, e.g. Bugum in Dagomba and Jentigi in Gonja, and commented:

No non-initiate is allowed into the Bagre room during these performances. In order to dramatise the situation some of the guides are asked to act as non-initiates who have stealthily entered the room to steal the food and drink. They are then chased out of the room with burning brands. When they get lost among the dancers, the fire is thrown into the crowd. The significance of this, I think, is to demonstrate to the initiates what would happen should any outsider actually dare enter the Bagre room to spy or to steal food.

Outside, the non-initiates are given their own food, yams, beans, and bambara beans, which they cook themselves (W. 4507), emphasizing their separateness and yet their participation as members of the same community who have contributed food, and neophytes too.

About half an hour later the neophytes emerge and walk round three circles, first round the xylophones and then round the house. This is the occasion when the bells, which had earlier been untied from the gourds, are 'hidden' by the guides (when their charges are 'dead') and then found by them when they recover. As the neophytes go out to find the bells, they sing:

> Give us way, give us way,
> *yi ngmaa guɔ ku ti yee*
>
> a twisting way.
> *na gɔ̃ gɔ̃ gɔ̃*

This is an appeal to the non-members dancing outside to let them pass. As they walk around the house the neophytes' eyes are covered (W. 4519) and their heads put under the arms of the guides. The neophytes are asked, 'Do you know the place you'll meet Bagre?' (W. 4521) and they walk slowly round the house, singing:

> Let's creep out,
> *yi gũũ gu yie*
>
> let's creep out,
> *yi gũũ gu yie*
>
> like creeping creatures.
> *na guura guuru.*

On the third occasion they stop and collect the bells that have been hidden in the outside wall, and as they return to the room they sing

> Beware of the house posts,
> *yi bɔɔ ni lue*
>
> beware of the crooked posts,
> *yi bɔɔni lue lu' gɔn gɔn*
>
> the crooked posts of [Depep's] house.
> *Depep yir puɔ lu' gɔn gɔn.*

Small pots of beer without any yeast are carried in procession, one for each neophyte. This is the point at which is sung the song

> The Bagre beer pot is small and empty.
> *bo dãã duli na kpol kpol*

When the neophytes have returned to the room, the women follow with the beer. More is allocated to the senior members (*bo ma minɛ dãã*) and all get down to the business of drinking. When they have finished, all come out once more, singing

> Let's go outside and enter again.
> *yi i ka ti yung ti bɔ̃ lɛ kpɛ*

They walk round the xylophone and finally return to the room for more instruction.

The whole process of killing and reviving the neophytes continues almost until daybreak. They are left lying for an hour or so before being revived with the Bagre medicine. Only the senior members are concerned with this part of the ceremony; the junior ones stand by to whitewash the neophytes. First their bodies are whitewashed on one side as they lie on the floor of the room. Even the slats of the small xylophone have white crosses painted on the end. Later they are woken up, killed again, and turned over so that they can be whitewashed on the other side as well. As before, the whitewashing is a further test of earlier behaviour.

7. The neophytes and their guides sit waiting after the shaving of their heads (Birifu, 1970)

The neophytes are sworn not to reveal what has happened to them during the ceremony, lest they incur great suffering, as is brought out in the following songs:

(If you) say (reveal the secret), your head breaks in two,
yel ka zu wɛl gele

Say and your stomach bursts.
yel ka puɔ pur mhaba

The song continues in the same vein for several verses.

Finally the neophytes are allowed to go to bed, while the guides roam around the clan sector where the Bagre is being performed, worrying every adult in the area for payments. This they do till dawn. At the house, the xylophone plays on while spectators dance. It has been a day of tribulation for the neophytes and their kin; tomorrow is their day of celebration.

Day 3. Bagre Day (Bo muna)

The guides are up early the next morning, continuing their rounds of all the houses of the patriclan and forcing people to give them gifts. If these are not forthcoming they get hold of the individual in question and swing him up and down until he relents. In Lawra, the collecting is yet more vigorously carried out and the guides go round to every house, shaking the rattles used by the elders and drinking any beer they find, unless the woman who owns it first gives them money. If she has neither beer nor money, *o ya paar*, 'she'll pay with her vagina'.

When they have finished collecting for themselves, the guides return to get the equipment needed to bathe and shave the heads of the neophytes, that is the razor, water, and shea oil. When these are ready the Bagre elder arranges for the Black Bagre to be repeated three times (W. 4870) and about mid-morning they start to shave, bathe, and anoint the neophytes. The shaving of the head is carried out on persons going through various rites of passage, but it is especially associated with the treatment of widows at funerals (Goody 1962: 61). For the bathing, each Bagre guide brings a chunk of sun-baked earth, picked from the ruins of an old house; this is his seat, which has later to be destroyed. The neophytes are bathed sitting on the brick, where they are brought guinea corn porridge to eat and guinea corn beer to drink. They eat and drink naked, sitting between two members. The clothes they have been wearing (which have been few and old) are cut off them and thrown into a hole (*bo yaar*, the Bagre grave) because they are 'dirty'. And for the first time (as far as the neophytes are concerned), their food is accompanied by meat and flavoured with pepper. It is the senior members that eat first and it is they who get the head of each pot of beer brought to them by the guides, in order to make it cool for the others. As they sit there, the White Bagre is recited three times and further instruction is given about the purchase of Bagre medicine (W. 4827) and the use of the horse acquired in this way to carry old men to the performances; the initiates are also told about their duties to others as well as ways of recognizing members and of deceiving outsiders (W. 4962). When the meal is finished, guns are fired and the neophytes run inside the room one by one as women line the way and ululate as each goes by. Holding a knife in the right hand, the guides go first to demonstrate the way to run elegantly. The neophytes follow, imitating this manner of majestic locomotion.

Once inside, the neophytes sit beside their corresponding senior member who is already in his place. Now it is the Black Bagre that is recited to them, the story of the Creation. It is told three times in all, but parts are cut out the second time, and the third is a much abbreviated version.

After the last recital of the Black Bagre the neophytes are dressed by their guides with the clothes provided by their parents or guardians. As they come out, led by the Speakers, they sing:

> Make way,
> make way for the neophytes to pass.
> *yi ngmaa guɔ ku ti yee*
> *yi ngmaa guɔ ku ti bɔbɔ tɔl*

They circle the xylophone three times and then burst into a lament:

hee wuyee	Alas
hee wuyee	alas
hee wuyee	alas
e-he yaa yee, e-hee yee	alas, alas, alas

The xylophone players now drop the Bagre tunes and play other songs for the dancers. Meanwhile the guides rush their neophytes over to the west of the open area[1] and then hurry them back to the front of the house where they take their seats for the gift-giving ceremony. Again it is as if they were being put through a funeral ceremony, even mourning for their dead selves.

When I arrived at Baaperi about 4.30 p.m., the neophytes had just come out and were sitting on chairs and stools, dressed in their best, the women in front, the men behind. One of the late chief's daughters held an umbrella over her brother's wife as she ate her millet porridge and was generally fussed over.[2]

When the meal was finished, everybody returned to the room for more reciting and more singing. As the time came for them to emerge, there was much excitement among the large crowd that was building up, with people coming from all over Birifu, and as far afield as Tanchera and Nadoli, some twenty miles south. The guides gathered at the entrance to the room, or rather at the special doorway that was cut in the wall of the courtyard on Bagre Eve. Here again is another striking similarity with the funerals. For when the corpse is taken from his room to the funeral stand outside, a special exit is made in the wall, though it is not as wide as the Bagre one (Goody 1962: 77).

As the neophytes came out the guides held a brush in one hand and a basket in the other (W. 4972); the brush consists of a single strand of the grass (*saar*) used for sweeping and the basket is the one in which the grain has been collected. The neophytes come out, preceded by their senior members, and the guides sweep the 'dirt' from their backs, 'sweeping away the bad things (*bebe*) that had caught them', the trouble that had made them become initiated. As they come out, they sing, telling the dancers to make way for them.

The male neophytes are now given the bows and arrows which they had left in their own rooms throughout the ritual sequence. In their right hands they carry knives, on the end of which are maize cobs to prevent them doing any damage; they also carry the bells, which they knock against the open palm of the left hand.

[1] It is possibly at this time that the neophytes' gourds are broken; the parallel with the breaking of the calabash which has been used to whitewash a widow was pointed out to me by one young man who recognized this as a kind of test, *pol* (2473).

[2] I do not know whether this meal was a substitution for the naked lunch. There was a strong feeling among educated LoWiili against nudity and this was beginning to make itself felt even in ceremonies of this kind.

As they reached the xylophones, they walked around them, singing:

> Give us way, a twisting way.
> *yi ngmaa gu ko ti gõ gõ gõ*

Three times they walked round the xylophones, while some of the onlookers joined in, dancing as they went. They broke off and went over to a tree some forty yards away, then all turned round together and rushed back to take their seats on a line of tree-trunks resting upon supporting poles that had been prepared for them to sit on. The baskets, which had already been used for several purposes, were now set down at their sides for people to throw in their contributions of money and delicacies such as *niiri* (light brown seeds used for soup) or *kpogo* (small white rings made from cassava flour).

People crowded round the new members bringing cocks for the males and guinea fowl for the females. With these birds, they proceed to 'sweep' (*pir*) the neophytes, brushing them across the shoulders, first the left, then the right, across the chest, and finally beating the head of the fowl against the log on which they were sitting (*ba vaarana*). The birds are killed unless the guides can rush forward and save them (W. 4997). One of these fowls from each neophyte is usually given to the owner of the xylophone and of the large gourd drum. The guides take the rest to the 'Bagre mother' with whom they are shared.

While the giving of gifts goes on, the women ululate, the men fire guns, the dancing continues, and the noise and excitement are intense. The whole performance is a display of wealth and prestige which is particularly marked now that a new system of stratification is emerging. By far the majority of those present were to be found around the woman married into the late chief's house. Partly these were her husband's brothers, probably the only people who were in paid jobs and at the same time had access to some recently acquired inheritance. Partly they were friends or supporters who had received favours in the past. The contrast was great between the mass of guinea fowl received by these fortunate few and the meagre offerings of some of the less well-connected persons present.

When the excitement died down, the neophytes were led back into the room for more instruction and were later released to return home or to dance and drink with their lovers or spouses. They are now members of the Bagre association and it only remains to tie up the ends of the ritual.

Day 4. *The End of the Dance* (Bo gyingyiri)

The last day of the Bagre Dance is known as the End of the Dance, the literal meaning being 'the day of the leaping feet'; it is put aside for drinking, dancing, and for courting girls and it is then that many marriages are arranged. In Lawra the same day is called *Bara dɛ nyuɔr*, 'dog tracks his prey with his nose', the implication of which is that the neophytes have successfully completed their initiation.

During the day-time, both the Black and White Bagre are recited to the neophytes, who spend most of the day listening to and taking in the words.

I arrived at Baaperi at about 5 o'clock on 27 December and the neophytes had already emerged from the room where they had sat right through the recitation of the Bagre. They had finished crying to the Bagre deity and the new members were now sitting on the rooftop, wearing normal clothes, and were being addressed by a Speaker. Before it got too dark, he led them in procession down the ladder, shaking a rattle as he went. Each new initiate was led by a senior member who was singing a song, the words of which were first enunciated by the Speaker. Around their necks hung the bell which will remain there until the final ceremony, the Bagre Bells, which follows shortly. Then the bells, which are 'like an egg' (W. 5063), are washed and the neophytes are warned that it is a great offence to commit adultery (W. 5072).

In their hand the neophytes carry a knife or long dagger. The knives again recall funerals where sextons carry them into the grave to make sure no wandering soul is buried with the corpse; 'they are like corpses', I was once told (A. 11). These knives are carried around until the neophytes make their final appearance in the local market, an act which brings them back fully into the life of the community.

The neophytes are given further instruction at this time, being told specifically about the role of the sister's son and why he is entitled to a share of Bagre food (W. 5076). This statement includes a classical justification of matrilineal inheritance which is not now practised in Birifu, although some are aware that certain of their ancestors did so; it is a justification phrased strictly in terms of intergenerational tensions. The neophytes are again encouraged to learn the Bagre myth and even to incorporate passages from other people's versions (W. 5210). They are also encouraged to ask questions as the only way of learning (W. 5351 and 5420) and the Speaker answers certain set queries about the relationship between God and gods (W. 5248) which are dealt with more fully in the Black Bagre, the importance of which is strongly emphasized (W. 5297 ff.).

The neophytes and their companions take part in two special dances and when they are finished go a short distance away where they receive some last brief words and then set off to their own homes. After having been given beer to drink, they are virtually free to act as normal people. On one such occasion I sat drinking beer on the rooftop of the Bagre house when some of the new initiates came to join us; their humble and silent demeanour now gone, they entered fully into the ordinary conversation. One of my companions started shaking the bell tied round a girl's neck—a forbidden act which can in theory bring great harm, but which was now treated as a joke.

At this point in the ritual sequence, the Maale performances were taking place a week (six days) behind the Baaperi ones and the End of the Dance came on 2 January. Again I arrived at about five o'clock when the recital in the room had already taken place and the neophytes were sitting over their beer. Soon they came out of the room to dance, though only for a short time because a funeral was taking place in another lineage of the same clan. The final ritual occurred when the neophytes were called to the rooftop where they clustered around the granary as a fowl was sacrificed to the Bagre deity. After half an hour they came down the ladder singing the song which, in Lawra, gives the day its name:

Bara dɛ nyuɔr, fã, fã, fã

I had earlier translated this as 'Dog track his prey with his nose', but the *bara* can also refer to the knife used for shaving their head: the 'nose' is the hair.[1]

---

[1] My original translation was 'The neophyte gets a nose' but K. G. corrected me. He also gave an alternative version of this song and comments:

bara wõna nyũũ yee
bara wõna nyũũ na vã vã

The song was followed by the lament:

> *hee wu yee, ayai, ayai.*

The words of this song simply indicate that the end has come; the xylophone now changes to play *bine*, the music that was played up to the time of the big dance. Various songs are sung to the music, including

> Bagre matters are like that,
> *bo yele ngmen lɛ*
>
> turning, turning, turning;
> *gyiri, gyiri, gyiri*
>
> Bagre matters are like that,
> *bo yele ngmen lɛ*
>
> always bringing death.
> *ma ku kû.*

The *gyiri, gyiri* appears to refer to the 'leaping of feet', but there is also the implication that the dance is now ended, the fire is dying down. The leaper is tired and weary.

The neophytes leave and go off to the house of their guide, where they drink the Guides' Beer, made from malt given by the neophytes. Afterwards they returned to the Bagre house to eat food prepared with the fowl slaughtered to the Bagre deity. The meal over, they are free at last to go back to their own houses, though not yet to sleep with their husbands or wives. This they can do only after Bagre Bells, which closes the performances for the year.

Meanwhile the senior members go home with the chickens they have gained, which can be used for sacrifices to the ancestors, to the beings of the wild, or to the guardians. But if the bones are swallowed by another fowl, it too will be for Bagre; 'Bagre things / you can't mix / with things of the hoe' (W. 5490–92).

> *bar' daa wõ nyũũ na vã vã*
> *bar' daa wõ nyũũ na vã vã*

The dog smells an awful smell. 'Here the "dog" is the knife used in shaving the neophytes' hair the day before. The smell refers to the dirty hair which they had been carrying for the past 6 weeks or more. The shaving of the hair takes away evil and sin from the neophytes.'

Bagre Gifts (Bo tuor)

The pattern of reciprocal relationship between clan sectors and lineages is very complex in all the ceremonial activity of the LoDagaa. In my earlier account of the funerals (1962) I tried to elucidate part of the total network that joins neighbouring groups. Similar networks are found throughout the Bagre. Directly Maale had finished the Bagre Dance on 2 and 3 January, their closest lineage in the clan sector (Ngmanbili Gorpuo) started to brew beer for Bagre Gifts (*Bo tuor*) in each of their compounds. *Tuor* here means 'load'; *fu tuo bɛ na*, 'you give them gifts', 'dash them' in West African English. People from all over the settlement trooped along to make small presents of money (cowries) and were given beer to drink in return. When the visitor's clan perform Bagre, the present recipients will go to greet them in the same way and increase the sum that has already been given. This escalating reciprocity ensures a wide participation, over time as well as space, in the performances of any one group.

On such visits a person has to pay special attention to female kin who have married there. On one occasion I visited the house where the sister of my assistant's father had married. No sooner had we sat down to drink than she directed a torrent of abuse at him because no one from her natal home, four hundred yards away, had come to visit her and when her nephew did appear, he came empty-handed. This was no playful abuse; the woman was very serious and my assistant most upset; she relented only when others tried to calm the situation down and when he promised to send something to her later on. It was not the monetary exchange that mattered as much as the respect, the recognition of a relationship, that such a gift implied; and such a recognition is particularly important for a woman who has married away.

This gift-giving is essentially an extension of the prestations that take place at the Bagre Dance itself, when the neophytes are sitting outside the Bagre house dressed in their finery. There is a long-term reciprocity about all these gifts, which build up during the lifetime of the individuals involved. On this whole process my collaborator, K. Gandaa, offered the following comments:

This ceremony resembles Christmas. But the reciprocity at Christmas differs from that at Bagre Gifts in that it is not automatic. If Naayili have Bagre, then every person in Naayili will expect gifts from people in the other sectors who are either friends, in-laws or relatives. These gifts range from sixpence to several pounds, from fowls to cows and from food to clothes. It depends upon the giver's wealth and upon the number of persons to whom he intends to give presents.

It should be emphasized that Bagre gifts accumulate with interest. If I have received a gift of five shillings from a relation or friend, he will expect more than this from me when his Bagre comes round. I may double the amount to ten shillings. My brother Tisep's senior sister from Naayili, who was married to the headman of Baaperi, Fainye, looked upon me as her favourite brother. When we first had Bagre she gave me two shillings. Although I was still in school I increased the amount until, by the end of 1951, she had received one pound from me as her Bagre gift.

The Bagre gifts begin on Bagre Day and continue until the last ceremony is done. Those who were unable to give their friends and relatives gifts during the Bagre Dance can do so during Bagre Bells. On each occasion the recipient of the gifts gives his benefactor a pot of beer as well as food.

In the present instance, however, the gift-giving is a lineage not an individual affair. Individuals give to individual neophytes at the Bagre Dance. But on this occasion it is an adjacent lineage that is the recipient of the gifts and that brews beer to give the givers. As in so many ceremonies, whether funerals, Bagre, or other occasions, the network of reciprocal gifts and services is extended to include lineages not directly concerned. A group performs only some of the tasks involved in the funeral of one of its members; in fact, they never bury their own dead. Neither do they recite for their own Bagre, nor receive all the gifts involved. There is often the equivalent of an incest taboo on 'doing it oneself', or 'going it alone'; the *bricoleur* cannot work only for himself. In this way other segments of the community are involved in an almost deliberate way. Such phraseology stands in danger of confusing manifest with latent function, but the idea of a local community consisting only of one clan or lineage is at odds with the ideas and practice of the LoDagaa. A typical clan history, for example, tells how the ancestor of the local lineage arrived in a certain area and found it satisfactory. Then he called for his joking partners (from another clan) to come and join him, so that they could help each other and 'make hot things cool'. The gift-giving of the Bagre society, like many other facets of the ceremonies, emphasizes this same theme.

Bagre Bells (Bo gbelme)

The final ceremony of Bagre is the one where the neophytes, now fully fledged members of the association, are formally brought back into the community once again. It occurs a week or so after the Bagre Dance and is so called because at this time the bells they have been given are ritually washed. All the remaining fowls donated during the course of the series of ceremonies are sacrificed to the Bagre deity. The entire White Bagre is recited three times and the initiates have their hair trimmed round in a circle, not shaved off completely but not yet worn quite normally.

In Maale, Bagre Bells took place ten days after the End of the Dance. But three days before that, sacrifices had again to be made to the Bagre deity, at the time the malt was collected. Although I did not attend this ceremony I met a contingent returning from Maale: a man from Tanziiri, who had taken guinea corn to the Bagre house, brought back a basketful of dead fowls which had been slaughtered on the shrine. These they were now going to distribute to their lineage members. The day following the collecting or measuring of the malt (*kεε wuur*, or *kεε lɔm*), the women began to brew the beer.

The whole morning of the ceremony of Bagre Bells itself is taken up with washing the bells in a small pot of beer (W. 5593). This is done with a fibre called *bir* and some special medicine. The latter is then put in the baskets which the neophytes have used for so many purposes and thrown away on a midden. Before the washing takes place they are once again questioned about whether they have broken any of the taboos, and specifically whether they have had sexual intercourse. When they have confessed or denied this, they drink their customary small pot of beer and come outside to have their heads shaved again by the guides. They return for more recitation and later emerge for an evening meal and a short dance. Taking more of the small pots of beer, they go back to the room where they continue to be instructed for the rest of the night.

As after the previous ceremony, the neophytes are told about the further stage of advancement, namely, the Black Bagre, and they are encouraged to learn the present recitation and its associated procedures. They are also given a chance of asking questions about Bagre matters and a number of these are posed and answered in

8. The Bagre members search for the bells at the foot of the baobab tree that is associated with the guardian spirit of the clan (Birifu, 1970)

9. The neophytes are finally led around the market place, dressed up in their finery
(Birifu, 1970)

the myth itself. These have to do with the conquest of death (W. 5610), with procedures (W. 5671), with the consequences of breaking the taboos (W. 5744), with precedence (W. 5775), with the cause of deaths that follow Bagre (W. 5827), with conjugal quarrels (W. 5843), with thefts (W. 5877), with hate (W. 5900) and love (W. 5909), with the order of the ceremonies (W. 5929), with rituals of pregnancy (W. 5953), with the recitation itself (W. 5971), and with the relationship between God, man, the beings of the wild, and the Bagre (W. 6008).

Bagre Bells is followed by another hunt of the same kind that took place after the Beating of the Malt. Wild animals are again divided into those given to Bagre and those given to the house; the text gives three of each on this occasion (W. 5719 ff.), namely:

House	Bagre
boar	partridge
grass-cutter	rabbit
porcupine	antelope (*wala*)

As compared with the previous list (W. 3439–63), the guinea fowl and squirrel are missing, a fact that is as likely to be by accident as by design.

It is a week later, but essentially part of the same ceremony, when the new members are dressed up in gay clothes, faces powdered, a knife or sword in the right hand, and are led off to the local market. Essentially this final rite, which winds up Bagre for the year, is an act of aggregation, bringing the neophytes back into the life of the community and displaying them to all and sundry in the most public of places. Those who have been withdrawn from society, painted as corpses, made silent as the dead, killed by poison, and then revived with the help of the Bagre are now brought fully back into social life.

Although it is not strictly part of the Bagre sequence, it is customary for houses that have put new members into the association to brew beer as a thanksgiving to the household shrines. This ceremony is known by the generic term of *Bon paal dãã*, since 'first fruits' will be offered to the various supernatural agencies, to the Earth (*tengaan*), the River (*man*), the Hill (*tong*), the beings of the wild (*kɔntɔmɔ*), and to the various medicine shrines (*tiib*). Now that the neophytes have successfully emerged through the ceremonial sequence, other supernatural agencies are thanked for their help in looking after crops and people.

The Second Grade (gan dãã), The Beer of the Leather Bottle

There is one further ceremony to which I need to refer, although it is not part of the present sequence. It is the ceremony that inducts initiates into the ranks of the second-graders and makes them senior members. The senior rank is for men only, although in Tom (LD.) I heard of a diviner having prescribed the Black Bagre for a woman client and she was duly admitted. But she was certainly past the menopause.

This grade is known as Black Bagre (*Bo sɔɔla*) or else as 'taking the Bagre container' (*Bo gan*); at this time the neophyte receives the leather bottle holding a number of marked cowries; this container is specifically for divination, though only in special circumstances, such the death of a member. But its possession is often used to distinguish the second grade. The ceremony itself is sometimes known as *gan dãã*, Beer of the Leather Bottle; the process of acquisition is described as *de gan*, to take the *gan*, and the recitation of the Black Bagre is known as *gan ngmeb*, literally, 'hitting the *gan*'.

The initiation into the second grade is a much shorter and less public affair than the White Bagre. It takes place in the dry season, about March or April, after the White Bagre Ceremonies are all over and when the dawadawa has begun to flower. Those who are about to be promoted go round to all the houses of the village as well as to kin and friends outside, saying

Come tomorrow and measure the malt,
ka yi bio wa de kɛɛ iɔng

the beer of the Bagre bottle will be brewed the day after tomorrow.
bɔ gan dãã duura dayere.

I have never myself attended one of these ceremonies but in one I knew of, some twenty people took part, all from the same clan section. Beer is brewed and chickens are sacrificed at the usual places, to the Earth, to the ancestors, and to the Bagre deity.

The ceremony begins in the evening when people have returned from the farm and continues the whole night long; during this time they hear the Black Bagre, repeat it, and recite it. Three weeks before the beer is brewed, the section concerned recite the Black Bagre in the open, on the rooftop of the Bagre house. This is a kind of practice session, which even non-initiates may apparently hear.

At the ceremony itself a great deal of beer is drunk during the course of the night and in the morning members are given the *gan* in which their marked cowries are kept. The bottle should be carried everywhere an initiate goes. Teachers I knew carried them to training colleges and the late Chief of Lawra had a special bag made which he could put under his smock and so carry his gear to all official meetings. When you are a senior member and have the Bagre medicine, you should not really travel at all and Lawra people, who are stricter about this, say that if you go south to Kumasi, either as a labour migrant or in some other capacity, you should never stay there longer than a month. Indeed it was also said that the chief of Lawra had deliberately made his sons into senior members so that they would stay with him and not go off to work in the south.

Great emphasis is placed on retaining the bottle and if it is lost the whole settlement is searched. If the container cannot be found, then the owner should in theory be initiated all over again; it is possession of the accoutrements that proclaim one a member.

The bottle is kept in another piece of equipment given to senior members at this same time, that is in the special shoulder-bag known as *bag kyur*. This bag is specifically linked with the kind of formal divination that Bagre members carry out, and second-graders are often known either as *bo kyurdem*, owners of the bag, or as *gandem*, owners of the leather bottle. Such divination by the senior members is done at the foot of the funeral-stand of a fellow member, on each of the three days before burial takes place. After the burial the Bagre joking-partners take away the dead man's medicine (*kyüli tǐ*) and bury it in an anthill so it will be destroyed: a man's personal medicines are usually thrown away. Here the burial is accompanied by an offering; three fowls are killed and divided amongst the second-graders present (2473). For an important member, an animal such as a goat may be killed, the head, skin, and hind leg going to the senior of the second-graders present, the man who has been in charge of the divining sessions (2476).

Bagre medicine, usually obtained at the special ceremony held after the Bagre of Beans, can also be acquired at the Beer of the Leather Bottle, and this is sometimes done in order to save time. This medicine, which is kept in a long-necked gourd hanging from the rafters of the byre, can be obtained only by a household head who needs it before he can sponsor any children for Bagre.

Although the Bagre gear is used to divine at the foot of the funeral-stand of any senior member who may die, Bagre is not, as Labouret thought, a 'fraternity of soothsayers'. Diviners use a small gourd, cowries, and a bell to communicate with the beings of the wild. But they are inducted in quite a different fashion. The overlapping is part of the proliferation of ritual thought and expression that Nadel noted as characteristic of the Nupe of Northern Nigeria. Among the LoDagaa too the magico-religious sphere is marked by a process of continuous creation that leads to polysemic ritual acts, to changing rites and to overlapping functions. Indeed more than other modes of social activity, ritual needs constantly to be reinforced against failure, against unbelief and disappointment. Promises of eternal life, hopes for the conquest of death, tend to lose their initial impact and despite the continual willingness of man to suspend his disbelief, the impulse is to look for other gods; for alternative solutions are ever-present, especially in those religions that are not tied by the written word to a static holy order. It is this theme of searching for the way that dominates the greater part of the myth connected with the second grade, namely, the Black Bagre. It is this myth, together with its counterpart, the White Bagre, that I present in the rest of this volume. The notes attempt to explicate points that have caused me some difficulty and those that are likely to be obscure to the reader. But I have tried to avoid over-frequent, over-obvious, and over-abstract comments on vocabulary, metaphor, and symbol, since these tend to detract from one's understanding by interrupting the flow of the original.

BIBLIOGRAPHY

ACHEBE, C., *Things Fall Apart*, London, 1958.

BALFOUR, H., 'Ritual and secular uses of vibrating membranes as voice-disguisers', *J. R. Anthrop. Inst.*, *78*, 45–69, 1948.

BINGER, L. G., *Du Niger au golfe de Guinée*, Paris, 1892.

FINLEY, M. I., *The World of Odysseus*, New York, 1954.

FORTES, M., *The Dynamics of Clanship among the Tallensi*, London, 1945.

—— *The Web of Kinship among the Tallensi*, London, 1949.

FORTIER, J., *Le Mythe et les contes de Sou en pays Mbaï-Moïssala*, Paris, 1967.

GIRAULT, R. P., 'Essai sur la religion des Dagara', *Bull. IFAN*, *21*, 329–56, 1959.

GOODY, J. R., *The Social Organisation of the LoWiili*, London, 1956.

—— *Death, Property and the Ancestors*, Stanford and London, 1962.

—— *Comparative Studies in Kinship*, Stanford and London, 1969.

GRIAULE, M., *Conversations with Ogotemmêli* (Fr. ed., 1948), London, 1965.

HOLAS, B., *Les Masques Kono*, Paris, 1952.

LABOURET, H., *Les Tribus du rameau Lobi*, Paris, 1931.

LEIRIS, M., *La Langue secrète des Dogons de Sanga*, Paris, 1948.

MEILLASSOUX, C., DOUCOURÉ, L., and SIMAGHA, D., *Légende de la dispersion des Kusa* (Epopée soninké), Dakar, 1967.

RADCLIFFE-BROWN, A. R., *The Andaman Islanders*, Cambridge, 1922.

RATTRAY, R. S., *Religion and Art in Ashanti*, London, 1927.

STITH-THOMPSON, *Motif-Index of Folk-Literature* (rev. ed.), Copenhagen, 1956.

TAIT, D., *The Konkomba of Northern Ghana*, London, 1961.

ZAHAN, D., *Sociétés d'initiation bambara*, Paris, 1960.

PART TWO

THE BAGRE MYTH

THE WHITE BAGRE

TRANSLATION

Gods,
ancestors,
guardians,
beings of the wild,
the leather bottles
say we should perform,
because of the scorpion's sting,
because of suicide,
aches in the belly,
pains in the head.   10
The elder brother
slept badly.
He took out some guinea corn
and hurried along
to the diviner
who poured out his bag
and then said,
let's grasp the stick.
They did so
and he picked up 'deity'   20
and he picked up 'the wild'
and he picked up 'sacrifice'.
He picked up 'deity',
that was what
he picked up first.
He picked out 'deity'
and began to ask,
What 'deity'?
Deity of childbirth?
Deity of farming?   30
Deity of daughters?
Deity of grandfathers?
Deity of grandmothers?
Deity of the bowstring?

Deity of chicken breeding?
You reject them all.
Deity of meetings?
The cowries fell favourably:
it was so.
The elder   40
began to think,
got up quietly
and hurried off
to his father's house.
He called his children
to come,
and they came there
thinking to themselves
it was a call to eat.
They ran there,   50
met together
and the elder
got up and went out
to stand on a pile of earth.
Taking some ashes
and cold water,
he began to spurt it out,
spurted it over the children
saying,
'I spurt it over you.   60
If you see
shea fruit,
don't eat them.
If you see
new crops,
don't eat them.'
He told the children
they could go down.

When they got home
the elder   70
lay down to sleep
but tried in vain.
So he got up
and went again
to the diviner's house
to pour out the bag
and he asked him
about his fear.
'What sort of fear is it?'
'It is not fear.   80
Last night
when I lay down,
I didn't sleep.
That is why
I got up and came here,
came to ask
if you know
whether you can help me
in this matter.'
So he spoke   90
and went home.
He went back
and reached his house,
and as he got there,
see the children
who have gathered around.
In the evening
they came together
and he told them
he had been   100
to inquire
at the diviner's
and was told
it was the deity
that has come
from the front,
that is pointing
with the right hand,

that has come
to stay here,   110
that has come
bringing childbirth,
that has come
bringing good hunting.
He has not come to return.
So he spoke
and paused.
'And yet
you children
don't want to farm,   120
don't want to raise chickens.
You don't want
to possess
the truth.
And yet
the problems
are beyond us,
we, the initiates.
The first men
searched in vain   130
and they went
and deceived us,
we, the living ones.
They went away
and they should have
taken it [the Bagre] along
to the land of the dead.
But they left it
for us
and we search in vain.'   140
And so it was
that he took cold water
and took ashes
and said,
'It is good health
that I want.'
He spat out the water
so it spurted over them.

And he told them
to come   150
in the evening.
'For when he comes
back to this place,
he comes
with food.
He does not come empty-
    handed.
He points
with the right hand,
never with the left.
He comes   160
with the truth
and does not bring
falsehood;
so that our Bagre
will flourish.
However,
all power
lies with
the rain god.
The soil   170
is parched.
We cannot see
its fruits.
However,
the earth
is now pregnant.
How is she pregnant?
She is pregnant
because
the hot season   180
is here.
That is why
we know
the rains are near.
And if
the god
is a true god,

he will look after us
so we will get
the fruits of our farming.'   190
'How will we get them?'
'The rain god
will beget
and leafy things
come forth.
We will take these
to perform our rites.
This it is
that lies ahead of us.'
He spoke in this way   200
and stopped.
And then
he did something else,
came back again
and continued the ceremony.
The earth gave birth;
leafy things
burst out.
The old woman,
a thoughtful person,   210
gathered some bean leaves,
plucked them off their stems
and began to cook them.
She began to eat,
and the children
saw her
and wanted to eat.
She told them,
'Your father
will say something.   220
How can you
eat bean leaves?'
The children's father
came along
and when he got there,
she took something
and put it on the ground.

'What sort of thing?'
It was some food
he wanted to eat.   230
He raised his hand,
he raised it,
picked up some porridge,
dipped it in relish
and began to eat.
Then he saw the leaves.
'What leaves are they?'
'They're bean leaves.'
He asked
who cooked   240
that kind of soup.
So he spoke
and when he'd done so,
he stood up
and left the porridge
and the relish.
He went out,
climbed on to the roof
and called the children.
They came there   250
and he told them
to go out
and run round
to tell people
that the Black initiates
should come
the day after tomorrow
and take
these bean leaves
and do their work.   260
They went round
to tell the initiates
and when they had done so
they went off
to their father's farm.
The wise old woman
plucked some bean leaves.

When she had done so
she began to cook them,
and when she had finished,   270
she put down the pot.
They came there,
and when they had done so,
the old man
told them
to look at
the bean leaves.
As he said,
they forbade
these things,   280
but today
you see
bean leaves
in the soup.
Don't you see
the initiates
sitting close together?
Don't you see
guinea corn
which is now porridge?   290
Don't you see
malted grain
which is now beer?
They came there,
saw the food
and ate the lot,
these greedy people.
When they had finished
they made a noise
and the elder   300
told them
to stop.
They did so
and he asked them
to draw together.
They drew together
and when they came

he took
a stone
and sat there.   310
The Earth priest
then said,
'The Earth shrine
and the guardian
and the deity,
they told us
to perform Bagre
and therefore
we must take thought
and begin to do so.   320
Don't you see
it's the tail
we grasp?
That's what
we hold
and beg
for those growing things
which have not yet
grown ripe.
Give us help   330
so they will come.
That is why
we are here.'
And he spoke
and paused
and spoke again
so they might know
about the performance.
They know that
what is done   340
is but little.
'We will bury
the matter
that troubles us.
It seizes hold of us,
so that we beg
a head

that sits on our shoulders.
About those matters
that remain,   350
he will come
and tell us
that he does not come
to do us harm,
but speaks so as [to bring]
a peaceful house.'
Then we told the children
we had finished
and turned homewards
to the father's house.   360
And when we reach there,
what is it
that remains?
The yams
they also
belong to our Bagre.
However,
they are not yet full-grown,
so we must wait.
We wait,   370
and one day
the children's father
went to the bush
to farm.
He went there
and came
back later.
When he arrived,
see the wise old woman
goes over   380
to his in-laws' house
and finds
a yam,
digs it up
and returns
to the father's house.
She cooks it,

lifts it off the fire,
puts it down
and starts to eat.   390
Do you see
the children?
They see it
and cry out.
They cry out,
cry in vain,
for she tells them
they must wait
till their father comes
and meanwhile keep quiet.   400
They keep quiet,
and when he came
she took the yam
to give their father
and told him
that his in-laws
had sent him the yam.
And he replies, 'Well,
on account of this,
the children   410
nearly sinned.'
And he went up
and told the children
to go round
and inform
the initiates
that tomorrow,
they should come
and perform
the Ceremony of the Bean
    Flower.   420
They came there
two days later.
They came there
and sat quietly.
See the beer,
see the porridge,

see the yams,
see the beans
made into soup.
See the meat   430
they put in bowls,
and they say
that if a neophyte
can eat like a bull,
let him do so.
They spoke to
the White initiates
with their greedy big mouths,
and they got up
and poured the first beer. 440
The top of the beer
they poured and drank,
saying, 'The Speaker, he drinks
    beer.'
And they say:
'About the beer from on top,
I said to them,
drink, I have drunk.
So I say.'
They finished speaking.
Do you see the food?   450
They were eating
and when they had done so,
the White initiates,
those hawks,
they also finished.
They are so pleased
they start to make a din
and the elder
tells them
to shut up,   460
for they have gorged themselves.
They reply that
there is still more food.
He told them
to draw together

and when they did so
he told them
about the matter
that troubles us.
'This our land   470
became pregnant
but has not given birth,
so today
the yams
we dig out
are not full-grown
and look like
the heart of a cow.
You see,
we dig out a yam   480
and cook it on the fire.'
When these are cooked,
he tells them
to look
at the matters
that remain.
They came to say
that we should tell
the children
and then sat down again.   490
He takes some cold water
and some ashes
and prays.
He calls
upon God,
upon the Earth shrine,
upon the guardians,
upon the deities,
who all say we should perform
    Bagre.
That is why   500
we go out today
to take away the evil
so you can get what we need.
He gets up

and tells them
to go and return.
In the evening
they should come back.
'And when you come
you should come from
    the front   510
and not from behind.
And you should point
with the right hand,
never with the left.
You should come
with food,
never come empty-handed.
Do all this,
so that the produce
that has not yet   520
ripened
may grow well,
and we can then bring it along
and show it
to the children.
For we want them
to sit [together]
so we can bury
the matter
that troubles us.   530
Take hold of it
and follow its path;
for we still
beg for a chance
to find a head
that sits on our shoulders.'
So we spoke,
and when we had finished,
the White initiates,
those hawks,   540
came out
and made a din.
They went off,

went off
and left us
sitting there.
And they asked,
'What lies ahead?'
They finished speaking
and a thoughtful person   550
then replied
that 'What
lies ahead,
that which
remains,
we call it
the Ceremony of the Bean
    Flower.
This we hold on to
and follow
until we reach this point.'   560
One day
the elder
went to sleep
and put down his skin bag.
The elder
was a fool
to go off to sleep.
An old guinea cock
and his mate
last night   570
fought together.
He wanted to sleep with her
and she refused him.
He got up
the next morning,
walked around
among the guinea corn leaves
and saw
a bean flower
which he picked.   580
And his mate
hurried along

and said to him,
'What is it?
Let's eat it.'
He replied,
'Why was it
that yesterday
I asked you
to lie with me   590
and you refused me?
And now look at today.'
The two guinea fowl
were struggling
and found themselves
in front of the elder.
He saw the white flower
and, taking a stick,
hurled it,
crying, 'Oh,   600
my bag
has a hole in it.
My shell money
has dropped out
and the guinea fowl
is eating it.'
He threw [the stick],
picked it up,
and as he did so,
he realized   610
it was a bean flower.
He exclaimed, 'Well,
this is just the way
our children
might have sinned.'
The children
returned from the farm
and when they came,
he told them
they must run   620
round about
and tell

the Black initiates
and the White initiates.
When those hawks
hear the din,
[they'll come here].
So he spoke
to the children,
and they went out   630
and ran round
to announce that
the day after tomorrow
[they should come for the
     Beans].
They arrived there
and when they had come,
what did they do?
They asked
if it was about food.
And he replied   640
'Ah well,
it is in order
the fire
shouldn't blaze up.
We must release
the children
from their fast.
That's why
I've called you
to come   650
and perform
the Ceremony of the Bean
     Flower
and give [to the gods].
Don't you understand?'
And they replied, Well,
they'd thought
it was about food.
They finished speaking.
See the bean flower.
They perform their rites   660

and when these are done
they say,
'You see the guinea corn
turned to porridge,
you see the malted grain
turned to beer,
you see the beans
made into soup.'
And they told them
to repeat their words.   670
'Which words?'
They had thought
it was only about food.
And he replied that
the god
who came for us
said that
he has come
to eat.
He's not come to return.   680
'Because of this
I want you
to repeat the words.'
So they said:
'Gods,
guardians,
deities,
beings of the wild,
ancestors,
say we should perform.   690
Because of this
scorpions sting
and suicides happen.
Because of this
we've struggled
for many days
to remove the evil.
Now we come to today.
Won't we perform the Beans?
The beans   700

have turned
to soup,
the guinea corn
to porridge,
and the malted grain
to beer.
However
we say
to you, god,
this isn't much.   710
Since it is
the old path
we follow,
help us
so we can hold on to it
and follow it
and beg
a head
that sits on our shoulders.'
They finished speaking,   720
but the rites of the room remain.
The White initiates
finished eating
and made a din.
One of the elders
told them
to stop their noise.
They became quiet
and he said,
'The problem   730
that troubles us,
we are unable to solve;
uncertain as the milk
of a pregnant cow,
we must act
on our own
and come together
to know what
lies ahead of us.'
And the elder   740

asked,
'What is it
that remains
ahead of us?'
And they said,
the thing that remains,
they thought,
was that we'd turn back
and perform
[a certain] ceremony.   750
'What is that?'
'The Bagre matter,
that is
the Announcement of Bagre.
Because of this
we will turn back
and find out
about the Announcement of
   Bagre.'
Some of them
cried out,   760
'Oh!
How is it
that you first
carried on
without finding out
and now you turn back again
to get to this point?'
'This time
we turn
back again   770
to find out
the right way.'
And a certain man
said [to them],
'A great matter
this is,
so we'll search around
to know the reason.'
So they began again,

and said, 780
'About the Announcement of
 Bagre,
we did this before
and now come
to the shea fruit
and the shea nut.
Yet they say
the time is not ripe.'
So they said
'We'll perform
the ceremony of the shea
 nuts 790
and then we'll go on
in the proper order.'
'But if the season hasn't come,
how will we
get hold of
the shea nut?'
We told
the children
they should not
partake 800
of new crops.
It was a shea fruit
we told them
to bring back
and eat.
The weather is cool,
and the good farmer,
the good poultry breeder,
took his quiver
and his bow 810
and his hoe
and his axe.
He reached
the farm
and when he began to hoe,
he noticed some creatures.
What were they?

A large fruit-bat,
which is
one of our Bagre 820
elders.
He and his mate,
when darkness fell,
played together.
He wants the female
but his mate
refuses him.
So he gets up
in the dark
and goes 830
to the top of a shea tree
where he seizes a fruit.
He eats some
and then
puts it in his mouth
and comes down
to his mate.
When he gets there,
she sees it
and asks him 840
to give it her.
He refuses
saying,
'Why was it
that on our mat
I begged in vain
and you refused me,
then you see some food
and want it?'
The fruit-bat's mate 850
said to him
'Give me yours
and I'll give you mine.'
And the male
got angry:
'I won't give you.'
So he,

our Bagre elder,
ate it
and left the nut   860
which he threw away.
He threw it away,
and the farmer
finished farming
and he took his hoe
to go into the bush
for white ants.
He began to dig
but with no success.
So he went to the foot   870
of a tree,
where he suddenly saw
another mound.
He dug there
and when he had done so,
suddenly he saw the nut
that our Bagre elder
had left behind.
He took it,
came to his house,   880
and when he got there,
the elder,
Napolo,
was asleep.
His son came
with the white ants.
Then thirst
seized him
and he took his bag,
took a hundred cowries,   890
put them in his bag
and went off
to drink at his lover's house.
The elder,
Napolo,
was sleeping
when he heard

the noise of chicks.
He told people
to call his son   900
and they did so,
but with no success.
So he got up,
took some water
and some guinea corn
and went over
to where the chicks were.
He sat quietly
and began to feed them.
He did so   910
and when he had finished
he took part of the mound
and broke it in fragments.
When he had done so,
he took
another piece
and broke it.
When he had done so,
there remained the loose earth.
He said   920
he would pour it out.
He did so
and stirred it with his hand
and saw the shea nut.
And he cried out,
'Oh, oh,
the fire blazes up.
If we don't act,
the children will sin.'
And so   930
he picked it up
and put it in his bag.
The old woman's children
came along
and took it
and gave it
to a clever woman.

She took it
and knew what to do.
She cooked it   940
for three days
and when it was hot
she put it inside
a big cooking pot.
When she had done so,
she went out and told
the elder
and he said
she should keep it.
If he cannot   950
continue,
she should sell it
to pay for farm help.
She put it down
and he said
no one
should speak
about this
to the children.
So they said nothing.   960
And the son,
when darkness fell,
came away
from his lover's house
and reached home.
He was told
to go round
and inform
both the Black initiates
and the White initiates.   970
When those hawks
hear a din,
they'll come along.
They went out
and walked round,
saying,
the Announcement of Bagre,

[the time for] its malted grain
was tomorrow.
They went around   980
and when the second day
arrived
they took the malted grain,
together with a basket,
and brought them up
to the big rooftop
where they put them down.
And they said
they should put their hand in
and see if it was full.   990
They asked again,
saying,
'What becomes malted grain?'
And they replied,
'Guinea corn becomes malted
    grain.'
'What do they do to guinea corn
to make it become malted grain?'
And they replied,
'The loose grains
they sweep up   1000
and give to a clever woman
who does her work;
and when she has finished,
she takes a calabash,
winnows the grain,
and God's breeze
blows what's bad
away to the woods,
leaving what's good.
The wise old woman   1010
goes and takes
a brewing pot
and fills it
with water.
Three days later
she cuts some grass

and climbs up
to the roof
and then descends
to the front yard   1020
and sieves [the grain].
When she has finished
she climbs up
to the roof,
empties it there
and spreads it out.
When she has done so,
she takes the grass
to cover it over.
When she has done so,   1030
she takes a mat
and covers the lot.
Then she sprinkles some water
and in three days
she removes the mats
and when she has done so,
she takes her left hand
and plunges it in to see.
She does so
and finds the grain   1040
   sprouting,
so she kneads it
and when she finishes,
the wise old woman
thinks what to do.
She takes [the grain]
to put in a basket.
When she has done so
she gathers her things
and covers it again.
She covers over   1050
the basket
and three days later
she uncovers the grain.
When she has done so,
she takes it out

to get dry.
She lays it out
and God's breeze
blows upon it
so it dries.   1060
She takes the grain,
comes down
and shows it to me.
[I said that]
she should take it
and put it aside,
and if I am unable
to perform the Bagre,
I'll use it for farm help.
And so it happened   1070
that she put it aside
until the fire
blazed up again.
Then I called
and asked you
to look at the grain.
You looked
and told me
that you understood
what I had said to you.   1080
Look at the neophytes,
they put their hands
into the basket,
and measure their malted grain.
They know how to measure,
and do it with their left hand
and then with the right.
And they told
the elder
that there was not enough.   1090
But because of
the matter
that troubles us,
we will take it
to beg a head

that sits on our shoulders.
When they had measured it
some slender girls
took the malted grain,
climbed down from the
        roof,   1100
went outside
and walked round
to people's houses
to grind the grain.
When they had done this,
they hurried along
to their father's house.
What did they do there?
The affairs of God
bring great suffering.   1110
They took some pots
and followed each other
till they came
to the bank of a stream.
They found water,
clear water,
drew some and returned
to their father's house.
They knew their job
and took the grist,   1120
poured on water,
and then took out some
in order to fry it.
When they had done so
they mashed it together,
put it in a large pot
and poured on water.
And when they had done so,
what did they do?
They built up the fire   1130
so it would brew.
When it was done,
they got ready
to scoop it out.

They poured in water,
mixed it all together
and then strained it.
When they had done so,
they took the wort,
they took it,   1140
poured it in a large pot
and then went up
to the roof of the house
to lie down.
Early in the morning,
a featherless cock
was beating his wings,
beating them quickly.
The slender girl
jumped up quickly   1150
came out of her room
and hurried down.
In one large pot
she saw the beer
which she tasted to see
if it was ready,
and found it was.
As the beer was ready,
she got some firewood
and returned quickly.   1160
She took a gourd
and skimmed the liquid,
and when she had done so,
she poured it
in the brewing pots.
When she had done so,
she built up the fire
so that it simmered.
When it did so
she scooped some out,   1170
and when she had done so,
she scooped out the rest,
put it back in the brewing pots
and then built up the fire

so that it simmered.
Then she scooped it out
and when she had done so
she climbed up
to her father's rooftop
and lay down to sleep.   1180
She slept there
and when the beer was cool
the wise old woman,
who knows her job,
brings some yeast
and drops it in.
See how the beer
begins to ferment.
The slender girl
took some pots   1190
and poured it in.
The elder
hurries along,
takes the drinking gourds
which he counts for the
    neophytes.
When he has done so,
see the initiates
coming near.
The slender girls
carry the beer,   1200
climb up and go outside.'
See the malted grain
that has turned to beer.
See the guinea corn
that has turned to porridge.
See the leaves
that have turned to soup.
They came there,
the greedy ones,
and started to eat.   1210
See the elder
call them to silence
because of the malted grain.

They became quiet
and he said,
'You want food,
yet what about the seniors
who sit near you?
Why is it
you eat without giving
    them?'   1220
The senior guides,
who know their job,
come forward
and take their beer,
the top of the special pot.
They offer the Speakers
their beer to drink
and then these tell them
they've had their drink.
So the guides   1230
go back
to their beer
and drink the lot.
They make a din
and the elder
becomes thoughtful
and tells them to keep quiet,
then tells them
to wait awhile.
They do so   1240
and he asks them
if anything's left to be done.
They waited,
and he told us
that something does remain.
He said that
Bagre affairs
bring great suffering.
We begin it
and follow its path   1250
but find nothing.
Don't let this

be just for fun.
It is not like that,
so they should hold their
    tongues.
When they were quiet,
he took some cold water
together with ashes
and went over
to a mound of earth.   1260
He sat quietly
and told them
they must now keep their
    promise.
And they asked,
'What promise?'
And he replied
'Bagre affairs
bring great suffering
and we know not what to do.
They sacrificed to the
    ancestors,   1270
to the gods,
to the guardians,
to the deities,
to the Earth shrine,
in order to find the things
that remain.'
And they [he] said,
'The gods,
the ancestors,
the guardians,   1280
the deities,
wanted us to perform,
because of the scorpion's sting,
because of suicide,
and we removed the evil
up to this point.
The White initiates
began to argue
with us.

That is why   1290
I tell you
to hold your tongues.
The performing of Bagre
is a serious matter.'
He told the children
they should think
about what he says.
He finished speaking
and his companion
then said,   1300
'We don't rear chickens,
yet the Bagre affair
is an affair of chickens.
What will we do?'
The thoughtful one
replied,
'The fowls they will bring
to give you,
we'll take out
some of them   1310
to give the neophytes.
Some people
are fortunate.
We will pray
and distribute them.'
Don't you see
the elder?
He takes some fowls
and then speaks,
'The gods,   1320
the ancestors,
the guardians,
said we should perform,
because of the scorpion's sting,
because of suicide,
aches in the belly,
pains in the head.
The elder brother
slept badly.

We performed it all,   1330
up to this point.
But the question of chickens
is a difficult one.
You see the fowls:
look after them well,
watch them carefully.
For if they come to anything
you too will be something.
If they lay,
the eggs will hatch;   1340
the eggs
won't go bad;
the chickens
won't die;
all of them
will be
the same size,
like the brood of one hen.
And we will take them
and go back to perform   1350
the task that remains.
For this reason
we say that
you should keep
the fowls.'
How should they keep them?
And they replied
they should keep them
in the house.
This special fowl   1360
is called
the Beginning Fowl.
'Why beginning?'
'Beginning
we talk about
and yet you don't know the
      meaning.
The present Bagre
is a beginning.

And therefore
if someone else's hen   1370
should come
and lay
among its eggs,
they are forfeit.
All of these
will become
the Beginning Fowl's
own eggs.
We will take them
and perform   1380
our Bagre tasks.'
We finished speaking.
The White initiates
ran off home.
We told them
to go and wait
for the part
that remains.
And now we tell them
to return home   1390
and go round
to the Black initiates,
the knowing ones,
for they want them
to divine
in order to know
about the Bagre
matters,
how they are
and how they go.   1400
So they will consult
the ancestors
and the deities.
All these people come,
come along,
and they say
what they have to say
to the senior initiates.

God's breeze
came there 1410
and the place was fine.
And the raindrops
fell down,
down upon
the things
that had not yet grown.
There's guinea corn
and beans,
and bambara beans;
these are 1420
Bagre things.
Don't you see
how the rain makes
everything grow?
One day
the sun
beats down
upon the guinea corn
so that it ripened,
and the ground nuts too 1430
were ready,
and the bambara beans
matured,
and the beans
swelled with seed.
They went
and harvested
and spread it all out
so that God's breeze
blew on it. 1440
On the third day
they piled it
in a heap.
The elder
laughed out loud
and said, 'Well,
this year
the hoe

has really produced things
for the house.' 1450
So he got hold
of the children
and told them
to come there.
So they came there,
where the elder was,
thinking
it was about food,
and he said to them,
'The farming 1460
we did,
now we see
it's been fruitful.
Now we know
that the deity
brings the truth.
You people,
in two days' time
run round
to the Black initiates 1470
and to the White ones.
When those hawks
hear a din,
they'll come here.'
So they spoke,
and they went out,
ran round
and told everybody,
all the Black initiates.
When they had done so, 1480
then on the third day
they gathered
on the rooftop.
He sent
the senior woman
to fetch a basket.
She went down
into her room,

where she used her wits
and collected the malt.   1490
She climbed up
to the rooftop
and put it down.
The elder
called the members
to gather round.
Those greedy ones
began to think
it was about food.
They started to laugh   1500
and came over.
He told
the children
that the matter
which has troubled them
for so long
caused the evil,
the scorpion's sting,
the suicides,
aches in the belly,   1510
pains in the head.
For this reason
we farmed
for the fruits of the hoe.
And God
came to our help
and we had a harvest,
but not large enough
to deal with
the matter   1520
that troubles us
and we could not understand.
And therefore
we take a pile of guinea corn,
split it in two
and spread it out,
and the women,
who know their job,

take long sticks
and beat it   1530
so the grains fall off.
They divide them in two,
and a broken basket
they take up
on the rooftop
to winnow the grain.
God's breeze
blows the bad
into the bush,
leaving the good.   1540
They take it
and pour on water
to let it soak.
And they take this
and strain it,
climb up again
on the rooftop
to spread it out.
Then they say
they'll cut some grass.   1550
They do so
and go back
to the rooftop
and when they get there
they cover the grain.
Two days later
they take it
and uproot it.
Then they think,
and begin to knead.   1560
When they finish,
they said
they would collect it up.
They know their job
and once more they take
the old basket
and put it in
so the roots will wither.

And when they had done this
and the sun   1570
had shone upon it,
they poured it out
upon the ground.
They spread it out
and the sun
shone upon it
and they went up,
collected it
and returned
to the elder,   1580
who said, 'Very good,
I see it.'
They should keep it,
for the performance
is getting near.
They did so,
and when they had finished,
they all dispersed.
After they had done so,
the place   1590
was quiet.
'Why was it quiet?'
It is the dry season
that has arrived,
and they spoke, saying,
'The time
is ripe.
What is left
for us to do
for the Whitening
    Ceremony?'   1600
So they spoke
and the elder
instructed
the children
to go out
and tell
the Black initiates

to come;
as for the White initiates,
when those hawks   1610
hear a din,
they will come too.
They went out,
ran around
and informed
the Black initiates.
The White initiates
thought that
it was about food,
so they too came down   1620
and followed them.
The elder
went and called
his wife
to collect
the malted grain
and climb up
to the roof
and leave it there.
He said,   1630
'The time
has come
and therefore
we say,
the malted grain,
you should take it
to measure out
in the proper way.'
They take it
and climb up,   1640
carrying a gourd
along with them.
They do this
and dig their hand in.
They measure
and when they have done so,
they fill [the gourd]

to overflowing,
and again they fill it
to overflowing;   1650
and they fill it yet again
and again it overflows.
They do this three times
and they speak, saying,
'It's not enough.
But God
troubles us,
so we'll take it
to beg a head
that sits on our shoulders.'   1660
They finished this
and took the grain
and gave it
to the women.
They took it,
and when they had done so
they went down
to the rooms below
and used their wits.
They ground it,   1670
they ground
the lot;
then they cooked
the beer.
They cooked
the beer
and after they finished,
two days after,
they all
came there   1680
and saw the malted grain
that was beer,
saw the guinea corn
that was porridge,
saw the beans
that were soup.
They saw

the elders
sitting
and went over.   1690
[These told them]
to go round
and ask people
to come quickly;
because of the children
who were fasting,
they should come quickly.
They came
and when they got there,
they took their beer   1700
and wanted to drink.
But they said,
'Wait a while,'
so they stopped,
and the elders
collected the fowls.
The eldest neophyte,
his fowls
were eight.
And he said,   1710
'The gods,
guardians,
ancestors,
deities,
say we should sacrifice,
because of the scorpion's sting,
because of suicide.
The elder one
slept badly.'
So he spoke.   1720
Therefore,
this fowl,
take it
and give it to the Earth;
take it
to give the guardians,
together with the ancestors,

so they may eat.
If you think
that the Bagre   1730
has no problems,
let the first chicken
fall on its back.
They take
the first fowl,
cut its throat
and it's accepted.
When it's accepted,
they take another fowl
to give to the Earth,   1740
and it falls favourably.
They laugh softly
and go inside
and choose a fowl
to give to the ancestors,
and choose a fowl
to give to the guardians,
and climb up to give to the
    deity,
together with the gods.
They all fall favourably.   1750
After the fowls are accepted,
the guides
then say,
'For the fowls,
that's enough;
it's enough;
now to the eating.'
The guides
start to eat
and the elders   1760
call them
to stop.
When they have done so,
they tell them
that, as for the special beer,
the elder

has not yet drunk it,
yet you want
to drink it first.
So they spoke   1770
and they were afraid.
They took their beer,
took the head
of the special beer
and came over
to us, the senior initiates.
We drank a little
and left it to them
so they could drink.
They proffer drink to the
    neophytes   1780
and when they have done this,
all the guides
go in to eat,
eat their fill,
everyone snatching from each
    other.
When they had finished,
they made a din
and the companion
told them
to stop a while,   1790
and they did so.
They thought that
this business
was the same
as we had done before.
The elders
then told them
that today
was the Whitening Ceremony
and there was work   1800
to be done.
And they exclaimed, 'Oh,
what kind of work?'
They replied that,

for the neophytes,
we should find
shea oil,
together with
some string of fibre,
together with   1810
small gourds.
And if we want
to get these,
we should go out
and search
for fibre.
The old woman
laid out her fibre.
We stole them
but told her   1820
and she asked
for the money.
She asked
for how much?
Twenty cowries.
From a dry skin bag
I took out
exactly twenty.
We did this
and when we had finished   1830
we came to a place
where we went down
to the bank of a big river.
See the gourd,
hanging on the vine.
We pick it
and return
to the house,
to the Bagre house,
where we put it down   1840
and cut a hole.
When we have done this,
we remove the inside,
we take it out,

and leave the good,
then pile them together.
The elders [said]
that 'Today,
this very day,
is the one   1850
they call
the Bagre Eve.
You will have
much work
until the break of day.'
So he spoke,
and then told them
their tasks.
'What tasks
does he give us?'   1860
'The Bagre oil
with a head pad
and a round gourd,
that is the task
he gives us.'
Those people,
using their wits,
announced that
the fire hurried near.
And they told   1870
the neophytes
that 'Today
is a bad day
and yet a good one.
When we took you
as neophytes,
we told you
that you must not
pollute yourselves.
The day   1880
has come today.
If you have
slept with a girl
and hide the fact,

then when they whiten your
   nose
and whiten
round your mouth,
you can never be anybody
in this Bagre society.'
They ask this   1890
three times.
You deny it.
The Bagre sponsors
ask again
three times.
You deny it.
The Bagre guides
use their wits.
They take some string
and the gourd,   1900
put them together
and take the bag
and tie string around it.
When they have done so,
they use their wits,
take the shea oil
and pound it.
Then they take
some millet husks,
they take them   1910
and drop them
into the oil.
When they have done so,
they tell them
to take the string.
'You take the string.'
And they ask,
'Neophyte,
have you confessed
everything?'   1920
And he declares
that he has done so.
And he asks

'Shall I mark?'
He asks
three times.
And the reply comes,
'Yes, mark.'
So I take him
and give him   1930
to my companion.
He also asks
three times
and the reply comes,
'Let them mark.'
So they marked,
and when we had marked
and had finished doing so
we took our oil
and said   1940
we'll mark round the mouth.
And he was afraid
and said, 'Oh,
why mark my mouth?'
And he replied
he would mark
your gossiping mouth,
but that
he'll leave
your eating mouth.   1950
They say this
and take the oil
and then they mark,
mark lines on you,
the criss-cross lines.
When they have done so,
they tell you,
'If you should go out
tomorrow
and sit down   1960
and look at
your brother,
then if he speaks to you,

don't answer.
If he laughs at you,
don't laugh.'
When he had spoken
and come to an end,
he says again,
'Today   1970
they have smeared you with oil.
If you have a wife,
don't go near her.
If you are a woman
and have a husband,
don't go near him.
If you are unable
to do this,
speak
and they'll withdraw you.   1980
You've all sworn
that you can do this,
you spoke
and finished,
and they've whitewashed you
and finished.'
When the time came,
the elder
stood up
and called upon   1990
God.
'God,'
he called
three times
and turned
to tell them
that God
has come down to earth
wearing his things,
his heavy attire.   2000
'He came down
and he said
that he came for food

and not to return,
that he points with the right
    hand,
never with the left,
that he approaches from the
    front,
never from behind.'
And he then said,
'You have heard   2010
that he brings food.
You have seen
the food
that comes.'
The guides
took the bells,
covered the gourds
and tied them together.
And he said,
'That gourd,   2020
if it breaks
your head will split.
Everyone
knows
about this,
that if it breaks
then your head will split.
It's like breaking your own
    head.'
So we should grasp it
and hold it   2030
gently.
And the guides
then said,
'When dawn comes
you will go
and beg
guinea corn.
If you are thirsty
and want water,
don't drink   2040

when your guide
can see you.
If there is
a big stream,
climb down,
put down your gourd,
cup your hands,
scoop up some water
and drink it.
If you know   2050
that the guide
is approaching you,
you must get up,
come away
and continue on your path.
However,
if it happens
that you want
to defecate,
then wait   2060
till he passes,
and crouch down.
When you get up,
take a short cut
by crossing
the fields
and again go out
in front of him.
He will then get up
and see   2070
that you're still
in front.
If you allow
anybody at all
to see you
drinking water,
he will cry, "Oh,
I see a neophyte
drinking water."
That isn't good.   2080

And therefore
we always hide
when we drink water,
and hide
when we eat anything.'
He spoke,
having shown them what to do,
and when he had done so,
he returned
to the Bagre performance   2090
and showed them
this too.
When the time
arrived,
he got up
and took
a broken basket
and put it
in front of you
and said,   2100
'This is your begging basket.
Tomorrow, he'll set it down
for you.
The people
who like you
will bring
twenty cowries
to put in
your basket.
If there is enough,   2110
then they'll be able
to continue
the Bagre ceremony.'
He put it down
and they threw in a lot,
and when they had done so,
he took it
to give to the Bagre elder, '
who took it all
and collected it together.   2120

He spoke, saying,
when the guinea corn
is ripe,
it is this [money]
he will use
to continue
the Bagre ceremony.
'We take
a basket
to put in your hand,   2130
so you can go out.
When you beg,
what they give,
whatever it may be,
take it.
If it is earth
they scoop up,
take it.
For that is
our Bagre way.   2140
Do you understand?
When you go out
and beg
and get
guinea corn,
bring it here
and I'll collect it
and keep it,
so that you can go round
and beg some more,   2150
because it's not enough.
But it is God
that makes him suffer,
that's why they say
they'll take it
to beg a head
that sits on their shoulders.'
They keep it
and when it comes
to the time,   2160

they take it,
and say, 'Well,
the old women's children
should take it
and thresh it
and put it
in a large vat.
It's not enough,
but I couldn't help it,
and I'll take   2170
some extra
to add to it,
so we can continue
the Bagre ceremony.'
Thus he spoke
and when he had done so,
they said,
well, yes,
they understood.
And he took [the corn]   2180
and kept it
and when
this had been done,
they still went round.
One day
the elders,
the thoughtful ones [said]
they cannot
permit you
to take   2190
your gourd
and walk round.
So they will take it
and keep it.
And they took it
and kept it.
Their fellows
said, 'No,
they cannot
take the gourd   2200

and keep it.'
When they said this,
and finished,
he asked,
'What can we do?'
He said,
'The gourd
is like an egg
for us.
We cannot   2210
put it down and leave it.
We will take it
and go round.
This thing
you told us
to take out;
with it
we'll go round.
And if there is
work to be done   2220
with it,
we shall do it.'
So he spoke
and when he had done so,
he said to us,
'The guinea corn
that we collected
by going round
is enough
to perform this affair.   2230
However,
as for the fowls,
that matter
is difficult.'
And he asked,
'What shall we do?'
And he replied.
'Just as
I earlier
begged   2240

for guinea corn,
in the same [way]
go out
and beg
for chickens.'
He finished
speaking.
'I tell you,
if you go out tomorrow,
when you get up,   2250
take along
your younger brother,
a small boy,
to follow you
as you go round
and beg.
If you see
just a few—'
'A few what?'
And he continued,   2260
'A few small chickens.'
And they said,
'And now
you're
a hawk;
if you're leading the way
and come to a house
where no one is about,
then take
a fowl.   2270
If you see
someone is around,
in that case
don't take it
but rather ask.
If he should
give it you,
take it.
If he doesn't
give it you,   2280

then leave him.
So I told them.
When day dawns,
you get up
and I give you
a chicken basket
and a boy
to follow you
around.
You arrive   2290
at a house,
you see a fowl,
you seize it.
He shouts at you,
you leave it
and go home.
You told them
and they say
it is not so.
If you   2300
should go
and seize it,
and they snatch it back,
don't be angry.
Wait a while
and ask for it.
If he happens
to be
a member,
he can't take it back   2310
and leave you empty-handed.
If he
is a non-member
and takes it,
leave it
and go on.
For the fowl
he took back,
it cannot
survive.'   2320

About our ceremony,
the elders
told us
to come closer.
We did so
and they said, 'Well,
this thing
we have begun
and have come
to the Whitening   2330
    Ceremony.
We want
(now we've reached there)
to get
to know
God's
dwelling-place.'
Then the companion
rose to his feet
and said
he believed   2340
that God
is here
on earth,
where we walk.
And one man
then exclaimed,
'Oh, no.'
He went on to say
he believed
that God   2350
is there
in the sky
where we look.
And he said,
'No, no,'
He said again
he believed
that God
is there

in front 2360
where he points.
And the other said,
'God
is not there.'
And he said,
'I believe
that God
is there
behind me
where I turn.' 2370
And the other said,
'God
is not there.'
And he said,
'God
I believe
is there
on my right side.'
And the other said,
'He is not there.' 2380
And he said,
'God
I believe
is there
on my left side.'
And the other said,
'He is not there.'
So he asked him,
'Where then
can God 2390
be,
he who troubles us
and the children
and the women?'
And the companion
said, 'Well,
about God,
we hear his name
without knowing him.

Yet today 2400
you ask me
about God's
dwelling-place.'
And he replied, 'Well,
I must ask,
because yesterday
I heard
you call
and shout out
and say, 2410
"God,
I hear you
when you call."
And you said,
"God,
he hears
and will descend."
That's the reason
I now want
to discover 2420
the place
from which he comes.
However,
if it is all right,
we can
go on
with whatever
remains to be done.'
The companion
then asked, 2430
'What is it
do you think
remains to be done?'
He replied,
'In our Whitening Ceremony,
I think that
the part which remains
for us to do,
that is

the Beating of the Malt.'   2440
And he said,
'My companion,
you know this
and yet
you ask me about God.'
He replied, 'Well,
about God,
you should still
show me
the place   2450
where he is.
They should pause
to find out
about God
and the place
where he is.'
The being of the wild
wanted to tempt them.
He came
and descended,   2460
declaring
that he
was God
in the Bagre house.
He said this
and gave them a lead,
showing them
what to do.
For the Bagre,
which they did not know   2470
how to perform,
he'll teach them
one way to do it.
And they said, 'Yes,
he should teach them.'
The being of the wild
got up
and stood.
He asked

'In the Bagre Dance,   2480
on the Eve of Bagre,
what will they do?'
They said
that they wanted
the day
to come
so that they
could find someone
who will teach
the children   2490
what to do.
And he said that
the being of the wild
had brought some medicine.
The Bagre medicine
in a gourd,
he set it down
and said
that this medicine,
whenever   2500
the day comes,
they should put the medicine
into water
for three days,
bring it out
and put it on the fire
for three days,
then anything
that is hot,
it will make cool,   2510
and anything
that is cool,
it will
make hot.
He said this
and they took it.
What should they do?
He told them
he would teach them

what to do,   2520
so they can see
what it is
that lies inside.
They took [the medicine],
put it on the fire,
took it off,
put it in water;
for three days
they kept it there.
The tempter being   2530
came there
and said
they should take
the gourd,
remove some medicine,
put it down,
and stamp on it
till it breaks,
take it out,
put it in water,   2540
and then
use this
to feed
one person;
then you can see
whatever
is there.
So they took it,
stamped on it,
broke it,   2550
and took the pieces,
put them in water,
and fed it
to someone.
Within three minutes
he was dead.
He died
and the being
went back

to the woods.   2560
He went there
and the elders
exclaimed, 'Well,
as you saw,
he performed something
in front of us
and we took it
and this was the result.
What can we do
to put matters straight?'   2570
The companion
got up
to find out
the place
the being went.
He got up,
ran off
to the woods
and looked for
the place where the being   2580
was staying.
He saw him
in a room,
sitting there,
and he said, 'Look,
that business
which you performed,
and showed us how to do,
we did it
and death   2590
has struck us.'
He replied, 'Yes,
all this is so.
But what
did I tell you
would happen?'
And the man said,
'You didn't say.'
The being

spoke again.   2600
'Did I not give you
the medicine?
You should
have followed
what I showed you.
I told you
that hot things
it would make cool
and cool things
it would make hot.'   2610
So he spoke
and when he had done so,
he followed the man
back home
to his father's house.
He saw the corpse
lying there
and told
the people
he wanted   2620
to teach them
the Bagre
which they perform.
'But look,
since that man
lay there,
is it a whole week?'
And they replied,
'It's not a week.'
And he said,   2630
'If it is
three days
today
since he died,
why does his flesh not rot?'
And they replied
that they didn't know.
And he said
they should wait

till he asked them   2640
something.
And he went on to ask,
if one of them
should die,
how many days
before he rots?
And they replied,
within three days
he'll rot.
The being of the wild   2650
told them
he wanted to teach them.
'But you people
who were to follow me,
didn't follow me well.
That is why
I didn't show you.
But this matter,
it is
in all Bagre   2660
the most important.
It is
because
of this
that the neophytes
are afraid.
Because
of this
the Black initiates
are afraid.   2670
Because
of this
the guides
are afraid.'
So he spoke
and went over
and placed
his mouth
over the ear of the corpse.

He rolled his tongue 2680
and then said
they should watch.
See the dead man
rising up.
He stands up
and he says
if they want
this medicine,
they should take
exactly twenty cowries 2690
and a male roan.
That is how
they always buy the medicine.
So he spoke
and they brought
the antelope
and exactly twenty cowries
to pay the being.
When they had done so,
what'll they do next? 2700
They went along
during the night
to his house
and he sat down
to teach them
about the medicine.
Well, then,
when they were begging
for God's help,
he heard them. 2710
It is he
who is God.
If anyone
knows his ways,
he will prosper.
If anyone
does not know them,
he cannot
succeed.

So he spoke 2720
and when he had done so,
the elder
said he thought that
in the Black Bagre
he earlier
saw something
about arrow poison.
Perhaps with this
they will kill
the neophytes. 2730
He replied, 'No,
it is not so.
This medicine,
the medicine in his bag,
this was what
his ancestor
left for him
to look after.
The cool medicine
was this one. 2740
The hot medicine
was this one.
Both these
are then
the things
which are able
to cause death
and also
revive the dead.'
So he spoke 2750
and went on to say, well,
if it is
medicine to revive the dead,
he has it.
If it is
medicine to cause death,
he has it.
He finished speaking.
And then

he wanted the medicine   2760
but it is
on Bagre Eve
they will brew it.
'Being of the wild,
you've still got that man.'
'Who is that?'
'It's the companion
that you keep,
leaving us all alone.
As it is,   2770
you have the companion,
and Bagre Eve
cannot be changed,
it cannot be
postponed
to a free day.'
However,
when Bagre Eve
came along,
the being   2780
allowed his child
to come
to the Bagre house
and see
how the neophytes
were doing.
So he spoke
and he came
and saw the neophytes
and how quickly the fire   2790
   blazed up.
The small being
sat quietly
and watched.
They got up
and said
they should kill the neophytes.
They started beating them
in order to kill

the neophytes
and they all lay there.   2800
The elder
got up,
shook his rattle
and sang a song.
'Death kills,
alas, death kills
and no one questions.'
They sang three times
and got up again
and stopped.   2810
Then they sang,
'They lie scattered about the
   room
and no one questions.'
They sang three times,
stopped,
and then they sang,
'Let them bring a hundred
to pay for the neophytes.'
They sang three times
stopped,   2820
and then sang,
'Be careful of the roof post,
someone's house has a crooked
   post.'
They sang this three times
and said,
'The Bagre bag
hits a fowl,
so it falls on its back, back,
   back.'
They finished this
and then said,   2830
'Death kills, alas,
death kills.
The Bagre god saves us,
so death won't kill.'
They did this, three times,

and then sang,
'Let's go outside
and see the neophytes.'
They sang this
three times,   2840
became tired of it
and stood up
and began to go out,
shaking their rattles,
and then sang again,
'Bend, bend your knees,
bend as low as you can.'
They finished this
and then sang,
'We draw out   2850
an old tooth.
We draw out
a witch's old tooth,
we draw out.'
They finished
and then they sang,
'We take away
an old ladder,
we take away
a witch's old ladder,   2860
we take away.'
They finished singing
and then turned,
came back
to the room
and went in.
In that room
the guides
used their wits.
During the night   2870
they took the bells
from the room
and went out
to the wall
and buried them there.

When they finished,
they returned to the room.
When they went
inside the room,
they came   2880
with the bells
and sang
into the ears
of the neophytes,
so they would hear
and get up.
They sang but weren't heard
and they asked,
what will they do
about this?   2890
The small being
came up to them,
felt them
and said,
'They're cold
and can't get up.'
And they said, 'Well,
what can they do?'
The companion
and his being of the wild   2900
came along
to the house.
Into the room
they came
and seeing blood,
cried, 'Oh,
what is this?'
And they replied,
the business
that was to happen   2910
on Bagre Eve,
that is what
they were told to do.
But they did it in vain
and made an error.

He said, 'Well,
in this Bagre
where have we reached?'
And they replied
that they didn't know.   2920
Look at the fellow
who asks,
'In this Bagre
have you done the Beating of
    the Malt?'
And they replied, 'No,
we haven't done this.'
'How did it happen,
that when Bagre Dance
came along,
on Bagre Eve   2930
you killed these people?'
And he went on to say,
'In Bagre killing,
they don't kill with a club,
they don't kill with arrows,
they kill
with wits
and with medicine.'
So he spoke
and the members   2940
were afraid.
What could they do?
Then the small being
got hold of them
and taught them
how it is
they should kill the neophytes.
'Everything
comes
from God.   2950
He it is
brings
evil
and good.

He it is
brings
sins
and pleasure.
He it is
brings   2960
tears
and laughter.
He it is
brings
poverty
and riches.
It is God
who brings
life
and death.'   2970
They asked him,
'How is it
that you God
created people
and gave them life,
yet others can take it away?'
So he spoke
and the child
replied, 'Well,
if you want   2980
everything
on earth,
God
will give you.
However
God
we hear
has a house.'
And one of them [asked],
'Where is the house?'   2990
So he spoke
and stopped.
The senior members
were still worried

about the dead
that were lying there.
One of them
felt [a neophyte]
and exclaimed,
'They're already cold.'   3000
So he spoke
and the small being
took his medicine,
put it in his mouth
and chewed it to pieces,
then spurted it out
over their heads.
When he had done this,
he pressed his mouth
against their ears   3010
and rolled his tongue.
They woke up
and he said, 'Well,
now they're awake,
have they all awoken?'
They all woke up,
and when they had done so,
he said, 'Now,
let's finish
the part   3020
that remains.'
'What part is that?'
And he replied,
'As you reached
the Whitening Ceremony
without doing the Beating of
  the Malt,
and jumped
to Bagre Eve,
you ruined the performance,
ruined it completely   3030
and got nothing.'
And so
he got up

and taught us
to perform
the Bagre ritual.
The time has come
for the Beating of the Malt;
it comes,
and the neophytes   3040
walk round with their gourds
and fetch water,
water from the river.
They fetch it
and bring it
to an open space.
They sit down there
all together.
The guides
were sent   3050
back home
to fetch some guinea corn
and they returned
to the open space.
The members
sat there
and began to speak.
And they asked,
'What did they say?'
And they said, 'Well,   3060
as the matter
now stands,
what can we do?'
The elder
told them
to wait
and he would pray.
And he said,
'The gods,
ancestors,   3070
guardians,
deities
say we should perform.'

However,
we searched in vain.
They said
it was on account
of the scorpion's sting.
The elder brother
slept badly,   3080
so he took some guinea corn
and went off
to the diviner
to get him to pour out his bag.
He said
he should draw near
so they could divine and see.
He drew near
and they sat together
and he asked   3090
about the problem.
He picked up 'deity'.
And they asked,
'Was it the deity of the wilds?'
'No.'
'Was it the being's deity?'
'No.'
'The grandfather's deity?'
'No.'
'The grandmother's deity?' 3100
'No.'
'The brothers' deity?'
'No.'
'The children's deity?'
'No.'
And then they asked
if it was the deity of meetings.
The cowries
fell favourably.
So we got up   3110
and followed that deity.
We followed
and came to today.

We got up
but the children
didn't know what to do.
So the companion
entered the woods
to look for
the thing we needed,   3120
the Bagre thing.
But for the children
the time
came near.
It came near
and they got up
to do their work
and they killed the children.
We saw
they'd done wrong   3130
and we searched in vain.
However
the being
had told us
to take
some powerful medicine
and put it in water
for three days,
then hot matters
it would   3140
make cool.
And if we took
that powerful medicine
and put it on the fire,
for three days,
then cool matters
it would
make hot.
So we took it,
and still keep it,   3150
but the children
didn't know
and they came along

and spoiled the ritual.
We came back from the
　woods
and returned
to see the dead.
We saw it
and when we had done so,
because of it,　　　　3160
we turned back
and began
to retrace our steps
in order to know
the things
that remained
to be done
and tell the children.
So it was
that we revived them　　3170
and took them again
to show them
the path.
And so we arrived
at today
and reached
the Beating of the Malt.
We emptied out
the guinea corn,
emptied it all out.　　3180
Don't you see
it lying here
in the open space?
We got sticks
and threshed it
till all the grain
dropped on the clearing.
And they said
God's big flat roof,
that is the clearing.　　3190
And God
then took

the river water
to soak it.
On that day
it changed
and we uprooted it.
They uprooted it,
and when they'd done so,
we went home　　　3200
and reached
the house.
What can we do,
for we've looked in vain?
They replied, well,
they should all come there.
They came
to the house.
The guides
got hold of the neophytes　3210
and sat them on the stool.
When they'd done so,
they took
some beer
and porridge
and came along
and ate their fill
and were pleased.
They got up
and made a din;　　　3220
the companion
hushed them
and they stopped.
He said
that Bagre
is not for noise.
So they should hold their
　tongues
and listen
and watch.
So he spoke　　　3230
and they listened.

He said,
'The food
you have eaten,
some matter remains
to be settled,
yet you eat the lot
and make a din.'
So he spoke
and went on,   3240
'The task
that remains
is a small one,
yet a big one.
But the neophytes,
we initiate them,
yet they make a din
and we teach them in vain.
Until today
you've been searching 3250
for God
but when I ask
you're unable
to tell the place
he is.
You see,
the Bagre
we perform it,
but we don't see
what lies ahead.   3260
However,
in this Beating of the Malt
we'll acquire
the knowledge,
we'll get to know
a certain matter
which we wait for,
a certain matter
which is in front of us
and is behind us too.' 3270
Thus he spoke,

and when he'd finished
we turned around
and went back
to the house.
We got there
and sat down.
We sat down
and the time came
for us to get up.   3280
What time was that?
Time for the Beating of the
  Malt.
And we said,
'A big problem
lies ahead of us
that you don't know about.
It is today.
We begin
and want to teach
the children,   3290
together with the women
and the men.
However
the Bagre
once reached
Bagre Eve
and you did something
that wasn't right.
And so,
this time,   3300
all of you,
try your hardest
so that when it comes,
we are not put to shame.
We'll finish the Bagre,
and then know
what to do.'
They went home
and when the time
had arrived,   3310

one neophyte,
a skilful hunter,
went to the bush.
A male antelope,
with his horns held high,
was coming
nearer.
He shot
and when he did so,
the arrow struck.   3320
When it struck,
what did he do?
He hullooed
and it ran
away
into the bush
and fell to the ground.
When it fell,
the senior members
were thinking   3330
they'd get meat;
the boy's mother
was thinking
she'd get meat;
the boy's father
was thinking
he'd get meat.
When they brought
the dead animal
to the father's house,   3340
they said
to the boy's father,
'There's no meat for you;'
and to the boy's mother,
'There's no meat for you.'
Then they were noisy
and began to quarrel.
They sat on the ground
and gave thought
and conferred.   3350

He spoke, saying,
'How is it
that you bear a child,
and suffer greatly,
you suffer,
and yet somebody else
takes his things
without having suffered.
If this is so,
I can't accept it.'   3360
And the others replied,
'That's how it's done.'
And again they went
outside the house
and conferred together
saying, 'Well,
as it's like this,
we'll take
the meat
and give to the mother.'   3370
The elders
stopped arguing
and thought again
and said, 'Well,
about this meat,
if the boy's mother
is a member,
and the boy's father
is one too,
then the matter   3380
is settled.
You must leave
the meat
and the neophytes
will take it
and go along
to the Bagre house.'
They sat together
and decided what to do.
They took out some meat,   3390

a hind leg,
they took it out
and gave it
to the father;
and the fillet
to the mother.
And he said, 'Well,
it's for the suffering.'
She took it
and laughed,   3400
saying, 'All right,
that's fine.'
Then they made
the neophytes
hunt around
to kill something.
They brought this back
to give the elders
so they could eat.
But we put some aside   3410
for another day,
because these things
are indeed
our Bagre things.
What Bagre things?
Well, this goes into
the Bagre soup.
So they said,
and finished
and then spoke again,   3420
'All you neophytes,
if you go hunting,
and don't kill anything,
nevertheless,
even if this goes on
for a thousand years,
when you do kill something,
you must pay it to the Bagre.'
'Why is it
that they do this?'   3430

'The children's
pollution
they are taking away.'
So they spoke,
and told of our gravest matter.
And they said 'Wild boar,
we forbid.'
They said,
'Porcupine
is not one   3440
of our Bagre things.
The grass-cutter
is not one
of our Bagre things.
The wild guinea fowl
is not one
of our Bagre things.
However
if you kill a rabbit,
this is one   3450
of our Bagre things.
If you kill
an antelope,
this is one
of our Bagre things.
If you kill
a partridge,
this is one
of our Bagre things.
If anyone kills   3460
a squirrel,
this is one
of our Bagre things.'
They spoke in this way
and then stopped.
The neophytes
roamed around
and killed
some animals,
then came and paid them   3470

to the Bagre,
to the senior members.
There still remain
many matters.
'What is there
that lies in front of us
that we don't know?'
And they told them
what remains.
There remains   3480
the Bagre Dance.
One day
the elder
slept and said afterwards
that the Bagre
which was coming
had now come.
Don't you see
the White initiates,
how they're laughing   3490
and getting impatient
for the day to come.
They get impatient
and begin to think.
'What is it
that they're thinking about?'
It's the food
for their greedy mouths,
that's what they want.
That is why   3500
they are hoping
the day will come quickly.
And they said that,
about the [collecting of the]
  Malt,
they should go out
and tell
the elders
to come and perform
the [collecting of the] Malt.

They went out   3510
to go and tell
the Black initiates
and the White initiates,
the ones who are
the hawks,
that they should come and listen.
This is what
they said.
In two days' time
they came along.   3520
That old woman
took a basket,
filled it with malted grain,
right to the very top,
and climbed up quickly
on to the rooftop.
She got there
and the Bagre officials
took their gourds,
plunged in their hands   3530
and began to measure.
They measured
the malted grain
and each neophyte
had two baskets
full up with grain.
They brought these along
but the grain
was not enough.
Still, because of   3540
the matter
that troubles us,
we will take it
and beg a head
that sits on our shoulders.
So they spoke
and measured [the grain].
They went home
and reached

their father's house.   3550
And then
the old woman,
who knows her job,
took the grain
and ground it
so it turned to grist.
She took guinea corn
and turned it to flour.
Then she took
the grist,   3560
put in water,
then mashed it,
poured on more water,
and then scooped off
the liquid
and poured it
into a large pot,
mixed it up
and brewed it.
The slender girls   3570
built up the fire
and it simmered away.
Then what did they do?
They scooped it out
and poured it into vats.
In the evening
they slept;
they got up
at cock-crow
and took off the liquid   3580
and said, 'Well,
this beer,
let's taste and see
if it's sour.'
They tasted it
and it was sour;
so they scooped the rest
into other pots
to cook it.

They cooked it again   3590
at dawn;
they finished cooking,
and when it came to the time
that the sun was high,
they scooped it out
into the vats.
The wise old woman
got up again
and took
her thing.   3600
'What thing?'
The yeast
it was.
They added it
and the beer swelled up.
And they took
the flour
that became porridge.
Night fell
and two days later   3610
they came back
and saw the flour
that was now porridge,
they saw the malt
that was now beer,
they saw the leaves
that were now soup.
And the cow's flesh
they took
and put it in dishes.   3620
When they had finished,
don't you see
the Bagre guides?
For the elder
stood up
and told them
to gather round.
They gathered round
and took

the small Beginning fowls 3630
and the big fowls
all together
to the Bagre house
in order to kill them.
They wanted to kill them,
so they called
the White initiates.
They came there,
and they said, 'Well,
the thing 3640
we told you
that was coming
but had not yet come,
it has come today.
Let us invoke Bagre
and repeat
that the gods,
the ancestors,
the guardians
the deities, 3650
said we should perform,
because of the scorpion's sting,
because of suicide.
The elder brother
slept badly,
so he took out some grain
and hurried along
to the diviner's.
He didn't refuse
but poured out his bag 3660
and took the stick.
He took the stick
and took out 'deity'.
He took out 'deity'.
Which deity?
Deity of the beings,
it rejected.
Deity of the wild,
it rejected.

Deity of the grandfather, 3670
it rejected.
Deity of the grandmother,
it rejected.
The brother's deity,
it rejected.
The deity of meetings
it accepted.
You've seen what we've done
to take away the evil,
right down 3680
to today.
So it is
the fire blazes up
and we want
to consider
this matter
to see what's to do.
Well then,
the thing
that we call 3690
guinea corn,
is a thing of Bagre.
And bambara beans,
these too
are also
things of Bagre.
And beans
are also
things of Bagre.
And the chicken 3700
is also
a thing of Bagre.
Today
is the very day
when we want
to understand
and finish
the matter
we talked about.'

The guides 3710
saw the food,
became impatient
and wanted to eat.
But he hushed them
and they were quiet.
He began to sit down
and then told
the neophytes
that the sun
which is setting 3720
is a man's sun.
As for the neophytes,
terror
seized them
and they sat down
and began to think.
The senior members
drank some beer
and then stood up
and said 3730
to the neophytes
that the food
they eat,
if that is
the deity
in truth,
then the food
can't harm their insides.
Their heads can't ache,
their bellies 3740
will be well.
When they piss,
it'll come like rain.
When they shit
it'll come like the antelope's,
in small round balls.
If our girls
or our boys,
our old women

or our old men 3750
are two-faced
and come along
to Bagre,
it is then
the Bagre deity
will act.
If a neophyte
doesn't confess
and it troubles him,
we will find out 3760
in the Bagre.
And the string
which we tie
round your heads
this night,
because of this
we sit and wait.
If a neophyte
breaks a rule,
if a neophyte 3770
cannot sleep,
if a neophyte
strikes anyone,
then today
let him tell all.
They told
the neophytes
what to confess.
They asked them to confess
and the elder 3780
sat silently
and then spoke, saying
that they know
the Bagre medicine
will be brought
into the room.
They took it,
brought it in,
and put it down in the middle.

And the elder 3790
then spoke, saying
that the business
they did before
was not well done.
And they asked,
'Why wasn't it well done?'
'About the medicine:
you killed the neophytes
but didn't possess the medicine,
and killed neophytes with 3800
clubs.
That's not the way.
And therefore
I say to you
the medicine that comes
into the room,
watch what to do.'
The medicine was brought in
and as it came,
people followed with water
and sprinkled the man 3810
as he entered
into the room.
The neophytes were afraid
and the elder
told them
that the medicine
is not a big thing,
but it has great powers.
They put the medicine aside,
and in the evening 3820
they told
the guides
to look after their neophytes,
to look after them today.
So he spoke,
and the guides asked,
'How will we look after them?'
And he told them

that today
they'll kill the neophytes, 3830
really kill them.
The neophytes
became afraid,
and he said, 'Well,
it's nothing,
and yet it's something too.
I say that today
they will kill you.
If anyone has done wrong
and doesn't admit it, 3840
then when they kill you,
they can't revive you.
And that day is today.'
Some among them
confessed freely,
[saying] that
'Since the time
you made us members,
I did wrong.'
'What did you do wrong?' 3850
Then she replied
that she'd slept with a man.
Then they asked the men,
'What about you?'
And they also replied
that they had done wrong.
Some had slept with women,
some had quarrelled;
all these are Bagre prohibitions.
So they announced 3860
they would leave them aside,
and then said
they'd initiate the others
and separate them off
and allow them to sit down.
They sat down
and the elder
told them

to bring a certain branch.
They brought it　　　　3870
and he told them
to bring cold water.
And when they brought
the cold water,
he spurted it over the medicine.
And he said
that today's
day
is an evil one
and yet　　　　3880
a good one.
Today
is a joyful day
and yet a bitter one.
Today
is a cool day,
and yet a hot one.
The neophytes
today
will get their deserts.　　　　3890
He said this
and then told them
to take the fowl
and draw together
around the medicine
so we may ask the way.
They took
the fowl
with its basket.
'What sort of fowl?'　　　　3900
A red cock.
They came
and he told them
to repeat the prayer
and ask the way.
They spoke,
saying,
'The ancestors,

the guardians,
the gods,　　　　3910
the beings of the wild,
the Earth shrine,
wanted to perform a sacrifice,
because of the scorpion's sting,
because of suicide.
The elder brother
slept badly,
so he took out some grain
and hurried along
to the diviner.　　　　3920
And then
he will go
and see
that we are instructing
you neophytes.
Do you understand
that this
very day
is the killing of the neophytes,
this very day.　　　　3930
This day
you see the medicine
that lies in the centre.
That is what
we will use
today.'
And he said, now,
the Bagre,
they should leave it a while.
They did so　　　　3940
and he said:
'Put your hand in your bag.'
They did so
and they told
the members
to take out something.
They did so.
'What was it?'

'The great leather bottle
we took out.'   3950
And they said
the initiates
should open it.
They did so
and he said
'This affair
is such
that we look in vain.
Therefore today
you'll ask the way,   3960
so we can carry out a certain
    task.'
He spoke
and then told
the guides
to do their business.
The guides
asked,
'What business?'
And he then said,
'The big fowl's egg   3970
will hatch today.
And now
the bell
which is tied
inside the gourd,
let them untie it
and put it on the ground,
so that we know
what is the matter
today.'   3980
They untie it
and when they had done so,
he said, 'Now,
let the initiates
throw their cowries
so they can see.
And if the deity

is following,
when they throw the cowries,
they'll fall favourably,   3990
and they'll initiate the neophytes
this very day.
About the Bagre,
as they said,
they have performed Bagre
last year
and this year,
up till today,
the day of your Bagre
    performance.'
They said, 'Well,   4000
we understand.'
They threw the cowries
and the shells
fell favourably.
They did so
and went over to the medicine;
when they got there,
they said, now,
they should grasp
the medicine.   4010
The elder,
who knows so much,
told them
to open it.
They did so,
and the elder
roared out,
saying:
'It's poison
I've inhaled'.   4020
He said,
'Instruct
the initiates
so the Bagre can be performed
    today.
For the poison

is a cool one,
and yet a bitter one;
it is a good poison,
and yet an evil one.
However, like　　　4030
an elephant in the swamp
and like
a hippo in the river,
it can kill him
today.'
So he spoke
and told them
to play the xylophone.
They played it,
they played the xylophone　4040
and they beat the drum;
they did this
so it blended together.
He said this
and then told them
to pour out the medicine.
When they had finished,
he told the guides
to draw near.
They did so　　　　4050
and he said,
'That's the way.
However,
don't let
the Bagre
take place
as you did
last time.'
Again they poured out the
　　medicine
and he shouted,　　　4060
saying,
'The poison is cool
and yet bitter;
like a bushcow in the tall grass

and a lion in the swamp,
it will kill him.'
Terror
took hold of
the neophytes
and they cried out.　　　4070
In a little while
they brought out
some cudgels.
They came
into the room
and the neophytes
cried out:
'Alas,
today
we're lost.'　　　　4080
So they spoke
and we told
the guides
to bring some potsherds.
They brought them
and came
and [we] put in the medicine,
telling them
not to let
it touch　　　　4090
the neophytes' mouths
but to hold it still.
They did so
and the elder
selected one man
to sit on the stool.
And he asked,
'Have you got it?'
and they replied
they had it.　　　　4100
And he asked again
'Have you got it?'
And they replied
they had it.

And he asked again,
'Have you got it?'
And they replied
they had it.
They said this,
and he asked again,   4110
'What did he say they have?'
They replied
'The stuff that kills neophytes.'
Then he said
that each initiate
should let his neophyte confess.
After a while
the elder sat down
and roared out,
saying   4120
the poison would kill him.
And he said,
'Put out the light.'
They did so
and only darkness remained.
He asked
the members,
all of them,
had they got it?
They had it,   4130
so he roared out
twice.
The neophytes were weeping
and he said
the seeds for the medicine
should be ground up.
They did this
and when they had done
he asked, had they finished?
And they replied   4140
that they had.
'The killing of the neophytes
has arrived.'
So he spoke

and stopped.
He pulled the medicine gourd
nearer to him,
grasped it
and put it on the ground.
Then he shook his rattle   4150
and said
the neophytes
should be held.
They held them,
drawing
their cudgels
nearer to them.
The neophytes were weeping.
However
the elders,   4160
who know everything,
burst out laughing.
And then
the senior member
got up and caught
the senior neophyte,
held him
and roared out.
He roared out,
saying, 'The poison   4170
is a bad one.'
And he told the guides,
'Don't let it touch the neo-
    phytes' mouths.'
So he spoke
and told the neophyte.
He took out some medicine
and blew it,
so the neophyte
became drunk
and lay down.   4180
He told
the guides
they should all

go in [and take some medicine].
They took some
and blew it,
so all got drunk
and lay down.
They felt their skins
and said,   4190
'They're no longer warm.'
They sang a song,
and when they had done so,
they laid them down,
singing again,
'Death kills,'
three times.
Then they said,
'Death kills, the Bagre god
    saves us,
so death can't kill.'   4200
They sang again,
'All lie down in the room,
and no one questions.'
They sang again,
'Let them bring a hundred
to pay for the neophytes.'
They sang again,
'Whose house timbers
are crooked, crooked?'
They sang again,   4210
'Look here,
take heed of this,
today is an evil day.'
They then sang,
'Let everybody laugh,
for today is a day of laughter.'
They sang again
and when they'd done,
they said
they'd divine with a fowl.   4220
They cut the fowl's throat
and it fell on its back.

Again they sang,
'The Bagre bag strikes the fowl
so it falls on its back, back, back.'
So they sang,
and when they'd finished,
the elder
spoke, saying,
'About the matter   4230
we struggle with,
what shall we do?
See here,
about this matter,
we've searched in vain
and still the dead
lie down, so many.
What shall we do?'
What did they do?
They begged God   4240
to revive the neophytes.
So he spoke
and then told them
to go outside.
They went out
and then came back
and reported
they had gone out
and could do nothing.
They should go out again   4250
to solve
the matter
that troubled them.
They got up
and conferred together.
What should they do?
One of them
spoke up and said
he would solve it.
We should all   4260
enter the room,
take the bells,

and the things of the beings,
and shake them and see.
The elders
smiled gently
and said
'If it's true,
really true,
it'll help us.' 4270
And they went in
and entered
the room
and sat quietly.
The senior guide
began to speak
to the elders.
He said, 'Well,
what we've discovered,
we've come to show you.' 4280
'You guides,
do it so we can see.'
And he told them
to give him the bell
to shake so the neophytes
would rise.
He shook it,
but shook in vain,
and went back
to the elders
and told them 4290
he had failed.
The elders
laughed quietly
and said, 'Right,
they had failed.
So the dead would rot
because of their failure.'
Then they said once more,
'About your problem,
[you] should confer with 4300
one another.'

They did so
and the elder said
they should wait.
He went over
to the senior neophyte:
'If you go to a tree
and climb it,
you'll come down the same one
    you climbed.'
And he went on,
'The neophytes 4310
have been lying there
right down to this minute.'
And he told them,
'The tree you climb,
you'll also come down.
These are sound words.
But over the neophytes,
we have failed,
and we sweat on their account.
If a guide 4320
committed a sin,
and touched them,
causing today
to be like this,
then let that person with some-
    thing to say
speak up.'
We told them,
and the members
then said,
'Now look 4330
at you
White initiates.
None of you is able
to revive them.'
So they spoke
and when they had done,
they took the bells
from the guides;

they shook the [bells]
and put their mouths   4340
to the [neophytes'] ears
and then rolled their tongues.
Up they got
and when they had done so,
each asked his neophyte,
'Yesterday where did you go?'
They replied
they didn't know the place.
When they'd got up,
they told them   4350
to listen
to the song of waking.
'They say
initiates are always eating.
So one leaves the cows in the
    byre,
one leaves the sheep in the stall,
one leaves the wife with her
    vagina,
and they all congregate in some
    one's house,
and cook their food together
and give each his share   4360
and eat quickly and leave.
But the Bagre god's matters,
see how they trouble us,
and yet you say, initiates are
    always eating.'
They finished singing
and said,
'Neophytes,
by today
they will have put you through
all this business.   4370
We have killed you
and revived you.
But if it happens
to spill out of somebody's mouth,

the one who talks, his head will
    split open;
the one who talks, his belly will
    burst,
the one who talks, his life will be
    short.
For, he said,
this comes from our ancestors.
They always buy   4380
this Bagre medicine
with a stallion
and 100,000 cowries.
If you don't know Bagre,
you have to go
and hire a member
who'll come along.
He it is
who will give you
the knowledge   4390
of Bagre affairs,
and you too
will give him
some food.
Moreover,
if you don't know,
one fine day
your child
might argue
with your Bagre elders.   4400
This matter
is a serious one.
It is our bowstring
and the breeding of animals
and it is the hoe
and it is trading.
Moreover,
if you don't realize
the Bagre god
has come to your house,   4410
then only an orphan

will remain
among the ruins
before the Bagre god
manifests himself.
He will make you
sacrifice
two cows,
six sheep,
three goats,   4420
and fifty fowls.
If you sacrifice these,
you will then be at rest
and can get to know the Bagre.
The neophytes
will become members
and go to Bagre.
They mustn't eat
like vultures.
Moreover,   4430
in this Bagre of ours,
a neophyte
may be knowledgeable
and learn to recite,
but when you go to Bagre
and sit down,
if they don't
ask you to speak,
then do not
open your mouth.   4440
And in Bagre,
if you go there
and see
an Oil Bagre member
who tries to speak,
let him do so.
If you should go
and come across
an Oil Bagre member
on his way to Bagre,   4450
then wait;

if they ask you
to speak,
then say, 'Well,
I understand,
but as for speaking,
some other time.'
'Why is it
you refuse?'
'An Oil Bagre man   4460
is present
and that's
the reason
you refuse.
When you become
a member,
you should follow
the Bagre
and its ways.
Then if it troubles
someone,   4470
you can help him
on the day.'
So they spoke,
and when they finished,
they got up
and sang
in the long room,
and taking the rattles
and taking the bells,
they shook them   4480
and sang a song.
'Give us way
so the members can pass.'
They gave us way
and we went out
and sang again,
'Draw back, draw back,
so the members can pass.'
They sang
and came to an end   4490

and the guides
ran in,
snatched a burning brand
and threw it [outside].
In the Bagre matters
that we are performing,
they come out
and throw this [brand]
at the non-members.
We go   4500
outside
and the non-members
cook beans,
bambara beans
and yams,
which they eat
till they can eat no more.
They start to dance again.
They dance
and when they've finished,   4510
we go out
around the house
three times
and then go in again.
At the beginning,
as we were going out,
the guides
took the neophytes,
covered their faces
and said,   4520
'Neophytes,
do you know
the place
we'll meet
the Bagre?'
They reply, 'No.'
And they say,
'It is today
you'll understand about Bagre.
The Bagre   4530

comes from the ancestors.
The first men had it;
it was their evil affair,
and yet their good one.
When they were buried,
they should have taken it along,
but they left it behind
and now it troubles us,
bringing death
and the sting of scorpions.   4540
You see this Bagre;
they say that all the members
should wait
till daybreak
to know what
is there.
For we Dagaa,
our greatest possession
is Bagre.
Our most serious talk   4550
is about Bagre.
If you're not a member,
you'll never hear
about your grandfathers'
affairs.
And in Bagre,
our elders
are many.'
'What do you mean by many?'
'You saw that   4560
in the Bagre
there was the large fruit-bat.
He's our Bagre
elder.
The belibaar bird
is one of our Bagre creatures.
The kyaalipio bird
is one of our Bagre creatures.
The large frog
is one of our Bagre creatures. 4570

The damdamwule bird
is one of our Bagre creatures.
The crown bird
is one of our Bagre creatures.'
'What's an elder?'
'I tell you,
all winged creatures
and the featherless cock.'
'Why are these
our Bagre creatures?'   4580
'See the large fruit-bat,
which is one of our Bagre
    creatures.
When we begin our Bagre,
we don't know the time.
The big fruit-bat
is the one
who shows us the time.'
'How does he do this?'
'He will know
by the shea fruit.   4590
He will know the time
to fetch the fruit
in the night,
to eat it and leave the nut;
then we know its the right time.
So we include it among our
    Bagre creatures.
As for the featherless fowl,
we don't know the time
to go to farm.
In the wet season,   4600
we want
to farm.
It's farming time,
and the farmers
go to sleep.
Early in the morning
the featherless fowl
beats his wings.

The boys get up
and go to the farm.   4610
As for the damdamwule bird,
we don't know the time
when rain will fall
and we can sow.
We go on
and the rain stops
and we still sow.
We don't know that sowing
should have finished.
As for the damdamwule,   4620
when a big rain falls,
and we take out
the guinea corn
and go to sow it,
don't you hear them
clicking their mouths
and then start
to clear their throats?
We sowed,
we sowed in vain,   4630
and they told us
that the clearing of their throats
we ignored;
for the guinea corn
we sow
when they clear their throats,
it can come to nothing.
When this takes place,
we should no longer
sow the guinea corn,   4640
that's why we take this bird
and include him
among our Bagre creatures,
together with the featherless
    fowl.
As for the belibaar bird,
as we reach the dry season,
we don't know when it'll come

but the belibaar bird
always knows the time.
If he comes   4650
from the rain side
and flies
where the sun sets,
then the dry season is upon us.
It is time
to cut the guinea corn.
When we've done this,
he and his mate
will come by
and show us the time.   4660
It is then
we begin [Bagre]
and to prevent the neophytes
    from sinning
we tell them
what is forbidden.
That's why
we take
the belibaar bird
and include it in Bagre.
As for the kyaalipio bird,   4670
in the Bagre
it is beer
they always brew.
And the kyaalipio bird,
just at dawn,
when the slender girls
are sleeping,
he passes by
and cries out,
"Don't let a boar muddy   4680
    the water."
They get up,
fetch water
and bring it
to carry out their Bagre.
That is why

we take
to include in Bagre.
The male crown-bird
at the top of a tall tree
is sitting.   4690
Our Bagre
has to do with fasting.
He sits
on top of a tall tree;
the time comes
and he calls out,
"Bagre members
Bagre members
Bagre members."
When he does this,   4700
we'll get up
at midnight.
We get up
and give food
to the children.
They eat
and go off to sleep again.
They get up,
and begin to fast
until we perform the Bagre.   4710
That is why
we include it
in our Bagre creatures.
And see here,
an old guinea cock
is also in our Bagre,
for he too
shows us
the time
to perform Bagre.'   4720
'What time does he show
to us?'
We don't know the time;
however,
when the bean flowers

have come,
he and his mate
quarrel
at night.
They get up   4730
and he goes into
his big farm.
He is angry
and wants
his food.
He goes there
and sees the beans
and plucks some
and returns.
The elder   4740
who sees this
cries out, "Well,
because of that
our children
were about to go astray."
So he spoke
and called them
to teach the Bagre matters
and all the taboos.
This is the reason   4750
we treat the bird
as our Bagre elder.
If you choose certain things
and people don't know why,
they'll always be asking,
'Why is it
you include winged creatures
in the Bagre?'
'That is why,
at White Bagre time,   4760
they teach you
the reason
they are Bagre creatures.
Our Bagre
has a mother

and a father.
I repeat,
it has a mother and father.
The father is rain,
the mother is earth.   4770
Do you know the reason
I say this?'
They replied, 'No
we don't know.'
'I ask this
and you don't know.
When rain
falls down
upon the earth,
it moistens the land.   4780
The old men
go out to hoe,
they hoe,
and get crops.
When they get them,
they perform Bagre.
That is why
rain is father
and earth is mother.
Do you understand?   4790
You understand now.
We continue the Bagre
and come at last
to Bagre Day,
and find ourselves at this point.
Do you understand?
One of these days
a boy
will go out and recite
about the performance   4800
of Bagre
and its truths.
Now Kusiele
are the Bagre joking partners
of Kpiele.

If those people
don't know Bagre,
and you initiate them
and teach them,
the stallion   4810
will be paid
but not the hundred thousand.
If Kusiele know it
and initiate our Kpiele children,
we will pay
the stallion
but not the hundred thousand.
The way they pay for Bagre
has a reason.'
'What's the reason?'   4820
'An old man
who can't walk about,
if they pay a horse
that'll give him a mount
to go to Bagre.
That is why
we go and take a stallion.
The hundred thousand
is for the malted grain
and the fowls   4830
that you'll use;
and the guinea corn
that you'll use.
That's the reason for the
   hundred thousand.
Have you understood?
As for you neophytes,
when you're finally initiated
and three years later
you're still alive,
then Bagre guards you.   4840
If you live two years
and then die,
a Bagre death
has killed you.

If you live two and a half years
and then die,
Bagre is involved.
If all you neophytes
turn out well,
then we'll be able   4850
on the day
to help each other.'
So they spoke
and then returned
to the White Bagre.
'It is the White Bagre,
it is Bagre Day;
we begin
to teach
the children   4860
and the women
and the men.
We go in again
to the long room.
You see the food,
you see the meat.
It is beer
we drink
and make a din.
The many matters   4870
to be performed in the room,
we recited them
and completed all.
And now
we turn again
to take the food.
We have eaten.
Neophytes,
you have eaten.
Senior members,   4880
you have eaten.
Ancestors,
you have eaten.
Guardians,

you have eaten.
Deities,
you have eaten.
Together
you have eaten.'
The next day   4890
they say,
'The day
has come
and we know
your kindness.'
'What is kindness?'
'Kindness
means a good heart.
Kindness
has things to give to others.   4900
Kindness
loves everybody's child.
Kindness
respects the weak.
You respect them
and today
they will come
with their fowls.
You will go out
and wash yourselves   4910
and anoint your bodies.
And now
I will teach you
something.
You all see.
The neophytes
should watch.'
He raised his hand
and said,
'Do you see anything?   4920
What is it?'
One fool
said, 'It's a hand.'
He said, 'No,

you say that,
but instead
something else is there.'
He asked the wisest neophyte,
to call out
its name.   4930
He replied
'Benima
knows that;
I don't know.'
He said,
'That is just
Bagre lies.
For see,
today
you are now members.   4940
You people
will go out
and one day
you'll see the moon
standing there.
If someone says
"Do you see the moon?"
Don't turn and look,
but say
you saw it   4950
days ago.
You say this
so they think you saw it,
but you didn't.
And so it is,
if you and a non-member
see the new moon,
then say
you saw it days ago.'
And so   4960
they always say,
'It is Bagre lies'.
Bagre Gyingyiri
is performed tomorrow.

We have come
to the next day,
and they told
the guides
to bring
a broom   4970
and a small basket,
and take them to the room.
When they send out the
    neophytes,
you'll sweep off the dirt
into the little baskets
and then sweep
yourselves
and depart.
Hurry them so they run;
and when they go outside, 4980
they sing a song,
'The razor smells something,
quick, quick, quick.'
They go and sit down,
and when they sit,
their friends
bring cocks
which are for Bagre.
And lovers
bring guinea fowls   4990
which are for Bagre.
Young girls
bring dawadawa
and the men
bring cocks.
They beat them,
beat them on the ground.
The guides,
the strong guides,
go and take   5000
some of them
to their place
and collect them together

to be used for Bagre.
When they finished
they told the neophytes,
'Today
you are raw Bagre members
and these Bagre matters
must never come from
    your mouth.   5010
If it does so,
it's Bagre you hurt.
For Bagre
is from our ancestors.
For Bagre
is a fine thing.
For Bagre
is a thing that kills.
For Bagre
is a thing that gives life.   5020
For Bagre
is a thing of the bowstring.
For Bagre
is a thing of the hoe-handle.
For Bagre
is a thing of chicken-rearing.
For Bagre
brings peace.
If you also get
to know   5030
the Bagre,
it brings you riches.
In the old days
the people
didn't know it
very well.
If someone did,
he was like a chief,
a rich man
and every kind of chief.'   5040
So he spoke
to the members.

'The Black Bagre,
you can't leave aside.
You always recite
for three days,
three days
and three nights.
And the White Bagre
they recite   5050
for three days
and three nights
and finish.
You don't stop there
in Bagre;
it's like an antelope's leg,
running one way, then another.
That's what I say
the Bagre is like.
Now, you'll go home   5060
and the bell
which you have,
it's like an egg.
In two days' time,
if we're strong enough,
we'll take it
to cleanse.
If you wear the bell
and you're a woman
or a man,   5070
and you commit adultery,
you wrong the Bagre.
If a man spoils a woman,
you will find
a separate place for them.
Now we come
to the sister's son;
don't you see
the Bagre food—
the senior sister's son   5080
is taking by force
some beer,

porridge
and meat?
He seizes it
and eats.
When they eat like this,
you know
that one day
these may be your own
  people.   5090
If you've got a mother
and she kicks you out,
you go to your father.
If your father kicks you out,
you go to your mother.
That's why
the sister's son
is not a person to be played with.
Your clan brother
and sister's son   5100
are all the same
to you.
I'll tell you this
so you understand.
About the sister's son,
in the old days
a brother
and a brother
looked after their father.
These brothers   5110
went out
with the father
into their farm
to hoe.
The sister's son
wandered round
to the farm
where he saw
the two brothers.
They and their father   5120
were hoeing.

As they were hoeing,
[the father] told
them to stop.
The sons
became angry,
measured the farm
and divided it
into strips
with their father.   5130
He said, "Well,
I'm weak
and can farm no more.
I farmed and fed you
till you became men.
How is it possible
that you and I
can hoe the same?"
But they divided the farm
and finished their strips.   5140
The sister's son
saw his uncle,
in the heat of the sun,
farming alone.
He was an old man,
but look at the children,
sitting down after hoeing.
So the boy,
the sister's son,
takes a hoe   5150
and goes over
to his uncle's strips.
He farmed them
and when he'd done so,
the uncle
got up
and told
his sister's son
and his children
that he preferred his   5160
  sister's son

to his children.
One day,
when he is no more,
the sister's son
will take his property.
If the sons
try to seize it,
they'll die.
That's the reason
the sister's son   5170
always takes property
and we say nothing.
That's what we tell
the neophytes,
the new neophytes,
so you know about the sister's
  son.
But about Bagre
we tell you
that you'll complete the Bagre
at Bagre Bells,   5180
when they'll wash them
and then you've finished.
If there's a small boy
among you
who has some sense,
and goes
to someone's Bagre
and sits,
its not for food you go.
You will go   5190
and sit
and look
and listen
how it is
they perform.
Bagre
is all one;
nevertheless
the way it's performed

is different.   5200

If you hear people

reciting Bagre,

you'll adopt

their way

and one day,

when you recite

the Bagre,

you'll include this.

When you recite,

you include that in your   5210
  Bagre.

You do so,

then greet

their elders

and their distant ancestors.

You will greet them,

greet their guardians,

greet their Earth shrines,

then recite Bagre.

If you leave

the Bagre room,   5220

you will go

outside

and pray

to the Earth shrine

and then return.

You'll find

you're able

to speak.'

A neophyte

then asked   5230

'Who brought Bagre?'

They said,

'The first people did.'

He asked again,

'Who was that?'

They said,

'It was the younger brother.'

And he asked again,

'What do they call god?'

They said,   5240

'A god is here

and God is there.'

The neophyte asked:

'The one

we follow

in this matter,

is it God we follow

or is it a god?'

He spoke

and the elder   5250

said, 'Well,

we follow

God.

He is the senior

but we can't see him.

It is a god

who comes down to people.

That's what we call god.'

'Do our elders

say that   5260

God's child

is the one

we follow?'

He then said, 'Yes,

we follow him

and so reach God.'

So he spoke

and the neophyte

asked again,

'All these things,   5270

how can you

know them all

and be able

to teach them?'

They said

they had performed

the White Bagre

up till today.

'Moreover,
the Black Bagre   5280
is similar to this.
People take you,
both by night
and by day,
for three days.
If you are clever,
you'll put it
in your head
and know it all.'
Then he asked,   5290
'Black Bagre
and White Bagre,
which comes first?'
The neophyte asked
and they told him,
'Black Bagre
is the senior.'
And they said,
'It is senior
because that one   5300
we knew
before we knew the White
      Bagre.'
The wise neophyte
then said,
'But why is it
you didn't first
perform
Black Bagre for us?'
The old man said, 'Well!'
He laughed out loud   5310
and went on,
'If we want to perform Bagre,
first of all
we recite
the Black Bagre
in order to see
and then continue.'

The neophyte
asked again,
'Why is it   5320
you recite it
without
our knowledge?'
The elder
replied,
'If you are not a member
how can they show you?'
He said,
'But you know that
you will initiate us   5330
into Bagre?'
He said, 'Yes,
I know
I will initiate you
into Bagre.
But it is like
the milk of a pregnant cow.
They cannot
show you
before you are initiated.   5340
We are betwixt and between;
that's the reason
I don't show you
the Black Bagre.
If you give it thought
and want to know
about Bagre,
you'll try
to ask
about Bagre matters.   5350
If you don't ask,
you can't know Bagre.'
He said, 'Well,
look here,
you said
when they teach
people

the Bagre,
we always take
a stallion   5360
and a hundred thousand.
Why is it
they always do this?'
So he asked,
and they replied
'There's a reason.
You see,
someone
went into
the wilds   5370
for three years
and then returned.
When he came back,
he said
they could see
that his hairs
hadn't been cut
for three years.
However,
he brings a matter   5380
that is troublesome
but teaches many things.
So it is
in our Bagre matters,
some [beings] come
from the hill-top,
and some come
from the water,
from the river.
It is   5390
to the river people
they pay
the stallion,
and it is
to the hill people
they pay
the hundred thousand.

If you know [Bagre]
and teach people
of another patriclan,   5400
you'll take
the stallion
and the hundred thousand.
If you don't do so,
you'll go blind.
If you don't do so,
your voice
will change.
Now you understand
the reason.   5410
That's why
we say
that if a child learns,
he will be able
to protect himself.
However,
if you don't know,
you too can ask
and they'll teach you
the Bagre.   5420
If it is lost
they will find it,
but only through sweat.
That's why
we say
that the children
should learn
the Bagre,
so that one day
we'll help one another.   5430
You now know
White Bagre,
today;
there remains
Black Bagre.
The man who breeds chickens
and farms well,

he is the one
who'll become
a Black initiate.   5440
However,
if you
always attend,
you'll get to know
the White Bagre.
If you're
an eater,
you'll get to know
the guide's
duties.'   5450
'Neophytes,
you understand?'
The elder
then said
he wanted
to go home:
'What is left
to be taught,
you should teach the children.'
He went home   5460
to his father's house,
taking
his meat.
The meat of the medicine
belonged to him;
the Black initiates
don't eat it
until they have the medicine.
He brought
the fowls   5470
and threw them down
in front of his house,
and cared for them
until they laid eggs.
'Well now,
this is what you'll do
with these fowls.

You'll give them
to your father's shrine
and to the wilds   5480
and to the guardians.
But the meat,
eat it, leaving the bones,
which you must bury.
Don't allow
a fowl
to swallow them
or it'll become
a Bagre fowl.
Bagre things   5490
you can't mix
with things of the hoe.
If you do this,
they'll spoil
and only senior members
can eat them;
non-members
can't do so.'
They went home
and walked round freely   5500
and a week later
they'll prepare for Bagre Bells.
Because of this,
no one can sleep with a woman.
So they spoke,
and two days later
they told
the Bagre mothers
to bring the neophytes.
They took   5510
the neophytes
up to the rooftop
and sat them down.
And they said, 'Well,
neophytes,
it is today
you finish Bagre,

and yet you don't.'
So they spoke,
saying, 'Well,   5520
you see
the Bagre
they've performed so far.
Many things
have been consumed.
Up to now,
the malted grain
and the fowls,
one man's fowls
amount to a hundred;   5530
the malted grain,
you know how many baskets?
Well, they amount
to twenty-five.
They sent you through
and you came out
today.
If one of you learns,
learns it
and gets to know it,   5540
it'll benefit him.
If they catch you,
make you sit on the chair
and you have no medicine
  [with you]
and they pay you
three thousand
and a black fowl,
you'll take it.
Take out the medicine money,
and then   5550
you and your fellow members,
you'll know
what to do.
They don't spend it
hurriedly.
Spending Bagre things

hurriedly
will kill the neophytes.
It changes the neophytes' voices.
This is what   5560
they teach you
today.'
They will again ask
your children
today.
They tell
the neophyte
that if he's slept with a woman,
he should speak out;
they'll still wash his bell,   5570
for there's a special rite to be
  performed.
'If you don't speak out,
but conceal it
through shame,
then one day
you'll be really ashamed.
Guides,
ask the neophytes.'
They asked
about their sins,   5580
and they confessed.
Again they asked
the neophytes
to confess.
They said, 'Well,
you've confessed
today,
now they'll wash the bells.'
So they spoke
and went on, 'Well,   5590
take the bells
from off your necks
and put them down.'
They took a vat of beer
and collected

the bells,
set them down
and washed them.
The elder
picked up　　　　　5600
a bell
and put it in the middle,
saying, 'Well,
if anyone
now has
a question,
let him ask it today.'
One neophyte
stood up
and said, right,　　　　5610
he wanted to ask
how it was
they know so much,
and yet death
still kills?
He replied, 'Well,
knowledge
came from
the ancestors.
And death too　　　　5620
comes from
the ancestors.
The problem
you pose
is an old one.
It is
death
that came first,
and Bagre
followed.'　　　　　5630
'How then
can it
drive away
death?'
And he said, 'Now,

if you want the truth,
Bagre
is a grave matter.
You grasp it
with both hands,　　　5640
following it
in the right way;
watch it
with your eyes,
and don't let it go.'
The elders
then took
the beer
and washed the bells,
put them down　　　　5650
and sat on the ground.
Just now
they want
to ask
a question.
'We take you out
today;
in the Bagre,
what have we taught you?'
If a neophyte　　　　5660
can get up
and recite
the Bagre
as they have done,
they'll give him a cow.
[The neophytes] said
[the elders] wanted
to laugh at them
and they asked,
what could they know?　5670
They said
that they first took them
and collected
some guinea corn
and malted it.

They were told
to go out
and tell the senior members
to come
and take the flour.   5680
[The members] laughed
saying, well,
they knew nothing.
'How is it
you don't know
about the time
when the Bagre god
picked on you,
and we started you on the way;
and yet you know   5690
about taking the flour?
Nevertheless,
the Bagre
we've spoken about,
we'll teach you
in the Black Bagre.
If you happen
to find someone
who knows Bagre,
and he teaches you,   5700
it is he
who owns
your food.
He owns
your drink.
When he teaches you
everything,
then he'll teach you
the Black Bagre.
If he is able   5710
to make a bell,
then you know
he can twist a bangle.
But now
today

you'll go down,
hunt around
and go into the bush.
If you see a partridge
and kill it,   5720
it's for Bagre.
If you kill a rabbit,
it's for Bagre.
If you kill an antelope,
it's for Bagre.
However,
if you kill a boar,
it's for the house.
If you kill a grass-cutter,
it's for the house.   5730
If you kill a porcupine,
it's for the house.
Are there any more questions?'
[The neophytes] replied, 'Yes,'
and then asked,
'You said earlier
that you'd beg a head
that sits on our shoulders.
That's what I don't understand
and want to find out   5740
   about.'
They replied, 'Look,
that's not a proper question.'
And then another asked,
'Well now,
the person
who sinned against Bagre
and didn't confess,
and then came out
of Bagre,
is there anything   5750
that can happen to him?'
They replied, 'Yes,
there is something,
for you'll go blind.

If you don't go blind,
you'll become a leper.
If you don't
speak up,
you'll wither away.
If you don't speak up,   5760
you'll become lame.'
So they spoke
and one [neophyte]
said, 'Look,
there was a woman
who said she'd slept with a man.'
He said this
and they heard
and said nothing.
They asked   5770
the neophytes,
'Who has anything to say?'
They replied
that they wanted to ask this:
'When you're
a member
and go
to a performance,
and your elder
is not present   5780
but only you
are sitting there,
and they bring food
and give it you,
can you eat it?'
They replied, 'Yes,
you can eat it.'
He asked again,
'But if you
go to the Bagre   5790
and your own
elder
is not present,
and they ask you to recite,

what will you do?'
They replied, 'Well,
you yourself
will recite
and in the middle
you'll greet the members,   5800
greet the ancestors,
greet the Earth shrine.
If you're a Kpiele
and see a clansman
at the Bagre,
he's your brother.
If you're a Kusiele
and see a clansman
at the Bagre,
he's your brother.   5810
If you're a Bekuone
and see a clansman
at the Bagre,
he's your brother.
If you're a Yongyuole,
and see a clansman
at the Bagre,
he's your brother.
You won't
be afraid   5820
in the Bagre.
You will recite
the Bagre
until it's completed,
and then go home.'
Then someone asked,
'If you've been initiated,
and get home
and die,
did Bagre kill you?'   5830
They replied, 'Yes'.
They want
to tell you
that if you live

three years
and then die,
Bagre is the cause.
So they spoke
and when they had finished,
they said, 'Well,   5840
do you understand?'
Then one asked,
'If you've been initiated
into Bagre,
get home
and fight with your wife,
will they make you pay Bagre
    again?'
And they said
they can't do that.
And they said again,   5850
'Do you understand?'
Then one asked,
'If you've been initiated,
and get home
and your child
should die,
is Bagre the cause?'
They replied, 'No.
that's not the case.'
Then another asked,   5860
'If you've been initiated,
get home,
and your wife leaves you
to marry someone else,
can he take her from you?'
And they replied, 'Yes,
he can take her.'
He asked again,
'If he's been initiated today
and sees someone's wife   5870
who wants him,
can he take her?'
And they replied, 'Yes,

he can.'
Then one got up
and asked again,
'If he gets home
to find
that he has put something down,
gone through Bagre,   5880
and then can't see it,
has the Bagre god taken it?'
They replied,
'If you go home
and can't find something
and it's been lost,
if you swear
to the Bagre god,
he'll kill
your housepeople.   5890
If your kinsman took it,
he'll kill him.
If it's someone outside,
he'll kill him.
However,
if you
are silent,
the Bagre god will follow the
    man.'
Then another asked,
'If a man and I dislike   5900
    each other
and I go home
and he has something
that he gives me,
should I eat it?'
They replied, 'Yes,
eat it.'
Then another
asked again,
'If he goes home
and sees the lover   5910
he used to have,

but someone else has now taken,
should I fight with that man?'
They replied, 'No,
you shouldn't fight with him.'
And they said again
that they want
to tell you
about the question;
they said   5920
if anyone has
a question,
it should not be
on any topic whatever;
they want
the questions
to be about Bagre.
Then another asked
that as between
the Whitening Ceremony   5930
and the Beating of the Grain,
which comes first?
They said, 'Now,
what sort of a question is that?'
and continued, 'The Whitening
  Ceremony
always comes first.'
Then one said
that as between
the Announcement of Bagre
and Bagre Beans,   5940
which comes first?
They replied,
'Don't you understand
when they say "announce"?
Announcing,
that is
what they do to begin with
and always comes first.'
Then another asked,
'Elders,   5950

excuse me,'
and continued,
'Well now,
when a man's an initiate
and his wife stops menstruating,
they pour water on her.
Why is it
they do this?'
They replied, 'Well,
it's an old path   5960
they follow;
they don't want
someone to talk
and this comes
to the girl's
hearing.
That is why
some water
is poured over her.'
Then another asked,   5970
'When you go
to someone's Bagre
and see
an elder
at the Bagre house,
and the old man
is reciting Bagre
and getting tired,
what will you do?'
They replied, 'Well,   5980
when you see
the elder
getting tired,
you can't take over
the recital.
You'll wait,
and when he realizes he's tired,
he'll call someone's name
and that man will take over.'
Then another asked,   5990

'Well, now,
if you're young
and an initiate,
and there's an elder
who's an old man
and joined after you,
and you both go to Bagre,
and the food is brought in,
who'll eat first and give the
     other?'
They replied, 'Well,   6000
if you're younger
but were a member first,
he'll follow you.'
Then another asked,
'The beings of the wild
and God,
which of them brought Bagre?'
They replied, 'Well,
God created them,
put them on earth   6010
and they sat there empty-
     handed.
However,
the younger one
and his elder brother
were living together
when the younger one
went and disappeared
and they thought he was fooling.
He came back
and taught us   6020
all this.
God created us
but gave us nothing
and when we were hungry,
we had to find food to eat.
However,
the younger brother,
he it was

who brought
this matter   6030
and taught it to us.
That is why
we always say
it's the ancestor's
affair.'
So he spoke
and when he'd finished,
[the neophytes] said, 'Now,
does God
know about Bagre?'   6040
They asked
and he replied, 'Yes.
It was God
who created us.
Everything
we say,
he hears.
Everything we do,
he sees.
Because   6050
he created us
and knows all about us.
And God
told us
he would have come
for all to see,
but the reason was
that if he came here,
he could not do his work.
For if anyone's kinsman   6060
were about to die,
he would ask,
"Why does [God] kill [my]
     kinsman?"
If someone's kinsman died,
he would come
and ask me to revive him.
If someone was ill,

they would come and ask [me]
to cure the sickness.
If someone   6070
is struck by another,
he will come and say,
"Kill the man who struck me."
That is why
God
doesn't want us
to see him.
He is near
and yet far.
That is why   6080
he said, "Well,
he would send a person
to come
who is more powerful than us
   all."
Our forefathers
said that,
about this person's matter,
which we searched out in vain,
the first men
told it   6090
to our forefathers
and they understood it.
And we children,
we have now seen it.
If you're a member,
the forefather's things
you'll always hear them,
you'll always know them.
But if you're not,
even if you're clever,   6100

you cannot
get to know
everything.'
They told
the neophytes
and they understood.
You have heard
the Bagre
to the end.
What is left?   6110
God's matter
remains;
the Black Bagre
will come.
In that
they will explain
these matters
to you.
Do you understand?
That is   6120
Bagre knowledge
and Bagre seeing
and Bagre hearing
and Bagre eating.
He will eat.
This is why
we recite some
and leave the rest.
We say
to the chicken-rearers   6130
and to the farmers,
'Initiates,
let's close the meeting.'

SUMMARY OF THE WHITE BAGRE

Invocation (1). The elder brother is troubled by the supernatural powers and goes to consult a diviner (11). The diviner relates his difficulties to the deity of meetings who is associated with the Bagre society (37). The elder returns home, calls his children together and prohibits them from eating the shea fruit and other new crops (40). He sprays the children (The Asperging of the Neophytes) (55). He is again disturbed in his sleep and returns to the diviner (70). He goes home and when his children come from their farms, he tells them about the deity that is troubling them and that they must now begin the performances (90). The Bagre is something we have inherited from our fathers but it would have been better had they taken it along with them to the land of the dead (129). He pours a libation and sprays water over them (141). He tells them to return in the evening (149). Food depends upon the rain god (166). The rains came and the old woman collected some bean leaves, cooked them and began to eat (206). The children wanted to do likewise but the old woman warns them against eating the leaves (215). The elder comes to eat, sees the bean soup and knows it is time to call the Bagre members together again to carry out the Bagre of Beans (223). They come and he frees them from the pro- hibition on bean leaves (272). They have a feast (285). When they have finished eating, the elder addresses the Earth shrine, saying that they have just begun to perform the rites of the Bagre society, for which they need much food (336). He predicts the coming of the deity (352). The next stage of the ceremony requires yams which are not yet ready to eat (364). One day, when the father has been late in the fields, the old woman gets hold of a yam and roasts it (375). The children want to eat it but she warns them (391). When the father comes, he is given a piece of the yam and realizes it is time to call the initiates together (401). The senior initiates eat and drink first (436). When they finish eating, the elder addresses them, saying there is still not enough food (458). They roast some yams and then he prays again, asking for help (479). One day the elder was sleeping. An old guinea cock and his mate quarrel over a bean flower and drop it. The elder wakes and picks it up, thinking it is money he has dropped (561). Then he realizes that it is time to call the initiates together again (613). They gather there to perform the Ceremony of the Bean Flower and he tells them to repeat the invocation after him (635). They do so (685). The rites in the room remain (720). The elder addresses them, asking them what comes next (730). That is the Announcement of Bagre (753). They decide to leave this and go on to the matter of the shea nuts (781). A man goes to the farm. In a near-by tree a large fruit-bat and his mate have a quarrel and he drops a shea nut which falls to the foot of the tree (807). Looking for a white ant hill to take to feed his chickens, the farmer finds one under the tree and accidentally takes the shea nut as well (862). His father finds the shea nut and realizes it is time to call the initiates together again (903). The old woman's daughters first make it into shea butter (933). Then the initiates are warned to start collecting malted grain for the Announcement of Bagre (966). They ask about making malted grain and it is explained to them (993). They collect the grain (1076). Some slender girls distribute the grain for people to grind (1098). Then the women fetch water and begin to brew the beer (1111). The neophytes are called together again (1196). Seeing the food, they start to eat (1204). The elder stops them, saying it is first the turn of the senior initiates (1214). The guides get their beer and start to make a noise (1221). The elder quietens them and tells them something remains to be done (1237). They must repeat after him the invocation, praying for good crops so that they can finish the ceremony (1251). One of them asks about the chickens they will need (1301). Each of the neophytes has fowls, so they may breed chickens for the later performances (1307). Any eggs laid in the same nest become Bagre property (1352). The people disperse again (1382). The ancesters and deities help to provide the crops required (1392). Rain comes (1409). The sun ripens the guinea corn and the beans (1423). The harvest is a good one (1436). The elder calls the neophytes and tells them to warn the members to come in two days' time (1451). When they come together, the old woman is sent to bring some grain (1479). The grain is threshed (1523), and winnowed (1533). They make it germinate (1541). They take it to the elder (1578). It is now the dry season (1589), and time for the Whitening Ceremony (1599). The members are called together (1601). The elder's wife carries malted grain to the roof, so they may see if it is enough (1624). When they have measured it, they give it to the women (1661), who prepare beer (1673). Two days later the members come together again (1678). They sacrifice a fowl to the Earth, the guardians and the ancestors (1724). The fowl falls auspiciously (1734). Other fowls are killed (1739). The guides start to eat greedily and are stopped, as the senior members have not yet drunk (1757). The guides eat and create a hubbub (1780). The elders tell them to keep quiet and explain that there is work to be done (1792). They must get whitewash to paint the new members, as well as string and small gourds for each of them (1806). The fibre for the string was purchased from the old woman for twenty cowries (1817). The gourds were found by the river bank (1833). The next part of the ceremony is of great importance (1849). This is the time they stop the neophytes from having sexual intercourse (1869). When the warning has been given, the guides prepare the small gourd for the neophytes (1899). The gourd is given to them (1924). Then they are shown some 'oil' (whitewash) and are told they will have criss-cross lines painted on their bodies (1939). On the following day they must go out decorated in this manner and sit in silence (1956). The elder calls upon God, whom he announces will come down to earth and bring food (1987). The guides then tie bells on the small gourds and warn the initiates that to break the gourd is like breaking one's own head (2015). The neophytes are given the bells, and told to go out and beg guinea corn from the neighbouring houses (2029). Prohibitions are put on the neophytes concerning the way they conduct themselves as they walk around (2038). The elder then gives them each an old basket in which to collect the grain (2092). They beg grain and bring it to the elder (2114). He instructs them about begging (2121). They are instructed about the gourd and agree to carry it all the time (2178). They are told there is enough guinea corn but the fowls are too few (2224). They should go round and beg for some (after the Beating of the Malt) (2238). The way they do this is then explained (2247). They then ask where God is (2321). They discuss the matter and eventually the being of the wild comes and pretends that he is God, and tells them what to do in the ceremony (2457). The being of the wild tells them about his medicine (2493). They treat the medicine as he had told them (2517). The being of the wild returns and shows them how to complete the preparation of the medicine (2528). He tells them they should give it to someone to see how it works (2540). They do so and he dies at once (2555). The being of the wild returns to the woods and the elders try to discover what has happened (2558). The younger one goes off to find the being of the wild (2571). He finds him and tells him that his medicine has brought death (2582). The being of the wild replies that he warned them this would happen (2592). He accompanies the younger one back home (2613), and explains that he wants to teach them Bagre (2620). He asks why it is that the man has been dead three days and yet the corpse shows no sign of putrefying (2630). This is the most important part of the Bagre (2659). Because of this, all Bagre members are afraid (2663). He breathes in the ear of the corpse and raises him from the dead (2676). He offers to sell them the medicine (2687). They pay him what he asks (2694). They go to his house and he explains that he heard them asking about God (2707). He declares that he is God (2711), and they should follow his ways (2713). The elder is worried lest they kill any neophytes with the medicine (2722). The being explains that there are two medicines, the cold and the hot (2731). They ask him to allow the younger one to come back to help supervise on Bagre Eve when they make the medicine (2764). He sends his child, the small being, along and he watches quietly (2771). They start to kill the neophytes (2794). The elder shakes his rattle and they sing a number of chants (2801). They go outside the room, singing more songs (2835). Then they return (2862). The guides had buried the Bagre bells. They got these and rang them while they sang in the neophytes' ears (2870). But they do not get up (2887). The small being feels them and they are cold (2891). The younger one and his being approach and ask what has happened (2899). They say they did as they were told but must have made an error (2908). Upon inquiry, they find out that they have performed this ceremony in the wrong order (2916). Moreover they should not kill people with clubs or arrows but with wits and medicine (2933). The small being then tells them that it is God from whom all things flow, including life and death (2943). They ask how it is that if God gave people life, others can take it away (2972). The small being replied that God could give them anything on earth but that he also has a house elsewhere (2978). He is asked where God's house is (2989). Before he could reply, the elders say they are worried about the dead (2991). The small being spits medicine on to their heads (3002), and brings them back to life (3012). They then return to perform the part of the ceremony they had omitted, the Beating of the Malt (3018). The neophytes fetch river water and take it to an open space (3037); and then fetch guinea corn (3044). The elder repeats the Invocation (3064). He tells how the elder brother divined and found that a deity was troubling them (3079). It was the deity of meetings (3109). Then today we did not know what to do and the younger brother entered the woods to find out (3117). Then they killed the children, following the being's instructions (3128). While we were finding out about this in the woods, the others killed the neophytes and we returned to find them dead (3155). And so we are performing the ceremony again (3161). Now we spread out the grain (3178), and thresh it (3184). Some guinea corn is changed to malt (3191). They return to the Bagre house (3200). The guides set the neophytes on a stool (3209). The companion reprimands them for making so much noise (3221). Something more remains to be done (3230). They come to the Beating of the Malt (3261). One neophyte goes hunting and kills an antelope (3309). But Bagre members and their kinsfolk quarrel about the division of the meat (3327). It is for Bagre members, but kinsfolk eat first (3373). All the neophytes go hunting and the meat is used for the coming ceremony (3403). They list the wild animals that are used in Bagre (3436). They prepare for the Bagre Dance (3480). The white initiates gather to eat (3488). They prepare the beer (3503). They prepare the soup (3609). The neophytes are called and they prepare for a sacrifice (3628). They recite the Invocation (3645). They list the food that is used for Bagre (3688), the guides become impatient (3710), the neophytes become afraid (3722), especially about the food, but are told that only those who have broken Bagre taboos need fear (3730). The neophytes confess their sins (3779). The members prepare to give the neophytes the Bagre medicine, which will kill them (3785). But they will resurrect those who have done no wrong (3837). They prepare to sacrifice (3891), again reciting the Invocation (3908). The initiates put their hands in their skin bags and take out the Bagre containers (3942). They untie the bells from the necks of the containers (3972), and throw some of the cowries from them (3983). The poison is tested (4019). The lights are extinguished (4122), they prepare the medicine (4133), and the guides blow it on the neophytes, who fall asleep (4181). The guides sing the Bagre songs (4192). They discuss what to do about the dead (4226). They pray to God to help revive them (4239). They shake their bells, but in vain (4259). But the senior members wake them up (4340) and question them (4347). They sing the song of waking (4350). The neophytes are told to keep the Bagre secrets (4373). Bagre is an old thing, which must not be forgotten (4378). It is expensive to revive (4416). The neophytes should learn the Bagre (4421). But they should not recite it unless asked (4434). Don't do so if an Oil Bagre speaks (4441). They finish (4473), sing a song (4476), and leave the room (4488). The guides throw a burning brand at the spectators (4491). The spectators eat their fill (4502). The neophytes walk round the house (4511). When they return, they are told of the importance of Bagre (4527). They are taught about the Bagre animals, whose actions tell them when the ceremonies should be performed (4556). About the fruit-bat and the shea fruit (4581). About the featherless fowl and the time to go farming (4597). About the damdamwule bird and the end of planting (4620). About the belibaar bird and the approach of the dry season (4645). About the kyaalipio bird and the brewing of beer (4670). About the crown-bird and feeding the children (4688). About the old guinea cock and the bean flower (4714). The father of Bagre is rain, the mother is earth (4769). For it is they who bring the crops we need for Bagre (4779). On teaching Bagre (4800), and paying for it (4819). On deaths due to Bagre (4836). They get down to eating (4876). They discuss kindness (4890). The neophytes are taught to lie about seeing the moon (4931). They prepare for Bagre Gyingyiri (4963). The guides prepare to brush off the neophytes as they leave the room (4967). The neophytes sit outside and receive gifts from their friends (4984). Secrecy is enjoined on members (5005). Reciting Bagre is important and brings rewards (5029). The neophytes are told to look after their bells, which will later be washed, (5060) and to observe the taboo on adultery (5068). They discuss the role of the sister's son, and the reasons for matrilineal inheritance (5078). At Bagre Bells the bells will be washed (5177). On learning about other people's Bagre (5183). The neophytes ask questions about Bagre, God, and god (5229). In Black Bagre, the second grade, they will receive more instruction (5279). On Bagre and the payments to the beings of the wild (5383). Later on, the neophytes can join the second grade, the Black Bagre (5434). The elder goes home and takes his fowls (5459). Bagre fowls have to be specially treated (5482). The neophytes go home and later reassemble for Bagre Bells (5499). The advantages of Bagre membership are explained (5538), and the one who can recite it is especially valued (5542). The neophytes are asked if they have had sexual intercourse (5566). They confess (5582). They take off the bells and wash them in the beer (5589). The neophytes are invited to ask questions (5603). One asks about death (5610). The elders wash the bells again (5646). Any neophyte who can recite Bagre is offered a cow (5652). The neophytes are questioned about procedure (5669). They are then told to go and kill a wild animal (5714). They are asked if they have any more questions (5734). The neophytes ask about breaking Bagre taboos (5744). They ask about precedence (5772), about deaths following Bagre (5826), about conjugal quarrels (5842), more about deaths (5852), more about wives (5860), about thefts at Bagre time (5876), about hatreds at Bagre time (5899), about lovers at Bagre time (5907). They ask about the order of ceremonies (5928), about the pregnancy ritual (5949), about reciting Bagre (5970), about precedence over food (5990). They ask about the roles of God and the beings of the wild (6004). They are told how the first men discovered Bagre through contact with the beings of the wild (6008). They ask about God's role, and are told why he could not dwell on earth (6038). But he sent Bagre down to us (6080).

NOTES TO THE WHITE BAGRE

1. This invocation is repeated at various times during the course of the recitation and addresses most of the main categories of supernatural being in the LoDagaa cosmology. An alternative version of part of the invocation recorded in Tom (LD.), began:

Tingani	Earth shrine,
kpimɛ	ancestors,
siuwɛ	guardians,
weni	deities,
ka bɔɔr	say we should perform.
sɔɔn dɔɔb	Failure of childbearing
kure pime	suicide,
dunɔ nɔn	the scorpion's sting,
sɔɔn kuur	failure of farms,
ka tɔ kpɛ̃ɛ	caused the elder one
ga fãã na	to sleep badly,
u zɛ u pie	so he seized ten cowries
zɔ kyene	and hurried off
gubasob zie	to see a diviner

I have translated *ngmin* as god; the root is found again in sun. But some of the LoDagaa also use *wen* (as in Tallensi *naawun*, God or Heaven) to refer to the Bagre god (*bo wen*), showing perhaps a LoBirifor influence. *ngmin* and *wen* are cognates. As both words occur in the *Bagre*, I translate *wen* as a deity and *ngmin* as god, but I do not think there is any difference between them (773).

The LoDagaa employ the term *naangmin* (i.e. 'head' *ngmin*) to refer to the (high) God. In the Bagre recital, *ngmin* in the singular sometimes seems to have the same reference but the LoDagaa certainly differentiate between the two concepts. *ngmime* are found here on earth in the form of shrines: *naangmin* has no such shrine, does not descend to earth and communicates to man only through intermediaries. The attempt to establish a shrine to him (B. 3590 ff.) was unsuccessful.

2. *Kpiin* (pl. *kpime*) are (i) the dead, and more particularly (ii) the ancestors and (iii) ancestor shrines. I have discussed this aspect of religious life in *Death, Property and the Ancestors* (1962).

3. *Siuwe* (LD. *sigra*) are not a separate category of being. Any shrine or ancestor may 'climb' (i.e. demand an association with) an individual and become his tutelary or guardian spirit. But there are also 'clan' tutelaries, which are independent foci of cult activities, although the only time I know of these being approached nowadays is during the Bagre. The word is cognate to the Tallensi *sɛɣɔr*, which Fortes translates as 'spirit guardian' (1949: 90). The Bagre deity (*wen*) was described to me as the 'great guardian' (*sigkpɛ̃ɛ̃*) (773).

4. *Kɔntɔme* I have elsewhere called hill and water sprites but here refer to as 'beings of the wild'. Such beings are widespread in West Africa (e.g. the *mmoatia* of Ashanti and the *kɔlkpaaris* of the Tallensi) where they are usually called 'fairies' or dwarfs, but this term has too childish a set of associations for the English reader. The *kɔntɔme* are the denizens of the bush or woods as distinct from the cultivated lands inhabited by humans. They are in closer touch with the supernatural world, both hindering and helping man in his endeavours. For the LoDagaa, they are an essential intermediary between gods and men, and stand halfway between them in the cosmological schema.

5. The leather bottle (*gan*, lit. skin, or *kpo*) is a small container made from hide, in which senior members of the society keep the cowries which they use for divination. Each second-grader (Black Bagre member) is given such a container, together with twelve marked cowries. However, among the LoWiili divination is normally carried out in connection with the beings of the wild and cowries are used as an auxiliary technique to divination with the wooden stick (see note, line 15).

6. I have understood *maale* here; this verb I translate as 'perform' (e.g. Bagre), but it also means to 'sacrifice', 'repair', 'make good'.

7. In this invocation man seeks the (mystical) cause of certain of humanity's recurrent scourges. The sting of scorpions, suicide, stomach pains and headaches, these are standard reasons for consulting a diviner as, like most misfortunes, they indicate something else is wrong. 'Suicide' here is by stabbing oneself with an arrow; some suicide by hanging (*yɔɔlo tie*) also occurs.

11. The two 'first' men are known throughout as *tɔ kpɛ̃ɛ̃* and *tɔ ble*. *Tɔ* (pl. *taaba*) means 'one member of a group of equals' and is often used in conjunction with a category noun e.g. *pɔɔyaa taaba*, fellow 'daughters' of a lineage. The most accurate translation would perhaps have been 'fellow' or 'companion', but I found these words too awkward in English. I usually refer to the two men as 'the younger one' and 'the elder one', but the original sometimes speaks of them as brothers. Whereas *tɔ* is used in everyday speech, *tɔ ble* and *tɔ kpɛ̃ɛ̃* are used only in Bagre. For another West African reference to two brothers, see Fortier, 1967: 31.

12. Sleeping badly is the sign of mystical trouble and usually prompts a visit to the diviner.

13. It is said that in the old days a bunch of guinea corn heads of the kind saved for seed (*kagyin*) were used to pay for a divining session. Nowadays it is cowries or metal currency.

15. The diviner first throws some cowries in order to make a preliminary check. But the main divination is done with a short forked stick and a number of material objects, bones, oyster shells, pieces of wood, stones from the river or from a shrine, which the diviner keeps in his skin bag. Each of these represents a particular mystical agency such as a deity (*ngmin*), or some feature of the sacrificial procedure which indicates what should be done, e.g. 'sacrifice' (*bɔɔr*, LD. *bagr*). All divination points to

sacrifice, which forms part of nearly every communicative act directed to the mystical powers, though it is not the only form of such communication.

The diviner clears a piece of ground in front of him, empties the contents of his skin bag on to the space, and then recites his invocation at the same time as shaking his rattle. The client then grasps the bottom of the stick with his right hand while the diviner holds the forked end with his left (hence *gobasob*, 'master of the left-hand'). Moved by the beings of the wild working through the consultant, the stick alights upon various objects from the diviner's gear and thus points to the cause of the trouble. The diagnosis is then confirmed by throwing cowries from the leather bottle.

20. For deity (*wen*), see line 1.

21. The 'bush' (*wiɔ* or *mwɔ*) is the dwelling-place of the beings of the wild; the word 'bush' is often used in Africa both for savannah and for orchard bush. I have often translated it as 'woods' but here I prefer 'wild'.

29. The 'deities' listed here are some of the many shrines that individuals may acquire. As is later emphasized, the Bagre has to do with the major goals of the peoples in this region—childbirth, farming (referred to as the 'hoe-handle'), shooting (referred to as the 'bow-string' and including both war and the chase), and the raising of livestock (referred to as 'chicken breeding', because this is how a man's stock is always reckoned to begin).

These values are not of course confined to this people; and it would be wrong to talk of them as LoDagaa 'values', since it gives a false particularity to their 'culture'. They clearly share these aims with many other neighbouring groups (and indeed most agriculturists) and this quasi-universality of aim is one of the basic reasons behind the migration of shrines such as Tigaari and cults such as the Bagre from one group to another.

37. Meetings (*kpaaro* or *kpaartiib*) are mainly ceremonies. Funerals apart, the Bagre performances are the major occasions when members of a local community come together, for drinking, dancing, eating, and for ritual activities. The phrase 'deity of meetings' seems to imply a recognition of one of the Bagre's main sociological functions.

38. 'Falling favourably'. If the cowries are thrown one by one from the container the even shells should fall in the same way (up or down) as the previous odd one.

44. 'His father's house' is presumably 'his own compound', where the ancestor shrines would rest in the byre. Hence it is also his father's house, even if the latter had not actually lived there; there is a presumption of residential continuity between generations, even if local movement and distant migration occur in practice. More usually this phrase identifies a woman's natal home.

49. In many sacrifices there is a motivational split between those in trouble, who come to give, and the spectators, who come to take.

54. The pile of earth represents (indeed is) the Earth shrine (*tengaan*)

though it also serves as an altar to the ancestors. The widow stands on such a pile at her husband's final funeral when making an exculpatory oath concerning his death (Goody 1962: 245).

55. The ashes and cold water are both methods of making 'hot' things 'cold', i.e. cooling down a dangerous situation. The joking partners, who help to control the bereaved during the burial ceremony, are also known as *tɛmpɛlodem*, 'people of the ash' (Goody 1956: 81).

57. Spurting (*puɔra*) is a 'ritual' gesture, similar to the scattering of water by priests in the Christian religion; it is central to the first of the Bagre ceremonies.

60. With these words the Bagre ceremony begins, and the prohibitions which the aspirant members (or neophytes) have to observe are formally recounted to them. The White Bagre text is at once a recipe for the ritual, the performance of the ritual itself, and an explanation of that ritual. This particular ceremony is known as *Bo* (or *Bag*) *puɔru* and the neophytes are called to the house where Bagre is being performed, the house of one of the 'Bagre mothers' (*Bo ma*). There they sit on the roof and are told of the taboos which are first enforced and later relaxed as the whole series of ceremonies progresses. For a similar example, see A. R. Radcliffe-Brown, *The Andaman Islanders*, Cambridge, 1922.

62. The first prohibition is on the soft sweet fruit that forms around the shea nut. This tree grows wild, though rights in its produce are often vested in 'alloidal' land-owners. The nuts are used to make 'shea butter', used for an unguent and as a cooking-fat. Formerly it was an important export from the savannah to the forest. The shea fruit ripens before the cultivated crops and it is taken as an indication of when the performances should begin. The ripening of the fruit is later linked to the role played in Bagre by the fruit-bat and a set of (forbidden) animals is associated with a set of (forbidden) foods.

68. 'Going down', because they were gathered on the rooftop and would have to descend by a ladder.

75. The second visit to the diviner is apparently to confirm the proper time for the performance.

106. This is the Bagre deity, who comes in front of a man, that is comes with the truth. It is only a coward or a liar that sneaks up from behind. Another interpretation of these lines is that the deity will not leave us (*n wana nyiu*, I have come to stay. Also *o wan zina*, he is coming to stay; *o wan wa zĩ*, he has come to stay).

108. K.G. thinks this should be *tuuri*, follows, i.e. 'he comes on the right (or favourable) side', while I have understood *tuɔri*, to point. In this I follow my original information. It is interesting how the interpretation of so central a passage can differ among knowledgeable men who come from adjacent clan sectors. See J. R. Goody, *The Social Organization of the LoWiili*, 1956, p. 70.

112. 'Birth', 'hunting'—the other main desiderata in Bagre are 'farming' and 'breeding' (livestock).

118. The elder one stops speaking but then turns to address the neophytes, telling them that if the Bagre deity has come, then they should set to in order to produce the crops and livestock required for the ceremony.

124. The 'truth' (*yel miong*) is the opposite of 'lies' (*ziri*); *yele* here means speech and *miong* is a reflexive form (*ma miong*, myself). *Yele* is perhaps the equivalent of what French students of the Dogon translate as *parole* and what their translators have rendered into English either as speech or as the word—quite properly, as the ambiguity is present in French. Among the LoDagaa (as I suggest with all unwritten languages) the concept of a 'word' (as distinct from a 'name') is hardly conceivable, though educated LoDagaa use the term *yel bie* ('child of speech', 'a bit') in some such way; however it is more properly translated as 'sentence' or 'phrase'. In my view the concept of a letter and a word (and indeed phoneme and morpheme) are dependent upon literacy. I have briefly mentioned this point in a critique of Griaule's book, *Conversations with Ogotemmêli*. If my suggestion is right, then 'In the beginning was the Word' is a non-oral formula: so that when Griaule is translated as 'The first word and the fibre skirt' (1965: 16), 'speech' would be preferable. On the other hand it will be clear from an examination of the present text that *yele* refers to the content as well as to the medium. So that I have also translated the word as 'affair', 'matter', at times as 'trouble'. It will be readily understood that since speech is the only means of communicating complex matters (for there is no alternative to oral intercourse), the separation of the form and content of utterance is neither relevant nor possible.

129. 'Forefathers' are *diõdem* (*diõ* = early, ancestral); alternative *dɛungdem*. I use 'ancestors' to translate *kpime*; *sããkum* (grandfather) is sometimes used in the same way (especially in the plural *sããkum mine*).

136. Although I have taken this passage as referring to Bagre, it could also refer to death.

137. The Bagre ceremony is seen as an imposition upon, as well as a benefit to, mankind. Not only does it involve the expenditure of much food, time, and labour, but the very fact that we have inherited it means that we have to perform it. To do otherwise would be to invite retribution from the deities concerned. But here is a further level of ambiguity, since (as will become increasingly clear) we do not know whether these ceremonies contain truth or lies. Indeed, we know that they are partly lies. The approach to these ceremonies is much more sophisticated than most discussions of 'primitive thought' would allow, especially when these are based upon a radical dichotomy of the kind used by Lévy-Bruhl or Lévi-Strauss.

152. This passage appears to refer to the coming of the Bagre deity, since similar phrases are used at other such times. But it could perhaps refer to the Bagre members.

169. The growth of crops is dependent upon the rain, which is associated (like everything else) with 'spirit' or 'god' (here *ngmin*); through the sky, rain is also closely linked to God. Shrines to the rain appear on the roofs of some houses, usually above a room wholly devoted to shrines; this 'rain-roof' (*saa garo*) is forbidden to women and children. But the shrine has to do with lightning more than with rain itself.

170. At a later point the male rain and female earth are counterposed. The Earth is never *ngmin*, though the rain is (or has). Rain is associated with the sky and the sun. The concepts of god (*ngmin*) or God (*naangmin*) and sun are related in a fairly obvious fashion, as elsewhere in the region, but it should be insisted that the actors often deny such a relationship when it is put to them.

188. Lit. 'keep us together'.

197. Lit. 'to follow and bring along'. If I send a man for someone else, *o biero wa*.

203. No mention is made of what he did but the reference is probably to some instructions given to the initiates.

209. An old woman (*pɔɔ nyɔ̃ɔ̃*) appears both as the female companion (or wife) of God and as the consort (or wife) of the elder brother. In both cases she performs the complementary female tasks, such as cooking food and brewing beer.

211. Bean leaves are forbidden to aspirants as are certain other new crops. They are one of the first new crops to appear and hence one of the first from which the neophytes have to be protected.

249. The elder brother realized that since the bean leaves were ready to be plucked, the next phase of the ceremony must be begun straightaway. So the neophytes are told to call together the initiated members. Two day's warning is required to brew the beer.

259. *Biõ* (*biõõ*) or *bieng* are beans; *bion* (*bionn*) is an alternative to *bion vaari*, bean leaves. This ceremony should really be called the Bagre of Bean Leaves.

288. The basic food of the LoDagaa consists of porridge and beer, both made from guinea corn (*sorghum*). The initiated members eat a meal of this, prepared from grain provided by (or on behalf of) the neophytes; then they get down to work.

297. *Di nõ wuro sob* is a greedy person; the word *wuro* is used only in exclamatory phrases, e.g. *a wuro te te te te*, that's a loud noise.

309. The stone is any stone used for addressing the Earth shrine. Each parish or ritual area has its own Earth priest (Goody 1956: 91 ff.), but here the term may refer to the leader of these rites acting in the capacity of master of the Earth.

321. That is, the end. We are just beginning.

333. The Bagre members pray for the crops they need to perform the ceremonies.

344. That is we pray (beg) for wisdom, for good fortune. 'Bury' is here 'to get rid of'.

349. The Bagre deity will tell us about what lies ahead and still remains to be done.

364. Yams (*dioscorea sp.*) become ripe between July and September when the tubers (*nyu kpiri*) are dug out from the mounds and detached from the vines leaving room for the smaller seed (*nyu wele*) to develop. The main harvest is in late November and early December when the tubers are brought to the house. In this area yams are something of a luxury food.

377. *N lieb puori*, I turn back.

379. *Biε*, wise, wonderful, strange; but apparently 'evil' in some contexts (B. 5383).

381. Possibly his wife's father's house (the old woman digs up the yam) but from the standpoint of the gift it is more likely to be his daughter's husband's house.

394. *O kŏnena dib iɔng*, he cries out for food.

412. The neophytes ('children') are called to the rooftop of the Bagre house before every phase of the ceremony. This particular ceremony is known as the Bean Flower (*Beng puru*).

420. *Puru*, flower(s); *puor*, to greet; *puɔ(r)*, belly; I have heard the title of this ceremony translated as 'Greeting the Beans'.

441. Each neophyte is accompanied by a White Bagre member (a first-grader) and sometimes by a Black Bagre member (a second-grader). In this ceremony the White Bagre members drink the top of the pots of beer in the name of the ritual officiants, i.e. those seniors capable of reciting the text and known as the Bagre Speakers (*bo nɛtuuri*). Other initiates learn the text and may take over (see W. 5970), but only the older, more experienced members are known by this title.

454. Hawks are full of greed, for they swoop down to seize young chicks.

476. For underground vegetables, *ã nyɛ̃na*, it is ready (*a bɛ nyɛ̃ sɛrɛ* or *a bɛ wumɛ*, it's not yet ready); *bi* is used for fruit, beer, and for meat; for corn, *a piola*, *a kwona*. *Nyɛ* also means to lay eggs or to defecate.

487. It is the officials telling members to go and instruct the neophytes.

503. The major categories of supernatural agency are called upon to help get the crops and livestock needed for the performances.

508. The two previous injunctions of this kind (W. 104 and 152) are spoken to the deity, but here it appears to be the initiates that are so addressed.

561. So far the text has taken the form of a guide to the ceremonies. Here it enters upon a narrative which explains the association of the old guinea cock with Bagre, and specifically with the bean flower. The link has to do with ceremonial (or liturgical) time-keeping.

597. The white bean flower was in the guinea cock's mouth.

603. The shell money consists of small white cowries (*cyprea moneta*) originating in the Indian Ocean; a man would normally keep them in the skin bag slung over his shoulder, a woman in the basket (*tiib pele*) she carries on her head.

641. An expression of surprise.

662. It is the elders addressing the neophytes; in line 674 the elders become singular and refer to the reciter. This kind of switch is very common and consistency in respect of numbers, tenses, and mode of speech (direct or indirect) is not very important. This relative lack of attention to consistency is partly a function of the context of recitation and partly an aspect of oral converse. In the situation of the ceremony, the recital jumps from telling about the performance to addressing the neophytes; it jumps from the time of the first men to that of the present, for the first initiation is also the present one and the elder brother is also the present 'mother of Bagre'. And the reciter represents the second-graders as well as speaking for himself and the ancestors. But the written sentence invites and receives a closer scrutiny than the spoken word; writing irons out a certain roughness in the texture of speech.

675. The idea of a god 'coming for us' is not to be ascribed to culture contact (though we can rarely rule this out as a possibility). Gods are there to help as well as to harm, and they move between heaven and earth.

683. 'The words' (which I use to translate *tu a nɛ*, lit. follow the mouth) are the *bag* (*bo*) *kab*, the invocation with which the recital starts and which calls upon the various categories of supernatural agency to help in the performance of Bagre.

710. The food we bring barely suffices.

721. The LoDagaa do not distinguish in words between *ritus* and *mos*, between rites and other forms of behaviour. I have used rites in order to get away from repeating 'thing', 'doings' (e.g. Greek *dromenon*).

737. *Ma taa*, cluster together; *man taa*, consult together.

739. The uncertainty of the solution offered is stressed throughout. Are we being deceived?

781. There is a good deal of uncertainty about the order of the ceremonies, and much of the text of the White Bagre depends on this.

809. The accoutrements are the ones a man takes to the field, the basic tools for carrying out the productive processes.

825. Once again, as with the guinea fowl and the bean flower, it is the female's refusal to copulate with the male that leads to a dispute. As a result of the quarrel, the Bagre members get what they are looking for, the object that is now forbidden to the neophytes.

849. Sexual intercourse and the provision of food are closely intertwined; the reciprocity is clearly expressed in lines 852–3.

867. The mounds made by white ants are collected in the woods to feed to young chicks. The first mounds he digs contain no ants.

883. Napolo was the name of the founding ancestor of the reciter's lineage; in the Black Bagre Napolo is the son of the 'younger one', i.e. God's child.

890. In the early 1950s (and even today) beer was nearly always purchased for cowries rather than for the official metal currency of West Africa. This was because women found it more useful to have cowries which they could use not only for traditional payments where currency would have been inappropriate (for funeral contributions and marriage prestations) but for the purchase of cheaper grain (guinea corn) in the neighbouring Ivory Coast. By the use of cowries they evaded the problems arising from the introduction of 'national' currencies and it is still true today that many border areas prefer to deal in such 'international' media of exchange rather than in more restricted national currencies.

893. Women brew beer on different days of the (six-day) week and it is to their houses that men repair when they return from the farm. Naturally the better one knows a woman the more likely she is to reserve you a pot of beer; most women have a regular clientele which includes their 'lovers' (*sɛn*). In my experience the term *sɛn* (lover, mistress) does not necessarily signify a sexual relationship; it is used as a word of generalized endearment, like 'love' by bus conductresses in the north of England.

931. *Ir* (falling tone), to get up; *ir* (rising tone), to pick up.

933. The old woman's daughters take over because the making of shea butter is a woman's task.

941. This Bagre phrase sometimes means 'for a short time', but here a longer period seems to be indicated.

953. *Kazikuɔra*, a guinea corn farmer; but *kuɔra* (pl. *kuɔbɔ*) on its own can refer to a person (e.g. an affine) who comes to help on the farm.

978. That is the time when they bring the malted grain to use for the beer.

986. The neophytes and their guides (who are first-graders) bring their grain to the rooftop of the house where the Bagre will be performed. They are asked to put their hand in the basket of malted grain to ensure that it is a full one.

997. There follows a detailed description of the making of guinea corn beer (or peto), the stages of which are very similar to those for all forms of beer. I should add that this lengthy description has no educative function for anyone present, since the process is well known to everybody. It is simply a description of one of the basic cultural processes.

999. There is one type of guinea corn that is called *kpaluɔra gyɛlɛ*, after the name of a small bird that builds its nest on the ground.

1069. The one who proposes to hold the Bagre provides the guinea corn for the beer, stating that if he cannot get the rest of the goods needed for the performance, he will use the grain to provide beer for the men whom he calls to hoe his farm.

1081. After the description of how the malted grain is made, we are now back at the first part of the ceremony, where the guinea corn is measured.

1098. In terms of generation the 'slender (or tall) young girls' are opposed to the 'wise (or strange) old women'. By implication they are her daughters, at least in a classificatory sense; they are also the unmarried (or recently so) as distinct from the married. In the Black Bagre the same phrases are used to describe the denizens of heaven as are here used for the inhabitants of earth.

The plural form of the noun is shown here by the adjective alone e.g. *baala*, sing.; *baali*, plural; *baalo*, adverbial form. See also *pɔɔ* (or *deb*) *wobo*, tall woman (man), pl. *pɔɔ woyr*; *deb nyããng*, pl. *deb nyããn*, old man; *bi faa*, pl. *bi faar*, bad child.

1104. When the grain has germinated and dried, it then has to be ground into flour (grist) on the granite grinding-stone (*niɛr*) found in the long room (*kyaara*) of most houses (for a description of the LoDagaa house, see Goody 1956; 38 ff.). The grain is sent round to all the houses in the neighbourhood so that the arduous job of grinding can be done by more people and done more quickly.

1145. The making of beer takes two days and requires the full attention of the brewer who has to get up earlier to brew the beer a second time. Here is an explanation of why the featherless cock is associated with the Bagre; it is he who wakes the slender girl.

1162. *Wel* (D. *wuɔl*) differs from *yaa* (1137) in that you only scoop out the liquid and leave the solid. *Kuɔri* is also to scoop out (completely).

1194. A half of a gourd or calabash is the usual drinking vessel.

1206. *Birɛ*, leaves for soup; but *biyr* or *byur* when used for string.

1212. *Kyɔri*, to walk in single file; *kyuuri*, to silence someone.

1218. To sit near can be expressed by *kɔɔ*, *piele*, or *gbo*.

1226. The Speakers are the reciters, the *bo nɛtuuri*; they repeat the earlier ritual with the beer. *Biõ* is to offer something without meaning a person to accept it.

1260. For the mound of earth, see note for W. 54.

1313. Some people are fortunate in being able to rear chickens. The neophytes are given a Beginning Fowl to look after and breed chicks for use in the ceremonies.

1362. The *tĩĩ* in 'the Beginning Fowl' appears to be cognate with *ti* in the opening phrase of the Black Bagre.

1395. The Black initiates (or second-graders) have the leather bottle (*gan*) containing the marked cowries used for special divination (though only in the context of the ceremonies themselves).

1409. The rain and the wind are associated with God, who is concerned with the heavens.

1419. Bambara beans or *voandzeia subterranea* (*singbile*) get ripe in November.

1437. *Gur*, to fold, to pull close to; here, to harvest.

1440. *Tɛ* is an unusual expression for the wind blowing; it refers to shooting with a bow.

1466. The deity has fulfilled his promise.

1522. The goods required for supernatural purposes are never sufficient to meet the needs of man or god. Men are always in debt to the gods.

1523. This section on malting the grain should logically come before that on the brewing of the beer; K. G. commented independently that it appears to be displaced.

1543. *Bura*, to get wet; *bul*, to grow.

1600. The Whitening Ceremony is the *Bo pir* (also known as *Bo byur*). This is the occasion on which the initiates are painted in stripes.

1670. This verb (*gbẽ*) is only used for grinding the malted grain; the set of grinding terms include *gyieri*, *gbõ*, *'yer*.

1733. The chicken that falls on its back is accepted; otherwise it is refused.

1743. The Earth shrine is always outside, the ancestors' inside. The guardians are often at the foot of the ancestor shrines in the byre, though the category is a wide one and can include other shrines. The deities are usually on the rooftop, hence the climb up; the Bagre deity is sometimes known as the *buur kɔkɔr wen* (*ngmin*), the deity in the neck of the granary, for it is usually placed in the top part of the granary that rises above the roof.

1769. The White initiates are again reprimanded for discourtesy towards the ritual officiants, members of a higher grade.

1775. The food is thrown in the middle and everyone grabs.

1807. At the Whitening Ceremony the initiates are painted with stripes of whitewash and set outside the community. They are treated in a manner similar to a widow, though the latter are whitened all over (Goody 1962: Plate 16); the initiates on the other hand look more like skeletons than ghosts. The shea oil is to whitewash their bodies, the string to tie round the head (as with widows) and the gourds are kept until the neophytes have been safely initiated and are then broken.

1818. Women traditionally wore a series of bands around their waists, made either of fibre or goat hide, the former having been soaked in water. The fibres stolen by the initiates have presumably been collected to make into waist bands. Female neophytes normally wear disposable bands plaited from the fibre of guinea corn stalks (*gyimue*), since these are all destroyed at the end of the ceremony.

1828. *Lizer mwõ*, twenty itself; *miong* is used for a person.

1834. These are small wild gourds, needed as containers for Bagre medicine.

1852. Bagre Eve (or Night) is the name given to one of the days of the later ceremony called Bagre Dance. Here the name seems out of place; it is possibly a mistake of the reciter, a mistranslation of mine (e.g. in the tense), or an alternative appellation for this night when there is so much work to be done.

1861. The 'Bagre oil' is the whitewash; the gourd is later broken; the head pad (a circle of plaited grass) is used to carry heavy loads but in this case the gourd is placed on it; gourd, *kuɔr*, but half (a calabash), *ngman*.

1879. They must not have sexual intercourse which is here especially polluting but always carries the implication of the interchange of dirt.

1889. The painting in whitewash, as in funerals, is a kind of silent oath whose effectiveness is guaranteed by the Earth from whence the chalk comes (Goody 1962: 58).

1903. The string is made from the fibre.

1919. *Kyiiri fu puɔ*, to swear, pour out your belly, confess.

1924. The guide asks the neophyte whether he is spiritually ready to have his body marked with the whitewash, known as oil.

1950. He'll stop him from talking but not from eating.

1955. The criss-cross lines, the marks round the mouth, are characteristic of Bagre and the Bagre deity, who is addressed as *ngmin nyɔtuon* (the god with the mark between the eyes) and *ngmin sɔr goba* (the god with the black and white stripes) at the beginning of the Black Bagre. The first is identified with the younger one (B. 5253), the second with his elder brother (B. 5256). For the painted initiates, see Labouret, 1931: Plate 31. *Bangyiri* is a diagonal cross, *garagyiri* is a right-angled one.

1972. The initiates are prevented from talking until the next ceremony and are once again prohibited from polluting themselves through sexual intercourse, even with legitimate partners.

1991. The Bagre god is here spoken of as God. All beings are in some sense created by God, and hence are refractions of him. But this formulation gives them too little independence.

1999. *Yɛri* is to carry a bag; *su* is to put on (a shirt).

2003. To bring food. As is shown in W. 2014, we owe the produce to God, to the Bagre god.

2016. The bells are mentioned for the first time. These objects, made of iron, are used for communicating with (calling upon) the beings of the wild, who are closely connected with the Bagre ceremony and are indeed a central feature of the cosmological scheme of the LoDagaa. The bell is tied to the gourd by means of the string (fibre). The gourd has to be guarded as one's own head; indeed it *is*, in a sense, one's head. To point with the left hand is to lack respect.

2042. You have to keep away from the guide because he may be 'dirty', having slept with his wife; the guides are only required to abstain on the days of the performance themselves.

2059. *Baangyira*, from the Hausa; LoDagaa is *samani*.

2065. *Bharena a mwo puo* is to go off the road into the 'bush', to be lost.

2085. The neophytes are told that during the time they are whitewashed they should not allow people, even their guides, to see them perform the functions of eating, drinking, and defecating. While they cannot prohibit such behaviour, as they can talk and sex, they can at least conceal it. In this way, they become in a sense non-human: to be human is (paradoxically) polluting, certainly shameful; they may be polluted by their guides who have been having sexual intercourse.

2099. The guide will put the basket down, so that people can make contributions for Bagre expenses. *O na bina* would be the correct form as I have translated this.

2197. The fellows are the helpers. They object to the elders taking the gourds away.

2216. They take the gourd out of the bag (*ira*).

2299. You go home and tell your people, and they say you should not have walked away.

2333. *Siɔna* (or *shɔɔn*) implies obligation; *a siɔna* (LD. *seyna*) *ka n kyen Father yiri diã*, I ought to go to the Father's house today (R.T.).

2424. *Ol wa ira, on kyen*: if he wants, he can go.

2448. *Fu naa ti věna kyeni*, you should have waited (or refused) to go.

2456. The search for God is a constant theme of the two Bagre myths, and it is a search for direct communion with God as well as with other gods. But the search is constantly confused by the intervention of the beings of the wild, who are intermediate (but not intermediaries) between man and god. The beings make their first appearance (in W. 2457) as tempters; in the Black Bagre they also appear as the originators or transmitters of human technology.

2509. The hot and cold imagery noted at W. 55 appears again in a very direct way.

2521. Original: *ka ti gyirɛ*.

2571. It is clear from line W. 5237 that it is the younger of the two first men who gets up and goes into the woods to see the beings of the wild, just as it is he who visits both them and God in the Black Bagre. But it is of course the elder of the two who first consults the diviner about what should be done (W. 11).

2578. The beings are denizens of the wilds, the bush; they live on hills, in rivers, and in woods.

2649. Three days is the normal period during which an adult corpse is displayed before burial.

2687. The roan antelope is here the beings' equivalent of the horse with which humans acquire the Bagre medicine from another group (W. 5353 ff.). The twenty stands for twenty thousand.

2728. *n mang fu tã no dɛ*, I think that perhaps you took it; *al tã wa yi*, perhaps because of that. *Kaapaɣ* (L D.) is another way of translating 'perhaps'.

2803. The rattle made from a bottle-shaped gourd is used for purposes of ritual communication, rather like the bell.

2807. The songs are standard Bagre songs, taught to the neophytes.

2817. That is, a hundred cowries. But this stands for 100,000.

2822. The stick refers to a man who might be listening.

2823. The flat roofs of these compounds are supported by strong posts dug into the ground. If these are crooked, the house may fall.

2826. This is the goatskin bag, like an ordinary bag a man carries on his shoulder, in which an initiate always takes his gear.

2834. This song represents the central belief of the neophytes at this stage. Later they are disillusioned.

2841. *Ba bɔng* (or *bɔ̃*) *gu* usually means, 'they failed to understand' (i.e. they did not know), but here it means 'they are fed up'.

2847. A song sung as they re-enter the room. You have to bend to avoid hitting your head.

2854. Then the witch can no longer attack; she cannot eat flesh without her teeth.

2871. A more usual form is *de gbeliir* (pl.).

2874. *Par* or *pule*, at the foot of, would be more usual.

2886. First rattles, then bells are used to try and revive the recumbent neophytes.

2921. The original man (*tɔ*, a word I have sometimes translated as 'companion' or 'fellow') is identified in the current proceedings with the persons conducting the Bagre. He has returned with the beings of the wild, for the ceremony cannot be performed without him (1490).

2950. The tempter beings, having pretended to be God, admit his omnipotence.

2978. The original is 'child', referring to the 'small being of the wild' (W. 2891, 2943). But in the key to the Black Bagre, a difference is made; the thieving god (*ngmin naayuo*) is the being's child (*kɔntɔmbie*), while the lying god (*ngmin gagara*) is the small being (*kɔntɔmble*). See B. 5263–8.

3046. At this phase of the ceremonies the neophytes are often physically separated from other people, being assembled on a piece of open ground away from the compounds.

3104. The list here is different from the earlier account of the elder brother's session with the diviner; note that deities (*ngmin*) are attached to individuals (like the Tallensi *yin*, Fortes 1949: 227 ff.) as well as to categories.

3167. A sense of dependence on the Bagre medicine is aroused in the neophytes by the account of the earlier killing, when their predecessors could be revived only by the direct intervention of the 'child' of the being of the wild. This is why they had to retrace their steps through the maze of ceremony in order to see where they had made an error.

3189. The flat surface of the clearing is compared to the rooftop where crops are normally threshed. But the sites of old ant hills which can be cleared to form a cement-like surface, are sometimes used for outdoor threshing.

3197. Loosened the germinating grain by uprooting it. They take some grains of guinea corn, put them in a container (nowadays a bottle) and say that they will change them into something else. Secretly they substitute some malted grain and display it to those present (1498).

3203–4. K. G. suggests the insertion of a line: *ti ba tu ala.*

3211. The stool (*kɔ*) is used by the reciter and also for the neophytes.

3282. *Sɔ̃ɔ̃* or *sɔŋ* (high tone), time; with a low tone, to spoil (vb.). *Bɔɔr* (high), want, find; *bɔɔr* (low), Bagre (adj. form, *bɔɔ*, but I have usually rendered this *bo*, which also occurs).

3302. From the Hausa. The LoDagaa is *maal fõ.*

3312. A more usual word for hunter is *nakpaana*; I have been told that the *nabɔl* is less expert than the *nakpaana* (1502).

3338. This passage emphasizes the fact that Bagre cuts right across kinship ties; indeed it provides a temporary substitute because, for the duration of the ceremony, the neophytes are under the care of the Bagre 'mother' and 'father' rather than their own. It is to the Bagre elders (for whom kin terms are sometimes used) that the obligations otherwise owed to close kin are now due. And the neophytes are now propelled into a wider sphere of social action, though this cannot be seen as an intrinsic part of the developmental process since many of the neophytes are either too young or too old; in any case a fair number of people are never initiated. The neophytes are propelled into the society of Bagre members, but kinship and association membership overlap, and the final solution takes both into account.

The other point to emerge is that the distribution of meat emphasizes the bilaterality of kinship as well as the unilineality of descent, for both mother and father are allocated their share. A hind leg (*gbɛr*) is the father's share in most distributions; and the fillet (*sie*) goes to the mother ('the waist' is where a woman suffers in childbirth and in menstruation). See Goody 1962: 174 for a parallel distribution of funeral meat, the flesh of the Cow of the Rooftop.

3398. *Walhala*, from the Hausa.

3406. As at a funeral, where it is a case of 'taking out the dream' (Goody

1962: 129 ff.), the neophytes are sent on a hunt. A hunt forms part of many ceremonies in West Africa (e.g. the Den festival of Senyon Kupo in Gonja). Here the meat is used to prepare a special meal; a neophyte's first kill after joining belongs to the society, though this obligation applies only to certain animals.

3504. Collecting the malt (*kɛi wuur*) precedes every ceremony.

3562. *Sãã* (high tone), to mash; *sãã* (low), father.

3587. *Yaa*, scoop; *yaana*, take out of water; *yana*, be tired (through work), giving rise to the regular greeting *yani, yani*.

3692. The wild animals having been specified, the same is now done with the crops and livestock associated with Bagre.

3721. The night will be only for the brave.

3751. 'Two-faced': lit. having two bellies, being a witch. Only those who have neglected the instructions but failed to confess will be harmed. The medicine kills all, but revives those who have confessed or not sinned.

3786. The calabash is normally kept in the byre.

3800. It is a recurrent story that people trying to learn about Bagre kill their neophytes with clubs.

3845. *Wõ* implies that they were forced by internal pressure to confess: *o wõrena*, he talks without wanting to. K. G. suggests the insertion of a line, *ti yel*.

3869. A branch of the *yolingpuo* tree.

3949. The leather bottle is given to second-graders and is used for divining.

3970. The big fowl's egg refers to the gourd.

4030. The medicine kills and brings to life again. It is as dangerous as a large animal.

4038. The xylophone is played at every gathering, and there is a special kind for playing Bagre songs, the *Bo gyil* or *Lo gyil prumo* (Goody 1956: 23).

4066. These are more threatening animals than the elephant and hippopotamus.

4073. These are throwing-sticks used to bring down birds and small animals; *gbulu* is a large stick used for dancing and for stunning cows before they are slaughtered (also *gulangu*).

4080. *Wɛ*, to rot away; figuratively to be lost, abandoned, i.e. *tengaan yiina fu pur, a la so ka fu wɛ*, the Earth shrine has stopped following you, that's why you are lost.

4096. The *bo kɔɔra*, at this point the *bo lonluɔre*, the Bagre joking partner, will sit on the stool.

4125. Darkness, confinement, fasting, noise, and threats all serve to induce a state of fear, which gives way to relief; both induce a sense of dependence.

4180. The neophytes are told to lie down by their guides.

4189. The members hold the neophytes as they fall; then they touch them with the backs of their hands to see if they are warm.

4263. 'The things of the beings' are the bells (or possibly the rattles).

4300. *Man*, consult openly (or narrate); *mul*, consult secretly (also a children's game of hide and seek); *waali*, whisper.

4308. You try to reverse the process of 'killing', presumably by using the same medicine.

4320. The guides also have to observe prohibitions on their behaviour, but much more limited than those for the neophytes.

4342. The child of the being of the wild previously woke them in the same way.

4355. So involved are the members in their Bagre performances that they fail to pasture their livestock or sleep with their wives.

4377. The realization that the neophytes have not really been killed and revived has to be kept from non-members.

4403. Bagre helps people succeed in their various occupations.

4415. If you are called upon to perform Bagre and fail to do so, your house will be ruined. This fate was said to have overtaken the house of Diiyir in Kyaa.

4438. Provision is made for new members to learn to recite the text of Bagre. In some parts, they hand a cow's tail to the one who should take over the recitation (1534).

4444. Oil Bagre is somewhat different from the form (*Bo pla*) which makes use of whitewash instead of shea oil.

4477. The long room (*kyaara*) is the main room of the house and the one where the rites are performed.

4499. The opposition between initiates and non-members is constantly stressed both in joking and in limited violence of this kind. The latter are provided with separate food.

4525. When the neophytes have been killed and revived again, their bells are collected by the guides who hide them in the outside wall of the house. The neophytes are then blindfolded and led around the house three times. On the third time round the guide stops both his neophyte, and the senior member who accompanies him, near the place where the bell is hidden and asks them to find it. Here the bells represent the Bagre deity who is believed to descend to each and everyone at this place. Hence the question 'Do you know the place we'll meet (or find) the Bagre?'.

4547. 'Dagaa' is not the usage I would have expected in this context since the Bagre ceremony is more typical of the Lo people to the West.

4560. The Bagre animals are listed here and their role is explained (W. 4581 ff.).

4595. N.B. *mhãã na*, cool; *mana*, the right time.

4613. N.B. *saa ba waari*, during the rains; *saa ba wai*, the rains didn't come.

4680. This phrase imitates the bird's cry and refers to the girls' lateness at the water hole.

4738. *Kpɛlo* (or *bhɛlo*) *vaar*, to pluck leaves; *kaara vaar*, to break off a leafy branch.

4803. Kusiele is the name of the patriclan who are joking partners of Kpiele, the clan of the reciter of the present text.

4892. N.B. *bibiir*, children; *bibir*, day.

4896. N.B. *na ngmin*, what? *naangmin*, God.

4962. The Bagre lies are ways of misleading the non-members, reinforcing solidarity by unimportant but communal gestures. But there is constant concern with time throughout the text, with liturgical time, the appropriate moment for the next ceremony.

4963. *Gyingyiri* refers to the tired way people dance on the last day of the 'Bagre Dance'.

4978. The neophytes finally emerge from the room and are swept clean of polluting 'dirt'.

4979. Watch them run, for they have been sitting a long time.

4982. The meaning of this song is obscure. One commentator thought the goat with its bad smell referred to the spectators outside, but the words are distinct; *bura*, goat; *bara*, razor, or male hunting dog. The neophytes have been unable to shave their heads for six weeks and are now shaved with a very sharp razor.

4984. All the neophytes sit down on logs at the entrance to the compound, where they receive gifts from kith and kin, from spouses and lovers.

4991. Guinea fowl are the normal gift from males to females, cocks from males to males.

4997. The beating on the ground is a gesture of respect. The initiates do not keep the gifts for themselves; these go to the guides and others. But the initiates as receivers have to make reciprocal gifts at the ceremonies in which the givers are involved.

5039. *Na* is chief or head; it applies to the foreign chiefs of centralized states and, among the LoDagaa, to the leader in almost any kind of activity.

5044. Or 'you can't stop there' (K. G.).

5056. N.B. *wal piɛl*, white duiker; *wal piel*, the horse-like roan antelope.

5067. The reference is to the next ceremony, Bagre Bells.

5074–5. This passage is ambiguous. I had first thought 'the other or separate place' referred to the home of the mother's brothers, often used as a refuge. This would have provided a link with what follows. K. G. thinks this unlikely and offers the present suggestion. It can mean a separate place in terms of the Bagre, or it can refer to 'a separate burial place' accorded to certain categories of wrongdoers (Goody 1962: 142 ff.). I had not myself heard of such a separation taking place in relation to sexual offences, although the compounding of these with the breaking of Bagre prohibitions clearly results in a more heinous sin.

5077. For an analysis of the role of the sister's son, see my paper, 'The mother's brother and the sister's son in West Africa' (1959), reprinted in *Comparative Studies in Kinship* (1969).

5105. This story offers an explanation of matrilineal inheritance, although it is many years since this form of devolution was practised among the LoWiili and then only by a few of the inhabitants of Birifu.

5130. The father could not keep pace with his more vigorous sons.

5235. N.B. *anu*, who (sing.), *tã bolo*, who (pl.); strictly this should be in the plural.

5237. The role of the junior brother is explained in the Black Bagre.

5261. 'God's child' is explained in the Black Bagre (B. 1041 ff., 2285). My reciter declared that 'God's child' was the rain; the reference in 5259 to *ngmina* is also to rain, in his view; others (K. G.) suggest 'sun'.

5314. Black Bagre is recited when the Bagre begins, but not before the neophytes.

5337. That is, uncertain.

5371. 'Three years' is a standard expression for a long time. The reference is to the younger brother. A sojourn in the wilds is the usual way in which new shrines and ritual techniques are learnt (see R. S. Rattray, *Religion and Art in Ashanti*, London, 1927, pp. 38 ff.).

5397. The payments for learning Bagre are the property of the beings of the wild.

5478. *Wɛri*, referring to the beings of the wild (pl., *wio*, sing., hunting).

5594. Although they speak of a vat (*sing*), the pot used for the ceremony is always a very small one.

5613. A return to the central theme of the Black Bagre.

5714. A further hunt is organized (see W. 3409).

5811. Bekuone and Yongyuole are the two other clans found in Birifu.

5867. The general problem here is that the sexual restrictions and joint ceremonies of Bagre may raise difficulties for a conjugal relationship; nor are the possibilities confined to those laid out here, for any diviner may declare, when consulted, that *Bo wen* is the cause. An example that occurred when I was in the area concerned the daughter of Dire, 'headman' of Kyaa, who had married into Depep's house (the Maale 'headman'). She returned to her father's house to become a neophyte and was sent back to her husband straight after Bagre Bells. But instead she went to Namɔɔ of Naayili that very day, when the Bagre had hardly finished, and remained there as his wife. Depep was very angry with his in-laws, for if you give someone your wife to look after (*kyiine*), you expect her back. The responsibilities of a guide (*bokyiini*) are very much in people's minds, especially when they are not observed. A fellow clansman of Dapla's looked after his wife in the Bagre ceremonies but took her back to his own house afterwards; again the death of Malka's sister was attributed to her having slept with her guide. It would be better, I was told, if female neophytes were looked after by their own husbands (or by other women, though this is not possible).

5881. N.B. *bɔ gu*, can't find; *bɔ̃ gu*, don't know.

5956. That is, when she becomes pregnant.

6003. Again Bagre may reverse the normal order of ranking. Seniority in terms of membership of the association overrides seniority due to age.

6053. This passage is very revealing both about human relations and concepts of the supreme God.

6084. The parallels with Middle Eastern concepts of the godhead are close. The one who was sent is the Bagre god.

6089. 'The first men' (*dɛungdem*) are differentiated from people's ancestors, (*kpime*). There are four main time levels indicated by reference to the people who lived in them: (i) *diongdem*, or *dɛungdem*, are 'the first men', i.e. the elder and younger 'brother'; (ii) *tengkuridem*, 'people of the old country' (or the past) I have translated as forefathers, whereas *kpime*, 'ancestors', are all 'the dead'; (iii) *sããkum mine*, 'grandfathers', referring to ascendants who were earlier inhabitants of their present habitat; (iv) the present.

6122. Grammatically this would be clearer as *ti i a bɔ*, etc.

6128. That is, the Black Bagre.

6131. That is, we say to all present.

6133. *Kpo* is to knock the leather bottle (*gan*) and loosen the cowries, so that one can shake them out one by one to know the truth. In the recital of the Bagre, the initiates shake out all the cowries three times as a final gesture. So that the phrase in effect means 'let's close the meeting' (*kpo gyɛlɛ* is to break an egg; *kpoor libie wuɔ puo*, to empty money from the bag).

THE BLACK BAGRE

TRANSLATION

In the beginning was god,
the god of the initiates,
and their gods,
the god who comes,
the god with the mark between
   the eyes,
the god with white and black
   stripes,
the god with the white arse,
the thieving god,
the lying god,
the troubling god.   10
He was always troubling that
   one
in the big byre,
that man and the younger one.
Look at the younger one,
the thoughtful one.
He hurries out
of the big byre's door
and takes the path.
He sees something.
What is it?   20
It is *Base*,
against a wall.
So he greets it,
greets it softly,
and when he has done so,
he then sets off
on a meandering path.
He walks along
and quickly reaches
the river bank,   30
where he sees something.

It's a large canoe,
with a smaller one,
which he greets softly.
When he has done so,
he sees the reeds
which he also greets.
When he has done so,
he sees a person.
What sort of person?   40
It's a river person,
carrying a small quiver.
He sees a woman
who is wearing leaves.
He greets them both,
greets them softly,
and they showed him
   something.
What sort of thing?
Do you see that stone
which he shows him?   50
When he has done so,
he shows him the canoe
which he begins to enter.
When he has done so,
the large canoe
begins to move.
Then fear
got hold of him.
What does he do?
He asks what to do   60
and is then shown.
What is he shown?
He takes a stick
and begins to throw it.

He takes a stick
which he quickly throws to him;
he takes a small stick
and shows him
how to paddle.
He begins to move,   70
moves the boat
and sees the way
to cross the river.
He gets across
and when he has done so,
he puts his small left hand
into his bag
to take out some string.
When he has done so,
he sees something else.   80
He sees an axe
hanging on his shoulder.
He takes it
and sees some leaves
on a slender tree.
He cuts this down,
and when he has done so,
into the river bank
he knocks it.
When he has done so,   90
he sees something else
on the river bank.
What sort of thing?
A croaking frog
which he greets,
greets softly.
When he has done so,
he starts to climb up
and catches some vines,
tugging at them gently.   100
He hurries up
and saw something else.
It was a reed,
which he greets softly.

On the river bank
there was an old man
with a pipe.
Do you see the dogs?
When they see someone,
they try to bite him.   110
The old man
calls them to heel
and they make no noise.
See the younger one
starting to greet,
greeting softly.
The old man answers,
and when he has done so,
he then asks me
what I want.   120
And I tell him
that the affairs of God
trouble me greatly.
The old man
spoke again,
'What can I do?'
God's affairs
bring great suffering.
What shall I do?
I was going out   130
but I saw something
in the dark wood.
Then I saw a being child
and began to run.
They started to call,
they called out to me
and when they'd done so,
they spoke and asked me
what I wanted.
And I told them   140
that the affairs of God
began to trouble me;
they troubled me greatly,
me and the elder one.

They overpowered me,
put me on the path
and I entered the woods.
For many days
I hurried here.
They overpowered me　　150
and I came here.
He finished speaking
and the being children
turned and caught him.
They held him gently
and made him sit.
When they'd done so
they took some guinea corn
and showed it him.
'Do you know this?'　　160
'No, I don't.'
And they told him
it was food.
Do you see the being child
begin to eat it?
He did eat it
and found it pleasing.
Do you see the man
dipping his hand in,
beginning to eat,　　170
putting the food in his mouth,
starting to chew?
Does it please you?
He said it does so.
So he spoke
and when he'd done so,
the being child
told him
to stop
and they'd bring some flour.　180
They brought some
and he asked them,
'What's that?
Is it ashes?'

He was told
to sit and watch.
He sat there
while the being child
fetched some water,
poured it on the flour,　　190
and began to mix it.
When he'd done so,
he took out his hand,
began to lick it,
and it tasted good.
Then the being child
said to him,
'Eat and see'.
He began to eat
and when he'd done so,　　200
he said,
'It's true.'
[The being] asked him
if he knew about guinea corn.
He answered, 'No',
and asked
'What made guinea corn?'
and they replied,
'God created guinea corn.'
When they had spoken,　　210
what did he do?
He took a stone,
took it,
and then took something else.
What sort of thing?
It is iron.
He broke the stone
and found the ore.
This he took
and began to leave.　　220
He went off
and reached his house.
He got there
and showed the man:

'Do you see that?'
When he'd shown him,
what did he do?
He told him
to watch well,
so he did so.   230
He took the stone,
took some logs,
took all these
and piled them together.
He took the ore,
the iron ore,
and stacked it on top.
He sees more [wood]
and piles it on.
He fires the wood—   240
'What made fire?'
He took a stone,
a white stone,
and another small one.
Do you see the kapok?
He puts this between them
and holds the big stone
in his hand.
He hits them together,
and when he does so,   250
see the spark
that lights the kapok.
The younger one
felt afraid.
What's this thing?
As he watched,
[the being] took the fire.
See the grasses
catching fire.
He takes these   260
to the large logs
and puts them underneath.
Do you see what
he is building?

When he has finished,
he takes a funnel
and puts it in the middle.
When he has done so,
he takes some earth
and pours on water.   270
When he has done so,
he takes a hoe.
When he has done so,
he mixes the swish.
When he has finished,
what does he do?
He plasters the iron
until it is covered,
and takes some earth
and begins to build.   280
When he has done so
he builds a chimney.
When he has done so
he takes a skin.
When he has done so
he begins to get up.
When he has done so
he puts his left hand
into the granary,
takes out some string   290
and begins to fasten [the
    bellows].
When he has done so
what does he do?
He calls his son
to come quickly
and sit there
so they can start.
He sat there
and watched quietly.
Then he told the boy   300
to press the bellows,
so he pressed till they hissed.
He told the boy

that he should try hard.
When he had done so,
do you see the iron?
The iron reddened
and he took it out.
He took his hammer
and began to beat it.   310
When he beat it,
he did so in vain.
What did he do?
The small being
then told him
he would put it back.
He put it back
and when he had finished,
he tried again
and the iron reddened.   320
When it had reddened,
he began to beat it.
When he had done so,
what did he do?
The affairs of God
bring great suffering.
What did he do?
He beat it flat.
What did he do?
He took his hammer   330
and put it down.
When he had done so,
with his hand
he grasped the iron.
The small being
thought to himself
and then spoke,
'Do you see that thing?'
'What is it?'
'A little iron rod.'   340
He took this [rod]
and bent it by beating.
When he had done so,

the small being
showed him
how to hold it.
He took
the iron.
When he had done so,
he told him   350
to pick up his hammer.
When he had done so,
he told him
to raise it up.
When he had done so,
he began to smite
and smote gently.
When he had done so,
see the boy,
he was told   360
to take up the sliver of iron.
He did so
and gave a name
to this piece of iron.
He called it 'chisel'.
He chiselled to try it
and when he'd done so,
he chiselled softly.
When he'd finished,
he took the hammer   370
and began to strike,
to strike till it bent.
When he had done so,
the left-handed one
laughed softly.
The younger one
sat quietly
and watched.
He watched
and said, 'That's why   380
the elder one
suffers greatly.'
[The being] took the hoe

and fixed a handle
by driving it in.
When he had done so,
he showed the younger one
how to pick it up.
So he took it.
The affairs of God   390
bring great suffering.
What did he do?
The small being
told him
to bend down.
He did so,
and he showed him
how to hold the hoe.
He held the hoe,
held it gently,   400
then he showed him
how to bend right down.
He did so,
and he told him
to cut the earth.
The affairs of God
pass understanding.
The younger one
then asked
the small being   410
to take the hoe,
cut the earth,
and make a farm.
When he had cut
the earth's surface
and made a mound,
he took some guinea corn
and began to plant.
When he'd done so,
some time later,   420
see God's child?
He came there
and began to laugh.

When he finished,
the small being
asked him,
'Why are you laughing?'
And he replied,
'It's the affairs of God
I'm laughing about.'   430
Then the younger one
began to think,
sat silently
and saw what to do.
He then said
he would greet
his great-grandfather,
and his guardian
and his ancestors
and the Earth shrines.   440
This was the matter
that made him speak.
He began to get up
and when he'd done so,
he spoke again,
greeting the Earth shrine,
greeting god,
greeting the ancestors,
greeting the guardian,
greeting the beings.   450
When he'd done this,
he saw something
of great importance.
Earth and rain,
the rain is male
and the earth is female.
When the time comes,
see the rain;
its penis rises
and bursts forth.   460
See the earth,
a fully grown maiden,
who is about to bear.

A slender tree
is brought forth.
It is the earth's child
that is born.
That old man
laughed softly.
When he had done so,   470
the younger one
came back
and now asked,
'What shall I do?
The affairs of God
bring great suffering.'
And he was told
that the slender tree,
he must grasp
and climb up quickly   480
to God's house.
He grasped the tree
but couldn't climb it
and fell on his back.
Then the spider
galloped over
with his feet flying
and said that
the great man
should sit on the ground.   490
He sat a while,
he sat quietly.
And the spider
took out some rope,
put it round his waist,
and then said
the great man
should grasp the rope.
When he had done so,
he spoke again,   500
'To God's house
we'll climb.'
They began to climb

to God's house.
The old man
was lying there.
They saw him
on a cow's hide.
They reached the place
and began to greet him,   510
'Good day.'
Do you see the dog?
It's a huge dog,
with a leopard
and a lion
and an elephant
and a duiker
and a hippopotamus
in a small pond.
See the hippopotamus.   520
That old man
in his wisdom
turned and said
that our ancestor
should come forward.
When he came,
he took some earth,
and pressed it together.
When this was done,
he spoke again   530
and called a young girl,
a slender girl,
to come there too.
She came over,
and when she had done so,
he told her
to take a pot.
She took it,
and stood up with it.
Then he told her   540
to look for okro
to bring to him.
He chose a piece,

put it in his mouth,
chewed it to bits,
spat them out
into the pot.
He did all this.
Do you see the man?
That old man   550
told him
to mix the earth.
When this was done,
the slender girl
he instructed
to pour the okro water
over the earth.
When he had spoken [to her],
he told the man
to take his left hand   560
and plunge it in the earth.
When he had done so,
he told him
to withdraw his hand,
and he did so.
Then what did he do?
He told him
to come nearer.
He did so.
A tom cat   570
and his mate
started to get up.
The old man
told them to lie down
and keep quiet.
A male fly
and his mate
who came there
shat on top.
Two days later   580
the tom cat
and his mate
hurried there

and scraped at the earth.
See the child
crying there quietly.
What shall I do?
The affairs of God
bring great suffering.
And he told   590
the woman
they should hurry back
to God's house
and God
then asked
our ancestor,
'Whose child is it?'
See the child,
how he resembles
the great man.   600
He laughed softly
and when he had done so,
he asked,
'What is this?'
And he replied,
'It's a child.'
'Who owns the child?'
The old man
then said,
'You own the child.'   610
'Where did I get it?'
He replied,
'You begot the child.'
The younger one
asked again,
'How did I do so?'
The old man
laughed softly.
When he had done so,
he asked,   620
'What shall I do?'
See the woman,
the slender girl,

who hurries over
and says,
'In that case,
don't I own the child?'
The old man
asked her,
'Well, where did you get it?' 630
The slender girl
thought to herself
and spoke again,
'My okro water
I poured out
over the earth.
It was from inside there
you took out the child.'
The old man
replied that 640
the slender girl
should hurry over.
She reached the place,
in front of the old man.
The old man
called his wife,
a wise old woman,
who came out
to do her work.
What work [was that]? 650
She broke off some leaves
and when she'd done so,
she instructed
the slender girl
to do the same.
She picked up the child.
When she had done so,
what did she do?
She began to carry it,
and when she had done so, 660
she started to walk
along the road.
The wise old woman

told her
not to hurry.
Didn't she know
that the blood
remained in her belly?
The slender girl
began to laugh 670
and asked her,
'What kind of blood?'
And she replied,
'Wait till we get home.'
They reached there
and began to sit down.
When they had done so,
the wise old woman
knew what to do;
she told 680
a young girl
to take a large pot
and put it on the fire.
She put it there
and filled it with water.
The wise old woman
got some leafy branches
and broke them in bits.
When she had done so,
she put them in the large
pot. 690
She lit the fire,
and when she had done so,
what did she do?
The fire blazed up,
and they took the leaves,
turned them over,
and when they had done so,
[the pot] was now boiling.
The wise old woman
went out quickly, 700
called the slender girl
to lay the child down.

She laid it down
and hurried over.
The wise old woman
poured the water
from off the leaves
and took some kapok,
dipped it in
and quickly pressed   710
the slender girl
on her groin.
She pummelled it
and the slender girl
saw something.
The wise old woman
knew the truth.
Do you see the blood
coming out?
The slender girl   720
became
afraid
and exclaimed,
'Why is it
the blood comes
out of my belly?'
The wise old woman
asked her, saying,
'That child,
where did you get it?'   730
And she replied,
'Out of the earth
that we dug up
and there was the child.'
[The old woman] told her,
'From your own belly
I took the child.
You and who
dug for the child?'
And she replied,   740
'I and a certain man.
He is called

the younger one.
We are the people
to whom the old man
allotted
this small task.
It was God
in his wisdom [told us]
to collect some earth,   750
and told us
to collect some okro.
We brought this to him,
and he took the okro,
chewed it in bits
and spat it in a pot.
We poured in water,
and emptied it over the earth.
The male cat
saw us   760
and began to get up.
Our old man
clicked his tongue
to silence it,
then did this again
so it lay down quietly.
When it had done so,
he told us
to pour and mix [the okro
    and earth].
When we had done so,   770
we turned and left.
A male fly
and his mate,
with all their cunning,
came there
and began to play.
When they had done so,
the male cat
came along
and scraped [the earth].   780
When he had done so,

he saw the child.
The old man
sat there holding it.
I went to him
and saw a man.
It was the younger one.
I greeted him,
and saw the child.
So I thought to myself   790
and began to joke,
saying that the child
belonged to me.
Wise old woman,
I took the child,
brought it here,
and you told me
how I should
break off some leaves.
When you had broken   800
   them,
we started to leave
and you told me
not to hurry,
because I wasn't aware
there was blood
in my belly.
It was the truth
you told me.
Because now
I see the blood.   810
Do I own the child,
or does the younger one?'
The wise old woman
then told her
to rest a while.
She did so,
and her belly healed.
What did she do?
The affairs of God
bring great suffering.   820

One day
see how the younger one
passes by
to the house of his friend.
At this time
the child
was walking along.
The younger one
came back
and retraced his steps.   830
The child saw
the younger one
and began to cry
to be taken along.
The child's mother
he then asked,
'Whose child is it?'
And the mother
replied,
'I own the child.'   840
And the younger one
then said,
'I own the child'—
about the same child.
The wise old woman
hurried there.
They made so much noise
that the wise old woman
hurried to see.
She ordered them   850
to stop quarrelling.
They did so
and she asked the girl,
the slender girl,
'Who owns the child?'
'I own it,
but the younger one
wants to snatch it.'
And she asked him,
'Why do you do this?'   860

And he replied,
'I own the child.'
The wise old woman
laughed loudly
and said
that one child
is causing two people
to quarrel.
'Wait a while
so that I can go   870
to the cow's hide
where that old man
is lying.'
They reached the place
and the wise old woman
began to greet him,
'Good day.'
The old man
returned her greeting.
When he had done so,   880
he asked,
'Is it fear [that brings you]?'
'No, no,
it isn't fear.
It's about that child
we have come
to see you.'
The old man
told them
to keep calm.   890
And he asked
the slender girl,
'What caused this quarrel?'
And she replied,
'The child is mine
but the younger one
wants to snatch it.
That's the cause.'
He laughed loudly
and when he had done so,   900

he began to ask
the younger one,
'What caused this quarrel?'
And the younger one
too replied,
'The child is mine
and the slender girl
wants to snatch it.
That's the cause.'
The old man   910
laughed loudly
and said,
'Slender girl,
where did you get the child?'
And the slender girl
answered,
'I got it here.'
And he asked
the younger one,
'Where did you get the
    child?'   920
And he said,
'I got it on the road.'
He told them
to wait a while.
They waited silently,
and when they'd done so,
he began to ask
the slender girl,
'Where did you get the child?
How is it   930
you own the child?'
Again he asked
the slender girl
and again she said,
'I own the child.'
Once again he asked,
'Where did you get it?'
And she replied
it was she got the okro.

'You took it,   940
chewed it in bits
and put them in the pot.
I poured it
over some earth
which turned into a child.'
'Who owns the earth?'
The slender girl
kept quiet.
What did he do?
He asked the child,   950
'Who owns you?'
And that child
laughed quietly
and replied,
'My father
is the younger one.'
'How is it,'
he asked him,
'that you know
your father   960
is the younger one?'
See the child
who laughs quietly
and begins to run.
He runs over
and grasps the man
around his thighs.
The younger one
laughed softly.
The old man   970
asked him again,
'Who owns the child?'
And he too said,
'I own the child.'
'How is it
that you know
you own the child?'
And he replied,
'There I stood,

when the spider,   980
my brother,
galloped over
with his feet flying.
The time arrived,
and a great thing,
a black cloud
filled with rain,
burst forth
on to the earth
which became pregnant   990
and gave birth
to a slender tree.
Weighty matters
troubled me.
What could I do
on this earth?
I sought in vain,
thought to myself,
and I decided
that I'd climb up   1000
to God's house.
So then I grasped
the earth's child,
that slender tree.
I began to climb
but tried in vain
and fell on my back.
It was the spider,
my brother,
galloped over   1010
with his legs flying
took out some rope,
tied it round his waist,
and told me
to take hold.
I began to climb,
caught hold of the rope
and he pulled me up
till we arrived

at God's house.   1020
The old man
[lay] on the cow's hide
and we greeted,
"Good day."
He returned the greeting
and when he had done so,
he asked me
what I wanted.
And I said,
"Everything,   1030
that's what I want."
He showed me
the being's child.
I saw him
when he showed me.
At God's house,
the old man
on the cow's hide
asked me
many questions.   1040
I answered him
and when I had done so,
he told me
to stand there
and start to hoe.
When I did so,
a small mound
I heaped up.
In all his wisdom,
he called a girl,   1050
a slender girl,
to bring a pot.
She brought it
and the old man
took some okro,
chewed it in bits,
spat them in a pot,
put in some water
and poured it on my earth.

When he had finished,   1060
we began to leave.
A male fly [and his mate]
came there;
they played their games
and when they'd done so,
they began to leave.
A male cat
and his mate
came there;
they scraped away the earth 1070
and took the child
from out of my earth.
That is how
I know
the child is mine.'
The old man
laughed loudly
and knew what to do.
He took a stalk of grass,
removed the pith   1080
and gave it to the man.
He took another
and gave it to the woman,
having done the same.
When he had done so,
he told them
to look at an object,
at a small bowl.
'You, woman,
you claim   1090
the child is yours.'
She agreed,
'The child is mine.'
Then he asked the man,
the younger one,
'Whose is the child?'
He also replied
the child was his.
So he told

the slender girl 1100
to urinate
down the stalk.
'Don't let it
splash about.'
So she pissed
but it splashed about.
When she stopped,
he told the man,
to urinate
down the stalk. 1110
'Don't let it
splash about.'
The man pissed
and it all went in.
When this happened,
he said,
'Slender girl,
you took the pot
and when you brought it,
you saw a person 1120
with a hoe,
who hoed the earth.
I own the okro,
and in my wisdom
poured it on top.
The younger one
begins to mix it.
When he had done so
you all went away.
When you had gone, 1130
a male fly
and his mate
came there.
When they had played,
a male cat
and his mate
came there.
They scraped away the earth
and took out the child.

A bitter argument 1140
ensued between you
and has continued.
You are the man
who left his village.
Great trouble
troubled him
and he hurried up
to God's place.
I, the great man,
helped him 1150
to find a child,
that child there.
It belongs to him.'
He took the child
and gave it to the younger one
who hurried down,
down to the Earth.
What did he do?
At last he reached
his father's house. 1160
What did he do?
Many problems
troubled him.
He took the child,
showed the guardian,
showed the gods,
showed the Earth shrine,
showed the ancestors.
When he had done so,
look at the child. 1170
The time has come.
Earth and rain
know their business.
[A cloud] burst forth
and the land was wet.
He took a hoe
and began to leave
for the farm.
What did he do?

The younger one 1180
hurried out
and saw the child
with his hoe.
He was pleased,
and asked the child,
'What is this?'
He replied
'Isn't it a hoe?'
and told him
he was going to farm. 1190
The child's father
laughed softly
and said
that's what he wanted.
He said this
and walked away.
Just then a scorpion
bit the child.
The child cried out,
and the father 1200
hurried out
and asked the child
'Why are you crying?'
It was a scorpion
that bit the child.
Fear gripped
the younger one.
He took some guinea corn,
took his bag,
took his quiver, 1210
took his bow,
took his axe,
and rushed out,
out of the doorway.
See the guinea corn
in his hand.
He showed the ancestors,
and the guardians,
and the gods.

When he had done so, 1220
he then went out.
He saw the path,
the meandering path.
He hurried to reach
the diviner's house.
The dog barked
and he hushed it.
The dog was quiet
and he asked the man,
'Is it fear?' 1230
And he replied,
'It's about my son
whom I brought down
from God's house.
I hurried down
and the rains had come
and he started to hoe.
Then a scorpion
bit the child.'
See the slender girl 1240
at the diviner's house.
She rushed out,
out of the doorway.
The younger one
saw the woman,
recognized her,
greeted her
and greeted the diviner.
When he had done so,
the woman said, 1250
'Where are you going?'
And he said,
'It's my child.
A scorpion
bit him.
It was fear
that seized me
and I came along
to the diviner's house.'

The slender girl　　　1260
laughed loudly
and then said,
'That child,
what is
he called?'
He laughed softly
and replied,
'My child
is called
Napolo.'　　　　　　1270
The slender girl
said, 'Well,
then it's my child.
Where did you find
that Napolo?'
And he said
she should wait a while
and keep quiet.
The diviner
took down his bag,　　1280
stroked his head,
took his axe
and his quiver
and his bow,
put them at his feet.
When he had done so,
he put his hand
in his bag,
took out something
and then asked　　　　1290
the younger one,
'Shall I put it down?'
The younger one
laughed loudly
and told him
to take it out.
When he'd done so,
he put in his hand,
brought out something;

it was a bell.　　　　　1300
When he had done this,
a male figure
and a female,
he took out
and placed on the ground.
Then he told
the younger one
to look at the ground.
He looked there.
Then he told him　　　1310
to look at the leather bottle.
He looked at it,
and when he had done so,
[the diviner] said
he would pause a while.
He did so,
then he took the bottle
and knocked the neck.
When he'd done so,
he told him　　　　　1320
to look at the ground.
He did so
and asked the bottle,
'Why is it
that at dawn
my friend here
came to see me?'
The bottle
then replied,
'It is the deity.'　　　　1330
He asked
'Which deity?
The grandfather's deity?
The grandmother's deity?
The brother's deity?
The daughter's deity?
The deity of the wilds?
The being's deity?
The deity of childbirth?

The deity of meetings?' 1340
At this it agreed.
See the younger one
who spoke, saying,
'Is that what
was going
to kill my son?'
He began to greet
and then got up.
He got up slowly
and began to go. 1350
At the doorway
he met some mat weavers,
and some reed gatherers,
and some firewood collectors
and some girls
and some little boys.
He greeted them all
and when he had done so,
he saw the path
and started off. 1360
See the object,
the being's bag,
which asked him,
'Why did you
greet my master
and not greet me?'
So he sat down quietly
and began to greet.
The bag answered,
answered softly, 1370
and he went to the path,
started to leave,
but saw something else.
What was that?
In the byre
there's the ancestors
and the guardians
and the deity
and the beings.

There is *Base*, 1380
the owner of the house.
He greeted them again.
When he had done so,
he hurried out.
The affairs of God!
He saw the path,
the meandering path,
the path to his father's house.
He started off
and hurried along 1390
the road to the house.
What shall I do?
He sat down,
sat quietly
and began to call
to his child
to come there.
He hurried out,
came out quietly.
'Who's calling me?', 1400
the boy
begins to ask,
'Who's calling me?'
When he asked,
the boy's father
spoke to him, saying,
'It's me that's calling.'
'What shall I do?'
Some time later,
the slender girl 1410
walked down the path,
the main path,
and was passing by
when the boy
saw his mother
and called out
'Mother,
where are you going?'
The boy's mother

replied,   1420
'I'm not going anywhere,
just passing by.'
And the boy
ran over
to his father's side
and said [to him],
'It's my mother.'
The boy's father
asked him,
'Where does she come
     from?'   1430
and he replied,
'I don't know.
A woman passed
and I know
she's my mother.'
The boy's father
said [to him],
'You have no mother'.
The boy
laughed softly   1440
and asked his father,
'Have you seen anyone
who has no mother
and yet has a father?'
The boy's father
then said,
'Many problems
still trouble me
and I don't yet know [the
     answers].'
The boy's mother   1450
was passing by.
See the boy
beginning to cry,
'My mother
is going by.'
The boy's father
became angry.

Again he asked the child,
'Who is your mother
that's going by?'   1460
'My mother
is the slender girl.'
The boy's father
hushed the child.
The boy's mother
hurried over
and when she got there,
she tried to take him.
The boy's father
said to her,   1470
'I won't give him to you.'
When he had spoken,
the boy's mother
laughed loudly
and said,
'Because of the child,
I can't let the matter drop.'
But she departed
and stayed away.
That boy   1480
had much sense
in his head.
One day
the younger one
went outside
into the woods.
He saw a being of the wild
who had a bow,
a quiver
and some arrows.   1490
He greeted him
and when he had done so,
the being of the wild
inquired,
'What do you want?'
He replied,
'You people caught me

and I came to the woods
and you taught me
many things,   1500
but you didn't teach me
about this one thing.
The being of the wild
laughed softly
and then said,
'Let's go home.
Follow me.'
He followed him home
and the being of the wild
told him,   1510
'What you want to make
can be made by children.
See my child.
Sit quietly by him
and he'll make it for you.'
He sat there.
The being's child
got some twine,
his axe
and his knife.   1520
He went to the woods
to cut some sticks,
bamboo for the bow.
When he'd done so,
he tied them together.
When he had done so,
he hurried back
to his father's house.
He dropped the bundle
and when he had done so,   1530
he saw the man,
the younger one.
He took his knife
to cut the bamboo.
He chose one stick
and when he had done so,
he split it into slivers.

When he'd done so,
what did he do?
He began to scrape it,   1540
and when he'd done so,
he took out another
of the bamboo sticks.
When he'd done so,
he took his axe
and began to shape it.
When he'd done so,
he took the fibre,
and laced it together.
When he'd done so,   1550
he stood up
and bent it with his foot,
bent it so it was right,
then fastened the bowstring.
When he'd done so,
he drew the bow
and let it go, ping.
He took the man
and went along
to the blacksmith's house.   1560
When they reached there,
see the small hoe,
see the axe,
a blunted axe.
When they reached
the blacksmith's house,
they began to greet him,
'Good day.'
He answered them
and when he had done so,   1570
he asked him,
'Is it fear [brings you]?'
'Oh no,'
and he said,
'The being of the wild
brought me
and I came along

to your house.
I came here
and greeted you.   1580
It's not fear;
it's the being's child.
Yesterday night
I got up,
went to the woods
and began to look
for what I needed.
It was medicine
I was looking for.
The being of the wild,   1590
I saw him
carrying things;
he was heavily laden,
and I said to him,
"What is that?"
And he told me,
"That's a quiver,
and that's a bow."
From his great knowledge
he told me.   1600
This is what
I said to him,
"You showed me
many things
at the time
when you caught me,
but you didn't show me
the bow and arrow
and the quiver."
When he had spoken,   1610
the being of the wild
went off
and led me
till we reached
his father's house.
He made his child,
a male child,

go into the woods.
See the stick
he cuts and takes.   1620
He began to show him,
and when he'd done so,
he got up,
bent the bow
and told me
to come along
to your house.
So we came.
The problem
I bring to you   1630
is the one
I have just recounted.'
See the being's child.
The being's child
took the axe
and gave it to the smith.
Then the blacksmith
called his child,
his male child,
who hurried out.   1640
He told him
to sit on the ground.
When he got there,
he was sent off again;
he ran out
of the byre door,
and saw something.
It was a dry shea log
to which he set fire.
When he had done so,   1650
the fire blazed up.
When it did so,
the male child
began to think.
Cold water
he brought outside;
cold water

he poured out,
all over the fire.
When he had done so,   1660
he took the charcoal
out of the fire
and hurried up
to his father's place.
And the smith
said to him,
'Wait a while.'
He waited a while
and when he had done so,
he told the being's child   1670
to bring the axe
and the hoe.
He brought them along
and he took the axe,
put it in the fire,
took the charcoal
and covered the axe.
When he had done so,
the blacksmith
called to his son   1680
who hurried over.
And he told him
to climb [on the forge].
He climbed up
and when he had done so,
he took the skin,
the skin of a goat,
and got out some string
from the small granary.
When he had done so,   1690
he knelt down
and began to tie [the skin].
When he had done so,
he took a pot,
broke off the neck,
and fixed it
on the end of the funnel.

Then he tied on [the skin],
and when he had done so,
he told his son   1700
to sit on top.
He climbed up
on top of the forge
and he told him
to hold the bellows.
He began to blow
and God's breeze
came blowing out
of the forge's mouth.
He pressed the left
    [bellow];   1710
it began to blow
and God's breeze
came blowing out,
out of both funnels.
See the forge.
The blacksmith
made him blow,
and he blew
till the axe got red.
He got the tongs   1720
and picked it up,
placed it gently
on top of the anvil
and began to strike.
As he struck it,
he flattened the iron.
When he had done so,
he took out his chisel
and began to shape it.
When he had done so,   1730
see the reed,
the greatest reed.
He fixed it on
and gave it a name.
The name was 'arrow.'
The small being

and the younger one
took the arrow
and the bow
and went home   1740
to the father's house.
The small being
told the younger one
to take the path
to his father's house,
that meandering path;
the younger one
started out
and saw some people,
beings of the wild.   1750
He greeted them,
greeted them softly,
and when he had done so,
he took the path
to his father's house,
that meandering path.
He hurried along
to his father's house.
See the child,
the male child,   1760
run to meet him.
When he did so,
the headstrong boy
saw something
that his father carried,
and asked,
'What is that?'
The boy's father
said to him,
'It is yours.   1770
Wait till we get home
and I'll give it you.'
When they arrived there,
at the father's house,
the boy's father
took the quiver

and the bow.
When the child
saw the bow,
he laughed softly   1780
and said,
'That's my father.
He has brought a bow
and a quiver.'
The boy's father
took the bow
and went outside
on top of the midden
and stood quietly.
There was a tall okro
    plant;   1790
he took the bow
and an arrow
and began to aim
at the okro plant.
The arrow struck
the tall plant.
The boy
saw this,
laughed softly
and hurried over   1800
to his father's side
and began to cry,
'Give me the bow
and the quiver
and the arrows.'
The boy's father
took the bow
to give the boy.
The boy grasped the bow,
took an arrow   1810
out of the quiver,
fitted it to the bow
and began to shoot,
shot till he'd had enough,
then began to laugh.

The boy's father
left the bow
for the child
who took it
and went inside.   1820
The boy's mother,
that slender girl,
had a broom
that she took
and began to sweep
the main room of the house.
She began to sweep
and the child
took the bow
and started to shoot   1830
at his own mother,
at the leaves she wore.
He hit her smack,
and the boy's mother
jumped up
and beat the child.
The boy's father
became angry
and said,
'Don't you ever   1840
beat the boy again.'
The boy's mother
left the child alone.
Two days later
the boy's father
went to his farm
in order to hoe,
and then came back
to his father's house.
See the boy   1850
with his bow.
He sat there,
wanting to play.
Then the boy
took the bow

and an arrow.
The boy's father
lay down to rest
and when he had done so,
see the boy   1860
take the bow
and an arrow.
Up to his father's balls
he went,
and at his balls
he began to shoot.
He shot at them
and hit them smack.
The boy's father
was seized with anger   1870
and jumped up to beat him.
The boy's mother
said to him,
'Oh no,
don't beat the boy.
How long ago was it,
how long today,
that I hit the boy
because he shot me,
and you told me   1880
not to beat him.
When he shot you,
did you leave him be?'
The boy's father
said to her,
'I won't take the child.'
And he hurried out,
out of the doorway,
leaving the child.
See the doves   1890
at the foot of the mortar,
eating guinea corn.
See the creature,
God's creature,
it's a hawk,

that dives down
and attacks the dove.
See the dove
lying there.
See the child   1900
running over
with his bow
and his arrows.
He shot till he tired,
then clicked his tongue
and when he'd done so,
he took the dove
with the arrow in it
and went over
to his father's side.   1910
He said to him,
'See my dove
which I shot and killed.'
The boy's father
began to laugh
and beat his chest
and declared,
'I begat a child,
a powerful child.
One day to come   1920
he'll give me help.'
When he had spoken,
he took the dove
and began to pluck it.
He took a leg,
he took the loins
and gave them
to the boy's mother.
He took a leg
and kept it himself.   1930
The boy's mother
laughed softly
for she was happy.
The boy's mother,
when darkness fell,

asked the father,
'What shall we do
to get another child
in addition,
so there'll be two?'   1940
The boy's father
said to her,
'The day after tomorrow
I will go
to my elder's place,
to the spider
who will help us
to climb up
to God's place
and get a child.'   1950
Day had broken
and the boy's mother
went to the woods
to fetch firewood.
She searched till she came
to a well-wooded bank.
When she got there
she saw a creature;
a boa constrictor
and his mate   1960
were playing there.
At this the woman
broke out laughing.
The boa constrictor
called the woman
to come near
and he asked her
why she was laughing.
And she answered,
'It's nothing,   1970
except the playing
gave me pleasure.
That's why I laughed.'
The boa constrictor
said to her,

'Do you know this pleasure?'
And she replied,
'No, I don't.'
And he told her
to sit there.   1980
She sat quietly.
The boa constrictor
slept with his mate.
They did their work
and the woman saw
and asked him
to sleep with her too.
He slept with the woman
and she got up.
When she had done so,   1990
she told him
his play had pleased her.
When she had said this,
the snake told her
if she played that game,
she'd give birth
to many children.
Then the woman
got up and ran off
to her own house.   2000
She reached there
and told the man
that she'd seen something,
a certain game.
And the man asked,
'What game was that?'
And she replied,
'Wait till I show you.'
She went to lie down
and called the man.   2010
He came there
and lay down too,
and then the woman
showed him what to do.
And the man

enjoyed it too
and laughed softly,
saying
it was true
the game was pleasing.   2020
Two days later
the man got up
and said to her,
'Let us go
to God
and beg for a child.'
But the woman
refused
and told him
she wouldn't go.   2030
'You discovered the game
that was so pleasing,
yet you want to go
back to God?
Let's play it again.'
So the man came
and they played the game
for six whole days.
See the woman;
two days later   2040
she cooked some beans
and her belly swelled.
At daybreak,
see the woman
still all swollen.
See the man,
it was fear
that came upon him.
He asked her
what they should do.   2050
And the woman
replied to him,
'Let's wait a while.'
And the man
told the woman,

'Let's go off
to God's place
and find the cause
of the swollen belly.'
Then the woman   2060
told him
she wouldn't go.
See the man
sitting quietly,
asking the cause.
Then the woman
told him
to leave it
and come and play.
'This belly of mine   2070
doesn't pain me.'
Two days later
her belly ached
and she began to wail.
The younger one
sat there quietly
and then got up
and hurried out
to see the being
and asked him,   2080
'Look at
this matter
that's troubling me.'
The being of the wild
hurried over
with his skin bag,
his leather bottle,
with his bell,
his carved figures,
his guardian,   2090
with his stones,
and his wild fruit pod.
He emptied them out
and when he'd done so,
he told him

to draw near.
And when he'd done so,
he said to him
they should grasp the stick.
When they'd done so,   2100
they greeted each other.
When they'd done this,
he took his left hand.
See the stick.
'What sort of stick?'
The handle of an axe
he took,
and when he had done so,
he told him,
'Take hold of it too',   2110
and he held it.
The being of the wild
held the stick,
held it and it shook.
The being of the wild
revealed to him
that he saw something,
and he asked him
what it was.
And he replied,   2120
'Your wife's belly
is aching;
that's why you came here.
That was why
I took my bag.
Wait while I throw
and you'll see the cowries.'
So he threw them.
See the cowries,
two up, two down.   2130
Then he said,
'It is true.
My wife's belly
ached so much.
That's why

I declared
I'd climb to God's place
to ask him about it.
Then a thought
came to me 2140
and I said
I would come
to ask you
to find out.
That's why
I came here.'
The being of the wild
said to him,
'There's nothing wrong.
A person 2150
is coming to you,
a new person;
it is this
that God
in all his wisdom
gave to the woman
in her belly.
Therefore
run back home.'
And the man 2160
stood up,
went out
and ran home
to his father's house.
He got there
and heard crying;
a baby
was crying out,
and he asked,
'Whose child 2170
is crying
in my house?'
He rushed in
and saw the woman
holding a child.

It was fear
that seized him,
and she said,
'Wait a while
and keep calm.' 2180
And when he did so,
the little old woman
told him
to wait a while.
'About this matter,
it was God
in all his wisdom
who made the woman
go into the woods
where she saw something. 2190
She began to play,
she stopped,
and her belly
became great with child.
And so this person
came to you.'
See the man
laughing softly,
and he said,
'The first child 2200
that I have,
it was God
that gave me.
But that other one,
I ask you,
who gave it me?'
The little old woman
then said,
'God gave it you.
That is why 2210
the slender girl
went to the woods
and saw a large snake
which showed her
how to play.

When the game was over,
my child helped him.
That's how it is.
Do you understand?'
The boy's father   2220
spoke again,
'That child,
I will give him
the name
of Der.
God didn't give me,
so I call him Der.'
The little old woman
thought to herself,
then hushed the man.   2230
The man became quiet,
and the little old woman
spoke, saying,
'The name
of Der
is not for him.
His name
is Number Nine.'
The boy's father
asked the woman,   2240
'Why is it Nine?'
And she replied
that it was not God
who gave him
the name
of Nine.
The man agreed,
and when he did so,
she continued,
'That child,   2250
I gave him
the name of Nine,
because you'll have
ten children
born after him.'

See them there,
they had children
amounting to ten.
The little old woman
laughed softly   2260
and asked,
'How many are there?'
And they replied
'There are ten,
in addition to Nine
and God's child.
See them all;
God's breeze
blows upon them
and they grow up.   2270
And when they have grown
see the man.
One day
he took bowstrings
and bow staves
to make some bows.
When he had done so,
he shared them out
and when he had done so,
they said to him,   2280
'Well and good,
now teach us to shoot.'
He took a bow,
hurried out
and called God's child
to come out
with his bow.
He came out
with his bow
and he told them   2290
to look at
the tall okro stalk.
He shot at it
and hit the stalk.
Two days later

the younger one
went out hunting
with his children.
They hurried along
to the thick woods.   2300
When they reached there,
they saw an antelope.
They began to shoot
but didn't hit it.
They stood there,
and God's child
fitted an arrow
to his bow
and began to shoot.
When he did so,   2310
he hit the antelope
and began to run,
to run after it.
He reached
the edge of a hole,
went down
and saw some beings.
What did he do?
One of the beings
asked him,   2320
'Who was it
shot our heifer?'
Fear it was
that seized God's child;
he stood there
while they pulled out the arrow.
When they had done so,
they asked him again,
'What did you put on it?'
and he said   2330
he didn't put anything.
The beings of the wild
then told him
to wait a while.
He waited

and sometime later
they led him
away
to the door of their room
where they told him   2340
to sit a while.
They cut some leaves
and brought them over
for him to taste.
He did so.
They were shea leaves,
which were not bitter.
They cut more leaves,
some dawadawa leaves,
and brought them over   2350
for him to taste,
and they were not bitter.
Then they took
some ebony leaves
and brought them over
for him to taste.
They took other leaves
and mixed them together
for him to taste,
and they were not bitter.   2360
Then strophanthus leaves
they brought along
for him to taste.
He began to taste
and found them bitter.
One of them took these leaves,
took a broken pot
in order to boil them,
took the strophanthus
and dropped it in.   2370
When this was done,
he lit a fire
and took an object.
What was that?
The head of a cobra

which he dropped in
and began to cook
until it boiled.
He told him
to bring the arrow.   2380
He took out an arrow
and handed it to the being.
The being's child
took the arrow
to the strophanthus.
The hot fluid
was smeared
on the arrow.
When he had done so,
he told him   2390
to look at this plant
and when he went home,
he should show his father,
the younger one.
He hurried home
to his father's house,
and when he reached there,
he showed the younger one.
When he had done so,
he told him,   2400
'So it came about
that the being of the wild
took me off
into the woods
and showed me
how to brew poison.'
When he had shown him,
the boy's father
fitted an arrow
to his bow   2410
and told him,
'It's a lie,
it's nothing at all.'
And God's child
said to him,

'Taste and see.'
He began to taste
and his tongue blistered.
He took an arrow,
got up to go   2420
out of the door
when he saw a fowl.
He gave it to a child,
a small boy,
to shoot so he could see.
He began to shoot.
See the fowl
which fell on its back,
was about to die
and then dropped dead.   2430
See the child
go tell his father.
Two days later
he took his quiver
with his arrows
to cut strophanthus.
A cobra's head
was cut off
and put in the poison.
He began to heat it   2440
and when it boiled
he took the arrows,
many people's arrows,
laid them down,
and spread on the poison.
When he had finished,
what did he do?
Two days later
he told them
to go out hunting.   2450
They did so
and saw an animal;
a large roan
and its dam
were standing there.

See the child;
it's God's child
with his sharp eye
who began to shoot.
He hit it smack   2460
and the arrow held.
The male roan
fell down.
He hallooed,
and the boy's father
hurried up
and saw an object,
the dead roan.
He laughed softly
and said to him,   2470
'Let's go off home.'
When they reached
the father's house,
what did they do?
They told the women
to fetch the meat;
so they hurried there,
saw the meat
and began to laugh.
They carried it off   2480
and hurried home.
The younger one
told them
to wait a while
and keep quiet.
He took a leg
which he kept himself.
He took the loins;
the mother has that.
He took the neck   2490
for the meat carriers.
He took the back
to give the grandfather.
He took the guts
to give the women.

He took the head
to give his friend,
and he told him,
'If you kill one yourself,
keep the head   2500
and give it to me.'
He finished speaking
and two days later,
they went to the farm
to hoe.
They saw some game.
What sort of game?
It was a buffalo
with its calf.
They stood quite still.   2510
God's child
came closer,
moving stealthily,
then drew his bow;
at the buffalo's
shoulder
he aimed and shot.
See the poison
climbing up,
out of her nostrils.   2520
She fell there
and as she fell,
they ran over.
The boy's father
began to laugh,
laughed softly
and then said,
'Look at that,
and I've got no bow!
If only I'd known   2530
wild animals
were here,
I'd have brought my bow.
See God's child,
the other day he killed [something]

and he comes here
again today
and kills another.
And I've no bow!'
They hastened back   2540
to their father's house
and told the women
to fetch the meat.
Some young girls
went along,
saw the meat
and began to laugh;
they picked it up
and carried it home.
But the buffalo calf   2550
they left behind;
they said
they'd leave it a year
so it could grow
and then they'd kill it.
They left it
and two days later
they went to the farm
and saw the calf
eating grass.   2560
They began to laugh,
and the small buffalo
began to cry
and then said,
'My mother's debt
I will redeem.'
See that one;
three years
have passed
when one day   2570
the younger one
and his sons
went back to the woods
to hunt for meat.
They returned with it

to their father's house
and finished the meat.
Two days later,
they went to the farm
and began to hoe.   2580
When they'd finished,
some young girls
brought them beer
which they sat and drank.
They drank the beer.
Do you see a creature
behind their backs,
stealing upon them?
What sort of creature?
A young girl   2590
of surpassing beauty.
They saw a woman
and called her
to come over.
She hurried there
and they said to her
'See the girl;
go and call her
to come over.'
She called the young girl   2600
to come there
and when she did so,
God's child
declared,
'That's my wife.'
And Number Nine
said the same.
And the younger one
told them
he would take her   2610
to be married
to his youngest son.
The girl
told them
to wait.

They waited
and she took a small stick,
began to measure
two hundred paces,
and stuck it in the ground.   2620
When she had done so,
she told them
to shoot at the stick.
'The one
who's a real man
and hits it,
he's the one I want.
I don't want
to marry a man
whom one day   2630
someone will overpower.'
They began to shoot
and the younger one
shot first
but didn't succeed.
He then said
that his last born
should shoot and see.
But he too missed.
See the child,   2640
he begins to shoot.
God's child
drew back his bow
and began to shoot
at the little stick.
He hit it
and then said,
'I'm the one
my father begat.'
The young girl   2650
caught hold
of God's child
and embraced him.
When she did this,
see the woman,

how pleased she was.
They began to farm,
and when they'd done so,
don't you see someone?
What sort of a person?   2660
The little old woman
came along
to the farm
and then asked,
'Young men,
what are you doing?'
And they replied,
'Nothing at all.
That young girl
came to us   2670
and told us
she wanted
the young men
that were good shots
to see who were men.
God's child
put on his wrist-guard
and began to shoot
like a man.
And she said,   2680
"That's the one I want." '
The little old woman
took the girl
and led the way
back to the house.
They reached
the father's house,
and the little old woman,
with her great knowledge,
watched the girl,   2690
understood her,
and clicked her mouth.
'That young girl,
she's not a woman.'
But the younger one

had told her
to take her home.
She took her home
and they reached
the father's house.   2700
In the evening,
see the young men
come from the farm
and arrive back
at the father's house.
The younger one
then told
God's child
to take the girl
into his room.   2710
He took the girl
and they entered in
to his room.
He fetched a skin,
an antelope skin,
and told her to sit,
but she refused.
Then he fetched
a roan skin
and told her to sit,   2720
but she refused.
Then he fetched
a duiker skin
and told her to sit,
but she refused.
Then he fetched
a lion skin
and told her to sit
but she refused.
Then he fetched   2730
another antelope's skin
and told her to sit,
but she refused.
Then he fetched
yet another antelope's skin

and told her to sit,
but she refused.
So he went and fetched
her mother's skin,
a buffalo skin,   2740
and threw it down
on the ground.
The young girl
hurried over,
sat on it
and began to weep.
God's child
asked the woman
why she was crying.
And she replied   2750
that she wasn't crying;
the little old woman
had lit a fire
and the smoke
got in her eyes,
so that the tears
came streaming out.
She finished speaking
and it was dark.
They lay down   2760
and she asked her husband
what his name was,
and he replied,
'My name is
God's child.'
And he asked the girl,
'Your own name,
what is it?'
And she replied,
'My name is   2770
Suffering.'
And he said
it was a good name.
She asked the man,
'Husband,

how did you manage
to kill
such big animals?'
And he replied
'Well, I know how to kill.' 2780
And she asked,
'What do you kill with?'
And he replied,
'With bow and arrow.'
And she asked,
'And if it's
a dangerous animal
that wants to kill you,
what would you do?'
And he replied,   2790
'I'd burrow into the ground.'
And she asked,
'And what if it follows you?'
And he replied,
'I would fly up in the air.'
'And if it follows?'
'I'd turn into a leaf.'
'And if it does the same?'
'I'd turn into a blade of grass.'
'And if it still does the
    same?'   2800
And he replied,
'I would turn into a ——'
The old woman
said to him,
'Be careful.'
And the man stopped.
The young girl
then asked,
'What was it
the old woman   2810
told you
and you stopped?'
And he replied,
'It was nothing.'

When he had said this,
see the young girl,
she had asked in vain,
then stopped and lay down.
Before daybreak
God's child,   2820
who is a farmer,
got up in the twilight
and began to go
to his farm.
And he told
the little old woman
to take out some millet
so they could pound it
to give to his new bride
to grind and bring to him. 2830
She took out the millet
to give to the girl.
They pounded it
and took the grains,
gave them to the woman
to grind and take
out to the farm.
She ground them,
and when she'd done so,
she began to leave.   2840
Some slender girls
also started to go
and she said to them,
'Oh no,'
they should wait.
They went back home
and she took the flour
and put it in a basket
which she carried on her head.
When she reached   2850
the edge of the farm,
she saw a small thicket
where she stopped
and changed to a buffalo.

With the load on her head,
she hurried on.
God's child
stood up and stared,
took his bow
and his quiver,   2860
drew out an arrow,
began to shoot,
shot and missed.
She came up,
ready to kill him.
God's child
burrowed into the earth
and the buffalo
burrowed there too.
He flew into the air   2870
and the buffalo
flew up in pursuit,
wanting to kill him.
He turned and came down
and changed to a leaf,
and the buffalo
did the same,
wanting to kill him.
He changed to a blade of grass
and the buffalo   2880
did the same,
wanting to kill him,
but without success.
What did he do?
He came to a clearing
and when he got there,
the buffalo
wanted to kill him,
but without success.
He changed to a needle,   2890
got into her tail
and hid there.
The buffalo
searched in vain.

She couldn't see him
and went off to the woods.
When she got there,
he fell out [of her tail]
and when he did so,
the buffalo   2900
began to cry
and said,
'God's child
is a real man;
if he hadn't been,
I'd have killed him
because of my mother
and the way they laughed at me.
However,
the old woman   2910
told him to be careful
and he was.
If he hadn't been,
I think that
this very day
I'd have killed him.'
That is why
the old woman's
advice
you can't   2920
neglect.
And the young men
then asked
'Why is it
that old woman's advice
should not
be neglected?'
Don't you see
God's child,
who spoke again.   2930
'You yourself know
that you can't
do anything.
That's why

you ask
such questions.
Don't you see
that when we go
into the woods
and stay a long time,　　2940
and then come out,
it is our father,
the younger one,
who asks us
about our hunting—
to choose the best man
from amongst us.
When he had asked him,
see the child
wearing his wrist-guard.　　2950
As for that question
which you asked me,
you're a wicked youth;
to know nothing
is a bad thing.
When you do something
and it's finished,
if it comes out well,
you'll know about it,
and if it comes out badly,　　2960
you'll still know
all about it.'
When he had said this,
he went on.
'As for the question
you asked me,
it's about that matter
I'm talking to you.
If you want
to know the reason,　　2970
do a bad thing,
then watch and see.'
When he had spoken so,
he went on.

'Headstrong boy,
if you do something
and they teach you in vain,
one fine day
you'll come up against
some problem　　2980
that'll really teach you.'
When he had said this,
he went on,
'This matter
that we have [in hand]
is a weighty one.
It troubles us
continuously.
What is it?
Our Bagre　　2990
is the grave matter
that troubles us,
together with the girls
and the men
and the women.
What shall we do
about this?
The first people
owned this [ritual],
and when they were
　　buried,　　3000
they should have taken it with
　　them.
But instead they left it for us,
so it troubles us
and we know not what to do.
Young girls,
young men
and old people,
it troubles us all
and we searched in vain.
We didn't know　　3010
and so began to go astray.
The ways of our ancestors,

how can you run
and leave them?
It is for this reason
that we performed this [ritual]
but did so in vain.
Of all the elders
including the younger one,
it is the younger one   3020
who is our great man,
and had his problem.
The beings of the wild
came out and took him
and led him off
into the woods,
where they showed him
many things.
They taught him everything,
except about death.   3030
But we had heard
about death.
It was the younger one
who taught us
how to hoe,
taught us
how to eat,
taught us
how to brew beer,
taught us   3040
how to grow guinea corn,
taught us
how to kill wild animals.
When he had finished,
one day
we watched
the younger one
as he died.
Fear struck us,
we didn't know what'd
    happened.   3050
We seized hold

of a creeper.
We got hold
and began to pull.
But we pulled in vain
and left it for the children,
who then took it.
See the boy
thinking to himself
about the problem   3060
that we couldn't solve.
He discovered
[the Bagre] was to do with God
and the beings of the wild
and we searched in vain.
So we returned
to our father's house.
That man
who knows so many things,
knows about this matter   3070
which we said
was God's affair.
So that one day
we'll save one another
and we'll know
what the first people
were unable to solve.
And then we'll grasp it,
grasp it with the right hand,
never with the left,   3080
so that we'll act truthfully,
not in a deceitful way,
and we'll begin to see
what the truth is
and not tell lies.
The forefathers
searched in vain,
and as a result
we also searched in vain,
accepting   3090
those lies

from the lips of the first people,
from their lying lips,
which they had followed
    fruitlessly
before turning to maggots,
and going back to the earth.
Then we came along
and also said
we would follow
the old ways.   3100
But we did so in vain.
We followed in vain,
got together
and conferred about
the ways of our forefathers,
and then we found out
about many problems
which confront us.
What confronts us?
Don't you see farming,   3110
which came to us?
It's a great boon
that God gave us.
Do you see that
which we feed to our children
and to the women too?
We feed them;
it's with the help of the hoe
that you feed people.
And then they asked,   3120
'Why is it
that a girl
cannot farm?
Do you know the reason
why it is so,
that women
cannot farm?'
The little old woman
asked them
to wait a while   3130

and keep quiet.
Then she said,
'This is the reason
why a girl
cannot hoe.
She is
the one who cooks.
She is
the one who sweeps.
She is   3140
the lighter of fires.
She is
the fetcher of water.
She is a member
of another person's house.
That's the reason
we do not let
young girls
do any hoeing.'
The young man   3150
asked us again,
'How is it
that girls
belong to another person's
    house?'
And the old woman
laughed softly
and then said,
'A young woman
is unable
to stay in your house.'   3160
'Why is it
she can't stay
in your house?'
'She's not a man.
She gives birth
and brings increase to the
    house;
when she has given birth,
for two years afterwards

she sits in a room
and suffers.'   3170
When she finished speaking,
the young man
laughed softly,
and when he'd done so,
he started off home.
The great man
went to his house
and the little old woman
took the path home
and went on her way.   3180
Do you see something,
something that kills,
which they had showed
to the [younger] one?
'What's the thing that kills?'
And he said,
'It's strophanthus
that they showed him
and boiled it for him,
to kill wild animals.'   3190
The young boy
began to leave
and the old woman too
found her path
and off she went.
The [younger] one's
very own child,
a brave child,
was called
Deri.   3200
'Who is Der?'
He is
a person
who was born,
then dies
and comes back,
and then they bear again
and again he dies;

he is the one
they call Der.   3210
He is
a young man,
that's why
they gave him a bow.
He went out
to the open grassland,
hunted in vain
for wild animals,
then returned home.
His wife was present   3220
in the house.
He arrived
and thirst
gripped him.
What was he to do?
He didn't know.
So he called his wife
to fetch cold water
for him [to drink].
See the wife: 3230
she became angry
and refused to bring water.
Anger took hold
of Deri.
He fitted an arrow
to his bow
and shot himself.
When he did so,
the strophanthus,
which makes the poison,   3240
rose and came
out of his nostrils
and killed him.
When he died,
see his wife
crying bitterly.
Many people
heard the wailing,

hurried there
and saw the corpse.   3250
Some didn't know
that an arrow
was able
to kill people.
They thought
that only a wild animal
was able to kill.
But they saw how it was
and afterwards,
two days later,   3260
they took Der,
put him in a room
and buried him.
When they had done so,
they took their bows,
took their arrows
and their quivers,
and they insulted each other
and began to quarrel.
See the men   3270
coming out.
Then that man
drew back his bow.
They were insulting each other
when, after a while,
one of them shoots,
shoots a man.
See the fellow,
God's son,
who laughs softly,   3280
fits an arrow
to his bow
and begins to shoot.
He shoots
and a young man
is felled by an arrow.
You see this?
And they say

that's how it is.
And yet   3290
when someone's
words offend you,
you take a stick
and try to hit him.
Do you see
it's the truth
that lies there?
Do you see them?
Two days later
the girl   3300
wore her long dress
and went to the market.
When she got there,
see [two] young men
about the same size,
one is Ziem
and the other is Naab.
They see the girl
and how pretty she is.
They say to each other   3310
that they will have her.
So they send a slender girl
to call her over.
She called her over
and when she came
she sat herself down.
She sat down quietly
and they got some beer,
filled a calabash,
gave it to her.   3320
She begins to drink.
See her husband,
red with anger,
coming over.
See his bow
and his quiver.
He comes over
and starts to flick

on his wrist-guard
so it makes a noise.   3330
And he said,
'It is fear
takes hold of Naab,
and Ziem too,
and they don't know what to do
except sit quietly.'
They sat quietly,
but his anger
was uncontrollable.
See the husband   3340
start to aim.
He shot at Ziem,
he shot
and killed him.
When he lay dead,
the old women
told them
to stop all this
and hold back,
and they began to wail.   3350
See the people,
so many people,
running there.
They saw Ziem
lying dead,
and didn't know what to do.
What did they do?
Ziem's clansfolk,
the young men,
were longing to fight,   3360
and the woman's husband
and his clansfolk,
they also came,
longing to fight.
They met together
in the open grassland
and began to shoot,
and shot till they tired.

See the dead
piled high on one another.   3370
The old women
began to wail.
The elder
came out
and put on his wrist-guard.
He reached the place
and told them
to stop all that.
They did so
and then he said,   3380
'In this affair,
one single girl
has killed many youths
and the husband
has also died.'
And they said,
'If you are able
to sit quietly and learn sense,
your reason will return.
What sense?   3390
The sense I speak of
is that over one woman
they killed many men.
This is the reason
all the elders
are sitting together,
thinking what to do.
They came out
and shouted loudly
to tell them all   3400
to keep quiet.
When they were quiet,
what did he say?
[The elder] told them,
'The being of the wild
taught us
about many things,
but with one exception.

And that was
about death.   3410
He taught us
about that poison;
he showed us strophanthus,
which we use to kill
wild animals
for food.
But this evil matter
which has come upon us,
what is it?
It happened   3420
that Deri
went hunting;
he went to the woods
and returning home,
asked for water.
But when he did so,
he didn't get it
from his wife.
Anger
took hold of him,   3430
so he didn't know what to do.
Taking out an arrow,
he shot himself
and died.
We saw this
and we said
a brave man had died.
We got up
and started to play
with his arrow.   3440
Look at the dead
now upon us.
If the youth had been a man
and had gone
to play with a woman,
he wouldn't have gone
and played
with arrow matters.

This death
that killed our children,   3450
we call it
God's death.'
The [younger] one
then said
it wasn't God's death
that troubled us.
'What trouble
comes amongst us?'
'It is that
shooting yourself   3460
with an arrow
or cutting yourself
with a knife,
a person, who is a real man
and has sense,
will be much afraid
of such a death.
If anger seizes you,
and you're a real man,
you go out   3470
and take your axe,
and your bow,
and your knife,
and your arrow,
and wear a quiver,
and go into the woods
taking your anger with you.'
'And what sort of thing
will you do there?'
'A male animal   3480
when you meet one,
kill it,
cut off the head
and hurry home
to your father's house.
Then they'll know
that you are
indeed a real man.'

One day
the younger one   3490
called his children
and his wives
and told them
to be quiet.
When they were quiet,
he spoke, saying,
that they call
upon God
but don't know him.
And he continued,   3500
'When you die
you will know God.'
'How is it
that you know God
only when you die?'
And he replied,
'During the time
when you're on earth
you speak of many things.
When you die,   3510
you will understand
the words you speak.'
And he said
'About God,
when you die,
it's then you'll see him,
like the younger one
and the spider,
and know God's place.
[God] told us   3520
that the child,
he created,
and the man,
he created,
and the girl,
he created,
and the old woman,
he created them all.

He created them,
but what do they give him? 3530
They give him nothing.
And he told them
to find a fowl
and catch it,
and take a pot,
fill it with water
and put it [on the ground].
They took an empty pot
and put it [on the ground].
When the time arrived,   3540
the rain came
and raindrops
fell into the pot.
They collected this,
then went to the river bank
where they saw something.
What was it?
An oyster shell.
They collected this
and came to the house.   3550
Then they went off again
into the woods
where they saw something else.
What was it?
The leaves of a tree.
What leaves?
Ebony leaves.
They cut these
and the [younger] one
hushed them,   3560
and when they were quiet,
he told them
to dig for roots.
They did so,
and when they'd finished,
they went home.
When they reached
their father's house,

they saw something else.
What did they see? 3570
A large tree.
They dug up some roots,
all digging together.
The elder,
who tells great lies,
told them
to take the roots
and twist them together.
They twisted the [roots]
and when they had done so, 3580
he told them
that one thing remained.
And they asked,
'What is that?'
'The mahogany tree,
its roots belong
to the beings of the wild.'
And they said,
'What shall we do?'
And he told them 3590
they should go
to the foot of the tree
and dig for roots
and add them to the rest.
They dug these up
and [he] told them
to twist them together
and put them in water.
'In what water?'
And he said, 3600
in the water
that came from the raindrops.
They should put them in
and bring a cock
to sacrifice and see.
And they asked,
'How shall we kill it?'
He replied,

'If you kill it
and the cock 3610
falls on its side,
you will know
that it's a kind god.
If it lies
on it's belly,
you will know
that it's not
god at all.
If it falls
facing upward 3620
on its back,
you will know
that this
is god.'
So they killed the cock.
A being of the wild
made a cloud of dust,
covered them all
and came there
to sit beside them. 3630
As they killed it,
he stretched out his hand,
caught the fowl
to turn it over.
The female being
told him
to turn it on its belly.
He said to her
he didn't want to.
'I've done nothing, 3640
and yet you call
my name,
so why should I spoil it.
That's the reason
I caught the fowl
and turned it face upwards
on its back.'
The elder

laughed softly
and took a calabash; 3650
he with his lying mouth
put water in it,
and with his hand
knocked it to see.
When he had done so,
what did he do?
He spoke, saying,
'This ritual
we performed
and it helped us, 3660
and we knew
that it held the truth.'
See the being of the wild,
he turns around.
What did he do next?
He didn't know,
got up quietly
and went on his way.
When he had gone,
they saw the place 3670
that was now clear
and we couldn't help
starting again
to perform it.
We performed it
and told the children
and the women
that this matter,
any child
who is clever 3680
should get hold of
and put in his head,
because he thinks
that one day
we can help each other.
'How help each other?'
'To do this,
we speak

to the children.
We say 3690
that all of them
cannot succeed in this,
but one child
amongst [them]
will know all.'
We finished speaking
and saw
there was a thing
we couldn't understand,
for many things 3700
are involved in it.
'What are these things?'
'We saw
that the male bat
is one of our Bagre creatures;
the damdamwule bird
is also one
of our Bagre creatures;
the male crown bird
is also one 3710
of our Bagre creatures;
the male kyaalipio bird
is also one
of our Bagre creatures;
the belibaar bird
is also one
of our Bagre creatures.
They are many
but not so many.'
And we said, 3720
'Since it is like this,
let us perform it
and get it over.'
The speech
was finished.
'Beings of the wild,
you came back
at the break of day.

You came back
and you troubled us.'   3730
'Troubled us how?'
Our bellies ached,
our heads ached.
Since they ached
and we know not what to do,
we ask the beings.
'I believe
you created us,
and put us on earth.'
They laughed softly   3740
and we asked,
'Did they create us?'
And they answered 'Yes'.
When they said this,
the [younger] one
asked again, saying,
'There's a certain thing
which they said
was the great thing
that created us.'   3750
And the being
asked him,
'What sort of thing?'
And [the younger] said,
'We hear his name
but know nothing of him.'
And [the being] asked,
'If you've heard his name,
what is it?'
And he replied,   3760
'His name
is God.
I, the younger one,
was the man
who knew his home
a long time ago.
I came down
to the Earth shrine,

and other people
were there   3770
whom they called
beings of the wild
and you silenced my question.'
And the being
laughed again
and asked,
'Why is it
you mention
the Earth shrine?'
The [younger] one   3780
sat on the ground
and touched the earth
to show him.
And he said,
the younger one,
'It was I,
and the elder one,
we were two.
We two,
we came   3790
and stopped at a place;
this place
was a flat rock.
We stopped there
and had no house
and no room
to sleep in.
So we went
to learn something
at God's house.   3800
We spoke with him
and when we had done so,
we found the path
and went home.
Now you've heard
the matter that relates to God.
The elder one
lay down at night

and said
he was in pain   3810
and I thought
it was a joke.
Shortly afterwards
he was on the point of death.
He died
and after his death,
I left him
lying there,
saying,
I will go   3820
and lie beside him.
I did so,
and in three days
the corpse began to rot
and I still lay
resting there.
His body putrified
and after it had done so,
on one occasion,
during the night,   3830
someone else
came there
and called to me
to come down here.
I did so
and he took me
into the woods
for three years.
He showed me
many things,   3840
and after he'd done so,
I went back home.
Some time later
he returned
and came to my place
to teach me
what it was
that I should do.'

'What was it?'
'He said   3850
I should build the walls of a
    house
and when I did so,
he asked me
what I would do next,
and I told him
that I knew
what to do.
And he said,
"Do it so I can see."
[I tried   3860
and failed,]
so he took a post,
fixed it in the ground,
and when he had done this,
he told me
to get some grass
and cover it over,
so that if rain came
it would protect me.
The being of the wild   3870
then told me
to wait a while.
I did so
and he took a post,
and fixed it in the ground.
After he'd done so,
he took another log,
brought it over
and put it on top.
He put it on top,   3880
and after he'd done so,
what did he do next?
The [younger] one
watched what he was doing.
What did he do?
He went out,
got what he wanted

and came back.
Many sticks
he placed criss-cross.　　3890
When he had done so,
he took some of these
and laid them on top.
When he had done so,
he took some earth
and covered it all over.
He did this and gave it me
so I could live there.
What shall I do?
He told me　　3900
to watch what he did.
I watched.
He took some earth,
covered the top,
and when he had done so,
he told me
to climb up and see.
I climbed up
and stood there,
and became afraid.　　3910
"Don't let me
fall through."
"But it won't break."
The sky became dark,
and when it did so,
the rain came
and it stood firm.
I slept there
and was happy.
One matter remained　　3920
that still troubled me.'
'What is it
that still troubles you?'
I said,
'My elder [brother]
died there
and I abandoned him

to stay here.
What shall I do about him?'
The being of the wild　　3930
replied, saying,
that to this place,
one year hence,
he should take a fowl
and go and sit
on the flat rock
and call his name,
his elder [brother's] name.
When he had so done,
he should think about　　3940
the thoughts
he has in his head
and kill the fowl.
'I thought about them
and killed the fowl
and the fowl fell down.
What was I to do?
I didn't then know
what to do
about that fowl.'　　3950
The being of the wild
told him
that when it fell down
he should sit and watch it.
'If it turns on its belly,
you know that
your elder [brother]
is angry with you.
If it should fall,
legs in the air,　　3960
on its back,
you know that
he agrees with you.'
When he had spoken,
that man
accepted the fowl
which fell on its back.

T

He laughed softly
and got up to leave.
The small being   3970
then asked him,
'What was the name
of the place
you went to?'
He turned and stood there
and thought,
thought to discover
the name of the place.
He couldn't think of it
and laughed softly,   3980
and said that
his elder brother
slept there.
'It is
as if it were
the skin of the earth (*teng gaana*).
Therefore
I'll call it
my Earth shrine (*tengaan*).
And that is why   3990
people know it
by this name.
If you stay in one place
and leave for another,
you always wait
till they find
a minor Earth shrine
   (*tengaanble*)'.
'What is this shrine?
'You will ask'
them to take   4000
a certain stone
to give you,
and you put it down
at the place you live.
It will be
the Earth shrine,

and it is that
they call
a minor Earth shrine.
Do you understand?'   4010
They finished speaking,
and when they'd done so,
they then asked,
'We want
to know
who created man?
We saw
a person
who called himself
a being of the wild.   4020
We ask the meaning
of a being of the wild?'
And he replied,
'I cannot tell
the meaning of the name
they gave to us,
but let us play.'
'What kind of game
shall we play?'
We sat down   4030
and he took something
and put it in a gourd.
We didn't know
what he took out,
but it's like water.
He told us
we should drink some
and we said
we wouldn't drink it.
And he said   4040
I should taste and see.
I took some and tasted
and it was good.
And he said
I should sip it.
So I drank a little

and it was good.
He asked me to drink,
and when I had finished,
he also drank.   4050
He had said earlier
that he could not tell
the meaning of his name
so I could understand.
But right now
he wanted to speak
about that matter
to me.
What did he say?
He then said   4060
that his name
was *kɔntɔme* [being of the wild]
and the meaning
is that
'he cannot come near you.'
So he spoke,
and when he'd done so
[the younger one] began to
   laugh.
When he had finished,
the [younger one] turned   4070
   to him
and asked,
'Is it you
whom they call so?
Was it you created man?'
And he replied,
'It was I
who did so.'
When he had spoken,
what should we do?
God's affairs   4080
bring much suffering.
Let us attack
one problem first.
We asked

about the affairs of God,
whose name we hear
but don't see.
And we asked again,
'Who created man?'
and he replied,   4090
that he created man.
When he had finished,
we asked again,
'Who is it
that they call
God?'
And he replied,
that if we say
it is God,
then it's a lie.   4100
If God
exists,
then it is he
who is God.
And we knew all this
to be a lie.
We didn't know what to do
and retraced our steps
to find out
who created man.   4110
We traced back
till we came
to the younger one,
for it is he
that was the first man,
and he told us
it was God
that created man
and the beings of the wild
and the fowl   4120
and the leaves
and the animals
and all things;
and stones

and guardians
and deities.
What shall we do
to know his ways?
Then one man . . .
'Who was it?'   4130
It was Napolo,
the younger one's
eldest son,
who said,
'I hear what you say,
I have heard it all.
However,
will you please
excuse me
while I say something.'   4140
They were quiet
and he went on,
'I heard what was said
and the thing
that I say
is not meant to humiliate you.'
Then he asked a question,
asked the children,
asked the women,
asked the men,
'If you say   4150
it was God
who created us,
then he created us
to do what?'
We said,
'The question
you ask
is a sound one.'
And he said,   4160
'God
created us
and put us on earth,
saying

that we should
obey his commandments,
fear him,
respect him
and follow his word.'
And [God] said   4170
there's a certain person
he created,
whom we cannot see.
And when he
gets to know us,
none of our affairs
can go right.'
And we asked,
'What person is that?'
And he replied   4180
that [you] people
should accept
what he has said.
'You say
that you agree.
You agree
and then go and ask again.'
'What is it
we should do
to follow your word?   4190
What is it
that we should do
to respect you?
What is it
that we should do
here on earth
to fulfill your ways?
For you say
those people
were created by you   4200
and put
upon earth.'
'If you people
accept my word,

then you reject theirs.
If you agree
with my word,
this affair of yours,
you'll understand
and perform.
Two days later,   4210
see the people
[gathered] there.
They came there
to deceive you.
They deceived you
and you say
you'll follow them.
You follow them
and you say
that if you follow them,   4220
you'll find the truth.
You followed them
and I withdrew my hand.
Some day
you will come
and tell me
about something you see
there on earth.'
So he spoke.
The distant ancestors,   4230
those people
who lived first,
they rejected his words.
They rejected that way
and followed the beings.
They continued to do so
and came to this point.
God's child
asked them a question.
He asked them,   4240
asked them quietly,
'What happened
there on earth?'

'We said
we would follow
your words.
And we began to follow them,
and as we were doing so,
a certain person
deceived us, saying   4250
that if we follow him,
we would know the truth.
And we followed him
and thought that
the truth
lay there
and we could understand it.
But we followed in vain.
What single thing
did you give us?   4260
The things of God
are many
that you taught us.
A hoe it was
you gave to us.
We had it with us
when we descended
to earth.
And you said
we should keep it,   4270
for it is something
that one day
could help us.
We kept it
and we reached
the earth.
We kept it
and it is the one thing
that helps us.
The being of the wild   4280
deceived us
to go into the woods,
where he took us,

changed us to what he wanted,
and turned our senses.
So that the elders,
those first people,
went off
to God's country
and reached that place.'   4290
God's child
began to ask them,
to ask a question:
'What did you say
to God?'
We said
we had agreed
to follow
his words,
that we would   4300
respect him
and we would
fear him.
So we said,
but came upon
a being of the wild
who told us
that if we followed
his own words,
we would discover   4310
the truth.
We followed,
and when we had done so,
we turned again
and said
we would follow
your words as well.
But we had forgotten how
and searched in vain
and came to you again   4320
at God's house.
And we said
that you and your words,

we will respect them
from today.
But, we said,
right now
we are unable
to repair the harm.
So we asked   4330
what we should do.
And you said
there was something;
you would lead us
and help us to understand.
And we began to think,
to sit and think.
And you said
that about this matter,
you must wait a while.   4340
A certain person
came to us
and wanted to question us.
And we said,
ask so we can see
what is peeping out.
What is peeping out?
It's a stone [from the Earth
    shrine]
which came there
and said   4350
'God,
you created me,
put me on earth
and told me
that God's children
are many,
but we cannot
understand one another.
So you spoke, saying
that all of us   4360
can speak,
but we can't understand

each other's tongues.
However,
one day
the younger one
slept beside me
with his elder [brother].
They lay there
and the elder one   4370
came near to death.
He died there
and when he did so,
the younger one
went off to the woods
and left us.
We lay there
for three years
before he returned.
One day,   4380
with another person,
he came up to me.
They came there
and he took something.'
'What sort of thing?'
'It was a fowl,
a live fowl.
He then came
right up to me
and sat beating   4390
till I ached,
but I said nothing.
Why was it
I said nothing?
You [God] said
I shouldn't speak
to my fellow beings.
Even if he makes a fire,
I should keep quiet
and lie there.   4400
Yet all of you
who speak

of many matters
on this earth,
you will come
to my place.'
So he spoke;
it was the first people,
who went there.
He spoke,   4410
and when he had done so,
he began to ask,
'About what matter
did he talk to God?'
He said,
'When you created me,
did you say I could speak
with anyone?'
And he replied,
'I didn't say so.'   4420
And he asked again,
'When you created me,
did you say
I should get up
and go to people
and talk with them?'
And he replied
that he didn't say so.
And he asked again,
'When you created me,   4430
did you say
I should have life
to give to people?'
And he replied
that he didn't say so.
'Well now,
one day
the younger one
brought a companion
and came here;   4440
this red-head
came and took up

one of my stones
and beat me
until I cried.
Yet you said
we mustn't
understand one another's
speech.
So it happened;   4450
I said what I had to say
and he did not understand,
but went on beating me.
And when he had finished,
instead of leaving me,
he picked up
the chicken
and cut its throat.
He took the blood,
poured it on my head,   4460
and after he'd done so,
he said that,
if I am anything at all,
if I have life,
I should watch over him
and see he comes to no harm.
Still I remained silent,
and God's raindrops
fell down,
beat upon me   4470
and cleansed me.
They did so,
and two days later
the younger one,
the red-headed man,
came back again.
They came here
with a chicken
and again beat me
till it hurt   4480
and I began to cry.
But I cried in vain

for they continued to hit me.
When they had finished,
they took the blood
and poured it over me again.
That's the reason
I came
to God's place.
You are God   4490
and have great wisdom.'
And [God] said
we should sit down.
They sat there
and when they had done so,
what did you do?
The affairs of God
bring great suffering.
And God
took something   4500
as large as the sun,
put it over our head
and said,
'Look at that'.
And he replied
he was looking at it
and saw
it was a skin.
And he said,
'The thing you earlier   4510
told me about,
this is it.'
[The younger one] said,
'I am lost.'
And [God] asked,
'How did you get lost?'
He replied,
'Someone
led me astray.'
'Who did?'   4520
And he replied,
'The small being it was,

he led me astray.'
And he said,
'The being of the wild,
did you hear of him
on earth?
Did you see him
walking around?'
And he replied   4530
that he didn't see him.
'Did you hear him
speaking
to you?'
And he replied
that he heard him.
'You and who else?'
And he said,
'I alone.'
And God said,   4540
'Did he come to your house?'
And he replied,
'He came
to that place.'
'Did the women see him?
Did the children see him?'
And he replied
that they didn't see him.
'How was it
they didn't see him?'   4550
And he answered,
'I alone
can see him.'
Thereupon
he said,
'Since you saw him
on your own,
call him over here.'
He called,
called his name.   4560
The being
was sitting near,

but he called
and there was no reply.
There was no reply,
and when this happened,
God spoke
and said,
'But you claimed
you understood his speech   4570
like he understands you.
How is it
that he didn't answer?'
And he replied,
'I don't know.'
Then God
himself
called [the being's] name
and he answered.
And [God] told him   4580
to come and hear
what they were saying.
He came over
and stood on his own
and [God] told [the man],
'Stand up and repeat
what you told me.'
And he replied,
'I said
you created me   4590
and put me on earth
and told me
to obey your words,
to fear you
and to respect you.
You told me this,
and then said
you would create a person
who would come and deceive
    me.
And he came   4600
and told me

that he too obeys your words,
so I thought that,
if I obeyed him
I was also obeying you.
I obeyed
but did so in vain,
for he deceived me,
spoke his words,
went into the woods   4610
and led me astray.
This is what
I told you.'
The being of the wild
used his cunning
and asked God,
'God,
when you created me
and put me on the earth,
did you tell me   4620
to speak to people?'
He replied
he didn't tell him.
'Why was it
that that man
came and told
this to you?
Let me ask so I can understand.
When you created me,
did you tell me   4630
that mankind
would see me?'
'I didn't say so.'
And he said,
'When you created me,
did you tell me
that mankind
could understand me?'
'I didn't say so.'
And then he said,
'When you created me,   4640

did mankind and I
live together?'
And he said,
'You lived together.'
'How then
could I deceive him
and spoil your plan?
He it was
of his own accord   4650
who abandoned you.'
[God] said,
'Now that
you've come to my place,
do you know
what to do?'
He replied,
'I don't know.'
And [God] told him   4660
to sit there.
He sat down
and when he had done so
[God] took something hot
and put it over his head.
'Younger one,
you walked round and saw;
when you saw how it was,
you should have spoken
so that we
could abandon the beings.   4670
But you didn't speak.
Because of this
we know
that our beings
are both bad
and good.'
'Why are they bad?'
They said,
'The [elder] one
who died and went away,   4680
he saw

the evil things
they brought
upon him.
And we
cannot abandon it.'
'Why is it
we cannot abandon it?'
And they said,
'As our elder,   4690
the younger one,
suffered,
so we also
must suffer.'
When they finished,
God's child
asked once more,
'If a person
walks in front of you
and says that   4700
he is going
far away,
and he goes
and you follow,
and he gets lost,
and you know
that he is lost,
then, to get to where you're
    going,
will you follow him?'
And he replied,   4710
'If I knew the place
I was going,
I wouldn't do so.'
'How was it then
that you knew
he was lost
and yet you followed him?'
'It was
an ancient affair,
the grandfather's affair,   4720

the grandmother's affair,
the agemate's affair.
The [younger] one
brought his ritual,
which became a problem
and troubled him.
But it is he
who owns us.
So it was
that we search in vain   4730
and suffer greatly
but still follow
the [younger] one's path.
Yet we know
that one day
it will harm us.
The reason
that you cannot
abandon it
is that when your elder   4740
is in trouble,
you don't forsake him.
And so it is
that we follow
the being of the wild.
We know that
the first men
went astray
and that one day
we'll suffer for it.'   4750
'How did it happen
that we met a being
who was our companion,
yet came to deceive us
and we searched in vain?'
'Ancestor,
it is because of you
that we cannot
abandon it.
That is why   4760

we could do nothing
except be afraid.
We followed him,
knowing that
one day
we'll suffer for it.
Do you understand?'
'What happened to us
so that we went astray
and came to this point?'   4770
One day
a certain person
came and said,
'What happened
that we
went astray and came to this
    point?'
And we replied,
'One of our people
whom we were following
went astray.   4780
That's why
we too are lost.'
And that person
then asked,
'If you took a path
and went along it,
many of you together,
and lost your way
in the woods,
then realized   4790
you had gone astray
but knew the way home,
would you go back?'
He replied
he would turn around,
go back
and tell people about it
so they could go out
and try to find them.

So he began to turn back,   4800
to turn and take the path
to his father's house.
He began to go home
and walked along
and went into the woods.
And he followed a person,
the very being
who wanted him to stray
and who said,
'My friend,   4810
wait a while.'
The man stood still
and [the being] told him
that he had something
to teach him.
And he replied,
'There was another person
you taught,
my master, the younger one,
and he went astray.   4820
I heard about him,
how he is there
in the land of the dead
and undergoes
great suffering.'
'What sort of suffering?'
'He rejected God,
rejected his words,
rejected his works.
Yet it was he that created   4830
    you,
moulded your body,
gave you legs
gave you breath,
and gave you a head
so that you breathed.
You breathed,
yet rejected his words
and followed your friend.

Your friend
knows what work   4840
he will do.
It was on account of this
that you [found yourself]
going astray.'
'That is how
I went astray.
I was going home
and met a man
who told me
I should obey him.'   4850
When he finished speaking,
what did he do?
'Do you see that person?'
'Which person?'
'The male being
with all his cunning,
he deceived the boy
and he stands there,
waits around,
waits for nothing.'   4860
'The being of the wild,
how did he get
that name?'
'Do you see
how the man turns around
and starts to follow him?
He follows him
into the woods.
Do you see the man
burst out laughing?   4870
He follows the being
and goes astray.'
'Why has he gone astray?'
'The being of the wild
took him along
into the woods.'
'What did he do there?'
He took an object

a dry skin bag,
he took it   4880
and took some stones
and some roots,
an oyster shell
and some cowries,
mixed them together
and then said
that he saw something.
'What was it?'
He heard the question
and tried to find out   4890
through divination.
And he said,
'Wait till I divine,
divine and find out!'
He took the diviner's stick,
struck the ground
and said,
'Your ancestor,
the younger one,
is in God's country,   4900
and it's happiness
that he feels there.'
So he spoke.
See the man,
how happy he is.
'What did he do?'
He laughed softly
and turned again
and saw the path,
the path of helpfulness,   4910
which he followed.
'Which path?'
And he said,
'Down that path,
if you follow it
and know it,
you will help
many people.'

And he told him
to speak so he would   4920
  know.
And he began to divine
and told him
to put his hand in his bag.
He raised his hand
and put it in the bag.
When he had done so,
what did he do next?
He told him
to take out an object.
What was it?   4930
He took out
my leather bottle,
the Bagre container.
And he told him
to tap it.
After he'd done so,
he put it down gently
and took a bell
and a guardian
and a rattle.   4940
He took [the rattle],
held it in the air,
then put it on the ground,
held it up on his right side,
then on his left.
When he had done so,
he said
he would shake and see.
He stroked his head
and after he'd done so,   4950
he greeted the beings,
greeted God,
and greeted his bag.
And after he'd done so
he greeted *Bara*
and then *Base*.
After he'd done so,

he saw the way ahead
and said that
he greeted the Bagre elders,   4960
greeted the White members,
greeted the Black members,
greeted the hill,
greeted the pool,
greeted the open lands,
the red-headed people
and the black-headed ones.
He greeted them without delay
and went on his way
to the river bank.   4970
'It was the old man
with the pipe in his mouth
and I greeted him
without delaying.
Red-headed people
and black-headed ones,
I saw them all
and greeted them together
and hurried out
to take the path,   4980
and in a thick copse
there I met
the old man,
pipe in mouth,
and I greeted him
and his children,
both the black-headed
and the red-headed ones,
I greeted them all.
When I had done so,   4990
I hurried on,
took the path
until I reached
the top of a high hill
where I greeted
both the red-headed
and the black-headed ones,

and their initiates,
both the White ones
and the Black.   5000
I greeted them all
without delaying
and I turned again
and ran back
till I reached
the white cave
and his children,
both the red-headed ones
and the black-headed.
I greeted them,   5010
and when I had done so,
I found the path
to my father's house.
I ran there
and when I arrived,
do you see something
of great importance?
It is *Bara*
and the guardian
and the deity   5020
and the god
and the being.
I greeted them all,
all of them together.
They are not cowries
that I can sit counting
one by one.'
He arrived there
and when he'd done so,
he took a bell,   5030
put it on the ground
and then said,
'It's the truth
I want to tell
the children.
In this affair
that we perform,

whose way
do they follow?'
And some said   5040
it was the way of God.
And others
said that
it was the beings' way.
He took his leather bottle
and he said,
'If it is
God's way,
the cowries will tell me.'
He watched the cowries   5050
and they denied
it was God's way.
And he said,
'If it is
the beings' way,
the cowries will tell me.'
He threw the cowries
and they fell favourably.
And he said,
'If you [ever]   5060
said that
the brother
was lost,
he's lost no longer.'
A certain matter
pressed upon him.
He performed it,
and when he did so,
what didn't he get?
He got food,   5070
got cows
and sheep
and goats
and chickens
and women,
he got them,
got them all.

In God's country
what is there
to surpass this?   5080
Because of this,
the children
turned their heads
to face the beings,
they turned their hands
to hold out to the beings.
They caught them
and began to greet.
They greeted them,
and when they had done
    so,   5090
they left this matter
and turned to another.
What matter was that?
And they said,
'As we are here
on this earth,
what can we do
to beg a head
that sits on our shoulders?
How can we   5100
[learn to] speak
the truth
so that it helps us?
Do you understand?'
And they said,
'If you want this,
you will walk
in your grandfather's
footsteps
and follow them.'   5110
So it was
that we followed in vain
and began to run,
began to go off
and enter the woods.
That person

who led the grandfather
that begat us,
told us
to follow him.   5120
We could do nothing
but follow.
And we heard of a matter,
a new matter.
'What matter was this?'
A farming matter,
a birth matter,
a bow matter.
That is why
this matter   5130
we said
was a new one.
What can we do
about birth?
What can we do
about farming?
What can we do
about shooting?
We didn't know.
And we said again   5140
that we would ask
at God's place.
God's child
became angry
and said,
'That man there
who showed the path
for you to follow,
and you followed,
he is your God.   5150
Because of this
we Dagaa people
know we are lost.
We know this.'
Therefore
they said,

'If you ruin something,
ruin it completely.'
And so,
see the child   5160
who forsook
God's way,
he asks,
'If you bear a child,
does he follow that path,
the path of the beings?'
They answered
and agreed, yes,
that's what they do.
'If you bear a child,   5170
the being's path
is the one he follows.
If you marry a wife,
the being's path
is the one she follows.
About the ways of God,
we hear his name
but we have ruined it.
It came to pass
that we ruined it,   5180
ruined it completely.
Do you understand?'
'But this matter,
our Bagre matter,
which we are seeking,
why is it
we seek it?'
And they said,
'We want
to know what to do.   5190
What can we do?
We do not know.
We searched in vain,
and so go out
to collect our initiates;
and when we have done so,

we divine for them,
but without success.
And we come back
and sit together.'   5200
'What matters
do we talk about?'
'Meeting matters
we discuss together.'
'And when we have done so,
what do we do?'
'The affairs of God
bring great suffering.
Do you understand?'
'If we always call   5210
upon God's name
and he answers,
why should we forsake his
    path?'
'This is the reason
we turned back,
wanted to ask,
divined together,
but divined in vain
and turned again,
like an antelope's tracks   5220
running across the ground.'
'What can we do?
If we lost our senses
and fell into error,
what can we do
about this matter?'
'To us
God [himself]
gave sense
to hold on to,   5230
but we failed to do so
and fell into error.
So it is
that we begin **Bagre**
by asking God

that many should be there.
The god who comes,
that one
is our god.
He is   5240
the truthful god,
who taught us
what to do,
so all was well with us.
The god with a good heart,
that one
is the spider
who showed us
God's place.
The god with the mark between
    the eyes,   5250
he is
a human being,
the younger one.
The elder one,
he is
the striped god.
God's child,
he is
the tom-cat
and his mate.   5260
The god with the white arse,
he is
the male fly
and his mate.
The thieving god,
he is
the being's child.
The lying god,
he is
the small being.   5270
The troubling god,
he is
the elder one's stone.
And so

we assemble
our children [for Bagre],
sit them down
and give them knowledge.
Then a child
who is thoughtful   5280
will know the matter,
which at this time
we still perform,
so that one day
we may help each other.
These things we do,
though they can't banish death.'
'But this our matter,
I had thought that
it was able   5290
to overcome
death?'
'It can't do that.'
I acquired this sense
to protect myself
but it has changed
into a troublesome sense
for us.
It is I
who had this sense,   5300
but it changed
into a lying sense.
I had this sense
but it changed
into a treacherous sense.
I had this sense
but it changed
into an untruthful sense.
Too much sense
is the thing   5310
that ruins a man's head.
Too much foolishness
is also what
ruins a man's head,

though not as readily.
On account of this
we searched in vain
and then turned back.
Then he said,
'How did we   5320
change our sense again?
What sense
could change
a troublesome sense?
What sense
could change
a treacherous sense?
What sense
could change
an untruthful sense?'   5330
And he said,
'My sense
could change
an untruthful one;
this was what
said one thing
and then denied it.'
He finished speaking
and began to cry out
and the people   5340
became quiet.
They did so
and began to speak
about what had finished.
What matter was that?
The suffering matter.
What matter?
The treacherous matter.
What matter?
The untruthful matter.   5350
And who
is your untruthful person?
The being's child
is my untruthful person.

He it was
who deceived me
about the ways of God
so I fell into error,
and one day
I suffered greatly.   5360
If you ruin some matter
and offend your fellows,
you can make it good.
If you ruin some matter
and offend God,
you can do nothing.'
'What was it
that offended God?'
'It was rejecting his words.'
'What was it   5370
that offended God?'
'It was leaving his ways.'
'How was it
I went astray
from God's path?'
'I declare
it was
the spider
who is the one
who knows God,   5380
and I began to follow.
When I did so,
an evil person . . .'
'Who is
your evil person?'
'The being's child,
he is
my evil person,
whose evil
led me astray,   5390
whose evil
ruined my thoughts.'
And now
the younger one

reached God,
who made him undergo
much suffering.
'What suffering?'
'He rejected his words;
that is why he underwent 5400
much suffering.'
'What suffering?'
'The suffering,
that is
going astray.
I knew
I had to suffer.'
Children,
do you see?
Children, 5410
do you hear?
Women,
do you hear?
This thing
which must be hidden,
is hidden with us.
If I teach you,
and teach you everything,
hold it
with your right hand, 5420
hold it
in front of you,
hold it
with pleasure.
And so
he told the children,
in this matter
he doesn't follow
the lying person.
In this matter 5430
he doesn't follow
the untruthful person.
In this matter
he doesn't follow

the treacherous person.
He follows
the boy
who is thoughtful
and is always there
to teach you. 5440
This takes
three years.
You know
the affairs of God
bring great suffering.
But I hold it,
keep it in my hand
and look after it.
I understand
in two days' time 5450
we'll enter
the White Bagre room.
I understand
in three days
we'll enter
the White Bagre room.
I think that
on the third day
we'll enter
the White Bagre room. 5460
When I go in,
if a young lad
begins to speak
and does so well,
he's like an old guinea cock
which begins to peck,
pecks and leaves for others,
pecks briskly.
This is what
pleases me, 5470
for the children
to know it.
We will greet
you, Bagre god;

we will greet
you, being's god;
we will greet
you, Bagre guardian;
we will greet
you, being's guardian.   5480
And that is why
I say to you,
in this room,
it is a many-sided matter.
I cannot
teach you it all.
To show you
would take
three years,
or even six.   5490
That's why
they call it
the Black Bagre.
It is
a matter of childbirth.

That's why
they call it
the Black Bagre.
It is
a matter of bows.   5500
That's why
they call it
the Black Bagre.
It is
a matter of farming.
That's why
they call it
the Black Bagre.
It is
a matter of chicken-
    breeding.   5510
That's why
they call it
the Black Bagre.
And now it is finished,
I tell you.

SUMMARY OF THE BLACK BAGRE

Invocation (1). The two men are troubled by the supernatural powers and the younger sets off in search of a solution (11). He meets a river being who shows him how to cross the river (39). On the other side he meets an old man who asks him about his troubles (106). In the forest beyond he meets the beings of the woods (131). These beings of the wild show him how to eat corn (153), and how to cook porridge (177), and how to smelt iron (212), and how to make fire (240). They build a smelter (263). They forge an iron tool (309). They called it a chisel (364). They make a hoe (370), and show him how to use it (393), and how to grow corn (410). The younger one then decides to approach the supernatural powers (431). When he has prayed to them, he sees the rain and the earth having intercourse (451). The earth gives birth to a slender tree (464). He tries to climb up to the skies by way of the tree (479). He falls down, but is helped by the spider (485). They find the old man in the skies, surrounded by animals (505). The old man tells him to bring some earth (521). Then he calls a slender girl and shows them how to create children out of the earth (530). The old man's wife, a wise old woman, shows the girl how to care for the child (645), and how to deal with the afterbirth (663). She tells her the child came from her belly (735). The girl argues and tells the story of how she came by the child (741). One day the younger one passes by and sees the child (821), which he then wants to take with him (832). They argue about the ownership of the child and the old woman hurries up to find out what the quarrel is all about (839). She suggests they take the matter to the old man (872). The old man asks the girl about the cause of the quarrel and she tells her story (893). He asks the same question of the younger one (901). As they cannot agree, he asks the child, who replies that the younger one is his father (950). The younger one tells how he found the child in the skies (978). The old man adjudicates the ownership of the child by seeing whether the man or the woman can urinate more accurately down a hollow reed (1079). The younger one wins and is awarded the child (1111). He takes the child to his house (1154). He shows him his shrines (1164). The wet season comes and the child starts to farm (1171). This pleases his father very much (1185). But a scorpion bites the child (1197) and the younger one hurries off to see a diviner (1207). There he meets the girl who again claims the child (1240). The younger one consults a diviner, who lays out his gear (1279). He diagnoses a deity as the cause of the trouble (1330); it is the deity of meetings, that is, of Bagre (1340). The younger one thanks every one concerned (1347), including the diviner's bag (1357). He then goes home and calls his son (1384). Later on the boy sees the girl and recognizes her as his mother, despite his father's objections (1408). But the mother leaves without him (1472). The younger one goes to the woods and meets a being of the wild (1483), whom he asks to teach him how to make a bow (1501). The being then sends his child to take the younger one to the blacksmith's house in order to get some arrows (1559). He tells the blacksmith how the being's child taught him to make the bow, which he brings with him (1576). The smith tells his child to make some charcoal (1631). Then he works the forge's bellows (1678). He heats a worn axe-blade and beats it into an arrow point, which he fixes to a reed (1720). The being's child and the younger one return with the bow and arrow (1736). When the younger one arrives home, his son rushes out to meet him and inquires about the bow and arrow (1759). The younger one shows his son how to shoot (1790). The boy gets hold of the bow and shoots his mother while she is sweeping the room (1809). The father stops her from beating the child (1836). Two days later the boy shoots his father (1849). This time the mother stops him from beating the child (1871). A dove eating corn at the foot of a mortar is killed by a hawk (1890). The boy thinks he has shot the dove and takes it to his father (1906), who shows him how to divide up the meat (1922). The mother asks how they will get another child (1931). The father says he will go and see God about it (1941). Meanwhile the woman goes into the bush and sees a boa constrictor and his wife playing a game (1952). She asks the snake to play the same game with her. He does so, she is pleased, and he tells her that this is the way to get children (1984). She goes home and shows the man what to do. He too is pleased (2007). The man still wants to go to see God, but the woman refuses (2025). Sometime later her belly swells (2040). The man becomes afraid and wants to see God, but the woman tells him not to worry (2045). Sometime later her belly aches and he goes to see the beings of the wild (2072). The being divines for him and says that his wife has given birth to a child (2084). He goes home and finds a baby crying (2160). The old woman tells him God gave it to the girl (2181). He refuses to believe this and wants to call the child Der (2199). The old woman repeats that God sent him and his name is Number Nine, because ten children will follow him (2230). They have ten more children, and all grow to manhood (2257). One day the father gets God's child to show them how to shoot (2273). Later they aim at an antelope and miss it (2297). God's child shoots the antelope and in searching for it comes across some beings in a hole in the ground (2305). They show him how to make poison for his arrows (2332). He goes home and shows his father, who refuses to believe him (2397). He goes into the bush and shoots a roan antelope (2448). The father divides the meat in the proper way (2486). Some time later they see a buffalo and her calf (2503). They kill the buffalo but leave the calf (2521). Some time later the younger one and his sons see a beautiful girl near their farm (2578). The sons want to marry her (2600). She gets them to have a shooting contest (2616). God's child hits the target (2643). The little old woman takes the girl to the father's house (2661). She becomes suspicious of the girl (2688). God's child returns from the farm and takes her to his room, where she refuses to lie on any of the skins (2710). When he produces the buffalo skin she bursts into tears, for it is her mother (2739). She asks him how he killed the buffalo (2760), and what would he do if a dangerous animal tried to kill him (2786). In reply to her questions,

he tells her of his various stratagems, until the old woman warns him
(2804). One day God's child goes to the farm and asks his wife to
follow with some food (2819). She avoids her companions, follows him
and changes into a buffalo (2844). She charges her husband, who shoots
and misses (2862). He escapes by adopting the stratagems he had told her
about (2867). She does exactly the same until he comes to the point where
the old woman stopped him. Then he changes into a needle and hides in
her tail (2878). She gives up the search and he gets away (2893). So you
should take the advice of the old woman (2917). Why? ask the young men
(2922). Because even God's child, who knows more than all of the children, didn't know this (2928). They are reprimanded for their ignorance
(2955). The narrator explains about Bagre (2981). It is something that
troubles us (2990). It came from the first people who left it behind when
they died, and we didn't know what to do (2998). It is the younger one's
way we follow (3018). The beings took him to the woods and showed him
everything, except about death (3023). Then he showed us how to hoe,
to eat, to brew beer, to grow corn and to kill wild animals (3031). Then
one day he died and we were afraid (3045). We didn't know what to do
and tried in vain to find an answer (3049). Then we realized that the
Bagre was the affair of God and the beings of the wild (3061). So we
returned home, to learn about Bagre, to get to know more than the first
people (3066). For we had followed their lying ways and did so in vain
(3089). But they have taught us some things such as farming, which came
from God (3110). They ask why girls cannot farm (3121). Because they
cook food, sweep, make fires, fetch water, and build up people's houses
(3136). How do they build up other people's houses? (3152). Because they
must give birth and suffer (3165). They all disperse homewards (3171).
About arrow poison (3181). The younger one's son, Der, goes hunting
(3196). When he returns, he calls for some water (3218). His wife refuses
to bring it to him (3230). So he commits suicide (3237). Many people
come to the funeral. They now realized that arrow poison could kill a
man (3247). There is a quarrel (3265). A man is shot (3274), and God's
son has his revenge (3278). Two days later a girl goes to the market (3299).
She is invited to drink by two twin brothers, Ziem and Naab (3311). Her
husband approaches angrily (3322). He shoots Ziem (3342). This starts
a fight between the two kin groups (3358). An old man brings the fighting
to a stop (3376). The elders get together and inquire into the cause of the
matter (3394). It started with Der's suicide (3420). Suicide is not a man's
way out (3459). If you are angry, go out and shoot a wild animal (3468).
One day the younger one tells his children that they will know God when
they die (3489). God created man. But they give him nothing (3520). So
they made a shrine for God (3534). They catch a cock to sacrifice (3604).
If it falls with legs outstretched, they know the shrine is really for God
(3619). The being of the wild turns the cock so that it is accepted (3625).
The elder finds the matter confirmed by the being's deception (3648). As
a result, they go on with the performances (3669). The children should
learn it well, so they can help each other (3678). He speaks of the Bagre
animals (3702). There is more trouble on earth caused by the beings of

the wild (3726). The beings are asked if they created man, to which they agree (3740). The younger one asks about God (3747). He tells how he went to God's place and came back to the Earth shrine and found the beings (3763). The being asked what the Earth shrine is (3776). The younger one tells how he and the elder one dwelt on a flat stone. They had nothing and went to God's place to find out about this (3802). Returning home, the elder one died. The younger one lived with the corpse until it putrified (3810). One day one of the beings called him into the woods, where he spent three years and was taught many things (3829). He returned home and the being showed him how to build a house (3843), and how to make a flat roof (3863). He inquired about his elder brother (3922). The being told him to sacrifice a fowl every year, which he does (3929). The being asked what the name of the place was, and he replies, *tengaan*, he sleeps on earth. He explains about the Earth shrine (3968). They ask who created man and what are beings of the wild (4014). The being explains in a roundabout way (4019). The being says that he created man (4072). But we know from the younger one that God created all things (4105). Napolo, the younger one's eldest son, asks a question (4133). 'Why did God create us?' (4153). He created us to do his bidding (4165). And he put someone on earth to see to our troubles (4170). These were the beings of the wild (4198). God replies that if you accept his word then you must reject that of the beings of the wild (4202). The ancestors rejected God's word and followed the beings of the wild, so he withdrew (4230). Napolo asks what happened on earth (4237). We met a certain person who deceived us and we followed him in vain (4244). It was God who gave us the hoe (4264). The beings deceived us and we went off to visit Heaven (4280). We had agreed to follow God (4297), but were deceived (4306). They asked how they could repair the harm (4326). God replied that he would show them a way, but that meanwhile someone else wished to speak (4334). It was the Earth shrine who says, God created me, and put me on earth (4348). But I cannot speak to humans, nor they to me (4357). One day the two men came and slept on me. The elder died and the younger one took to the woods (4364). After three years he returned with some other people and they made a sacrifice to me (4378), but I didn't speak (4392). Two days later they came again and performed another sacrifice (4472). Because of this I came to see God (4487). God arranges to protect the Earth shrine from people by means of a skin (4498). The younger one announces that he is lost. God asks how? He says the being of the wild led him astray (4510). God asks the younger one if he saw the being on earth (4524). The younger one replies that he had heard him; he came to his house (4531). To test him, God asks the younger one to call the being to come over (4556). But he does not come (4564). How is it, God asks, that you can claim to understand his affairs, yet he did not answer when you called him? (4567). God called him and he came (4576). At God's behest, the younger one repeats what he had said earlier, that God created him (4586). But the being had deceived him (4599). The being admits he was created by God but asks how he could deceive a fellow creature, whom God had made so different (4614). He claims the younger one left God of his own accord (4647). God addresses the younger one, asking him if now that he has come to see him, he knows what to do. He says that he does not know (4652). Younger one, when you wandered and saw how things were, you should have warned the rest of us, so that we would abandon the beings. For they are bad as well as good (4666). Why bad? (4677). Because the elder one had died, after suffering greatly (4678). So we cannot abandon his path (4686). God's child asks why it is that you follow someone who has gone astray (4695). Because it is a traditional affair, we follow it even though we suffer (4718). When an elder is in trouble, you don't forsake him; so we follow the beings (4741). We went astray and will suffer for it (4769). On his way he met the same being who first led mankind astray (4802). He speaks to the being about leading his master, the younger one, astray (4817), and leading him to deny God (4827). But the being succeeds in leading the son astray too (4851). He takes his diviner's bag and empties the contents on the ground (4878). He says that the younger one is happy in heaven and that his descendants should follow his way (4904). He continues to divine (4921). He begins by greeting all the supernatural beings (4951), the old man with the pipe (4971), the high hill (4994), the white cave (5006), and the shrine at the father's house (5018). Then he takes the diviner's bell (5030) and divines with the cowries to see whether this is the way of God or of the beings (5040). The cowries show it to be the way of the beings, not of God (5053). So they are lost no longer (5062). By following this matter, he got food, animals, and women, as much as is to be found in God's country (5067). So now the people turned and followed the beings (5081). But they are still worried about the truth (5093). They are told, 'If you want what the younger one had, then you must do what your grandfather did' (5105). They heard of a new matter that concerned farming, birth, and the bow (5123), and they went to ask God about it (5140). But God's child is angry and says that the being is their God (5143). That is why we are lost, completely lost (5150), and follow the beings' path (5166). So they begin to perform the Bagre (5193). Why did God let us lose our senses? (5222). God gave us sense and we failed to use it (5227). So we begin Bagre by praying to God that other gods should be there (5233). These gods are explained (5237). We teach the initiates these things (5274). But they cannot banish death (5287). His sense has changed (5294). It was the being's child who deceived him and made him offend God (5353). He rejected God (5357). This is what caused them to suffer (5390). The initiates are asked if they understand (5408). They are taught how to hold the leather bottle containing cowrie shells which they are given during the Bagre ceremony (5417). The initiates are encouraged to learn the Bagre (5436). Two days from now they will perform the white Bagre (5450). Even a young lad can recite (5461). But to teach all about the Black Bagre would take a long time (5483). It is for birth, hunting, farming, and raising livestock (5995).

NOTES TO THE BLACK BAGRE

1. I find the construction of the opening phrase obscure; K. G. first suggested, 'For the sake of God', a modification of my own translation. Girault gives the opening phrases of Bagre as follows (1959: 333):

mwin tî	Dieu était au commencement.
mwin bo n'o?	Que fit Dieu?
mwin yoghri	Dieu donna une impulsion.
yoghrè īr nibè:	Celui qui donne l'ébranlement créa les hommes:
kã kworbè	le cultivateur de mil,
nō gwōlbè	l'éleveur de poulets.

The sentence *o tin a yir*, means 'he laid the foundation of the house'; *ulɔ ti ku ti*, 'he began it for us'. This translation is therefore adopted here.

It does seem to be God that is being addressed. Lines 5234 ff. read:

> we begin Bagre
> by asking God
> that many should be there.

This passage is followed by the key to the gods that appear in the invocation.

An alternative version of the opening was given to me by K. G. as a comment upon the key to the end of the Black Bagre (B. 5265). I reproduce it all because of its great interest. Note the counterpoint behind the insults and praise names offered to God (or god), and the association of dead and living, made explicit in the notes. He writes: 'I do not think the description of God as a thieving god has anything to do with the non-initiates (*dakume*) who steal the bambara beans on the eve of Bagre Night. . . . To me, *ngmin naayuo*, although literally a thieving god, is a sort of exaltation of the God, *ngmin*, the God with many features. This appears in the Birifu version as:

ngmin ti	god began,
bɔbɔ ngmin	the god of initiates.
maa buɔl fu	I call you,
fu sɔɔ baar	you answered me.
kã n lɛ tu	Then I insulted you,
ngmin gagaara	a lying god,
ngmin naayuo	a thieving god,
tu lɛ zu	I abused and greeted you,
ngmin po paal	a loving (fulfilling) god,
ngmin nyɔ tuɔn	a god with mark between the eyes.
faa yel ka	You told me
kã nyɔɔ bɛrɛ	to approach the 'elders'.
bɛrɛ bɛ nyinɛ?	Where are the elders?
liɛb bufulɛ	Turned to maggots

liɛb kpɛ teung	and gone back to earth.
faa yel kaa	You told me
kã nyɔɔ bili	to approach the young ones.
bil be nyinɛ	Where are they?
liɛb bufulɛ	Turned to maggots
liɛb kpɛ teung	and gone back to earth.

In this Birifu version the *bɛrɛ* and *bili* link the White and Black Bagre together. In the White Bagre it was *tɔ kpɛ̃ɛ̃* who could not sleep because in a vision he had seen God who told him wonderful things about Bagre. So the next day he went to the diviner to inquire. But now *tɔ kpɛ̃ɛ̃* (plural, *tɔ bɛrɛ*) has turned into maggots and entered the earth. Similarly with *tɔ ble* (plural, *tɔ bil*).

Each section of Birifu will begin Bagre only if the elders of the section receive a vision from the *ngmin* (god) telling them to do so. Here *bɛrɛ* are the elders of yesteryear—i.e. forefathers, ancestors, etc. Similarly *tɔ bil* are the youngsters of yesterday but the forefathers or ancestors of today.'

An earlier version from the same source began:

ngmin ti	god began,
sããkum ngmin	grandfather's god,
makum ngmin	grandmother's god,
ma buol fu	I call you,
ngmin po paal	god with a good heart,
ngmin sɔɔ goba	the god with stripes.
fu sɔɔ bar	You answered me
kã n lɛ tu	and I abuse you,
ngmin naayuo	thieving god,
tu lɛ zu . . .	I abuse and greet.

2. The invocation used in the Black Bagre represents a radical shift from the invocation in the White. There the major categories of supernatural agency were addressed. They were addressed in a double capacity, both as causes of the present difficulties and as the sources of help in the ceremony which was aimed at solving those problems. Here it is the god of the initiates that is addressed together with the other agencies appearing in the myth. The 'key', in a very deliberate sense, is provided at the end (B. 5233). Meanwhile it should be said that 'the god who comes' is there revealed as the Bagre deity.

The other named deities addressed also refer to the Bagre ceremony. 'The mark between the eyes', 'the black and white stripes', and 'the white arse' all refer to the way in which the neophytes are treated when they are whitewashed. The epithets, thieving, lying, and troubling, link up with other aspects of the Bagre (see B. 5265 ff.).

12. The byre is the only room of a LoWiili house that has an external door; the room does not communicate with the rest of the house. It is here that the ancestor and other shrines are to be found.

13. In the White Bagre, it was the elder of the two companions (brothers) who began. Here it is the younger one.

21. *Base* is a clan shrine as well as a medicine shrine. In B. 1381 it is described as 'the owner of the house'.

23. I translate the verb *puoru* as 'greet', though it also means to pay one's respects to a person, to pay him obeisance, to thank, or to worship. In itself the verb is devoid of hierarchical significance, though it is always the junior who first 'greets' the senior. 'To greet softly' is to approach someone in a respectful manner. In this context, it does not mean that the younger one sacrificed to the shrine *Base* but rather that he acknowledged it. Indeed the term is not used for a major sacrifice, though *bun puoru* ('a thing of greeting') does describe an initial offering made to pave the way for a subsequent transaction of greater substance (Goody 1962: 405); this category would include small offerings of grain made to all household shrines when the harvest is gathered in or the kind made when a man sets out upon a journey. In B. 446–50 the greeting of the supernatural agencies is apparently purely verbal, the equivalent of an invocation (*kaab*, which I also translate as 'pray').

32. The canoes used locally are dug-outs. Formerly any traveller in the wet season would need to make a river crossing either by canoe or by holding on to a large gourd (Binger 1892: ii, 81). It is a canoe that transports the dead to the other world across the River of Death (Goody 1962: 371 ff.).

41. One of the beings of the wild that inhabit the river.

44. Leaves draped from the rear of the waist were the usual wear among the 'pagans' of the savannah country, though 'Mossi' cloth, purchased from itinerant traders from the north, was worn on special occasions. The leaves are as characteristic of a woman as the quiver is of a man.

49. The stone is a stepping-stone on which he treads before entering the dug-out canoe. I have altered my original wording, which was *kure* (iron).

53. The form 'begins to' (*iɔng na*) is a recurrent formula of Black Bagre. In both texts such phrases punctuate the composition, though perhaps this is also a device for giving the Speaker time to think what follows. I have been told that the formula *iɔng na* is used regularly in the White Bagre and *irɛ na* in the Black, but the present text does not bear this out.

70. The being of the wild paddles the canoe across the river. *Vuur* is the usual word for paddle.

82. This is the usual way of carrying the axe-adze, which is used as a defensive weapon.

89. The stick used to moor the boat.

94. The frog and the reed are river objects; I am not aware of any other significance the LoWiili attach to them here, though the former is included among the Bagre animals (W. 4569). *Pure* is a type of tree with a sour fruit which is used as a laxative; I might have mistaken this for *kpurɛ*, a grove by a river or swamp. N.B. *tɔ* = to pound, *tɔɔ* = to pull.

106. The old man reappears later in his proper abode, that is, heaven.

117. The line is too long for the rhythm.

119. This is one of many shifts of person and similar changes between direct and indirect speech. In analysing a literary work, one would be correct in demanding a specific 'functional' explanation for any such change. The very nature of the written medium demands a high degree of consistency in these respects, the work itself being constantly open to retrospective checking on the part of both author and reader. But oral delivery moves in a single direction for both reciter and audience; moreover the immediate context of transmission is of far greater significance. The shifts to the first person are partly the result of the reciter switching from reporting a scene to acting it, and the significance of such changes may lie in the field of reciter–audience reaction, desire to obviate boredom, or to impress upon the initiates the importance of the occasion and the lesson, and upon other considerations of a similar kind. The consistency, one might say rigidity, that characterizes literate forms is not a requirement of oral composition, at least to the same extent.

128. In Tallensi, *Naawun yɛla ba mar' wɔmhug*; M. Fortes suggests 'God's doings bring great burdens'.

129. The encounter with the 'old man' is a brief one. Having crossed the river the younger brother goes deeper into the forest where the beings show him the main elements in man's technology. The river has some similarities with the River of Death since God's dwelling place, in one sense, lies on the other side. So that the encounter with God perhaps establishes his role as creator and in this sense superior to the beings of the wild. The relationship emerges more clearly towards the end of the narrative.

133. The 'key' which is provided at the end (B. 5233) differentiates between three 'beings of the wild'. The being himself (*kɔntɔme*), the child of the being (*kɔntɔm bie*), and the small being (*kɔntɔm ble*). I did not at first realize that a tripartite distinction was being made and, owing to the similarity of the written forms *bie* and *ble*, and of the abbreviations used, I may have made a mistaken attribution in dealing with these characters.

145. Overpowered me spiritually so that I began to wander off the normal path.

151. The younger brother appears to be telling God the story of how he found himself in the forest. But there is another shift from description to participation and he begins to enact rather than recount the events he experienced. God is set aside until later.

154. 'Caught' is also a metaphorical usage describing the influence of supernatural agencies on a man when they want him to establish a shrine in their name.

158. Guinea corn: the word is also used more generally for grain.

159. This is not a myth of agricultural origins alone. Man owes all his technology to the beings of the wild, including the bow.

167. The line is too long for the rhythm.

169. His right hand, of course.

184. The LoDagaa would smile at this suggestion. For them the deeper meaning of this passage has to do with man's dependence upon supernatural agencies even for the basic productive and reproductive processes.

212. Low-grade iron ore (laterite) is widely distributed in West Africa and smelting occurred almost everywhere. There was a lot of iron produced among the LoDagaa, judging by the extent of the remains of recent smelting operations.

246. *o'a, o ba*, he has (high tone on *ba* makes it negative).

296. K. G. suggests an extra line: *o'a yel kaa*.

299. *kpib, gbili*, quiet.

302. *fɛɛ* represents the air rushing out of the bellows.

327. *mhuɔli*, to beat flat; *ɔɔla*, to bend up.

334. He held the iron with his tongs (*kyeba*); the sense is cut short.

342. Or *gwoli*, to spring round (R. T.).

374. The term 'left-handed' (*gobasob*) is used to describe diviners and smiths; the former grasp their divining sticks with their left hands.

380. The line is too long for the rhythm.

421. 'God's child' is the 'son' of the younger brother (see B. 1270), who is also called Napolo and was created during the younger brother's visit to heaven. Here it is perhaps a term for the younger brother. The original is 'god's child'; the phrase is sometimes used in a general sense, e.g. B. 4355–6, 'God's children are many'.

436. See B. 23. The verb *puoru* I translate as 'greet' and also as 'thank'; here it refers to the dead and hence implies worship, but the LoDagaa do not usually distinguish verbally between communication with the dead and communication with the living, except as far as 'prayer' (*kaab*) is concerned.

453. *dindam* refers to size; one can say of an elephant, *o ara dindam*. The word is used only of animals and men.

454. The analogy between vegetable growth and human fertility is drawn yet more clearly here than in the White Bagre.

464. Or possibly *woyo* (R. T.).

466. The earth's child, the tree, stands opposed to God's child, man, though God created all.

468. The last 340 lines (from 130) can be taken as an account to God of the younger brother's meeting with the beings of the wild. The story now reverts to the encounter with God himself. The intercourse of rain and earth gives birth to a slender tree which provides a ladder to heaven.

485. The spider (also *ngmindɛr* or *mundɛr*, a specific type of spider) is here, as elsewhere in the savannah country, a hero, even a trickster. In this particular scene it is his ability to produce a web that makes him so useful

to man. Spider tales, though not as numerous as in Ashanti, are told at night by groups of children and adults. But, writes K. G., they are not connected with 'Bagre reality' but are considered as 'fairy tales'.

487. Or possibly *kyã kyaari*, to stand astride something (R. T.).

489. The word *nikpɛ̃ɛ̃* is difficult to translate, since it means 'old man', 'big man', or 'elder'; the phrase 'big man', often used in West African English and in New Guinea pigeon, seems misleading here. It refers to an important person (see also B. 524, 596, 742, 4756).

492. *baalu* or *zuom* (adv.), sitting without moving or talking; here 'leave it quietly'.

508. In centralized societies in the region chiefs sit on skins, but the LoDagaa rarely do so.

512. The dogs were a feature of the first encounter with God; here God is again accompanied by some of the larger and more important wild animals.

527. The subject is God. He takes some earth in order to create (or re-create) humanity.

532. 'Slender girl' is of course a stock phrase in both parts of the Bagre.

537. The explicit associations of pot and okro are with container (vagina) and sexual fluids. The okro has a thick, white glutinous fluid which is often compared, in a ritual context, to semen and the white of an egg (Goody 1962: 113).

547. The imagery is of course of procreation.

560. The younger one is told to take his left hand, used for sanitary purposes and for other 'dangerous' tasks.

570. This could be cat or leopard, but *luɔra* is used for leopard in B. 514. *nanyu* is the LoSaala term for cat; in Birifu the word is *diubaa*.

576. Those with whom I have discussed the matter saw no special significance in the cat and the fly. 'The cat digs; the fly hovers around food, defecates and goes off again' (K. G.). 'Bagre food brings many flies; the non-initiates are like flies, coming only for food' (K. G.). None of these responses assign any specific relevance to these animals.

579. *nyɛ* (low tone), shit; high tone, see. The reference is to the laying of eggs (1111).

584. The meaning of the discovery (virtual creation) of the child by cats and flies is not understood by those with whom I have discussed this matter. Nor is it at all clear to me as an observer, though one could offer a comment about the participation of the animal world, wild and domestic, in the creation (or perpetuation) of mankind. N.B. *kuɔri*, to scratch; *'yeb*, to pinch, grip.

647. *biɛ*, wise, but also strange.

651. Every 'family' has certain leaves which it uses to prepare an infusion to bathe new-born children and their mothers.

712. In Tale *pɛn* is the vagina; here it is the pubic area of both men and women. The Waala call their pubic hair *pɛn kɔɔlung*, though in Birifu they prefer *yɔ kɔɔlu* for men (*pa kɔɔlu* for women). A man can say *n pɛn paala*, I want to urinate (lit. my *pɛn* is full).

774. M. Fortes points out that in Tallensi the equivalent would mean 'circling round and round'; but no such implication is present here.

776. The concept of *diɛnɔ*, play, here (as often) refers to sexual inter-course.

847. K. G. comments: 'This line is too long and out of place. It should have been line 845 and the reciter should have corrected it in the following way:

lɛ lɛura	Changing the theme,
maa yel ka	I said that
bi ma na	the mother
ni tɔ ble,	and the younger one,
bi bein iɔng	for the sake of a child,
baa iɔng na gɔ̃	they were about to quarrel.
pɔɔ nyɔ̃ɔ̃ biɛ	The wise old woman
duur wa ta	hurried over,
o'a nyɛ lɛɛ	saw what was up,
lɛ yel ka	and then said . . .'

851. *gɔmɔ* means dispute as well as noise; the two ideas are closely interwoven since most noise is human noise and indicates a quarrel.

981. This is not the only time when there appears to be an identification of the spider and the elder brother. See the references to the younger and elder brother going together to heaven in the later sections of the myth (B. 3802). But 'brother' is also used in a very general sense.

1033. It is clear from this passage that it is God who directs the younger brother to the 'child' of the being of the wild, by whom he is shown many things.

1059. The younger brother has the earth, the girl has the pot (vagina), God has the okro (semen).

1099. The test administered by God is somewhat weighted in favour of the man; it indicates male dominance and virilocal marriage rather than patrilineal descent.

1217. The guinea corn, which was to pay the diviner, is first shown to the household shrines.

1266. To 'laugh softly' is perhaps better translated as 'to smile'. As in English (and as with 'laughing loudly'), this act can generate mutual pleasure or interpersonal hostility.

1270. Concerning Napolo, see W. 883, B. 421.

1300. Concerning the bell, see W. 2016.

1302. The wooden figures are known as *baatibe* or *bɔtibe* and are used in divination (Goody 1962: 368).

1318. The neck of the bottle is knocked so that the cowries fall out and give the answer to the question. There are usually twelve cowries so that the answer is not simply limited to a binary yes–no, although the shells are also used for this more limited purpose (e.g. 'falling favourably').

1352. These are not specialist occupations; most people engage in all these tasks at one time or another. The reference seems to be to humanity going about its business.

1445. The duality of parenthood is continually stressed throughout the Bagre.

1502. That is, about the bow.

1537. The bamboo is sometimes grown in clumps near houses and sometimes taken from the woods. The 'bow-string' is made of a sliver of bamboo and is fixed to the bow by leather loops. To tighten the 'string' ready for shooting the bow-stave has to be bent and the leather loop raised a notch, a task requiring a lot of strength.

1564. The 'small hoe' and the 'blunted axe' are discarded tools, the iron of which is then used for making arrows.

1664. The smith's son is charged with making the charcoal used in the smithy.

1685. K. G. comments that the narrator appears to have got the sequence out of order. When this happens, he should alert the audience to his mistake by introducing a comment like the following:

ala ba baari	This is finished.
ti'a bar ala	We leave this
lɛ lɛɔɔra	and go back.
sããnsob no	The smith
de o gani	took a skin,
burdaa gan	the skin of a he-goat,
ir o miur	and a rope
boor kpil puɔ . . .	from a small granary . . .

Then l. 1700 should read:

ka ba naa	This is where
ka ti dɔɔ tua	we left off.
yaa nyɛ bie	You saw the boy
o'a ir zî be	go and squat down
a sãan zu iɔng	at the head of the forge.

1732. The greatest reed of all is the one used for the shafts of arrows.

1735. Here as elsewhere in the text the process of naming an object (or a person) is seen to be a significant aspect of the process of creation.

1772. The gift of a bow makes a child into a man, or at least a male; young boys will be seen shooting small animals with their bows; little girls play different, less aggressive games.

1814. N.B. tɛna nyir, he shot and missed; o tɛna puni, he misfired.

1815. The boy achieves manhood by shooting.

1826. Lit. the big room's dust (LD. *saγr*, pl. *sagɛ*).

1832. The leaves cover her pubes from the rear, which is where the sexual approach is made. M. Fortes points out that the shooting of the arrow may carry the added meaning of incest. Certainly it is paralleled (B. 1866) by the Oedipal aggression of the son against the father—a direct attack upon his virility. This account of the growth of God's child is a paradigm of individual development, the attainment of manhood by differentiation from one's parents, a process that inevitably involves conflict between the generations.

1833. If you hit something soft, the usual expression is *o tɛna ngmib*; if hard, *o tɛna ka bageng*.

1886. The father temporarily rejects his son when his virility is threatened.

1905. The clicking of the tongue is a sign of victory, a kind of ululation.

1910. Father and son are reconciled when the latter proves himself as a hunter and the farmer understands that he can depend upon him in old age. He has become a man and accepted his responsibilities. The flesh of the dove is divided between both parents who now think of having further children.

1956. See note for B. 94; *man tuur*, river bushes, climbing plants; *man nyɔrɛ* (LD.), roots of river trees (*nyɔi*, roots or nostrils).

1959. The snake is a creature of the earth, often associated with its shrines; the spider, with its high-strung web, has closer links with the sky, though he plays the part of an intermediary (as a 'brother' of the younger one) between man and God, between earth and heaven. He is 'the god with the good heart' (B. 5245), though he is also accused of leading mankind astray (B. 5378).

1972. I'm pleased, *n yangan* (skin) *nome*, or *n puɔ* (stomach) *pɛlɛna*.

1983. The verb 'sleep' (*gan*) is used here rather than 'copulate' (*nyib*).

1988. The association of snake and penis are of course widely reported from many cultures; here it is quite explicit.

2065. Possibly divining.

2074. *ngme kyɛl*: a man does this as a sign of triumph, e.g. when he has killed an animal in the hunt. The phrase is also used of a call of alarm for both men and women. But when women express joy they will ululate (*kuyiir*). Woman will also *la heli* (giggle), especially when drunk; young girls do the same when wanting to attract the attention of boys.

2092. These are the contents of the diviner's bag. The fibre is used by women for weaving baskets (R. T.).

2207. Possibly *biɛ*, wise, but elsewhere I read *ble*, little.

2227. 'Der' is the name given to a child whose elder sibling has died. It is often thought to be the same child coming back again, not only the 'soul' (*sie*) but the 'body' (*yangan*, 'skin') as well. One way of telling a returned child is by its body marks.

2316. K. G. comments that the sequence of the story seems to require the insertion of a passage like the following:

naangmin bie	God's child
o'a tu ulɔ	followed him
zɔ ti kyeni	and hurried along
bɔɔ nuɔr iɔng	to the opening
a ti nyɛ	where he saw
kɔntɔmbiiri	the beings of the wild.
on in ngmin?	What will he do?

2322. The wild animals of mankind are the domestic livestock of the beings of the wild (see W. 2690).

2361. *Strophanthus* is the active ingredient of the arrow poison.

2445. For this lineage ceremony, see Goody 1956: Plate 5 and p. 69.

2501. Earlier the dove was divided (B. 1930); among the LoDagaa, this is rarely a domestic animal, but it feeds domestically and is attacked by a wild predatory creature, the hawk. Here the 'first' formal division of game takes place, a pattern for all future distributions. Note how the norms of reciprocity among friends (*ba mine*) are more specifically tied to direct return than are those among kin; one is direct, the other indirect exchange.

2508. The following long incident is a type of transformation story found widely throughout the world. The hunt of one individual by another through a series of physical transformations is a common theme of folklore in West Africa as elsewhere. Many examples are given in Stith Thompson's *Motif-Index of Folk-Literature* (revised, Copenhagen, 1955–8) under heading D. 615. 'Transformation combat. Fight between contestants who strive to outdo each other in successive transformations.' An example of a different kind from West Africa is found in the legend of the Dispersion of the Kusa, where 'le héros-magicien', Jagu Marê, transforms himself in order to attack the tyrant, Garaxe. 'Il se transforme en deux najas noirs qui allèrent s'introduire dans les deux babouches de Garaxe à Kélampo' (Meillassoux 1967: 122–3).

2510. *dɛu*, from *dɛungdem* (*dẽdẽ*), to stand straight; *kyen daadaa*, to go straight, at once. The word is also used for truthfulness, uprighteousness.

2555. The diverging interests of men and animals, of hunter and hunted, of killer and prey are clearly recognized in this narrative which generates a certain sympathy for the victims of man's search for food. I have argued elsewhere that such attitudes lie behind the animal taboos often called totemic (1962: 101, 120); I refer to those prohibitions of the kind found generally throughout Africa.

2563. The crying of the young buffalo is contrasted with man's laughter; laughter indicates both pleasure and superiority (see B. 2908).

2591. The buffalo calf who has changed (*lɛba*) into a young girl.

2620. Archery practice (*tɛfa*) is a common sport among the LoDagaa.

2649. There is some recognition of biological heritage even though a man belongs to the patriclan of his *pater* (social father, i.e. mother's husband) rather than his *genitor*.

2677. The wrist-guard gives protection against the bamboo 'bow-string' flicking against the wrist.

2731–5. I am ignorant of the English names for the different types of antelope.

2771. Proverbial names are very common among the LoDagaa.

2827. It is usually millet (*pennisetum*) that is eaten in the farm; the flour is mixed with water to make a browse.

2845. A new bride will normally be accompanied by a band of young girls.

2849. Women carry even the smallest 'loads' on their heads, often in their personal basket.

2921. The wisdom of old women is widely recognized among the LoDagaa. Those who have stayed in one house know as much about the shrines and medicines as the lineage members themselves; they have helped 'to build the house' by giving birth to children and are anxious to protect it from danger.

2933. You can't do anything on your own.

2937. This passage appears to be a 'wrong lead'; the narrator starts off on a certain tack and then decides (B. 2951) that he has not finished with the earlier theme.

2941. The original read *ti m'a wa yir*, which means 'we do come home'.

2947. LD. *sɔyo*, middle.

2950. The gesture is one of pride as a hunter.

2981. LD. *sey*, to satisfy.

3052. *ɔra* is probably *Landolphia senegalensis*, a wild rubber plant which has an edible seed. It is used as a fibre for tying bundles of firewood and for fastening the roofing sticks on a thatched hut. It can also be used in funeral ceremonies as a 'rope' to restrain the bereaved. The reference is clearly to death and it is suggested to me (by K. G.) that 'like the creeper, death never ends'. We tried to root out death but failed. 'We tried to save ourselves'. But there is possibly a further reference to divination (1310).

3095. *bufulɛ*: 'an insect that sucks blood'; 'if the floor of your room is not well beaten (to give a hard surface), these animals will come out of the ground at night and suck your blood. If your children urinate on their mats or in their rooms, you will find these animals there. When found, they are buried at once.' These are maggots that feed on people's flesh and breed in damp places; they seem to epitomize the fear of the bad things of the earth.

3096. Contrary to many assumptions about societies of this kind, there is no automatic respect given to the ways of the ancestors; these are not always right.

3103-4. Literally, 'we sat on the ground and turned back to follow the leg of the first men'; if you make a mistake, you turn back to find out what went wrong.

3107. K. G. thinks that this should read 'our problems are solved by farming'. I had earlier translated it as 'and then we saw the many matters that had come to us', i.e. farming, given to us by the younger one.

3135. The sexual division of labour is laid down.

3145. The division of labour is linked to the principle of marrying-out.

3152. The conflict between a woman's natal and affinal ties is openly recognized in this series of questions and answers.

3237. The beginning of suicide.

3277. The beginning of war.

3289. The myth is much concerned with the introduction of weapons, death, and fighting into the world. The present section treats first of suicide and then of feud.

3301. The long dress (*ganzuole*) is worn by girls who are unmarried or who have not yet given birth; from in front of the waist hang long strings of plaited grasses which reach down to below their knees.

3302. Particular markets recur every six days; they are meeting-places for people from miles around who come to make purchases, sell goods, consume food, and drink beer. It is also the place where 'debts' tend to get settled, though the market shrine places a heavy sanction on any bloodshed (Goody 1956: 104).

3306. These are the names given to twins, Ziem being the first-born.

3313. A girl is approached through a female intermediary.

3322. 'Husband' seems here to have the significance of betrothed.

3329. He flicks the bowstring against his wrist guard in a threatening fashion.

3331. 'And he said'. The narrator intersperses a comment. But K. G. thinks the phrase, '*faa nyɛ ala*', 'you see this', would be better here.

3353. People literally run to funerals, anyhow as they approach the stand where the corpse is displayed (Goody 1962: 97).

3389. The beginning of peace.

3448. One possible implication is that sex is a substitute for war. But more specifically perhaps it is suggested that a man could gain his ends more subtly than by fighting.

3452. 'God's death' is a phrase also used when an old man dies (Goody 1962: 209); it refers to an accidental death, one for which no other supernatural cause has to be found.

3468. The younger brother advocates that those in a suicidal frame of mind should take out their anger on wild animals. The slaughter of animals is recommended as a substitute for the slaughter of self.

3502. K. G. suggests this line would be clearer if split as:

> *fu na bɔɔ na*
> *ti bɔɔna naangmin*
> *baa lɛ soor*

3519. The other world is sometimes referred to in ordinary speech as God's country (*naangmin teung*); the idea expressed here is present elsewhere in LoDagaa thought.

3530. In Africa the creator God is rarely the object of sacrifice or similar offering.

3532. This formula looks like one for creating a rain shrine (*saa ngmin*), i.e. the pot for rain water, the oyster shell from the river, the leaves of ebony and mahogany trees. The shell and leaves are both linked with the beings of the wild. Tree-roots are associated with many shrines; indeed the word *tiib* (shrine) has an etymological connection with 'tree'. The clan elders who look after the hunting shrine are sometimes spoken of as 'the great tree-roots', since they go out to dig up the roots needed for the clan medicines.

3594. K. G. suggests that the following two lines be inserted:

> *baa ti tu*   They went and dug
> *wa iɔng puɔ*   and added them to the rest.

3627. This could also mean that he turned into a cloud of dust. In any case he was invisible to the human beings.

3633. It is because of the possibility of interference by other agencies that one can never be completely sure of communication of this kind.

3637. If it lands belly downwards, the fowl is rejected by the supernatural agencies.

3652. The reference appears to be water divination but I have never seen this used among the LoDagaa.

3663. The sacrifices appeared to have been accepted when in fact they were refused.

3706. These are actual birds but I do not know their zoological names. The *kyaalipiɔ* keeps away from water except at night; the *belibaar* sings sweetly, often high in the sky.

3737. The myth returns to the question of whether it was the beings of the wild or God who created man; the beings still claim they did so.

3747. A general question running through this dialogue relates to the problem of evil. 'If you, God, created us, why do you cause us trouble?'

3768. Earth shrines are found in every settlement and play a major part in maintaining social control (Goody 1956: 91 ff.).

3793. *pan* is a door; here the word is used to indicate flatness.

3826. Another recurrent theme is that death passes our understanding.

3873. The house that man is shown how to build is the flat-roofed kind common in the area.

3938. The younger brother makes the archetypal sacrifice to the ancestors.

4009. On the levels of Earth shrine, see Goody 1956: 91 ff.

4065. 'come near', 'reach', 'touch', often figuratively: *'ka o lɛ ta fu, fu na baara ʑaa ti tu*; if he gets through to you, you will leave all and follow him' (R.T.).

4146. *fuɔr (gyin)*, to tempt, tease, belittle, irritate or annoy; e.g. *fu fuɔrɔ o na*, you are teasing him (or her); *bibile ba fuɔrɔ o ma i*, a child does not tease his (or her) mother.

4170. There is a shift from a report of God's words by Napolo (God's child), eldest son of the younger brother, to a direct confrontation between God and his interrogators.

4179. This is, of course, the being of the wild. God establishes his position as creator, even of the beings who deceive mankind by claiming omnipotence.

4213. These are the beings of the wild.

4229. God explains how he came to withdraw from human affairs, here the Bagre. He withdrew because man rejected God.

4238. The discussion shifts back to Napolo and the interrogators.

4252. See B. 4179.

4260. As I have translated this line, it appears to be addressed to the beings.

4264. This is the first mention of the hoe having been brought down by God. He appears to be the ultimate source even of the technology the beings reveal to man.

faa has the significance of 'already': 'you had already given a hoe to us.' Yet the beings showed them how to make it. In this respect the use of the hoe parallels the creation of children.

4320. These visits to God are not mentioned earlier in the text (unless one makes certain assumptions about the identity of the spider).

4341. The 'certain person' is the Earth shrine; the 'us' seems to refer to the company assembled in front of God.

4364. The incident recounted by the younger brother is now approached from the standpoint of the Earth shrine.

4367. i.e. slept on the ground beside the shrine.

4376. From one standpoint the dead belong to the Earth in which they are interred.

4391. It is usual for the sacrificer to strike the altar with a knife or with a stone, dividing up his prayer into rhythmic units of the same kind as the lines in the present text.

4410. God now addresses the Earth shrine.

4413. The narrator interposes a question.

4441. Red hair, attributed to the younger one, is a not uncommon feature of the area.

4508. God put a covering over the earth to protect the Earth shrine (*tengaan*); this latter word, of which the text earlier gives a different etymology (B. 3984), is probably derived from the word for skin (*gan*); see Tait 1961: 35 n.i. and Girault 1959: 339 where it is translated as 'the earth's crust'.

4513. There is now a shift from the problems of the Earth shrine to those of the younger brother.

4553. 'Seeing' ghosts and other supernatural agencies is a highly regarded attribute, possessed only by few people.

4555. God addresses the being of the wild; he wishes to test him to see if he understood the speech of men and whether he could have deceived them.

4664. The sun presumably.

4675. The beings of the wild are not alone responsible for man's rejection of God.

4682. *yel bier*, pl. *yel bebe*, sins.

4686. It is the Bagre they refer to.

4696. God's child is addressing his father, the younger one.

4771. The person referred to appears to be one of the neophytes who is asking the Bagre elders why they continue to follow the wrong path. They explain (B. 4817) that not only the younger one but others too were led astray by the beings.

4819. *daana* is a Waala word meaning 'master' (i.e. *sob*). It is the younger one who is suffering in the other world.

4823. As I have elsewhere explained, the notion of punishment after death is accepted by the LoDagaa (1962: 371 ff.).

4826. God appears to be addressing mankind (see B. 4842).

4835. To breathe and to live are virtually the same concept in LoDagaa.

4901. The being of the wild tells his descendants that the younger one is not suffering in the other world. The descendant then agrees to follow the path the beings of the wild have suggested, namely Bagre. So the descendant divines with the Bagre bottle and goes to greet the supernatural agencies, especially the dwellings of the beings of the wild. In doing so he also meets the old man with the pipe, God.

4941. This is how a diviner will call upon the beings of the wild and other helpers.

4948. He shakes out some cowries.

4951. The word for 'greet' and 'thank' are the same. Again, the greeting is part of the usual divining session.

4955. Like *Base*, *Bara* acts as a clan and medicine shrine.

4966. This phrase means 'everyone'; according to those with whom I discussed the point there is no special significance in the division between red and black. The local people sometimes refer to themselves as *Dagaara zu soola*, 'Dagaa black heads', but this is not in opposition to heads of another colour. However, an opposition between black and red (the translations are only approximate) does appear in the naming of matrilineal sub-clans (Goody 1956: 83). The red heads can also be the beings of the wild (K. G.; 1383); in this case the black heads will refer to humans.

5006. The white cave refers to the 'place of the clan guardian' (*siura zie*) of the Kpiele patriclan, to which the reciter belongs. It is a shallow shelter in the scarp above Kyaa (Birifu), which cattle use as a lick.

5041. Here the argument about whose way Bagre follows becomes more precise. Is it God or the beings? Divination shows it to be the latter, for man has forsaken God. But Bagre is still valuable because it brings food, livestock, and property in this world, rather than riches in the next. Not only does it help 'birth' but, more concretely, existing members benefit from the contributions of new initiates; and its performance is always the occasion for the expenditure and transfer of much property.

5143. Although he follows a certain path, man still seeks the truth from God. But this suggestion angers Napolo (God's child) who points out that they have rejected God. We continue to perform Bagre, knowing that we have fallen into error.

5224. *n bura*, I make a mistake, *n tulina*.

5233. This passage explains the invocation to the Black Bagre, where they call upon God and the other gods. 'The god who comes' is the Bagre god. 'The god with the good heart' (the spider) is omitted in this version of the invocation. 'The god with the mark between the eyes' is the younger one, this mark being made on many ritual occasions, for example, during the Whitening Ceremony. The striped god (the black and white stripes of the invocation) is the elder one; again this refers to the whitening of the neophytes. God's child is the tom cat and his mate; this I don't altogether understand as God's child is also the child created by God, that is, Napolo. The god with the white arse is the male fly and his mate; the reference is to the neophytes sitting in the dust without stools. The being's child (*bie*) and small (*ble*) being are here differentiated—and are thought of as a thief and a liar respectively. Finally, 'the troubling god' is the Earth shrine, associated with the elder one.

5259. 'By pawing at the ground, they opened the way' (1392).

5263. 'God sees us as flies, small things, copulating' (1393).

5265. The 'thieving god' because the non-initiates steal the bambara beans (1393).

5268. The 'lying god': the small being of the wild told us that if they performed Bagre, no one would die, but it wasn't true (1393).

5271. As for the 'lying god' (1393).

5287. The initiates are now told that the Bagre medicine does not have the power attributed to it in the White Bagre.

5337. That is, he was saved by recognizing reality as it was.

5422. The reference is to the Bagre container, which the initiates now receive.

BƆƆ PLA

ngmini / kpime / siuwe / kɔntɔme / game / ka bɔɔr / dunɔ non /
kure pîîme / ɔɔr puur / ɔɔr zuri / ka tɔ kpɛ̃ɛ̃ / gana fã̄ã̄n / ir a kyi / ir
zɔ kyena / gobasoba / k'o zur lɔb / ti yel ka / k'o ir ba nyɔɔ / ti ba
nyɔɔ / k'o ir weni (20) / k'o ir wiɔ / k'o ir bɔɔr / un ir wena / olɔ
ba nu / k'o dɔ̃ɔ̃ iri / on ir weni / ka ti iɔng na soor / bon weni / bidɔɔ
weni / kakuɔr weni / pɔɔyaa weni / sã̄ã̄kum weni / makum weni /
tamiur weni / no guol weni / yaa zɔɔri / kpaartiib weni / ko lo
sɔɔ / lɛ na yaa / nikpɛ̃ɛ̃-aa (40) / iɔng tiɛro-a / k'o ir a zom / duur
ti ta / o sã̄ã̄ yir puɔ / ti buɔl biir / ka ba wa ka / ban kyeni ti ta /
ba ba man ka / nandi woro / ban zɔ kyena / ti lɔng ta / nikpɛ̃ɛ̃-ya / o'a
ir yi / a tampuor zu / tɛmpɛlo-a / kuɔ̃ bhaaro / wa iɔng na puɔri /
o'a puɔri-a biiri / ti yel ka / k'on puɔr yi-aa (60) / yin wa nyɛ /
tã̄ã̄ma-yaa / yi ta dire / yin wa nyɛ / bun paala / yi ta dire / o'a yel
ko biiri / ba yi siu / ban ti taa yira / nikpɛ̃ɛ̃-na / o'a iɔng na gã̄ /
o'a gã̄ gu / o'a lɛ iri / lɛ liɛb kyeni / a gobasob zie / k'o ti zuu lɔb / ti
lɛ soor-aa / ka dã̄bie-wabna / bon dã̄bie / dã̄bie banai (80) / zaa
na-yaa / ka n gã̄ / n ba gure / alɛ na / ka n ir wa ka / wa yel ka-yaa /
fũ bɔɔra / fu kaa mɛ / a yel nya puɔ / on yel lɛ-aa / o'a liɛb kuli /
on liɛb kul-aa / o'a ta yiri / on ti ta / faa nyɛ biiri / ka ba wa tai-
ya / zimani / ba'a lɔng taa / ko yel ka / k'o kyena (100) / ti bɔ bɔɔ /
ka gobasob / k'o yel ka / ka wen-yaa / ka wana / ni nĩo / ka wana /
tuɔri goba / ka wana / ni aro / ka wana / ni dɔɔb / ka wana / tamiur /
o ba wani liɛbo-a / o na yel olɛ / on yel wa baara / tikyɛ-a / ka yi
biira / ba buɔr na kɔi (120) / ba buɔr na guole / yi ba buɔra / na
tɛr / yel miɔng / tikyɛ-a / ka yele-aa / i yɔɔ zuo-aa / a ti bɔbɔ-aa /
ka dɛungdem / bɔ̃ɔ̃ wa gu / ti kyen / ti bel ti-ya / tin na vuurɔ-
aa / ban ti kyier-aa / ba naa ti-a / tɛr kyeni / a ba teung / ti pã̄ã̄
bar / ko ti-a / ka ti bɔng gu (140) / alɛ na / k'o wa de kuɔ̃ bhaaro /
iɔng tɛmpɛlo / ti yel ka / a iɛng bhaaro / ka n bɔɔr / o'a puɔri-a /
ka waar ba / ti yel ba / ka ba wa / ka zima / k'o wa waa / lɛb wa
ka / k'o wana / dib-a / k'o ba wani kɔ̃ɛ / k'o tuura / nu duro / k'o
ba tuur gobai / k'o wana (160) / yel miɔng / k'o ba wani / ziri-e /
ka ti bɔɔra / ka nyɔɔ vla / tikyɛ-a / a zaa kpɛung / be na / sa ngmin
zie / ti a zie / o kona / ti ba nyɛ / o bome-ya / tikyɛ-a / a teung /
o tɛra puɔ / o tɛra puɔ ni bo / o tɛra puɔ / olɛ no-a / tulo (180) / na

man ta / olɛ no-a / ka ti bɔng ka / ti ben o puɔ / ka ol wa i / a
ngmin-o / a wa ni yel miɔng-ya / o na tiɛ ti na / ka ti nyɛ-a / a kuur
bomo / nyɛ ni bo / a sa ngmino / na dɔɔ-ya / ka bõ vaar / a ba wa /
ti na nyɔɔ na / a tu biɛri ni / a olɛ-ya / na dõõ ti nio / on a yela
lɛ-a (200) / wa baara / tikyɛ-a / lɛ liɛba / wa nyɔɔ / iɔng na tu / a zie
ba dɔɔ / a bom vaar / a ba yi / pɔɔ nyõõ / tiɛro sob / o'a nyɔɔ a bɛng
vaar / o'a bhɛl ala / o'a iɔng tulo / iɔng na di-a / ka bibiira / ba nyɛ
ala / ba buɔr na dib / k'o yel ka / a yi sãã / na yele yele-a (220) /
yi in ngmin / di bɛng vaari / bi sãã na / o'a wa ta / on wa ta / ba de
bomo / wa bin baar / bõ bonu / bundiri na / k'o buɔr na di / o'a de
a nu / on de a nu-a / o'a ngmaa saab / su ni ziɛr / o'a iɔng na di /
wa nyɛ vaar / bonu vaar / beng vaar ba na / k'o yel ka / ka anu
duu (240) / a ziɛr nyɛ taaba / o na yela / wa baar-a / ti ba iri / bar
a saab / ni a ziɛr / ti ir yi-a / ba do a garo / ti buɔl a biiri / ban wa
ta / ko yel ko ba / ka ba yi-a / ka zɔ yɔ-aa / yele-a / ka bɔɔ sɔɔli / ka
ba yi-a / ka dayere bio / ka wa de / ka bieng-na / ka bar ka (260) /
ba ba yɔ-aa / yel a bɔbɔ / ba yel wa baara / ti wa ta / a sãã yir
puɔ / pɔɔ nyõõ biɛ / wa bhɛl a bion vaar / o na bhɛl-a / o'a iɔng tulo /
on iɔng a tulo-a / ti bini / ba wa wa / ban wa ta / nikpẽ̀ẽ-na / o'a
yel ka / ka ba nyɛ-a / a bion vaara / on yel ka / ka ba kyiiro-aa /
olɔ no-a (280) / a diẽ / yaa nyɛ / a bion vaari / a ba i ziɛr / yi ba
nyɛ / a bɔbɔ / baa zin lɔng taa / yi ba nyɛ / kyi-a / a ba i saabo /
yi ba nyɛ-a / kɛɛ-a / a ba i dãã / ban wa ta / baa nyɛ dibo / ban di
wa baara / a nandi woro / ban di baara / ti iɔng na gõ / ka tɔ-ya (300) /
lɛ yel ka / ka ba bar gõmɛ / ban wa bar gõmɛ-a / k'o yel ka / ka ba
tɔɔ ta / ban tɔɔ ta / ba ta be / k'o de-a / a kuur-aa / zini-a / a
tengaansoba / ti yel ka / ka tengaani / ka siuwe / ka weni / ka ba
yel ka / ka bɔɔr / lɛ na yaa / ka ti iɔng tiɛro-a / ka ti iɔng na tu (320) /
faa nyũ / a o zuur-nu / ka ti nyɔɔ / olɛ no-a / ka ti nyɔɔ / ti zɛlɛ-a /
ka bõ buurɔ / na kyɛ-a / na ba yi-a / fu sõa-ya / ka ba yi / alɛ nɛ-
yaa / ka ti be ka / k'o yeli-a / wa baari-a / ti lɛ yel k'o / fu bɔng ka /
ba na tua / ba bɔɔna / a la puori-a (340) / a ba zẽbom-ye / ti ũũ-
yaa / a bomo-a / na tul ti-a / wa nyɔɔ ti-a / ka ti zɛli-a / a zu-a /
na dɔɔla nyu / ti a bomo / na kyɛ puori a / o na wana / wa yel ko
ti / o ta / wa iɔng tulo-e / o yeli-a / yi bhaaro / ka ti yel ko a bibiir /
ka ti a baara / ti liɛb kula / a sãã yir puɔ (360) / k'o ti ta / bonu / kyɛ
niu / nyuur-a / na-i-a / a ti bɔɔr bom / tikyɛ / o ba yi-e / tin ma
kyɛli-a / tin kyɛli baara / daar kɔng-yaa / bii sãã / o'a yi ga wiɛ / na
ti kɔ / on gaa-yaa / wa waar-a / a puori-yaa / wa tai-ya / faa nyɛ
pɔɔ nyõõ biɛ / o'a kyeni (380) / o diɛm yiri / ti nyɔɔ-a / a nyuuro-aa /

o'a kpiri / o'a wa tani / a sãã yir puɔ / o'a duuli / o'a to / bin-
yaa / iɔng na uɔbi / faa nyɛ / bibiiri / ba nyɛ ala / ba ba kõno / ba
na kõn-a / kõ bɔng gu / o'a yel ka / ka ba vẽ / ka ba sãã wa / ka ba
i gbili-a (400) / ban i gbili-a / k'o wa ta / o'a de a nyuur / ko a bii
sãã / ti yel ka / ko diɛm / ka ko a nyuur / ko yel ka ai / ka lɛ na /
ka bibiiri / ka irɛ na sõõ / ti ir-a / yel a biira / ka ba zɔ yɔ-aa / ka
yel-a / a bɔbɔ-aa / ka ba la yi bio / ka ba wa / ka wa de-a / a bɛng
puru (420) / baa wa ta / a dayere bio-aa / ba wa ta / zĩ baalo-a / faa
nyɛ dãã / faa nyɛ saab / faa nyɛ nyuur / faa nyɛ biẽng / a ba i ziɛr /
faa nyɛ nɛn / ba iɔng na lari / ti yel ka / ka bɔble-a / na dire ba
wona / k'o dire / baa yeli / a bɔɔ pɛlɛ / ni ba nandi nɛ / ba ira /
ngmaa dãã (440) / a dãã kpẽẽ zu / ba ngma nyuu / ka bɔɔ k'o nyu
a dãã / ba na yela / ka dãã kpẽẽ zu / ka n yel ka-ya / ba nyu, n nyuna /
n yel lɛ-a / ba yel baari / ya nyɛ dib / ba dire / ban di wa baara /
bɔɔ pɛlɛ-a / na dabɔɔ nibɛ / ban di wa baara / nũɔ ba kpe ba / ka ba
iɔng na gõ / ka nikpẽẽ-na / yel ba-a / ka ba bar gõmɔ (460) / a ni ban
nandi woro / ba ba yel ka / ka dib aminɛ na / k'o yel ka / ka bɛ tɔɔ
ta / ban tɔɔ ta / o'a yel ka / ka yel nya / na fɛrɛ tia / ti tɛung nya /
tɛra puɔ-a / o ba dɔɔ-ɛ / ti diẽ-a / a nyuura / ka ti kpira / a ba nyẽi /
ti kpɔɔ na / na naab sukyira / ya nyuu / ka ti kpiri (480) / wa iɔng
tulo / ban iɔng tulo-a / ti lɛ yel ka-ya / ka ti gyir-a / ka a bome-a /
na kyɛ a puori-a / ka ba wa yel ko ti / ka ti yel ko-a / a bibiir / ti lɛ
zĩ / ti de kuõ bhaaro / iɔng tɛmpɛlo-aa / ti kaaba / buɔli-a / ka
ngmin / ka tengaan / ka siuwe / ka weni / ka bɔɔr / alɛ na-yaa (500) /
ka ti yi diẽ / ire na bebe / ka yi nyɛ bomo / o'a iri / yel ka-ya / ka
yi wa / ka zima / ka ba la lɛ waara / ka ba waa / ni nĩo / ba taa wa
waar ni puori-e / ka yi tuuri-a / duro-a / ba ta tuuri gobai / ka yi
wani / na dib-a / yi ba wa ni kɔĩ / yi i-a / ka kuur bomo / na kyɛ-
a (520) / ba i-ɛ / kaa i vla / ka ti de wa / a wiili ni-a / a bibiir / ti ti
buɔra / ka ba zĩ / ti unu yaa / a bomo / na fɛrɛ ti / yi de-o / tuno
a sor / ka ti kyaan / lɛ zɛlɛ a sor / ka ti nyɛ a zu / lɛ dɔɔla a nyu /
tin yela / ti yel wa baara / ti bɔɔ pɛlɛ / ni dabɔɔ nibɛ (540) / ba yi /
iɔng na gõ / ba kyeni / ba kyeni wa baari / ti kyɛ ti / ka ti zĩa / ti ba
yel ka / ka bon kyɛ nio / n yel wa baar / tiɛrosob-ya / yel ka-ya / ka
ala na / na be a nio / ka ala na / na kyɛ-a / ala na / a bɛng puru /
ti na nyɔɔ-a / a biɛrɛ-ya / waar-ya (560) / daar kɔng-ya / ka nikpẽẽ
o'a gã / bin o wuo / nikpẽẽ-a / dãbol nu / ko gãna / kõõ dakora / ni
o pɔɔ / zãã daar / ba zɛb ta / o'a bɔɔra pɔɔ / ka pɔɔ ba zɔɔri / k'o
ir-a / bibio-a / o'a yɔ yuɔri / a ka vaar puɔ / o'a wa nyɛ / a bɛng
puru / o'a pɔri (580) / ka pɔɔ-ya / duuri ti ta-a / ti yel ka / ka bono /

k'o i ba di / k'o yel ka / ka dabora / ka zãã / ka n zɛl fu / a gaal
iɔng / ka fu sib ma / ti yi diɛ̃ / pɔɔ ni daba / ba ba zeɔɔr ni / wa
wa yi / a nikpɛ̃ɛ̃ niu / o'a nyɛ pla / o'a de daa / o'a lɔbo / ti yel
ka aa (600) / ka mãã wuo / ni puo / ka a libie / ka yire / ka kyiin /
dire / o'a lɔb bari / o'a ti de / on de-a / o'a nyɛ / k'o i bɛng puru / k'o
yel ka-ai / ka lɛ na ka / ka ti bibiir / ka irɛ na sɔ̃ɔ̃ / ka bibiiri / wa yi
puo puɔ / wa ta-ya / ko yel ka / ka ba zɔ-yaa (620) / ka yɔ-aa / ka
yele-a / a bɔɔ sɔɔli-a / ka ni bɔɔ pɛlɛ / ka dabɔɔ nibɛ / ka ba la wa
wõ gõm / [ka ba wa ka] / on yel lɛ-a / a bibiiri / ba ba yi / zɔ yuɔri /
a yel ka / dayere bio / [ba wa de biɛng bar] / ba wa ta / ban wa
tai-ya / ban in ngmin / ba yel ka-ya / ka nandi na / k'o yel ka-ya
(640) / ka sɛɛ / ka lɛ na / ka ka vũũ / ta dire / ka ti ira / bibiiri /
na sɔ̃ɔ̃ / ka lɛ na / k'o buɔl ba-a / ka ba wa / wa de-a / a bɛng puru /
ka i bar / ba ba nyãã / ka ba yel ka õ / ka ba mãn ka / ka dib na / ba
yel wa baari / faa nyɛ bɛng puru / ba tu ba tub (660) / ban tu wa
baara / ka ba yel ka / yi nyɛ kyi / ka liɛb saabo / yi nyɛ kɛɛ / ka liɛb
dãã / yi nyɛ biɛng / ka i ziɛri / ka bɛ yel ka / ka ba tu ba nɛ / ka bono
nɛ / ba ba tiɛr ka / nandi na / k'o yel ka-ya / ka ngmina / na wa ti
iɔng / yel ka ya / k'o wana / a nã di / k'o ba wa liɛb-o'a (680) / alɛ
na-ya / ka n bɔɔra / ka yi tu a nɛ / ka ba yel ka / ka ngmini / ka
siuwe / ka weni / ka kɔntɔme / ka kpime / ka bɔɔr / ka ala na / ka
dunɔ nɔn / ka kure pĩĩme / alɛ na-ya / ka ti tɛra / a daar zaa / ira
bebe / wa yiin diɛ̃ / ti k'o i-a biɛng / a biɛng (700) / lɛ liɛba / a
ziɛri-a / ka kyi / liɛb saab-ya / ka kɛɛ-ya / liɛb dãã / alɛ na / ka ti
yel ka / ka fu ngmin / a ba shɔɔ bome / ti on i-aa / a sor kura / ka
ti tuur-a / fu na sõõ tina / ka ti de-aa / a tuni-yaa / a zɛli-yaa / a
zu / a dɔɔl nyũũ / ba yel wa bar (720) / ti kyɛ kyɛ diu / bɔɔ pɛlɛ /
ba di bar / ti iɔng na gõ / ka tɔ ya / yel ka-yaa / ka ba baar gõmõ / ba
bar zoom / k'o yel ka-yaa / ka yel nyɛ-aa / na fɛrɛ ti-aa / ka ti bɔ̃ɔ̃
gu / k'o ina naa pɔɔ biro / ka ti piɛn / tina in na / ti miɔng-aa / ka
ti man taa / bɔ̃ɔ̃ a bom / a be-a ti nio / ka tɔ-yaa (740) / lɛb yel ka /
ka boono / ka kyɛ-a / ka ti nio / ka ba yel ka / ka bom na kyɛ / ka
bɛ tiɛra / ka tin liɛba / a nyɔɔ / a bom-nya / boona bom / a bɔɔr
bom / na i-a / a bɔɔr wuora / lɛ na-yaa / ti na liɛba / ti bɔ-a / a bɔ
wuor / ka ba minɛ / yel ka-ya (760) / ka 'õ' / kaa in ngmin / ka fu
dõ̃ɔ̃ / waara / ba bɔi / ti lɛ liɛb / wa ta / a sɔ̃ɔ̃ kõ / ti na lɛb / lɛ liɛb
puor / ti bɔ / kaa i a ib / ka kõ-yaa / yel ka-yaa / a yel kpɛ̃ɛ̃ / ba
nu / tina bɔn / bɔ̃ɔ̃ a zie / baa lɛ nyɔɔ / ti yel ka (780) / a bɔɔ wuora /
tin dõ̃ɔ̃ baara / ti tana-ya / a taama / kyuunɔ / ka ba yel ka / ti'a
tai / ka ba yel ka / ti na nyɔɔ na / a tãã kyuun yele-aa / kyier ni-a /

an tu lɛ ya / a zie ba bhaana / ti na in ngmini / wa nyɛ / a taa
kyuun / tin yela / ka bibiir / ka ba ta / wa dire-a (800) / a bun
paala / a taama ba na / ka ti yelɛ / ka ba la liɛba / irɛ na di / zie ba
bhaani / kakuɔr bie / no guol bie / o'a zie o lɔɔ / long ni tam /
long ni kuur / long ni lɛr / ba ti ta / a puo puɔ / ira na kɔ /
ba nyɛ bomo / bono bomo / zɔ̃zɔ̃ kpɛ̃ɛ̃ / olɛ no-a / i'a ti bɔɔr (820) /
nikpɛ̃ɛ̃ / olɔ no pɔɔ / zi lio iɔng / ba diɛna ba diɛno / o'a bɔɔr a
pɔɔ / ka pɔɔ-a / o'a zɔɔri / ko ira / a zi lio / o'a kyeni / a tãã tiɛ zu /
ti nyɔɔ a tãã̃m / on di-a / tikyɛ-a / iɔng o nuɔro / wan wa tan / o pɔɔ
zie / wa tani-aa / pɔɔ ba nyɛ / yel ka-yaa (840) / k'o i ko / k'o sibo /
ti yel ka / ka aano / tĩĩsɔɔ iɔng / ka n zɛl fu gu / ka fu sib / ti wa
nyɛ n dibo / lɛ bɔɔra / ka zɔ̃zɔ̃ pɔɔ / yel ka-yaa / i kum-a / ti mi
i kob / ka daba / o'a ir suuri / n ba kurɔ fuɛ / ti un i-a / a ti bɔɔr
nikpɛ̃ɛ̃ / o'a di-o / di kyɛ kyuun (860) / o'a de lɔbo / o'a lɔb baari /
ka kuɔr bie na / on kuɔr wa baara / ir de kuur / o'a kpɛn muɔ /
tambir iɔng / o'a ir kyɛ / on kyɛ bɔ̃ gu / ti ir kpɛ-a / a tiɛ pule / o'a
nyũũ / a tambir / o'a kyɛ / on kyɛ baar / ti gyir nyɛ bomo / ka ti
bɔɔ nikpɛ̃ɛ̃ / o'a bari / k'o de-a / wan a yira (880) / wa tani-a /
nikpɛ̃ɛ̃ banu / napolo banu / o'a gã be / ka bie wa tana / a tambir
na / kuɔ̃ nyuur na / ba kpɛ-o / k'o de a wuɔ / o'a de koba / iɔng
a wuɔ mi / o'a kyeni / o sɛn dãã zie / ti nikpɛ̃ɛ̃-a / napolo banu / on
gã-a / wa wona / liliir gɔ̃mɔ / ko yel ka / ka ba buɔl bie (900) / ban
buɔl bie / buɔl bɔ̃̃ gu / k'o ira / ɔng kuɔ̃-a / iɔng kyi-a / ti tan-ia /
a liliir zie / zĩ baalo / ti irɛ na iɔng / o'a iɔng ba / on iɔng baara / o'a
ir tambiri / o'a tɔ ngmɛri / on ngmɛr baar / ti lɛ de-a / a yen-a /
o'a ngmɛri / on ngmɛr wa baar / o'a kyɛ tambir sɔɔ / ko yel ka (920) /
k'o kyir iɔng / on kyir iɔng na / o'a ton gyɛli / o'a nyɛ kyuuni / ti
yel ka / ka ai / ka vũũ tan duuri / ti ba irɛ / ka bibiir na sɔ̃̃ / lɛ
na-yaa / k'o ir u-aa / iɔng a wuɔ puɔ / pɔɔ nyɔ̃̃ biiri / ba wa ta /
o'a de-a / ti ko-a / pɔɔ kyila / ko de-a / bɔ̃̃ a bɔɔm / o'a iɔng
tulo (940) / sambar ata / o'a tuli / k'o de-a / iɔng duu puɔ / on iɔng
wa baara / ti yi ti yela / a nikpɛ̃ɛ̃ / k'o yel ka / k'o bin sɛr / ka o lɔ
wa / wa bɔ̃ gua / k'o de da / ka kɔni kuɔrbɔ / o'a bini / ti o yel ka /
ka nir zaa / k'o ta wa yel / kur-a / a bibiiri / ba i gbile (960) / a bie
na / zie ba sɔbɔ / ko yi-a / a sɛn dãã zie / wa ta-a / k'o yel kua / k'o
yɔ-aa / ka yela-a / ka bɔɔ sɔɔli-a / ka na bɔɔ pɛlɛ / ka na dabɔɔ nibɛ /
ka ba la wa wɔ̃ gɔ̃ / ka ba wa / ba yi / yuɔri / yele / ka bo wuor /
kɛɛ / iɔng na bio / baa yɔɔ yel ba (980) / dayere bio / ba wa ta / ka
ba de kɛɛ / ba iɔng piɔ / ba ti tani / a garo zu puɔ / bina / ti yel ka /
ka ba de nu / ka tɔ̃ ka ba nyaa / baa lɛ soori / ka ba yel ka / ka boonu

i kɛɛ / ka ba yel ka / ka kyi i kɛɛ / ba in kyi ngmini / ka a liɛb kɛɛ /
ka ba yel / ka boor bɔ̃ɔ̃ gyɛlɛ / ka ba piira (1000) / ka ko pɔɔ kyila /
ka o nar o naru / o'a nɔɔr baari / o'a de ngmani / ir
na yɛli / a naangmin sɛb na / o'a de bebe / kpɛni kaling wiɔ puɔ /
ti kyɛ vla / a pɔɔ nyɔ̃ɔ̃ biɛ / o'a de-a / siuni-a / ti iɔng salɛũ puɔ / ti
i kũɔ̃ iɔng / bibie ata / k'o ngmaa muo-a / wa duni-a / a gar zu
puɔ / o'a siuu / a dundɔr puɔ (1020) / o'a kyuori / on kyuor wa
baara / o'a doni / a gar zu / ti kyir bina / ti nyɔɔ yɛri-a / on yɛr baar /
ti de muo-a / lɛ pɔɔ-yaa / on pɔɔ wa baara / o'a de sɛn / ti pɔɔ-ya /
o'a kyɔr kũɔ̃ / bibie ata-ya / o'a nyɔɔ yuo / on yuo wa baara / o'a
liɛb goba / k'o tɔ̃ nyɛ / o tɔ̃ nyɛ-a / a ba buli (1040) / o'a iɔng na
nɔ̃ / o nɔ̃ wa baara / pɔɔ nyɔ̃ɔ̃ biɛ / na iɔng tiɛru-a / o'a liɛb de /
iɔng piɔ puɔ / on iɔng wa baar / ti wob o bomo / o'a lɛ pɔɔ / on
pɔɔ baara / a piɛ puɔ-a / bibie ata / ko nyɔɔ yuo / on yuo wa baara /
o'a de / o'a diɛli / on diɛli baara / naangmin sɛba / ba ngme / ka
ko-yaa (1060) / k'o de-a / wa siu-nia / wiili ma-a / [kan yel-aa] /
k'o de-a / leb ti bin / ma wa-ya / wa bɔ̃ gu / n ku kɔni kɔrbɔ /
ala na-a / k'o bina / ka vũũ-ya / o'a ta duuri / ka n buɔl yi / wa yel
ka / ka yi nyãã-a / yi ba nyɛ-a / soor ma / yi ba nyɛ a yele / n yel
ko ya (1080) / faa nyɛ bɔbɔ / ka ba liɛb nu / tɔ̃ piɔ puɔ / ti iɔng ba
kɛɛ / bɔ̃ɔ̃ a iɔɔm / ba tɔ̃ duro / ti tɔ̃ guba / ti lɛ yela / a nikpɛ̃ɛ̃ / ka
a ba shɔɔ bome / ti on ia / a yela / na fɛrɛ ti-a / yin den lɛ / soori
zu / na dɔɔla nyũũ / ban iɔng baara / pɔɔbil bhɔlɔa / ba de-a / zɔ
siuni-a (1100) / a yɔ̃-a / ba zɔ yɔni / a nibɛ yie / ba iɛraa / ba iɛraa
wa baari / duuri wa tani / a sãã yir puɔ / ba in ngmini / a naangmin
yele / na wa wuro / ba de yoi / zɔ tu ta / ti tani-a / a kulkpɛ̃ɛ̃ nuɔr /
ba nyɛ kũɔ̃ / kũɔ̃ vlana-a / ba ɔng wa tani / ba sãã yir puɔ / ba na
bɔ̃ɔ̃ ba bomo / ba de kɛɛ zɔ̃ (1120) / iɔng kũɔ̃ puɔ / ba i aminɛ / ba
i kyĩĩ / ban kyĩĩ wa baara / ba bul lɔng ta / ba iɔng duu puɔ / ti
i kũɔ̃ iɔng / ban iɔng wa baara / ba in ngmin / ba iɔng vũũ / ka i
na bii / a ba bii / ba nyɔɔ-a / yaa wa baara / ba iɔng kũɔ̃ / ba iɔng
taa / ti ir kyuori / ban kyuori wa baara / ba ir dãã zie / ban ir wa
baara (1140) / ba iɔng siung puo / ti liɛb ti do-a / a sãã yir zu / ba
i na gãã / zie ba mhãã / ka kpakpol nɔra / o'a ir ngme / o'a duur
ngme / pɔɔbil bhɔla / ko vaa na vulɔ / o'a iri / ti dur ti siu / siung
kpɛ̃ɛ̃ puɔ / o'a nyɛ dãã / k'o lɛn nyãã / ka dãã miina / a dãã ba mii /
an mii-a / o'a ir daari / duur wa lɔbo (1160) / o'a de ngmani / i na
wuɔli / on wuɔli wa baara / o'a kyir iɔng / o'a iɔng duu puɔ / on
iɔng wa baara / o'a iɔng vũũ / ka ba kara / on ka wa baara / k'o
nyɔɔ wuɔli / an wuɔli wa baara / o'a kuor dãã sɔɔr / o'a iɔng duu /

o'a iɔng vũũ / ka wa kara / k'o nyɔɔ yaa / on yaa wa baara / ir do
a / a sãã yir zu / o'a irɛ na gã (1180) / o'a gã be / dãã ba mhãã / pɔɔ
nyɔ̃ɔ̃ biɛ / na bɔ̃ o bomo / o'a wan dãbil / o'a iɔng be / faa nyɛ / ka i
puuru / pɔɔbil bhɔla / o'a de yue / o'a dɛr iɔng baari / nikpɛ̃ɛ̃-a / duur
wa ta / o'a nyɔɔ ngmama / mani a bɔbil / on man wa baara / faa
nyɛ bɔbɔ / ka ba wa ta / pɔɔbil bhɔla / ba de dãã (1200) / do ti yini /
faa nyɛ kɛɛ / ka liɛb dãã / faa nyɛ kyi / ka liɛb saab / faa nyɛ birɛ / ka
liɛb ziɛr / ba wa ta / nandi woro / ba i na di / faa nyɛ nikpɛ̃ɛ̃ / o'a
ir kyuuri / ka kɛɛ iɔng / ba bar kpibo / ko yel ka / yin bɔɔr diba /
ti-a bɔɔ bɛrɛ / na zin kɔɔ yi-a / yin in ngmin / ti di ti kpɔ̃ (1220) / ka
bɔɔ kyiin bɛrɛ / na bɔ̃ ba bomo-aa / ba wa ta / ba ba ngma ba dãã /
dãã bɛrɛ zuri / ba biɔ̃ ni bɔbɔ / ka ba nyũũ dãã / ka ba yel ka ya / ka
ba nyuuna / bo kyiin bil / ba liɛb ti ta / ba dãã iɔng / ba nyu ti
baar / ti iɔng na gɔ̃ / ko nikpɛ̃ɛ̃ na / na iɔng tiɛru / o'a kyɔɔr ba / ti
yel ka ya / ka ba kyɛli ka / baa kyɛli sɛri (1240) / k'o lɛ yel ka ya /
ka bom kyɛ naa / ka ba vɛ̃-ya / k'o yel ko ti / ka bom na kyɛ / ti yel
ka ya / ka bɔɔr bomo / na wa woro / ka ti nyɔɔ ya / tuur a gbɛɛ /
bɔ̃ɔ̃ gure / ira ia / ka i nũɔ ib zie / a ba i lɛ / ba'a bar kpibo / ban
bar wa baara / ko ɔng kuɔ̃ mhaaro / ni tɛmpɛlo-ya / liɛb ti tani-a / a
teung sɛr zu (1260) / zin baalo-a / ti lɛ yel ka ya / ka ba tu nuɔr / ka ba
yel ka / ka ba tu bonu nuɔr / k'o yel ka / a bɔɔr yel / na wa wuro /
ka ti bɔ̃ɔ̃ gu / yi tu ku a kpime-a / lɔng nia ngmina / lɔng ni siuwe /
lɔng ni wen-a / lɔng ni tengaani / ka ti nyãã bomo / n na kyɛ / ka
ba yel ka / ka ngmini / ka kpime / ka siuwe (1280) / ka weni / ka
bɔɔr / ka dunɔ nɔn / ka kure pĩĩme / ti ira bebe / wa ta diã / ti a bɔɔ
pɛlɛ / ngmiera nɔkpɛn / ni yia / ala na / ka n yel ka / ka ba bar
gɔ̃mɔ / ka ti nyɔ bɔɔr / on i yel kpɛ̃ɛ̃ / o'a yel ko biir / ka ba tɛr
tiɛru / a iɔng / on yel wa baara / ti tɔ-ya / yel ka ya (1300) / ka tin
ba guole / ti a bɔɔ yele-a ya / ia nuur yele-a / ti na in ngmin / ka
tiɛrusob-a / lɛ yel ka ya / ka nuur ba na wana / wa ko yi-a / ti na
iri-a / aminɛ / ko a bɔbil / kɔ̃ɔ̃ zu-a / wa i vla-a / tin yɛrena ya /
ti koba / fu bai nyɛ / ka nikpɛ̃ɛ̃ / o ba nyɔ nuuri / ti lɛ yel ka ya / ka
ngmini (1320) / ka kpime / ka siuwe / ka bɔɔr / a dunɔ nɔn / kure
pĩĩme / ɔɔr puur / lɔng ni zuri / ka tɔ kpɛ̃ɛ̃ / wa gana fããn / ti tina
nyɔɔ-a / wa tɔ ka / ti a nuur yele-a / na i kpɛung-a / fun nyɛn a nuur
anya / kaara / maali iɔng yaa / ka ala wa i bom / fu mi na in bom /
ala wa lɔba / wa ti wio (1340) / ka gyɛlɛ-a / ba kpole / ka liliir / ba
kpimai / a zaa kpo / na ara-a / zɛn ta ya / na n'ɔ buura / ti na de
na / a biɛri nya / a bom na na kyɛ / ti a yele / ti na yel ku yi-a / ka
yi na bara / a nuo / in ngmin bara / ka ba yel ka / ka ba na bara /

a yir puɔ / ti n'ɔ tuo-na (1360) / o yuɔr nu'a / tĩĩtĩĩ nuɔ / boonu
tĩĩtĩĩ / a tĩĩtĩĩ-a / tin a yeli-a / ka yi ba bɔ̃ɔ̃ a par / a bɔɔr na i a /
a bun tĩĩra / ole no-a / a nir nuɔ / wari-a / wan lob iɔng / o gyɛlɛ
puɔ / a sɔngna / a zaa ya / ina / a tĩĩtĩĩ nuo / gyɛlɛ / tin na de na /
tuuri-aa (1380) / a ti bɔɔr yele / tin yel wa baara / bɔɔ pɛlɛ / baa
zɔ ti kuli / ti ti yel ka / ba ti kyɛlɛ / a ngmãã-a / na kyɛ-a / ka ti lɛ
yel kuba / ka ba kuli / ti yi yɔ kyen / a bɔɔ sɔɔli zie / yɛndem nibɛ /
ka ba bu / a bɔɔri / ka ba bɔ̃ɔ̃ / a bɔɔr / yele / na i lɛ a / na kyier
lɛɛ (1400) / ka ba ti nyɛ-a / ka kpime-a / ani-a wen-a / ba zaa nibɛ
wa wa / wari-a / ba yeli / a yeli / ko a bɔɔ bɛrɛ / a ngmin sɛba / o'a
i a zie / ka zie viɛli-a / ka sa bir / lɛ lona / iɔng / a bomo / na kyɛ-a /
kyi-bana / ni biɛ̃ũ / ni singbile-a / na i-a (1420) / a bɔɔr bomo /
yi ba nyãã / a saa ba maali / kaa viɛli-a / daar kɔ̃ / ka mutong-a / wa
ti ngme / iɔng a kyi / ka kuɔ̃ yi-a / a simie / a mi ba bii / a singbile /
mi ba bii / ka biɛ̃ũ / mi wɔ̃ ya / ba nyɔ-a / guri / bin bari / a ngmin
sɛb / a ba tɛ iɔng (1440) / ka dayere bio / baa vaari / a kaduora /
nikpɛ̃ɛ̃-a / o ba la / ti yel ka ɔ̃ / ka yuona ya / a kuura / k'o wana / a
yiri / ti lɛ nyɔɔ-a / a bibiiria / yel ko ba-a / ka ba wa ka / ba wa ta /
a nikpɛ̃ɛ̃ pule / ba ba mang ka / ka dib na / k'o yel ko ba / ka a
kɔba (1460) / ti na kɔ-a / ti nyãã na ya / ka viɛla / ka ti bɔ̃ɔ̃ ka ya /
ka wena / o wan na ye miong / ti yini-a / wa yi dayere bio / yi zɔ
yɔ-a a / a bɔɔr sɔɔli zie / nii bɔɔ pɛlɛ / dabɔɔ nibɛ / ba la wa wɔ̃
gɔ̃n / ba na wana / ba na yela / ba yi / zɔ yɔɔ / yel ba zaa / a bɔɔ
sɔɔli / ba yel wa baari (1480) / dayere bio / ba wa ta / a gar puɔ /
k'o iɔng-ya / pɔɔ sɔ̃-a / o'a de piɔ / siu ni-a / a dio puɔ / o'a nar
o naru / ti vaa o kɛɛ / do ni-a / a garo zu puɔ / ti bini-a / ka nikpɛ̃ɛ̃-a /
o'a buɔl a bɔbɔ / ka ba tɔ ta / nandi woro / ba ba man ka (1500) /
ka dib na / ba iɔng na la / ti tɔ tai-ya / k'o yel ka ya / ka bibiir / a
yel-la / na fɛr ba / a kori zaa / kaa ira bebe / dunɔ nɔn / kure pĩime /
ɔɔr puur / ɔɔr zuri / ala na-yaa / ka ti kɔ yaa / a kuur bomo / ka
naangmina / tu ti puori / ti nyaana / ta ba zɛ bom-e / ka ti na tun
i na / a yele-a (1520) / na fɛra tina / ka ti bɔ̃ gu-a / ala na yaa / ka
ti nyɔɔ a kaaduora / ngmaa ya / bini yaa / ka pɔɔbɔ / na bɔng ba
bomo / ka ba de daa bhɔla / ba fɔbi / ka yi-a / ka ba ngmaa / pɛ
zɔɔ ya / ba doni / a garo zu / ba yɛli / ngmin sɛb na / ko de a bebe /
kpɛn a wiɔ / kyɛ viɛli (1540) / ti a de-a / iɔng kuɔ̃ / ka bur ya / ka
ba de-a / kyuori-ya / lɛ doni-ya / a garo zu / ti bini / ti yel ka / ka
ba ngmaa muɔ / ba ba ngmaa / wa tani / a garo zu / ba tani / ba
pɔɔ / dayere bio / ka ba nyɔɔ / lɛ lɔɔ / ba iɔng tiɛru / lɛ iɔng na
nɔ̃ (1560) / ba nɔ̃ wa baari / ba yel ka / ka ba na woba / ba bɔ̃ɔ̃ ba

bomo / ka ba lɛ de / pɛ zɔɔ ya / iɔng ya / ba uri / ban uri wa baara /
ka muna / ba tɔ a / ba kyiri / bin teung / ti nyɔɔ yɛr / a muna / o ba
ngme / ka ba do-a / woba-a / lɛ ti tana / a nikpɛ̃ɛ̃-a (1580) / k'o yel
ka ɔ̃ / k'o nyãã na / ka ba bina / ka yele-a / na ta duura / ba bini /
ba na bina / ti lɛ yaari / ba yaari baari / a zie / o ba kyɛli / kyɛli ni
bo / a uon bana / ba yi / ka ba yel ka / ka zie / na uɔra / boonu kyɛ /
ka ti na i / a bɔɔ biɔ (1600) / ka ba yel ka / ka nikpɛ̃ɛ̃ / k'o yeli / a
bibiiri / ka ba yi-a / ka yela / a bɔɔ sɔɔli-aa / ka ba wa ka ya / ka na
bɔɔ pɛlɛ / dabɔɔ nibɛ / ba la wõ gɔ̃mɔ-aa / ba na wana / ba yi / zɔ
yɔɔ / yeli / a bɔɔ sɔɔli / bɔɔ pɛlɛ / baa man ka / ka dibna / ti mi siu
pɔɔ (1620) / ti ta-ya / ka nikpɛ̃ɛ̃ / o'a buɔli / a pɔɔ / k'o de-a / a kɛɛ /
doni-a / a garo zu / ti bini / ti yel ka / ka zie-a / na ngmɛ anya / ala
na ya / ka ti yel ka / a kɛɛ / yi de-aa / mani-a / a mano / ka ba de-a /
wa doni (1640) / ba de ngmani / ba iɔng / ba iɔng be / ti tõ ba
nuri / ba mani / ban a baara / ba iɔng / ka kyiri / ba iɔng / ka
kyiri / ba lɛ iɔng / ka lɛ kyiri / sambar ata / ba yel ka / ka ba zɛ̃
bire / ti a naangmin-aa / na fɛrɛ ti-aa / ti na de na-aa / sɔr i zu-aa /
na dɔɔlo nyuu-aa (1660) / ban i baara / ba lɛ de / lɛ ko-a / a pɔɔbɔ /
ba de-aa / ban de-aa / lɛ siu ni-yaa / ba dir puɔ / nar ba naru / ba
gbɛ̃ / ban na gbɛ̃-a / baari-a / ba duu / a dãã / ba na duu-aa / a dãã /
baa baari / ka dayere bio / baa wa / wa ta (1680) / baa nyɛ kɛɛ / ka
i dãã / baa nyɛ kyi / ka i saab / baa nyɛ biɔng / ka i ziɛri / baa nyɛ /
ka nibɛrɛ / baa zĩ / ka ba wa ta / [ba yel ka] / ka yi zɔ yɔ / yele-a / ka
ba wa fɔ̃ɔ̃ / ka bibiir / ni a nɔ tuo / ka ba wa fɔ̃ɔ̃ / ka ba wa ya / wa
ta ya / ba de dãã (1700) / bɔɔr na nyu / ka ba yel ka / ka ba alɛ / ban
ara / nibɛrɛ / ba de nuuri / a bɔbil kpɛ̃ɛ̃ / nuur ya / nuur ani / yel
ka ya / ka ngmini / ka siuwe / ka kpime / ka weni / ka bɔɔr / ka
dunɔ nɔn / kure pĩime / ka tɔ kpɛ̃ɛ̃ / gana fãã / on yel lɛ-a (1720) /
tikyɛ-a / a nuura / ka fu na de-a / ko a tengaana / ti de-a / kpe ko
siuwe / lɔng ni kpime / ka ba di-a / fũ wa nyɛ / ka bɔɔr / ba tɛra
yele / a n'ɔ dɛ̃ũ / on na lon puɔr / baa de / a no dɛ̃ũ / baa ngmaa /
o'a lo / on lo-iya / ba de nũɔ / ba ko a tengaan (1740) / o ba lo
kpai / ba la muɔr / ti ba kpɛ / baa ir nuɔ / ko a kpime / ba ir nuɔ /
ko a siuwe / ba do ko a weni / lɔng ni ngmini / a ba lo kpai / a na
lo kpai-a / bɔɔ kyiin biir / ka ba yel ka / a nuura / kaa shɔɔna / ana
shɔɔ-aa / a ba kyɛ dibo / bɔɔ kyiine / ba ba dire / ka nibɛrɛ (1760) /
iɔng na kyɔɔri-a / baa bari / ban bari-a / ka ba yel ka / ka dãã kpɛ̃ɛ̃
zu ya / ka nipkɛ̃ɛ̃ / ba nyue / ti yi buɔr / na nyu / ban yele-a / baa
zɔ dãbie / baa de ba dãã / ba ngmaa a zu / dãã kpɛ̃ɛ̃ zu / wa tani-a /
ka ti bɔɔ bɛrɛ-aa / ka ti nyu bõ gu / ti bar ko ba / ka ba nyu-ya / baa

tu na bɔbɔ (1780) / ban tu baara / ka bɔɔ kyiin bil / baa kpe dibo /
ba di bõ gu / ti zɛ kur-kuri / ban zɛ kur-kuri / ti irɛ na gõ / tɔ banu / lɛ
yel ka / ka ba bar sɛr / baa bari / ka ba man ka ya / ka yel-nya / ka
lɛ ngmɛna / a tin dõõ ira / ka nibɛrɛ / lɛ yel ko ti-a / ka diẽ bibira /
na bɔɔ biɔ / ka tomo-a (1800) / ben be / ka ba yel ka ai / ka bono
tomo / ka ba yel ka / ka bɔɔbil / ka ti bɔ-aa / a kã / ka ni-aa / a
mie / ka ni-aa / a kɔi / ka ti ni bɔɔr / ka ti bɔ-a / ti na yin / a ti bɔ /
ti a nyɛ biur / pɔɔ nyõõ-a / bin o biur / biur tin zuni-a / ti yel-a
(1820) / o a sɔri / ka libie / on sɔr baara / a ngmina? / ka lizɛri-a /
wɔɔ kong puɔ / n ba ira / lizer mwõ / tin ira / tin ir baara / ti wa
taiya / tin su-ya / a kul kpẽẽ nuɔra / faa nyɛ ngmama / ka wõ ya / ka
ti pɔraa / wa tani-aa / a yiri-aa / a bɔɔ yiri-aa / ti a bini (1840) / ti
ngmaa a nɛɛ / tin ngmaa baara / ti ba ira bebe / tin ir baara / ta
kyɛ viɛl / de lɔng ta / nibɛrɛ [baa yel ka] / ka diẽ-a / bibir-nya / olɛ
nu / ka ba buɔl / bɔɔ tĩĩsɔɔ / yi na ton / a tomo / ti yiini bio / o na
yel lɛ-a / o'a ko ba / o tomo / bon tomo na / ka o ko ti (1860) / a bɔɔ
kã-ya / ni taasir-a / ni kuɔr-a / ala tomo na / k'o ko ti / ka balɛ / nar
ba naru / ti wa yel ka / ka vũũ tan duuri / ka ba sooraa / a bɔbil-a /
a diẽ bibir / bibir faano / ti lɛ i bibir vla / ti na nyɔɔri ya / a bɔɔr
ya / ti yel ko yi-a / yi ta / wa irɛ diɔre / a bibir-a (1880) / olɛ na diẽ /
ka fũ wa / gani pɔɔ / ti wa sɔɔli bara / ka ba la tũõ fu nyuɔr / ka ba
la wa / tũõ fu nuɔr / fu kon i nirɛ / a ti bɔɔr puɔ / ba soori / sambar
ata / fu zɔɔri / bɔɔ ma / o ba soori / sambar ata / fu zɔɔri / bɔɔ
kyiin bil / ka ba nar ba naru / ba de mie / ba de kɔi (1900) / lɔng
ta ya / de ba wuur / ba ba gyiri / ban gyiri wa baara / ti nar ba
naru / baa de ba kãã / tɔ ka ta / ka ba de-a / ziɛ ur / ban de-a / wa
iɔng / a kã puo / ban iɔng baara / ti lɛ yel ka ya / ka ba de a mie /
yina de a mie / ka ba yel ka / ka bɔɔble / fu kyiirina / a fu puɔ (1920) /
k'o yel k'o kyiirina / a o puɔ / k'o yel ka / n tuõ / o'a soori / sambar
ata / ko yel ka / ka fu tuõ / ka n de-a / ko-ya / ma tɔsob-a / ko
soori / sambar ata / ka ba yel ka / ka ba tuõ / baa tuõ / tin tuõ-a / wa
baari-aa / ti-a i ti kãã / yel ka ya (1940) / ti ngmaara nuɔr / dãbie
ba kpɛ-o / ko yel ka ai / ka ngmaa nuɔr ngmin / k'o yel ka /
k'o na ngmaana / a fu nɔ iɛru / tikyɛ-a / bara / a fu nɔ dira /
ba yel lɛ / ti de a kã ya / pãã ngmaa / pãã ngma fu / ngma bangyiri /
ban ngmaa bangyira / ti yel fu ya / ka fũ wa yi-a / a bio-a / wa ti
zĩ-a (1960) / wa nyɛ-a / fu yebe-a / ko iɛr sɔɔ fu-a / fu ta wa sɔɔre /
o lo wa la sɔɔ fu / fu ta wa laarɛ / o na yel lɛ-aa / o'a wa baari / ti
yel ka ya / a diẽ bibir-a / ba zɛ fu kã-ã / fũ wa tɛr pɔɔ / ta wa piɛlɛ
u-ɛ / ka fũ wa i pɔɔ / ti wa tɛr daba / ta wa piɛlɛ u-ɛ / ka fũ-a / kun

tuõ i-a / yel / ka ba bar fu (1980) / yi zaa ba kyiiri / ka yi na tuõ na /
yin yele-a / wa baara / ka ba zɛ yi-a / wa baara / zie wa mani-a /
nikpɛ̃ɛ̃-a / ko ir ar-a / ti buɔli-a / ka ngmini / ka ngmino / o ba
buɔli / sambar ata / ti lɛ liɛba / lɛ yel ka ya / ka ngmina / ko wa
siuna / ka yɛra o yele / ka zaa zɛ̃zɛ̃ (2000) / ka wa siuni / ka ti yel ka /
ka dib na ko wa / k'o ba wa liɛbɛ / k'o tuura duro / k'o ba tuuri
gobai / k'o wan nio / o ba wan puore / o na yela / ka yi wõ-a / k'o
wanna dib / ya nyɛ / a dibo / a ba wa / ka bɔɔ kyiin bil / ka ba de
gbelme / baa pɔɔ a kuɔri / ti lõn ya / ti yel ka ya / ka a kuɔr nya
(2020) / k'o ulɔ wa ngmɛra / ka fu zu na ngmɛra / ti nibɛ zaa / bɔɔ
ka / yel nya / ka ulɔ ngmɛr baari / ka fu zu ngmɛri-aa / o mi na
ngmɛr o miõ zu / ka ti nyɔ-a / tɛri-aa / zaa zom / ka bɔɔ kyiinɛ /
ba yel ka / ka zie wa kyila / ka fu wa kyier-a / wa zɛlɛ-a / a kyii-a / kuõ
nyuur wa kpɛ fu-a / ka fu wa buɔr kuõ-a / fu ta wa nyure (2040) /
ka bɔɔ kyiina / wa nyɛrɛ / ka olɔ wa i-a / kul kpɛ̃ɛ̃ / fu na siuna-
ya / bin a kuɔra / ti maal fu nuuri / ɔng ni a kuõ-a / nyuu ya / ka fu
wa bõõ ka / a bɔɔ kyiini-a / tara fu-naa / fu na ira / lɛ yi-a / a kyier-a /
ti kyɛ-a / ka fũ wa / wa buɔr-aa / bangyira / fu na vɛ̆na (2060) / k'o
tɔli-a / ti fu dɔm / ka fũ wa ira / fu na ngmaana / ti bhara / a muɔ
puɔ / lɛ ti de-a / a o niõ / k'o wa iri-a / ti nyɛ fu / ka fu kyãã be /
a o niõ / fũ vɛ̃ / ka nirza / wa ti nyɛ-a / a fu kuõ nyuba / o na yel
ka ai! / ka ba nyɛ bɔɔ / na nyuur kuõ / aba viɛlɛ (2080) / lɛ na yaa /
ka ti ma sɔɔli / nyu kuõ / sɔɔlia / di bom / o'a yeli /
wiil ba-a gbɛɛ / o'a baari-a / ti nyɔɔ-a / a bɔɔr yele-a / wiil o-a / wa
baar / ka zie-a / wa mani-a / k'o ira / a de / pel zɔɔ / bina / a fu
nio / ti yel ka (2100) / ka fu zɛl pele nu / bio o ba bini / ko fu-a /
ka fũ nira / na nɔn fũ yele-a / wa wani / a lizɛr-a / wa iɔng a fu /
pele puɔ / ka wa i yɔɔ / ka ala na / na tuni / a bɔɔr yele / o ba bini /
ba iɔng na yɔɔ / ba iɔng baari / k'o de a / ko a bɔɔ kpɛ̃ɛ̃ /
k'o de / bin lɔng taa (2120) / ti yel ka ya / ka kyi-a / wa baara / ka
alɛ na / ka bona / na tuuri / a bɔɔr yele / ti de / a pele / o ba iɔng
fu numi / ka fũ yini-aa / ka fũ wa zɛlɛ / ka ba la wa kub / bom
zaa / fũ de / ka tɛnɛ na / ba ɔng ko fu / na de / ala na / a ti
bɔɔr bom (2140) / ya nyɛ-a / fu na yi-a / zɛlɛ-a / fun nyɛ / a kyi /
wani / n de lɔng ta / bina / ka fu yɔ / zɛlɛ iɔng ni / an ba zɛmbiira / ti
naangmin / na fɛra wora / ka ba yel ka / ka ba de lɛ / ka sɔri zu /
na dɔɔla nyũũ / ba bini / ka wa ta / a sõõ-aa (2160) / ka ba de-aa / yel
ka õ / ka pɔɔ nyõõ biir-a / ka ba de ya / ka va ya / ka iɔng-aa / a
siũ puɔ / ka ba warɛ / kan bõ gu / ti de a / a anya / iɔng puɔ / na
tu / a bɔɔr yele / o na yel lɛ-aa / wa baari-a / ka ba yel ka / ka õ /

k'a ba wõ-ana / ti o de-a (2180) / ba bini / ba bin / wa baara / ti ba
yuɔr / daar kɔ̃ɔ̃-aa / nibɛrɛ / tiɛrudem-aa / ka ba kun tuõ / bar / ka
fu tɛr / a fu kuɔr / yuɔri lɛ / ka ba na dena / ka bini / baa de / bini /
kaa taba / yel ka ɔ̃ / ka ba kun tuõ / de a kuɔr (2200) / bine / ba na
yel lɛ-aa / a wa baara / k'o yel ka / ka ti na in ngmin / k'o yel ka /
a kuɔra / na i a gyɛla / a ti zie / ti kun tuõ / bin barɛ / tina tɛr-aa /
yuɔri-a / a bom nya / fu na yel ka / tin na ira / tin lɔ̃ / yuɔri-a / ka
alɛ-a / saa i tomo (2220) / ti na lɔ̃ na / tono ni / o'a yel lɛ / on yel
wa baara / ti yel ko ti-a / ka kyi-a / ti na nyɛ-a / a yuɔra / ka shɔɔn /
a yel tuub / ti kyɛ-a / a nuur-aa / ala yele na / ia kpɛung / k'o yel
ka / ti na in ngmin / ko yel ka / lɛ yi na / dɔ̃ɔ̃ / zɛlɛ-a (2240) / a
kyii-a / alɛ na / ka yina lɛ / zɛli / a nuur / o na yela / wa baara / ti
yel k'o ba / ka yi ni wa yi biõ / wa ira / fu tɛr-aa / fu yɛble / bida-
bleno / k'o tu fu puor-aa / a yuɔr-aa / zɛlɛ-a / fũ wa nyɛ / a blã-a /
bonu blã / k'o yel ka (2260) / a n'ɔ bil blã / ka ba yel ka / a pam-
paniyãã / fu in / ziɛra / fu wa de nio / wa ti ta yira / ka nir ba piɛl
be / fu na de na / a nuɔ / fũũ wa nyãã / a nir wa piɛl be / a la
ilɛ-aa / fu na bara / ti zɛli / olɔ wa nɔ-aa / wa ko fu-aa / fu de / ti
olɔ ba / ko fu-aa (2280) / fu bar-o / n ba yeli / bio ba viɛ / faa iri /
ka n ko fu / a kaso / ni bie / o'a tuur fu / zɔr yuɔri / fu mãã ta / a
yiri / f'a nyɛ nuuri / f'a nyɔɔ / k'o ba tani / ka fu bari-a / ti lɛ wa
kuli / f'a yeli / ka ba yel ka / ka lɛ banai / ka fũ-a (2300) / wa kyeni /
wa nyɔɔ-aa / ka ba la wa faa / ta wa irɛ suure / fũ vɛ̃-aa / ti zɛli / olɔ
wa / wa i / a bɔɔ / o kũ de / ti bar fuɛ / ti olɔ / wa i dakume / wa
de-a / fu bar / ti kyier-a / ti a nuɔ / o na de-a / o kun / baa-i (2320) /
ti yele-a / a ti nibɛrɛ / ka ba yel ka / ka ti tɔɔ ta / ka ti tɔɔ ta / ka
ba yel ka ɔ̃ / ka bom nya / ti na nyɔɔ-a / a wa tani / a bɔɔ biɔr / ti
bɔɔra / ka ti na ta ka / a ti shɔɔn / ka ti bɔ̃ / a naangmin / zie / ka
tɔɔ ya / ir ara / ti yel ka / k'o tiɛr ka (2340) / ka naangmina / k'o
bena / a teung zu / ti na kyiera / ka kɔ̃ɔ̃ / yel ka / ka ɔ̃, ɔ̃, / k'o lɛ
yel ka / o tiɛru / ka naangmin / k'o ben / a salon zu / tin gyira / k'o
yel ka / ka ɔ̃, ɔ̃, / k'o lɛ yel ka / k'o tiɛru / ka naangmin / k'o bena /
a o nio (2360) / o natura / k'o yel ka / ka naangmin / ka ba be be / k'o
lɛ yel ka / n tiɛr ka / a naangmin / o bena / n puori / n na liɛb
tori-aa / k'o yel ka / naangmin / k'o ba ka be / k'o yel ka / naangmin /
n tiɛr ka / o bena / n duro loor / k'o yel ka / k'o ba ka be (2380) / k'o
yel ka / naangmin / n tiɛr ka / o bena / n guba loor / k'o yel ka /
k'o ba ka be / k'o lɛ soor ka ya / ti nyinɛ-na / ka naangmin / be-a /
fɛrɛ ti / lɔng na biiri / lɔng na pɔbɔ / ka tɔ yaa / yel ka ɔ̃ / ka
naangmin / ti na wõ o yuɔr a / ti ba bɔng o-a / ti fu yi diã (2400) /

soor ma / a naangmin / na yi zie-na / k'o lɛ yel ka ɔ̃ / a shɔɔn ka
n soor / zaa na yaa / ka n wõ-aa / ka fu buɔl / i gɔ̃mɔ̃ / ti yel ka
ya / ka naangmini / ka n wõ ya / fu na buɔla / ti fu yel ka / ka
naangmin / k'o wonaa / ko wa siu / ala na / ka n pãã bɔɔr / ka na
bɔng-a (2420) / a zie-na / o na yi-a / ti kyɛ-aa / ka ala wa i lɛ-aa /
ti pãã ba / tuur / a ala / na kyɛ / ka tɔ / lɛ soora / ka boonu / ka fu
bɔng / na kyɛ-aa / ko yel ka / tin bɔɔr biɔra / n tiɛr ka / bom na
kyɛ / ka tina i-a / olɔ na / a kɛɛ ngmier (2440) / ko yel ka / ka tɔɔ /
fu na bɔng lɛ-a / ti kyɛ / soor ma a naangmin zie / ko yel ka ɔ̃ / a
naangmin-a / yi naa ti-a / wiil mana / a zie / o na ba-aa / ka ba
ara / ti bɔ̃ ya / a naangmin / a zie-a / o na be-a / ka kɔntɔmɔ / o'a
bɔɔr ba gyinu / o ba wa / wa siu (2460) / ti yel ka / ka olɔ nu / a
naangmina / a bɔɔr yir puɔ / o na yeli-a / ti nyɔɔ ba-aa / ti wiil
ba-a / lɛ ba na irɛ / a bɔɔr-yaa / ti ba bɔ̃ / alɛ ba na tu / k'o na wiil
bana / sor kɔ̃ɔ̃ / k'a ba yel ka ɔ̃ / k'o wiil ba / kɔntɔmɔ / o ba iri /
ir ari / ti yel ka ya / ka bɔɔ shɔɔr tomo (2480) / a bɔɔ tĩĩsɔɔ daar / ka
ngmin bana i? / ka ba yel ka yaa / ka ba bɔɔr-aa / ka a daar / wa
taiya / ka bana / bɔn nira / k'o wa wiil ba / a bibir / lɛ ba na i-a /
o ba yel ka / ka kɔntɔmɔ / k'o wana tĩĩ / bɔɔ tĩĩ / an ni kuɔr / wa
bina / ti yel ka / ka tĩĩ-a nya / ka bala (2500) / wa yi a lɛ daar / ka
ba ia tĩĩ nya / iɔng kuɔ̃ puo / bibie ata / lɛ ir-a / lɛ iɔng vũũ puo /
bibie ata / ti bom zaa / na tulɔ-aa / o na tuɔ̃n i ka mhãã / ka bom
zaa / na lɛ mhãã / on lɛ / tuɔ̃n i k'o tulɔ / on yel lɛ-a / ka ba de-a /
ka ban in ngmin / k'o yel ka / k'o na wiil bana alɛ / ka ba na tu
alɛ (2520) / ti i ti nyɛ / a bom / na be a puɔ / ka bɛ de-a / iɔng
vũũ-a / wa ir o-aa / lɛ iɔng kuɔ̃ mi-aa / bibie ata / ba bini / kɔntɔmɔ
gyina / o ba wa / wa yel ka / ka ba de-a / ka kuɔra / ka ira tĩĩ bla /
ka ti bini / ti nɛ̃-aa / k'o ngmɛri-aa / ka ti iro-a / iɔng kuɔ̃ mi-aa (2540) /
ti kyɛ-a / de-a / a i tuuli / ni bo-yen-a / ka yi nyɛɛ-a / a bom / na be
be / ban de-aa / ban nɛba / k'o ngmɛri / ka ba de-a / iɔng kuɔ̃ mi /
ti tu la / a nir kɔ̃ / sambar ata / o'a kpi / on kpi-a / kɔntɔmɔ-a / o'a
lɛ kpɛɛ / o kɔlingwiɛ puɔ (2560) / o na kpe-a / ka nibɛrɛ-a / yel ka
ɔ̃ / ka yin nya / on wa tua / ko ti-a / ka ti de-a / ko wa i anya / tin
in ngmini / ka iib i-a / tɔ banu / o ba iri / biɛri / a zie-na / kɔntɔmɔ
na be-a / o'a iri / mi zɔ kpɛ / a kɔlingwiɛ puɔ / ti bɔɔra / a kɔntɔmɔ
zie (2580) / o na be-a / o'a wa nyũũ / o dio puɔ / k'o zĩ be / k'o yel ka
ai / ka a tomo nya / fun tɔ̃ ko ti-a / ti wiil ti a ibo / ti tuna / ka i kũũ /
a ko ti / k'o yel ka ɔ̃ / ka in lɛ / ka tikyɛ-a / o dɔ̃ɔ̃n yel ka bonu / ko
yi / k'o yel ka / k'o ba yel yele / k'a kɔntɔmɔ / lɛ yel ka (2600) / n ba
dɔ̃ɔ̃ ku-yi / a tĩĩ / ti yini-aa / yi na ta tuna / alɛ na n yel ko yia /

ti n yel ko ya / ala i yel tulo / a na mhãã na / ka i yel bhaaro / a na
tulɔ na / on yel lɛ / wa baara / ti tu daba / kula / o sãã yir puɔ /
a ba nyɛ kũ / k'o gã / k'o yel ka / ka nibɛ / k'o bɔɔra (2620) / k'o
wiil ba / a ba bɔɔr / ba na ma nyɔɔ-a / ti nyɛ-a / a niri-nya / na
gan ka / o tan daa? / ka ba yel ka / k'o ba ta daai / k'o yel ka / ka
bibie / ata na / a diɛ / o na kpi-a / ti in ngmin ba puɔ̃ / k'o yel ka /
ka ba mi ba bɔ̃ɔ̃-ɛ / k'o yel ka / ka ba alɛ / k'o soor ba-a (2640) / yel
kɔ̃ɔ̃ / ti lɛ yel ka / ka ba nira / na ma kpii-a / ka bibie angmina /
k'o ma puɔ̃ / ka ba yel ku-a / ka bibie ata / k'o ma sɔngna / ka
kɔntɔmɔ / yel ka ya / k'o bɔɔra k'o wiil-ba / ti yini / na tu n puɔri /
yi ba tu n puor vla / ala na vẽ-a / kãn ba wiil yi / a ma yel nya / o
ina / a bɔɔr (2660) / yel kpẽ̃ẽ̃-no / ti-a nya / olɔ nu-a / na vẽ-a / ka
bɔɔble / zɔ dãbie / olɔ nu-a / na vẽ-a / ka bɔɔ sɔɔli / zɔ dãbie / olɔ
nu-a / na vẽ-a / ka bɔɔ kyiinɛ-a / zɔ dãbie / o na yel lɛ-aa / ti kyena /
ti kpa / o nuɔr-aa / a toor puɔ / ti kuura (2680) / ti yel ka / ka ba
gyirɛ / faa nyɛ kũ / o'a lɛ iri / on ira / k'o yel ka / ka ba la wa bɔɔra /
ka tĩĩ anya / ka ba de-a / a lizɛr miɔ̃ / ani wal piel da / ala na ya / ba
ma daa a tĩĩ / o na yel lɛ-a / ba wani / a wal piel da / ani lizɛr miɔ̃ /
ba ya a kɔntɔmɔ / ban ya wa baara / ban in ngmin (2700) / baa
kyeni / tĩĩsɔɔ daari / a o yir-aa / k'o ti zĩ-aa / ti wiil ba-o / a kyile
tĩĩ / ka ɔ̃ / ka bana soora / a naangmin yele-aa / k'o wɔ̃-ana / ko
olɔ na / a naangmin / ka nira / wa bɔ̃ɔ̃ o tub / ka ma nyɛn vla / ka
nira / ba bɔ̃ɔ̃ o tuba / o kun tuɔ̃ / nyɛ vlai / on yel lɛ-a (2720) / a wa
baara / nikpẽ̃ẽ̃ / o'a man ka / bɔɔ sɔɔli puo / n dɔ̃ɔ̃ / nyãã / yɛbɛ
yele-a / ala tãna / ba ma kuni / a bɔbɔ / k'o yel ka o / ka ala banai /
ka a tĩĩ-na / o wuɔ puɔ tĩĩ / ka ala na / ka sããkuma / bar k'o / ka o
tɛra / a tĩĩ bhaar / olɔ na anya (2740) / a tĩĩ tulu / olɔ na anya / ka
zaa / ina / a boma / na na tuɔ̃ / ku kũũ / na lɛ na tuɔ̃ / siung kũ / on
yel lɛ-a / ti yel ka ɔ̃ / ka al wa i-a / a kũũ siung tĩĩ / a ben o zie /
alɛ wa i-a / kũũ kurɔ tĩĩ / a ben o zie / o'a yel baari / ara be-a / o na
bɔɔra tĩĩ-a (2760) / tikyɛ-a / ka bɔɔ tĩĩsɔɔ / ban na duula / kɔntɔmɔ /
fu ba tɛra deb nya / a ano deb nya / a tɔ banu / ka fu tɛri / ti kyɛ
ti / an i lɛ-a / ka fu tɛri tɔ / ti bɔɔ tĩĩsɔɔ / na ba lɛɔrɔ / ka ti na tuɔ̃ /
liɛb barɛ / iɔng bi zɔɔlai / ti kyɛ-a / a bɔɔ tĩĩsɔɔ / ba wa ta / ka
kɔntɔmɔ-a (2780) / bar o bie-a / k'o wa-a / a bɔɔ yira / ka wa nyɛ-a /
a bɔbɔ / na ira lɛ / on yel lɛ-a / o'a wa ta / nyɛ bɔbɔ / vũũ ba tan
duri / ka kɔntɔmble-a / zin zoma / ti gyirɛ-a / ka ba ba ir / yel ka
ya / ka ba kurɔ bɔbɔ / ka ba'a ngmiere / ka ba ku-a / a bɔbil /
bin-aa (2800) / ti ka nikpẽ̃ẽ̃-a / ira / dɔm o sinshiura / ti ngmaa
yielo / ka kũ kuna / yee kũ ku / ka soora kai / baa ngmaa olɔ

sambar ata / lɛ iri-a / lɛ bar-a / ti lɛ ngmaa / ka vini gã gã dio / ka
sooro ba kai / ba ngmaa sambar ata / lɛ baari ya / ti lɛ ngmaa ya /
ka ba wani kuba / ka ba ya bɔbɔ / ba ngmaa sambar ata / ba bari
(2820) / ti lɛ ngmaa / ka ba bɔng ni luue / ka o sob yir puɔ lu gɔn
gɔn / ba ngmaa sambar ata / ti yel ka ya / ka bɔɔ wuɔ / ngme nuɔ /
na kpa kpa kpa / ba bar ala / ti lɛ yel ka / ka kũũ kuna yee / kũũ
ku / ka bɔɔwen faa bar / ka kũ ta kuɛ / baa baar lɛ sambar ata / ti
lɛ ngmaya / ka ba iri yi yõõ / ka ti nyɛ bɔbɔ / ba ngmaa olɔ / sambar
ata (2840) / ba bɔng gu / ba iri / ba irɛ na yi / ka ba lɛ dɔm sinshiura /
ti lɛ ngma yielo / ka ba gũ gũ gbɛ / na gura gura / baa bari / baa
lɛ ngmaa / ka ti viri kpiru / sɔɔr nyin kora / ka viri [kpiru] / sɔɔr
nyin kora / ka ti viri [kpiru] / ba bar olɔ / ti lɛ ngmaa / ka ti ir
bar / dɛr kora / ka ti ir bar / ka sɔɔr dɛr kora (2860) / ka ti ir bar /
ba ngmaa wa bar / ti lɛ liɛba / lɛ kyena / a dio puɔ / na ti kpɛ / a dio
nya / bɔɔ kyiin bil / ba nar ba naro / a tĩĩsɔɔ daari / baa ũũ gbelme /
a dio puɔ / yiini-a / a dakyin zie / ti ũũ yaa / ban wa baari-a / ti kpɛ
dio puɔ / ba ti ta / a dio puɔ / ba mi ba kpɛ (2880) / ni gbelme / ba
ngmaa yielu / a iɔng yaa / a bɔbɔ toori-a / ka ba wõ / ka bana iri /
ka ngman bõ gu / ka bɛ yel ka / ka ban in ngmin / ka yel par-nya /
kɔntɔmble / ba tɔɔ ta / ba siir kaa / ti yel ka / ka ba bhaan / ka ba
kun tuõ ire / baa yel ka õ / ka ban in ngmin / ka tɔ ya / ni o
kɔntɔmɔ (2900) / ba ba waari / wa ta yiri / a dio puɔ / ba a kpɛɛ / ba
nyɛ zĩĩ / [ti yel] ka ai / ka bono i / ka ba yel ka yaa / ka yel nya /
ana wa ta / a tĩĩsɔɔ daari / ka ala na / ka ba yel ka ba tu / ka ti tu
bõ gu / ti bur bur / ko yel ka õ / ka bɔɔra / ka nyinɛ ti ta / k'o yel
ka / ka ba ba bɔnge-ye (2920) / faa nyɛ tɔ / k'o yel ka / ka bɔɔr
yin ngme kɛɛ ngmier / ka ba yel ka õ õ / ti ba ngmei / ti in ngmin / ka
bɔ sɛur / wa ta / a bɔɔ tĩĩsɔɔ / ka yi kua nibɛ / k'o lɛ yel ka / ka bɔɔr
kuba / ba ba ma kuni daai / ba ba ma kuni pĩĩ-ye / ba ma kuna / ni
yɛ̃ / ani tĩĩ / o na yel lɛ-a / ka bɔbɔ (2940) / dãbie ba kpɛ ba / ban
in ngmini / ka kɔntɔm ble-a / lɛ nyɔ ba / ti wiil ba / alɛ-a / ban na
ku a bɔbɔ-a / ka a zaa / ka a yina / naangmin zie / olɔ nu-a / wani-
a / tõ faa / ani tõ vla / olɔ nu-a / wani-a / yel bebe / ani yel nuɔ /
olɔ nu-a / wani-a (2960) / kon / ani laar / olɔ nu-a / wani-a / nõõ / ani
tɛru / olɔ naangmina / olɔ wani-a / nyɔvuɔri / ani kũũ / ka ba lɛ
soor o-a / a in ngmin / ka fũũ naangmin / ira nibɛ / iɔng nyɔvuɔr /
ti ka kõõ mo tuõ ngma / on a yele-a / ka bie na / mi yel ka õ / ka
fũ bɔɔra (2980) / ka bom zaa / a teung zu / naangmin-a / na ka
funa / a ma / a naangmin / ti wona / k'o tɛra yir / ka isob yel ka /
ka nyinɛ naa yir be / o'a yel lɛ / on yel wa baara / ka bɔɔ bɛrɛ / ba

mirɛ / a kun / bana gã / a kõ ya / lɛ mhe ka / ti yel ka ai / ka ba faa
mhaa (3000) / o na yel lɛ-a / a kɔntɔmble / o'a de o tĩĩ / iɔng o
nuɔri / ti uɔb k'o ngmɛri / ti puura / a ba zuri / on puur wa baara /
ti liɛb o nɛɛ / kpa a tobo puɔ / o'a kuuri / baa iri / k'o yel ka õ /
ka bana ira / ba zaa ba ira / ka ba zaa ba iri / ban ir baara / ko yel
ka õ / ka ti lɛ biɛra / a yel ngmaara (3020) / na kyɛ / bonu yel
ngmaara / k'o yel ka / yin wa ta / a bɔ biɔra / ba tuõ ngme kɛɛ /
ti ba lo-a / a bɔ tĩĩsɔɔ / yi ba sɔng yele / a sɔng zɔɔla / ta nyɛ
bome / lɛ na / ko lɛ ira / tɛr tia / turi-a / a bɔɔ yele / ana lɛ wa /
a kɛɛ ngmiera / a ba wa ta / ka bɔbɔ (3040) / ba yuɔri ni ba kɔi / ɔng
ni kuõ / man kuõ na / ba na ɔng lɛ-a / wari-a / gbangbala puɔ / ka
ba wa zĩ be-a / zĩ lɔng ta / bɔɔ kyiin bil-aa / baa tõ ba / ka ba
kuli-a / ti vuõ a kyi / wa tani / a gbangbala puɔ / bɔɔkar bil / ka ba
zĩ-a / i ba de nuɔr / ka ba yel ka ya / ka bon nuɔri / k'o yel ka õ (3060) /
a bom-a / na ngmɛ anya / tin in ngmin / ka nikpɛ̃ɛ̃ / lɛ yel ka / ka ba
vɛ̃ / ka k'o de nuɔr / o'a yel ka / ka ngmini / kpime / siuwe / weni /
ka bɔɔr / ka tikyɛ / ka ti bõ gu / ti ba yel ka / ala na-a / dunɔ nɔn / tɔ
kpɛ̃ɛ̃ / gana fãã̃n (3080) / na o ir u kyi / kyeni-a / a gobasob zie /
o'a zu lɔbi / ti yel ka / k'o tɔ taa / ka ba soor nyɛ / ka o tɔ taa / ba
zin mhan ta / ti soori-a / ka bɔɔr / o'a ir weni / ka ba soor-yaa / ka
wiɔ wen bi / o'a zɔɔri / kɔntɔm wen bi / o'a zɔɔri / sãã̃kum wen bi /
o'a zɔɔri / makum wen bi (3100) / o'a zɔɔri / taaba wen bi / o'a zɔɔri /
bibiir wen bi / o'a zɔɔri / k'o pãã soor / ka kpaartiib wen bi / ka
bie-aa / kaa lo sɔɔ / ka ti ira / ti zɔ biɛra / tin biɛra-ya / wa tɔ diɛ̃ /
ka ti ira / ka bibiira / ban ba bɔng / ti tɔ-ya / kpɛ o muõ-a / ti
bɔɔra / a bom bɔɔra (3120) / a bɔɔr bom / ti biira / a zie / ba piɛli /
on piɛli / ka ba ira-a / tõ ba tomo-ya / wa kuni biiri-a / ka ti wa
nyɛ-a / ka ba kpɛ tule / ka ti bõ gu / ti kyɛ-a / a kɔntɔmɔ-aa / dõõ
yel ka yaa / ka tin de-aa / a tĩĩ biɛr-aa / ka iɔng kuõ mi-aa / ka bibie
ata / ka yel tulu-aa / k'o na tuõ na i (3140) / ka o bhaaro / ka tin
de-aa / a tĩĩ biɛr kõõ ya / ka iɔng vũũ ya / ka bibie ata / ka yel
bhaar / o na tuõ na / kaa i tule / ti-a de / kyaan bini-a / tia bibiiri /
ba a bɔnge / ti ir-aa / sɔng a sori-aa / ka ti yi a muɔ / wa ta yaa / taa
nyɛ kuni / ti nyɛ alɛ-a / ti ba nyãã / ala na (3160) / ka ti lɛ liɛba /
lɛ nyɔɔ-aa / lɛ biɛri-aa / ka ti na bõõ / a bomo-aa / na kyãã̃ni-a / a
niõ-a / ka ti wa yel ku a bibiiri / ala na-ya / ka ti wa siung ba / lɛ de
ba / lɛ wiili-aa / a soi / ti yi diɛ̃ / bibira / ti a ta / a kɛɛ ngmier / ka
ti kyiraa / a kyi / tin na kyiraa (3180) / yi ba nyãã / ka ba bini /
a gbangbal puɔ / ti iɔng dãbie / a fɔb / ka ti a ii-a / a gbangbal
puɔ / ti yel ka ya / ka ngmin gar kpɛ̃ɛ̃ / a gbangbala ba nu / ti a

ngmina / lɛ de-a / a man kuõ-a / ti a iɔng / a daar nya / ka lɛ lieba /
taa lɛ lɔɔ / baalɛ lɔɔ / ban lɔɔ-a / ka ti kuli-a (3200) / ti tani / a
yiraa / tin in ngmin / tu bõ gu / ti yel ka ɔ / ka ba ta ka / baa ta /
a yiri-aa / bɔɔ kyiin bil / baa nyɔɔ bɔɔbili / baa ziil ba a kɔɔ zu / ban
ziil wa baara / ti de-a / a dãã ya / a saab ya / wa tani-a / baa di bõ
gu / ka i ba nuõ / ka ba ira-a / iɔng na gõ-ya (3220) / ka tɔ-yaa / o'a
kyuur ba / ka ba bari / k'o yel ka / ka bɔɔr / ka ba i gõm / ka ba
gõmɔ-a / ka ba kyɛli-a / ka ti gyirɛ / lɛ o na yela / ba kyɛli / o'a yel
ka / ka dib / yin di baara / a yel na kyaan / a puɔr-a / ti yi di bar /
ti iɔng na gõ-aa / o'a yel lɛ / ti yel ka (3240) / a yele / na kyɛ-a / yel
blã nu / ti i yel yɔɔ / ti a bɔɔ-a / ti na nyɔɔ-a / ka ba gɔn-aa / ka ti
wiili gu / wa yiina diɛ̃ / ti yin bɔɔra / a naangmina / tin soora / ka
yi ba tuõ / yel a zie / ona be-aa / yin nyɛ-a / a bɔɔra / tin nyɔraa /
ti ba nyɛ / a nio (3260) / ti kyɛ-a / a kɛɛ ngmier nyɛ puɔ / ti na
bõõna / a yɛ̃-nya / tin bõõni-aa / a yel kõõ / ti na gu-a / a yel kõõ /
na be a ti nio-aa / ti be-a ti puori-aa / ti-a yele / tin yel baara / ti
lɛ liɛba / zɔ kula / a yira / ti ta ya / t'a zĩ / ti na zĩ-a / a sõõ ba ta /
ka ti na iri (3280) / bonu sõõnu / a kɛɛ ngmier sõõ / tin yel ka ya / ka
yel yɔɔ-a / be na ti nio / ka yi ba bõõi / ola na diɛ̃ / ka ti ira / bɔɔr
na wiila / a bibiir / lõõ ni pɔbɔ / lõõ ni dɔɔr / ti kyɛ-a / a bɔɔra / na
dõõ ta / a bɔ tĩĩsɔɔ / ka yi tõ alɛ / a ba ia 'ibɛ / ti kyɛ / pampana
nyãã (3300) / yi zaa kpo / yi i a niã / ka wa ta ya / ka vĩĩ ta kpɛ yi-ɛ /
ti baara bɔɔr / ti bõõ lɛ-a / ti na i-a / baa kuli ti ta / ka zie / ba
mani / ti a bɔɔble-a / nabɔl bie / o'a kpɛ wiɛ / wal piel da / na tuo
iilɛ / o'a waari / wa tara / o'a tɛ / on na tɛ-a / pĩĩ ba nyɔɔ (3320) /
a pĩĩ na nyɔɔ-a / o in ngmin / o'a ngme kyɛli / o ba duuri / ti
kpɛni-a / a wiɔ puɔ / o'a lo / on lo-a / ka bɔɔ bɛrɛ / tiɛru ka / ba
nyɛn nɛni / ka bi ma-ya / tiɛru ka / k'o na nyɛn nɛn / ka bi sãã /
tiɛru ka / ba nyɛn nɛn / ka ba wa tani / a wɛ dũõ / a sãã yir puɔ (3340) /
ka ba yela / ka bi sãã / k'o nɛn ba ka bei / ka bi ma / k'o nɛn ba
ka bei / ba iɔng na gõ / zɔɔr ba wa / ka ba zĩ teung / ti iɔng tiɛru-a /
ti ba mani / k'o ba yel ka / bonu vɛ̃ / ka na dɔɔ bie / di ni dɔi / di
ni dɔi yɔɔ / ti nir wa de / a o bomo / ni iɛn bhaaru / ka ala i lɛ-a /
k'o ba sɔɔre (3360) / ka ba yel ka ya / ka a tub tubna / ka ba la
yi-a / a yong-aa / ti ar manta / ti yel ka õ / ka an ngmɛ̃ lɛ-aa / ka
ti na de naa / a nɛn-aa / ko a bi ma / ka nibɛrɛ / baa bar gõmɔ / ba
gyur bari / ti yel ka õ / ka nɛn yaa / a bi ma / wa i bɔɔ-aa / ka bi
sãã / mi wa i bɔɔ-aa / ona in yel (3380) / yel bhaaru / yi na bara /
a nɛn yaa / ka a bɔɔbil-a / ka ba de a nɛn yaa / ti tani / bɔɔ kpɛ̃ɛ̃
yir-a / baa zĩ lɔng ta / ti bɔng bomo / ba ira nɛni / a gbɛro-a / ka

ba ula / lɛ ko / a bi sãã / tikyɛ siɛ / ku a bi ma / o yel ka ɔ̃ / ka ba
walhala iɔng / o ba de-o / o ba la (3400) / ti yel ka ɔ̃ / kaa viɛla / ti
ba i-a / ka bɔɔbil-a / ba yuɔri / kun bomo / wa lɔng taa / kurɔ ba /
ka ba dire / tikyɛ bin aminɛ / a ni-daar iɔng / ka ala na / ka i-a / a
bɔɔr bomo / bɔɔr bõ bonu / ala na-ya / i a bɔɔ ziɛr / baa yeli / bana
yela / ti yel ka ya (3420) / ka bɔɔble zaa / fũ wa yi yɔ̃ / ba ku
bom-yaa / tikyɛ-a / al wa kɔɔr / yuomo tur / ti saa ko bom / fu na
yana a bɔɔr / bonu vɛ̃ / ka ba tuur alɛ / a bibiir / diɔra / ka ba mi ir /
ban wa yela lɛ-a / ka ti lɛ yel oora / ba yel ka dobaa / ti kyiiru nu / ba
yel ka / ka siɛ̃ni / o ba ka be (3440) / ti bɔɔr bom puɔi / sã sir / o ba
ka be / ti bɔɔr bom puɔi / we kõɔ̃ / o ba ka be / ti bɔɔr bom puɔi /
tikyɛ / nir wa ku sɔng / o ben be / ti bɔɔr bom puɔi / ka fũ wa
ku / wala / o ben be / ti bɔɔr bom puɔi / ka fũ wa ku / kɔrĩ / o ben
be / ti bɔɔr bom puɔi / nira wa ku (3460) / gbel / o ben be / ti bɔɔr
bom puɔi / ba yel lɛ / ti a are / bɔɔbil-a / ka ba zɔ yɔ / ku-a / a duna /
wa ti ya / a bɔɔr / ku a bɔɔ bɛrɛ / ti pãã kyɛ / a yel yɔɔ / banu be
be / a ti nio / ka ti ba bõɔ̃-ɛ? / ba na yela / bom na kyɛ-a / a ba
kyɛ (3480) / a bɔɔ shɔɔr / daar kõɔ̃ / a nikpɛ̃ɛ̃ / gã ti wa yel / ka bɔɔr /
na waara / na wa ta / fu ba nyɛɛ / bɔɔ pɛlɛ / ka ba laari / ti zɛ̃zɛ̃
nɛ / kaa ta fɔ̃ / ban zɛ̃zɛ̃ nɛ / ti ba tɛri-a tiɛrɛɛ / bonu iɔng na / ka
ba tiɛrɛɛ / a bondiri-na / ni ba di nɛ / ka ba bɔɔra / ala na (3500) /
ka ba tiɛrɛɛ / ka ta fõɔ̃ / ka ba yel ka / ka kɛɛ-yaa / ka ba yi-a / ka
yele-a / a nibɛrɛ / ba wa nyɛ / a kɛɛ / ba yi / yɔ yeli / a bɔɔ sɔɔlia /
ni a bɔɔ pɛlɛ / na i-a / a dabɔɔra / ka ba wõ / lɛ na / ka ba yela / ka
dayere bio / ka ba wa (3520) / kaa pɔɔ nyɔ̃ɔ̃ na / o'a de a piɔ / vaa a
kɛɛ-ya / iɔng ka shɔɔ / ko duuri dona / a gar zu-ya / ba ti tani / bɔɔ kar
bɛrɛ / ba de ba ngmama / iɔng ba nuri / ti irɛ na mani / baa mani /
a kɛɛ-ya / bɔɔble zaa / ni pɛliir ayi / ni kɛɛ / baa wani / t'a kɛɛ-a / ba
zɛ̃ boma / t'on i-a (3540) / a bom na / fɛrɛ ti-a / tin de naa / sɔri
zu-aa / na dɔɔla nyũũ-aa / ban yel lɛ-aa / ti man baar / ba ba siu
zɔ kuli / ba ti ta / a sãã yir puɔ / tikyɛ / pɔɔ nyõɔ̃ na / na bõɔ̃ o
bom-aa / ba de kɛɛ / ba gbɛ̃ / ka liɛb zɔ / ba de kyi / ka liɛb zɔ / ba
de-a / a kɛɛ-a (3560) / iɔng kuõ̃-a / ba sãã kɛɛ / iɔng kuõ̃-a / lɛ mali-
yaa / a kɛɛ kuõ̃ / iɔng i-ya / ba siung puɔ / ti dɔm-aa / ti duuli-yaa /
pɔɔbil bhɔla / ba iɔng vũũ / kaa kara / ban in ngmin? / ba nyɔɔ
yaa / iɔng siung puɔ / zie ba mhãã / baa gã / wa iri-aa / zĩ lio iɔng / ba
wuol dãã (3580) / ti yel ka ɔ̃ / ka a dãã ya / ka ba lɛn nya / kaa
miina? / baa ba lɛn o / kaa ba mii / ba nyɔɔ yaa / yaa iɔng / ba duur
ya / ti lɛ duuli / a zi lio iɔng / ba duul baari / ka zie ba mani / a mutõ
tuo / ba nyɔɔ yaa / a ba duu puɔ / pɔɔ nyõɔ̃ biɛ / k'o lɛ iri-aa / de-aa /

o bomo (3600) / bonu bomo / dãbil na / i-a bomo / ba iɔng / kaa
fu-a / ka ba de-aa / ba zɔ̃-a / ka liɛb saabo / zie ba sobi / dayere bio /
ba wa ta / baa nyɛ zɔ / ka i saabo / baa nyɛ kɛɛ / ka i dãã / baa nyɛ
birɛ / ka i ziɛri / a naab nɛn / ba de-a / iɔng laaliir (3620) / ba na
iɔng laaliir baar / fu bɛ nyɛ / a bɔɔ kyiinɛ / ka nikpɛ̃ɛ̃ / o'a ira / ti
yel ka / ka ba tɔɔ ta / ka ba tɔɔ ta / o'a nyɔɔ / a tĩĩtĩĩ nɔ bili / ni a
nɔ bɛrɛ / lɔng taa / a bɔɔr yiri / na ku-a / bana bɔɔr kuba / baa
buɔli / bɔɔ pɛlɛ / baa wa ta / ti yel ka ɔ̃ / ka bomɔ (3640) / tin dɔ̃ɔ̃
yel ka / o tara na-ya / ti ba taa / olɔ na diɛ̃ / ti kaab bɔɔr / ti pãã
yel ka / ka ngmini / ka kpime / ka siuwe / ka weni / ka bɔɔr / dunɔ
nɔn / kure pĩĩme / tɔ kpɛ̃ɛ̃ / gana fãã̃n / ti ir kyi / zɔ kyena / gobasob
zie / o'a zɔɔre / ti zu lɔb (3660) / k'o nyɔɔ / k'o nyɔɔ-a / k'o ir weni /
o na ir weni / bonu weni? / kɔntɔm wen bi? / k'o zɔɔr / wiɔ wen
bi? / k'o zɔɔr / sããkum wen bi? / k'o zɔɔr / makum wen bi? / k'o
zɔɔr / taaba wen bi? / k'o zɔɔr / kpaartiib wen bi? / k'o lo sɔɔ /
yaa nyãã ka ti turi / ire ni bebe / wa yi naa (3680) / a diɛ̃ / alɛ na / ka
vũũ ta duuri / ka ti bɔɔra / ka ti mana / a yele-a / nyɛ lɛ / tikyɛ /
a boma / ti ma yel ka / ka kaab nu-a / kaa ia ti bɔɔr bomo / ka
singbile-a / ala na / ka mi i / a ti bɔɔr bomo / ka biɔ̃ / ka mi i / a ti
bɔɔr bomo / ka nuɔ-a (3700) / ka mi i / a ti bɔɔr bomo / a zãã / bio
na diɛ̃ / ka ti bɔɔra / ka ti bɔng / ti baari / a ti yele / ti na yela / ti
bɔɔ kyiina / baa nyɛ dibu / zɛ̃zɛ̃ nɛ-a / bɔɔr na di / ti a kyuur ba /
baa bar kpibo / ti irɛ na zĩ / ti yel-a / a bɔɔbil-ya / ka mutong nya / na
kpiɛra (3720) / ka daba muna no / kaa bɔɔbil-a / dãbie / ba kpɛ ba /
ka ba zĩ-a / iɔng tiɛru / bɔɔ kpɛ̃ɛ̃-ya / o'a nyu dãã / ti ir ara / ti yel
ka / ka bɔɔbil-a / ka bondiri-a / ban dir-a / ka ka olɔ wa / i wena /
sirzaa-ya / kaa-bondiri-a / a kũ bɛ ba puurɛ / ba zuri kũ biɛrɛ / ba
poi (3740) / na ina po vlai / ka ba duuri / na saa / ti bɛ nyɛra / wal
piel bin / zaa wiriwiriwiri / ka ti pɔble / ni dable / pɔɔ nyɔ̃ɔ̃ / ni da
nyɔ̃ɔ̃ / wa tɛra puor ayi / wani-a / a bɔɔr ya / olɔ no / ni bɔɔ wena /
na lɔng kpɛ / ti bɔɔble-a / mi wa kyiiri gu / t'a a won-o / ti na
bɔɔna (3760) / a bɔɔr puɔ / ti a miur-aa / ti na lõ-a / a yi zumi-ya /
a tĩĩsɔɔ-nya / alɛ na / ka ti zĩ kyɛlɛ / bɔɔble-a / wa sɔng o puɔ /
bɔɔble-a / wa gana fãã̃n / ka bɔɔble / wa ngme nira / a diɛ̃ bibir-a /
ko na yela zaa / ba yele / bɔɔbile / ba kyiiro / bana kyiir o-aa / ka
a nikpɛ̃ɛ̃ (3780) / lɛ zĩ zom / ti yel ka ya / ka ba bɔ̃ɔ̃na / a kyile / ka
olɔ nu / na kpɛ a diom / ka ba dea / kpɛni / ti bina sɔ̃ɔ̃ / tia nikpɛ̃ɛ̃ /
k'o yel ka / ka tomo / ban dɔng tõ / kaa ba tõ vlai / ka ba soor / kaa
in ngmin ba tõ vlai? / ti a kyile-aa / yi dɔ̃ɔ̃ kuna bɔɔbila / ti ba kpɛ
kyile / ti ku a bɔɔbɔ ni daar (3800) / a ba tu sore / lɛ na / ka n yel ka /

a kyile na kpɛ-a / a diõ-ma / yi gyirɛ 'ib / a kyile ba kpɛ / a kyile
na kpɛ-a / ka ba tuuri kuõ / ti mirɛ a sob / k'o kpiɛni / ti ta ni / dãbie
ba kpɛ bɔbɔ / ka nikpɛ̃ɛ̃ / yel ka ya / ka a kyile-a / ka bom kpɛ̃ɛ̃ ba
nuɛ / ti tono tom bɛrɛ / a kyile baa bini / a zaanuɔra bana (3820) /
ka ba yel ka ya / ka bɔɔ kyiinɛ / ka ba kaar ba bɔɔbɔ zie / ka a
diɛ̃ / on a yel lɛ-a / bɔɔ kyiine lɛ soor / ka ba kaa ni bo? / k'o yel
ka ya / ka diɛ̃-na / ba kurɔ bɔɔbil / a yel miõ kub / a bɔɔbili / ba zɔ
dãbie / k'o yel ka õ / ka ba i yele / ka ti lɛ i yel / tin yel ka diɛ̃ / ka
ba kurɔ yi-na / ka nir wa di sõõ / ti wa ti sɔɔli (3840) / ka bala wa
ku fu-a / ba kũ lɛ tuõ fu siung-ye / a daar na ni nya / ka bamina-a /
wõ-yaa / ka-ya / alɛ yaa / yi na irɛ ti a bɔɔra / n sõõn / bona fu
sõõ? / k'o yel ka ya / k'o sõõn daba / ka ba lɛ soor dɔɔr / ti yini
mi? / ka ba yel ka / ka ba mi sõõn / baminɛ sõõn pɔbɔ / baminɛ zɛb
ni nibɛ / ti alza ia bɔɔ kyiiru / ba yele (3860) / ka ba bar ba zõm /
ti yel ka ya / ka ba na tuna bɔɔbil sɛr / ti tuur ba-a / bar ka ba zĩ
ba yõ / ba zĩ / ti a nikpɛ̃ɛ̃ / o'a yel ka / ka ba wan yelingpuɔ / baa
wani / k'o yel ka / ka ba wan kuõ bhaaru / ka ba wa tani / a kuõ
bhaaru-a / k'o puura kyile / ti kel ya / a diɛ̃ / bibiri / bibir faa no /
ti i-a (3880) / bibir vla / a diɛ̃ bibira / bibir nuõ-nu / ti i bibir
tuo / a diɛ̃ bibira / bibir bhaaro-nu / ti i bibir tulu / bɔɔble-a / a
diɛ̃ / o tɛra o zu / o'a yel lɛ / ti yel ka ya / ka ba de nuɔ / ka tɔ
tani-a / ka kyile iong / ka ti zɛli sor / ba de / a nuɔ / na kaso / nɔ
boonu? (3900) / nɔr daziɔ ba i-oo / baa tani / k'o yel ka ya / ka ba
tu nuɔr-aa / ka ti zɛli sor / baa de nuɔri / ti yel ka yaa / ka kpime /
siuwe / weni / kɔntɔme / tengaani / ka bɔɔr / kure pĩĩme / dunɔ
nɔn / tɔ kpɛ̃ɛ̃ / ka gana fããn / o'a ir o kyi / gani-a / a gobasob
zie (3920) / ti kyɛ / o na kyena / o'a nyãã / ka ti tu kaa / a yi bɔɔbil /
yi wõna / ti a diɛ̃ / bibiri / a bɔɔbɔ kub / bibiri / a diɛ̃-a / yaa nyɛ
kyile / na bin yi sõõ / a yele na nya / ka ti na tu / a diɛ̃ / ti lɛ yel
ka õ / ka bɔɔr / ka ba bar sɛr / baa bari (3940) / k'o yel ka / ka ba
tõ wuur / baa tõ / ko yel ka ya / ka bɔɔbɔ / ka ba ir bom / ba ba iri /
bonu bom? / a gan kpɛ̃ɛ̃ no-a / ka ti ir o-aa / ka ba yel ka / ka
bɔɔbɔ / ka ba tɔ nyũũ / ba tɔ / k'o yel ka / ka yel nya-a / na ngmɛ-
anya / ka ti bõ gure / ti a diɛ̃ bibiri / yi na zɛli na soraa (3960) / ka ti
tu tub kɔɔ / o na yela / ti lɛ yela / bɔɔ kyiinɛ / ka ba nar ba naru /
bɔɔ kyiinɛ / ba ba soori / ti nar banu? / k'o ba yel ka ya / ka nɔ
kpɛ̃ɛ̃ gyɛlo / ka wiɔra diɛ̃ / ka tikyɛ-a / a gbelme-a / na be-a / a kuɔr
nuɔr iong / ka ba lhor / ti ir bin teung / ka ti bõõ-a / a bom / a diɛ̃
bibir (3980) / baa lhori / ban wa baara / k'o yel ka õ / ka bɔɔbɔ / ka
ba gba bie / ka ba nyɛ / ka ka wenu-a / wa tu ba sora / ka ba na

lɔba bie / ka lo vla / ka ba nyɔɔ bɔɔbɔ / a diɛ̃ / a bɔɔr / ba na yel
ka / ba nyɔɔra bɔɔr / a diyɛ̃ zaa / wa yi naa yuõna / a diɛ̃ bibir / ba
bɔɔr nyɔɔb / ba yel ka ɔ̃ (4000) / ba wõn / baa lɔb bie / ka bie-a /
o ba lo shɔɔ / an lo shɔɔ-aa / ka ba ta kyile / ka ba ta-ya / ka ba
yel ka ɔ̃ / ka ba nyɔɔ / ka nyɔɔ kyile / nikpɛ̃ɛ̃-a / na bɔ̃ɔ̃ wuuro /
k'o yel ka / ka ba tõ yuo / ba tõ / ka nikpɛ̃ɛ̃ / k'o uori-aa / ti yel
ka / ka lɔɔ / ka na ir do u-aa (4020) / ti yel ka ya / ka ba tu ko /
a boobili / ba bɔɔr na nyɔɔra diɛ̃ / ti tikyɛ a lɔɔ-a / ka lɔɔ bhaaro nu /
ti i lɔɔ tuo / ka lɔɔ vla no / ti i lɔɔ faa / ka tikyɛ-a / a dalingpuɔ
wɔb / ka ni-aa / a mangbul iɛn / k'o na ko-onaa / ka diɛ̃ / o na yel
lɛ-aa / ti yel ka / ka ba dɔm gyil / ba dɔm-i / ban dɔma gyila (4040) /
ka ba iɔng kuɔr / baa iɔng / kaa lo shɔɔ / o na yel lɛ / o'a yel ka / ka
ba pur a tĩĩ / ka ba pura / k'o yel ka bɔɔ kyiin bil / ka ba tɔɔ ta /
baa tɔɔ ta / ko'a yel ka / kaa ib na lɛ / tikyɛ-a / yi ta wa ia / ka
bɔɔr / lɛ wa tu / a kori / yi dɔ̃ɔ̃ tua / ba lɛ pura tĩĩ / k'o lɛ uori (4060) /
ti yel ka / ka lɔɔ bhaaro / ka ti i lɔɔ tuo / na mɔgar naab / ani
dalingpuɔ gbeun / ka o na ku-una / dãbie / ba kpiɛri / a boobili /
ka ba kon / blã puɔ-yaa / ka ba wan / gbul bɛrɛ / ba tani / a dio
puɔ / boobili / ba koni / ka ai / ka diɛ̃ / ka ba wɛna (4080) / bana
yel lɛ-a / ti ba yel ka / ka bɔɔ kyiinɛ / ka ba wan sɛɛ / baa wani /
wa tana / ka ba iɔng tĩĩ / ti yel ko ba / ka ba ta i-a / ka o piɛl / o
boobil nɛɛ / ka ba tɛr zom / baa tɛri / nikpɛ̃ɛ̃-a / o'a ir olo / bɔɔ
kɔɔra banu / ko yel ka / ka ba tɛra? / ka ba yel ka / ba tɛra (4100) /
k'o lɛ soor / ka ba tɛra / ka ba yel ka / ba tɛra / ko lɛ soor / ka ba
tɛra / ka ba yel ka / ba tɛra / ban yel lɛ-a / k'o lɛ soor / ka boonu
k'o yel ka ba tɛra? / k'a ba yel ka / a boobɔ bom kura / k'o yel ka /
ka bɔɔ zaa / ko ma maal kaa o boobile vla / ka blã puɔ-a / ka nikpɛ̃ɛ̃
zĩ-a / ti uori / ti yel ka (4120) / ka lɔɔ na ku-una / ti yel ka ya /
ka ba kpiira vũũ / baa kpiira vũũ / ti kyɛ lio / k'o yel ka / ka
boobɔ / ka bɔɔ zaa / k'o tɛra? / ba lɛ tɛri / k'o lɛ bɔ̃ɔ̃ lɛ uori /
gbaa
ayi / ka bɔbɔ kon / k'o yel ka / k'a tĩĩ bir / ka ba niɛ̃ / ba ba niɛ̃-aa /
ban niɛ̃-aa / k'o yel ka, ka ba baara / ka ba yel ka (4140) / ka ba
baara / ka boobɔ kub / ka pãã tana / on na yel lɛ-aa / wa baara /
ti tɔɔ kyile-a / ko ta / k'o nyɔɔ-a / bin teung / ti dɔm sinshuura / ti
yel ka / ka boobil / ka ba nyɔɔ ba / ba nyɔɔ / ti ba tɔɔ / a gbul
bɛrɛ / ka ta yaa / ka boobil kuon / tikyɛ-a / nibɛrɛ-a (4160) / na bɔ̃ɔ̃
wuuro / ba laari / tikyɛ-a / a bɔɔ kpɛ̃ɛ̃-a / k'o ir nyɔɔ-a / a boobil
kpɛ̃ɛ̃ / ba tɛri / ti uori / o na uori-a / ti yel ka lɔɔ / ka lɔɔ faano /
ti yel ku'bɔɔ kyiinɛ / ka ba ta wa ira ka wa kpiɛr a boobile nɛ̃ɛ̃ɛ̃ / o'a
yeli / ti yel ku a boobile / ti i a tĩĩ-a / o'a piɔli / ka boobile / o'a kuoli /

o'a gã (4180) / ti yel ku-a / a bɔɔ kyiine / ka ba zaa / ka ba kpɛ [i a
tĩĩ] / ba zaa ba i tĩĩ / ba ba piɔli / ba zaa kpo ba kuoli / ba gã /
k'o bhe iangan kaa / ti yel ka / ka ba kyaan tulɛ / ka ba ngmaa
yielu / baa ngmaa yielu-u / ti gaal bari / ti lɛ ngmaa yielu-a / ka
kũũ kuna / sambar ata / ti lɛ yel ka / ka kũũ kuna bɔɔ wen faa bar /
ka kũ ta kuɛ (4200) / ti lɛ ngmaa a yielu / ka vin gã gã dio / ka sooro
ba kai / ti lɛ ngmaa a yielu / ka ba wan kuba / ka ba ya bɔɔbɔ /
ti lɛ ngmaa a yielu / ka ano yir lue na / na gɔn gɔn / ti lɛ ngmaa
a yielu / ka ya / ka ba bɔɔni yel / ka diɛ̃ bibir yel faa nu / ti lɛ
ngmaa / ka ba zaa ba laar / ka diɛ̃ bibir laar bio na / baa lɛ ngmaa /
ban wa baara / ti yel ka / ka ba pɔl nuɔ (4220) / ba ngmaa nuɔ / ka
nuɔ lo kpai / ka ba lɛ ngmaa yielu / ka bɔɔ wuɔ ngme nuɔ / na kpa
kpa kpa / baa ngmaa ulɔ / wa baari / ti nikpɛ̃ɛ̃-a / yel ka ya / ka
yele-a / na pɔɔ ti / ka ti na in ngmini? / ka nyɛ-a / a yele / ti bɔɔn
gure / ka tikyɛ a kũn / na gã shɔɔ anya / ka ti na in ngmin? / ka ba
na in ngmin? / ka ba na zɛli naangmin (4240) / ka ba ba siũ-a
bɔɔbil / o ba yel lɛɛ / ti ba yel ka ya / ka ba yi yong / ba ba yi / ti
wa kpɛ / yel ka / ka ba yina / ka ti nar gu / ka ba lɛ yi-a / ka ti bɔ̃ɔ̃ /
a bom na-a / na be be-a / ba ba iri / ti ar man / ka bana in ngmin? /
ka kɔ̃ɔ̃ yaa / yel ka yaa / ka ulɔ nyɛ na bom / ka tina (4260) / kpɛ
na diomaa / ti de gbelme / na i-a kɔntɔme bomo-a / o'a dɔm nyɛ-aa /
ka nibɛrɛ / ba la murɔ / ti yel ka / al wa i lɛ / sizaa / kaa na wia ba
na / ka ba kpɛ-aa / ti taa / a diomaa / zĩ zom-aa / ka bɔɔ kyiin
kpɛ̃ɛ̃-a / o'a de nuɔri / yel ku a bɛrɛ / k'o ba yel ka ɔ̃ / ka pampana
nyãã / yi nyũũ (4280) / t'a yi bɔɔ kyiinɛ / yi na tun ka ti nyɛ-aa /
k'o yel ka / ka o ku gbelme / ka ba dɔm, ka bɔɔbɔ na ira / o ba
dɔm-u / dɔm bɔ̃ gu / ti lɛ ta yaa / a nibɛrɛ zie / ba [yeli] / ka ba
bɔ̃ɔ̃n gu / ka nibɛrɛ-aa / ba la murɔ / ti yel ka ɔ̃ / ka ban bɔ̃ gu-aa /
ka ban puɔ̃n / ka ban faa bɔ̃ gu-aa / ti lɛ yel ka ya / ka yi yel nyaa /
ka ba mul taa (4300) / baa muli / ka nibɛrɛ yel ka ya / ka ba vɛ̃ / ti lɛ
ta / a bɔɔbil kpɛ̃ɛ̃ zie / ka fu wa nyɔɔ tiɛ / do-a / ka ba na kaa na
la fu na lɛ siu / ti yel ka ya / ka bɔɔbil-aa / ba ba gãã / wa ta i iɛr
nya / ti yel ka / a tiɛ fun do-a / ka ba na fu na siu-a / yel vla na /
tikyɛ-a bɔɔbil / tina bɔ̃ gu-aa / ti haana ni ba / ka bɔɔ kyiini
nu (4320) / wa irɛ diɔra / ti nyɔɔ baa / ka wa yi diɛ̃ / ngmɛ-aa nyaa /
ti kɔ̃ɔ̃ wa tɛr yel na yela / ba yeli / ka ti yel ba / ti bɔɔbɔ-ya / yel
ka ya / ka yi nyɛ / a yini-a / bɔɔ pɛlɛ / kɔ̃ zaa ba tuɔ̃ / na tuɔ̃ siung
ba / ban yel lɛ-a / baa baari / ti lɛ de a gbelme / a bɔɔ kyiinɛ zie /
baa dɔmi / ti de ba nɛ-a (4340) / ti iɔng ba tobo / ti kuur / ba ba
iri / ban ira / ka nya ma soor o bɔɔ / nyinɛ fu zaa kyen / ka ba yel

ka / ba ba bɔng zie ba na kyena / ba na ir baara / ba ba yel ka /
ka ba won / a siun yielu / ka ba yel ka / ka bɔɔbɔ ma dire na / ka
nya ma bar o nii ni zɔɔ / ka nya ma bar o piir ni zɔɔ / ka nya ma
bar pɔɔ ni paar / ti wa lɔng taa nir yir / ti ba lɔng taa bonderi /
ka ti i iɔng taa nuuri (4360) / ka ti zɛ korkor ti ir / tia bɔɔ wen
boma / yi na nyɛ kaa fɛri tia / ti yel ka bɔɔbɔ na dire-aa / ba ngmaa
baari / ti yel ka ya / ka bɔɔble-a / a diɛ̃ / bom tu yiã / a yel nya
puɔ / ti na ku yi-a / lɛ siun yi-a / ka ul wa ira-a / wa ti yel ku nira /
ulɔ wa iɛra o zu wɛl gele / ulɔ wa iera ko puor pur bhaba / ulɔ wa
iera ko nyɔvur mi na ngmaana / k'o yel ka yaa / ka tengkori zaa bom
na / ka ba ma dana (4380) / a bɔɔ tĩĩ-ya / ni wur daa-aa / an ni tur
kuba / ka fũ ba bɔ̃-aa / fu na kyeni / ti tuo bɔɔ yaa / ko wa bɔ̃ɔ̃ /
ola na-aa / na kurɔ fu / a bɔɔm / o bɔɔr yel / fũ-aa / mi na ku-o
na / a dib / tikyɛ / fũ ba bɔ̃ɔ̃i / a fu bible-a / ni daar kɔ̃ɔ̃ iɔng-yaa /
wa ngmier nɔkpɛn / ni a fu bɔɔ ma yirdem (4400) / ti a bom
nyan / bɔ̃ kpɛung-nu / o in a ti tamiur / ti ia guolu / ti ia a kuur /
ti ia da yɛru / tikyɛ-aa / fũ ba bɔ̃ɔ̃-aa / ka bɔɔ wena-aa / wa kpɛ yi
yiri-aa / bibil boyen / na kyɛ-a / a dabuo puɔ / tikyɛ ka bɔɔ wen /
pãã yi / o na ina-a / ka fu maal / nii ayi / piir ayuɔb / iɔng buur
ata (4420) / iɔng nuur lizɛɛ-ayi-ni-pie / ka fu maali-a / ti pãã zĩ
teung / pãã bɔ̃ɔ̃ na bɔɔr / bɔɔble-a / wa yi-a / wa kyen bɔɔr / o'a
dire-a / na sinduura / tikyɛ-a / a bɔɔr nyɔɔb puɔ / bɔɔble-a / wa
tɛr yɛ̃-aa / wa tɛr nuɔr-aa / wa ti kyen bɔɔr-aa / a ti zĩ-aa / ka bala
ba / kub nuɔr / ta wa irɛ / wa de nuɔre (4440) / tikye a bɔɔr-aa /
yin wa kyena / ti nyɛ-aa / bɔ kã soba / ka lɔ de nuɔr / yin na bar
una / yin wa kyena / ti tuor / bɔɔ kã sob / k'o kyen a bɔɔr / fu na
vɛ̃na / ka bal wa yel ka / ka fu de nuɔr / ka fu yel ka ɔ̃ / n wɔ̃na /
tikyɛ a nuɔra / ni daar kɔ̃ / bonu vɛ̃ / ka fu zɔɔr? / a bɔɔ kã (4460) /
na be be-aa / ala na / vɛ̃-a / ka fu zɔɔr / ti fu wa yi-a / a bɔɔra / fu
na tura / a bɔɔr / sora / al wa won nira / fu na faa-ona / ni daar /
baa yel lɛ / ba baari / ti iri / ba ngmaa yielu / a kyaar kpɛ̃ɛ̃ puɔ / ti
de sinshuura / de ni gbelme / ba dɔmu (4480) / ti ngmaa yielu /
ka ba ngmaa vuɔr ku ti / ka bɔɔbɔ tɔl / ban ngma ku ti / ka ti yi
a yeong / ti ta ti lɛ ngmaa / ka ba tɔɔ yi puor / ka bɔɔbɔ tɔl / baa
ngmaa / wa baari / bɔɔ kyiin biiri / baa zɔ kpɛ / zie vũũ daari / baa
lɔbi-ii / a bɔɔr yela / tin ira / ka ba ma yi-e / ti lɔba / a dakume /
tina yi-a (4500) / a yɔ̃ / dakume-a / baa duu biɛ̃ũ / ani singbile / ni
nyie / ka ba di-a / ba ba di bɔ̃ gu / ti lɛ kpɛ diɛnu / ban diɛna / baa
baari / ti ka ti yi-a / viiri a yira / sambar ata / ti lɛ wa kpɛ / ti a
paalu-aa / ti na yire-aa / bɔɔ kyiine / yaa pɔɔ bɔɔbɔ / ba nimie /

ka ba yel ka (4520) / bɔɔbili / yi bɔɔna / zie / ti na pɔɔ / a bɔɔr-
aa / ka ba yel ka ɔ̃ ɔ̃ / ka ba yel ka ya / ka diɛ̃ bibira / yin na bɔ̃ na
bɔɔr / a bɔɔra / tengkuri bom nu / dɛ̃ũ dem tɛr ona / k'o i ba yel
faa / ti i ba yel vla / ban wa kpɛ teung / naa ti tɛr kpɛni / ti bar ku
ti-aa / k'o dɔɔn ti-aa / kurɔ a kun / dunɔ nɔn (4540) / nyãã bɔɔra /
ba bu yel ka bɔɔ kara / ka ba vɛ̃-a / ka zie viɛ / ka ti bɔng bom / na
be be-aa / a ti dagara / yel kpɛung / naa bɔɔr / a ti iɛr kpɛung /
in a bɔɔr / fũ ba i bɔɔ / faa wonai / a fu sã̃akum minɛ / yele-i / ti-a
bɔɔr-aa / a bɔɔr nibɛrɛ / ba yɔɔ mɔ na / yɔɔ mɔ ni bo? / ya nyãã
(4560) / a bɔɔr-aa / zɔ̃zɔ̃ kpɛ̃ɛ̃ / ulɔ ni-aa ti bɔɔr / nikpɛ̃ɛ̃ / bɛlibaar /
o i na ti bɔɔr nir / kyaalipiɔ / o i na ti bɔɔr nir / kpan kyaaro / o i na
ti bɔɔr nir / damdamwule / o i na ti bɔɔr nir / burngmaan / o i na ti
bɔɔr nir / nikpɛ̃ɛ̃ ni bo? / n yel ka / a bon piurɛ / a ni kpããkpol nɔra /
boonu vɛ̃ / ka i a ti bɔɔ bom? (4580) / nyɛ a zɔ̃zɔ̃ kpɛ̃ɛ̃ / a ona i a ti
bɔɔ bomo / ti ti nyɔɔra bɔɔr / ti ba taraa sɔ̃ɔ̃ / a zɔ̃zɔ̃ kpɛ̃ɛ̃ / ulɔ nu /
bɔ̃ɔ̃ a sɔ̃ɔ̃ ku ti / boonu k'o bɔ̃ɔ̃ni? / o bɔ̃ɔ̃ni-na / a taan / o na bɔ̃ɔ̃
a sɔ̃ɔ̃ yaa / wa naa taan-aa / a tĩĩsɔɔ / wa di ti ti bar-a / ka ti bɔng
ka zie mana / lɛ na ka ti de ulɔ iɔng a bɔɔr bomo puɔ / a kpããkpol
nɔra / ti ba bɔ̃ɔ̃-a a sɔ̃ɔ̃ / ka ti na kɔ-a / a zie ba mana (4600) / t'a
bɔɔra / a kuɔbu / an i kuoba / ka kuɔrbie / wa iɔng guɔ̃ / zie ba
mani / kpããkpol nɔraa / o'a ngme kpekpe iɔng / a bie ba iri / o'a
gaa wiɛ / damdamwule / ti-a bɔng a zie sɔ̃ɔ̃-i / a saa ba waari / ka
ti bur / kyier ni-a / ka saa war / ka ti kyãã burɔ / ti bo bɔɔ ka burɔ /
in bum baarai / damdamwule (4620) / saa son ba lo / ka ti iri-aa /
a kyii-a / gaa ni buru / fu ba wɔ̃ / ka ba kyiirɛ / lɛ ba / diɛr ba
kukɔi? / ka ti buri-aa / bur bɔ̃ gu / ka wa yel ka / ka ba kukɔi
diɛru / ka ban gɔ̃ɔ̃ baara / kaa kyii-a / ti na bura / kaa diɛra kukɔi-a /
ka a kũn ia iibɛ / o'a yel lɛ / ka ti bar kyii / a buru (4640) / lɛ na ka
ti de-a / iɔng-a / a bɔɔr bom puɔ / a ni a kpããkpol nɔra / bɛlibaara /
a uun ba yi / ti ba bɔ̃ɔ̃ a zie na kyier lɛ / ti bɛlibaara / a ba tara a sɔɔ /
k'o wa yi-a / a saa par / ti wa kyier / a muna kpɛb zie / a wun yin
baar / a lɛ sɔɔ na / ti ma ngmaa kyii / tin ngma baara / ulɔ ni o pɔ̃ɔ̃ /
ba wa tɔlɔ / wiil ti a sɔ̃ɔ̃ (4660) / lɛ na / ti ti irɛ / ka bɔɔbil naa sɔ̃ɔ̃ / ta
iɔng ba / a ba kyiiru / lɛ na ya / ka ti de-a / a belibaar / ko i a ti
bɔɔr bom / kyaalipiɔ-ya / a bɔɔri / mã dãã na / ba ma duu / ka
kyaalipiɔ / zi lio iɔng / pɔɔbil bhɔlu / baa gure / ka wa tɔlɔ-yaa /
ti kon-a / ka duo ta sɔ̃ɔ̃ kuɔ̃-i (4680) / baa iri / ti ɔng kuɔ̃ / wani / ka
i-a ti bɔɔr bomo / alɛ na / ka ti de-o / iɔng ti bɔɔr puɔ / burngmaan
daa / ni o ti woo zu / o'a zĩ be / tia a ti bɔɔra / nɔ tuo bomo / o'a
wa zĩ / a ti woo zu / zie ba mani / k'o ba buɔli / ka bɔɔ kara / bɔɔ

kara / bɔɔ kara / o na buɔl lɛ-aa (4700) / tia iri / zie ba pĩĩ / t'a iri /
de a saaba / ku a ba bibiir / baa di / ti lɛ gã / ban wa iri / tɛra ba
nɔ tuo / ka ti wa i a bɔɔr / alɛ na yaa / ka ti ma iɔng / ko i a ti bɔɔ
nir / ti nyɛ-a / a kãã dakora / o mi ina ti bɔɔr bom / a o mi-a / wa
wuul ti na / a sɔ̃ɔ̃ / ka ti na i bɔɔr (4720) / bonu sɔ̃ɔ̃ na ku wiil /
a ti zie? / ti-a bɔ̃ɔ̃ a sɔ̃ɔ̃-i / tikyɛ-a / bɛng puuru-a / wa taya / o ni
o pɔɔ-a / ba zɛbu / a tĩĩsɔɔ / baa iri / k'o kpɛ-a / a o po kpɛ̃ɛ̃ puɔ /
suur ba kpɛ-o / k'o ti bɔɔri / o bondiri / on na kpɛ-a / ti nyɛ
biɛng / o'a bhɛli / wa tani-a / a nikpɛ̃ɛ̃-aa (4740) / o'a nyɛ / yel ka ai /
ka lɛ na ka / ka ti bibiiri / ka irɛ naa sɔ̃ɔ̃ / o na yel lɛ-a / o ba buɔl
ba / a wiil ba bɔɔr tubu / wiil ba a kyiiru zaa / lɛ na vɛ̃-a / ka ti ma
de-o / ko i-a bɔɔr nikpɛ̃ɛ̃ / fu irɛ bomo / ka nibɛ ba bɔ̃ɔ̃ a para / ba
na ma yel ka / ka in ngmin / ka ba de bom piuri / iɔng bɔɔr puɔ /
lɛ na vɛ̃ / ka bɔ pla daar (4760) / ka ba ma wiili-yi / a bom na vɛ̃ / ka
i a ti bɔɔ boma / ti-a bɔɔra / o tɛra o ma / ti tɛra o sãã / n yel ka /
k'o tɛra o ma ni sãã / a sãã nu saa / ti a ma nu teung / yi bɔɔ na
par / n na yel lɛ-a? / ka ba yel ka ɔ̃ ɔ̃ / baa bɔɔ-i / n na yel lɛ-a /
ka yi ba bɔ̃ɔ̃-a / a saa no-a / o lɛ wa wa / a teung-a / o ba ma
mhãã (4780) / ka nibɛrɛ / ba yi kɔ / ba na kɔ-a / ba nyɛ bomo /
ba na nyɛ bomo / a nyɔɔ a bɔɔra / alɛ na / ka saa i sãã / ti ka teung
i ma / yɛ wõn ala? / yi na wõ alɛ-a / ti ti na tuura bɔɔra / wa ta
ka-ya / a bɔɔ muna bio-a / ka a ngmɛ a-nya / yi ba wõ-a? / ka ni
dar iɔng / ka bible-a / wa yini nuɔr / a tuura (4800) / a bɔɔra / ni
o yel miɔ̃ / ti-aa Kusiele / a ti bɔɔr lɔnluɔrɔ naba / a Kpiel biiri /
bala-a / ba bɔng bɔɔrɛ / ka fu wa nyɔɔ ba-a / wa wiil baa bɔɔra /
a wur daa / ka ba na ya / ti bar a tur kuba / ka Kusieli mi wa
bɔng / mi wa nyɔɔ ti Kpiele biir / a wur daa / ti mi na ya / ti bar
a tur kuba / ba na yara bɔɔra / a tɛra par / par ni bo? (4820) / da(b)
sõ / na ba buɔr kyier-a / ka ba la ya a wur daa / ulɛ nu k'o ma zɔm /
kyeni a bɔɔr / lɛ na vɛ̃-a / ka ti kyen ka ti de a wur daa / ti a tur
kuba / a kɛɛ ni / a nuur / fu na sɔ̃ɔ̃ / a kyii-a / fu na sɔ̃ɔ̃ / ala naa
tur kuba / ma yira wõ? / ti a bɔɔbila / bal wa iri yi baara / ka yin
wa yi yuomo ata / ti kyaan tɛr nyɔvura / a bɔɔr tu funa (4840) /
fũ wa i yuomo ayi / ti wa kpi-a / a bɔɔr / kũũ na ku fu / ka fu i
yuomo ayi ni yuon ngmãã / ti wa kpi-a / a bɔɔr bom ben be / ka
bɔɔbil zaa / wa ti yi vla / ti zaana bɔɔr a / ni daar iɔng / ka ti faa
taa / ban yela / yel lɛ wa ta / a bɔɔ pla / a bɔɔ pla bano / a bɔɔ
mutong / ti na nyɔɔ-a / ti wiili-a / a biira (4860) / lɔ̃ɔ̃ ni pɔbɔ /
lɔ̃ɔ̃ ni dɔɔr / ti lɛ kpɛ-a / a di kpɛ̃ɛ̃ puɔ / yaa nyɛ dibu / ya nyɛ
nɛni / dãã ba naa / ka ti nyuu / iɔng na gɔ̃ / ti yel yɔɔ / na be diom /

ti a iɛr / wa baar / tikyɛ / lɛ liɛba / nyɔ dib / ti a di / bɔɔbili / yi a di /
bɔɔ bɛra (4880) / yi a di / kpime / yi a di / siuwe / yi a di / weni /
yi a di / yi a lɔng taa / di-a / bio ba viɛ / ka ba yel-a / a diɛ̃-a / bibir
ba wa / ka ba bɔng yaa / a fu ni-yɔɔnu / ni-yɔɔnu na ngmin? /
ni-yɔɔnu naa / a pu pla / ni-yɔɔnu naa / na tɛr bom ku-a nira (4900) /
ni-yɔɔnu naa / na nɔ nir bie-aa / ni-yɔɔnu naa / na iɔng nibaal
nir / fu iɔng ba-a / ti a diɛ̃ bibira / bala wa waara / ni a nuura / fu
na yiina / a so fu kuɔ̃ / a zɛ kã / ti-a / n na wiil funa / bom kɔ̃ /
yi zaa kpo nyɛ / bɔɔbili / ba gyirɛ / k'o shɔɔ o nu / ti yel ka / yi
nyɛn boni? (4920) / boonu? / a dãbol-i / ba yel ka ka nu no / k'o
yel ka ɔ̃ ɔ̃ / ka nu ba nũɛ̃ / ka-yaa / ka bom ben be / o'a buɔl bɔɔbil
kyiira / k'o buɔli / o yuori / k'o yel ka / ka Benima / a ulɔ na bɔ̃ɔ̃ o /
ka n bɔ̃ɔ̃ gu / k'o yel ka / ka a nyɛ̃na / a ti bɔɔbɔ ziri / ana nyãã /
diɛ̃ / yi in a bɔɔbɔ (4940) / yini yaa / wa yi-a / daar kɔ̃ɔ̃-a / wa nyɛ
kyuu-a / k'o ara / ka nir wa yel ka / ka fu nyɛ kyuu / taa wa lɛɔr
kaarɛ / ti yel ka / ka fu nyuu na / daar zaa / fu na yel lɛ-a / ka ba
man ka fu nyuu na / ti fa nyuu-e / lɛ na / yin ni a dakume / ba wa
nyɛ a kyu / yel ka / ka fu nyuu na daar zaa / ka lɛ na (4960) / ka ba
ma yel ka / a bɔɔbɔ ziri na / bɔɔ gyingyire / a ba i bio / yi-a yi /
a bio ya / ka ba yel ka / ka bɔɔ kyiinɛ / ka ba wani-a / saara / ni
pel-liira / ka wani diom / ka bala wa yina bɔɔbila / a diɔr zaa yina
ngmaa / yin iɔng a pele puɔ / ti piiri-a / ba miɔnga / kyiɛr ni-a /
yin ti dɔm ba zɔn nyɛ / ka bala wa yi-a yong-aa (4980) / ka ba
ngmaa yielu-a / ka bura wõ nyũũ / fãã fãã fãã / baa kyeni ti zĩ /
ban na zĩ-a / ka ba minɛ / baa waari nuuri / a ti bɔɔr bom na / sɛn
minɛ / ba war kyiini / a ti bɔɔr bom na / pɔɔbil-a / waari kal /
ka dɔɔr / waari nuur / baa varaa / ban varaa / bɔɔ kyiinɛ / bɔɔ
kyiin kpɛung banu / o'a dere (5000) / a ala / a ba zie / iɔng ni-a /
ka ti lɛ tuura ti bɔɔr / ban wa baara / ti yel ka bɔɔbila / a diɛ̃ bibir-a /
yi in bɔɔ kari / ti-a bɔɔr yele / a ba yire yi nɛɛ-i / ala wa yi-aa / bɔɔr
u fu ngmir / ti-a bɔɔr / tengkori bom nu / ti-a bɔɔr-aa / yel vla nu /
ti-a bɔɔr-aa / kũũ kub bom nu / ti-a bɔɔr-aa / nyɔvur bom nu (5020)
ti a bɔɔr-aa / tamiur bom nu / ti-a bɔɔr-aa / kukur bom nu / ti-a
bɔɔr-aa / no guol bom nu / ti-a bɔɔr-aa / yel maal bom nu / ka fũ
wa / wa bɔ̃ɔ̃ / a bɔɔr mi-a / a in na bom / ka tengkori-aa / ka nibɛ /
ba dɔ̃ɔ̃ bɔ̃ɔ̃-a / yɔɔ-i / ka nirɛ wa bɔ̃ɔ̃-a / o'a ma in na naa / ti i libie
na / ti bom zaa nalu (5040) / o na yel lɛ-a / ku a bɔɔbɔ / ti-a bɔɔ
sɔɔla / fu kun tuɔ̃ barɛ / fu ma ngme na / a bibie ata / mutɔng ata /
tĩĩsɔɔ ata / ka bɔɔ pla / ba na ngme na / mutɔng ata / tĩĩsɔɔ ata /
ti baari-a / fu kun tuɔ̃ barɛ / ti a bɔɔr-aa / a in wal piel gbɛɛ /

ma nɛb lɛ tuli wa / lɛ na ka ti ma yel ka / ka bɔɔr i / yin na zɔn
kul-aa (5060) / ti a gbelme nyɛ na / yi na tɛra / k'o in na gyɛla / ka
dayere bio / tin wa nyɛ fɔ̃ɔ̃ / tina wa de ona / a piɔ bin / fu wa iɔng
gbelme / ka pɔɔ na fu-a / ka daba na fu-a / ti wa sɔ̃ɔ̃ pɔɔ / fu sɔ̃ɔ̃
na bɔɔr / ka daba wa sɔ̃ɔ̃ pɔɔ / yi na gɔ̃ɔ̃-na / a zie kɔ̃ɔ̃ bar / alɛ na /
a arba / yi bɛ nyɛ / a bɔɔ dib na / arbil kpɛ̃ɛ̃ na (5080) / ba fu faa / a
dãã / lɔ̃ɔ̃ ni saabo / lɔ̃ɔ̃ ni nɛni / o'a fu faa / ba di / ban na di lɛ-a /
yi bɔ̃ɔ̃ ka / nin daar iɔng / yi nibɛ na ba / fũ tɛr ma-aa / ka o la
zɔɔr fu bara / fu ma kye na sãã zie / ka fu sãã wa zɔɔr fu bara / fu
ma kye na ma zie / ala na ya / ka arbile / o ba i bon diẽnai / a fu
yir yɛbɛ / ni a arbile (5100) / ba zaa in boyen / a fu zie / n na yel
a lɛ-a / yi a wõ / arbile-a / a tengkori / yɛbɛ / ni yɛbɛ-a / ba tɛra ba
sãã / ka ba yuɔra / ba a yi / ani ba sãã / ba kyen puo puɔ / a ti kuɔri /
ka arbile / wa yɔɔ kyeni / a puo puɔ / ti nyɛ-aa / bibiir ayi / bala
ni ba sãã (5120) / ka ba kuɔri / bana kuɔr-aa / k'o yel ka / ka ba ir /
ka bibiiri / baa ir suuri / ba nyɔɔ a puo / ba ngmaa / ngma nɛɛ / lɔ̃ɔ̃
ni a sãã / ko yel ai / maa ni baala / n kun tũõ kɔi / maa kɔ uu yi /
ka yi wa pɔli / ka wa irɛ yini ngmin / na i ngmini ka ti / kɔ zɛ̃taa? / ka
ba ngma ba puo / ba kɔ baari (5140) / ka arbile-na / wa nyɛ o
madaba / k'o be mutɔng puɔ / kuɔri / da nyɔ̃ɔ̃ ba nu / ti nyɛ bibiiri /
baa kɔ baar ti zĩ / ka bie-aa / arbile-aa / o'a kyen ti de kuuri / o'a
nyɔɔ o madaba / nuɔri / o'a kɔ / wa kɔ baari / ka madab-a / o'a iri /
ti yel ka / k'o arbile / naa bibiir / o nɔ na arbile (5160) / gɔ̃ɔ̃ a
bibiir / ka ni daar kɔ̃ɔ̃ / ka ulɔ ba kabe / ti-a arbile / wa de bomo /
ka bibiir / wa nyɔɔ faa / ka bana kpina / lɛ na / ka arbile / ma ira
bomo / ka ti i gbili / le na ka ti ma yel k'o-aa / a bɔɔbila / bɔɔbil
paali-a / ka yi wõ arba par / ti-a a bɔɔr-aa / ti na yel ka-aa / yin wa
yi a bɔɔra / a bɔɔ gbelme (5180) / bal wa piɔ / ka yin wa yi / ka
bible-a / boyen / wa be be / wa kyena / nir bɔɔra / ti zĩ-aa / a ba
i dib na fu kyene / fu na kyeni-aa / ti zĩ-aa / ti bɛlɛ / ti won / a lɛ /
ba na tuura / a bɔɔra / yel boyen / tikyɛ / a tu tuuri / in dindimɛ
(5200) / fu wa wõa / a nibɛ minɛ ngmeb / fu na de-na / a ba dema /
ka daar kɔ̃ɔ̃ / fu wa ngmiera / a bɔɔra / wa ti ngme alɛ iɔng / fu na
ngmena / a iɔng fu bɔɔr puɔ / ti fu wa ngmiera / fu na puora / a ba
nibɛrɛ / na-a kpiin kora / fu na puor bana / puora ba siuwe / puora
tengaamɛ / ti ngme-a bɔɔr / fũ wa ti yi-a / a bɔɔ diom (5220) / fu
na yire / a yõ-a / ti tɛra nuɔr / k'o tengaan / ti lɛ kpɛ-a / fu na
nyɛna / a nuɔr / k'o wa / ka bɔɔble / o'a soori / anu wana bɔɔr? /
ka ba yel ka / dɛ̃ũdem wan / k'o lɛ soora / dɛ̃ũdem na anu? / ka ba
yel ka / dɛ̃ũdem na tɔble / k'o lɛ soor ka / boonu ba buɔla ngmin? /

ka ba yel ka (5240) / ka ngmin be na / ka naangmin be be / ka bɔɔble
soor / ka ya / ka tin tuura / a yel nyɛ-aa / ka naangminu ti tuur /
bii ngminu ti tuur? / ko yel ka ya / nikpɛ̃ɛ̃ banu / yel ka ɔ̃ / ka tin
na tuura / ka naangmin / o in nikpɛ̃ɛ̃ / ka ti kũ nyuu-e / ti ngmina /
na siu nibɛ / le na ti buɔlɔ ngmin / ka ti nibɛrɛ / yela ka (5260) / ka
naangmin bie-aa / ka olɔ / ka ti ma tu bii? / k'o lɛ yel ka ɔ̃ / ti ma
tuura ulɔ / ka pãã ta naangmin / o'a yel lɛɛ / ka bɔɔble / lɛ soor-aa /
ka yel yɔɔ anya / fu na ma in ngmin / wa bɔ̃ɔ̃ a zaa / wa tuɔ̃ / wa
wiil? / ka ba yel ka / bana tu-a / a bɔɔ pla / wa tɔ diɛ̃-aa / tikyɛ-a /
a bɔɔ sɔɔla (5280) / a mi ngmɛ̃ na lɛ / ba ma de funa / a tĩĩsɔɔ / ani
a muna / a bibie ata / ka fũ i yɛ̃ sob / fu na den iɔng / a zu puo / wa
ti bɔ̃ɔ̃ ni-aa yel / k'o lɛ soora / a bɔɔ sɔɔla / ni a bɔɔ pla / buor de
nio? / bɔɔble ba soori / ka ba yel ka / ka bɔɔ sɔɔla / ka o lɔ na kpɛ̃ɛ̃ /
ka ba yel ka / ka ona i-a kpɛ̃ɛ̃-aa / olɔ nu (5300) / ka ti bɔ̃ɔ̃ / wa bɔ̃ɔ̃ a
bɔɔ pla / bɔɔbil kyila bano / k'o yel ka / ka tikyɛ a i ngmin / ka yi ba
de nio / nyɔɔ ti / a bɔɔ sɔɔla sɛr? / ka nikpɛ̃ɛ̃ yel ka ai / o ba laar / ti
yel ka / a tin bɔɔr na i-a bɔɔr / ti ma de nio-o / a ngme-aa / a bɔɔ
sɔɔli / nyɛ sɛr / ti pãã irɛ / bɔɔble / o'a lɛ soor / ka tia i ngmini (5320) /
ka yi ngme / ka ti ba tuɔ̃ / wiil ti? / ka nikpɛ̃ɛ̃ / o'a lɛ yel ka / ka fu
ba i bɔɔ / ti ba lɛ wiil fu? / k'o yel ka / ti fu na bɔ̃ɔ̃ ka / fu na wa
nyɔɔ ti na / a bɔɔra? / k'o yel ka ɔ̃ / n bɔ̃ɔ̃ ka / n na nyɔɔ yi na /
a bɔɔr / ti o ma ina / na puɔ biru / ba kun tuɔ̃ / a wiil fu / ti bɛ i
yi sɛrɛ (5340) / ti ma pɔ̃ zɛtaa / lɛ na vɛ̃ / ka n ba wiil fu / a bɔɔ
sɔɔla yele / ti fu wa iɔng tiɛru / bɔɔr nabɔng / a bɔɔr yele-aa / ia
nia / sooro-aa / a bɔɔr yele / ka fu ba soore / fu kun tuɔ̃ bɔ̃ɔ̃ bɔɔrɛ /
k'o yel ka ɔ̃ / ka ya / a yin yel ka / ka ba la wiila / a nira / a bɔɔra / ka
ti ma de-na / a wur daa (5360) / ani a tur kuba / boona vɛ̃ / ka ba
ma de alɛ? / o'a soori / ka ba yel ka / kaa par ben be / fu na nyãã /
a nir-a / na kpɛɛ-aa / a kɔlingwiɔ / a yuomo ata / wa ti wa-a / on
wa wa / o'a yel ka / ka ba nyɛ / o zu kɔɔlu na / ba pɔ̃i / yuomo ata /
ka tikyɛ-aa / ka yel kɔ̃ na k'o wan (5380) / a nãn fɛrɛ-aa / ti wiili
yel yɔɔ / alɛ na-a / ka bɔɔr yele / ka minɛ yire-a / tɔ̃ɔ̃ zu / tikyɛ
aminɛ yire / kuɔ̃ puɔ / a man puɔ / ka man puɔ-a / dem-aa / ka ba
ma ya / a wur daa / ka ti kyɛ a tɔ̃ɔ̃-a / dem-aa / ka ba ma ya / a tur
kuba / ka fũ wa bɔ̃ɔ̃ / wa ti wiil nibɛ / a dɔɔb yuo (5400) / fun de na /
a wur daa / ni a tuur kuba / ka fũ ba i lɛ-aa / fu na zɔ̃ɔ̃ na / ka fũ
ba i lɛ-aa / fu kukɔr / na liɛba / yin faa wɔ̃ / a para / lɛ na ya / ka ti
yel ka / bible wa bɔ̃ɔ̃ / o tɛr / guni o miɔ̃ / ka tikyɛ-a / ka fu mi ba
bɔ̃ɔ̃ / fu mi na soora / ka ba wiil fu / a bɔɔr (5420) / al wa bɔra /
ba mã bɔɔ na / hani zaa / lɛ na / ka ti yel ka / a bibiira / ba bɔ̃ɔ̃-aa /

a bɔɔr yele / ni daar iɔng / ka ti faa taa / ti yi bɔɔ na / a bɔɔ pla /
diɛ̃ / ti pãã kyɛ / a bɔɔ sɔɔla / ti nɔ guol bie / na i kakuɔr bie / olɛ
nu-a / na wa i / a bɔɔ sɔɔla (5440) / tikyɛ / ka fũ / wa yuɔra / fu na
bɔ̃ɔ̃ na / a bɔɔ pla / ti fũ wa / i didire / fu na bɔ̃ɔ̃ na / bɔɔ kyiinu /
baa yele / bɔɔbili / yaa wõ / ti nikpɛ̃ɛ̃ / yel ka / k'o bɔɔra / k'o ta
yir / ka ti-a ngmãã na kyɛ-aa / ka ba na wiila / ka yi wiil ku-a bibiir /
o'a kuli (5460) / o sãã yiri / ti tani-a / a nɛni / a kyile nɛn / ulɔ so
ala / bɔɔ sɔɔla / ba ɔɔr-ai / see bala na tɛr kyile / o'a tani / a nuuri /
lɔb bari / a yir dundɔri / ti bɛlɛ-a / ka wa lɔb gyɛlɛ / ka tikyɛ-a / lɛ
fu na i na / o nuur alɛ / fu na ku-ana / a fu sãã kpime / ni a wɛri
(5480) / ni a siuwe / tikyɛ a nɛna / uɔb kyɛ kɔbɔ / ũũ ba / ta irɛ /
ka nuɔ / wa de vɔlɛ / on na liɛba / a bɔɔ nuɔ / a bɔɔr bom / a ba
dɔɔlɔ / kuur bom zue / fu wa iɔnga / a ma sɔ̃ɔ̃na / bɔɔ bɛrɛ yõ / bala
na di / tikyɛ dakume / baa dirai / ba ba kuli / ti yuɔri (5500) / ti
diɛntɔɔ / ba na iɔng gbelme dãã / ana i lɛ / ka kɔ̃ zaa ta gã ni pɔɔ /
ba yeli / dayere bio / ba yel ka / ka bɔɔ ma minɛ / ka ba wan bɔɔbili /
baa wa doni / a bɔɔbili / a gar zu puɔ / zĩ-a / ti yel ka ɔ̃ / bɔɔbili / a
diɛ̃ / yi yina bɔɔ / ti ba yie / ba yel lɛ / ti yel ka ɔ̃ (5520) / ti yi nyɛ /
a bɔɔr / ba na tu yi-a / yel yɔɔ na / ka ba sɔ̃ɔ̃ bar / tikyɛ ka yi yia
diɛ̃ / a kɛɛ-a / ni a nuura / ni boyen nuur / a ma tan kuba / ti a
kɛɛ-a / yi bɔ̃ɔ̃ na pari / a tan / pɛr lizɛr na nu / ba tu yi / yi wa yi /
a diɛ̃ / kɔ̃ zaa na zana / o lɔ wa zana / wa ti bɔ̃ɔ̃ (5540) / a na
wiɛ-oa / bala wa nyɔɔ fu / wa ziil kɔɔ zu / ti faa tɛr kyile / ka ba wa
ya fu / tur ata / iɔng ni nɔ sɔɔla / fu na dena / ir kyile libie / tikyɛ /
fũũ na fu bɔɔ taaba / yi bɔ̃ɔ̃ / lɛ yi na ia / ba ba dire / fufue / a
bɔɔ / di fufu / a kurɔ na bɔɔ / a lɛɔra bɔɔ kukɔr / alɛ na (5560) / ka
ba wiile / a diɛ̃ / ba na lɛb a soori / a yi bibiir / a diɛ̃ / ka ba soor /
bɔɔble / ulɔ wa gani pɔɔ / k'o yel / ban na kyãã piɔ o gbelme / ti-a
tɛr tub ba tu / ti fũ ba ye lɛ-a / ti sɔɔli bar / ti yel ka vĩ / ni daar
kɔ̃ / vĩ na kpɛ fu na / bɔɔ kyiinɛ / yi soor bɔbɔ / baa soori / ba
dɔɔri (5580) / baa kyiiri / ba lɛ soori / ba pɔɔbɔ / baa kyiiri / ka ba
yel ka ɔ̃ / yin na kyiiri-a / a diɛ̃ / ban ba piɔ na gbelme / ba yel lɛ /
ka ba yel ka ɔ̃ / yi ira gbelme / a kukɔi iɔng / a wa bin / ba de siung
kpɛ̃ɛ̃ dãã / ba de / gbelme / baa bin / ti ba piɔ / nikpɛ̃ɛ̃ / k'o de-a
(5600) / a gbelme-a / bin sɔ̃ɔ̃ / ti yel ka ɔ̃ / ka kɔ̃ɔ̃ zaa / wa tɛra /
sooru-a / u soora diɛ̃ / ka bɔɔble / ir ar-aa / ti yel ka ɔ̃ / k'o bɔɔr k'o
soor / ka ba in ngmina / bɔ̃ɔ̃ shɔɔ anya / ti-a kũũ / kyãã kurɔ ? / k'o
yel ɔ̃ / ka bɔɔm / a yina / a dɛ̃ũdem / ti kyɛ a kũũ (5620) / ami yi
na / a dɛ̃ũdem / ka tia bomo / fu na tɛra / bom kura nu / ulɔ nu-a /
a kũũ / ulɔ dɔ̃ɔ̃ yi / ka bɔɔr / wa tu puor / ona in ngmini / na tuɔ̃ / a

duu / a kũũ bar? / ti yel ka ɔ̃ / ka ba la bɔɔr yel miɔ̃ / a bɔɔr yele /
yel kpɛung nu / yi na nyɔɔ ona / ni nur ayi (5640) / tuur-i / ni nio /
bɛlɛ u-aa / ni nimie / ta wa bara o-ɛ / ka nibɛrɛ / baa de / a dãã / piɔ
gbelme / lɛ bina / ti pãã zĩ teung / ka pampana-nyãã / ka ba bɔɔra /
ka ba na de-a / soora / a tin iri yi-a / a diɛ̃ zaa / a bɔɔra / boonu ti
wiil fu? / ka bɔɔble (5660) / wa tuɔ̃ ir / wa wiil / a bɔɔr / a lɛ bana
i-a / ka ba na ku ona naab / ka ba yel ka / ka ba bɔɔra / ba laar / ti
yel ka / boonu ba bɔng? / ka ba yel ka-ya / ka paalu ban na ire
ba-aa / ka ba ira / a kyi / ka kyi i kɛɛ / ka ti yel ka / ka ba yi / yel
bɔɔ bɛrɛ / ka ba wa / ka wa de zɔ̃ bar (5680) / ka ba laar / ti yel ka
wi / ka ba ba bɔ̃ɔ̃-aa / ka in ngmini / ka fu ba bɔ̃ɔ̃ / a lɛ daari / a bɔɔ
wen / na ir fu / ka ti tɛr tuni-a / ti wa bɔng / a zɔ̃ baru daar? /
tikyɛ-a / a bɔɔr / tin yeli-a / tin na wiil yi na / a bɔɔ sɔɔla / ka fũ
wa / wa nyɛ̃ nira / na bɔ̃ɔ̃ bɔɔra / k'o wa wiil fu a bɔɔr (5700) / ulɔ /
so-aa / a fu dib / ulɔ so / a fu nyuub / ti ulɔ wiil fu / wa ti baar / o na
wiil fu na / a bɔɔ sɔɔla / ulɔ wa ti tuɔ̃ / wa ti kur gbelme / fu bɔ̃ɔ̃ ka /
o na tuɔ̃ viire bɔng / tikyɛ / a diɛ̃ / yi na siuna / a zɔ yuɔra / a kpɛ
muɔ / fu wa nyɛ-ãã kɔri-ya / wa ku (5720) / bɔɔr bom nu / ka fũ wa ku
sɔ̃ɔ̃ / bɔɔr bom nu / ka fũ wa ku wala / bɔɔr bom nu / tikyɛ-a / fũ
wa ku duo / yir nɛn nu / fũ wa ku sasir / yir nɛn nu / fu wa ku siɛ̃n /
yir nɛn nu / ti bonu yi tɛr na soor? / ka ba yel ka ɔ̃ / ti soori / a yin
dɔ̃ yel ka / ka yin an soora zu / a dɔɔla nyũũ / o la na ka n ba bɔ̃ɔ̃-ɛ /
ti yel ka n soor nyɛ (5740) / ka ba yel ka ɔ̃ / ka ba i soor-oɛ / ka kɔ̃ɔ̃
lɛ soor / ka ti kyɛ-a / ka nir / a sɔ̃ɔ̃-a bɔɔra / ka tuɔ̃ yele / ka ti yi
vla / a bɔɔr puɔ / ka yel kɔ̃ ben be / na la yi-o? / ka ba yel ka ɔ̃ / ka
yel kɔ̃ ben be / ka fu na zɔ̃ɔ̃na / ka fu ba zɔ̃ɔ̃ɛ / ka fu na ngman kuɔn /
ka fũ / ba yele / fu na in nisaal kɔ̃ɔ̃ / ka fu ba yele (5760) / fu na
gbɛra / ba ba yeli / ka ni boyen-na / yel ka ɔ̃ / pɔɔ ba nu / yel ka o
sɔ̃ɔ̃n daba / o'a yeli / baa wɔ̃ / ti i gbili / ti soori / a bɔɔbili / ka anu
tɛr iɛru? / ba yel ka / ka ba bɔɔra ka ba soor / ka fũ-a / a i bɔɔ / ti wa
kyena / a bɔɔr zie / ka fu nikpẽɛ̃ / ba ka be (5780) / ti a fu yɔ̃ɔ̃ / wa
zie a bɔɔr / ka ba wan bondiri / wa kub / fu na din bii? / ka ba yel
ka ɔ̃ / ka fu na dina / ko lɛ soora / ka tikyɛ fũ / kyena bɔɔra / ka fu
yir / nikpẽɛ̃ / ba ka be / ti ba ko fu nuɔr / ka fu na in ngmin? / ka ba
yel ka ɔ̃ / fu na / dena nuɔr-aa / a tu ta sɔ̃ɔ̃ / a puɔra bɔɔbɔ (5800) /
puɔra kpime / ti puɔra tɛngaan / ti fũ wa i Kpielɛ bie / wa nyɛ Kpielɛ
nir / a bɔɔr zie / fu yɛbɛ nu / fũ wa i Kusielɛ bie / wa nyɛ Kusielɛ nir /
a bɔɔr zie / fu yɛbɛ nu / fu wa i Bɛkuɔnɛ / wa nyɛ Bɛkuɔnɛ bie / a bɔɔr
zie / fu yɛbɛ nu / fu wa i Yɔngyuɔlɛ / wa nyɛ Yɔngyuɔlɛ bie / a bɔɔr
zie / fu yɛbɛ nu / fu ba la zɔr / dãbie (5820) / a bɔɔr puɔi / fu na

ngmiera / a bɔɔr / kaa wa baar / ti fu kul / ka kɔ̃ɔ̃ lɛ soora / ka fũ wa
yi a bɔɔr / wa ta yir / wa kpi / ka bɔɔra ku fu bii ? / ka ba yel ka ɔ̃ /
ka ba bɔɔra / ka baa yel ku yi / ka fũ ba yi / yuomo atai / ti wa
kpi-a / ka bɔɔr yel ben be / baa yeli / baa yel baar / ti yel ka ɔ̃ (5840) /
ka yaa wõ ? / ka kɔ̃ lɛ soor / ka tikyɛ fũ wa yi / a bɔɔr / wa ta yir / ka
fũ na fu pɔɔ wa zɛb taa / ka ba na lɛ de ma na bɔɔr yab-bii ? / ka ba
yel ka / ka ba kun tuɔ̃ lɛ de-i / ba yeli / fa wõ / ka kɔ̃ɔ̃ lɛ soor / ka fu
yi a bɔɔr / ta yir / ka fu bie / wa kpi-a / ka bɔɔr yel na ku bii ? / ka
ba yel ka ɔ̃ ɔ̃ / ka al ba nai / ka kɔ̃ɔ̃ lɛ soor (5860) / ka fu yi a bɔɔr / kul
ti ta a yir / ka fu pɔɔ yi / ti kul nir / k'o na sɔɔna de ? / ka ba yel ka ɔ̃ /
k'o na dena / o lɛ soor / ka o lɛ yi a bɔɔra diɛ̃ / ti nyɛ nir pɔɔ / k'o bɔɔr
u-aa / k'o na dena bii ? / ka ba yel ka ɔ̃ / k'o na tuɔ̃ de / ka kɔ̃ɔ̃ lɛ ira /
ti lɛ soora / ka o lɛ kul / ti nyɛ o bom / o na bina / ti irɛ-a bɔɔr (5880) /
k'o wa kul ti bɔ̃ gu / a bɔɔ wen de bii ? / ka ba yel / ka fũ wa kula / ti
bɔ fu bom gu / k'o bɔra / fũ wa yel ka / ka bɔɔ wen ben be / o na
kuna / fu yirdem / al wa ia fu yirdem na / a na ku bana / al wa ia muɔ
puɔ nibɛ na / a na ku bana / tikyɛ / fũ-a / wa i gbili / a bɔɔ wen na
tuna a sob / ka kɔ̃ɔ̃ lɛ soora / ti ma ni nir ba dɔ̃ɔ̃ nɔnɔ taa-i (5900) /
ti n wa kula / k'o wa tɛra bom / wa kuma / n na den di bii ? / ka ba
yel ka ɔ̃ / ka fu na de na / ka kɔ̃ɔ̃-a / lɛ soora / ka olɔ kul / ti nyɛ o
sɛn / on dɔ̃ɔ̃ tɛra / ka nir wa de / n na zɛbi na o sob bii ? / ka ba yel
ka ɔ̃ ɔ̃ / fu kun tuɔ̃ zɛbi-a sobe / ka ba lɛ yel ka / ka ba bɔɔra / ka ba
yel ku yi-a / a sooru-aa / ba na yel ka (5920) / nir wa tɛra / k'o sooro /
ka ba i / bom zaa sooru-ɛɛ / ba bɔɔra / ka fũ wa sooro / fu soora bɔɔr
yele / ka kɔ̃ɔ̃ lɛ soor / ka-a / a bɔɔ biɔr / a ni kɛɛ ngmier / ka a buor ma
de nio ? / ka ba yel ka ɔ̃ ɔ̃ / ka sooru na lɛɛ ? / ti ba yel ka bɔɔ biɔr /
olɔ nu ma de nio / ka kɔ̃ɔ̃ lɛ soor / ka-a / a bɔɔ wuor / a ni biɛ̃ũ (5940) /
ka a buor ma de nio / ka be yel ka / ka o'a ma wõ / ban ma yel ka a
wuora ? / ka wuor / o ina / bom na i paalu-aa / ka ulɔ nu ma de nio /
ka kɔ̃ lɛ soor / ka nibɛrɛ / ka ba i o gafura / ti yel ka / ka tikyɛ-a / on
i a bɔɔble / ka o pɔɔ wa ngma siɛ / ka ba wa kyiir kuɔ̃ iɔng / ka
boona / alɛ ? / ka ba yel ka ɔ̃ / ka tengkuri sor kɔ̃ɔ̃ naa lɛ (5960) / ka ba
ma tu / ka ba ba bɔɔr / ka ba iɛrɛ / kaa wa lo / a pɔɔble / toore / ka a
la na so / a kuɔ̃ / ban ma kyir iɔng baa / ka kɔ̃ɔ̃ lɛ soor / ka fu wa
kyen / nir bɔɔr / wa ti nyɛ-a / nikpɛ̃ɛ̃ / k'o be a bɔɔr yir / ti a da
nyɔ̃ɔ̃ / wa ngmiera bɔɔr / ka fu wa nyɛ k'o bal / ngmin fu na i ? / ka
ba yel ka ɔ̃ (5980) / ka fũ wa nyɛ / a nikpɛ̃ɛ̃ / k'o wa baala / fu kun
tuɔ̃ de / a o nuɔrɛ / fu na vɛ̃na / ulɔ wa bɔng k'o baala / o na buɔla
nir kɔ̃ɔ̃ yuor / k'o ir de-o / ka kɔ̃ lɛ soor / ka tikyɛ-a / fũ i bible / ti
i bɔɔ / ti nikpɛ̃ɛ̃ / i da nyɔ̃ɔ̃ / ti wa biɛr i bɔɔ / ka yi zãã lɔng kyen bɔɔr /

ka bondiri wa wa / anu na di kyɛ ko a tɔ? / ka ba yel ka ɔ̃ (6000) / a
fũ na i bible / ti de nio ia bɔɔra / fũ nio k'o tuur / ka kɔ̃ɔ̃ lɛ soor /
a kɔntɔmɔ / ni a ngmin / an wan bɔɔr? / ka nikpẽẽ yel ka ɔ̃ / ka
ngmin ir bana-ya / bin teung zu / ka ba zĩ zɔɔla lɛ / tikyɛ / ka tɔ ble /
ka ni tɔ kpẽẽ / wa ti zĩ ba zima zie / ka tɔ ble / wa ir zɔ bɔr / ka ba
yel ka olɛ bɔ̃ɔ̃ ti irɛ / ti wa wa / wa wiil ti (6020) / o yel anya / a
ngmin ir ti / ti ba lɛ ku ti bom zaa / ka a bondiri kɔ̃ wa kpɛ ti / ti ma
nyãã na ti di / tikyɛ-a / a tɔ ble / olɔ nu-a / a wani-a / a yel anya / wa
wiil ti / ala na / ka ti ma yel ka / a dɛungdem / yele na / o'a yel lɛ / on
yel wa baara / ka ti yel ka ɔ̃ / ka ngmin / bɔɔn bɔɔr yel bii? (6040) /
ba soori / k'o yel ka ɔ̃ / ka ngmin / ka ir ti / ka tin yel / ti yele-a / k'o
ma wõ-a na / ka ti bom zaa tin ira / o nyɛrɛ-a na / ka tikyɛ-a / on ir
ti-a / o lɔ bɔ̃ɔ̃ a ti zĩma / ka ngmina / yel ka / k'o na wa na / ka nir
zaa nyɛ / ka ti bonu vẽ / ka ulɔ wa ka / k'o kun tuɔ̃ tõ tome-i / ka
nisaal nir (6060) / na wa kpiura / o ma yel ka / ka i ngmin k'o kurɔ
o nir? / ka kɔ̃ɔ̃ nir kpi / on na wan / wa yel ka n siung k'o / ka kɔ̃ɔ̃
biɛr / ban wa yel ka / k'o ira baalu bar / ka kɔ̃ɔ̃-a / nir ngme-oa / on
wa yele ka / k'o ku a sob / lɛ na / ka ngmin / ba bɔɔr ka / ti ta nyuue /
o piɛl tina / ti zãã ti / alɛ na (6080) / k'o yel ka ɔ̃ / k'o na bara nir / k'o
wa / o na tuɔ̃ ti zaa kpẽũ / a tengkuridem-a / yela-a / ka nir nya yele /
ka ti bɔ̃ɔ̃n gure / a dɛungdem / ba na yel ko-a / a tengkuridem / ba
wõ / ti biir / ti ba nyãã / fũ i bɔɔ-a / a tenkuri yele / fu ma wõn / fu
ma bɔɔn / ti fu ba i bɔɔ-a / ti saa tɛra yẽ (6100) / fu kun tuɔ̃ / bɔ̃ a
yele / a zaai / ba yeli / bɔɔbili / ba wõ / yi na wõ-a / a bɔɔ yele-a / ti
baari-a / tikyɛ boonu / a ngmin yele / na kyɛ-a / ka bɔɔ sɔɔli / wa
ta-ya / a lɛ puɔ-na / ka ba na yele / a yele / k'o yi-a / yina wõ? / a
bɔɔra (6120) / o yẽ na nya / ti ia bɔɔr nyɛb / ti ia bɔɔr wõm / ti ia
bɔɔr dib / on na dia / olɔ nu-a / ka ti yel-aa / ti wa kyɛ a pari / ka ti
wa yel ka / noguol bie / kakuɔr bie / bɔbɔ / yi kpo a gan

BƆƆR SƆƆLA (NGMINTI)

ngmin-ti / bɔbɔ ngmin / ka ba ngmini / ngmin ka wa / ngmin
nyɔtuɔn / ngmin sɔr goba / ngmin par pla / ngmin naayuo / ngmin
gagara / ngmin biila / o na biil anya / zɔɔ kpɛ̃ɛ̃ puɔ / tɔ ni ble / faa
nyɛ ble / iɔng tiɛr-ua / duur ka yi / a zɔɔ kpɛ̃ɛ̃ nuɔr / iɔng na de sor /
ti lɛ nyɛ bom / bom bono? (20) / ka base nu / lan dakyin / k'o iɔng
na puor / k'o puor baalu / on puor wa baara / ti paa nyɛ soor / mɔl
mɔl iɔng / o'a de sori / o'a duuri ta / man nuɔr iɔng / o'a nyɛ bomo /
ar kpɛ̃ɛ̃ / lõ ni ble / k'o puor baalu / on puor wa baara / ti nyɛ
gyimuda / ku mi puoro / o puor wa baara / o'a nyɛ niri? / ni
booni? (40) / a man nir nu / k'o yɛr o lɔɔlee / o'a nyɛ pɔɔ / k'o sɛ
vaari / o'a iɔng na puori / puor baalo / ba wiili bomo / ka bon
boono? / faa nyɛ kuur / k'o na wiili / on wiil wa baara / ti wiil aro /
k'o iɔng na kpɛ / on kpɛ wa baara / ar kpɛ̃ɛ̃ na-aa / k'o iɔng na
ngmaa-a / ka dãbie iɔng / le kpɛ-o / on in ngmin? / k'o lɛ zɛl sor-aa
(60) / o'a wiil sori / wiil ngmi ngmin? / o'a de daa / iɔng na lɔbo / o'a
de daa / ti duur lɔb ku / k'o de dale / k'o wiil oa / a duuru / k'o iɔng na
ngmaa / o'a ngmaa aro / o'a nyɛ sori / iɔng na gõõ / o'a ta be / on ta
wa baara / k'o liɛb guble / o'a tõ wuɔ / o'a ir miuri / on ir wa baara /
ti lɛ nyɛ bom (80) / o'a nyɛ lɛri / lɛ dɔɔl o bɔɔ / o'a de ulɔ / o'a nyɛ
vaar / tile mhuɔl / k'o kyɛ olɔ / o'a kyɛ wa baari / a man nuɔr iɔng /
o'a iɔng na kpa / on kpa wa baara / ti wa nyɛ bomo / a man nuɔr
iɔng / bom bono? / kpan kyɔɔra? / on wa puora / kan puor baalo /
on puor wa bara / ti iɔng na yi / o'a nyɔɔ purɛ / k'o tɔɔ baalu (100) /
ti dur na yi / o'a nyɛ bomo / gyimuda / k'o puor baalu / a man nuɔr
iɔng / ni kpɛ̃ɛ̃ ba no / iɔng tɔɔla / faa nyɛ bari / ka nyɛ niri / iɔng na
dũ / ni kpɛ̃ɛ̃ naa / o'a kyɔr bari / ka bari bar kpib / faa nyɛ ble / ko
iɔng na puori / puor baalu / ka nikpɛ̃ɛ̃ wa de soobo / on soor baara /
ti lɛ soor ma / ka bon kan bɔɔr? (120) / kan lɛ yelu-a / ka naangmin
yelo / iɔng n fɛru / nikpɛ̃ɛ̃ na-a / lɛ yel ka / ka na in ngmin / a
naangmin yele-a / na wa uro / n in ngmin? / ka lɛ iɔng na yi / n ba
nyɛ bomo / tuu zong puo / ka nyɛ kɔntɔmbie / iɔng na zɔ / ba iɔng
na buɔl / ba na buɔl ma / ba buɔl na baara / ti lɛ soor ma / bonu kã
bɔɔr? / kan lɛ yel ba (140) / naangmin yelua / iɔng n fɛru / o'a fɛra
ma / ma ni kpɛ̃ɛ̃ nu / o'a nyɔɔ ma / ti iɔng ma sori / kan wa kpɛ
muɔ / bi yɔɔ iɔng / ka n dur wa ta / ba na tuõ maa / ka wa kpɛ ka-a /

on yel wa baara / ka kɔntɔmbiira / lɛb nyɔɔ bie / ba ba nyɔɔ baalu / ti
iɔng na ziil / ba ziil wa baara / ba de kyi / ti lɛ wiil-uwa / fu bɔ̃ɔ̃
una? (160) / ɔ̃ ɔ̃ ye / ka ba lɛ yelu-a / ka bondiri na / faa nyɛ
kɔntɔmbie / k'o iɔng na uɔbu? / on uɔb wa baara / ka iɔng na i nuɔ
iɔng / faa nyɛ dɔ / k'o tɔ̃ i ala / iɔng na uɔbu / o'a iɔng o nuɔri / o'a
nyɔ uɔbu? / faa nyɛ nuɔ / k'o yel ka lɛ na ka / on yel lɛ iɔng / on yel
wa bara / kɔntɔmbie-a / lɛ yelua / ko lɛ bar ka / ka ba wan zɔ̃ (180) /
baa wa tani / iɔng na soori / boon anya? / a tɛmpɛlo bii? / k'o yel
ka / zi nyɛle / o'a zĩ be / kɔntɔmbie-a / o'a de kuɔ̃ / o'a kyir iɔng zɔ̃ /
ka iɔng na bu / on bu wa baara / o'a ir nu / ti iɔng na lɛn / ko lɛn ka
yurru / ka kɔntɔmbie-a / lɛ yelua / ko uɔb nya / o'a iɔng na uɔbu /
on uɔb wa baara (200) / ti yel ka / lɛ na ka / o yel ka ya / k'o ba bɔng
kyi-e / o yel ayi / ka ba yel ka / bonu ir kyi? / ka ba yel ka ya / ngmin
ir kyi / k'o yel wa baar / ka fun in ngmina / o'a de kuur / o'a de ulɔ /
ti lɛ de bom / bun bonu? / o ina kuura / o'a ngmɛr kuuri / o'a nyɛ
yɛ̃ / o'a de ulɔ / ti iɔng na kyeni (220) / o'a lɛ kyeni / wa tan yiri / ti
ta be-ya / ti wiil dɔ / faa nyɛ ya? / on wiil wa bara / o in ngmin? /
o'a yel ka / iɔng gyiru / k'o iɔng na kaari / o'a de kuuri / o'a de
dããngmara / o'a de ala / o'a tɔɔ lɔng ta / o'a de yɛnɛ / o kur yɛ / ti
dɔɔl be / a nyaa minɛ / wa wa iɔng / o'a iɔng vũũ (240) / bonu ir
vũũ? / o'a de kusibɛ / kusi pla ba na / ni o ble / faa nyɛ goni? / o'a
de iɔng sɔ̃ɔ̃ / o'a de kpɛ̃ɛ̃ / iɔng o numi / o'a ngme ta / on ngme ta
ya / faa nyɛ vũũ / ka nyɔɔ goni / ka tɔ ble nya / ko iɔng dãbie / bom
boonu / k'o iɔng na kaar / o'a de vũũ / nyɛ muɔ baalu / o'a nyɔɔ
vũũ / o'a de olɔ (260) / a dããngma bɛrɛ / o'a iɔng be / faa nyɛ bomo /
k'o mɛ bin / o bin wa baara / ti de kur vuɔr / wa bin o puɔr / on bin
wa baara / ti wa de tɛnɛ / o'a iɔng kuɔ̃ / on iɔng wa baara / ti wa de
kuur / on de wa baara / ti iɔng na bu / on bu wa baara / on in
ngmin? / o'a fɔb kuri / on fɔb pɔɔ baara / ti ba de tɛnɛ / ti iɔng na
mɛ (280) / o mɛ wa baara / o'a mɛ iɔng suuli / on mɛ wa baara / o'a
de gani / on de wa baara / ka ti iɔng na ir / on ir wa baara / ti liɛb
gublɛ / o'a tɔ̃ bon puɔ / o'a iro miuri / ka ti iɔng na lɔ̃ / on lɔ̃ wa
baara / on in ngmi ngmini? / o'a buɔl o bie / k'o zɔ wa ta / k'o wa zĩ
ka / ka ti na tɔ̃ tomo / o'a zĩ be / ti bɛlɛ kpib / o'a yel ko bie (300) /
k'o fuur k'o nyɛ / ko fuur ka fɛɛ / ko lɛ yel ko bie / ko iɔng gankyɛ /
on iɔng wa baara / faa nyɛ kuri / ka kur ba muɔ̃ / o'a ir ulɔ / o'a de
zɛr / ti iɔng na tɔ / o tɔ wa baara / tɔ bɔ̃ gu / on in ngmini? / ka
kɔntɔmble-a / k'o lɛ yel ua / k'o lɛ iɔng / on lɛ iɔng nɛa / on iɔng wa
baara / ko lɛ iɔng gankyɛ / ka kur ba muɔnɛ (320) / on muo wa
baara / wa iɔng na tɔ / wa tɔ wa baari / o'n in ngmini? / naangmin

yele / na wa uro-a / on in ngmin? / o'a tɔ k'o mhuɔli / on in
ngmini? / o'a ir o zɛri / iɔng na bini / on bin wa baara / ti ba ir nu /
ba nyɔɔ a kuri / ka kɔntɔmble / iɔng tiɛro-aa / ka lɛ yelua / k'o nyɛ
bom / bon boonu? / kur daalee (340) / k'o de ulɔ-aa / ka tɔ guɔl / on
tɔ guɔl baara / ka kɔntɔmble-a / lɛ wa wiilo / a nyɔɔb-aa / o'a nyɔni /
a kuri / o'a nyɔɔ wa baara / ko yelua / ko de a zɛr / on de wa baara /
ko lɛ yel kaa / ko shɔɔ k'o nyãã / o'a shɔɔ wa baari / ko iɔng na tɔ / o'a
tɔ baalu / on tɔ wa baara / faa nyɛ bie / o'a yel ulo (360) / k'o de kur
piɔ / on de wa baara / wa iɔng o yuori / iɔng o kuri / ka kyiira no / ko
kyi ko nyãã / o'a kyi wa baari / on kyi baal-ua / o'a kyi wa baara / o'a
de o zɛri / ti iɔng na ngme / ngme guɔl iɔng / o'a guɔl wa baara / ka
sã goba / wa la murɔ / ka tɔ ble / o'a zĩ baalu / ti iɔng gyiro / on
gyirɛ-a / ka yel ka lɛ na ka (380) / ka a tɔ kpɛ̃ɛ̃ / ka nyɛra wuuri / o'a
ira kuuri / o'a iɔng kukuri / o'a ngme kpa iɔng / o'a kpa wa baari /
lɛ wiil tɔ ble / k'o de kaa nyaa / o'a de ulɔ / naangmin yele / na wa
uro-a / on in ngmini? / kɔntɔmble-a / lɛ yelua / k'o ir gago / on ir
gago / ko lɛ wiilu / a kuur nyɔɔb / o'a nyɔɔ a kuuri / o'a nyɔɔ
baalua (400) / o'a lɛ wiilu / k'o gũni / o'a gũ wa baar / k'o lɛ yel ka /
k'o ngmaa a teung / naangmin yele / n ba bɔ̃ɔ̃-ɛ / tɔ ble-a / na yel
kua / kɔntɔmble / o'a de kuuri / o'a ngmaa a teung / ngmaa puo
iɔng / o'a ngmaa wa baari / a teung tɛnɛ / k'o tɔɔ lɔ̃ taa / o'a ira kyi /
o'a iɔng na buri / o buri wa baara / sambar ata (420) / faa nyɛ
ngminbie / o'a ta be / ti iɔng na la / on la wa baara / kɔntɔmble / lɛ
soor ka ya / ka bono so lar / k'o yel ka yaa / naangmin yele / ka alo
so laari / ka tɔ ble / o'a iɔng tiɛro / o'a zĩ kpibo / o'a nyɛo yɛng / na
yel ka yaa / ko na puora / k'o sããkum kora / ka lɔng ni siuwe / ka
lɔng ni kpime / ka lɔng tengaama (440) / ka yel nya iɔng / o'a haa o
nɛ / ti iɔng na ir / on ir wa bar / lɛ yel ka ya / o'a puor tengaani / ti
puor a ngmin / ti puor kpime / ti puor siuwe / ti puor kɔntɔme / o
puor wa baari / o'a nyɛ bomo / dindamno / teung ni saa / a saa i
daba / ti teung i pɔɔ / zie ba mhani / faa nyɛ saa / o'a iɔng yɔlee /
o'a puor lɔro (460) / faa nyɛ teung / pɔɔsar kpɛ̃ɛ̃ / o'a nyɛ puɔ /
tilee wule / o'a wa yi / teung bie bano / ko ti doo / nikpɛ̃ɛ̃ banu / o'a la
murɔ / on la wa bar / ka tɔ ble / lɛ wa ta / lɛ yelua / ko na in ngmin? /
naangmin yela / na wa uro-a / k'o lɛ yel kayaa / ka tilee wule / k'o na
nyɔɔ na / ka dur ti do (480) / ka naangmin yir / o na nyɔɔ tiɛ / do bɔ̃
gu / lɛb lo kpai / ka sɛlngmindɛr / ka iɔng o gbɛɛ / iɔng kye kye / wa
yel ka / ka nikpɛ̃ɛ̃ / ko lɛ zĩ teung / k'o zĩ bar sɛr / o'a zĩ baalu /
sɛlngmindɛra / k'o ir biuri / iɔng o siɛ / ti yel ka / ka nikpɛ̃ɛ̃ / k'o
nyɔɔ miuur / k'o nyɔɔ wa bar / k'o lɛ yel ka (500) / naangmin yiri /

ti na dona / o'a iɔng na do / a naangmin yir / nikpɛ̃ɛ̃-noa / na gan
be / ba'a nyũũ / naa gan puo / ba'a ta be / iɔng na puori / zani
yaani / faa nyɛ baa / ba song bano / lɔng ni luɔra / lɔng ni gbeung /
lɔng ni wɔb / lɔng ni waala / lɔng ni iɛn / gbatɛr ble / ba'a nyɛ
iɛn (520) / nikpɛ̃ɛ̃ banu / na nar o naru / wa yel ka / ka nikpɛ̃ɛ̃-na /
k'o wa ka / k'o wa ta / o'a de teni / tɔɔ lɔng taa / on lɔng wa baara / ti
lɛ yel ka / ti buɔl pɔɔble / pɔɔbil mhɔla / k'o wa ka / o ba wa taa / on
na wa baara / k'o lɛ yel ka / k'o de yuɔr-aa / o'a de olɔ / ir ari / k'o lɛ
yelua (540) / k'o nyɛ saaluɛ / k'o de wani / o'a ir beini / iɔng o nuɔri /
ti dun k'o ngmɛri / o'a puur iɔng / iɔng o yuori / on iɔng wa baara /
faa nyɛ daba? / nikpɛ̃ɛ̃ ba nu / k'o lɛ yel-ua / ko maala tɛnɛ / on maal
wa baara / pɔɔbil mhɔla / o'a lɛ yel-u / k'o kyir a saalu / iɔng a tɛnɛ /
on yel wa baara / k'o lɛ yel daba / k'o ir goba (560) / tɔ̃ a tɛnɛ puɔ / on
tɔ̃ wa baara / k'o lɛ yel ka / k'o ir nu / o'a ir nu / o na in ngmini? /
o'a yel o / k'o lɛ wa ka / o'a lɛ wa ta / nanyu daa / lɔng ni pɔɔ / kaa
iɔng na iri / nikpɛ̃ɛ̃ banu / o'a kyuur ala / kaa baar zom / ka naazuɔ
daa / lɔng ni pɔɔ / wa ta be / nyɛ iɔng ni / ka dayere bio (580) / ka
nanyu daa / ni o pɔɔ / duur ta be / wa kya lo / faa nyɛ bie / ko kon
be zom? / n pãã in ngmin? / naangmin yele / na wa uro-a / ko lɛ yel
ka / ku o pɔɔ / ka ba duri ti ta / naangmin yiri / ka naangmin na / ko
lɛ yel ya / ka nikpɛ̃ɛ̃-na / an so bie / faa nyɛ bie / na ngmɛ taa ni /
a nikpɛ̃ɛ̃-na (600) / k'o la murɛ / o la wa baara / ti lɛ yel ka / ka bom
boonu? / ka ba yel kaya / ka bie banu / an so a bie? / ka nikpɛ̃ɛ̃-na /
lɛ yel ka / ka fũ so bie / nyinɛ ka n pɔɔ? / k'o lɛ yel ka / ka fu dɔɔ
bie / ka tɔble-a / lɛ yel ka / in ngmin dɔɔ? / ka nikpɛ̃ɛ̃-na / o'a la
baalu / on la wa baara / ti lɛ yel ka (620) / ka n na in ngmin? / faa
nyɛ pɔɔ / pɔɔbil mhɔla / k'o duur wa yi / k'o lɛ yel ka / ka alai lɛ /
ma so bie / ka nikpɛ̃ɛ̃-na / lɛ soor-oa / nyinɛ fu pɔɔ? / pɔɔbil mhɔla / o'a
iɔng tiɛru / ti lɛ yel ka / n saalo kuɔ̃ / n kyir iɔng / a tɛnɛ puɔ / al puɔ
bana / ka fu ir bie / ka nikpɛ̃ɛ̃-na / lɛ yel ka (640) / ka pɔɔbil mhɔla /
ko duur wa ka / o'a wa ta be / nikpɛ̃ɛ̃ nio / nikpɛ̃ɛ̃ na-a / buɔl o pɔɔ /
pɔɔ nyɔ̃ɔ̃ biɛ / o'a wa yi / nar o naru / bono naru? / o'a kar o vaari /
kar wa baari / ti lɛ yel ka / ka pɔɔbil mhɔla / ka ta ira lɛ / k'o de
bie / o'a de wa baar / on in ngmin? / o'a iɔng na piɔ / on piɔ wa
baara (660) / ti iɔng na kyeni / o'a de sori / pɔɔ nyɔ̃ɔ̃ biɛ / o'a lɛ
yel-ua / k'o kyiɛr shɔɔr / ko ba bɔng ka / zĩĩ be na / a o puɔri / pɔɔlɛ
mhɔla / o'a iɔng na la / ti lɛ soor ka / ka bono zĩĩ? / k'o lɛ yel ka / vɛ̃
ka ti ta yir / ba'a ta be / ba iɔng na zĩ / ba'a zĩ wa baari / pɔɔ nyɔ̃ɔ̃
biɛ / o'a bɔng o bomo / ti lɛ yel ka (680) / ka pɔɔyaa-ble / k'o de a
siung / ka dɔɔ vũũ zu / o'a de ba dɔɔl / o'a iɔng kuɔ̃ / pɔɔ nyɔ̃ɔ̃ biɛ-a /

o'a de o vaari / o'a nyɔɔ kari / on ka wa bar / iɔng siung puɔ / gbɔɔ
vũũ iɔng / ban iɔng wa baara / on in ngmin? / vũũ ba nyɔɔ /
ba de vaari / ba nyɔɔ liɛbo / liɛb wa baari / ka ba tuli be / pɔɔ nyɔ̃ɔ̃ biɛ-a /
duur kɔɔ yi (700) / buɔl pɔɔle mhɔla / k'o gaal bie / on gaal bie-a / ti
duur wa ta / pɔɔ nyɔ̃ɔ̃ biɛ-a / o'a pur kuɔ̃ / a vaar puɔ / ti de gõn / o'a
tõ be / o'a duur wa tani / pɔɔle mhɔla / o pɛn iɔng / o'a nɛ̃ be / pɔɔle
mhɔla / o'a nyɛ bomo / pɔɔ nyɔ̃ɔ̃ biɛ / ni a yel miɔng iɔng / faa nye
zĩĩ / ka yi be / pɔɔle mhɔla (720) / dãbie iɔng / na kpɛ-o / o'a yel ka /
nyinɛ na / ka zĩĩ yi be / n puori? / pɔɔ nyɔ̃ɔ̃ biɛ / lɛ yel-ua / ka bie
nya / nyinɛ fu pɔɔ / k'o lɛ yel-ua / tɛnɛ puɔ na / ka ti ga ir / faa nyɛ
bie / lɛ yel ka / fu puɔmi na / kan ira bie / fũ ni ano / ga ti ir? / k'o
lɛ yel ka (740) / ma ni nira nikpɛ̃ɛ̃ kɔng / o yuɔr-ua / ka tɔ ble / tin
na ba / ka nikpɛ̃ɛ̃-yaa / na o tõ ti / ni yel ble kɔng / ti naangmin nu-a /
na nar o naru / ka ti ɔng ti tɛnɛ / ti lɛ yel ti-a / ka ti ɔng ti saalu / ka
ti ɔng wa tani / o'a de a saalu / o'a dũ k'o ngmɛri / o'a puur iɔng
yuɔri / ti ɔng kuɔ̃ iɔng / ka ti kyir iɔng tɛnɛ / ka nanyu daa / o'a nyɛ
ti ari (760) / ti iɔng na ir / ka ti nikpɛ̃ɛ̃-yaa / o'a kyuuri o baari / o'a
bar zomi / ti lɛ kyuuri / k'o lo be gbili / on lo wa baara / k'o lɛ yel
ka / ka ti kyir nyɔɔ taa / tin kyir wa baar / taa liɛb na kyeni / naazuɔ
daa / ni o pɔɔ / kyil ba kyilu / baa ta a be / ti iɔng na diɛ̃ / ban diɛ̃
wa baara / ka nanyu daa / o'a mi ta be / o lɛ kyaa lɔb (780) / o kyaa
wa baar / ti nyɛ a bie / ka nikpɛ̃ɛ̃-na / k'o tɛr zini / kan wa ta be / ti
gyir nyɛ nir / k'o tɔ ble / n ba puoru-a / ti nyɛ bie / kã iɔng tiɛru /
ti iɔng na diɛni / ti yel ka bie-a / maa so ulɔ / pɔɔ nyɔ̃ɔ̃ biɛ / n de na
bie / n de wani / ka fu lɛ yel ma / ka n i ngmin / kan kar vaari / n kar
wa baar (800) / ti iɔng na kyen / ka fu lɛ yel ka / ka n kyier shɔɔ-taa /
ka n ba bɔng ka / ka zĩĩ be na / n puori puɔ / yel miɔng naa / fu yel
kum / pampana nyãã / n nyɛ zĩĩ / maa so bie / bii tɔ ble / pɔɔ nyɔ̃ɔ̃
biɛ / lɛ yel ka / ko bar sɛr / o'a bar sɛri / ka puɔ bhãã / on in ngmin? /
a naangmin yele / na wa uro-a (820) / daar kɔng iɔng / faa nyɛ tɔ
ble / wa kyen tɔli / o ba yiri / a lɛ daar / ti bie na / mi kyiera / ka tɔ
ble-a / lɛ wa iɔng / ba liɛb wa tɔli / bie ba nyɛ / a tɔ ble / ti iɔng na
kõ / k'o de-o / bi ma na / k'o yel ka / an so bie? / bi ma na / ko yel
ka / ma so bie (840) / ka tɔ ble / mi yel ka / ma so bie / a bi bein
iɔng / pɔɔ nyɔ̃ɔ̃ biɛ / duur wa ta / ba iɔng ba na irɛ gõ na / ka pɔɔ
nyɔ̃ɔ̃ biɛ / on duur wa nyɛ lɛ-a / lɛ yel ka / ka ba baar gõmɔ / ban bar
wa baar / o'a soor pɔɔble / pɔɔble mhɔlu / an so bie / ma so bie / ti tɔ
ble / bɔɔr na faa / ko lɛ soor tɔ ble / boono so? (860) / ko mi yel ka /
ma so bie / pɔɔ nyɔ̃ɔ̃ biɛ / o'a la kpai / ti lɛ yel ka / bi bein iɔng / ka
nib ayi / zɔɔri taa / yi vɛ̃ sɛra / ka n lɛ kyena / na gan puɔ / nikpɛ̃ɛ̃

banu / o'a gã be / ba iɔng na ta / pɔɔ nyɔ̃ɔ̃ biɛ / wa iɔng na puori /
zaani yaani / nikpɛ̃ɛ̃-na / o'a de yaani / on de wa baara (880) / ti
iɔng na soor / dãbie iɔng? / ai a-yi / dãbie bana-i / a bii nya yele / ka
ti wani / a fu zie / ka nikpɛ̃ɛ̃-na / ko lɛ yel ka / ka ti bar baalu / o'a
iɔng na soori / pɔɔlɛ mhɔla / bono so zɔɔro? / ko lɛ yel ka / ma so
bie / ka tɔ ble / bɔɔr faa / al so gɔ̃mɔ / wa la ma kpai / o la wa
baari (900) / ti iɔng na soor / ka tɔ ble / bono so zɔɔro / ka tɔ ble / ko
mi yel ka / ma so bie / pɔɔle mhɔla / bɔɔr na faa / al so gɔ̃mɔ / ka
nikpɛ̃ɛ̃-na / la na kpai / ti yel ka ya / pɔɔle mhɔla / nyinɛ fu pɔɔ bie /
ka pɔɔle mhɔla / lɛ yel ka / ka ka kan de / ko lɛ soora / a tɔ ble / nyinɛ
fu pɔɔ bie (920) / ko yel ka / sor puɔ kan de / ko lɛ yel ka / ka ba bar
sɛr / ba bar ba kpibo / ban bar wa baara / k'o iɔng na soor / pɔɔle
mhɔla / nyinɛ fu pɔɔ bie / a in ngmini / ka fu so bie / o'a lɛ soori /
pɔɔle mhɔla / ko lɛ yel ka / maa so bie / o lɛ soor ka / nyinɛ fu pɔɔ? /
ko yel ka / o lɛ de saalu / ka fu de ulɔ (940) / dun ngmɛr iɔng / a yuɔr
puɔ / kan a kyir iɔng / tɛnɛ puɔ / k'o liɛb bie / anu so tɛnɛ? / pɔɔle
mhɔla / o'a bar ba zom / on in ngmin? / k'o lɛ soor bie / an so fu? /
bie ba nu / o ba la murɛ / ti lɛ yel ka / n sãã nu / a tɔ ble / a in
ngmin / o'a soor o / ka fu bɔng ka / fu sãã nu (960) / a tɔ ble / faa
nyɛ bie / k'o la zom / ti iɔng na zɔ / o'a lɛ zɔ ti kyeni / o'a nyɔɔ
dabo / gbɛr kpɛ̃ɛ̃ iɔng / tɔ ble banu / o'a la murɛ / nikpɛ̃ɛ̃-na / ko lɛ
soor tɔ ble / an so bie? / k'o mi yel ka / maa so bie / an in ngmin / ka
fu bɔng ka / fu so a bie? / k'o yel ka / maa no / sɛlngmindɛra (980) /
n yɛbɛ nu / iɔng o gbɛɛ / iɔng kyekye / zie ba mhãã / nikpɛ̃ɛ̃ banu /
dindamno / ba teung ni sãã / o'a pur lɔr o / o'a iɔng teung / puɔ ba
kpɛ / o'a dɔɔ bie / bie da bhɔl / yel yɔɔ-bana / iɔng n fɛru / n in
ngmini / a teung zu ka? / n ba bɔ̃ gu / ba iɔng tiɛru / n ba yel ka /
n na do na (1000) / naangmin yiri / n ba ti nyɔɔ / teung bie banu / tile
mhɔla / ti iɔng na do / do bɔng gu / ti liɛb lo kpai / sɛlngmindɛr
banu / n yɛb nu / iɔng o gbɛɛ / iɔng kyekye / o'a ir miuri / iɔng o
siɛ̃ / ti lɛ yel ka / ka n nyɔɔ miuri / n ba nyɔɔ miuri / ti iɔng na do /
o'a de ma / wa ti tani / naangmin yiri (1020) / nikpɛ̃ɛ̃ banu / naa gan
puɔ / k'o iɔng na puori / zaami yaani / o'a de yaani / on de wa
baara / ti lɛ soor ma / bonu kan bɔɔr / ka n lɛ yel ka / bɔ̃ zaakpo /
ul ka n bɔɔr / o'a wiil ma / kɔntɔmbie / n ba nyɛ ulɔ / o'a wiil wa
baara / naangmin iri / nikpɛ̃ɛ̃ banu / naa gan puɔ / ul soor ma / a yel
yɔɔ yele (1040) / n ba yel u / n yel wa baara / k'o yel ka / ka n ar
ka / ka n iɔng na kɔ / n kɔ wa baara / tɛnbil puri / ka tɔ lɔng taa / k'o
bɔng o bomo / ti buɔl pɔɔble / pɔɔle mhɔla / o'a yin o yuori / on yi
wa tani-a / nikpɛ̃ɛ̃ banu / o'a de saalu / o'a dun ngmɛri / puur iɔng

yuɔri / o'a iɔng kuɔ̃-mi / ti iɔng n tɛnɛ / on iɔng wa baara (1060) / ti
ba iɔng na kyeni / naazuɔ daa [ni o pɔɔ] / baa ta be / ba diɛ̃ ba
diɛnu / ba diɛ̃ wa baara / ti iɔng na kyeni / nanyu daa / mi nu o pɔɔ /
baa wa ta / ba kyaa lɔbi / baa ir bie / n tɛnɛ puɔ / lɛ na vɛ̃ / ka n bɔ̃
ka / ma so bie / nikpɛ̃ɛ̃ banu / lɛ la kpai / ti bɔng o bɔɔm / o'a de
muri / o'a puo vuɔri (1080) / wa ku daba / o'a de kɔ̃ɔ̃ / wa ku pɔɔ /
ti puora vuɔ-i / on tir baara / o'a yel ka / ka ba nyɛn bom / lalɛ
purɛ / fu pɔɔ ba ioo / fu yel ka / fũ so bie / o'a de sɔɔ / ma so bie / o
lɛ soor daba / tɔ ble banu / an so bie? / k'o mi yel ka / ka olɛ so bie /
k'o yel ka / ka pɔɔle mhɔla (1100) / k'o iɔng duuru / a mur puɔ / ta
wa vɛ̃ / ka yaar-ɛɛ / o'a iɔng na duuri / ka a yaar-ɛɛ / an yaar wa
baar / k'o lɛ yel daba / k'o iɔng duuru / a mur puɔ / k'o ta wa vɛ̃ /
kaa yaar-ɛɛ / dab iɔng duuri / ka zɑ̃ɑ̃ kpe / ma kpɛ wa baara / k'o lɛ
yel ka / pɔɔle mhɔla / fu de yuor / fu na wani-a / faa nyɛ niri (1120) /
lɔng ni kuuri / kuur bini tɛni / ma so saalu / nar o naro / kyir ala
iɔng / tɔ ble banu / iɔng na bu / on bu wa baara / ya kyen be / yi
kyen wa baara / ti naazuɔ daa / ni puɔ / mi ta be / ba diɛ̃ wa baara /
nanyu daa / ni o pɔɔ / ba ta be / ba kyaalo / ba ir bie / nɔkpɛn
banu (1140) / yin ngme iɔng taa / a ngme iɔng taa / daba ba ioo / yi
o teung / yel fɛro / o'a fɛru / ko duur wa ta / a naangmin zie / a
nikpɛ̃ɛ̃-naa / n ba song-u / ko nyɛ bie / bie nya ulɔ / ulɔ so o / ba da
bie / ku tɔ ble / ku duur wa tani / a tengaan zu / on in ngmin? / o'a
wa tani / o sɑ̃ɑ̃ yir puɔ (1160) / on in ngmini? / yel yɔɔ bana / iɔng
na fɛru / o'a de bie / wiila siuwe / wiila ngmini / ti wiila tengaani /
ti wiila kpime / on wiil wa baara / faa nyɛ bie / zie ba mhaani / teung
ni saa / baa bɔng ba bɔɔm / wa pur na mhɔro / zie be mhɑ̃ɑ̃ / wa de
o kuuri / iɔng na yina / o kɔb iɔng na / on in ngmini? / tɔ ble
banu (1180) / duuri wa yi / o'a nyɛ bie na / iɔng ni kuuri / ka nuɔ
ba kpɛ-o / o'a yel bie / ka boona nyaa? / k'o yel ka / ka kuur ba ioo /
ti yel ka / k'o na kyeni ti kɔni / bi sɑ̃ɑ̃ ba nu / lɛ la murɛ / ti yel ka / lɛ
kan bɔɔr / o'a yel lɛ / iɔng na gbɛɛ / teung nɔng ba nu / o'a dun bie /
bie ba koni / bi sɑ̃ɑ̃ ba nu (1200) / o'a duur wa yi / lɛ soor bie / bonu
so koni / nɔng ba ioo / na dun bie / dɑ̃bie ba nu / kpɛ tɔ ble / k'o ir
o kyi / ti de o wuɔ / ti de o lɔɔ / o'a de tɔm / o'a de lɛr / ti duur na
yi / a dundɔr nuɔri / faa nyɛ kyi / o nu puɔ / o'a de wiil kpiin /
wiil siuwe / ti wiil ngmini / on wiil wa baara (1220) / ti iɔng na yi /
o'a nyɛ soori / mɔl mɔl iɔng / o'a duuri ti taa / bɔɔbuurɔ zie / baa ba
woori / o'a kyuur bar / k'a baa bar kpib / o'a soor daba / dɑ̃bie iɔng
na bii? / k'o yel ka / n bie banu / kɑ̃ yini-u / naangmin yiri / duur
wa tani / zie ba mhɑ̃ɑ̃ / k'o iɔng na kɔ / teung nɔng banu / o'a dun a

bie / faa nyɛ pɔɔle mhɔla (1240) / a bɔɔbuur yiri / k'o duur wa yi /
a dundɔr nuɔri / tɔ banu / o'a nyɛ pɔɔ / iɔng o bɔɔmu / o'a puor
pɔɔ / ti puor bɔɔbuura / on puor wa baara / ka pɔɔ yel ka / ka nyinɛ
fu kyier? / k'o yel ka / n bie nu / nɔng ba nu / ul dun-u / dãbie
iɔng / na kpe ma / ka wani / a bɔɔbuur yiri / pɔɔle mhɔla (1260) /
k'o la na kpai / ti lɛ yel ka / fu bie nya / o yuɔr-aa / din ka bo? / o ba
la zom / ti lɛ yel ka / n bie yuora / din ka / napolo / pɔɔle mhɔla /
yel ka ai / maa so bie / nyinɛ fu pɔɔ / napolo ka? / k'o yel ka / k'o vɛ̃
sɛri / o'a bar kpibo / bɔɔbuur bie / ba yɔɔ wuɔ (1280) / ti gbaal o zu /
ti de o lɛri / lɔng ni lɔɔ / lɔng ni tɔm / bin o pulɛ̃ / o'a bar ala / o'a
ir nu / tõ o wuɔ / o'a ir bom / ti lɛ yel ka / ka tɔ ble / n bin bom? /
ka tɔ ble / o ba la kpai / ti yel ka / k'o bin ulɔ / on bin wa baara / ti
lɛ tõ wuɔ / ti ir bom / gbelme banu (1300) / k'o ir wa baar / bɔtiib
daa / lɔng ni pɔɔ / o'a ir ala / ir bin teung / ti lɛ yel ka / ka tɔ ble /
ko kaa teung / o'a kaa be / k'o yel ka / k'o nyɛ gan / o'a nyɛ gani / o
nyɛ wa baara / o lɛ yel ka / k'o alɛ sɛr / o'a bar zom / o'a de gani /
k'o tɔ nyũ̃ / o tɔ wa baara / ti lɛ yel ka (1320) / k'o kaa teung / o ba
kaa teung / k'o soor gan / bono so waab / zi lio iɔng / ka n ba nya /
wa n zie / gan ba ioo / lɛ yel koa / ka wen nu / k'o lɛ yel ka / bono
wen? / sã̃akum weni / makum weni / tɔ ni weni / pɔɔyaa weni / wiɔ
weni / kɔntɔm weni / bidɔɔ weni / kpartiib weni (1340) / ku lo sɔɔ /
faa nyɛ tɔ ble / ko yel ka / lɛ na ka / ka na ti irɛ / na ku n bie? / o'a
iɔng na puori / ti iɔng na iri / o'a ir baalu / iɔng na yi / a dio nuɔr
iɔng / sɛung vurbɛ / a mur karbɛ / i da bɔɔr be / i pɔɔbil prumɛ /
i dabil prumɛ / o'a puor ba / on puor wa baara / o'a nyɛ sori / iɔng
na yi (1360) / faa nyɛ bomo / kɔntɔm wuɔ / lɛ soor o / a angmin / kan
puori a dɔɔ na / ti ba puor ulɔ? / kãn lɛ zĩ murɛ / ti iɔng na puori /
a wuɔ ba sɔɔ / o'a sɔɔ baalu / k'o yi nyɛ sori / iɔng na kyeni / ti lɛ
nyɛ bomo / bom boono? / a zɔɔ puɔ bomo / kpiin ba nu / lɔng
siuwe / lɔng ni wen / lɔng ni kɔntɔme / basɛ na (1380) / yirsob banu/
k'o lɛ puor ba / on puor wa baara / ti duur na yi / naangmin yeli / o'a
nyɛ soori / mɔl mɔl iɔng / sãã yir soori / o'a iɔng na kyeni / o'a duuri
taa / a sãã yir soori / n in ngmin / o'a zĩ be / zĩ baalu / ti iɔng na
buɔli / bi dable / ku yi wa ka / o'a duur wa yi / wa yi baalu / an buɔl
ma? (1400) / a bie ioo / iɔng na soori / anu buɔl a? / on soor wa
baara / bi sãã banu / lɛ yel ka / maa nu buɔlɛ / n in ngmin? / ka iɔng
na kɔɔri / pɔɔle mhɔla / wa de soori / sor kpɛ̃ɛ̃ banu / k'o iɔng na
tɔli / bi dable / o'a nyɛ ma / o'a buɔlu-u / n maanu-u / nyinɛ fu
kyier / bi ma-naa / lɛ yel ka (1420) / na ba kyier zie / ka ka n tɔlɛ /
ka bi dable / zɔ duur ta / o sãã zie / lɛ yel ka / ma in manu / ka bi

sãã-naa / lɛ soor o / nyinɛ ku yi / k'o lɛ yel ka / n ba bɔng ye / pɔɔ ni
tɔlɔ / ka n bɔng ka / n manu / bi sãã-naa / lɛ yel ka / faa tɛr ma-i? /
bi dable / k'o la baalu (1440) / ti lɛ soor sãã / fu nyɛn nir / k'o ba tɛr
ma-i / ti tɛr sãã / ka bi sãã-naa / lɛ yel ka / yel yɔɔna / kyãã fɛrɛ ma /
ka ba bɔng sɛrɛ / bi ma-naa / k'o iɔng na tɔl / faa nyɛ bi dable / ko
iɔng na kɔ̃ / n ma nu / bɔɔra tɔlɔ / bi sãã-naa / faa nyɛ suuri / ti lɛ
soor bie / fu manu anu / bɔɔra tɔlɔ? (1460) / n ma bana / a pɔɔle
mhɔla / bi sãã-naa / k'o lɛ kyuur bie / bi ma-naa / o'a duur wa ta /
on wa ta / iɔng na de / bi sãã-naa / k'o yel ka / n ba kɔro fuɛ / on yel
wa baara / bi ma-naa / k'o lɛ la kpa-i / ti lɛ yel ka / ka bie iɔng / n
kun tuɔ̃ bar-uɛ / ti lɛ kyene / o'a zĩ be / bie ba ioo (1480) / o'a nyɛ
yɛ̃ / o zu puɔ / daar kɔ̃ iɔng / tɔ ble na / o'a yi yo / yɔ kpɛ muɔ / ti
nyɛ kɔntɔme / k'o tɛra tɔm / lɔng ni lɔɔ / lɔng ni piime / o'a puoro-
u / on puor wa baara / a kɔntɔmaa / lɛ sooru-a / ka bonu k'o bɔɔr? /
k'o lɛ yel ka / yi na nyɔɔ ma / ka n kpɛ muɔ / ka yi wiil ma / yel yɔɔ
zaa (1500) / ti yaa wiil ma / a bum nya iɔng / kɔntɔme na / o'a la
baalu / ti lɛ yel ka / wa ka ti kuli / ba tu o puri / tu ti kuli / kɔntɔme
na / o'a yel ka / ka bon yi na bɔɔr na maali / bibiir niba ma maalu /
nyɛ n bie / zĩ kɔɔ zom / k'o maal kub / o'a zĩ be / kɔntɔmbie / o'a de
miuri / lɔng ni lɛri / lɔng ni suɔ (1520) / yi kpɛ muɔ / o'a kyɛ daari /
tamiur daari / on kyɛ wa baara / o'a iɔng na lɔ̃ / on lɔ̃ wa baara / o'a
duur wa tani / o sãã yir puɔ / o'a too lɔb na / on lɔb wa baara / ti ba
nyɛ dɔɔ / tɔ ble banu / o'a de suɔ / tamiur iɔng / o'a ir ulɔ / on ir wa
baara / o'a iɔng na bhari / on bhar wa baara / on in ngmin? / o'a
iɔng na kuɔri (1540) / on kuɔri wa baara / o'a ir boyeni / a tamiur
daa / on ir wa baara / wa de lɛri / iɔng na pɛni / on pɛn wa baara /
o'a de miuri / o'a iɔng na kpari / on kpar wa baara / o'a ir ari / o'a nɛ
ulɔ / nɛ na lɛrɛm / o'a nyɔɔ duɔri / on duori wa baara / o'a iɔng na
tɛ / tɛ na pim / o'a tɛra dɔɔ / kyeni ti tani / sããsob zie (1560) / on ti
taa / faa nyɛ kule / faa nyɛ lɛri / lɛgbie ba nu / o'a ti tani / sããsob
zie / o'a iɔng na puori / zaa yaani / o'a sɔɔ yaani / on sɔɔ wa baari /
ti lɛ soor u / ka dãbie iɔng? / a ai / k'o yel ka / kɔntɔmo nu-aa / nu-a
de ma yaa / ka n wa / fu zie / n wa ta / n be iɔng na puori (1580) /
dãbie ba nai / kɔntɔmbie-nu / zãã tĩĩsɔɔ / kã̃ n ir lɛ yi / a ti-vaar
puɔ / ti iɔng na yɔ bɔ / n bon bɔɔra / tĩĩ ba na / ka n bɔɔr na bɔ /
kɔntɔma nu-a / maa nye ulɔ / o'a yɛri bomo / yɛri zɛzɛ / maa soor
ulɔ / boona anya? / o'a yel ma-a / ka lɔɔ na nya / ka tɔm na nya / on
bɔ̃ɔ̃ woro / o'a yel ma (1600) / ala na ya / kã̃ yel-ua / fu na wiil ma /
a yel yɔɔ / a lɛ daara / fun nyɔɔ ma / faa wiil ma / tɔm ni pĩĩ / lɔng
ni lɔɔ / on yel wa baar / kɔntɔmbie / a lana ya / ko de ma / ka ti wa

ta / o sãã yir puɔ / k'o iɔng o bie / bi dable / o'a kpɛ muɔ / o'a nyɛ
daari / kyɛ wa tani (1620) / o'a iɔng n wiilu / on wiil wa baara / o'a
iri ari / nɛ na duori / o'a yel ma / kan i ti wa / fu zie ka / tia wa wa
ta / a bom na / n wani-a / ola na anya / n yel koba / nya kɔntɔmbie /
kɔntɔmbie / o'a de lɛri / ku sããsoba / sããsob na-a / wa buɔl bie / bi
dable / k'o zɔ wa ta (1640) / k'o yel ka / wa zĩ teung / k'o wa ta / o'a
lɔ tõ-u / k'o zɔ yi / a zɔɔ nuɔr iɔng / ti nyɛ bomo / taan dangma / k'o
iɔng vũũ-a / iɔng wa baari / o'a iɔng na di / on di wa baara / bi
dable / o'a iɔng tiɛru / kuõ bhaaro / o'a ɔng ala / duur wa yini / kyir
ba iɔng / a vũũ zɛlɛ puɔ / iɔng wa baari (1660) / o'a ir saala / a vũũ
kpo piɔ / duur ti tani / o sãã zina zie / a sããsob na / lɛ yel ka / k'o
ka alɛ / o'a bar sɛri / on bar wa baara / k'o yel kɔntɔmbie / k'o wan
lɛri / lɔng ni kuuri / o'a wa tani / o'a de lɛri / iɔng vũũ puɔ / o'a de
saala / kyir pɔɔ lɛri / on kyir wa baara / sããsob na / lɛ buɔl bie (1680) /
k'o duur wa ta / k'o lɛ yel ka / k'o do zĩ ka / o'a do zĩ be / on zĩ wa
baara / ti de o gani / bura dãã gan / ir o miuri / boor kpil puɔ / on
ir wa baara / ti ir na gũũ / nyɔɔ na lõ / on lõ wa baara / o'a de o
yuori / ngma o nɛɛ / ti de ba pɔɔ / a sããn nuɔr iɔng / o'a nyɔɔ na lõ /
on lõ wa baara / ti lɛ yel bie (1700) / k'o zĩ ka / o'a ir zĩ be / a sããn
zu iɔng / o'a yel ka / k'o zuu iɔng / o'a iɔng na zuu-aa / ngmin piɛlu /
duur wa yi / a sããn nuɔr iɔng / o'a iɔng guba / lɛ iɔng na zuu / ngmin
piɛlu / lɛ wa yi / gbɛɛ ayi / faa nyɛ sãã / sããsob-na / iɔng k'o zuu / on
zuur ala / lɛr ba muɔ / o'a de kyaba (1720) / iɔng na nyɔɔ / wa nyɔɔ
baalu / a sããn kuur zu / iɔng na tɔ / tɔ wa baari / tɔ bhuɔl iɔng / tɔ
wa baari / o'a ir kyiira / iɔng na kyi / kyi wa baari / faa nyɛ muri / mu
kpẽẽ bana / o'a sɛl ulɔ / ti iɔng o yuor / ka pĩĩ-nu / kɔntɔmbie / ni tɔ
ble / ba de pĩĩ / lɔng ni tɔm / kul ti tani (1740) / a sãã yir puɔ /
kɔntɔmbie / yel tɔ ble / ku nyɛ sor / o sãã yir sor / mɔl mɔl iɔng / tɔ
ble na / iɔng na yi / o'a nyɛ nibɛ / kɔntɔmbiri / o'a puor ba / puor
baalu / on puor wa baara / ti ba nyɛ sori / o sãã yir sori / mɔl mɔl
iɔng / duur ti ta / a sãã yir puɔ / faa nyɛ bie / bi dable (1760) / zɔ
tuor u / on zɔ tuor u-aa / bibil bawono / o'a nyɛ bom / o sãã zie /
iɔng na soori / boonu anya? / bi sãã na / lɛ yel ka / fũ so ulɔ / vẽ ka
ti ta yir / ka n ku fu / ba ti ta / a sãã yir puɔ / bi sãã na / de lɔɔ naa /
lɔng ni tɔmu / bie banu / o'a nyɛ tɔmu / o'a la murɛ (1780) / ti yel
ka / n sãã nu / wani tɔmu / lɔng ni lɔɔ / bi sãã na / o'a de tɔmu / wa
yi yon / a tãpuor zu / ar baalu / saal daa bhɔl / o'a nyɔɔ tɔmu / ti
iɔng pĩĩ / iɔng na tɛ / na saal daa / pĩĩ ba nyɔɔ / a saal daa bhɔl / bi
dable / o'a nyɛ ala / o'a la murɛ / ti duuri ta (1800) / o sãã zie / iɔng
na kon / kuma tɔmu / lɔng ni lɔɔ / lɔng ni pĩĩme / bi sãã na / o'a de

tɔmu / o'a ko bie / bie nyɔɔ tɔmu / o'a ir pĩĩ / a lɔɔ puɔ / iɔng a
tɔmu / iɔng na tɛ / tɛ bõ gu / ti iɔng na la / bi sãã na / o'a bar tɔmu /
k'o a bie / o'a tɛr tɔmu / o'a kpɛni (1820) / bi ma banu / pɔɔle
mhɔla / saar ba ioo / o'a de ulɔ / iɔng na piiri / di kpɛ̃ɛ̃ sɔɔri / o'a
iɔng piiru / bie banu / ni o tɔmu / iɔng na tɛ / bi ma-na / o vaar
iɔng / o'a tɛ na kpib / bi ma-na / duur ka ira / ti ngme bie / bi
sãã-na / o'a nyɛ suuri / o'a yel ka / nin daar iɔng (1840) / ta la ngme
bie / bi ma banu / o'a bar bie / dayere bio / bi sãã banu / kyen puo
puɔ / ti ti kɔ / ti ir wa ta / o sãã yir puɔ / faa nyɛ bie / long ni tɔmu /
ba zĩ be / iɔng na dien / bie ba ioo / o'a de tɔmu / iɔng ni pĩĩ / bi sãã
banu / o'a iɔng na gan / on gan wa baara / faa nyɛ bie (1860) / o'a de
tɔmu / lɔng ni pĩĩ / o sãã lani / o'a ta be / a lan iɔng / o'a iɔng na tɛ /
tɛ a lani / tɛ na kpib / bi sãã-na / o'a nyɛ suuri / ir ngme bie / ka bi
ma-naa / lɛ yel ka / o'o 'i / ta ngme bie / dabor daara / dabor daa
diɛ̃ / kã ngme bie / bie na tɛ ma / ka fu yel ka (1880) / ka n ta ngme /
on tɛ fu-a / fũn bara? / bi sãã-naa / o'a yel ka / ma nyɔɔ bie / dur
yini / dundɔr iɔng / o'a bar bie / faa nyɛ ngmama / a tuɔr pari / kaa
dire kyi / faa nyɛ boni / naangmin bonio / ziɛra banu / dur wa siu /
ngme a ngmana / faa nyɛ ngmana / a ba gã be / faa nyɛ bie (1900) /
duuri ti ta / lɔng ni tɔmu / lɔng ni pĩĩ / tɛ bõ gu / ti lɔng ni kyuuru /
o'a wa baara kyuur / o'a de ngmani / lɔng ni pĩĩ / iɔng na kpɛni / bi
sãã zie / ti yel ka / nyɛ n ngmani / ka n tɛ ku / bi sãã na / iɔng na laa /
ti ngme o nyãã / ti yel ka / maa dɔɔ bie / bi gandaa / daar kɔng
iɔng (1920) / k'o faa ma / on yel wa baara / ti ba de ngmani / iɔng
na guri / o'a ir gbɛri / o'a ir siɛ / k'o a siɛ / bi ma na / ti de gbɛr / o'a
mi tɛri / bi ma na-a / wa la murɛ / nuɔ ba kpɛo / bi ma na / zie ba
sɔbu / k'o soor bi sãã / ka ti na in ngmini / lɛ nyɛ bie / lɛ iɔng puɔ / ka
ba i ayi? (1940) / ka bi sãã na / lɛ yel ka / ka dayere bio / n na kyena /
a nikpɛ̃ɛ̃ zie / sɛlngmindɛri / k'o nyɔɔ ti / ka ti lɛ do / a naangmin
zie / ti nyɛ bie / zie ba kyaa / bi ma na / ir ba kpɛ muɔ / o daar bɔbu /
bɔ ti kpɛ / man kpurɛ nuɔr / o'a ta be / o'a nyɛ bomo / zun banu /
lɔng ni pɔɔ (1960) / ba ba diɛni / pɔɔ ba nyɛ / iɔng na laa / zun ba
ioo / o'a buɔl pɔɔ / k'o wa ta / o'a soor ulɔ / boonu fu laar / k'o yel
ka / ka bom ba i-aa / ka ba diɛn na / irɛ ma nuɔ / ala na kã laari / ka
zuna / lɛ yel ka / k'o bɔɔn bom nuɔ / k'o yel ka / o' o' ye / k'o yel ka /
k'o wa zĩ ka (1980) / k'o wa zĩ bi-kpibo / zun ba ioo / o'a gani o
pɔɔ / ba tõ ba tomo / pɔɔ ba nyɛ / lɛ yel ka / k'o mi gani / o'a gani
pɔɔ / pɔɔ ba iri / ir wa baari / ti lɛ yel ka / ka a diɛnu numɔ na / on
yel wa baara / zun ba yel / ka ulɔ diɛn ni nya / k'o na dɔɔna / bi yɔɔ
za / pɔɔ ba ioo / ir zɔ kuli / o yir puɔ (2000) / ti ta be / o'a yel daba /

bom ka nyɛ / diɛnu kɔng / deb yel ka / bonu diɛnu? / ka o yel ka / vɛ̃
ka n wiil fu / o'a ti ga / ti buɔl daba / o'a ta ba / wa mi ga / ka pɔɔ
nɛ / o'a wiil tomo / dab ba nyɛ / ka numɔ o zie / k'o la murɛ / ti yel
ka / ka lɛ na ka / ka ka diɛnu numɔ (2020) / dayere bio / dɛb ba iri /
iɔng na yeli / ir ka ti kyeni / a naangmin zie / ti zɛl a bie / pɔɔ ba
ioo / iɔng na zɔɔri / ti yel ka / ka o'a kyiere / fu na nyɛ diɛnu / ka
numɔ nya / ti fu lɛ duori / naangmin zie? / ir ka ti diɛn / daba ba
taa / ba ba diɛni / bibie ayuɔbi / faa nyɛ pɔɔ / dayere bio (2040) / o'a du
biɛ̃ũ / o'a uɔb tiu / zie ba kyɛlɛ / faa nyɛ pɔɔ / k'o kyãã tiu / faa nyɛ
daba / dãbie bana / iɔng na kpɛ o / k'o lɛ yel ka / ka ba in ngmin /
pɔɔ ba ioo / lɛ yel ka / i ka ti zĩ / dab ba ioo / yel a pɔɔ / vɛ̃ ka ti
kyeni / a naangmin zie / ti bɔng a puor / tiub yele / pɔɔ ba ioo (2060)
lɛ yel ka / k'o kõ kyeni / faa nyɛ daba / k'o zĩ baalu / ti iɔng na soora
par / pɔɔ ba ioo / lɛ yel ka / k'o bar ala / ti ir ka ba diɛni / n puor
nya / ba ɔɔr ma-i / dayere bio / ka puor ba ɔɔri / o'a lɔɔr kyɛli / tɔ
ble banu / o'a zĩ bɛr zom / ti ir ka yi / duur ti kyeni / kɔntɔmbie zie /
ti soori u-aa (2080) / wa nyɛ ma / yel kɔng na / na dɔɔ maa / kɔntɔmbie / duur wa ta / lɔng ni wuɔ / lɔng ni kpo / lɔng ni gbelme /
lɔng ni bɔtibɛ / lɔng ni siuwe / lɔng ni kube / lɔng ni man uɔra / o'a
zuu bini / bin wa baari / ti lɛ yel ka / k'o tɔɔ ta / o'a tɔɔ ta / k'o lɛ
yel ka / k'o nyɔɔ ba nyɔɔ / ba nyɔɔ ta (2100) / baa puor ta / ban puor
wa baara / ti k'o liɛb guba / faa nyɛ daa / daa boonu? / lɛr kukur nu /
o'a de-o / on de wa baara / ti lɛ yel ka / k'o nyɔɔ iɔng ma / o'a nyɔɔ
iɔng u / kɔntɔmbie / ba nyɔɔ daa / ba nyɔɔ shɔɔ / kɔntɔmbie / ba
wiil o / k'o nyɛ bomu / k'o iɔng na soori / bom bonu / ka ba yel
ka (2120) / fu pɔɔ puɔ / na ɔɔra / ka fu wa ka / ala na so / ka n de
wuɔ / vɛ̃ ka n zuu lɔb / ka fu nyɛ bie / o'a zuu lɔbi / faa nyɛ bie / ka
lo gyirmɛ / k'o lɛ yel ka / ka yel miɔ̃ na / n pɔɔ puɔ nu-aa / ɔɔr o zaa /
ala na ya / ka n yel ka / n do naangmin yir / ti soor nya / faa nyɛ
tiɛru / lɛ wa ma (2140) / ka n yel ka / n na wana / wa soor fu / soor
bɔ̃ɔ̃ bom / ala na ya / ka n wani / kɔntɔmbie / lɛ yel u-aa / bom ba
nai / nir nu-aa / na wa fu zie / ni paala / ala na ya / ka naangmina /
bɔng o bɔɔm / de ku pɔɔ / iɔng o puɔmi / alɛ zũũ yaa / lɛ zɔ kula / a
nir na (2160) / o ba iri / o'a yi / zɔ ti kuli / o sãã yir puɔ / o'a ti ta /
wõ koni / ka bible / iɔng na kõ / ko yel ka / an so bie / k'o wa
kon / n yir ka? / o'a duur kpɛ be / o'a nyɛ pɔɔ / k'o tɛri bie / dãbie
ba na / iɔng na kpɛ o / k'o lɛ yel ka / k'o alɛ ka / o'a bar zomu (2180) /
on bar wa baara / pɔɔ nyɔ̃ɔ̃ ble / lɛ yel ka / k'o vɛ̃ sɛr / ka yel nya
iɔng / naangmin-ua / naru naru-u / tõ a pɔɔ / ko kpɛ muɔ / ti nyɛ
yele / wa iɔng na diɛni / on diɛn wa baara / k'o liɛb puɔ / lɛ kpɛ o /

nir ba no / wa fu zie / faa nyɛ daba / ko la murɛ / ti lɛ yel ka / a bie
nya iɔng-a (2200) / n tɛru a / naangmina-u / ku ma ulɛ / ti bie nya
na / n yel ka / anu kum? / ka pɔɔ nyɔ̃ɔ̃ ble / lɛ yel ka / naangmin
kum / ala na vɛ̃ / ka pɔɔle mhɔla / kpɛ a muɔ / ti nyɛ zuni / k'o wiil
o / a diɛnu nya / a diɛn wa baara / n bie o'a song-o / ala na anya / faa
nyɛ ala / bi sãã na (2220) / lɛ yel ka / a bie nya ulɔ / n na puora / o
yuɔr ka / ka Dɛr / naangmin ba kuma / ka dɛrua / pɔɔ nyɔ̃ɔ̃ ble /
iɔng tiɛru-aa / o'a kyuur daba / k'o bar kpibo / ka pɔɔ nyɔ̃ɔ̃ ble / lɛ
yel u-aa / k'a a yuor / na di dɛr-aa / k'o yuor ba nuɛ / k'o yuor di na /
ka piwai / bi sãã na / lɛ soor pɔɔ (2240) / bono piwai / k'o yel ka /
naangmin-oa / na dɔng ku o anya / iɔng o yuori / ka piwai / bie ba
soor / soor wa baari / k'o yel ka / ka bie nya naa / n puora yuora / a
piwai-a / yi na nyɛna / biir pie / dɔɔl ba zu / faa nyɛ ba / ba dɔɔ
biiri / ka ba i pie / pɔɔ nyɔ̃ɔ̃ ble / o'a la murɛ (2260) / ti yel ka /
angmin nibe / ka be yel ka / ba in pie / lɔng piwai / ni naangmin
bie / faa nyɛ ba / naangmin sɛb / wa ngme ba / baa i pɔlɔ / ban pɔl
wa baara / faa nyɛ daba / daar kɔng iɔng / o'a de tamiu-e / lɔng
tɛndɛɛ / o'a maal ala / maal wa baari / o'a põ ba / põ wa baari / ka
ba yel ka (2280) / a ba i yele / wiil ti a tɛb / o'a de tɔmu / duur ti
yini / buɔl ngmin bie / ko wa yi / na o tɔmu / o ba wa yi / ni o
tɔmu / o ba yel ka / ka ba kaar ka / a saal daa mhɔla / o'a tɛ o / o'a
pɔɔ saalu / dayere bio / ka tɔ ble / o'a yi yɔbu / lɔng ni biiri / baa
duuri ta / muɔ kpɛ̃ɛ̃ puɔ (2300) / ban ti ta / mure ba nu / iɔng na tɛ /
tɛ bõ gu / o'a ar be / naangmin bie / iɔng o pĩĩ / o tɔm iɔng / ti iɔng
na tɛ / on tɛ wa baara / o' a pɔɔ murɔ / k'o iɔng na zɔ / zɔ ti kyeni / ti
ta be / bɔɔ nuɔr iɔng / iɔng na kpɛ / o'a nyɛ kɔntɔmbiir / o in
ngmin? / kɔntɔmɔ-na / lɛ soor ka (2320) / an tɛ ma / nadɛr ble? /
dãbie-na / kpɛ ngmin bie / k'o ar be / baa vũɔ̃ pĩĩ / ban vũɔ̃ wa
baara / ti lɛ soor o / bono fui ɔng? / k'o yel ka / n ba iɔng bome /
kɔntɔmbira / ka ba yel ka / k'o vɛ̃ sɛr / o'a vɛ̃ be / on vɛ̃ wa baara / ba
nyɔɔ-o / ba tɛr tani / ba dio nuɔr iɔng / ba yel ka (2340) / zĩ ka sɛri /
ba kyen ka vaar / wan wa tani / k'o lɛn nya / o'a lɛn ulɔ / taan tiɛ
nu / o'a tɛr tuoi / ba lɛ kyɛ / do vaar ba nu / wan wa tani / k'o lɛn
ala / o'a tɛra tuoi / ba lɛ de / ga vaar bana / lɛ wa tani / k'o lɛn ala /
o'a de vaari / lɔng lɔng taa / k'o lɛn ala / a ba tɛra tuɔi (2360) / yebe
vaari / o'a wa tani / k'o lɛn nyɛ lɛ / o'a iɔng na lɛni / k'o tɛr tuo / ba
kɔ̃ɔ̃ ba de ulɔ / o'a de sɛr / wa wa duuli / o'a de yebe / iɔng ser puɔ /
iɔng wa baari / ti iɔng vũũ na / o'a de bomu / bom bonu? / dampan
zu / o'a iɔng be / ti iɔng na duu / ba kara ala / k'o yel ka / wana
pĩĩ (2380) / o'a de pĩĩ / tur ko bie / a kɔntɔmbie / o'a de pĩĩ / a yebe

kuɔ̃ na / a kuɔ̃ tulo / o'a de iɔng / a pĩĩ iɔng / iɔng wa baari / ti yel
ku-a / k'o nyɛ yebe / ka ulɔ wa kula / k'o ti wiil o sãã / a tɔ ble na /
o'a duur ti kuli / o sãã yir puɔ / o'a ti tani / wiil tɔ ble / on wiil wa
baari / k'o yel ka (2400) / ka lɛ na ka / ti kɔntɔmɔ / tɛr ma lɛ / ti kpɛ
muɔ / a ti wiil ma / lɔɔ dulu / on wiil wa baar / sãã ba ioo / de o
pĩĩ / iɔng o tɔmu / ti lɛ yel ka / ka zirina / k'o ba i bome / ka
naangmin bie / lɛ yel ka / k'o lɛn nyɛ / o'a iɔng na lɛni / zɛl ba vɔɔ /
o'a de pĩĩ / o'a ir yini (2420) / a dundɔr iɔng / o'a nyɛ nuɔ / o'a de
ku bie / bibil puri / k'o tɛ k'o nyɛ / o'a iɔng na tɛ / faa nyɛ nuɔ / ko
liɛb lo kpai / o'a de kũũ / o'a kpi baari / faa nyɛ bie / o'a kpɛ yel
sãã / dayere bio / o'a de lɔɔ / lɔng ni pĩĩme / o'a kyen kyɛ yebe /
dampan zu / o'a ngma wa iɔng / o lɔɔ puɔ / o'a iɔng na duuli (2440) /
ala ba kara / o'a de pĩĩme / a bi yɔɔ pĩĩme / o'a iɔng be / tikyɛ i
zɛlɛ / on zɛl wa baara / on in ngmini? / dayere bio / o'a yel ba / ka
ba kpɛ muɔ / ba-a kpɛ muɔ / ba'a nyɛ bomo / wal piel da / lɔng ni
pɔɔ / ba ar be / faa nyɛ bie / ngmin bie banu / nu tulu sob / o'a iɔng
na tɛ / kpi kpib iɔng (2460) / pĩĩ ba nyɔɔ / wal piel da / o'a lo be / o'a
ngme kyɛli / bi sãã na / o'a duur wa ta / wa nyɛ bom-u / wal piel
kũũ / o'a la na murɛ / k'o yel ka ya / ir ka ti kuli / baa ti ta / a sãã yir
puɔ / ban in ngmini? / ba yel pɔbɔ / ka ba kyen tuo nɛn / baa duur
ta be / baa nyɛ nɛni / baa iɔng na la / baa tuo ala (2480) / duur ti
tani / ka tɔ ble na / o lɛ yel ka / ka ba alɛ sɛr / ba bar kpibo / o'a ir
gbɛri / ulɔ so ulɔ / o'a ir siɛ / ma so ulɔ / o'a ir nyũũ / nɛn tuoro so
ulɔ / o'a ir ziuɛ / ku o sããkum / o'a ir nyɔbɔ / ku a pɔbɔ / o'a ir zu /
ku o ba / ti lɛ yel ka / fu mi wa ku / mi ira zu (2500) / wa kuma / o
yel wa baara / dayere bio / ba gaa puo puɔ / ba ti kuɔri / ba nyɛ nɛni /
nɛn bono? / wɛ naab ba nu / lɔng ni ble / ba ira ar dẽũ / naangmin
bie / duur ta be / liur ta be / ti iɔng na tɛ / wɛ naab na / o bɔɔ-
ngman iɔng / o'a gyir ba tɛ / faa nyɛ lɔɔ / a ba ir ti do / o nyɔi
puɔ (2520) / o'a lo be / on lo lɛ-aa / ba'a duur ta be / bi sãã nu-a /
iɔng na la / o'a la murɛ / ti lɛ yel ka / lɛ na ka / kã ba tɛr tɔmai / kã
da bɔng ka / wɛ bomo-aa / ben a ka / n ba de tɔmɔ / nyɛ naangmin
bie / daar dɔng ku / ti lɛ wa ka / a diẽ bibir / lɛ ku anya / ti n ba
tɛr tɔmɔ / ba duur ti ta (2540) / ba sãã yir puɔ / ba yel pɔbɔ / ka ba
kyen de nɛn / pɔɔbil ba na / baa kyen ti ta / baa nyɛ nɛn / baa iɔng
na la / ti de ala / kul ti tani / ti-a wɛ naab ble / ba ba bar ulɔ / ti lɛ
yel ka / ka ba bar yuon boyen / ka k'o ta naab / ka ba wa wa ku / baa
bar ulɔ / dayere bio / ba kyen puo / ti nyɛ naab ble / k'o ɔɔr o
muɔ (2560) / ba iɔng na la / wɛ naab ble-a / k'o iɔng na kɔ̃ / ti lɛ yel
ka / k'o ma san nya / k'o na yana / faa nyɛ alɛ / yuoma ata / al ba ta /

a daar kɔng iɔng / tɔ ble ba nu / ni o biiri / baa kpɛ muɔ / ti bɔ ba
nɛni / baa kul wa tani / ba sãã yir puɔ / ban uɔb wa baari / dayere
bio / baa kyen ba puo puɔ / ti iɔng na kɔ (2580) / baa kɔ wa baara /
pɔɔbil ba na / baa wan dãã / baa zĩ nyuuri / ban nyuura dãã / faa
nyɛ bomu / ba puori / k'o lan wa ta be / bom boono? / pɔɔsarble /
iɔng viɛlu / baa nyɛ pɔɔ / baa buɔl pɔɔ / k'o wa ka / o'a duuri ti
ta / ka ba yel-ua / k'o nyɛ pɔɔble / k'o buɔl u / k'o wa ka / ban buɔl
pɔɔble (2600) / o'a wa ta / on wa ta / ka naangmin bie / yel ka ya /
k'o pɔɔ-ono / ka piwai / mi yel ka o pɔɔ nu / ka tɔ ble / yel ka ya / k'o
na dena / ka ku yaa / k'o bi nyuɔra / ka pɔɔble / lɛ yel ka yaa / ka ba
alɛ ka / ba baar sɛri / k'o de dale / o'a iɔng na kyeni / gbɛɛ kɔɔr ayi /
o'a ba be (2620) / on ba wa baara / ti yel ka yaa / ka ba tɛ dale / ka
nirzaa yaa / na i dable / wa tɛ pɔɔ-aa / ulɔ ka n bɔɔr / n ba bɔɔr ka /
ka n kul daba / ni daar iɔng / ka ba tuõ o / baa iɔng na tɛ / tɔ ble
banu / ir tɛ sɛri / ti ba pɔɔi / o'a yel ka / ka o bi nyuɔri / k'o tɛ nya /
o'a tɛ pɔɔ ye / faa nyɛ bie (2640) / ba iɔng na tɛ / naangmin bie / o'a
tɔ o tɔmu / ti iɔng na tɛ / dale na / o'a pɔɔ ulɔ / ti lɛ yel ka / ka ulɔ
nu-aa / k'o sãã dɔɔ / pɔɔsarble / o'a kyen ti nyɔɔ / naangmin bie /
kang-kori ulɔ / on kor wa baara / faa nyɛ pɔɔ / nuõ ba kpɛ-a / ba
iɔng na kɔ / ba kɔ wa baara / faa nyɛ bomu / bon boonu (2660) / pɔɔ
nyõõ ble / o'a wa ta / a puo puɔ / ti iɔng na soori / bi pɔl bili / bono
yi irɛ / ka ba yel ka / ka bom banai / ka pɔɔble-nu-a / wa ti zie / ti
yel ka / k'o bɔɔra / ka bi dable / na iɔng zana / o'a nyɛ daba / naangmin bie / o'a iɔng zan / o'a iɔng na tɛ / a dable tɛbu / k'o yel
ka (2680) / ka lɔnu k'o bɔɔri / pɔɔ nyõõ ble / o'a de pɔɔ / ka be
denio / kula a yir / na ti ta / a sãã yir puɔ / pɔɔ nyõõ ble / na bɔng
o bomo / o'a gyir pɔɔ / nyɛ a pɔɔ-a / ti iɔng na kyuuri / pɔɔble nya /
o'a i pɔɔi / ti tɔ ble / na yel ka / k'o tɛr kuli / o'a tɛr kuli / ti tani / o
sãã yir puɔ (2700) / zimaan sɔng / faa nyɛ pɔlɔ / ba ir puo puɔ / kul
wa ta / a sãã yir puɔ / ka tɔ ble / o'a yel ka / ka naangmin bie / k'o
de o pɔɔ / ka kpɛn o diem / o'a de pɔɔ / ba ti tani / o dio puɔ / o'a
de gani / mure gani / yel k'o zĩ / o'a zɔɔr bari / k'o lɛ de / wal piel
gani / yel lɛ ko zĩ (2720) / k'o zɔɔr bari / o'a lɛ de / zipiu gani / yel
k'o zĩ / k'o zɔɔr ulɔ bari / o'a lɛ de / wɛnaa gani / yel k'o zĩ / k'o zɔɔr
ulɔ bari / o'a lɛ de / bur gani / yel ko zĩ / k'o zɔɔr ulɔ bari / o'a lɛ
de / siba gani / yel k'o zĩ / k'o zɔɔr ulɔ bari / o'a ir de / o ma gani /
wɛnaab gan banu (2740) / o'a wa lɔbu / lɔb bin teung / pɔɔble ba
nyɛ / duur ta be / o'a lo zĩ / ti iɔng na kõ / naangmin bie / o'a soor
pɔɔ / bon so koni / k'o lɛ yel ka / k'o ba kone / ka pɔɔ nyõõ ble-nu /
gbɔɔ o vuu / ka zuur ya / kpɛ ma nimie / ka nimie kuõ / wa yire / on

yel wa baara / zie be sɔbu / ba iɔng na gã (2760) / k'o soora sirɛ / ka
o yuor din ka bo / k'o yel ka ya / n yuor-ua / naangmin bie / o'a mi
soor pɔɔ / fu yuor-a / din ka boonu? / ko yel ka / n yuor-ua / ma nyɛ
wuur / k'o yel ka / k'o yuor viɛla / k'o lɛ soor ua / n sirɛ / fu ma in
ngmin / wa ti ku / a bom bɛrɛ nya? / k'o yel ka ya / ka o ma tuõ
ku (2780) / k'o lɛ yel ka / ku ni bo / k'o yel ka / tɔm ni pĩ / k'o yel
ka / ti ulɔ wa / i dun-faa / o'a bɔɔr fu kub / fu na in ngmin? / ko lɛ
yel ka / kãn mur teung / k'o yel ka / ti ulɔ mi wa mur / ko yel ka / ka
o yɔɔ do saa / k'o tur fu / kã liɛb vaa / k'o kyan tur / kã liɛb muɔ /
k'o kyan tuur (2800) / k'o lɛ yel ka / kã n liɛb mi— / ka pɔɔ nyõ̃ / yel
ka ya / faarin gyɔ / ka bie bar kpib / pɔɔsarble / ba iɔng na soori /
buono yelu / ka pɔɔ nyõ̃ ble / yel ku fu / ka fu lɛ i gbili / k'o yel
ka / bom ba iai / on yel wa baara / faa nyɛ pɔɔsarble / soor wa gu /
ti baar ti gã / zie ba kyɛli / naangmin bie (2820) / ka kuɔr bie / ir zi
lio / iɔng na kyeni / o puo puɔ / wa yel ka / ka pɔɔ nyõ̃ ble / k'o ir
a kyi / ka ba tɔ-aa / k'o ku pɔɔ saana / k'o iɛri wani / o'a ir a kyi / ku
a pɔɔble / ba ba tɔ / baa ir bie / o'a ko pɔɔ / k'o iɛr kyeni / a puo
puɔ / o'a ti iɛri / on iɛr wa baara / o'a iɔng na yini (2840) / pɔɔbil
mhola / ba iɔng na biɛlu / k'o lɛ yel ka / ka õ̃ õ̃ ye / ka ba vẽ sɛr / baa
lɛ kuli / ti o ba de zõ̃ / iɔng piɔ puɔ / a tuo zumi / ba ti tani / a puo
nuɔri / nyɛ to ble / o'a ar be / ti liɛb o naab / lɔng ni tuori / o'a duur
ti ta / naangmin bie / o'a ir gyir nyɛ / o'a de tɔmu / lɔng ni lɔɔ (2860)
o'a vuõ pĩ / iɔng na tɛ / o'a tɛ bõ gu / o'a ta be / bɔɔr o kub /
naangmin bie / mur kpɛ teung / ka naab na / mi muri kpɛ teung / o'a
ir iɔɔ / wɛ naab na / mi iɔɔ tu o / bɔɔr o kubu / o'a liɛb wa siuu / o'a
liɛb vaari / ka wɛ naab na / mi liɛbu vaari / a bɔɔr o kubu / k'o lɛ
liɛb muɔ / ka wɛ naab na (2880) / mi liɛbu muɔ / a bɔɔr o kubu / k'o
bõ gu / on in ngmin / o'a yi kyaa puɔ / k'o wa ta / a naabu / o'a bɔɔr
o kubu / k'o bõ gu / ti liɛb fumin / ir kpɛ o zuuri / o'a gã be / ka wɛ
naab na / bõ wa gu / o ba nyu ye / ti kpɛ o muɔ / on kpiɛr ti tara / k'o
yi lo / on yi lo baara / ti wɛ naab na (2900) / o'a iɔng na kõ / ti yel
ka / ka naangmin bie / ka bidaba nu / ka ulɔ ba i daba / n na ti ku
ona / n ma iɔng / ni n laab iɔng / tikyɛ yaa / a pɔɔ nyõ̃ ble / o faari
n gyɔ / o lɛ faa-o / ka a ba i lɛɛ / tin tiɛr ka yaa / a ziẽ zaa kpo / n na
ti ku ona / lɛ na vẽ / ka pɔɔ nyõ̃ / o nuɔri / nir kun tuõ (2920) / gõ̃
barɛ / ka bi pɔlɔ / lɛ soor ka / a in ngmin / ka pɔɔ nyõ̃ nuɔr / ba kun
tuõ / lɛ gõ̃ barɛ / fu ba nyɛ / ka naangmin bie / lɛ yel ka / fu tɔr
bɔng / ka fu kun tuõ / i bom zai / ala na / ka fu soora / a anya taba /
fu ba nyɛ / a tini / wa kpɛ muɔ / ti kuɔra (2940) / ti wa wa yir / ti
sãã banu / a tɔ ble / ko lɛ soor ti / a ti muɔ yele / o'a ir daba / a ti

sɔ̃ɔ̃ be / on soor wa baara / faa nyɛ bie / na iɔng zana / ti a fu sooru /
a fu na soor ma / fu in bibi faa / ba bɔng bom zaa / in yel faana / ka
fu wa i bom / i wa baara / wa nyɛ vla / fu na bɔɔna / ka fu lɛ ba nyɛ
vlai (2960) / fu na kyaana / lɛ bɔng ala / on yel wa baara / ti lɛ yel
ka / ti kyɛ sooru / fu soor ma / a yele na / ka n yel ku fu / fũ wa
bɔɔra / na bɔng a par / tõ tõ faa / ti bɛl nyɛ / on yel wa baara / ti lɛ
yel ka / bibil bawono / fũ tõ toma / ka ba wiil wa gu-a / daar kɔ̃
iɔng / fu na tuɔra / a yele ala (2980) / na shɔɔ fu-a / on yel wa
baara / ti lɛ yel ka / ka ti bom nya / tin tɛr o'a / i a bom kpɛ̃ɛ̃ / a fɛra
ti-a / a kori zaa kpo / bom boono? / ma ti bɔɔr bono / ia yel faa / a
fɛra ti / lɔng n pɔɔbili / lɔng ni dɔɔr / lɔng ni pɔɔbɔ / tin in ngmin /
a yel nya iɔng / ma deungdem / tɛra ba bom / wa ti kpiɛr a teung
(3000) / na lɔng kpɛni / ti bar ku ti / ka a fɛri ti / k'o bɔ̃ wa gu /
pɔɔbil naba / dabil naba / lɔng ni nibɛrɛ / ka fɛra ti / ka ti bɔ̃ gu / tin bɔ̃ wa
gu / ti iɔng na zɔ / a deung bomo / fun in ngmin / zɔ ti baar? / ala
na so / ka ti nyɔɔ-a / nyɔɔ bɔ̃ gu-a / tɔ bɛrɛ naba / ni tɔ ble / tɔ ble
banu (3020) / ti nikpɛ̃ɛ̃ / tɛri o bomo / kɔntɔmbira / ir nyɔɔ u-aa /
tɛra viiri / ti kpɛni muɔ / ti wiil-ua / a yel yɔɔ anya / ban wiil wa
baar / ti kyɛ kũũ / ka ti bɔ̃ɔ̃ ka / a kũũ nyɛ iɔng / tɔ ble banu / wa
wiil ti / a kɔbu / wa wiil ti / a dibu / wa wiil ti / dãã duubu / wa wiil
ti (3040) / kyi kɔbu / wa wiil ti / wɛ bom kubu / on wiil wa baara / ni
daar bio / ka ti gyirɛ / a tɔ ble na / k'o kpɛ teung / ka dãbie kpɛ ti /
ka ti bɔ̃ gu / ti ir nyɔɔ ala / a man ɔra na / ti nyɔ ala / iɔng na tɔ / tɔɔ
bɔ̃ gu / bar ku biiri / ka biir mi de / fu na nyɛ bible / na iɔng tiɛru /
ti bom nyɛ iɔng (3060) / ti na bɔ̃ gu-aa / o'a ti nyu-u / k'o i
naangmin yeli / ti i kɔntɔm yeli / ka ti tu bɔ̃ gu / ti lɛ wa ta / ti sãã
yir puɔ / daba ba ioo / bɔ̃ɔ̃ yel yɔɔ / o na bɔ̃ɔ̃ yela / ka ti yel ka /
naangmin yelua / ni daar iɔng / ka ti faa ta / ti a bɔng ala / a
dɛungdem na / na bɔ̃ wa gu / ti ti nyɔɔ ala / nyɔ ni duurua / ba
nyɔɔ ni guba (3080) / lɛ ari sirɛ-a / ba ar bɛlɛ / ti iɔng na nyɛ-a / yel
miɔ̃ yele / ba ngmara ziri / a dɛungdem-aa / na bɔ̃ gu / tia ngme
anya / ka ti bɔ̃ gu / ti nyɔɔ-ala / a yel ziri-a / a dɛungdem nuɔra /
zir nuɔra / be tu bɔ̃ gu / ti liɛb bufulɛ / lɛ kpɛ a teung / ti ti mi ira / mi
yel ka / ka ti na tuna / a dɛungdem yele (3100) / ti tuɔ̃ bɔ̃ gu / tin tu
bɔ̃ gu / tia lɛ zĩ teung / ti lɛb biɛri / a dɛungdem gbɛɛ / ti lɛ nyɛɛ / a
yel yɔɔ yele / na lɛ wa / boonu wa? / faa nyɛ kɔbu / na wa ti zie / yel
miɔ̃ na / ka na in ngmin ko ti / faa nyɛ ala / tia ur biiri / lɔng ni
pɔɔbɔ / ti na ur ba-a / a kuur ba-io / ka fu uu ni ba / ti lɛ yel ba-a (3120)
a in ngmin / ka pɔɔble ulɔ / kun tuɔ̃ kɔi? / fu bɔɔno buno / na i lɛ /
ka pɔɔbɔ / kun tuɔ̃ kɔ-a? / ka pɔɔ nyɔ̃ɔ̃ ble / le soor ka / yi ala ka / ba

bar zom / k'o lɛ yel ka / ka bom na vẽ / ka pɔɔble yaa / kun tuõ kə-a /
olɔ nu-a / a bondiri ire / olɔ nu-a / a sɔr pirɛ / olɔ nu-a (3140) / a
vũũ gbɔɔrɔ / olɔ nu-a / a kuõ ɔngnɔ / olɔ nu-a / nir yir nir / lɛ na
vẽ / ka ti kun tuõ-a / bar pɔɔble / k'o kuɔr a kɔb-ɛ / ka dable-a / lɛ
soor ti-a / bona vẽ / ka pɔɔble / i nir yir nir? / ka pɔɔ nyõõ na / lɛ la
baalu / ti lɛ yel ka / ka pɔɔble-a / k'o kun tuõ-a / zĩ a fu yiri puɔ
(3160) / bona vẽ / k'o kun tuõ / zĩ a fu yiri puɔ? / ulɔ i daba / o dɔɔra /
dɔɔ iɔng yir puɔ / un dɔɔna / yuom o ayi / zĩ a diem-a / ti dire a
dɔɔ-i / on yel wa baara / ka dable-a / o'a la baalu / on la wa baara / ti
iɔng na kuli-a / nikpẽẽ banu / gaa o yiri / ka pɔɔ nyõõ ble / mi yi de
soori / iɔng na kyeni (3180) / faa nyɛ boni / bom kuura banu? / ka
ba wiili / a tɔ / bɔɔnu bom kuura? / k'o lɛ yel ka / yebe nu-a / ka ba
wiil-u / ka ba duuli / k'o kun wɛ duni / a dable-a / iɔng na kyeni / ka
pɔɔ nyõõ mia / o'a mi de sori / on kyiera-a / ka tɔ / o bi dabanu /
gandaa bie / ka ba buɔl ua / ka dɛri (3200) / bonu-nu dɛr? / o in ya /
a nir / ban dɔɔ / ko kpi-a / ti lɛ wa / ka ba lɛ dɔɔ / ko lɛ kpi-a / ulɔ
nu-a / ka ba buɔl dɛr / o in na-a / dable-o / ala so / ka ba k'o tɔmu /
o'a yini / muɔ pla puɔ / o'a ti bɔ / a wɛ nɛn gu / lɛ wa yir / pɔɔ ba
ioo (3220) / ba be yiri / k'o wa ta / kuõ nyuur banu / iɔng na kpɛ-o /
o in ngmin / o'a bõ gu / ti buɔl o pɔɔ / kuõ mhaarua / wa kum ka /
faa nyɛ pɔɔ / o'a ir suuri / o'a zɔra kuõ / suur ba kpɛ / a dɛri / o'a de
pĩĩ / iɔng o tɔmu / o'a tɛ o miõ / on tɛ wa baara / yebɛ ba ioo / o'a
i lɔɔ-a (3240) / ir do o / piu u nyuɛ / o'a i kũũ / on i kũũ-a / faa nyɛ
pɔɔ / o'a lɔb kyɛli / ni yɔɔ niba / baa wõn kyɛli / zɔ wa ta / baa nyɛ
kũũ / ba minɛ ba bõõ ka / ka a pĩĩ-a / ma tuõ na / k'o a nirɛ / ba man
ka ya / wɛ dun tiɔna / k'o ma tuõ ku / baa nyɛ lɛ / ban nyɛ wa baara /
dayere bio (3260) / baa de dɛri / iɔng dio puɔ / ba ti ũũ / ban ũũ wa
baara / ti de ba tɔmu / de ba pĩĩme / lɔng ni lɔɔri / baa turɔ taari /
baa iɔng na gɔm / faa nyɛ dɔɔr / baa yi be / daba ba ioo / o'a kyaar
tɔmu / baa turɔ taari / sambar ata / ayen ba tɛ / o'a tɛ niri / faa nyɛ
daba / naangmin bie / o'a la murɛ (3280) / ti kyaar o pĩĩ / lɔng ni
tɔmu / mi iɔng na tɛ / o'a tɛ be / bi pɔl banu / lo ni pĩĩ / faa nyɛ ala /
ka be yel ka / k'o lɛ na / ka tikyɛ-a / ka niri / ma yel ka kpɛ fu / ka fu
de daa / bɔɔr na ngmɛ / faa nyɛ anya / yel miõ banu / ka anya tɛr /
faa nyɛ ala / dayere bio / pɔɔsarble (3300) / na sɛ zuɔrɔ / o'a kyen
daa / kyen ti ta / faa nyɛ pɔɔlɔ / na pɔl zɛnta / ziɛm banu / ti naab
anya / ba nyɛ pɔɔ / na viɛl woro / ba yel ka / ba na bɔna / ba tõ pɔɔle
mhɔla / k'o ti buɔl-u / buɔl ku wa / wa ta be / iɔng na zĩ / on zĩ
baal-ua / baa de dãã / iɔng o ngmani / ban ku-a (3320) / k'o iɔng
na nyu / faa nyɛ sirɛ / su tulu sob / o'a wa ta / faa nyɛ tɔmu / lɔng

ni lɔɔ / o'a ta be / iɔng na ngme / a o zani / ngme na kpim / ti yel
ka / dãbie ba iaa / kpɛ naab-o / lɔng ni ziɛm / ka ba bɔ̃ gu / ti zĩ
baalu / ban zĩ wa baara / suur ba ioo / tɛr o gu / faa nyɛ pɔɔ sirɛ
(3340) / k'o iɔng na tɛ / o'a tɛ ziɛm / on tɛ wa baara / o'a i kũ / on
kpi lɛ-a / ka pɔɔ nyɔ̃ɔ̃ bil-a / lɛ yel ka / ka ba ala ka / ka ba vɛ̃ sɛrɛ /
o'a iɔng kyɛli / faa nyɛ nibɛ / ni yɔɔ niba / zɔ wa ta / ba nyɛ ziɛm / ko
i kũ / ka ba bɔ̃ gu / ban in ngmin / ziɛm yidem / bi pɔɔl nibɛ / kokor
iɔng (3360) / pɔɔ sirɛ na / o mi yidem-a / mi i yɔɔ / a kokor na / ba
tuor ta / a muɔ pla puɔ / iɔng na tɛ / tɛ bɔ̃ gu / faa nyɛ kũni / kpi
diɛl taa / ka pɔɔ nyɔ̃ɔ̃ bila / ba iɔng kyɛli / nikpɛ̃ɛ̃ banu / o'a yi be /
iɔng o zani / wa wa ta / ti yel ka / ka ba bar sɛr / ba ba bar zom / k'o
lɛ yel ka (3380) / ka yel nyɛ iɔng / ka pɔɔbil beini / wa ku pɔlɔ / pɔɔ
sirɛ na / ba ba ku / ka ba yel ka / fu na tuɔ̃ na / a zĩ zom / ka yɛ̃ lɛ
wa / bon yɛ̃ nu? / ti yɛ̃ n yel ka / a pɔɔ bein iɔng na / ka ba ku kun
yɔɔ / lɛ na vɛ̃ / ka nibɛrɛ na / zĩ lɔng taa / nar ba naru / wa wa yi /
ti iɔng na hieri / ti lɛ yel ka (3400) / ba bar gɔ̃mɔ / baa bar gɔ̃mɔ /
bono k'o na yel? / k'o yel ka / a kɔntɔm-a / na wiil ti / bon yɔɔ-ya /
ti bon bein-ɛa / ia boma / ulɔ nu kũũ / k'o wiil ti / a lɔɔ nyɛ yela-a /
k'o wiil ti a yebe-a / ka ti kurɔ ni / a wɛ dun-a / ka ɔɔr ya / ti yel faa
nya / na wa yi ti zu / ulɔ nu bono? / ulɔ nu-a (3420) / a dɛra / na
kyena a wiɔ / wa kul ti ta / on ta o yira / o'a zɛli kuɔ̃ / on zɛli kuɔ̃ /
a ba nyai / o pɔɔ zie / sur bɛ iaa / lɛ kpɛ o / k'o bɔ̃ gu / ti ir o pĩĩ / tɛ
o tuɔra / o'a yi kũ / taa nyɛ ala / taa yel ka / bi pɔl kũũ-na / ta ir ari /
iɔng na diɛni / a o pĩĩ (3440) / ti nyɛ kũni / na wa ti zu / bi pɔl wa
i bie / wa ti gaa / diɛn o pɔɔ-ya / o ta wa ti / wa diɛn-ya / a pĩĩ yele /
a kũ nyana / na ku ti biira / tin yela / ka naangmin kũũ na / ka tɔ
sob / o'a yel ka / a ba i naangmin kũa / wa fɛrɛ ti-ɛ / ti na fɛr taa / ulɔ
nu bonu? / ulɔ nu-a / tɛ fu tuɔra (3460) / ani pĩĩ / ngmaa fu tuɔra /
ani suɔ / ka nir wa i bie / wa bɔ̃ɔ̃ yɛ̃ / o zɔ dãbie / a kũ nya iɔng / suur
wa kpɛ fu-a / ka fu i daba / fu mã yi na / a de fu lɛra / lɔng ni tɔmu /
lɔng ni suɔ / lɔng ni pĩĩ-a / ti yɛr fu lɔɔ-aa / yi kpɛ muɔ / tuni fu
suura / fu na tun / bon tomo? / wɛ dun daa (3480) / ka fũũ pɔ ulɔ-a /
ti ti ku-a / ngmaa o zu / duur wa tani / fu sãã yir puɔ / ba na bɔ̃ɔ̃
na / ka fũũ-nu / ka i daba / ni daar kɔ̃ɔ̃-yaa / ka tɔ ble / buɔl o bira /
lɔng ni pɔɔbɔ / lɛ yel ka / ba bar zom / baa bar zom / k'o yel ka / ba
na buɔla / a naangmin-a / ti ba bɔ̃ɔ̃-oa / ti yel ka (3500) / ka fũ kpi
baara / ka fu na bɔ̃ɔ̃ naangmin / fu na in ngmin / a bɔ̃ɔ̃ naangmin /
ka fu wa kpi-a / k'o yel ka / a lɛ daara / fu na ti yuɔra / a yele
yele-a / fũ wa kpi-a / fu na nyɛ na / a fu yel bie za / baa yel ka / ka
naangmin-a / ka fu wa kpi-a / ka fu na nyuuna / ka ma tɔ ble-a / ani

ngmindɛr / ti bɔ̃ɔ̃ a naangmin zie / k'o yel ti-a (3520) / ka bible-a /
o lɛ iru / a daba-a / o lɛ iru / a pɔɔble-a / o lɛ iru / pɔɔ kpɛ̃ɛ̃-a / olɔ
ir ba zaa / on ir ba ya / bon ba ku / baa ku bome / ka ba yel ka / ka
ba nyɛ nuɔ / ka ba lɛ nyɔɔ nuo / ka ti de yuor-a / ka ɔng kuɔ̃ iɔng-a /
ka bin ya / ka lɛ de yuor zɔɔla / ka bin ya / ka ka zie wa mani (3540) /
ka saa ba wa / ka sa bie kuɔ̃ / ka kpɛ yuɔri / ka ba de ala / ba tani
man nuɔri / ba nyɛ bomo / bom boono? / zɔ̃-zɔ̃ piə nu / baa iru / ba
tan yiri / baa ti ta / a muɔ nuɔr puɔ / ba nyɛ bomo / bom bono? /
a ti vaar banu / ti buor vaar? / ga vaar bana / baa kyɛ na iɔng / tɔ ba
ioo / o'a kyuur ba (3560) / ba bar zom / k'o yel ka / ka ba tu a nyu-ɛ /
ba tu a nyu-ɛ / ban tu wa baara / baa tan yiri / ba ti tani / a sãã yir
puɔ / ba nyɛ bomo / bom bono? / ti sõng na / baa tu o nyu-ɛ / baa
tu lɔng taa / nikpɛ̃ɛ̃ banu / zir ngma bɛrɛ / k'o yel ka / ka ba de
nyu-ɛ / ka gur lɔng ta / baa gur lɔng ta / ban gur lɔng taa (3580) /
o'a lɛ yel ka / ka bom bein kyɛ / ka ba lɛ soor ka / ka bom bono? /
kakal tiɛ / ka o nyu-ɛ / ka kɔntɔm bom nu / ka ba yel ka / ka ti in
ngmin / ko yel ka / ka ba ti ta / o par-aa / a tu o nyu-ɛ / wa iɔng
puɔ / ban iɔng wa baara / ti yel ka / ba gur lɔng taa / iɔng kuɔ̃ puɔ / kuɔ̃
buor puɔ? / k'o yel ka (3600) / ka kuɔ̃ ala / na i a sabie kuɔ̃ / ka ba
iɔng a puɔ / ka ti nyɔɔ nɔra / ka wa ku iɔng nyɛ / baa yel ka / ka ti
ku ngmin ngmini / k'o yel ka / ka yin wa ku-a / ka a nɔra / wa liɛb
lombora / fu bɔ̃ɔ̃ ka / ngmin pla nu / ti ka ulɛ / wa liɛb vɔɔl / fũ bɔ̃ɔ̃
ka / ngmina / ba nu-ɛ / ti ka ulɔ / liɛb lo kpai (3620) / ni o puora / fu
bɔ̃ɔ̃ ka / a bom nya / a ngmin-u / baa nyɔɔ ku / kɔntɔmbie / o'a ir
uuru / wa piu ba / ti wa ta / zĩ lan ba / baa ku wa baara / o'a liɛb
o nu / o'a nyɔɔ nuɔ / iɔng na liɛb / ka kɔntɔm pɔɔ / lɛ yel ua / k'o
liɛb vɔɔl-o / k'o yel ka ya / k'o o ba bɔɔra / ka n ba i bomi ya (3640) /
ka yi buɔli / a n yuor / ka n sɔng bari / alɛ na vɛ̃ / k'o nyɔɔ nuo / o'a
liɛb kpai / ni o puori / nikpɛ̃ɛ̃-na / o'a la murɛ / o'a de ngmani / ni
ziri ngma nɛ / ɔng kuɔ̃ iɔng / ti liɛb o nu / o'a tõ kaa nyɛ / on tõ kaa
nyɛ / on in ngmin / k'o yel ka / ka yel nya iɔng / tin i-oa / k'o tu
ti (3660) / ti bɔng ka / yel miɔ̃ bom nu / faa nyɛ kɔntɔmɔ / o'a lɛ
liɛbu / on in ngmini / o'a bɔ̃ gu / ti ir baalu / o'a kyen o zie / on kyen
wa baara / baa nyɛ zie / k'o i kyaa / ka ti bɔ̃ gu / ti lɛ nyɔɔ-a / iɔng
na tu / tin tu-aa / ti yel ka biir / lɔng ni pɔɔbɔ / ka yele nya iɔnga /
ka bible-a / wa iɔng tiɛru-a (3680) / k'o nyɔ-a / k'o kpɛ o zu / k'o tɛr
tiɛru / ni daar iɔng / ka ti faa taa / bonu faa taa? / ala nu ya-a / ka ti
yela / ku bibiira / tin yel kuba / ba zaa kpo / k'o yi a puɔ / ti bible-a /
na ben be / na i tiɛru sob / tin yel baara / ti lɛ nya / k'o lɛ i-aa / bon
bɔ̃ɔ̃ guura / ka yel yɔɔ (3700) / wa kpɛ o puɔ / bon i yel yɔɔ / ti ba

nyɛ aa / ka zɔ̃zɔ̃ daa / i a ti bɔɔr bom / damdamwulɛ / o mi i na /
ti bɔɔr bom / burngmaan daa / o mi i na / ti bɔɔr bom / kyaalipiɔ
daa / o mi i na / ti bɔɔr bom / belibaar / o mi i na / ti bɔɔr bom / ka
ba i yɔɔ / ti ba yɔɔ / ka ti yel ka (3720) / alɛ wa ngmɛ lɛ-aa / tin i na /
ti lɛ bar / tin yele-a / yel wa baara / kɔntɔmbira / ya lɛ wa / a zi lio
iɔng / yin wa ta / ya dɔɔn ti / dɔm ni bo? / puur ba ɔɔri / zuri ba
ɔɔri / an ɔɔr ti-a / ka ti bɔ̃ gu / ti soor kɔntɔmɔ / n tiɛr ka / yin ir ti /
bin teung zu / ka ba la murɛ (3740) / ti'a soor ka / ka bala ir ti? / ba
sɔɔ ɔ̃ ɔ̃ / ban sɔɔ wa baar / ka tɔ lɛ maali-aa / lɛ soori ba / ka bon kɔ̃ɔ̃
aa / ka ba na yel ka / ka bon kpɛ̃ɛ̃ nu-aa / ka i ti dɔɔru / ka kɔntɔmɔ-
aa / lɛ soor-aa / ka bom ngmɛ̃ ngmin? / ka tɔ yel ka / ti won o yuor /
ti ba nyɛ o ngmɛi / k'o yel ka yaa / fu wɔ̃ o yuora / o yuor di ka
bo? / k'o lɛ yel ka (3760) / o yuor nu yaa / ka naangmin / ka ma tɔ /
manu-a / bɔng o zie / a kori zaa / ti wa ta / a tengaan / ka nibɛ yaa /
mi be be-aa / ka ba buɔla / ka kɔntɔmɔ-aa / ka yi wa piu n sooru / ka
kɔntɔmɔ / ba lɛ la / ti yel ka yaa / ka boono / ka fu buɔl / ka tengaan /
ka tɔ (3780) / ba zĩ teung / ti nyɔɔ tengaan / o'a man-u / k'o yel
ka / a tɔ ble nu / a mãã yaa / ni tɔ kpɛ̃ɛ̃ / ti ni ayi / tin ayi / na ti wa /
wa zĩ zie / a zie na-a / kusir panu-a / ka ti zĩ be-a / ti ba tɛr yir-e / ti
ba tɛr dioɛ / nãn gai / ti ba kyeni / ti bɔn yel kɔng / a naangmin
zie (3800) / ti na yelua / a yel wa baara / taa ir nyɛ sori / na kyeni /
fu ba nyɛ ala / a naangmin yele / ka tɔ kpɛ̃ɛ̃ / o'a gan tĩɛ̃sɔɔ / wa yel
ka / kaa won o na / ka mang ka / diɛnu na / ka blã puɔ-a / k'o iɔng
na kpi / o ba kpii-a / on a kpii-a / ka n bar o-aa / a be ya / ti yel ka
yaa / n na lɔ̃ɔ̃ na (3820) / a tɛr gani / ka n tɛr gani / bibie ata / k'o
iɔng na puɔ̃ / kã kyãã̃n tɛr / gana gure / k'o wa puɔ̃ / on puɔ̃ baara /
daar kɔ̃ɔ̃ ya / tĩɛ̃sɔɔ bein-a / ka nir-ya / wa wa ta / wa buɔl ma / ka
n siu ka / n ba siu / k'o de ma / kpɛni muɔ-a / yuom ata / ti wiil ma /
a yel yɔɔ yele (3840) / on wiil wa baara / ti lɛ liɛb kyena / sambar
ata / k'o lɛ wa / wa n zie / wa wiil ma / a bom na / n na i lɛ / boono-
nu? / o'a yel ka / kan ngmaa yir / ka n ngmaa wa baara / ko lɛ soor
ma / ka n na in ngmin? / ka n yel ka / n bɔɔna / lɛ n na ia / k'o lɛ
yel ka / i kan nyɛ / n ba i (3860) / i bɔ̃ gu / o'a de daa / o'a ba teung /
on ba wa baara / ti yel ka / ka n ir muɔ / pɔɔ daa zu / ka saa wa
waara / k'o piu ma / ka kɔntɔmɔ / lɛ yel ka / kã kyɛli sɛr / n ba kyɛli /
k'o de daa / ba iɔng puɔ / on ba wa baara / ti lɛ de daa / wan wa
tani / de iɔng a zu / on iɔng a zu (3880) / iɔng wa baara / on in
ngmin? / ka tɔ na / kaar a ibu / on in ngmin? / k'o yi-a / ti naru
naru / kpɛni wa tani / da yɔɔ bana / o'a ba gangyirɛ / on ba wa
baara / ti de aminɛ / lɛ yɔɔli a zu / on yɔɔli wa baara / o'a de tɛnɛ /

o'a pɔɔ a zu / on pɔɔ kum-aa / ka n zĩ be / n na in ngmin? / k'o yel
ka (3900) / ka n kaara iiba / n ba kaari / o'a de tɛnɛ / o'a pɔɔ a zu / on
pɔɔ wa baara / ti yel ka / ka n do ar nya / n ba do ari / n ar wa baara /
ti iɔng dãbie / k'o ta wa irɛ / wa ka loi / k'o ba karɛ / zie ba sɔbu / zie
na sɔba / saa ba wa / o'a ar zom / n ba gã be / nuɔ ba kpɛma / bom
bein-ua (3920) / ar n woma / bom boonu / na ar fu wom / kã yele /
ka n kpɛ̃ɛ̃ / na kpi be-aa / ka n baar u-aa / ti wa zĩ ka / n in ngmin? /
ka kɔntɔmbie-a / lɛ yel-oa / ka be-a / ka yuon wa ta / k'o ir nuɔ / ka ti
zina / a kuur zu / ka ti buɔl o yuor-a / o kpɛ̃ɛ̃ yuor-a / ka ulɔ buɔl wa
baara / k'o tiɛru bomo (3940) / on tiɛra / a o puor puɔ / ka ti ngma
o nuɔ / n ba ti tiɛri / ti ngma a nuɔ / ka nuɔ ba lo / n in ngmin? / n
ba dɔng bɔngɛ / lɛ n na i-aa / ni a nuɔ nyɛ iɔng / ka kɔntɔme-o /
yel ka yaa / ka ulɔ lo wa baara / k'o zĩ gyirɛ / ka o wa liɛb vɔɔl puɔ / fu
bɔ̃ɔ̃ ka / ka fu kpɛ̃ɛ̃ / o zɔɔra fu yele / ti ulɔ-a / wa liɛb lo kpai-a
(3960) / ni o puor-a / fu bɔ̃ɔ̃ ka / o sɔɔn fu yele / on yel wa baar / ka
nir-na / o'a de nuɔ / o'a lo kpai / k'o la murɛ / ti ir na yi / ka
kɔntɔmble / lɛ soor-aa / fu na kyiɛri-a / a zie nya o yuor / din ka
bo? / k'o liɛb ar be / o'a iɔng tiɛru / tiɛr na bɔng / a zie nya yuor / o'a
tiɛr bɔ̃ gu / ti lɛ la murɛ (3980) / ti lɛ yel ka / ka o kpɛ̃ɛ̃ / na gã a
kaya / o i na / na-a / tengaana / ala i lɛ / n na buɔli na ka / n
tengaana / lɛ na vɛ̃ / ka ba buɔlɔ / ka tengaan / ka fũ zĩ zie-a / wa ir
zĩ zie kɔ̃ɔ̃ / fu mi vɛ̃na / ka ba bɔ-a / a tengaan ble / boonu a
tengaan ble? / fu ni yel a / ka ba ira (4000) / o kuur kɔ̃-a / lɛ ko fu-a /
ka fu de bin / a fu mi zĩ zie / o na i na / a tengaan / ulɔ nu-a / ka ba
buɔla / a tengaan ble / faa nyɛ ala / ba yel wa baari / ba na yel wa
baara / ti lɛ yel ka / ti bɔɔra / ka ti bɔng / boono ir nir? / tin wa
nyɛ-a / a nir nya / na iɔng o yuor / ka kɔntɔmɔ (4020) / ka ti soora
para / boono kɔntɔmɔ? / k'o yel ka / k'o kɔ̃n yele / a o yuor par / ka
ku tiɛ / ka ti diɛni / boono diɛni / ka diɛnu-a / ti zina / k'o wa ir
bomo / iɔng kuɔr puɔ / ti ba bɔ̃ɔ̃ bome / o na ir / ka a ngmɛ-na kuɔ̃ /
ko lɛ yel ti / ka ti i ka ti nyu / ka ti yel ka / tai nyuure / ko yel ka
(4040) / ka n lɛn nyɛ / ka n de lɛni / ka numɔ ya / k'o yel ka / ka n
fuor nyela / kã ba nyu kaa nyɛ / ka a numɔ / k'o iɔng ka n nyũ / n
nyũ wa baara / o'a mi nyũ / o dɔng yel ka ya / ko kɔ̃ yele / a o yuor
par / ka kama-a / i-iɛr nya-a / ko o bɔɔr na yela / a yel nya / kum
ma / o yel ka bo? / k'o yel ka ya (4060) / ka o yuor / ka kɔntɔmɔ-a /
k'o a par anya / ka ala na / ka o kũ ta fu-ɛ / on a yel lɛ-a / on yel wa
baara / ti iɔng na la / o'a la wa baara / ko lɛ liɛb ya / ti lɛ soori / a fũ
nu / ka ba buɔlɔ / ka fũ nu ir a nibɛ / ka o yel ka / ka ulɔ nu / ka ir /
on yel wa baara / tin in ngmin? / naangmin soru (4080) / na wa

uro-a / vɛ̃ ka ti nyɔɔ / a soor bein iɔng / lɛ soor-a / a naangmin
yelua / ti na won o yuora / ti tai nyue / ti a lɛ soori / boono ir nir / ko
yel ka / olɔ ir nibɛ / o yel wa baara / ka ti yel ka / a boonu / ka ba
buɔlɔ / a naangmin? / k'o yel ka / ka ti n yel ka / ka naangmin-ua /
ka zirina (4100) / ka naangmin-a / ka ba be / ka ulɔ nu-o / ka ia
naangmin / ka ti nyɛ ala-a / ka i ziri / ka ti bɔ̃ gu / ti liɛb biɛri / ka
ti bɔ̃ bom / na ir nira / tin biɛra / wa ti nyã / tɔ ble zie-a / ma ulɔ
nu / ia dɛung nir / ko yel ka / ka naangmina / ka ulɔ ir nibɛ / ka lɔng
kɔntɔme-a / ka lɔng ni nuur (4120) / ka lɔng ni vaar / lɔng ni dun /
lɔng ni bom zaa / lɔng ni kube / lɔng ni siuwe / lɔng ni weni / tin
in ngmin / wa ti bɔ̃ɔ̃ o yele? / ka nir kɔ̃ɔ̃ ya / ni boono? / napolo
banu / a tɔ ble / bidab kpɛ̃ɛ̃ / o'a yel ka / n won fu yel / n won wa
baara / tikyɛ-a / fũ yɔɔ ma / gafura / ka n lɛ yel yel kɔ̃ (4140) / o'a
bar zom / k'o yel ka / n won nuɔra / ti-a n yel / n yela / tin ba fuɔr
fuɛ / o'a de sooru / soora biri / soora bɔɔbɔ / soora dɔɔri / fũ na yel
ka / ka naangmin-a / ka olɔ ir ti-a / a un ir ti / ka ti ira boono? / ka
ti yel ka / ka fu sooro / fũ na soor anya / a viɛla ti zie / k'o yel ka
(4160) / naangmina / o na ir ti / bin a teung zu / o yela / ka ti ya / ka
ti tuur o nɛ / ka zɔr o dãbie / zɔr o viĩ / ti tuur o nuɔri / ti lɛ yel ka /
ka nir kɔ̃-a / ka k'o ir bin / ka ti ba nyɛrɛ-o / ka ti ulɛ-a / wa bɔng
ti-a / ka ti yel zaa / ka kun tuɔ̃ mali / ka ti lɛ sooro / ka ni boono? /
ko yel ka (4180) / ka tini-a / ka ti sɔɔr a nuɔr / o na yela-a / ya yel
ka / ka yi sɔɔna / yi ni sɔɔ-ya / ti lɛ soorua / boonu-a / ka tin na i /
tur a nuɔri / boonu / ka ti na i / a zɔɔra fu viĩ / boonu / ka ti na i / a
teung zu ka / a maal fu soori / ti fu yel ka / a nibɛ bala-a / fu ir ba
bin (4200) / a teung zu / ka yini wa / wa sɔɔ n nuɔr / yina zɔɔra ba
nɛɛ / ka yi sɔɔna / ka n nuɔri / yi yela nya-a / ya nyɛ ala / ya tu ala /
bibie ayi / faa nyɛ nibɛ / na be be-a / ba wa ta / ba iɔng yi bɛlu / ban
bɛlɛ yi-a / ka yi yel ka / ka yi na tu bana / ya tu ba / ka yi yel ka / ka
yi tu banu (4220) / ka yi na nyɛ na yel miɔ̃ / yi na tu baa / n ba ir
n nu / ti sɔng kɔɔ iɔng / yi na wa / wa yel ma / bom yin nyɛ / a
teung zu ka / o yel lɛ-a / sããkum kori / bɛl ba nibɛ / ia dɛungdema /
ba zɔɔr a nuɔri / ba na zɔɔr a nuɔri / ti tu kɔntɔme / ba wa kyeni / ti
ta be / naangmin bie / iɔng ba sooru / o'a soor ba (4240) / o'a soor
baalu / boonu kã i / a teung ka? / ka ti yel kaya / ka tin na tuna / ka
fu nuɔri / ti n iɔng na tu / ti na tuura-a / ka nir kɔ̃-nu / wa bɛl ti /
ka tin tu o-aa / ka tin nyɛ o yel miɔ̃ / tin na tuur o-a / ti mang ka /
ya / yel miɔ̃-a / bebe-a / ka ti na tuɔ̃ nyɛ / ti-a tu bɔ̃ gu / bon bom
beini / ka fu ku ti? (4260) / naangmin yele / na i yɔɔ / faa wiil ti /
kuur ba ioo / faa ku ti / ti na tɛr o-aa / wa lɔng siu nia / a teung

zu-a / ka fu yel ka / ka ti nyɔɔ-a / ka k'o i bom / ka ni daar kɔ̃-a / k'o
na wiɛ-ti / taa nyɔɔ-a / tini wa tani / a teung zua / ti na tɛr o-aa /
k'o i bom bein / wa song ti / ka kɔntɔmɔ (4280) / wa bɛl ti / ka ti
kpɛ muɔ / k'o nyɔɔ ti / liɛb o liɛbu / wa liɛb ti yɛ̃ / ka nibɛrɛ-a /
dɛung ba nibɛ / baa ti kyeni / a naangmin teung / ban ti ta / ka
naangmin bie / wa iɔng ba sooru / on liɛb soora / boonu yelu ka yi /
yel ko naangmini? / k'o yel ka / ka ti yel ka / ti na tuna / a o nuɔri? /
ti na zɔna (4300) / a o vĩĩ / ti na zɔna / a dãbie / ti yel wa baara / ti
wa ta / ka muɔ nir / k'o yel o yele / ka tin tu-ɔ / k'o nuɔra / ka ti na
nyɛ na / ka o yel miɔ̃ na / tia tu-o / tin tu wa baara / ti lɛ liɛb yaa / lɛ
yel ka / tin na tuna / a fu mi nuɔri / ti iɔng na yiiri / tia tu bɔ̃ gu / ti
lɛ wa ta fu (4320) / a naangmin zie / tia yel ka / fũ ni fu nuɔra / ka ti
na zɔna / a fu nuɔr diã / ti yel ka / ka diɛ̃ bibir / ti kun tuɔ̃ / lɛ maal
vlai / ka ti yel ka / ka tin in ngmin / ka fu yel ka / ka bom ben be /
ka fu na de ti-a / wa wiil ka ti nya / ka ti iɔng tiɛru / zĩ tiɛri / ka fu
lɛ yel ka / ka bom nya-a / ka fu na vɛ̃ sɛrɛ (4340) / ka nir kɔ̃ ya / wa
ti zie / wa bɔɔr ti sooru / ka ti yel ka / k'o soor ka ti nyɛ / bom na
sãã / boono sãã? / kasir oa / ba wa ta / ti yel ka / ka naangmini / ma
fu ir ma / bin teung zu / ti yel ka / ka fu ngmin biir / ti in yɔɔ / ka ti
kun tuɔ̃ / wono ta iɛru / fu na yel lɛ-a / ti zaa-ya (4360) / ti iɛrɛ na /
ti ba wona taa / iɛru-ɛ / tikyɛ-a / daar kɔ̃-a / tɔ ble banu / wa gã in
ple / lɔng ni kpɛ̃ɛ̃ / ba n gan be-a / a kpɛ̃ɛ̃ nua / o'a iɔng na kũa / o'a
kpii be / on kpii wa baara / ka tɔ ble / ir kpɛ̃ɛ̃ muɔ / ti bar ti / tia gã
be / yuom ata / ko wa wa yaa / a daar kɔng-a (4380) / wa lɔng ni
nir / wa n zie / baa wa ta be / ko de bomo / bom bono? / nuɔ banu /
ni o nyɔvuri / ko wa ta / a n zie / ti zĩ ngme ma / ka ɔɔr ma / kã n
ba yel yele / bono vɛ̃ / kã n ba yel yele? / fũ yel ka / kã n ta iɛrɛ-i /
n tɔ sob zie / ka ulɔ saa gbɔɔ vũ / n kyãã i gbili / ti gã ya (4400) /
tikyɛ-a yi zaa-aa / na yele-aa / a yel yɔɔ / a teung zu-aa / yi na wana /
a n zie / o'a yel lɛ / dɛungdem-a / ba na kyena / k'o soorɛ-a / on soor
wa baara / ti de yele / boono yel / k'o yel ku ngmin? / k'o yela ka /
fu na ir ma / fu yel ka n iɛrɛ / a nir zie? / k'o yel ka / n ba yel lɛɛ
(4420) / ko lɛ sooro / fu na ir ma / fu yele ka / n ma iri / kyen nir
zie / ti yel yel kuu? / ko yel ka / ko ba yel lɛɛ / k'o lɛ soor / fu na ir
ma / fu yel ka / n tera nyɔvur / na tuɔ̃ iɔng niri? / k'o yel ka / o ba
yel lɛ / lɛ na ya / ti daar kɔng ya / ka tɔ ble / o'a tɛra o nira / wa wa
tana (4440) / ko i zuziɔ / ko wa de-a / a in tɔ-ya / ti tuori ma / ka n
kono / ti fu na yel ka / ka ti ta / won taa / iɛru / ala na / ka n yel n
yele / ko ba wũai / ti tuɔr ma-a / on tɔ wa baara / naa bar ma / ti lɛ
de-a / nuɔ-a / ngma iɔng / o'a de zĩĩ / iɔng n zu (4460) / iɔng wa

baara / ti le yel ka / ka maa i boma / ka n na tera nyɔvur / ka n kaa
o zie / ka o ta nyɛ fai / ka n kyãã i gbili / ka ngmin sabie / ka ba wa /
a wa pɔbu / wa piɔ ma / an piɔ wa baara / dayere bio / ka tɔ ble /
lɔng ni zuziɔ / ba lɛ wa / wa ta be / lɔng ni nuɔ / le tuɔr ma / ka won
ma (4480) / ka n iɔng na kon / n kon bɔ̃ gu / ba la ngme ma / ba
ngme wa baara / ba de zĩĩ / le iɔng ma / ala na ya / ka n wani / fu
naangmin zie / fu in naangmin / ti bɔ̃ fu bɔɔm / ka o yel ka / ka ti
zĩ ka / ba ba zĩ be / ban zĩ wa baara / fu in ngmin / a naangmin
yele / wa war uro-a / naangmina-a / wa de bomo (4500) / k'o shɔɔ
mutong / k'o iɔng ti zu / ti yel ka / k'o nyɛ bomo / o yel ku-a / k'o
kaa nyɛ / on kaa nyɛ / gan ua / k'o yel ka / bon fu dɔng / yel kum-a /
ala na ya / k'o yel ka / n bɔra / k'o yel ka / bɔr ngmin bɔru? / k'o
yel ka / ka niru-wa / tɛr ma bɔri / ni boonu? (4520) / k'o yel ka ya /
kɔntɔmble / o lɔ i ka n bɔr / o lɛ yel ka / kɔntɔmble-a / fu wona a
yele / a teung zu? / fu nyũũ na / k'o yuori? / k'o yel ka / k'o ba
nyũe / fu nyũũ na / ko yel yele / kurɔ fu? / k'o yel ka / k'o nyũũ na /
fu ni ano? / k'o yel ka / ma n yɔ̃ / k'o yel ka (4540) / k'o wa fu yir
bii? / k'o yel ka / o wana / wa wa ta / pɔɔbɔ nyũũ na / ka biir nyũũ? /
k'o yel ka / ka baa nyũe / a in ngmin / ka ba ba nyũe? / k'o yel ka /
ma n yɔ̃ / ma nu nyɛrɛ-o / lɛ na-a / k'o yel ka / fu nyũũ-a / a fu
yɔ̃-a / buɔl k'o wa / k'o buɔlu / buɔl o yuor (4560) / ti a kɔntɔmɔ /
k'o zĩ piɛl be / k'o buɔluɛ / k'o zɔɔr buɔlu / o'a zɔɔr buɔlu / on zɔɔr
wa baara / ka naangmini / lɛ yel ka / ma fu yel ka / ka fu won o
yele / k'o mi won fu yele / ti fu in ngmin / ka o zɔɔra buɔlu? / ka o
yel ka / n ba bongɛ / naangmini / ko miɔ̃-na / mi buɔl o yuori / o ba
sɔɔ / k'o yel ka (4580) / wa wɔ̃n yele / ba na yele-a / on wa ta / wa
ar o yɔ̃ / k'o yel ka / ir yela / bom na fun yel ku ma / k'o yel ka / n
yel ka / fũ ir ma / bin teung zu / ti lɛ yel ka ya / ka n tuur fu nuɔr /
ka zɔɔr fu dãbie / ka zɔɔr fu vĩĩ / faa yel kumu / ti lɛ yel ka / ka fu
na ira nir / ka o wa bɛl ma nyɛ / o ba wa (4600) / wa yel yele / k'o
mi tuura fu nuɔr / ka n tiɛr mang ka / ma tu o nuɔra / n tun fu
dem / ti tuura / wa tu bɔ̃ gu / k'o bɛl ma / yel o yele / ti kpɛn muɔ /
ti vɛ̃ ka bɔri / alɛ na yi / ka n yel ku fu / ka kɔntɔme-a / na iɔng o
yɛ̃ / ti soor naangmin / ngmini / fũ ir ma / bin teung zu / fu yel
mana (4620) / ka n iɛrɛ ni nibɛ / k'o yel ka / o ba yele / ti in ngmin /
ka dɔɔ nya / wa yel yele / lɛ ku fu / vɛ̃ ka n soora nyɛ / fũ na ir
ma / fu yel ka / ka nisaal sɔɔla / k'o nyɛ ma? / ko ba yel lɛ / k'o yel
ka / fu na ir ma / fu yel ka / ka nisaal sɔɔla / o won n yele / k'o ba
yel lɛ / k'o lɛ yel ka (4640) / fu na ir ma / ma ni nisaal sɔɔli / ti lɔng
kpiɛri? / k'o yel ka / yi lɔng kpiɛri / ti i ngmini / kã wa bɛli nir / ko

sɔng fu sor? / olɔ nu-a / bɔ̃ɔ̃ o yɛ̃ / ti bar fu / k'o yel ka / pampaana
nya / fu na wa n zie / fu bɔ̃ɔ̃ lɛ / fu na i-a? / kã yel ka / n ba bɔ̃ɔ̃-ɛ /
ko yel ka / ko zī ka (4660) / o'a zī wa bari / on zī wa baara / o'a de
tulu / iɔng o zu / tɔ ble / fu na bɔɔr ti nyãã / fu na nyɛn lɛ / fu naa
yela / ku ti-a / ka ti bar kɔntɔmɔ / ti faa yel yele / ala na vɛ̃ / ka ti
bɔ̃ɔ̃ ka / a ti kɔntɔmɔ / yel faanu / ti i yel vla / yel faa na bo? / ba
yela / ka tɔ / na kpi kyena (4680) / k'o nyana / a yel bebe / bana i
uaa / a o zie / ti tini-ya / kun tuɔ̃ barɛ / bona vɛ̃ / ka ti kun tuɔ̃ barɛ /
ka ba yel ka / ka ti nikpɛ̃ɛ̃ / a tɔ ble / o na dire wuura / ti na ina /
dina wuur / ba na yel wa baara / ka naangmin bie / lɛ soor ka / ka
fũ ni nira / k'o denio / ti yel ka (4700) / k'o kyiera / ka zi zãã / ko
kyieri-a / ka fu tuura / ko ti bɔra / ka fu bɔng ka / o bɔra / a teung
fu kyiera / fu na tun bii? / ko yel ka / ma bɔ̃ɔ̃ zie / n na kyiera / n ba
sɔɔrɛ / ti a in ngmin / ka fu bɔ̃ɔ̃ ka / o bɔra / ti tuur / on ia / o yel
kora / a sãã̃kum bomo (4720) / a makum bomo / a taba bomo / ka
tɔ-a / o wa wana o bomo / ka wa liɛb yele / wa wõn ua / ti olɔ-a / so
ti-a / ala na / ka ti bɔ̃ gu / ti bɔ̃ɔ̃ ti tuo / ti kyaan tuura / a tɔ / ti bɔ̃ɔ̃
ka / nin daar-a / a na wõn tina / a bom na vɛ̃-a / ka fu kun tuɔ̃-a / bar
o-aa / a fu nikpɛ̃ɛ̃-a (4740) / ka yel pɔɔ ua / a zɔ ti bari / alɛ na vɛ̃ / ka
ti tuura / a kɔntɔmɔ / ti bɔ̃ɔ̃ ka ya / ka dɛungdem-o / ba la sɔng ba
sora / ka nin daar iɔng / a na wõn tina / a in ngmin / ka ti nyɛ
kɔntɔmɔ / ti tɔ sob-nu / ti wa bɛl ti-a / ka ti bɔ̃ gu? / nikpɛ̃ɛ̃ banu /
a fu iɔng na / ka ti kun tuɔ̃ / lɛ ban uwe / alɛ na-a (4760) / ka ti bɔ̃
gu-a / ti zɔr a dãbie / ti na tuuraa / ti bɔng ka ya / nin daar na / a na
wõn ti / faa nyɛ ala / bon i ti / ka ti bɔr bɔru / wa tan ka / ka nir
kɔng-a / daar kɔng-a / wa yel ka / ka boono i / ka ti-a / ka bɔra wa
ta ka / ka ti yel ka / ti niru-aa / ka ti tuur ya / k'o bɔra (4780) / ala
na vɛ̃ / ka ti mi bɔr / ka nir-na / lɛ soor-o / ka fu de sor-aa / kyier-aa /
ka yi i yɔɔ / ti bɔri-a / a bɔr kpe muɔ / ka fu bɔ̃ɔ̃ ka / fu bɔra / ti bɔ̃ɔ̃
fu yira / fu na liɛba wa kul be / k'o yel ka / k'o na liɛba / a liɛb kul /
ti yel a yele-aa / ka ba wa irɛ / ka ba yi bɔ / k'o iɔng na liɛba (4800) /
liɛb de sora / a sãã yir sora / o iɔng na kula / o'a kyieri / ti kpɛ muɔ /
ti tuor nir / wa i kɔntɔmɔ / na nõ k'o bɔra / k'o yel ka / n ba / ar ka
sɛr / o'a ar zom / ko olɛ yel ka / k'o nyɛ bomo / k'o wiil o-aa / k'o yel
ka / nir kõ-aa / k'o wa wiil lɛ-aa / n daana tɔ ble / k'o bɔra-a (4820) /
ka wõn o yel ua / k'o be be / a kpime teung / a nyɛrɛ / ka wuur / bona
wuur? / o zɔɔr ngmin-aa / zɔɔr o yele / zɔɔr o tomo / t'o lɛ ir fu / mɛ
fu iɔng / iɔng fu gbɛɛ / iɔng fu nyɔvuri / iɔng fu zu / ka fu vuurɔ /
ka fu vuura-a / ti zɔɔr o nuɔra / ka ti tu fu ba / fu ba na-a / o bɔɔn
o tomo (4840) / o na ton-aa / ti lɛ vɛ̃-a / ka fu-a / ar bɔru / lɛ na vɛ̃ /

n ba bɔri / ka ba lɛ kuli / ti nyɛ niri / k'o yel o yele / ka n tuur o
nuɔri / on yel wa baara / o in ngmin / faa nyɛ dɔɔ / dɔɔ boonu? /
a kɔntɔm dɔɔ-banu / k'o nar o naru / ti lɛ bɛl bie / o'a ari / iɔng na
bɛri / o'a bɛr bɔ̃ gu (4860) / kɔntɔmbie-a / boono so yuori / na di
kɔntɔma / faa nyu / dɔɔ ba liɛbu / iɔng o tuubu / o'a tuur u / kpɛ a
muɔ / faa nyɛ dɔɔ / k'o ba la be / ti tu kɔntɔmɔ / lɛ iɔng o bɔru /
boono so bɔru / ka kɔntɔmɔ / o'a tɛr u / ti kpɛ muɔ / on in ngmin /
o'a de bomu / wuɔ kɔ̃ banu / o'a de-o (4880) / o'a de kube / lɔng ni
nyuɛ / zãzã piɔri / lɔng ni libie / dɔm lɔng taa / ti le yel ua / k'o nyɛ
bomo / bom boonu? / o'a de a yele / o'a nyɔɔ bɔɔ / bɔɔbuur yele / ti
yel ka / kã vɛ̃ k'o buu / buu kã nyɛ / o'a ziɔ dagoli / o'a tɔ a teung /
ti yel ka / fu sããkumɔ / tɔ ble-nu / a naangmin teung (4900) / ma
nuɔnu / ko wõn be / on yela / faa nyɛ dɔɔ / nuɔ ba kpɛ-o / o in
ngmin / k'o la na zom / ti lɛ liɛba / o'a nyɛ sori / a sor faa na / ko
turia / boono sori / ko yel ka / ka sori nya puɔ / ka fu de-a / ka wa
bɔ̃ɔ̃ o-aa / fu na faani-na / ni yɔɔ / k'o yel ka / k'o yel k'o nyɛ (4920) /
k'o nyɔɔ yele / ti yel ka / k'o tõ wuɔ / o'a de nu / tõ o wuɔ-aa / o tõ
wa baara / on in ngmin / k'o yel ka / k'o ir bomo / bon boonu? / o'a
ir o / ma kpo-nu / bɔɔ kpo-nu / o'a yel ka / k'o tɔ o nyu / o'a tɔ wa
baara / o'a bin lɛ zom / ti de gbelme / lɔng ni siuwe / lɔng sinshiura
(4940) / o'a de-o / tur bar saa zu / o'a lɛ bin teung / ti lɛ tur duru
loori / ti lɛ tur goba / on tur wa baara / ti yel ka / k'o dɔm nya / ti
gbaal o zu / on gbaal wa baara / o'a puor kɔntɔme / ti puora ngmin /
ti puora wuɔ / on puor wa baara / lɔng ni bara / lɔng base / on puor
wa baara / ti nyɛ sor / ti yel ka / o puoro bɔbɔ (4960) / ti puor bɔɔ
pɛla / ti puor bɔɔ sɔɔli / ti puor a tɔng / ti puor a bule / ti puor a
gbangbaala / ni zur ziiri / ni a zu sɔɔli / ko puor be gu be / ti lɛ de
sori / a man nuɔri / nikpɛ̃ɛ̃ nu / iɔng tɔɔla / ka n puoro / ba gu-o-ɛ /
zu ziiri / ani zu sɔɔli / ka n nyɛn ba zaa / ka n puor lɔng taa / ti lɛ
duur yi / iɔng de sori (4980) / ti ta ya / a tu zɔng puɔ / nikpɛ̃ɛ̃ / iɔng
tɔɔla / ka n puoro / ni biir / zu sɔɔli / ni zu ziiri / ka n puor nyɔɔ
ta / be puor wa baara / ka n dur ka yi / lɛ de sori / wa wa ta / a tɔng
kpɛ̃ɛ̃ zu / n ba puor be / zu ziiri / ni zu sɔɔli / na ba bɔɔbɔ / bɔɔ pɛlɛ
niba / lɔng bɔɔ sɔɔli (5000) / ka na puor ba zaa / ba gu be / ti lɛ
liɛba / zɔr wara / wa ta i ya / bɔɔ pla ya / ni o bibiiri / zu ziiri / ni zu
sɔɔli / ka n puor ba / n puor wa baara / ti baa nyɛ sori / a sãã yir
iɔng / kan zɔ wa ta / n na ta be / faa nyɛ bomo / yel yɔɔ na / bara
no / lɔng ni siuwe / lɔng ni wen (5020) / lɔng ni ngmin / lɔng ni
kɔntom / k'o puor ba zaa / dɔm nyɔɔta / ba ba i libie / kun tuɔ̃ / zĩ
sor ba / on wa ta / wa wa baara / ti de gbelme / o'a bin teung / ti yel

ka / ka yel miɔ̃-a / ka n bɔɔr ka n yela / a biiri / yel nya iɔng / ti na
tuura / boonu yelo / ka ba wono-a? / ka ba yel ka (5040) / ka
naangmin yelo / baminɛ-a / yel ka ya / kɔntɔme yelu / o'a de kpo / ti
yel ka / ola wa i-a / naangmin yela / a bie kan kaar / o'a kaa bie / a ba
zɔɔri / a naangmin yele / k'o yel ka / ola mi i-a / a kɔntɔm yelua /
a bie k'o kaari / ti lɔb bie / ka lo sɔɔ / o'a yel ka / fũ banu (5060) / yel
ka ya / ka tɔ / k'a na bɔra / o ba i bɔru-ɛɛ / yel kɔ̃-a / ar o tub / o tu
ala-a / o tu wa baara / bon ko o ba nyɛ / o nyɛn dib / nyɛn ni nii /
lɔng ni piir / lɔng ni buur / lɔng ni nuur / lɔng ni pɔbɔ / o'a nyɛ ba /
nyɛ ba zaa / ti naangmin teung / bon ben be / na gɔ̃ anya (5080) / lɛ
na vɛ̃ / ka biira / baa liɛb nio / tur kɔntɔme / baa liɛb nu / tur kɔntɔme / baa nyɔɔ ba / ti iɔng na puori / ba na puor bana / baa puor
wa baari / ban baar ala / ti lɛ nyɛ yele / bono yele / ka ba yel ka / tin
be ka / a teung zu puɔ / tin in ngmin / soor ti zu / dɔɔla nyũũ? / tin
in ngmin (5100) / yela yele / yel miɔ̃ / ka ar ti zu / faa nyɛ ala / ka ba
yel ka / fu bɔɔr ala / fu na nyɔɔna / a sããkum / gbɛ-a / ti biɛri / alɛ
na ya / ka ti tu bɔ̃ gu / ti iɔng na zɔ / iɔng na kyeni / ti kpɛ muɔ / a
nir na-a / na tuur sãakuma / k'o dɔɔ ti-a / olɔ nu yel ka / ka ti tu
ulɔ (5120) / ka ti bɔ̃ gu / ti iɔng na tu / lɛ wa wɔ̃ yele / yel paala /
boono yelu? / ka kɔb yela-a / a dɔɔb yela-a / tamiur yela / alɛ na / i a
yele / tin yel ka / a yel paala / tin in ngmini / a nyɛn dɔbu / tin in
ngmini / a nyɛ kuɔb / tin in ngmini / a nyɛ tamiur / ti a bɔ̃ gu / ti a
lɛ yel ka (5140) / ka tin sora-a / naangmin zie / naangmin bie / wa i
suuri / ti lɛ yel ka / ka nir-na-a / na wiil a sora / kayi tuur-a /yin
tuur-ua / ko i a naangmin / lɛ na vɛ̃ / ka dagara bie-a / bɔ̃ɔ k'o bɔra /
o na bɔ̃ɔ lɛ-a / lɛ na vɛ̃ / ka ba yel ka / fu sɔng bomo / nari sɔng ku
tɔl / ala na ya / faa nyɛ bie (5160) / ka ba bari / a naangmin sori / ti
lɛ yel ka / fu dɔɔ bie-a / on tuura sori / o kɔntɔm sori? / ba na yel
lɛ-a / baa sɔɔ ɔ̃ ɔ̃ / baa nyɔɔ alɛ / fũ dɔɔ bie / a kɔntɔm sor / ala nu
k'o tuur / fu na kul pɔɔ / a kɔntɔm sor / ola nu k'o tuu / ti naangmin
yelua / ti ma wɔ̃ o yuora / ti sɔng u-aa / lɛ na vɛ̃ / ka ti sɔng-o (5180) /
sɔng ku tɔl / faa nyɛ ala / tia bom nya iɔng / a ti bɔɔr bom / ti na
bɔɔr-ua / bono iɔng na / ka ti bɔɔru / ka ba yel ka / ti bɔɔra / lɛ ti
na i-a / tin in ngmini / ka ti bɔ̃ gu / tin bɔ̃ gu-a / ti yi de sori / ngma
ti bɔbɔ / ta ngma bɔbɔ / ti ba buu ba / ti na buu bɔ̃ gu / ti lɛ wa ta /
zĩ lɔng ta (5200) / boni yelu / ka ti yel k'o taa / a kpaartiib yelu / ka
ti yel ku taa / ti yel wa baara / ti in ngmin / naangmin yele / na wa
uro-a / faa nyɛ ala / ti ni ma puora / naangmin yuora / ku ir sɔɔ / ti
na zɔɔra o yele / lɛ na vɛ̃ / ka ti liɛba / bɔɔra sora / ka ti buu ku taa /
ti buu bɔ̃ gu / ko lɛ liɛba / a wal piɛl gbɛɛ (5220) / nɛb kyun kyun /

tin in ngmin / ko i ti yɛ̃ / ka ti burbur / tin in ngmin / a yel nya
iɔng / tin ia / naangmin-ua / a iɔng ti yɛ̃ / ka ti tɛru-a / ka ti tɛru gu /
ti nyɔɔ tule / olɛ nu-a / ti ngmĩĩ ngmĩĩ a bɔɔra / a soori naangmin /
ka ba be yɔɔ / a ngmin ka waara / olɛ nu-a / ia ti ngmini / olɛ nu-a
(5240) / a yel mĩɔ̃ ngmin / wa wiil ti / lɛ tin a i / ka viɛl ti zie / ngmin
popaala / olɛ nu-a / a sɛlngmindɛr / na wiil ti / a naangmin zie / a
ngmin nyɔtuon / ola nu-a / a nira / a tɔ ni ble / a tɔ kpɛɛ-a / olɛ
nu-a / a ngmin sɔr goba / a ngmin bie-a / olɛ nu-a / a nanyu daa / na
o pɔɔ (5260) / a ngmin par pla / olɛ nu-a / a naazuɔ daa / ni o pɔɔ /
a ngmin naayuo / olɛ nu-a / a kɔntɔmbie / a ngmin gagara / olɛ nu-a /
a kɔntɔmble / a ngmin biila / olɛ nu-a / a tɔ kpɛ̃ɛ̃ kur / olɛ na ya / ka
ti nyɔɔ-a / a bibiir-a / a bin teung / ti iɔng ba wiil-ua / ka bible-a /
wa iɔng tiɛr-ua (5280) / wa bɔ̃ a yele / ti songna-ya / ka ti kyaan
tuur / ka ni daar iɔng / ka ti faa ta / tin yel alɛ-a / a ba duur kũ / tin
yele-a / ka n mang ka / an i lɛ-a / a na tuɔ̃ na / a kũ ? / a ba tuɔ̃i /
ma iɔng yɛ / gun in tuɔra / ka wa liɛba / yel wɔ̃n yɛ̃ / iɔng a ti zu / ma-
yaa / n tɛra n yɛ̃ ya (5300) / ka wa liɛba / ziri ngma yɛ̃ / n tɛra n yɛ̃
yaa / ka wa liɛba / nimili yɛ̃ / n tɛra n yɛ̃ / ka wa liɛba / gagara yɛ̃ /
yeng yɔɔ ya / olɛ nu-a / sɔɔn nir zu / dãmbol yɔɔ ya / alɛ na / sɔɔn
nir zu / ti ba sɔɔn yɔɔi / lɛ na ya / ka ti bɔ̃ gu / ti lɛ liɛb puor / olɛ
yel ka / tin in ngmini (5320) / lɛ liɛba yɛ̃ / boono yɛ̃-nu / na liɛba /
a yel wɔ̃n yɛ̃ / boono yɛ̃-nu / na liɛba / a nimili yɛ̃ / boono yɛ̃-nu / na
liɛba / a gagara / k'o yel ka / n yɛ̃ na / na liɛba / a gagara / ulɛ nu-a /
dɔng i boma / lɛɔr ba puor / on yel wa baara / ti iɔng na hiera / nibɛ
ya (5340) / ba bar gɔmɔ / ban bar gɔmɔ / ka n de n yel-a / a yel wa
baara / boonu yelua / a yel wun yelua / boonu yelua / a nimili yelu /
boonu yelua / a gagara yelu / a nu-a / a fu gaga nir ? / kɔntɔmbie-
na / n gaga nir / olɛ nu-a / wa bɛl ma / a naangmin soor puɔ / kan
wa song n tuɔra / ka nin daar iɔng / ka wɔ̃ ma (5360) / fũ sɔng yela /
song fu taba / fu na tuɔ̃ maal / fũ sɔng yela / sɔng naangmin / o ba
ka maal-uɛ / boonu na / na song naangmin / a zɔɔra o nuɔri ? / boonu
na / na song naangmin ? / fu na song a sora / boonu na / naangmin
sor / ka mã sɔng ? / olɛ nu-a / n yel ka / o sɛlngmindɛra / olɛ nu-a /
a bɔ̃ɔ̃ naangmina (5380) / ka n iɔng na tua / ka n tu wa baara / ka
nir biɛ-a / a nu-a / a fu nirɛ biɛ-a ? / kɔntɔmbie / olɛ nu-a / a n nirɛ
biɛ / biɛ ni bo / na song n sora / biɛ-ni-bo / on song n tiɛru-a /
pampaanaya / ka tɔ ble / ti tan naangmin / k'o iɔng wuura / ko
nyɛrɛ / boonu wuuri ? / o zɔɔr o nuɔri / ala so wuuri (5400)/ k'o
nyɛrɛ / boonu wuuri ? / a wuuri-ya / olɛ nu-a / o na song a sora / ka
n bɔɔn ka / n in wuur nir / biiri / yaa nya / biiri / yaa wɔ̃ ? / pɔbɔ / ya

wõ / a bum nyaya / na iɔng sɔɔl-ua / sɔɔli ti zie / ma wa wiil yia / a
wiil wa baara / yi nyɔɔ-a / nu duru (5420) / yi nyɔɔ-a / ni nio / yi
tɛru-aa / ka i laar / lɛ na / k'o yel ku a biir / a yel nya puɔ / o ba
tuur / zir ngma nirɛ / a yel nya puɔ / o ba tuura / gagar nirɛ / a yel
nya puɔ / o ba tuur / nimil nirɛ / o tura / bideble / ni iɔng tiɛru / ma
ara ia / a iɔng yi wiil-ua (5440) / tin de na / yuom ata / yi boona / a
naangmin yele / na war uro-a / ti ka n nyɔɔ-o / a iɔng n nu-o / ti
kaar o / n tiɛra / ka dayere bio / ti na kpɛni ona / bɔɔ pla dio / n
tiɛra / ka bibie ata / n na kpɛni ona / bɔɔ pla dio / n tiɛra / ka datɛrɛ /
n na kpɛni ona / bɔɔ pla dio (5460) / ma wa kpɛ / bible-a / wa iɔng
o nuɔra / k'o ti mana / kɔng da kora / ko iɔng na kyɛ-a / kyɛ k'o
niri / o'a kyɛ gugur / lɛ na ya / ara n suuri / ka biira / wa bɔɔ-a / ti
na puora / a fu bɔ ngmin / ti na puora / fu kɔntɔm ngmin / ti na
puora / fu bɔɔr siuwe / ti na puora / a fu kɔntɔm siuwe (5480) / alɛ
na ya / ka na yel k'o yia / a dio nya puɔ / o ina a yel yɔɔ yele / n kun
tuɔ̃ / wiil a zaa / maa wiil ku yi / a ina / yuom ata yelua / yuom
ayuɔb yelua / lɛ na ya / ka ba buɔla / a bɔɔ sɔɔla / o ina / bidɔɔ yelua /
lɛ na ya / ka ba buɔla / a bɔɔr sɔɔla / o ina / tamiur yel (5500) / lɛ na
ya / ka ba buɔla / a bɔɔr sɔɔla / o ina / a kukuur yel / lɛ na ya / ka ba
buɔla / a bɔɔr sɔɔla / o ina / a nɔɔ guol yel / lɛ na ya / ka ba buɔla /
a bɔɔr sɔɔla / tia baari / n yel ku yi

INDEX TO THE INTRODUCTION